THE FIXED TRILOGY

LAURELIN PAIGE

This book is a work of fiction. Names, characters, places, and incidents either are products of the author's imagination or are used fictitiously. Any resemblance to actual events or locales or persons, living or dead, is entirely coincidental.

ISBN: 0991379659
ISBN 13: 9780991379651

First edition May, 2013.

The following story contains mature themes, strong language, and sexual situations. It is intended for adult readers.

Also by Laurelin Paige:

Take Two

Coming Soon by Laurelin Paige:

Hudson

Free Me

Find Me

Star Struck

FIXED ON YOU

BOOK ONE

— CHAPTER —
ONE

I felt alive.

The alternating flashes of dark and soft lights, the throbbing pulse from an Ellie Goulding club mix, the movement of sweaty bodies dancing, grinding, enjoying each other—The Sky Launch Nightclub got into my blood and turned me on in a way that I hadn't let anyone or anything else do in quite some time. When I was there—working the bar, assisting the wait staff, attending to the DJs—I felt more free than at any other time of my day. The club held magic.

And, for me, healing.

For all its vibrancy and life, the club was a safe haven for me. It was a place I could attach myself without worry of going overboard. No one was going to sue me for focusing too hard or long on my job. But rumor was The Sky Launch, which had been up for sale for quite some time, was about to be sold. A new owner could change everything.

"Laynie." Sasha, the waitress working the upper floor, pulled me from my thoughts and back to my job. "I need a vodka tonic, a White Russian, and two Butterballs."

"Got it." I pulled the vodka from the shelf behind me.

"I can't believe how busy we are for a Thursday," she said as I worked on her order.

"It's the summer crowd. Give it a week, and the place will explode." I couldn't wait. Summer at the club was a total blast.

"That's when things around here get fun." David Lindt, the club manager, joined our conversation, a sparkle showing in his eyes as the bright white light that lit the bar illuminated his face.

"Real fun." I gave David a wide smile and winked while I placed the drinks on Sasha's tray, my stomach tensing with a flicker of desire.

He answered my wink with one of his own, stirring the flicker in my belly to a low flame.

David wasn't the love of my life—not even the love of the moment—but his shared passion for the club sparked something in me. My interest in learning more and moving up from bartending had seemed to interest him as well. More than one late night of showing me the ropes had ended in heavy make-out sessions. Though I hadn't been instantly attracted to him, his small stature, curly blonde hair and blue eyes had grown on me. Also, his keen business sense and exceptional management style were qualities I required in a man. And, truthfully, the lack of effect he had on my emotions provided half the draw. We had decent chemistry, but he didn't have me freaking out all over him like I had over other guys. He was safe and solid and that was my definition of the perfect man.

I rang up Sasha's order while David filled shot glasses—Todd's order, I suspected, another waiter standing next to Sasha. David rarely stepped behind the bar anymore, but we were short-staffed for the night and I welcomed his help. Especially with the way we were picking up. A regular and his friends had leaned against the bar waiting for my attention, and out of the corner of my eye, I saw a suit taking a spot at the far end of the counter.

I handed Sasha her ticket, but David stopped her before she could take off. "Hold on. While there's at least a few of us here, I think we should toast to Laynie." He passed around the shots he'd been filling. Tequila—my liquor of choice.

I peered at him suspiciously. While it wasn't unusual to have a shot or two while working a shift, it was always kept on the down-low, never in front of our manager and certainly not at his encouragement.

"No worries," David said, bumping my shoulder with his. "It's a special occasion."

With a shrug, I smiled and took the shot he offered me. "You're the boss."

"We're too busy for a proper toast, so let's just say this is to Laynie. We're proud of you, girl."

I blushed and clinked glasses as everyone around, including the regular customer and his friends, shouted out "hear, hear" and "cheers."

"Woo hoo!" I screamed my own excitement. I'd worked hard to get my degree. I was proud of myself too. I slammed the shot back, enjoying the burn as it lined my throat and spread through my veins. "Goddamn, that's nice!"

Aware that the crowd was getting antsy, Sasha took off with her order while David filled Todd's. I turned my attention first to the regular, a guy whose name deserted me. He leaned in to give me a hug, which I returned. I might not remember him, but I knew how to earn my tips.

"Four of whatever's on tap," he said, raising his voice over the music which seemed to have gotten louder in the last few minutes. "Where's Liesl?"

I handed him his first two mugs and began work on the next two. "Since she's covering all my shifts next week she has tonight off." That's right—this was the guy that usually flirted with Liesl, another bartender.

"That's cool. So what are you doing on your vacation?" With Liesl not around, Regular turned his charm on me. His eyes travelled to my breasts that were admittedly hard to miss. Especially with my low-cut neckline. I had some nice girls, who could blame me for showing them off?

"Absolutely nothing." I hoped my delivery sounded like I was looking forward to my vacation. Truth was I'd taken the time off so I could go home and spend time with my older brother. But only that morning, Brian had called the trip off, saying that he was too swamped with work. He wouldn't even be able to make it to my graduation.

I swallowed the emotions that threatened to show on my face. On top of being disappointed, I was terrified. Me with nothing to occupy my time was not an attractive me. I'd almost told David several times to go ahead and put me on the schedule, but every time I started, I felt like a total loser. Maybe a week off would be good for me. I could handle it. Right?

Now wasn't the time to fret about the week to come. I finished the transaction with Regular and slid down the bar to take care of the suit at the end of the counter.

"Now what can I get...you...?" My words trailed off as my eyes met the suit's, the air leaving my lungs, suddenly sucked out by the sight that met me. The man...he was...*gorgeous.*

Incredibly gorgeous.

I couldn't look away, his appearance magnetizing. Which meant he was exactly the type of man I should avoid.

After the numerous heartaches that had dotted my past, I'd discovered that I could divide the men I was attracted to into two categories. The first category could be described as fuck and forget. These were the men that got me going in the bedroom, but were easy to leave behind if necessary. It was the only group I bothered with anymore. They were the safe ones. David fell into this category.

Then there were the men that were anything but safe. They weren't fuck and forget—they were, "Oh, fuck!" They drew me to them so intensely that I became consumed by them, absolutely focused on everything they did, said and were. I ran from these men, far and fast.

Two seconds after locking eyes with this man, I knew I should be running.

He seemed familiar—he must have been in the club before. But if he had been, I couldn't imagine that I'd have forgotten. He was the most breathtaking man on the planet—his chiseled cheekbones and strong jaw sat beneath perfectly floppy brown hair and the most intense gray eyes I'd ever seen. His five o'clock shadow made my skin itch, yearning to feel the burn of it against my face—against my inner thighs. From what I could see, his expensive three-piece navy suit was fitted and of excellent taste. And his smell—a distinct fragrance of unscented soap and aftershave and pure male goodness—nearly had me sniffing at the air in front of him like a dog in heat.

But it wasn't just his incomparable beauty and exquisite display of male sex that had me burning between my legs and searching for the nearest exit. It was how he looked at me, in a way that no man had ever looked at me, a hungry possessiveness present in his stare as if he not only had undressed me in his mind, but had claimed me to be sated by no one ever again except him.

I wanted him instantly, a prickle of fixation taking root in my belly—an old familiar feeling. But that I desired him didn't matter. The expression on his face said that he would have me whether I wanted it or not, that it was as inevitable as if it had already happened.

It scared the hell out of me. The hair on my skin stood up as witness to my fear.

Or perhaps it rose in delight.

Oh, fuck.

"Single-malt Scotch. Neat, please."

I'd almost forgotten I was supposed to be serving him. And the idea of serving him seemed so sexy, that when he reminded me of my job, I nearly fell over myself to get his drink. "I have a 12-year-old Macallan."

"Fine." It was all he said, but the delivery in his low thick voice had my pulse fluttering.

As I handed him his Scotch, his fingers brushed mine and I shivered. Visibly. His eyebrows rose ever so slightly at my reaction, as if he were pleased.

I jerked my hand back, tucking it against the bodice of my sheath dress as if the fabric could erase the warmth that had already traveled from where he'd touched me to the needy core between my legs.

I never brushed fingers with customers—why had I done that?

Because I couldn't *not* touch him. I was so drawn to him, so eager for something I couldn't name that I'd take whatever contact I could get.

Not this again. Not now.

Not ever.

I moved away from him. Far and fast. Well, as far as I could get, curling into the opposite corner of the bar. David could serve the guy if he wanted anything else. I needed to be nowhere near him.

And then, as if on cue in the bad luck life I led, Sasha returned. "David, that group in Bubble Five is harassing the waitress again."

"On it." He turned to me. "You can handle it for a minute?"

"I so got this." I so didn't have it. Not with Mr. Draw-Laynie-To-Me-Whatever-The-Cost-To-Her-Sanity sitting at the end of the bar.

But my declaration was convincing. David slipped out from behind the counter, leaving me alone with the suit. Even Regular and his friends had joined a group of giggly girls at a nearby table. I scanned the dance floor hoping I could attract customers by glaring at the sea of faces. I needed drink orders. Otherwise, Suit might think I was avoiding him by hiding in my corner, which, of course, I was. But, honestly, the distance between us did nothing to dim the tight ball of desire rolling around in my stomach. It was pointless avoidance.

I sighed and wiped down the counter in front of me, though it didn't seem to need it, just to keep myself occupied. When I braved a glance over at the hottie who had invaded my space, I noticed his Scotch was nearing empty.

I also noticed his eyes pinned on me. His penetrating gaze felt more than the typical stare of a customer trying to attract the bartender, but knowing I had a tendency to exaggerate the meanings of other people's actions, I dismissed the idea. Summoning my courage, I forced myself over to check on him.

Who am I kidding? No forcing was necessary. I glided to him as if he were pulling me with an invisible rope. "Another?"

"No, I'm good." He handed me a hundred. Of course. I'd been hoping he'd give me a credit card so I could glean his name.

No, no, I was not hoping for that. I did not care for his name. Nor did I notice that his left hand was absent of any ring. Or that he was still watching my every move as I took the cash he'd given me and rung his order into the register.

"Special occasion?" he asked.

I furrowed my brow then remembered he'd seen our toast. "Uh, yeah. My graduation. I walk tomorrow for my MBA."

His face lit up in honest admiration. "Congratulations. Here's to your every success." He raised his drink toward me and downed the final swallow.

"Thank you." I was transfixed on his mouth, his tongue darting out to clean the last drop of liquid off his lips. *Yum.*

When he set his glass down, I reached out my hand to give him his change, bracing myself for the thrill of contact that would inevitably happen when he took it from me.

But the contact never came. "Keep it."

"I can't." He'd given me a hundred. For one glass of Scotch. I couldn't take that.

"You can and you will." His commanding tone should have rankled me, but instead it got my juices flowing. "Consider it a graduation gift."

"Okay." His demeanor took away my will to argue. "Thanks." I turned to stuff the money into my tip jar on the back counter, pissed at myself for the effect this stranger had on me.

"Is this also a goodbye party?" His voice called from behind me, drawing me back to face him. "I don't imagine you'll be using your MBA to continue bartending."

Of course that's what a suit would assume. He was probably some business type that shared the opinion of my brother—there were jobs worth having and jobs for other people. Bartending was the latter.

But I loved bartending. More, I loved the club. I'd only started my graduate work because I needed more to do. Something to keep me "occupied" was what Brian had said when he offered to pay for my expenses beyond what my scholarship and financial aid covered.

It was a good decision—the right decision since it essentially stopped my life from spiraling out of control. For the past three years I'd thrown my life into school and the nightclub. Problem was that graduation took most of my preoccupation away. And now bogged down with student loans, I had to figure out how to make ends meet without having to leave The Sky Launch.

But I had a plan. I wanted a promotion. I'd been helping with supervisory duties for the last year, but had been unable to get an official title since managers had to work full-time. Now that school was over, I was available for more hours. David had been grooming me for the position. The only wrinkle in my trajectory could be a new owner. But I wasn't going to worry about that. Yet.

Explaining my intent to strangers was never easy, though. How wise was it to use an MBA from Stern for a career in nightclub management? Probably not wise at all. So I swallowed before answering the suit. "Actually, I'd like to move up here. I love the nightclub scene."

To my surprise, he nodded, his eyes shimmering as he sat forward into the bright white light of the bar. "It makes you alive."

"Exactly." I couldn't keep back my smile. How had he known?

"It shows."

Hot, rich, and in tune with me. He was precisely the kind of man that I could obsess over, and not in the healthy way.

"Laynie!" The shout of the Regular from earlier drew me away from the intense gray eyes of the stranger. "I'm out of here. Wanted to say congrats again and good luck. And, hey, here's my number. Give me a call sometime. I can help you occupy your week off."

"Thanks, uh," I read the name he'd written on the napkin he'd handed me, "Matt." I waited until he'd walked away before tossing it in the trash under the counter, catching the suit's eye as I did so.

"Do you do that with every number you receive?"

I paused. It wasn't like I hadn't hooked up with customers before, but never with regulars. That was a rule. I didn't want to see them again. Too much temptation to go crazy over them.

But I had no interest in having that conversation with the suit. And with his eyes constantly on me, I finally believed that my attraction to him wasn't one-sided. Not when he'd tipped me so generously. "Are you trying to figure out if I'd throw away your number?"

He laughed. "Maybe."

His reaction made me smile and made the moisture between my thighs thicken. He was fun to flirt with. Too bad I had to end it. I placed my hands on the counter and leaned toward him so he could hear me better over the music, trying not to delight in the searing look he gave my bosom as I did so. "I wouldn't throw yours away. I wouldn't take yours at all."

His eyes narrowed, but the laughter from earlier still danced in them. "Not your type?"

"Not necessarily." Pretending I wasn't attracted to him was futile. He had to be aware of my reaction to him.

"Why then?"

"Because you're looking for something temporary. Something fun to play with." I leaned even closer to deliver my punch line—the one that would deter even the horniest of men. "And I get attached." I stood back up to my full height so I could take in his reaction. "Now doesn't that just scare you shitless?"

I'd expected to see panic flash through his face. Instead, I saw a flicker of amusement. "You, Alayna Withers, do anything but scare me." But despite his words, he stood, buttoning his suit coat as he did. "Congratulations again. Quite an accomplishment."

I watched him for far too long as he walked away, more crestfallen about his abrupt departure than I wanted to admit.

It took me a good five minutes after he left to realize I'd never given him my name.

— CHAPTER —
TWO

"Have you met the new owner yet?"

I glanced up from my clipboard at Liesl's backside as she studied the contents of the small fridge behind the bar, her cascading purple hair dancing with her movements. My brow furrowed. I hadn't forgotten about the new owner but had tried not to think about him, knowing I'd obsess.

Irritation at being reminded of him now filled my response. "When would I have met him?" I hadn't been at the nightclub since my graduation more than a week before.

Liesl closed the door to the fridge and shrugged. "I don't know. You could have stopped by or something."

She knew me too well. I'd stopped myself several times that past week from wandering over. It had been a battle, but I'd stayed away. "Nope. Actually, I spent most of the week at a spa near Poughkeepsie."

"Well, la de da!" Liesl raised a studded eyebrow. "Did you win the lotto when I wasn't looking?"

"Hardly. It was a gift from Brian." He hadn't bothered with a card, just an envelope containing the train ticket and voucher for the resort delivered to me by my doorman the morning of my graduation. It was thoughtful. And so very unlike my brother. Maybe it had been his wife's idea.

"How...nice." Liesl detested Brian and never bothered to hide it. One of the few people in my life who knew my history, she was fiercely loyal and always on my side. My brother, not so much. That automatically put them at odds.

"Don't sound so shitty. It *was* nice. I did a bunch of crap I'd never done before—horseback riding, rock climbing. Tons of spa treatments—feel my skin!" I held out my hand for her to feel. "My hands have never been this soft."

"You're not kidding. Baby smooth."

"It was good for me. Really. Exactly what I needed. Relaxing but still kept me preoccupied."

"Wow. Score one for Brian. Maybe he's finally growing up." Her voice lightened. "And how was your time not at the spa?"

Miserable. The five days at the spa had been perfect, but after the trip was over, I had to return to my real life, which meant an empty apartment and a mind that refused to stop working. "I'm glad to be back, if that's what you're asking. And I may have four or five files of new ideas for the club."

She laughed. "Hey, at least that's healthy obsessing."

I smiled sheepishly. "Healthyish." I searched for the Skyy Vodka that my report said should be on the shelf and marked its presence on my paper when I found it. There were benefits to an active mind. I always had perfect inventories and flawless presentations. It was in relating with people—men, to be precise—that obsessing had its disadvantage.

I leaned against the back counter and checked my watch. Fifteen minutes until opening. That meant fifteen more minutes before the lights went down and into club mode. The club with all the lights on made me vulnerable and bare and out-of-place. Even Liesl's sassy gossipy personality was muted as if someone had turned down her volume. We'd never have this conversation in club mode.

My eyes traveled across the bar, lingering on the spot the suit had sat in the last time I'd worked. It wasn't the first time I'd thought of him since that night. He'd known my name. Had he overheard it? Not my last name. He must have asked someone, although I hadn't seen him talking to anyone else. But maybe before I'd taken his order...I hadn't been paying attention to him. Maybe someone had told him then.

"Whatcha thinking?" Liesl cut through my thoughts, mimicking my lean against the counter.

I shrugged. She'd freak if I told her some random guy knew my name, assume that my safety was at risk. I, on the other hand, had distinct empathy for people who had the need to gather more information than they should. And I didn't want a lecture on would-be stalkers. I knew all about stalking.

But I could tell her other things about the mysterious stranger. "Last time I worked, this guy—" I paused, remembering how magnetically attractive the suit had been. "This incredibly hot guy, actually—gave me a hundred dollars for three fingers of Macallan. Told me to keep the change."

"And did he expect you to blow him after your shift?"

"No. I thought that was what he was about, but..." What had he wanted? He'd seemed so into me, or had I imagined that, swayed by my own intense desire for him? "I don't know. He left without trying anything." I'd meant to scare him off, but that hadn't seemed to be the reason he left. "It was...odd."

"Midnight masturbation material?"

"I'll never tell."

"Your face says it all."

Over the past week, he *had* entered my thoughts, wearing decidedly less than he had when I'd seen him at the bar. And while sexual fantasies were innocent enough for most people, thinking too much about any guy was never good for me and Liesl knew it. But I didn't need her lecture. As long as I didn't see him again—and chances were slim that I would—I'd be fine.

I moved to straightening things on the counter that didn't need to be straightened and changed the subject. "So the new owner...you've met him? What's he like?"

Liesl shrugged. "He's all right. Younger than you'd imagine. Like, twenty-seven or twenty-eight. Fucking rich. He's insane about clean-up, though. We've been calling him the Bar Nazi. He inspects everything, wiping his finger on the counters to make sure they're clean, like he's got OCD or something. Oh, and talk about masturbation material, he's psychotically hot."

Liesl thought any guy with a fat wallet who still had his hair was hot, so her statement didn't say much. But the Bar Nazi remark made me smile. The staff had been lax on cleaning standards for some time and could do with some tough love. At least, that's what I'd say if I were a manager. It gave me hope that the new owner and I might get along just fine.

I wondered about the man who finally ponied up the unreasonable asking price for the club. Not that The Sky Launch couldn't be worth it, but it needed some serious overhaul to stand out in the sea of New York City clubs. Would the new owner see the place's potential? How hands-on would he be? Would he leave the business under David's control?

"You'll meet him tonight." Liesl ran her barbell across her lower lip. "I guess he's a big deal in the business world. You've probably heard of him—Houston Piers or something like that."

My jaw dropped. "Do you mean Hudson Pierce?" I waited while she nodded. "Liesl, Hudson Pierce is only the most successful business man under thirty in America. He's like a god in that world." Hudson had been born into wealth with modern day Rockefellers for parents. The eldest son, he'd expanded the Pierce wealth tenfold. As a business student I'd been intrigued with a number of his dealings.

"You know I'm not into all that Who's Who bullshit." Liesl straightened to her full five-foot-ten plus three-inch heels height. "Though I wouldn't be surprised if he's on the Top Ten of, like, every Hottest-slash-Sexiest-slash-Most-Beautiful list in the world."

I bit my lip trying to conjure up an image of him in my head. I'd probably seen a picture of him somewhere, but I couldn't for the life of me remember what he looked like. I generally didn't pay attention to those things. But something tugged at the edges of my brain, something I couldn't quite grasp. A connection my mind was failing to make.

"Anyway," Liesl said, leaning back against the counter, "I think he's around. I saw him go into the offices earlier when you were grabbing napkins from storage."

I nodded, not sure if I was thrilled to meet Hudson Pierce or not. Part of me wanted to fan girl all over one or two of his more famous corporate decisions. And bouncing ideas off of him could be thrilling.

Or terrifying. What if I had nothing to suggest that he hadn't already thought of? Hudson Pierce didn't need my lame ideas to help him make the club thrive.

Unless he wasn't planning to be involved with the business.

But why would he buy the club if he didn't intend on being involved? In which case…

Crap. Before my visions of the future I desired went poof in my overactive imagination, I needed to meet Pierce and feel him out, whether I was intimidated or not.

I took several inconspicuous calming breaths then returned my focus to stocking the bar. Concentrating on my task, I pulsed absentmindedly to the techno strains that streamed over the sound system and let go of all my worries.

The music wasn't on normal business volume—we could talk comfortably without raising our voices—but it was loud enough that I didn't hear the office door open to the left of the bar. That's why I didn't notice Hudson at first. My back was to him and my gaze fixed above me as I reached for the Tequila Gold on the upper bar shelf. Even after I'd retrieved the bottle and turned around, my eyes first found David's. He scanned me from head to toe and I smiled, pleased that my tightly fitted corset hadn't gone unnoticed. He was the reason I'd worn the damn thing. I could barely breathe under its vice-like grip. But for the searing look he gave me, it was worth it, heating me to low simmer in the arousal department.

Then I met Hudson's stare and two things happened simultaneously. First, my arousal went full boil. Second, my brain finally made the connection it had missed before. Hudson Pierce was the suit.

Without meaning to, I scanned his body. The full view of him was even hotter, especially in the better lighting. Again he wore a suit, two-piece this time, a light gray that I'd almost call silver. It fit his lean body in such a sexual way that it felt obscene to look at him.

When my eyes made it to his face—his strong jaw, even more pronounced than I'd remembered, begging to be licked and kissed and nibbled—I found he was checking me out as well. The knowledge of this made my already warm face flush deeper. Though his gaze wasn't as intense as it had been when I'd first met him, his pull was just as strong, and I knew—absolutely unequivocally *knew*—that he desired me as much as I desired him.

David spoke first, his words coming at me through a haze, barely registering. "This is Laynie." I suspected his eyes hadn't left my bosom. "Um, Alayna Withers, I mean." Normally I'd be ecstatic that I had him so mixed-up and that his pants were visibly straining, but I was thrown by the new owner. More precisely, by how insanely he affected me.

"Hudson Pierce." Hudson's smooth, low murmur had me clenching my thighs together, my panties pooling with moisture. And if I thought he'd claimed me with his eyes the night we'd met, the surge that ran through me as he shook my hand deepened his possession. Almost like an invisible handcuff reaching out to bind me to him permanently. "Good to meet you properly, Ms. Withers."

"Alayna," I corrected, surprised at the low ache in my voice. "Or Laynie."

He dropped my hand, but his touch lingered on my skin, in my veins.

Pieces began to fit together. That was how he'd known my name. He'd probably come that night to check out his would-be staff. But that didn't explain his possessive staring. Maybe he was the type to think of women as objects. Maybe he took the definition of *owner* to a whole other level. The thought made my skin pebble in goose bumps.

And underneath that, panic crept into my gut.

I could not be this twisted up over my boss, the head honcho, the guy who would determine my fate at the club. Freaking out over him would end in serious consequences.

I placed a hand loosely over my belly, encouraging a deep diaphragmatic breath to calm my growing anxiety.

Hudson tilted his head and studied me. "I've heard many things about you. And witnessed your work." He paused, moving his gaze up and down my body once more, scorching my skin as he did. "But none of what I heard or saw prepared me to find you wearing this ensemble."

The color drained from my face. I wasn't sure where he was going with his statement, but from his tone, I felt chided. "Excuse me?"

"I would think a graduate of Stern looking for a career in management would be more appropriately dressed."

As quickly as I paled before, now I flushed, equal parts embarrassed and enraged. Sure my top was revealing, but he hadn't seemed to mind when he ogled me only a moment before.

Or maybe his ogling had merely been wishful thinking.

Shit. I'd imagined it all, hadn't I? That whole knowing he desired me—god, how had I so completely misread him?

Even in my error, I couldn't take his criticism without responding. Whether Hudson owned other nightclubs or not, I had no clue, but he was certainly wrong about what acceptable attire was. Eye candy was expected at a club. Hot girls drove in customers. "What I'm wearing is quite appropriate for a club staff."

"Not for someone working toward manager."

"Yes, even managers. Sex sells, Mr. Pierce."

"Not at an elite club. Not at the kind of club I intend to run." His authoritative tone resonated through my head, but then he lowered his volume and the words resonated through my bones. "You must know that women have a difficult time in the business world. You need to work to be taken seriously, Alayna. Dress sexy, not like a floozy."

I clenched my jaw shut. Normally I'm the type to argue well past the point of winning or losing—I'd had several heated debates in more than one of my graduate classes—but now I found myself flustered and at a loss for words. Hudson was right. I had ideas for the club—ideas that required people to trust my business savvy. I'd learned at Stern what it took to impress people and, to my credit, I'd hesitated when I'd purchased the corset, wondering if the open middle that revealed my midriff from the insides of my breasts to my belly button was *too* revealing. His words validated that fear.

Worse, I realized that what I'd thought was desire was something so much different. He wasn't claiming me, he was judging me.

My stomach dropped. There went any chance at promotion. How could I have been so stupid? Dressing for a guy instead of my career? *Stupid, stupid, stupid!*

I looked to David and discovered he was equally petrified at the transaction. "Um, yeah, Laynie," he said, attempting to recover. "Is that new?"

It didn't matter what David said. The glimmer in his eyes told me he appreciated my outfit. But he was with his new boss. He had to keep it professional.

And truthfully, I cared more about Hudson's opinion at the moment than David's. David was a category one attraction, after all. The kind of guy I didn't emotionally invest in. Hudson, on the other hand, was...

No, I wouldn't think about him like that.

I ran my tongue across my dry lips. "It is new." I hoped I didn't sound as ashamed as I felt. "I apologize. I misjudged." I also sort of hated Hudson Pierce. Even though he was in the right. He was an asshole with wandering eyes, just like all the other suits I'd ever met.

"I've got that lace pullover in my locker," Liesl offered. "It should tame you."

"Thanks. I'll take it."

Liesl whispered in my ear as she brushed past me toward the staff break room. "Though, if you ask me, you look damn fine!"

"Now that that's taken care of..." Hudson turned his attention to David. "I've changed my mind about returning this weekend." David visibly relaxed. But Hudson's next statement had him stiffening again. "I'll be back tomorrow. I can't be here until nine. Could you spare time for me then?"

I fiddled with the napkin holders, even though I'd already stocked them, not sure if I was supposed to be part of the conversation or if I should get back to my duties.

"Of course," David said, even though nine was when the club opened and wasn't really a convenient time to have a meeting.

"Good." Hudson turned to me and I froze mid-napkin shuffle. "Alayna, you'll be here as well."

Still ruffled from my disastrous mistake, I was uneager to accept the invitation—the demand, rather. But I'd have to get over my rough start if I expected to continue working with him. Not even sure he expected a response, I gave one anyway. "Yes, sir."

Hudson narrowed his eyes, so I couldn't be certain, but they seemed to have dilated. He scrutinized me as if deciding something—whether to fire me, maybe, or give me another shot. After several painful seconds, he simply nodded. "Tomorrow." Then he turned to leave.

David and I watched in silence as Hudson walked toward the club doors. At least, I watched, too distracted by the hint of tight rear end under the bottom of his suit jacket to notice what David was doing. Damn, Hudson looked just as good from the rear as from the front. If he was going to be in the club a lot I was going to have to start wearing panty liners.

The minute Hudson's gorgeous backside disappeared into the entrance area, David let out a sigh, reminding me of his presence.

I stared at him, wide eyed. "What the fuck?"

David chuckled. "I have no idea. I've only met with Pierce once before today and we haven't gotten much into anything besides me explaining our current business operations. He's certainly odd, though."

"Well, what do you expect, growing up with all that wealth and pressure to succeed?" Why the hell was I defending him? The man made me feel anxious and intimidated and humiliated. And maybe a little bit excited. Oh, and horny as all get out. I wasn't even going to acknowledge the fixation I knew I would have on him if I didn't get myself under control.

I took a deep breath, hoping to release the strange knot in my stomach that thinking about Hudson created. "I don't know what I'm saying. I guess we'll just have to wait and see."

"Don't worry, Laynie."

Remembering he was the one I was almost sort of dating, I met David's blue eyes, straining to recapture the certainty that he was perfect for me.

Misinterpreting my anxiety to be about my job, he continued. "Pierce has too many high profile assets. He won't want to spend too much of his time on the club. I'm sure he'll let things run pretty much as is with maybe some minor finessing. And as long as I have a say in it, you'll have a more significant role."

David grinned, more at my chest than at my face. "Want to stay and help close tonight?"

His playful change of attitude provided the assurance I needed. "I was counting on it."

AT FOUR A.M. the club shut down for the night, and David and I worked quickly and efficiently, splitting the managerial duties between us. When all the drawers had been counted and the money dropped in the safe, he dismissed the rest of the staff and sat behind his desk to finish up the reports. I perched on the desktop and swung my feet as I watched him work.

David glanced over at me and smiled before returning to his monitor. "Thank god you were behind the counter earlier. Who knows what else Hudson would have said about your outfit if he'd seen those pants?"

I glanced down at the black slinky pants that were so tight they gave me camel toe. They made me feel sexy, and for some reason that made me think of Hudson's dark expression when he'd first laid eyes on me. The expression I'd since convinced myself was imagined.

"Great. Now you're telling me I have to throw these out too?"

"Well, just don't wear them while you're working." He stood so he could reach the printer on the corner of the desk behind me. "For the record," he said as his arm brushed my waist. "I don't disapprove of this outfit in the slightest."

I, on the other hand, wanted to burn the whole ensemble. It had caused me nothing but trouble all night—drunk patrons thinking they could touch me and say things to me that they otherwise wouldn't.

But I'd worn it for David—for the moment when we'd be alone. This was it.

I put on a fake pout. "Too bad your opinion isn't the one that matters."

David leaned in close. "My opinion doesn't matter?"

"Actually," I said, grabbing his jacket by the lapels, "your opinion matters very much."

His voice lowered. "Then I think you look sexy as hell."

He covered his mouth with mine, plunging his tongue deep inside. I wrapped my arms around his neck and darted my own tongue between his lips. The arousal that had been ignited by the heated stare of Hudson Pierce hours earlier had remained just at bay throughout the night. Now it returned full force with David's kiss.

I moved my hands along his torso and downward to his pants. But when I began to fumble with his buckle, he pulled away.

I opened my eyes and startled. For a moment I'd expected to see the gray eyes of Hudson staring back at me instead of David's dull blue. What was wrong with me? Man, that Hudson could mess with a girl's mojo.

David caressed my shoulder. "We need to stop this, Laynie."

I blinked. "What do you mean? Why?"

"Look, I like you. I really like you. But..." He appeared to be struggling with himself. He dropped his arm from my shoulder. "If you're serious about getting the management position, do you really think we should be messing around? How would that look? I'm sure that Pierce wouldn't approve."

I hadn't thought about it quite like that. In my fantasies, David Lindt and Alayna Withers-Lindt ran The Sky Launch as a couple, driving the club to new and unbelievable success. The fantasy had never included a part where the rest of the staff and the club owner accused me of sleeping my way to the top.

"We could keep it secret," I said softly, not willing to let go of a vital part of my dream. Not willing to lose my safety net.

"It doesn't have to be forever. But for now, especially when I'm not sure what Pierce's plans are for me or for the club. I think we need to take a break."

"Sure." I forced a smile. I didn't want him to realize the extent of my disappointment. We hadn't even been dating. We'd barely been fooling around. Why did I feel so crushed?

I thought about what had drawn me to David in the first place. He wasn't the smartest guy I knew and not the hottest. I didn't even really know him all that well. And it wasn't as if I didn't have other options. I was an attractive girl working at an elite nightclub—I'd had plenty of opportunities for sex in the city. Yummy opportunities. Not anyone as yummy as Hudson Pierce, but yummy nonetheless.

I shook my head as I hopped off David's desk. Why did my thoughts keep leading back to Hudson? Even in the middle of a sorta-not-at-all break-up, I was thinking of him. And Hudson was exactly the kind of guy I shouldn't be thinking about. At all. Ever. Not if I wanted to maintain the modicum of control I'd managed to acquire in the past few years.

"Are you okay, Laynie?" David's voice brought me back to the present awkwardness.

Damn it. I'd been so sure of a relationship with David that I'd pictured us sending Christmas cards together. Okay, maybe I'd fixated on him more than I wanted to admit, but not so intently that I was going to wig out about ending it. The biggest bitch of the whole situation was that now I didn't have a safe guy to hide behind. Now I was vulnerable to notice other not-so-safe men. Men like Hudson.

Oh, god, was this the beginning of an obsessive episode?

No, I'd be fine. I had to focus on my promotion. I was stronger than this.

"Yeah. I'm fine. If you're almost done, I'm going to get changed."

David nodded. I hurried to the staff break room across the hall. Stripping out of my corset and tight pants, I changed into sweat shorts and a sports bra, stuffing the troublesome outfit into my duffel bag. Since there wasn't a straight subway line from Columbus Circle to my apartment at Lexington and Fiftieth, I usually ran it. Sometimes after a long shift I'd take the bus or cab, but with all the stressors of the night, I needed the cardio to direct my focus.

Fifteen minutes later, I hit the pavement, taking in the fresh morning air with the rest of NYC's early morning joggers. I loved the feeling of unity it gave me, even though most of the other runners were starting their day, not ending it as I was.

Quickly, I got into my groove, running along the south border of Central Park, but the steady rhythm of my body wasn't enough to drown the thoughts of David and my future at The Sky Launch. Wasn't enough to drown my thoughts of the gorgeous new owner who had demanded I meet with him later that night. Worry set in again. Was Hudson planning to fire me? Or did I still have a shot at promotion?

One thing was certain—I'd be a lot more thoughtful about my choice of wardrobe in the future.

— CHAPTER —
THREE

I took a cab to the club that evening, which had been a mistake. Unusual traffic had me arriving at three after nine. I hurried toward the office but was stopped at the upstairs bar by Liesl.

"David and hot owner boy are already in there," she said over the club music, playing with a strand of purple hair. "Hudson told me to have you wait here. He'll let you know when he wants you."

"Dammit! I'm not that late, am I?"

"No, they went in there about ten minutes ago. They have no idea what time you got here."

I relaxed, thankful that my exclusion from the meeting wasn't because I'd been tardy. I hopped onto a bar stool nearest the office and set my computer bag on the floor at my feet.

"Hold on, Laynie," Liesl said coming around the bar. "Let me see you."

I stood up again and turned around, displaying my bodycon dress. I'd picked it because the white tie color had a business style to it, but the tight black skirt said nightclub instead of office secretary.

"Fuck, girl, you look good!" Liesl's validation calmed me more than she could ever know. Or maybe she did know. She was a good friend.

"Thanks. I needed that. Especially after Mr. Disapproval last night."

"He is now known as the Bar and Wardrobe Nazi."

I laughed and hopped back onto my stool. The same stool Hudson had sat on the first time I saw him. "Hey, you know he's the suit I was telling you about, the one who gave me the hundred."

"You're shitting me!"

"I'm not. Do you think he wants me to blow him to get the promotion?"

"Would it be that bad if he did?"

"Yes. It would be utterly, wonderfully, horrible." But mostly it was horrible how not bad that idea sounded.

While trying to empty my mind of Hudson blowjob images, I surveyed the club. The place was slow, even for a Wednesday night. From the bar, I had full view of the ten bubble rooms that circled the perimeter of the upper level. The bubble rooms were The Sky Launch's highlight. Each room, round in shape, featured a glass wall overlooking the dance floor on the lower level, and had private access much like box seats at a stadium. They all had a curved seating area around a table, and fit eight people comfortably. The bubbles provided a relatively quiet and discreet area while still being very much part of the club. When the occupied lights were on, the outer walls of the bubble rooms glowed red. Only two were lit up. A shame. If the club had the kind of notoriety it could have, those rooms would fill within the first ten minutes of being open.

"God, I hope it picks up," Liesl said, draping her torso across the counter next to me. "I can't make it through a full shift at this pace. It's so boring!"

"I hope so, too." We should have been busting with the summer crowd by now. The lack of business made me feel more confident about my ideas for the club. I fidgeted, anxious to get in the office and share them with my bosses.

"What did you do today?" Liesl asked.

"I worked on a PowerPoint presentation all morning. I crashed about two."

Liesl narrowed her eyes. "You need more sleep than that, Laynie."

"Nah. Five hours is plenty." I actually felt pretty good. Gathering the best of my thoughts for The Sky Launch into a presentation had been very therapeutic, easing my concerns about my future at the club. Hudson couldn't fire me after he saw how much time and effort I'd put into the business, could he? Not if my ideas were good, and I knew they were.

I pulled my phone out of my bra cup where I kept it—no pockets in my skin-tight dress—and checked the time. It was almost nine-thirty. How long would they keep me waiting?

They walked out minutes later. I stood the moment I saw them, smoothing my dress down and looked to Hudson, eager for a sign of approval.

But the expression that met me took my breath away—an expression of total male power and dominance. Even in the dark of the club, I could make out his eyes as they perused me—the way he did every time we saw each other. Again I felt claimed by his overwhelming magnetism, my heart racing just at the sight of him. My legs turned to jelly and my knees buckled, tipping me forward.

Into his arms.

He caught me with a graceful ease that contradicted the solid body that held me steady. My hands clenched his dress shirt—how did my hands get under his jacket?—and I resisted the urge to run them across the firm pecs I felt under my grasp.

He mistook my motion, seeming to think I was searching for further stability. "Alayna," his voice flowed over me like liquid sex. "I've got you."

I've got you. Boy, did he.

"Laynie, are you okay?" David peered at me over Hudson's shoulder. Did he have to ask? Couldn't he see that I was drowning in lust?

"Yeah," I managed. "I'm, um, new shoes."

Hudson glanced down at my strappy rhinestone embellished sandals. "They're lovely." His voice came out so deep it rumbled and my belly knotted with the sound.

"Uh, thanks." I was breathless. And embarrassed when I realized I was still in Hudson's arms. I eased my grip and pushed myself into a standing position.

"Sorry we kept you waiting." Hudson's hands lingered on me until I was steady. "I had a few things to discuss with David privately."

"No problem." I still felt the burn of Hudson's hands on my bare skin. For distraction, I dove into business discussions. "I have so many ideas I'd like to share about the club. I put them into a presentation. I brought my laptop."

Hudson's lips curled with a hint of amusement. "How thoughtful. Set up a time with David. I'm sure he's very interested."

How thoughtful. As if I'd done something cute. Something only big boys did. How fucking patronizing.

My heart plummeted. I really shouldn't have been so disappointed. It wasn't as if I'd been asked to prepare anything. That had been my own hyper-focusing. In fact, I hadn't even known why I'd been invited to the meeting. Especially now that it was apparently over and I hadn't even been in on it.

"How about tomorrow, Laynie?" David suggested. "You're opening anyway. Why not come early? Does six-thirty give you enough time to present?"

"Yeah. I'll leave my laptop here if you don't mind." I bent to pick up my bag, but Hudson reached it before I did.

He handed it to David. "David, could you lock this in the office? I need to eat something. Alayna will join me. I've reserved one of the bubbles." His eyes narrowed as he surveyed the empty rooms. "Though it doesn't seem a reservation was required."

I tensed at Hudson's latest demand. Why wasn't David joining us? Did Hudson plan on firing me over pecan-crusted salmon? Was that what they had discussed privately?

Or maybe Hudson's interest in me was less business and more pleasure. The looks he'd given me had suggested it was, and after receiving the same expression on several occasions, I realized I may not have imagined it like I kept trying to convince myself I had.

And that was a scarier thought than being fired. Especially when I'd already felt a tug of fixation. I'd been so stable for the past three years—I couldn't open myself to get all obsessive over my hot boss. That was a disaster waiting to happen. I definitely should say no to the bubble room.

Except I hadn't given up on my promotion. And because there was a slight possibility that Hudson wanted to talk to me about that, I had to say yes to dinner, though my acquiescence hardly seemed necessary since he'd had his hand pressed against the small of my back directing me to one of the more private bubbles before I'd even agreed to join him. My body tensed under his touch, and my stomach twisted in a nervous knot that wasn't exactly unpleasant.

And I was very aware of the eyes that followed us, few as there were in the club, sure that many of them flashed with envy. Alone in a bubble room with Hudson Pierce? All the women in Manhattan should be jealous. Kinky things had been known to happen in those bubbles. I smiled at the possibilities.

Goddammit. What the hell was I thinking? The guy had invited me to dinner, not to his bed. Just because I was all gaga over him, reading sex into his every move, didn't mean he reciprocated. And the gaga needed to stop once and for all, even if he did reciprocate.

Inside the room, I turned on the occupied light out of habit. Usually a hostess would have done that when they seated the customer, but since we'd sort of skipped the whole hostess formality, I took it upon myself. And I had to do something with my nervous energy. Continuing the job, I grabbed a menu from the wall and handed it to Hudson who stood waiting at the edge of the seating.

He took the menu from me and gestured for me to sit. "After you."

It had been quite some time since I'd been in a bubble room off-duty and the reversal in my role combined with the "Fuck Me" aura that surrounded Hudson unbalanced me. I slid onto the plush cushion, gripping the table for support.

Hudson stayed standing, watching me intently for several seconds before he removed his gray suit jacket and hung it on the hook behind him. Damn. He was even hotter in only his fitted gray dress shirt. I bit the inside of my cheek, admiring his hard thighs straining against his pants' fabric as he sat down. God, he was so yummy.

God, I was in trouble.

He tossed the laminated menu on the table without looking at it. "I don't need this. Do you?"

"No, thank you, Mr. Pierce." I had the menu memorized. Besides, there was no way I could eat in his presence.

"Hudson," he corrected.

"No, thank you, *Hudson*." His eyes widened slightly when I said his name. "I've already eaten."

"A drink then? Though, I know you work at eleven."

I licked my lips, thinking more about the man sitting across from me than of thirst, wondering what he had in store for me. "Maybe an iced tea."

"Good."

Out of habit, I reached to press the button in the middle of the table to summon the waitress, but he beat me to it, our fingers colliding. I moved to pull my hand away, but he was quicker again, taking my hand into his. I inhaled sharply at the sensation of his skin against mine.

"I didn't mean to startle you. I was admiring your soft skin." But his eyes never left mine.

"Oh." I thought about saying I'd been to an amazing spa, but really, did he care? And besides, talking was difficult with that thing he was doing to my skin, burning it so thoroughly with his caress.

His phone rang and he let go of my hand. I pulled it to my lap, needing the warmth of my body once it'd lost the warmth of his.

"Excuse me," he said, taking his phone out of his pants pocket and silencing it without looking at the screen.

"You can take it if you need to." I could use a few minutes to gather my thoughts. Because, what the hell did he want with me? Not only was not knowing killing me, but the more time I spent with Hudson, the easier it was for me to think about him and his amazing gray eyes. And his hard body. And his smooth voice.

"There can't be anything important enough to interrupt this conversation."

And even smoother lines.

I opened my mouth to say something, but was interrupted by the door opening. Sasha entered with a tray of food and drinks. I watched as she set down a plate of sea bass and a glass of Sancerre in front of Hudson and a glass of iced tea in front of me. Hudson must have preordered, but how did he know I'd get iced tea?

He must have sensed my question. "I asked Liesl what you usually drank. If you had said you wanted something different, I wouldn't look quite so cool at this moment."

That earned him a smile. Whatever his game was, he was working for it. "Hmm, cool is not quite the word I'd use for you." Hot, blazing, volcanic. All of those words were much more appropriate.

"What word would you use for me then?"

I blushed and delayed answering by taking a swallow of my tea.

Thankfully, Sasha spoke at that moment. "Anything else, Mr. Pierce?" I raised my brow. Would he invite her to call him Hudson as well?

"We're good."

Nope. No first name basis for Sasha. Only me. Well, didn't that have liquid pooling between my thighs?

The door had just shut behind Sasha when Hudson asked again. "What word would you use for me, Alayna?"

The way my name sounded in his sensual voice brought goose bumps to my skin. "Controlled," I said, without hesitation.

"Interesting." He took a bite of his bass and I watched, hypnotized by the way his mouth curved around the fork. "Not that controlled isn't an accurate description of me. But I had thought from the look on your face that you would say something else."

I began to ask what he had expected me to say, but I wasn't certain I wanted to walk through that door he'd opened. He didn't press it, spending the next few minutes eating in silence.

Wanting to let him eat, I turned my body to look at the club below me. Even with my eyes averted, I felt Hudson's presence hanging on me like a cloak. I wondered about the man sitting across from me. Why had he bought The Sky Launch? What did he want from me? And the most intriguing question, how did I feel about this domineering male who bossed me and chastised me and made me want to climb on to his lap and rub against him like a kitten? Yeah, he was good-looking, but did I *like* him? Or was he just another rich pompous ass that I was inexplicably drawn to?

"I know why you agreed to dine with me, Alayna."

I turned back to face him and stilled, wondering where he was possibly going. First of all, I hadn't actually agreed to dine with him, if that's what this was. He'd sort of led me there. Secondly, many of the reasons I hadn't fought against coming with him would be embarrassing if he voiced them. They were numerous: to find out his plans for the club, to get a promotion, to make David jealous. To get in Hudson's pants.

No, not to get in his pants. That could not be on my list of reasons. Could. Not.

Hudson took a swallow of his wine, then wiped his perfectly formed lips with his napkin. "I have to be honest with you. I don't intend to help you with your desire to make management."

I fidgeted, not knowing if I should relax or be disappointed. On the one hand, that was probably the least humiliating reason he could have mentioned for me dining with him. On the other hand, there went my promotion.

"That doesn't mean you won't be promoted." Did Hudson have some sort of mind-reading capability? It would explain how he did so well in the business world. "David said you're quite capable, and I'm sure you'll get the position without my help. I may own The Sky Launch, but I am not your boss. David is your boss and will continue to be unless the business no longer thrives under his command."

Well, then. I could live with that. David had all but guaranteed me a place in management. Plan back on track. And it likely meant that Hudson wasn't planning on spending a lot of time around the club. I might have sighed audibly.

Hudson leaned back against the couch, draping his arm across the top. "But I didn't invite you here to discuss the club."

Finally. I swallowed. "Why did you invite me?"

A hint of amusement crossed Hudson's face. "Perhaps I like you."

I shuddered as a thrill traveled up my spine. But I didn't trust that he was merely trying to pick me up. He was taking too long to make his play, and that would never be Hudson's style. There was more.

God, I hoped there was more. If he was just trying to pick me up, what the hell was I going to say?

I took a sip of my iced tea, wishing it were something stronger. When I lowered my glass, I said, "Perhaps I'm seeing someone."

"You aren't. No man would let his woman wear the outfit you wore yesterday. Not in public, anyway."

The mention of the outfit I'd nicknamed trouble and the idea that any man would *let* me do anything ruffled my feathers. "Perhaps I'm not into controlling boyfriends."

His mouth twitched slightly. "Very well, Alayna." He cocked a brow. "Are you seeing anyone?"

Of course I wasn't seeing anyone, damn it. I looked at my lap, my expression telling Hudson all he needed to know. Why did this man make me so flustered? I was a confident, well-spoken woman on a normal day. But not around him.

I sat straighter, attempting to find some semblance of sure footing. "That isn't why you invited me, Hudson. You have an agenda."

"An agenda." Hudson made a sound that I think must have been his version of a chuckle. "Yes, Alayna, I have an agenda."

And then, instead of sharing his agenda, he changed the subject. "I presume you enjoyed your time at my spa last week."

Startled by absolutely everything he was saying, I attempted to follow the topic swing. "Oh, I didn't realize you owned…wait…" And the light went on. "The gift was from you?"

"Yes. Did you have a nice time?"

"No. Way." I'm pretty sure my jaw dropped. Actually, physically, literally dropped.

"No way?"

Realizing my remark hadn't expressed what I meant it to express, I tried again. "I mean, yes, I had a nice time—a wonderful time, in fact—but no way could you have done that. Why did you do that? You shouldn't have done that."

"Why ever not?"

A whole range of reasons ran through my head, number one being because it was creepy and psychotic. But I had been called both of those things many times and would not throw them easily at another person. I grabbed for the next reason. "Because that's big!"

"Not for me."

"But for me it is." How could he not understand? The vastness of it built in me like champagne bubbles in a newly uncorked bottle. "It's huge! And you don't even know me! It's completely inappropriate and unprofessional and unprecedented and inappropriate. And if I'd known it was from you, I never would have accepted it." This couldn't be only about getting in my pants. I could have been won over by much less, as ashamed as I was to admit that to myself.

Hudson took a deep breath, trying to remain patient. "It's not inappropriate at all. It was simply a gift. Think of it as a golden hello."

My voice was tight as I strained to keep myself from screaming in frustration. "But you don't give gifts like that to women who work for you unless you're running an entirely different kind of club."

"You're overreacting, Alayna."

"I'm not!" Finally his previous statement registered. "And what do you mean a golden hello? You mean, like a signing bonus?" Several of my peers had talked about the bonuses they'd been offered when they'd accepted their six-figure positions after grad school. Cars and stuff like that.

"Yes, Alayna." He tossed his hand in the air. "That's my agenda. I would like to hire you."

He couldn't have startled me more if he'd asked me to strip for him. Or maybe that's what he was asking. What exactly did he want to hire me to do? "I already work for you and I'm happy where I am."

"Again, I don't feel that you do work for me. I am not your boss. I own the establishment that you work for. That is all. Is that clear?"

Semantics. But I understood what he was attempting to do, separating himself from me and my job at The Sky Launch, so I nodded.

"This wouldn't affect your employment at the club." He removed his arm from the couch and sat forward. "Maybe hire is not the correct term. I'd like to pay you to help me with a problem. I believe you'd be perfect for the job."

The whole conversation had my head spinning, but he had my attention. "You win. My curiosity is piqued. What's the job?"

"I need you to break up an engagement."

I coughed, wondering if I heard him correctly, knowing I had. "Um, what? Whose?"

Hudson leaned back, his dazzling gray eyes flickering in the strobe lights. "Mine."

— CHAPTER —
FOUR

Hudson tapped one long finger on the table in front of him. "Close your mouth, Alayna. Although it's quite adorable to see you flabbergasted, it's also very distracting."

I closed my mouth. A million questions circled through my mind, too quickly for any to take shape. And somewhere behind all that, I registered that he'd called me adorable. I needed a drink, something stronger than iced tea. Hudson scooted his Sancerre toward me and I took it, grateful.

The wine gave me back my voice. "I didn't realize you were engaged." I blushed then, remembering all the dirty thoughts I'd had about Hudson and how I'd believed—okay, *hoped*—he had been flirting with me. I took another swallow of wine.

Hudson glanced out the window, maybe hoping to hide the torment that flashed across his face. "I'm not really." He turned back to me, his expression now reserved and emotionless as usual. "That's the problem. Neither Celia nor I are at all interested in the arrangement."

This relaxed me, for some reason. But it did little to clear anything up. "Then why not just break up with her?"

He sighed. "It's not that simple."

I gave Hudson my best dumb-it-down-for-me-dude expression. Apparently, it worked.

"Her parents have been friends with mine for decades. They have a specific plan for their daughter's life and they do not accept her choice to not marry me. If she broke it off, they'd cut her off emotionally and financially. That's not something I wish for my friend."

His explanation prickled me. Were we living in the early twentieth century with arranged marriages and shit? God, rich people lived such strange lives. I picked my words thoughtfully, careful to not show the extent of my irritation. "Never mind that parents shouldn't be controlling their grown daughter, they don't control you. Do they?"

Hudson's eyes blazed. "No. No one controls me."

His emphatic response had my body turned on. That command and authority, it was so...*hot.* I licked my lips, and then delighted as he zeroed in on the action. I hadn't imagined it. He *was* reacting to me. Maybe not as forcefully as I reacted to him, but the energy between us was real.

I crossed my legs attempting to ease the need between them. "I'm missing something."

He nodded. "I suppose you are." He retrieved the Sancerre from in front of me and finished it off in one quick swallow. Knowing we'd shared the glass sent another tingle to my lower regions.

"Alayna, if there is anyone in the world who has any power over me, it's my mother. My mother knows that I am...*incapable*...of love. She worries that I will...end up alone. A marriage with her best friend's daughter, at least, insures that won't happen." His words were measured and even. And just like every time he spoke, he hypnotized me with his voice.

"It would make my mother very happy to see me marry Celia. If it comes to Celia losing her entire life, then I'll willingly enter into a loveless marriage. However, I'd hate to rob her future of happiness she might find with someone else."

I shook my head, confused, overwhelmed, dazzled. "Where would I come in?"

He raised his brows. "Ah, see, if Celia's parents believed I was in love with another woman—"

"They wouldn't want her to marry a man who was in love with someone else."

"Exactly. And my mother would be so thrilled that I'd found someone I was happy with, she'd stop worrying about my future."

The idea of betraying someone who only wanted Hudson to be happy bothered me. But I was also extremely attracted to the sweetness of this hard, virile man in front of me caring enough about his mother and his friend to go to such extreme measures.

I also saw enormous potential for me to be made the enemy in the scenario. "So I'm supposed to be the floozy you're in love with."

His lips curved at the edges. "No one would ever mistake you as a floozy, Alayna. Even when you dress like one."

That damn trouble outfit again. I was burning it when I got home. Mention of it made me suddenly cold and defensive. I crossed my arms over my chest and leaned back—away from Hudson Pierce. "Why don't you hire a real floozy to put on your charade?"

He smirked. "My mother would never believe I'd fall for a floozy. You, however, have particular qualities—qualities that would make the story quite believable."

I didn't want to play this game anymore. My answer was no. But I couldn't help myself from asking, "What sort of qualities?"

His eyes darkened, and I was caught up in them. "You are exquisitely beautiful, Alayna, and also extremely intelligent."

"Oh." I dropped my hands to my lap, stunned. It was a good thing the wine was gone. I'd have slammed it, and I still had a shift to work.

Hudson broke the intense eye contact. "And you're a brunette. All three make you 'my type' so to say."

The absence of his heated stare was both chilling and releasing. I could think again, make coherent sentences. But I also wanted it back with a fierceness I couldn't explain.

"I sense your hesitation, Alayna, and I understand. Perhaps this would be a good time to discuss payment." I admired how he could move from moments of magnitude to straight business with such fluid ease. Me, I had whiplash. I didn't even have time to wonder what someone got paid to fake a romance before he continued. "I understand you have a substantial amount of student loans. I'd like to rid you of that debt."

I laughed. "That's way too much, Hudson." He had no idea how much I'd needed to get through school. No idea how heavy of a burden they were on me now.

"Not to me."

"It is for me." I sat forward, challenging him. "It's eighty thousand dollars."

"Eighty four thousand two hundred and six, to be exact."

I froze. How did he know that?

As he often did, he answered my unasked question. "I own the bank that holds your loans. I looked them up today. It would be very easy for me to have them written off. No actual money would exchange hands, if that makes you feel better."

"That's an awfully generous payment." Too generous. And just like I jumped to buy a lottery ticket whenever the pot got particularly high, I wanted to jump on his offer. But nothing that paid that well ended in good.

"It's worth it to me to see this project succeed, Alayna."

My answer was no. I'd already decided. It had to be no. There was too much risk at entering into an arrangement—any arrangement—with him.

But I couldn't help but want to know more of the details. "What exactly would you want me to do?"

"Pretend we're a couple. I'd invite you to several gatherings where my mother would see us together. I'd expect you to hang on my arm and behave as though we're madly in love."

"And that's all?" I couldn't imagine it would be that hard to pretend to be in love with Hudson. And that was the problem with the whole damn thing. Pretending to be in love with someone who already affected me so intensely was a big fat trigger for obsessing.

"That's all." His shoulders had visibly relaxed. He thought I was taking him seriously, that I was considering his ridiculous idea, and I almost wondered if I actually should.

I swallowed. For eighty thousand dollars there had to be more he expected. Since he wouldn't spell it out, I tiptoed around the topic myself. "This pretend relationship—to what extent would I be expected to perform?"

"Don't pussy foot about it. You're asking about sex." His eyes darkened again. "I never pay for sex, Alayna. When I fuck you, it will be for free."

There it was, the promise that I'd both longed for and feared. His stark declaration had me squirming in my seat. I had never been so aroused and so confused all at once. We were at my work, for Christ's sake! I had to start my shift in less than half an hour, and all I wanted to do was respond to his crude remarks with equally naughty behavior.

Somehow I forced my mouth to speak. "Maybe I should go."

"Do you want to?" It was an invitation to stay.

"I'm n-not sure," I stuttered. "Yes. I think I should." But I didn't move. I couldn't.

Hudson took advantage of my weakness, pressing me to indulge him with reasons. "Because you're uncomfortable with my proposition? Or because I told you that I'm going to fuck you?"

His profession had no less impact the second time. "I'm...yes. That."

He cocked his head, contemplating me with puzzled eyes. "But I'm certain that's not a surprise to you, Alayna. You feel the electricity between us. Your body language expresses it quite well. I wouldn't be surprised to find you're already wet."

My cheeks heated.

He flashed a wicked grin. "Don't be embarrassed. Don't you know I feel the same?" He shifted in his seat. "If you were to carefully read my body, you'd see the evidence."

I knew then that he was hard. My sex clenched with the knowledge. If my brain hadn't completely turned to mush I'd be in his lap by now, taking his length into my hands, sucking him off with my mouth.

Hudson seemed to find my misery fascinating. "Let's table my proposition to hire you for a moment and discuss this other thing further. Please understand that they are very separate from each other. I'd never want you to think my sexual desire for you was in any way part of a sham for my parents and their friends."

Ridiculous giddiness flowed through me. *Hudson Pierce desired me.* And I was going to wreck it all with my flabbergasted reaction. I furrowed my brows in concentration. "I'm—I don't know how to react to someone stating they desire me."

He frowned. Even with his lips curled down they begged to be kissed. "Has no man told you that before?"

I fumbled with my glass, caressing the beads of sweat that still accumulated from the pile of remaining ice. "Not in so many words. Actions sometimes. Certainly not so bluntly."

"That's a shame." He reached across the table and stroked a thumb across my hand, his touch making me dizzy. "I plan to tell you every chance I get."

"Oh." I pulled my hand away. It was too much, too fast. Maybe I could end up in Hudson's bed and it would be all right and I wouldn't freak out.

But this wasn't his bed. This was the club. And whether I freaked out or not, mixing work with sex was never a good idea.

Ah. Was that what David had been saying when he broke it off with me? What a moment for understanding to click in.

I put my hands on the edge of the table. "I, uh, I'm feeling a bit overwhelmed. I need to go. You've given me a lot to think about."

I stood and he did too.

"I wish you wouldn't. But if you must…" He sounded needy, reflecting how I felt.

I couldn't look at him. If I did, I'd stay. "I've got to get to work."

I moved to the door and placed my hand on the knob. But Hudson's palm pressed on the top of the door, holding it closed and trapping me between him and the wall.

He lowered his head to my ear. "Wait, Alayna." His breath tickled and burned simultaneously. I closed my eyes, taking it in, bearing it. "I apologize for overwhelming you. That wasn't my intent. But I want you to know that whether or not you decide to help with my situation, I will continue to seduce you. I'm a man who gets what he wants. And I want you."

Um, holy wow.

Turned on did not begin to describe how his statement made me feel.

Then his mouth was on me, nibbling at my earlobe. I drew in a sharp breath. Involuntarily, I let my head roll to the side, granting him better access.

And, man, did he take what I gave, nipping a trail down my neck, sending ripples of desire through my belly. I moved my hand off the doorknob and grabbed his arm to steady myself. He curled his other arm around me, his hand settling on my breast. I gasped at the contact, leaning in to his touch.

He kneaded my breast as he nuzzled his face in my hair. "I should have told you earlier," he said softly. "You look absolutely beautiful tonight. I can't keep my eyes off you. Serious and sexy wrapped into one package." He pressed against me and I could feel his erection at my lower back. "Kiss me, Alayna."

It was so hot how he used my name freely. As if it was his to use. And in many ways it was. Almost no one called me anything but Laynie. He'd claimed my name when he claimed me.

All that was left was for me to accept it.

His mouth was waiting as I turned my head. Instantly, he captured mine with his own and I whimpered. He slipped his tongue in possessively and skillfully, urging mine to come out and play. His kiss was just as demanding and confident as he was, his firm lips driving the tempo, stealing my breath and sending a firm buzz to my lady parts. *God, imagine his lips down there…*

I shifted my body, needing more contact, and instinctively, he turned too so we were face to face. Wrapping my hands around his neck, I pulled him deeper, wanting to feel him in every part of my mouth. He knew what I needed, licking and stroking into me, as his hands slid down to clutch my ass.

I wanted all of him. Screw my shift and any other excuse I'd made to myself during the course of the conversation. Even if it led to obsessing, I needed him inside me, and not only with his tongue. I rolled my hips against his, begging for him to touch me there, to ease the ache at my core.

Hudson responded, moving his hands from my behind to my shoulders. Then he gently pushed me away, breaking our kiss, but leaving his hands on my shoulders as if trying to hold me at that distance.

My mouth felt empty and cold as I struggled to calm my breathing. Hudson's breaths were equally ragged, and he panted in rhythm with me. As my brain returned from a state of blissful haze, I became uneasy, unable to understand his sudden retreat.

Recognizing my concern, Hudson moved his hand to brush my cheek. "Not here, precious. Not like this." His other hand wrapped around my neck and he pressed his forehead against mine. "I will have you beneath me. In a bed. Where I can adore you properly."

His statement was a promise. A sensual threat that had me itching to make it come to pass.

But I had to get to work. And he was right. A fast fuck in the bubble room would not nearly be enough for what I wanted with Hudson. No, *needed.* Hudson was far from what I wanted. But I'd gone beyond that now. I had to have him, bad for me though he may be.

I closed my eyes as Hudson trailed a hand down to my bosom and reached inside. My eyes startled opened when, instead of feeling his fingers on my breast, I felt my phone being removed.

He unlocked the screen and dialed a number. A moment later I heard his phone ring. "Now we have each other's numbers. I expect you to use it." He replaced my phone inside my bra cup, his eyes lingering on my cleavage before pulling me in to brush his lips across mine. "Call me when you're ready. Tomorrow."

He kissed me swiftly and then was gone, leaving me to wonder if I'd be "ready" to call him as soon as tomorrow. And if I could wait that long.

— CHAPTER —
FIVE

I woke up right before noon the next morning when I heard my phone buzz an incoming text. It was plugged in on the nightstand next to me, but I wasn't ready to wake up, having gotten to bed after six.

Lying with my eyes closed, I grinned into my pillow and recalled the events of the night before. The things Hudson had said to me, the way he'd kissed me, touched me—my heart sped up at the memory. Had all of that really happened? My obsessive relationship disorder made it really easy for me to imagine that things happened between me and others that actually hadn't. It had been several years since I had fallen into those old habits. Now, was I doing it again?

No, I wasn't making it up. I couldn't make up a kiss like that. It had happened. And I had wanted more to happen. But in the morning with distance and fresh eyes, I could see so much better how it shouldn't happen. As much as I wanted him, I was already thinking about him way more than was healthy.

I went through the steps of recognizing unnatural fixation in my mind:

Did I think about Hudson to the point that it affected my work or daily life? I'd certainly thought about him a lot after he'd left the club, but I'd managed to work my shift without a problem.

Did I think he was the only one for me? No way. In fact, I suspected I shouldn't be mixed up with him at all.

Did I believe I would never be happy if I didn't see him again? I'd be disappointed, but not devastated. Well, probably not devastated. All right, I'd be devastated.

Did I call him or visit him obsessively to the point of stalking? I didn't know where he lived or worked. If I was fixating, I'd have figured that out before I'd gone to bed that morning. I didn't even have his number.

Oh, wait, I did. But I hadn't used it. I was fine. For the moment.

Still, I couldn't help but wonder why he wanted to be with me. Hudson Pierce held celebrity status. He could date supermodels and pedigreed women—why would he want *me*? The lack of an answer kept me doubting what had really occurred between him and me.

And then there was his ridiculous offer to pay off my student loans in exchange for hanging on him like arm candy. How on earth did I qualify for that? If I were another type of girl, one with dollar signs in the eyes, I'd be all over his—what did he call it?—*proposition*. Fortunately, money didn't speak to me beyond what I needed for survival. The only temptation was the opportunity to spend more time with that delicious specimen of a man. But I'd already been through this—it was not a good idea.

Besides, if I'd understood him correctly, the option to spend time with him stood with or without accepting his job.

Not an option, Laynie!

It was a confusing idea anyway. Sleep with him without a relationship but pretend to have a relationship. Why not just have a relationship?

And there I was, already trying to make his offer more than it was.

I sighed and stretched my arms above my head. Clearly I wasn't going back to sleep and Hudson was too much to contemplate without coffee. I turned over and grabbed my phone to read my text, secretly hoping it was from him.

It was from my brother. *"Be there in twenty."*

I sat up, panicked. Did I forget a visit from Brian?

Scrolling through my texts I saw he'd sent one at seven in the morning. *"Court cancelled. Taking a fast train to NYC. We need to have lunch."*

I threw my phone onto the bed next to me and groaned. As my only living relative, I loved Brian with extreme depth and neediness. But his role in my life had transformed from sibling to caretaker when I was sixteen after the death of my parents, and in an effort to compensate for all he knew I'd lost, he'd alienated me in many ways.

He'd also saved me, and I'd be eternally grateful.

Plus he paid the rent for my apartment. So when Brian trekked out from Boston on a weekday to have lunch, I better be ready and waiting. Even though I knew a surprise visit couldn't mean anything good.

I took a deep breath and jumped out of bed. I didn't have time for a shower. Brian and the patrons of whatever swank place he took me to would have to settle for the smelly version of me. I pulled on a pair of taupe dress slacks and a cream blouse and sprayed myself with a generous amount of Pear Blossom Body Spray before throwing my long brown hair into a messy bun. I'd just located my keys and purse when my phone rang.

I pulled the door closed behind me and stepped toward the elevator as I answered.

"I'm outside your building," Brian said.

"Hello to you, too." Never any small talk for Brian. I hit the elevator call button and waited.

"Whatever, sassafrass. We have reservations in fifteen minutes at The Peacock Alley. Are you ready?"

I rolled my eyes at his restaurant choice. How unoriginal of him to pick the Waldorf. "Already on my way down. You know, you could have used the apartment buzzer instead of calling."

"But then you couldn't walk and talk like you are."

"And I'm about to lose you now as I get in the elevator. See you in a sec." I wasn't certain that the elevator would cause our call to drop, but I was facing a whole lunch hour with Brian. I needed the fifty-second reprieve.

"There she is," Brian said to no one when I walked out of the front door of my apartment building. The apartment had been Brian's pick since he was footing the bill, and I was sure that its proximity to the Waldorf had been half of the reason he'd chosen it. No one could mistake the place as classy, but the location was killer. My only gripe was the lack of a subway to the west side, but that only became a problem in bad weather.

"Hey, Bri," I said throwing my arms around him. "It's good to see you."

"You too." He pulled away and looked me up and down. "You look terrible, Laynie. Like you need more sleep."

"Gee, thanks." We started toward the restaurant. "I didn't get off work until five. Yeah, I'm a bit tired."

"Isn't it time you started working a more normal job? Something nine to five like?"

"I work nine to five. Just not the same nine to five you work." As if Brian worked nine to five. He was a workaholic, often burning the midnight oil working on his latest case. If his paralegal hadn't been his type, he never would have gotten married. The man had no social life. I'd be surprised to learn he had a sex life, even with a new wife.

"You know what I mean."

We'd only been together five minutes and he was already picking. If that was an indicator of how lunch was going to go, I'd rather skip the meal and get right to whatever bug was up his ass. "What brings you out here, Brian?"

He studied me, deciding whether to show his cards yet or not. He chose not. "Can't a brother come visit his only sister on a whim? I still feel bad for missing your graduation."

I hid my eye roll. He could have made my graduation if he'd wanted to, and we both knew it. But we had to play the game of happy family. "You're a busy hotshot lawyer. I get it."

"I sense the sarcasm in your voice, Laynie."

My brother excelled at reading people, making him a force to be reckoned with in the courtroom. "Okay, I was pissed you didn't come. Does that make you happy?" Actually, I'd been hurt. He'd had the date for almost nine months. How could I not feel low priority? "I'm over it now, though, so forget it."

We'd reached the hotel, which gave us the perfect chance to drop the subject. At the restaurant, we were seated right away, and I let the new environment transform me from outwardly brooding to introspective.

I deliberated for a long time about my menu choice, annoying Brian who knew what he wanted instantly. When the tempo of his leg bouncing under the table accelerated, I settled on a house salad. God, the man had no patience. He should take a lesson from Hudson.

The thought of Hudson brought warmth to my body and a furrow to my brow. Something was poking at the edge of my thoughts, something I couldn't quite grasp.

Brian chatted with me casually, keeping me from focusing on what perplexed me about Hudson. He briefly told me about a case he was working on and about the renovations he and Monica had done to their brownstone.

When he'd finished a decent portion of his meal, about the same time I thought I'd shoot myself over the banality of our conversation, Brian cleared his throat. "Laynie, I'm not here to catch up. I've been doing a lot of thinking about our situation lately and have realized that you're a grown woman with an excellent education. It's time for you to assume more responsibility for yourself. I'm not doing you a favor by enabling you."

I took a long swallow of my water, contemplating how to react to his sudden statement. Old connotations of the word "enable" stung me. Was he insinuating that I wasn't well? And how was I not responsible for myself? I was living and working in the Big Apple—if that didn't take responsibility, I didn't know what did.

Ever impatient, Brian didn't wait for me to choose my response. "I can't let you throw your life away at a nightclub. You are too vulnerable to work in that type of establishment."

The Sky Launch. Brian had never liked me working there, not from day one. But he'd accepted it because I'd kept out of trouble. Had he now forgotten? "I haven't had any issues since I've worked there."

"You had school to keep you occupied. You need something more challenging to focus on."

Never mind that I'd worried about the exact same thing myself, I was pissed. "Brian, I know how to handle my triggers. And what do you know about it? You never went to any support meetings."

His voice rose uncomfortably high for the serene surroundings. "Because I'm not your parent!"

That was the crux of the whole conversation. Brian had been forced into parenting me and I'd always suspected he resented me for it. Now I knew for sure.

He stared at his near empty plate. When he spoke again it was quieter. "Look, Monica's having a baby."

And everything clicked into understanding. I was being replaced. "Congratulations."

"I need to focus my energy and money on her and the baby. It's time for you to be grown-up." He straightened in his seat, as if to strengthen his position. "I'm not paying for the apartment anymore."

"But I can't afford to pay for the apartment! Not right now with my student loans about to be due." I was painfully aware that I sounded petulant and spoiled, but I had always assumed he'd help me for a while longer. It wasn't like he didn't have the money.

"Then maybe you better look for a better paying job."

"Brian, that's not fair."

"Think about everything I've been through with you and then talk to me about fair."

He couldn't have hurt me more with any other words. "I haven't had any problems in a long time," I whispered.

"You violated a restraining order."

"Over four years ago!"

"I'm sorry, Laynie. I can't support you anymore." His words were final. He'd made his decision; there would be no convincing him otherwise.

I saw what it had done to him, the years of caring for a mentally disturbed sibling. I'd known—I'd always known—but had never wanted to believe that my actions had hurt him so deeply. It stirred an old ache I had buried.

But I was also angry. I might not be fragile anymore, but I certainly wasn't steady on my own. Not financially anyway. I needed his support now as much as ever and as shitty as it was, he was my only family. I had no one else.

I threw my napkin on the table and, not sure if I hoped to sound more sincere or snotty, said, "Thanks, Brian. Thanks for everything." I grabbed my purse from the back of my chair and walked out of The Peacock Alley, careful not to look back. I wanted to appear strong and stoic. Turning back would give my brother a good look at my tears.

I let myself cry until I left the hotel. Once on the street, the city bustle and grit steeled me. I didn't need Brian. I could do it on my own. Sure he'd helped me foot the bill since my crazy antics had ran through all of my inheritance money, but support and responsibility was much more than throwing cash around.

I hurried back to my apartment, aware that Brian didn't try to stop me or call me. I spent the next hour behind my computer, figuring out my bills and expenses, searching for ways to make cuts. With a promotion at the club—which wasn't guaranteed—I could pay for my apartment. But I wouldn't be able to afford my student loans when they went into repayment the next month.

Brian had effectively trapped me. Not a bad strategy. The Laynie from a day before would have to give into his wishes, taking a job at one of the high paying corporate offices that had pursued me at graduation.

Fortunately, I had another option.

Taking a deep breath, I picked up my cell phone and pushed redial. God, was I really doing this? I was. And if I was honest about it, I was glad for the excuse. Maybe I really should have been thanking Brian.

The number Hudson had called the night before rang only once before he answered. "Alayna." His voice was smooth and sexy. Not sexy like he was coming on to me but like the sex he exuded naturally.

The confidence threw me. "Uh, hi, Hudson."

I paused.

"Is there something I can help you with?" I sensed he enjoyed my uncertainty. Why couldn't I display the same confidence he did? I never had anxiety issues at work or at school.

The thought of school jostled something and I blurted out the question that had niggled at me during lunch. "How did you know I was intelligent?"

I heard a creak and I pictured him leaning back in a leather chair behind an executive desk. "What do you mean?"

"You said I was…" I blushed, glad he couldn't see me. "Beautiful and intelligent—"

He interrupted me. "Exquisitely beautiful and extremely intelligent."

"Yeah, that." Having heard them before made his words no less effective. The matter-of-fact manner of his statement should have felt clinical and cold, but they were anything but. A shiver ran up my spine. I cleared my throat. "But you've barely talked to me. How do you know anything about my intelligence?"

He paused only briefly. "The graduate symposium at Stern. I saw you present."

"Oh." The symposium had been held a month before graduation and had featured the top students from the MBA program. Each of us had presented a new or innovative idea for a panel of experts. My presentation had been called *Print Marketing in a Digital Age*. I hadn't wanted to know who was on the panel, knowing that names would send me into obsessive researching and online stalking. Afterward, the experts and presenters were invited to a wine and cheese soiree, so that students could schmooze and corporate execs could make job offers. I'd presented for the experience. For the honor. I hadn't wanted a job, so I'd skipped the after affair.

Now I wondered what would have happened if I'd gone. Would Hudson have tracked me down? Was it entirely coincidental that he'd made an offer on the club I worked for around the same time as the symposium?

"Is that the only reason you called, Alayna?" His all-business words held a hint of a tease.

"No." I closed my eyes and clutched onto the side of my desk for support. Accepting his offer was harder than it should be. I couldn't help but feel it was too easy of an out—like I was selling my soul to the devil.

But I also felt a surge of excitement, a thick electric wave of freedom. "Your proposition—I'd like to do it. I'm saying yes." Remembering his other proposition to seduce me, I clarified. "Your offer to pay my student loans, I mean."

His chair creaked again and I imagined him standing, his hand thrust in the pocket of an Italian suit. Ah, yum. "I'm very happy to hear that, Alayna."

I shook the vision out of my head and waited for him to say more. When he didn't, I said, "So what happens now?"

"I have time in my schedule at four-thirty. Come to my office at Hudson Industries then and we'll finalize the details."

I'd get to see him in—I looked at my watch—two hours. My heart sped up. "Sounds nice. I mean, good. Sounds good."

He chuckled. "Goodbye, Alayna."

"Bye." I hugged the phone for several seconds after he hung up, mesmerized by this stranger's effect on me, wondering if I'd be able to pull off the scam he'd concocted, hopeful I'd be able to thwart his promised advances.

All right, maybe I didn't hope for that last one, but I wanted to believe I did. For my sanity's sake.

I also thought about the symposium, considering the possibility that Hudson Pierce had gone to greater lengths than he'd let on to set up this facade for his parents.

Maybe the thought should have scared me. But it only intrigued me more.

— CHAPTER —

SIX

Two hours turned out to be barely enough time to prepare for seeing Hudson. I spent a long time in the shower, shaving my legs and underarms and cleaning up my Brazilian, chastising myself as I did since there was no way Hudson was going to see my lady parts.

Then I stood in front of my closet for what felt like hours. I'd be going straight from Hudson's office to the club to meet with David then a full shift of bartending after that. I needed the perfect blend of smart and sexy with a dash of fuck-me-please—for work, of course. Finally I settled on a belted teal and black shirt dress. It was shorter than I would have liked for the business part of my plans, but still longer than most of the dresses I wore at the club. I pulled my hair into a low ponytail and kept my makeup to mascara and lip gloss. I looked good—fresh and natural.

Having been too distracted to ask Hudson where Pierce Industries was located, I had to Google it. Turned out the offices were near the One Worldwide Plaza, a straight subway shot to the club. From my apartment, I took a cab, not wanting to get sweaty. And, hey, I was getting eighty thousand dollars—I could afford a taxi to the West Side.

I'd been by the beautiful copper-topped granite and brick building many times, but never inside it. Pierce Industries took the top several floors, and I recognized some of the other tenants listed in the lobby as Pierce Industry subsidiaries. I got directions from the security guard and took the elevator to the top floor.

The lengthy ride gave me one more chance for a silent pep talk. *Three years sober, Laynie. You cannot fixate on him. You cannot obsess.*

But as I checked in with the pretty blonde receptionist, I felt an aching stab of envy because she got to work close to Hudson on a daily basis. God,

I was already in trouble. He didn't make it into the *Oh, fuck* category of attractive men for nothing.

"Miss Withers," the blonde said after notifying her boss I'd arrived. "He's ready for you."

I checked my watch—four-twenty-two. How long had Hudson been waiting? Did I get the time wrong?

The thick double doors behind the receptionist's desk opened, seemingly by themselves. She must have pushed a button somewhere. "Right through there," she said.

I stepped tentatively into the office. Hudson, who sat behind an expansive modern executive desk, stood when he saw me. "Alayna. Come in."

When I caught a full view of him, I froze. In his well-lit office, I truly saw Hudson Pierce for the first time. And he was gorgeous. He wore a pinstriped three-piece suit with a crisp white dress shirt and a plum and white striped tie. His black thick-framed glasses, which should have screamed nerd alert, had me slipping in my panties. He looked sharp and smart and commanding and…wow.

I swallowed. Twice. "Am I late?"

"Not at all." His sexy voice made my knees buckle and I suddenly regretted my high-heeled Mary Janes. "My last appointment finished earlier than I'd anticipated. Have a seat."

Determined to appear poised and with it, I straightened my stance and strode to the chair he gestured at in front of his desk.

"Hmm," I said, looking around after I was seated. The generous office space continued the modern décor throughout. Behind his desk were floor to ceiling glass windows giving a breathtaking view of Midtown. "Nice place. Not what I'd pictured, but incredible."

Hudson unbuttoned his jacket and sat down, brows raised. "You pictured my office?"

My cheeks grew warm. Now he thought I'd been thinking about him. I had been, but he didn't need to know. "I thought you'd be more traditional. But the modern really suits you."

A small smile crept on his face. "Actually, I have a designer. I have no idea what's modern or contemporary or traditional. She showed me pictures of things she thought I'd like and I nodded."

I grinned, knowing he was attempting to put me at ease, but my stomach bunched into knots. Hudson's office was unfamiliar territory for a nightclub bartender and we were meeting to discuss an unusual business deal. And he was so fucking hot, he dazzled me.

"I hope you don't mind if we get to business first."

"Of course not." If business was first, I wondered what would follow.

Nothing. Nothing would follow because when we were finished I would politely thank him and leave his office.

Ha ha, right.

"As I said earlier, I'm very pleased that you've accepted my offer. Before you officially agree, though, I want to make sure you understand exactly what I am asking of you. We tabled this discussion last night..." He paused and I suspected he was recalling the reason the discussion was tabled. At least, that's what I was thinking about. "So I neglected to mention a key point."

Hudson leaned back in his chair, placing his arms on the rests. "I'm a very high profile man, Alayna. Convincing my mother that we are a couple requires putting on a show for the world. That means you will be 'on duty', so to say, at all times. When we are together around other people, we will play the happy couple. When we aren't together, you must still act as though you're mine."

Was it my imagination or had he emphasized the words *you're mine*? Either way, goose bumps travelled down my skin.

"You can't tell anyone that we are not really in a relationship."

I creased my forehead and my mouth suddenly went dry. "I hadn't realized that."

"No, I suspected as much." He narrowed his eyes, gazing my reaction. "Are you still interested?"

I didn't really have a choice. Either accept it or give into Brian's wishes. Besides, whom would I want to tell? Liesl. And David. Was I still thinking about David with tall, hot, and devastatingly handsome sitting in front of me? Yes. Because David had the potential of being real. And frankly, I didn't know that I actually liked Hudson beyond the whole physical thing. I certainly shouldn't.

"How long would we keep up the act?"

"As long as we feel we can without imposing too much on our personal lives. The longer the better, obviously, but if my mother sees that I am capable of falling in love, she won't try to press me into a loveless marriage, even if you and I have 'broken up.'"

"Are you still interested?"

"It's eighty thousand dollars, Hudson. That's a drop in the bucket for you, but for me...I understand if I have to work for it."

He relaxed, nodding. "Good." Hudson pressed a button on his desk.

"Yes, Mr. Pierce?" The sweet timbre of the receptionist's voice filled the room.

"Send him in, please, Patricia." Hudson stood and pressed another button on his desk.

I'd heard her answer the phone as Trish when I'd arrived and I wondered if he was opposed to nicknames for people in general, or if he just knew the weight of using a proper name—the power it held over people.

The doors opened and a dark-haired, muscular man in a black suit walked in. If Hudson hadn't already sent my horny button into overdrive, I was pretty sure this guy would have set it buzzing.

"This is Jordan," Hudson said, crossing around to the front of his desk. Jordan nodded. "He's been assigned to drive you to and from work and anywhere else you may need to go."

Not that I wanted to turn down such a beautiful gift, but one thing I loved about NYC was alternate modes of transportation. My parents died in a car accident. Cars weren't my favorite. "I don't need a driver." Then, so I wouldn't seem ungrateful I added, "I usually get my exercise running home."

"Then he will drive you to work and follow you home when you run to make sure you arrive safely." Before I could argue, Hudson eyed me sternly. "Alayna, my girlfriend would have a driver. She'd also have a bodyguard. I'm willing to forego the bodyguard if you use my driver."

I took a deep breath. "All right."

"He'll be waiting downstairs to take you to the club when we've finished. Thank you, Jordan."

Jordan nodded again and then left the office. Hudson pushed a button and the doors shut behind the driver.

"And Alayna, wipe that look off your face. Jordan's gay. I wouldn't have hired him for you otherwise."

I folded my arms over my chest, embarrassed and chided. Also, I decidedly did not like Hudson. Beyond the sexual appeal, anyway. "Anything else?" I couldn't look at him.

He leaned back to sit on the front edge of his desk, his body close enough to touch without much movement on my part. "My mother is hosting a charity fashion show on Sunday. That will be our first outing as a couple."

"Okay." I crossed my leg over the other, his close proximity making me fidgety. And while I was so affected by him, I realized he'd been nothing but business since I'd arrived. Had his move on me the night before been a way to insure I'd accept his proposition? If so, he was a total ass.

"Your loans will be written off as of nine a.m. Monday morning. A written confirmation will be sent to you."

"Don't you want to wait and see if we pull this whole thing off first?" I hadn't meant to come off snotty. Well, not entirely. I was beginning to feel like a deal he was negotiating. I didn't like it.

"I'm really not worried about it, Alayna." Hudson seemed on edge as well. "But if you prefer, I'll postpone the write-off by one week."

"Fine, whatever. Do I sign some agreement or something?"

"I'd rather there isn't a paper trail on this."

"But if anyone questioned my loans being paid off—"

"I would pay off my girlfriend's loans." Of course he would. "And any other debt. Do you have other debt?"

"No." I had a Visa I'd charged up. He didn't need to know about that. "Is that all?"

Hudson shrugged, the gesture out-of-place for such an assured man. "Unless you have any other questions."

I hesitated to ask, but I had to know. "When we're together, in public, I mean, I can hold your hand and...kiss you?" I peered at him through my mascara thick lashes.

The corner of his lip twitched. "I expect you to. Often." Um, wow. "Anything else?"

Thinking about kissing him, I ran my tongue over my lower lip. "No."

"Then the business portion of this meeting is done." He stood and moved back around to his side of the desk. He removed his suit jacket and hung it on the back of his chair. Fuck—the vest, tight across his torso, showing his lean muscular middle—yeah, it was distracting.

Hudson stood in front of his chair and leaned on his desk, his palms flat in front of him. He stared at me for several seconds, and I itched to know what he was thinking. When he spoke, his tone was low and even. "In about two minutes, Alayna, I'm going to come around this desk and kiss you until you're wet and gasping for air."

Oh, wow.

"But first, let me clear up one thing that I suspect may be an issue. This charade is mostly about me convincing my mother. I will be saying and doing things—romantic things, perhaps—that are not genuine. I need you to remember that. Out of the public eye, I will seduce you. That will be genuine, but it can never be misconstrued as love."

"Because you're incapable of love." My voice sounded meek and flat.

"Yes."

Curiosity pulled me to lean forward. "Why do you believe that?"

Hudson straightened and removed his glasses, setting them on the desk. "I'm twenty-nine years old and have never had any inclination toward a woman other than to have her in my bed. I don't do romantic relationships. I'm married to my work." He walked slowly around his desk toward me. "That, and casual sex, are what fulfill me."

I sorted through the oddity of the situation in my mind. Hudson Pierce wanted sex. With me. But not a relationship. But he wanted his mother to believe he had a relationship. With me. So that she didn't realize her son was incapable of love. Which he was.

The whole thing had me spinning in a circle.

And the worst part was that I knew that I wasn't capable of the casual relationship he was demanding.

Except…I thought back on the other category two men I'd been involved with in my life—the men that I'd been too attracted to. Joe, Ian, Paul—they'd all wanted a relationship in the beginning. If they hadn't, if they had made a declaration from day one that they didn't want more, would it have made a difference in how attached I became to them later?

I was justifying and I knew it. With Hudson, I was an alcoholic walking into a bar but deciding I could withstand temptation as long as all the bottles were sealed.

It was a lie I decided to try to believe. "No romance? I can do that."

Hudson leaned back on the front of his desk again. He raised a brow, amusement in his eyes. "Are you also incapable of love?"

I met his gaze and ignored the little voice in my head telling me to run. "No, just the opposite. I love too much. Keeping love out of the equation is a very good thing."

"Good. No love."

He stepped forward and leaned toward me, a hand on each of my armrests, caging me. His stare was hungry, and a thrill ran through my body, as I realized I was about to be kissed.

But before that happened, I had to know something. When he moved closer, I put a hand against his chest. His very strong, rock hard chest. "Wait."

"I can't." But he paused. "What?"

He was inches from my face, and the lips I longed to nibble on kept my focus as I spoke. "Why me? You could have anyone you want."

"Awesome. I want you." He leaned in again, his mouth brushing mine, his breath heating my skin.

"Why?"

He pulled back. Not far, only far enough to look at me. "I don't know. I just do." His words came out a whisper, as if he rarely made statements of uncertainty, and I doubted he did. "From the moment I saw you…" He trailed off as he brushed his fingertips across my forehead, his eyes fixed intently on mine, and I briefly wondered which moment—the night of the graduation symposium or when he'd first seen me in the club?

Whenever he meant, his bewildered possessiveness was sincere, and when and why didn't matter anymore and the little voice screaming in my head was drowned out by the loud whooshing sound of desire pulsing through my veins. I leaned forward.

Hudson didn't hesitate for a second, meeting my mouth with his. As doubtful as his words had been, his lips were confident and firm. He moved a hand behind my neck to direct me, deepening the kiss, stroking my tongue with his own. He sucked and licked into me, sending shivers down my spine and I imagined his wet, hot mouth on other parts of my body. I sighed.

Without his mouth leaving mine, he pulled me to a standing position. This was better. I could press my body into him, feel his lust along my belly, get the contact that I yearned for. I ran my hands through his hair and down along the base of his neck, enjoying the tingles shooting through my limbs as he moaned against my lips.

A sharp buzzer made us both jump and pull away. I put a hand over chest, my heart beating rapidly from the scare and from the intense kiss.

Hudson grinned. "The intercom," he explained, his voice ragged. He moved behind his desk and pushed a button. "Yes?"

The secretary's voice poured into the room again. "I'm about to leave, Mr. Pierce. Is there anything else you need?"

"No, thank you, Patricia. You may go." He'd gotten control of his voice now. Amazing. I was still reeling.

Hudson put one hand on his hip and stared at me, as if wondering what to do with a problem in front of him. It both heated and chilled me simultaneously, to be looked at so intensely, to be considered so scientifically.

I hugged my arms around myself. "What?"

He shook his head. "Nothing." He grabbed his jacket off the seat chair and extended his hand to me. "Come, Alayna."

My body responded to his command before my brain could decide to. I took his hand, the warmth of it rekindling the fire he'd started in my mouth.

He led me to an elevator in the back corner of his office that I hadn't noticed before. Inside the car, he entered a code into the panel and we traveled what felt like one flight up. The doors opened to a fully furnished loft, styled in the same modern design as his office below. Floor to ceiling windows lined one whole wall. The theme was echoed throughout the sprawling space, glass walls partitioning off a dining room, a sitting area, and peeking behind half-drawn curtains, a bedroom.

I quickly looked away from the bed, scandalized by the wicked thoughts that flashed through my mind at the sight of his personal space, and met Hudson's gaze, aware of the amusement in his eyes. I flushed.

He walked to the kitchen and opened a cupboard pulling out two glasses. "Can I get you some iced tea?"

"Sure." I wondered if he always had iced tea or if he'd stocked it specifically for me. I followed him to the kitchen, climbing up onto a sleek metallic looking barstool. "You live here?"

He opened the freezer and grabbed a handful of ice cubes, dropping half in each of the glasses. "Sometimes I stay here. But I don't consider it my home."

I looked around the loft again, realization setting in. "Hudson! Is this your fuck pad?"

"Sometimes." He poured tea into our glasses and then turned to hand me one across the counter.

I took the glass from him, sipping eagerly, needing the moisture for my suddenly dry mouth. "And you brought me here because...?"

He took a swallow of his tea, and licked his lips. He raised a brow. "Why do you think I brought you here?"

A sudden thrill set in followed by a wave of panic. I wasn't ready for this, was I? I looked at my watch. There was no time. "Um, I have to leave for work in ten minutes."

"Twenty minutes. You have a driver."

I shifted, the inside of my legs feeling sticky and moist. "That's still not a whole lot of time."

Hudson came around the counter, took my tea from my hand and set it down with his. "Not a whole lot of time for what?"

My throat felt like it had closed, but somehow I managed weak words. "Are you going to make me say it?"

He grinned as he swiveled me around, then caged me against the bar. "No. Not now. If you say it I won't be able to resist you, and, as you said, there's not enough time. So instead I'll have to settle for a sample."

His mouth sealed over mine, consuming my lips and my tongue with heated frenzy. My hands crawled up his vest, yearning to be on his skin. I could feel the hard, broad muscles of his chest underneath my fingertips. Jesus, this man had to work out, the sculpted definition of his torso evident through two layers of clothing. I wanted to run my nails over his body, aching to discover if he had hair or was bare-chested, desperate to be naked against him.

Hudson didn't let the minor detail of fabric get in the way of his desire. He undid several buttons at my torso so he could slip his hand in and cup my breast. My nipples stood up as he flicked lightly at one with his thumb. Then he squeezed using just the right amount of roughness that I liked, causing me to sigh with pleasure into his mouth.

He placed his other hand on my bare leg and slowly traced up my limb. His touch was fire against my skin and I fidgeted under his caress wanting more of the burn, greedy for the inferno at bay. I opened my thighs for him, coaxing his hand upward with one of my own. He smiled against my lips as I willingly showed him my need—my insane craving for him.

And then his fingers were on me, pushing aside the thin material of my panties, reaching for the sensitive bud at my core. I moaned at his touch, his thumb circling the bundle of nerves with a skilled mixture of deep and gentle pressure. Feather light sweeps followed measured rubs. I was already writhing when he dipped a finger into my hot opening. I gasped, lifting my hips to meet his probe, out of my mind with the desire to come.

He murmured against my mouth. "Christ, Alayna, you're wet. Ah, so wet. You're driving me crazy with your sounds and how wet you are for me." He dragged my juice up and over my clit, then rammed two fingers inside me, luring a series of whimpers from my body. One more brush of my clit and I was over the edge, my orgasm spurring me to convulsions.

But even as I came over his hand, Hudson didn't stop his assault. "God, you come so easily." His voice betrayed his amazement and his own longing. "I have to make you do that again."

He slipped off my panties while I still shuddered. "Lean your elbows back on the counter," he commanded.

I did, grateful for the support it gave me. Then Hudson put his hands on my knees and spread my legs apart, opening me further. Before I realized what was happening, his fingers returned to my hole—three of them now—and his tongue was on my clit.

"Fuck!" I cried, unable to bear another climax, unable to live without it.

His skilled fingers fucked me, plunging in and pulling out in long, steady strokes as he sucked and licked at my cleft. I clutched the end of the counter behind me as I felt the ripple of another orgasm overtake me, all my muscles tightening, my core clenching around his fingers.

Still, he fed on me, lapping up the evidence of my ecstasy, caressing my tender nerves with his tongue with endless devotion. It was so much—too much. A third climax tore through me, right on the heels of the last. I threw my head back, trembling violently and cried out—a curse, maybe, or his name or unintelligible sounds, too mindless to identify the details of my cry.

When my vision cleared and my brain returned, I found Hudson holding me, whispering at my ear, my scent wafting off his lips. "You're so sexy, precious. So fucking sexy and soon I'm going to come with you just like that."

My fingers clutched at tufts of his hair.

"Soon," he promised. "And often."

— CHAPTER —

SEVEN

When I'd recovered enough to sit without support, Hudson left me, returning with a wet washcloth. I watched as he wiped the insides of my legs and my sex, the warmth of the cloth and the intimacy of the action transfixing me.

"Thank you," I said when he met my gaze, my gratitude extending beyond the cleansing.

He kissed me, my taste clinging to his tongue. Though sated, arousal began anew at the touch of his lips and the awareness of the bulge in his suit pants.

Too soon he pulled away. "You're welcome."

I followed him with my eyes as he walked to the bedroom and threw the washcloth in a tall, black laundry basket. When he looked back, he caught me staring and winked.

I blushed. The new familiarity he had with my body made me feel awkward. Scrambling to compose myself, I fumbled with the buttons of my dress. Then I slid off the barstool, found my underwear on the floor and stuffed them into my purse.

He raised a questioning brow as he straightened his tie.

"My panties are, um, soaked." I noted his expression of satisfaction. "I can't wear them."

A frown replaced his smile. "You can't work without them. Your dress is too short."

"I'll be careful. I don't mind."

"I do." Hudson approached me, putting his hands on my upper arms. "Alayna, you not wearing panties is very sexy. When I'm with you. I definitely don't think it's sexy knowing you're bare and surrounded by a bunch of grabby drunk customers." He was stern, as though he were reprimanding a wayward child. "In fact, it makes me very unhappy."

Well, well. Hudson had a jealous streak. Could he be any hotter?

But I couldn't have him infiltrating all aspects of my life. He'd already insisted on a driver. And weighed in on my wardrobe choices. I stood my ground. "I can take care of myself."

He folded his arms over his chest.

I mirrored him. "I'm not putting on soaking wet panties. I'll smell like sex all night and let me tell you what that does to a bunch of grabby drunk customers."

He scowled. "Leave them then. I can at least have them laundered."

I held out my panties for him. "If you wanted a memento all you had to do was ask."

He took them, his expression still tight. "I'm not keeping them. Excuse me a moment and I'll be ready to go." He disappeared into the bathroom, leaving the door open.

"You'll be 'ready to go?'" I hadn't expected him to be going with me. He didn't respond, though, or I didn't hear his answer over the sounds of water running.

"Did you say something?" he asked when he returned. He put on his suit jacket and held his hand out to me.

I took his hand, realizing he no longer smelled like me, his hands washed and his teeth freshly brushed. It was practical, but I deflated as he officially distanced himself from the passionate scene of moments before. "I hadn't realized you were going to the club."

"I am." He pulled me through a main door into a corridor with another elevator. This one, I guessed, led to the main lobby instead of his office. He let go of my hand and pushed the call button. "Is that a problem?"

I shrugged though I wanted to say, *Hell, yes it's a problem. You befuddle and dazzle and distract.* How could I present my ideas with Hudson's hot eyes on me, staring at his incredibly wicked mouth that had recently devoured me with such skill? Especially when his hot eyes and wicked mouth gave no indication that anything out of the ordinary had occurred.

Unwilling to be that honest but unable to let it go, I pushed. "Why did you have me meet you here when you could have met me at the club?"

"Privacy, Alayna. I can't imagine you would want to experience *that* at the club, would you?" The doors opened and he ushered me into the elevator. "Do you regret coming?" The smile in his tone emphasized the double meaning in his words.

"No," I answered quickly as he pushed the L button. "I regret *you* not coming." I couldn't think of a time when a man had let me take all the pleasure without receiving any of his own. It made me feel even more vulnerable in front of him.

"You'll have opportunities to rectify that."

And then thoughts of *rectifying that* raced through my mind, touching Hudson's naked body, his shaft in my hands...

My sex felt swollen and needy. Again.

Damn. Not what I needed at the moment. I had to get my head in the game. Which would be easier without the object of my desire standing next to me, his arm brushing at my shoulder. "Just after all your talk about not being my boss and all that, I didn't think you'd show."

"David may want advice. I should be there." He peered down at me. "Also, I'm curious. Is that going to bother you?"

"I wasn't prepared. That's all."

His eyes lit with understanding. "You're nervous."

"Yes."

He shifted behind me, wrapping me into his arms. "Don't be. You're perfect. You'll be perfect."

I sunk into him. That's what I'd needed—his touch after such an intimate act. I'd felt bereft and exposed. I needed reassurance, not just about the business presentation I was about to give, but about his feelings, or attraction, or whatever it was he had for me.

As we descended, I turned my thoughts to David and the presentation I was about to give. Oh, god, David. A new horror struck me. "Could we...?" I didn't know how to ask what I wanted to ask. "Do we have to, um, do the pretend thing today?"

"You don't want David to give you extra points because he thinks you're dating his boss."

"Right." And since I still might marry David one day, my sham with Hudson required delicacy. Though the idea of marrying David sounded less appealing than it once had.

"We can keep it under wraps for a day or two, if you'd rather."

"Thanks." Anxiety crept into my belly as I wondered how I planned to balance the men in my life and all the facets of my relationships with them: the fake romance with Hudson, the wannabe future with David, the severing of dependence on Brian, the real sex with Hudson, the possible promotion from David. I shivered and pulled Hudson's arms tighter around me.

He misread my anxiety. "You know what they say to do about nervousness," he whispered in my ear. "Imagine your audience naked."

I raised my brows. "You and David?"

"No, precious. Just me. That's an order."

Hudson's commanding tone sent a trickle of desire to pool between my thighs. Somehow I didn't think picturing him naked would be any help.

Jordan waited for us on the street in front of the building in a black Maybach 57. I'd never been in a luxury car and my natural reaction would have been to gush and salivate, but I held in my enthusiasm, trying to appear more unaffected than I actually was. I did recline my seat, taking advantage of the footrest, while Hudson attended to some work issues. He typed away on his Blackberry and made several phone calls.

I should have been focusing on my presentation, but listening to him conduct business fascinated me, his commanding tone and demand for respect radiated so naturally in even the simplest directives. Usually when he spoke like that to me, I felt shaken and off-balance. But when I witnessed him speaking that way to others, or perhaps because of what had transpired between us, I felt empowered. As if I could embody those qualities myself through osmosis.

We arrived at the club five minutes before the scheduled meeting. Hudson stayed in the car for a while, allowing me to go in first instead of together. In the office, I found David setting up my laptop.

"Hey," he said in greeting. "Are you ready to show off those brilliant brains of yours?"

I wondered if David knew about Hudson's plan to attend or not. Either way, I didn't want him to know I knew. "Should I start?"

"No, Pierce said he might come. You should give him a few minutes."

Hudson walked in seconds later. "David," he said, shaking his hand. "Alayna." He nodded at me, and I wondered if this was out of consideration to me, knowing that his touch drove me beyond distraction. Or did touching me do the same thing to him? I couldn't imagine that could be true—he compartmentalized so naturally, I had to think his thoughts were sincerely only on the moment at hand.

Beginning my presentation of ideas took the most effort, but with my PowerPoint slides to rely on, I easily fell into the zone, soon forgetting my audience. First, I focused on the operational aspects of The Sky Launch, items that threatened our competitiveness with other clubs, suggesting an increase in hours and days we were open, a retraining of key personnel, and a unified mode of operation between bartenders and wait staff. Then I moved to marketing recommendations, emphasizing a total rebranding with a spotlight on the bubble rooms.

I spoke for nearly an hour and a half. Sometimes David asked questions, and I answered confidently and succinctly. I knew The Sky Launch. I knew business. I knew what would make the club a rockin' place. I felt good.

Except for occasionally asking for clarification, Hudson remained quiet and attentive. When I finished, I looked to him, hoping for feedback or praise or a reaction of some sort.

Instead, he looked at his watch. "David, I have some place I need to be now. You can call me tomorrow if you want to discuss these ideas."

The endorphins of presentation performance weren't enough to shelter me from the defeat of Hudson's lack of acknowledgement. Had I completely sucked shit? Did smart girls turn him off? And where did he have to be at eight o'clock on a Thursday night?

Whatever. If Hudson didn't like it, then tough. He wasn't my boss, as he'd so vehemently pointed out. I didn't need his stupid validation. I'd been top of my class. I knew my stuff. I put my laptop away, fury leaking into my brisk movements.

"Thanks," David said.

"Great. Alayna?"

"What?" I may have snapped.

Hudson waited until I met his eyes to continue. "Walk me out, please."

I bit my lip as I followed him out the office door, knowing my attitude had been less than professional. At least he would chastise me in private.

We walked in silence down the ramp toward the entrance. The club didn't open for another hour and the place was empty except for a few employees preparing for the night.

When we neared the front door, Hudson pulled me into the coat-check room. I squealed in surprise.

"Alayna," Hudson growled, pressing me against the wall with his body, pinning my hands to my sides. His nose traveled along my jaw. "You were brilliant, do you know that?"

"No." My voice squeaked, his unexpected change of temperament throwing me for a loop. "I mean, I thought my ideas were good, but then you didn't say anything..." I trailed off in a moan as he nipped at my earlobe.

"I couldn't. I was too fucking turned on." He pushed his groin against my stomach, emphasizing his point and I fought off another moan. His warmth against me spread tingles throughout my body.

"Then it was good?"

"Oh, precious, do you really have to ask?" He pulled back to look at me. "You think smart—practical and yet outside the box." He leaned his forehead against mine. "And it drives me fucking crazy."

I felt giddy. I generally hooked up with men who were attracted to my body, not my mind. It elated me. I was also now sure that Hudson's attraction to me began at the graduate symposium at Stern. "So Hudson Pierce is into nerdy girls."

He alternated his words with hot kisses at my neck. "I'm into *you*—when you're nerdy, when you're flustered, when you're whimpering under my tongue."

Damn, Hudson knew how to hit my buttons—buttons I wasn't even aware I had. I shivered under his kisses. I longed to touch him, to run my fingers through his hair, to pull his body closer to mine. But he still had my arms pinned so I had to settle with telling him with words. "I'm into you, too."

He crushed my mouth with his, letting go of my arms to let his hands wander under my dress. He grabbed my bare ass squeezing and caressing my tender skin as he kissed me aggressively. My fingers flew to his face, and I cupped his cheeks as his tongue danced with mine.

When he pulled away, we were both panting. His eyes gleamed mischievously. "During your presentation—did you picture me naked?"

Always. I grinned. "I didn't have enough to go on. I haven't seen ya naked."

"I haven't seen you naked and that doesn't stop me from picturing." He scanned my body momentarily and growled. As if he were picturing me naked that very second.

His playful mood made me braver than I had been with him. "So when are we going to remedy all the seeing of naked bits?"

Hudson rubbed his thumb along my cheek. "Ah, now she's eager. After she's sampled the goods."

"I was always eager. Now I'm sure." I turned my mouth to nibble on his thumb and he raised a brow.

"What time do you work tomorrow?"

"Nine."

His eyes widened as my nibbles turned to sucking. "I'll make sure I'm done with work by five," he said hoarsely. "Come by the loft then. Take the main elevator to the penthouse. You'll have to enter the code: Seven-three-two-three. Repeat it for me."

"Seven-three-two-three."

"Good. I'll text it to you so you don't forget. Five o'clock. Don't eat. I'll feed you." He pulled his thumb from my mouth and gave me a swift kiss. "And I'll feed on you." He returned again for a deeper kiss.

He sighed when he pushed away from me. "Tomorrow, precious." He grabbed my hand and held it as long as he could while he walked away. Before he disappeared out of the coatroom he turned back. "Oh, and I assure you, bits is not an appropriate word for my naked parts."

I assumed that already from the outline in his pants.

Less than an hour after Hudson left, Liesl stopped me as I passed the lower bar. "Laynie," she said, nodding to a small bag on the counter. "Hot Stuff left that for you while you were pulling the cash drawers from the office."

I bit my lip. "Hot stuff? You mean Hudson?"

"Yeah." I had no idea what Hudson could have given me, and though I had been on my way to unlock the front doors and open the joint, I changed my direction and headed to the package.

A folded paper was taped to the outside. In neat block print he had written: *I can't let you go without.* I blushed as I peeked inside, suspecting I knew what I'd find. Sure enough, there were my panties—laundered and folded neatly. I didn't even want to think about what member of his staff got the job of cleaning the under things of Hudson's fuck buddies. But the fact he'd made it happen was kind of cute.

"So what the fuck, Laynie?" Liesl said, and I quickly closed the bag.

"It's nothing. I left something when I was at his office earlier." Internally I smacked myself. Next she'd question why I'd been in Hudson's office.

But that wasn't what she asked. "You left your panties at Hudson's office? Yeah, I looked. What did you expect from me?"

I rubbed a hand over my face. Liesl would find out soon enough. She'd find out the fake story, anyway. This was the perfect opportunity to tell her I was dating the man.

But I didn't. I couldn't. I wasn't ready to share him yet. I wanted to live with the genuine a little longer before I started playing the pretend. "Liesl, I promise I'll tell you. Just not tonight."

She breathed out an exaggerated puff of air. "Fine, whatever. But you better have juicy details when you're ready to spill."

"Deal," I said. I took the bag and its contents to the bathroom to put them on.

After I did, I caught myself smiling in the mirror. Maybe I'd been wrong about Hudson. He obviously wasn't the pompous asshole I thought he was. In fact, he was turning out to be a pretty decent guy.

Damn it.

— CHAPTER —

EIGHT

I woke up the next day with Hudson on the brain. Again. I'd never scheduled sex and knowing it was on the day's agenda made my belly tight and my pussy throb. But with the constant replay in my head of words he'd said, moves he'd made—my panic flag began to rise. I wondered as I had many times in my life if I was doomed to live either obsessing about my relationships or obsessing whether or not I was obsessing over them.

With three hours before I was set to meet Hudson at the loft, I had to address my anxiety. Otherwise I'd be too wound up by the time I saw him and I doubted even his magic charm could unwind me.

I decided to take a jog and quickly regretted it. Midday runs were brutal in the summer, especially when I'd become used to running in the cool of the morning. Halfway through my planned course, I gave up and slowed to a walk. None of it helped ease my mind—the heat, the exercise—I still couldn't stop wondering about Hudson, what he was doing and what he would do to me when I saw him.

By coincidence or subconscious effort, I found myself wandering over to the Unity Church where my old Addicts Anonymous group met. I'd discovered it at the height of my obsessive disorder—a place where atypical addicts got together to discuss everything from video gaming addictions to obsessive shopping. I'd moved away from attending on a regular basis since I hadn't had any attacks in several years, but maybe checking in now wouldn't be a bad idea.

I went inside and down to the basement meeting rooms, finding a session led by my favorite facilitator ending. I hung in the back until they'd finished, then made my way toward Lauren.

"Well, there's a sight I haven't seen in a while," Lauren said, throwing her arms around me in a friendly hug, her hair hitting me in dozens of long braids. "Should I be concerned to see you?"

"I don't know yet. Do you have any time to talk?"

"A bit. Wanna grab a cup of coffee at the corner café?"

"Yeah."

As we walked, I caught Lauren up on my graduation and the prospects of promotion at the club, as well as the blow Brian had dealt me with his retraction of financial support. Lauren had counseled me through many of my family issues and knew probably better than anyone about the intricacies of the relationship with my brother.

"Will you be okay without the help from Brian?" Lauren asked when we were seated outside, each with an iced coffee. Her subtext said she was talking about more than the money. Stressful situations led to relapses in mental health disorders, and she wanted to know if I was stable enough to hold up.

"Maybe," I said with a sigh. "I think so. Brian hasn't been much help with any of my crap except financially. And I've gotten the money worked out."

"You have? That's great. I'm sensing a 'but,' though."

"But there's a guy."

"Mm hmm." She sat back, her arms crossed over her chest. "Go on."

I paused, not really sure how to explain my relationship with Hudson, wanting to give details and knowing I couldn't. I tried to pinpoint exactly what concerned me and express it as simply as possible. "We work together. And I can't stop thinking about him."

"Is it David?"

Thinking about David now seemed odd. I'd mentioned David before in the group, when we'd started our occasional make-out sessions. Now he felt distant and in the past though he'd only put a hold on us two days before. "It's someone else."

Lauren cocked her head. "What sort of thoughts are you having about him?"

"Fantasies." I lowered my face to hide my blush. "Sexual fantasies."

"What else?"

"That's it."

Lauren shook her head. "You're not going to get me to say you're having problems because you're thinking kinky about a hot guy."

"But it's all the time. I mean, I wake up thinking about him, I go to sleep thinking about him, I'm tending bar and I'm thinking about him."

"But no stalking or calling him at work or emailing him incessantly?"

"No."

"Only sexual thoughts?"

"No, I replay things he's said to me in my head. I wonder what he's doing and thinking."

"Have you considered you might just like him?"

I took a swallow of my coffee. Up until the night before I had spent a lot of time considering that I didn't like Hudson. Except sexually. I always knew my female parts were drawn to him. But other than that, no, I hadn't considered it. I couldn't.

"Lauren, I can't like him," I groaned. "We…there's no chance with him."

"Are you sure?"

"Yes. We've discussed it."

She looked at me curiously. I searched for something more I could give her. "He doesn't do romance," I conceded.

"Lots of women get the hots for men that are unattainable. It's natural. It doesn't mean you're falling backwards. Stay realistic about the situation. If you feel he's consuming your thoughts to the point that it's affecting your daily routine, then you need to seek some help."

"So would sleeping with him be a bad idea?" If she said yes, I didn't know what I'd do. I didn't think I could cancel on Hudson. I wanted him too badly.

"Have you?"

"Not yet."

Lauren looked at me sternly. "But you're planning on it, right? Now, girl, sex with no intention of a relationship opens up a whole other host of problems that have nothing to do with addiction but certainly can add to it."

"Is it impossible to have meaningless sex?"

"I'm sure it's possible, I just don't know very many people who get away with it. And I don't mean to imply that you're not strong enough to deal with it, but, honey, are you?"

"It might get rid of the fantasies."

"Maybe. It also might make you latch on."

"Not to sound like a slut, Lauren, but I've had quite a few one-night flings in the last few years with no attachment issues."

"Then maybe you'll be fine. But your one-night things work because you don't see the guy every day after. You'll still see this guy after, right?"

My one-night flings worked because those guys were fuck and forget guys. Hudson, not-so-much. And I would be seeing him after. "Occasionally." Probably more than that. Truthfully, I didn't have any idea how much our little scam would require me to see Hudson. The charade was set to start Sunday, though, and he'd been intent on keeping the sex separate so I imagined that we'd be having a one day affair and then would move on.

Lauren studied me carefully. After a few minutes she shrugged. "I can't tell you what to do, Laynie. And I can't tell you that sleeping with this guy or not sleeping with this guy will make any difference in whether you do or don't fall into obsessive patterns. What I can do is be there for you and suggest that you come back to group for a while for some extra support."

Extra support was a good idea. Before we parted, I agreed to come to a weekly meeting. Then I hurried home to prepare for my evening because I had not agreed to cancel my sex date with Hudson.

AGAIN I AGONIZED about my wardrobe choice for my night with Hudson, finally settling on a black sequined cowl neck shirt and sequined striped shorts. Jordan dropped me off in front of the Pierce Industries building a few minutes before five. By the time I'd entered the elevator code and ridden up to the penthouse, I was shaking in my strappy three-inch heeled sandals.

It took at least one full minute before I could bring myself to knock on the loft door. Hudson opened it immediately, as if he waited just on the other side, but he had his cell phone to his ear. "Roger, I don't want to hear that we lost this company because my staff wasn't able to foresee the possibility of separation." He held the receiver away from his mouth. "Come in," he whispered to me. Then he returned to his call as he shut the door behind me.

I couldn't decide if his preoccupation with work made me more or less nervous, but I took the opportunity to check him out. He wore tailored black suit pants and a light gray dress shirt with several buttons open at the top, his tie hanging undone around his neck. I fixed on his exposed chest, picturing myself licking the patch of bare skin that I was seeing for the first time. God, if I was this enthralled by a few square inches, what would I do when he was naked?

He returned my stare, his eyes intense and dilated with want. The heat I always felt in his presence turned on full force and the moments he stood there on the phone felt like agonizing hours.

"Take care of it, Roger. I expect this to be resolved before I arrive on Monday." He ended the phone call without saying goodbye, tossing his Blackberry onto the table beside the front door, his gaze never leaving mine.

"Hi," I whispered, unable to handle the acute silence.

His lip curled slowly into a sexy grin.

That was all it took. One smile and I couldn't hold back any longer. I'd imagined the first move would be his, but it was me who moved to him, my mouth crashing against his.

His surprise lasted only a millisecond before he responded in kind. His previous kisses had been deep and passionate, but this one held no restraint as he plunged his tongue into the recesses of my mouth with desperate hunger. I met his eagerness with equal fervor, licking into his mouth, swooping my tongue across his teeth.

Without breaking our kiss, Hudson's hands moved under my shirt to palm my breasts through my bra. I gasped at the wonderful tingles that shot through my body under his gentle squeezing. My own hands fumbled with his shirt buttons, images of me ripping the damn thing off filling my mind.

Just as I'd completely opened his shirt, he pulled away, panting. "Jesus, Alayna. I want you so bad, I'm not behaving."

"Hudson," I said, closing the distance he'd created. "If this is misbehaving, please don't stop." I slid his shirt off his shoulders, letting it fall to the floor, then put my tongue on his chest and licked under his collarbone toward his nipple.

He groaned. "At least let me take you to a bed. If you keep this up, I'm going to fuck you against the door."

"That doesn't sound like the worst thing in the world," I murmured, but I let him lead me toward the partitioned bedroom.

"No, it doesn't." He stopped a few feet from the bed and pulled me into his arms. He nuzzled my neck as he said, "But I won't be able to savor you properly and I'll forever regret it."

He tugged the bottom of my shirt up and over my head then reached behind to undo the clasp of my lacey black demi-cup bra. When it fell off, releasing my tits from their C cup prison, I wanted nothing but to press my skin against his naked chest.

But Hudson wanted to gaze, mesmerized. "I imagined you'd have beautiful breasts, Alayna. But I had no idea..." He broke off, his voice choked. He pushed me back until my legs met his bed and I had to sit. Kneeling in front of me, Hudson flicked one breast with his tongue, cupping it toward his mouth with his hand, his other hand wrapped around my back.

With a growl, his mouth covered my nipple and sucked and tugged with pleasing pressure. I cried out at the jolt that accompanied his ardor, my cunt tightening. I clutched his hair as he feasted thoroughly, leaving me gasping and near orgasm before he turned the same attention to my other breast.

When he'd finished, he kissed his way down my stomach. "You're so responsive. I could spend all day sucking your gorgeous tits." He pushed me back on to the bed. "But there's so much of you to adore."

He gripped his fingers in the waistbands of my shorts and panties and pulled down. I arched my hips to help him. "My shoes," I said when my bottoms reached my ankles.

"I love them." He maneuvered my clothing over my high-heels. "I want them digging into my back when you wrap your legs around me."

I quivered at his sensual instruction. Not a particular lover, I enjoyed the way he told me how things would be, trusting that his way would bring us both pleasure.

"Lean on your elbows." I did and he bent one leg up then the other, anchoring my heels on the edge of the bed, my thighs open. He sighed as he slid his hands up the inside of my legs. "You're so fucking sexy like this. All spread out for me." My sex clenched and he smiled, running his fingers down my slit. "You want me. Look how your pretty pussy throbs."

No one had ever talked to me like that—so raw and crude. It was incredibly hot and savage and combined with the repeated tease of his fingers brushing across my pulsing bud, it wouldn't take much to bring me to convulsions.

As soon as his tongue replaced his fingers, grazing me with velvet licks, I unraveled, throwing my head back to let out a ragged cry.

"Again," he demanded gruffly, plunging three fingers deep inside me. My hands curled into the bedspread, not sure I could take another, wanting even more than his fingers. He stroked me, rubbing the inside of my walls as he returned his mouth to suck on my clit. When I'd reached the brink of climax again, shuddering under the building tension, he stretched his other hand up to my breast and tugged at my nipple with his fingers. I came violently, thrashing against the bed, my sex rippling around his digits.

As I lay shaking, I was vaguely aware of Hudson removing his clothing. I heard the drawer of the nightstand open and close and the rip of a condom foil. He shifted me backward on the bed, giving himself space to crawl over me. Then he settled between my legs, his hot staff pressing at my quivering entrance.

"You're ready for me," he said, leaning his weight on his forearms. He aligned his erection with my opening and entered me partway. "Jesus, Alayna," he hissed. "You feel so goddamn good."

I gasped as he invaded me. He was so big. Not sure if he would fit, I tensed, knowing that I had to relax if I had any hope of accommodating him. He adjusted my leg and that's what I needed. I opened to him and he sunk deeper, nestling in my tight channel.

I couldn't remember ever having felt so completely filled, not only because of his girth, but because of the way his eyes pierced mine as he stretched and moved within me. He circled his hips nudging his tip forward. "So good."

He pulled out slowly, almost the entire length of his cock, and I bemoaned the emptiness left behind. Then he flexed his hips and rammed inside me with a fierce stroke.

I cried out and he echoed with a low grumble of desire. He pressed his chest against me and captured my mouth, kissing me roughly with my taste on his lips as he pounded into me.

Even though he'd already taken care of me—twice—I was desperate for him to bring me to another orgasm. I rocked against him, meeting each grinding pulse of his hips, moaning and panting as I took each one of his blunt drives.

"Wrap your legs around me," Hudson grunted as he continued his assault.

I obeyed, having forgotten his earlier wish for me to do so. My heels hit against the back of his thighs, digging into him as he moved in and out of me, adding an additional level of eroticism. Lifting my legs also opened me further, and his cock bore deeper into me, hitting a spot within that ignited at each stroke.

My orgasm built from there, my body tightening and clenching and contracting around Hudson's pummeling thrusts. "I'm going to come," I groaned, already trembling.

"Yes," Hudson cried. "Yes, come, Alayna." My climax crashed through me, brought to a head by his coaxing. Seconds later, his own body tensed and jerked, releasing into me long and hard, my name spilling from his lips.

He fell onto my quaking body, our chests rising and falling in tandem. His head buried into the crook of my neck as I pulled my fingers through his sweat-dampened hair.

"I knew sex with you would be like that," he said, his voice almost a whisper. "Powerful and intense and fucking incredible. I knew it."

I swallowed, forcing down any emotion that threatened to show itself except for satiation. "Me, too."

— CHAPTER —

NINE

I must have dozed. When I woke, Hudson stood over me, pulling a comforter over my naked body.

"Sleep, precious," he said as I struggled to sit up. He'd put on a pair of sweats, but he still smelled like sex. My belly tightened in response to his scent. Would my lust for Hudson never be satisfied?

He brushed a kiss on my forehead. "I need to order dinner. Chinese okay?"

I stretched. "Sounds delicious."

"I'll call it in."

I watched his gorgeous backside as he left the bedroom, luxuriating in what was left of my post-sex high. God, I felt good. I hadn't been fucked like that in…well, ever. The care and attention Hudson delivered as a lover left little to be desired. Of course, that made me want him. Again.

I tugged the comforter tighter around me, an uneasy feeling creeping over me. I tried to dissect its source. The fact was I felt comfortable—too comfortable. My number one rule in avoiding unhealthy attachments was to avoid attachments in general. Getting comfortable was too close to attached. And there was no way I could get attached to Hudson.

A tenuous ball of anxiety began forming in my belly. I could stay through dinner, I decided, but I needed to be dressed and sitting at a table. And then, after the night was over, Hudson and I had to keep our relationship to business only.

Throwing off the blanket, I began to gather my clothes. I found my panties and slipped them on then reached for my bra.

"You're getting dressed?"

I jumped. Hudson was standing in the doorway, watching me, carrying his shirt and tie that he'd—um, *we'd*—discarded earlier in the main room. Suddenly feeling awkward at my near nakedness, I crossed my arms over my chest.

He tossed his clothes on top of the laundry basket then crossed his own arms. Hudson didn't appear to be hiding as I was, but looked like he meant to scold me. He raised a brow. "Are you in a hurry to leave?"

I shivered. His gaze and my lack of clothing made it hard to remember why I'd wanted to go. I looked away. He probably wanted me gone soon anyway, having already gotten what he wanted. We didn't have to pretend otherwise. "Guys don't usually want me to hang around after sex."

"That statement brings up so many issues for discussion that I don't know where to begin." He stepped toward me. "What is wrong with men to not…?" He shook his head. "Alayna, please don't group me with other guys you know. I'd like to think I'm not like most of them. And I don't want to know or think about you having sex with other men. I don't share."

Not meeting his eye, I picked up my shorts from the floor, ignoring the thrill that ran up my spine from his suggestion of possessiveness. "That sounds awfully relationshippy to me. I thought you didn't do relationships."

"I don't do *romantic* relationships. Sexual relationships are another thing entirely. Why are you getting ready to leave?"

Avoiding his question, I dove for my shirt at the foot of the bed, but Hudson beat me to it. "Stop," he said, holding my shirt out of my reach. He put his finger under my chin so that I would look him in the eye. His brow creased in confusion and his tone held sincerity. "I want you to stay. And, if you are so inclined, I'd prefer that you not be dressed."

I wanted to melt under his invitation, but I refused to be affected. "You're dressed," I said, crossing my arms over my chest again, sounding like a pouty child. The knot of anxiety was tightening, and I was grabbing at anything I could to try to stand my ground.

"As soon as the food's here, I'll be happy to lose the clothing. Would that make you feel better?"

"Yes." But that was my hormones talking. My hormones wanted him naked. And hard. And slippery with sweat.

But my brain wasn't sure it was a good idea. "I don't know," I corrected.

Still holding my chin, he brushed my cheek with his other hand. "What's going on inside your head, precious? Are you going to run off every time we have sex?"

He wanted to have sex with me again. My girl parts clenched at the thought. But, as my arousal piqued, so did the terror throbbing in my veins. Usually sex ended any interest I had in a guy. Except for before—when nothing ended my interest in a guy and I obsessed about them endlessly. And now—when every part of my body screamed with the need to have more of the man in front of me. Oh, fucking god, was I falling into old patterns?

I turned away. "I hadn't really thought this would be more than a one-time thing, Hudson."

He grabbed my arm and pulled me to him. "Alayna." He searched my eyes, looking for an answer I knew he wouldn't find because I didn't have the answers myself. "If you don't want to have sex with me again, you need to tell me."

"I do!" His hands on me, and his piercing eyes elicited the truth from my lips. "I do," I said again softly. I threw my arms around him and pressed my face against his chest, nuzzling his hard pecs. He returned my embrace. *So warm.* He felt so warm and safe and strong. Like he could shield me from whatever scared me. Like the reality of him—the reality of what he was to me—might be enough to keep me from needing more.

"What is it?" His voice was light. He stroked my hair, and my panic lowered half a notch. "Tell me."

Tears threatened and I was grateful he couldn't see my face. Was I doomed to live the rest of my life afraid of becoming close to people? To men? "I'm not good at relationships. Of any sort. I have…issues." What the fuck was I doing? Casual sex meant no sharing of inner secrets. But it felt good to say it.

"Like what?" Hudson's hands tangled in my hair, soothing me. "Does this have anything to do with that restraining order?"

The floor dropped from underneath me. I couldn't move. "You know about that?" No one knew about that. At least, very few people. Brian, my support group, Liesl had heard bits and pieces. But I would never have told Hudson. I broke free of his arms and fell onto the bed, burying my face in the blankets. "Oh, god, I'm so embarrassed!"

He laughed and lay on the bed next to me, his head propped on his elbow near mine. He rubbed his hand across my backside, massaging my tense muscles. It felt so good that, had I not been dying of humiliation, I'm sure I would have moaned.

When he spoke, his voice was low and at my ear. "I know intimate things about you, precious—the way you look and the sounds you make when you're about to come—and you're concerned about this?"

I groaned into the bed, half from misery and half from the pleasure I felt from his fingers on my back. I turned my head so he could hear me talk, but away from him so I wouldn't have to see his face. "It was a big deal. The biggest deal. Like my biggest secret. I thought my brother had buried it." I rose up on my elbow and turned to eye him. "And are you saying I should be embarrassed about how I look and sound when…you know?"

"I needed to know anything that might come up about my pretend girlfriend. It wasn't necessarily easy to find, but not incredibly hard. It's been buried now." He cupped my cheek, his eyes growing dark. "And never, never be ashamed of how you look or sound at any time, especially when you're about to come." He circled his nose around mine. "I'm honored to be acquainted with you in that way."

"I'm mortified." I let my head fall back on the bed, but stayed facing him. "About the restraining order, I mean. I don't know how to react to the other."

"Why?"

He ran his hand across my face and through my hair, each stroke setting off an electric charge that sparked in my core. It relaxed me and comforted me and made me feel like Jello. He could have asked me anything right then and I'd have surrendered. "Because it makes me feel all weird and tingly. And turned on."

"Fantastic." He grinned. "But I meant, why are you mortified?"

"Oh." I flushed. What I'd said in error was actually less embarrassing than what he had really asked. But since he was still stroking me with that magic hand of his that had more power than Chinese water torture, I answered him that, too. "Because it's evidence of my crazy. You know, when I said I love too much? The restraining order is part of that, and I like to pretend it never happened."

"Then it never did." He kissed my nose. "We've all done insane things in the past. I'd never hold it against you." He stopped stroking my hair, and looked somewhere beyond me. "Just another reason romantic love holds no interest for me. People get crazy with it."

Then he relaxed and focused back on me. "But going back to the heart of this conversation—why does that have a bearing on a relationship between you and me?"

I sat up, unnerved by how easily he dismissed my past behavior. "I freaked out, Hudson. About a guy." He wasn't taking me seriously and I needed him to understand. "Several guys, actually, but it was the last one that ended not well."

He sat up next to me, our shoulders brushing. "And do you think you're going to 'freak out' about me?"

I focused on my hands in my lap. "I really can't honestly tell you. I've stayed away from any relationships for a while so I wouldn't have to deal with it. Trying to have something now with you—it's uncharted territory for me." Truthfully, as scared as I was of falling into unhealthy patterns, I didn't want to end things with Hudson. And we would be working together. Even if the best course of action was to not sleep with him again, would I be able to resist?

I looked him in the eyes, wondering if I'd scared him off yet. Because as much as I knew he should run, I hoped he wouldn't. "I haven't freaked out so far. With you. And I don't want to not have sex with you again. I mean…" I turned away, blushing for the millionth time.

He wrapped his arms around me and nibbled on my ear. "You're adorable when you're flustered. I don't want to not have sex with you again either. So we won't do that. We'll have tons of incredible sex instead."

I let myself be held in his embrace. "I'm not saying yes, yet." But wasn't I? "I have to take this one day at a time." And what would I do if I woke up one morning completely obsessed with him? As if I could stop things with him at that point.

"Alayna, you might have to take this one day at a time, but I already know there will be tons of fucking between the two of us." He pulled me closer, and I melted at his words, at his touch. "In fact, I'm going to have to be inside you again before you leave for work."

I felt his erection at my bare belly. Instead of being surprised and ashamed that I still wanted him so very much, I decided to relish in it. "Like right now?"

He kissed me, deeply, his tongue taking over my mouth. Then, just as quickly, he broke away. "Not right now, precious. Dinner's almost he—" The intercom buzzed before he'd finished his word. He smiled as he stood. Then he headed to the front room, saying over his shoulder, "But your enthusiasm is super hot."

I smiled to myself, enjoying the residual tingle from our kiss. Fuck. Dinner was here and I wasn't dressed. Putting on my own clothes now would be a statement. Staying naked would be too. I sat up and eyed his shirt on top of the laundry basket. It would have to do as a compromise.

I pulled off my shorts and had barely finished buttoning his shirt when Hudson returned with a bag of food in one hand and two plates in the other. He scanned me up and down, a pleased glint in his eye. "If you have to be dressed, I completely approve."

Suddenly feeling playful, I curtsied. "Well, thank you very much, Mr. Pierce. I don't know what I'd do without your approval."

He grinned, crossing to the bed. "Should I undress? I said I would."

"Not if you want me to actually eat. I'd be much too distracted. And I already have a hard time with chopsticks."

Hudson gestured for me to join him on the bed. "Do you need me to feed you?"

"Hmm. Maybe."

We ate together, eating Mongolian beef and Szechuan chicken spread out over the bed. I struggled with my chopsticks, half of my food not making it to my mouth. Every now and then he fed me, and I let him, enjoying being cared for in a way I hadn't been in a long time, if ever.

"What are you doing tomorrow?" Hudson asked after he'd left and returned with two glasses of iced tea. "Before work, I mean."

I took a swallow, moved that Hudson chose to drink with me when he probably preferred wine. "I'm off work at three tonight. Or tomorrow morning, however you want to look at it. I'll probably sleep a good part of the day. I work at nine tomorrow night. Why?"

He reached over to feed me another bite. "I need to take you shopping. You'll need an outfit for my mother's charity event."

I practically choked on a water chestnut. "Oh my freaking god, one inappropriate outfit and you assume I can't dress myself. Seriously, I should burn it."

"That's not it at all. I happen to love that outfit and would be very disappointed to find you'd burned it. I actually hope to see you wearing it again. In private, of course." His eyes glazed, perhaps picturing me in the tight corset I'd worn that night I officially met him. "And I've adored every other outfit of yours." He tugged at the bottom of my shirt—*his* shirt—that I was wearing. "You have an excellent sense of fashion. But my mother would expect a girl I dated to be dressed…" He paused. "How should I put it?"

I kind of liked watching him struggle with his words for once. But he seemed miserable so I helped him out. "I get it. I need designer clothes." I paused, trying to decide if I was offended. "I guess if you want to take me out and buy me expensive clothes, I'm not going to argue."

His lips curled slightly. "That's a beautiful attitude. I'll pick you up at two. Plan to spend the day with me. And don't look at me like that—there will only be sex if you want there to be."

Of course I'd want there to be. But whether or not I thought it should happen remained to be seen. I let myself consider it. "How do you intend on this working, exactly? Do you text me when you want a booty call?"

"Sure. Or you can text me. Or we can arrange ahead of time like we did tonight." Hudson studied me. "What would you say to no condoms?"

I'd always thought condoms were a drag, but I hadn't ever been in a committed relationship where I could consider not using them. It struck me as odd that after one time I was having this conversation with Hudson. "I suppose if you're clean…I'm on birth control. I get the shot. My last STD test was a month ago and it came back clean."

"I am clean. I'm checked monthly. And I hate condoms."

"Then no more condoms."

He smiled and I caught my mistake.

"If I agree, I mean."

"Mmhmm." He stroked his hand up my bare thigh. Sexual tension hung in the air between us, but my brain screamed at me to be cautious.

I hugged my knees, casually pulling away from his touch. "You said you expected fidelity—can I expect the same from you? Or will you be using this loft with other women?"

Hudson moved our leftover dinner to the floor, clearing the space between us. Then he put a hand on each of my knees, pinning me with his eyes. "I'm not a slut, Alayna. This loft has been used for sex, yes, but I have it so I can be close to my office, not for fucking." He stretched a hand out to brush a strand of hair behind my ear. "I will be as faithful as I expect you to be."

His nearness, his touch, his promise of fidelity—it stirred my arousal, begging me to give in. But it also tugged at something much deeper, something both familiar and unknown, something I couldn't name or identify, and I knew if I tried, it—whatever it was—would come rushing up and consume me.

I scrambled off the bed. "I can't think about this anymore right now." I began gathering my clothing.

"Why are you panicking?" Hudson stood as well.

I turned to him, suddenly angry—with him, with myself, with my stupid compulsion to cling and drive people away, with my parents for dying and pushing me into that behavior. "You know, it's all very good and fine for you to say you want a committed sexual relationship. You'll have no problem remaining unemotionally involved—that's your default. It's not my default. Don't you see what you're asking of me might be impossible for me to deliver?" I rubbed at my eyes, hoping to stop any tears before they dared to fall.

Hudson reached toward me, but I stepped away. "The more we have sex, Hudson, the more I'm likely to latch on, and even if you were into that, you wouldn't be into the level that I latch. So, trust me when I say this has bad idea written all over it. Let's call this a wonderful—oh, my god, such a wonderful evening—and now we need to move on."

His mouth tightened into a straight line. "If that's what you need."

"I do." I hugged myself, embarrassed by my outburst. "And I need a shower. Do you mind?"

"Not at all. In there." He gestured toward the bathroom. "I'll bring you some towels."

He sounded distant, and I immediately regretted pushing him there. Already I missed the warmth of him.

In the bathroom, I threw my clothes on the black granite counter and avoided looking in the mirror, not liking who I'd see staring back at me. I turned the shower on extra hot, hoping the heat would relieve the chill that had settled on me, and climbed under the heavy spray.

In there, alone, water and steam embracing me, the tears came freely. I cried soundlessly, surrendering to the hollow loneliness that I had grown accustomed to before Hudson arrived to show me something new.

Absorbed in my self-pity, I didn't hear him enter the bathroom with the towels, and when he opened the shower door and slid in to join me, instead of cursing his obvious lack of respect for my wishes to withdraw from him, I abandoned myself and pressed my lips to his.

He responded without hesitation, kissing me with gentle aggression. When I pulled away to catch my breath, he reached for the bottle of body wash and poured a small dollop onto his hand. Then he began to wash me. He took his time, running his soapy hands over every inch of my body. At my breasts he lingered longer, squeezing and caressing them both, flicking across my nipples with his thumbs. I sighed into the pleasure.

When he'd thoroughly cleaned the top half of me, he bent to wash my legs, starting with my feet and moving up my long limbs. He moved so slowly, so sensually, massaging the suds into my skin, that by the time his fingers slid through the folds at the base of my belly, I was ready to beg. His thumbs brushed past my clit and I moaned.

He swept through my folds over and over, and I jerked at each teasing pass. "Hudson," I said, my teeth gritted, my pussy clenching with need.

"Is this what you want?" He thrust two fingers inside me, twisting them.

"Yes!" I gasped. "I mean, no. I want you."

His grin was wicked as he continued to grind into me with his fingers. "You'll have to wait. I'm enjoying making you wait."

I wanted to argue, but he added a third finger to his probe and gently squeezed my clit and speech became impossible. I moaned as I rocked back and forth, digging my nails into Hudson's broad shoulders.

Just when I'd reached the brink of orgasm, his fingers left my body. I opened my eyes and found him standing in front of me, holding the bottle of body wash. "I need to be washed too."

My body ached with yearning, but I was eager to explore him. I hadn't even fully taken in his naked body, having been too distracted in the bedroom and now in the shower. Lathering my hands up, I began as he had, at his shoulders, but I was too greedy to move slowly. Soon, I'd cleansed all but his cock. I stared at his giant erection, fascinated by its length and girth. He'd felt big, but I had no idea he was *that* big.

I swallowed. Hard.

"What's the matter, precious?" I sensed he was smiling, unable to move my eyes from the sight in front of me.

"Um, wow," I managed. "I'm a little intimidated."

"But it's already been inside you. You know it fits." His voice grew ragged. "Touch it, Alayna."

His command stirred me to movement. I circled my hands around his shaft and stroked his hot silky skin. He felt so firm, so powerful, so perfect. I moved my fist up and down, once, twice, and the third time, he leapt in my hands.

At the next stroke, he growled and hoisted me up, encouraging me to wrap my legs around him. He pressed my back against the tile wall, his mouth ravaging mine, and in one fierce thrust, he was inside me. I tangled my hands in his hair as he rammed into me, feeling every inch of his cock filling me and fucking me.

I cried as my orgasm shook through me, the tremors of it spreading all the way to my toes. Hudson quickened his pace, clutching tighter to my hips so he could pump through my sex as it spasmed around his steel shaft. Several strokes later he released with his own cry, his cock jerking inside me as he spurted hotly into my sex.

In that moment, I let myself believe we could be together like that, how he wanted, without becoming consumed, even though I was afraid that I already was.

— CHAPTER —
TEN

Anxious for our shopping adventure, I decided to wait for Hudson in front of my building. I'd expected Jordan and the Maybach, so I was surprised when Hudson pulled up driving a Mercedes SL Roadster.

I slipped into the passenger seat. "Nice wheels."

His lips curled up into a sexy grin as he eased the car out into traffic. "Glad you approve."

I didn't know where to look first—at the luxury sports car or at Hudson in his tight dark blue jeans and fitted maroon button down shirt. I hadn't seen him in casual wear, and, as good as he looked in his suits, this new look had my tummy fluttering.

Well, Hudson in general made my tummy flutter.

"So you drove yourself?" Normally, I'm not much into small talk, but the sexual undertone between us needed silencing. Especially because another morning of constantly questioning the healthiness of my Hudson relationship had led me to decide the day needed to be sex free. I needed to counteract any attachment with distance. Hopefully, I wouldn't chicken out when it came to telling him.

He glanced at me over his shoulder before he switched lanes. "Why does my driving surprise you?"

I shrugged, securing my seatbelt. "I figured you always had a driver." Not that he needed one. He navigated city traffic well and watching him handle the wheel was hot.

"What's the fun of having a cool car if you don't get to drive it?"

"Good point."

At the next stoplight, Hudson peeked at me over his Ray Ban Aviator sunglasses. "You look gorgeous, Alayna. As usual."

His voice oozed pure seduction, and I pulled at the hem of my blue shift dress, wondering if it had always been as short as it suddenly seemed. "Are you buttering me up so I'll let you choose what I try on?"

"I'll choose what you try on anyway."

"Of course, you will." He was paying, after all.

We drove in silence for a few minutes, exchanging occasional glances that held the entire weight of our attraction. Under certain circumstances, the flirting and tension would be fun, but not when I felt so off-balance and unsure.

I had to get my declaration over with. "Um, Hudson, could we keep today to shopping only?" I hoped to God he understood what I meant without spelling it out.

He did. A brief flash of disappointment crossed his face—or maybe it was my imagination. His voice seemed stiff when he said, "Whatever you want, Alayna."

Immediately, I regretted saying anything. The fun flirty mood vanished, and Hudson became reserved and withdrawn. I considered taking my words back, but really, how could I do that?

"We're going to Mirabelle's," he said after a few minutes, not looking at me.

"Mirabelle, your sister?" Hudson's sister, Mirabelle owned a popular designer boutique in Greenwich Village. It was the type of place you could only get into with an appointment, but from what I'd seen from window-shopping, the woman had mad fashion skills.

"Yes. Her friends are throwing her a baby shower today and so I'd hoped she wouldn't be at the shop. However, when she learned I was bringing my *girlfriend* in for a fitting, she insisted on being there to meet you. Which means we're officially on the job. Is that a problem?"

"Um, no, of course not." My palms started to sweat. It occurred to me that the hours I spent worrying if I had any impulse to stalk Hudson online should have been spent actually stalking him online. Then I'd maybe have some more info about the supposed love of my life. "What if she asks me things? About you? About us?" And how would we be able to pull off the image of a happy couple when the tension between us was palpable?

"Don't worry about it. I'll be there. Follow my lead." Hudson reached under his glasses and rubbed the bridge of his nose. "Frankly, you're unlikely to get a chance to speak at all. Mirabelle is somewhat of a talker."

"But...what do I *do*?"

"Just be my girlfriend."

"OH MY GOD, Hudson, you told me she was gorgeous, but I had no idea!" The perky brunette who stood in front of me was clearly Hudson's relative. They shared many of the same features—chiseled cheekbones and strong jaws and matching hair and skin tones. Where Hudson was broad and muscular, Mirabelle was petite, her small stature accentuated by the round belly that protruded in front of her.

Mirabelle continued talking as she scanned me up and down, circling around me and Hudson, who had held my hand since grabbing it right before ringing the service bell. "She is going to be so much fun to dress. She's got my favorite body type—all boobs and hips and—" She paused as she raised my already short dress. "Fantastic legs, Hudson!"

Hudson's wicked grin appeared as he squeezed my hand. "Yes, I'm well acquainted with Alayna's physical assets."

Heat ran to my face.

Mirabelle hit her brother playfully. "You're such a bad boy." Then she faced me and gasped, covering her mouth with her hand. "Oh my goodness, I'm talking about you in the third person. How could I be so rude! I'm so excited to finally meet you, Alayna! Hudson has told me so much about you!"

She threw her arms around me in a generous hug. I glared at Hudson over her shoulder, wondering what he'd said about me and how I'd let myself walk into this moment so unprepared. He shrugged in response and let go of my hand, no longer giving me an excuse to not embrace her back.

By the time Mirabelle released me, I'd realized I needed to stop fretting and get into character. I swallowed and gave her a wide smile. "Glad to meet you too. But call me Laynie."

"And you can call me Mira. Huds is way too proper." She wrapped her arm around mine, reminding me of the annoying popular girls in high school who walked down the halls with their hands clasped with their girlfriends. Though admittedly, it wasn't as annoying when you were the girl being clasped. "Okay, okay, okay, I can't stay long today which I regret immensely, so let's get started. I already have a million ideas for you."

I hadn't had a chance to look around, having been accosted by Mira at the entryway, but now I surveyed the shop. Though small, Mirabelle's held a wide range of women's clothing and shoes. The walls and furniture were all brilliant white, giving the room an air of elegance while letting the clothing on display pop like art.

"Are we shopping only for Mom's event?" Mira asked, her forehead creased as if pondering where to start.

Hudson kept his hand at the small of my back. Despite knowing that the gesture was part of the show staged for his sister, the electricity that always accompanied his touch ran up my spine. "Specifically for the fashion show, but let's see what else we can find. Whatever Alayna loves, we'll buy." He gazed at me with a look that could only be described as adoration. God, he was good.

Mira's attention was on us so I made sure to return Hudson's stare, fighting to not lose myself in his intense, gray eyes. "Aw, thank you." I added sugar to my usually unsweetened tone. I turned to Mira. "Hudson spoils me. I don't deserve him."

Hudson began to protest but was interrupted by a buzz on his phone. "Excuse me." His eyes narrowed as he read his text.

Mira ignored him and gathered clothing over her arm. "This and this, oh and this will be perfect on you!" She called toward the back of the store. "Stacy, can you start us a room?"

A tall, skinny blonde appeared out of an office in the back. She took the clothing Mira handed her. "Which room do you want to use?" Although she spoke to Mira, Stacy stared longingly toward Hudson. Longingly enough to make me wonder if they had a history or if Stacy wished they had a history.

I snuck my own glance at Hudson. He was still typing things into his cell phone, his brow furrowed and his mouth pulled in a tight line.

"The big dressing room please. Laynie, this is my assistant, Stacy." Mira drew the blonde's attention back to her. "Laynie is Hudson's girlfriend so make sure she gets VIP treatment."

"Certainly," Stacy said with a bright fake smile, her eyes shooting daggers in my direction.

When Stacy had retreated out of earshot, I leaned into Mira. "Your assistant seems not to like me very much." I paused. Should I say more? I decided yes. It was the real me that wanted to know about Stacy and Hudson, but girlfriend me would want to know too. "And she seems to like Hudson an awful lot. Is there something between them?"

Mira hesitated, not looking me in the eye. "Ignore her. Stacy's totally been in love with Huds for forever, even though she's completely not his type. Nothing to worry about. It's actually comical."

She seemed like she may have been holding back, but on the other hand, maybe she was just awkward about talking girl crushes with her brother's girlfriend. I decided on the latter when Mira lowered her voice. "Did you notice how Hudson didn't even give her the time of day?" She giggled.

"I did." I giggled too. For real. I liked Mira.

Mira continued gathering clothing and accessories. "Hudson, what do you think about these?" She held up a pair of strappy heels.

Without looking up, Hudson grunted his response. "Uh huh."

I bit my lip, wondering what had him preoccupied. He'd been determined to pick clothes for me, and I knew he wanted to play up the sham for his sister. Instead, he'd been on his phone since we'd arrived. A small part of me feared he was passively-aggressively dealing with my no sex declaration by avoiding our situation. But then again, Hudson wasn't ever passive about anything.

Mira didn't approve of his lack of attention either. "Huds, it's the weekend. Put your Blackberry away." She nudged him with her elbow. "You finally have a girlfriend. Are you trying to run her off?"

Hudson finished his typing and raised his head. "Hmm?"

I stepped in front of him and put my hands on his biceps—his perfectly sculpted biceps. "Listen to your sister and stop with the working."

He pocketed his phone and wrapped his arms around me. "Are you feeling ignored?" His face had relaxed, but his eyes still showed signs of distress.

"You're going to make me think you have another girl." Maybe he did have another girl. I'd nixed the sex and maybe he was now going through his contact list.

I shoved the idea out of my mind and rubbed my nose against his. Then, because I couldn't help myself, I lowered my voice and asked. "Is everything okay?"

"It's work." He nuzzled his face against mine, but not before he glanced at Mira to make sure she was watching. His phone buzzed in his pocket again. He pulled it out, leaving one arm wrapped loosely around me. His body stiffened under my hands as he read his text. "I'm sorry, baby, I have to make a phone call."

Baby? In my head, I rolled my eyes.

Mira actually did roll her eyes. "Come with me, Laynie. He can make his boring call. Let's go try some of these things on you." She took my arm, ready to lead me to the dressing room.

Hudson paused his dialing. "Hold on a second, I'll join you."

Mira shook her head. "We'll come out and show you her outfits. Don't worry."

"Mirabelle, I'm not leaving Alayna alone with my over-enthusiastic little sister."

I vacillated between gratefulness for Hudson's protection and suspicion that he didn't want me alone with Mira for reasons of his own. I leaned toward suspicion, but that may have been because I'm suspicious by nature.

Mira glared at her brother. "You're not coming in the fitting room. That's just...wrong."

Deciding that I could handle her fine on my own, if that was indeed the reason he meant to keep us apart, I pulled away from Mira's grasp and leaned into Hudson. "I'll be fine, H." I shortened his name partly out of the need for something more familiar to call him and partly to irritate him. "Take care of whatever you need to."

"H?" he questioned so only I could hear.

I whispered in return. "Go with it, *baby*." I meant to only give him a peck, but when my lips brushed his, he pulled them in for a deeper kiss—a kiss that felt much more involved than necessary if it was only for Mira's sake.

The afternoon went quickly as I tried on nearly every item in the boutique. Mira helped me dress, pairing each outfit with appropriate shoes and accessories. I had always loved trying on new clothes, but I'd never looked or felt as good as I did wearing Mira's choices. I felt like a model.

At each outfit change, she'd parade me out for Hudson who smiled and nodded in between talking on the phone. Occasionally he'd shake his head in disapproval, usually when an outfit was slightly risqué. And a few times I saw the glint of desire in his eyes—the one that had claimed me on the night I met him. Those outfits were the ones I set aside as my favorites.

When we'd already selected a dress for the fashion show, plus a stack of additional outfits, Mira held up a long black evening gown with a corset bodice. "We've saved the best for last," she said.

Though the idea of wearing a corset around Hudson had me slightly anxious because of my first encounter with him, I'd never seen anything so exquisite as the gown Mira held, and I knew before I'd even put it on that it would be gorgeous.

Mira helped me remove my bra then lifted the dress over my head, pulling it down over my bust. "So Hudson told me you met at some college thingy," she said as she began to thread the laces.

I swallowed. I'd assumed that Hudson would have told people we met at the club, but this made more sense. It gave the fictional Alayna and Hudson time to fall in love. Still, it threw me off for a moment, and I paused before answering. "Yeah, it was a graduate symposium at Stern."

Mira tightened another lace. "I have to know, was it love at first sight for you too, or just him?"

So he'd claimed love at first sight. *Nice touch.* "Definitely for me too."

I saw Mira smile behind me in the mirror. "It's all so romantic. How he wanted to hire you and you already had a job, so he bought the club you work at to get closer to you."

I sucked in a quick breath, shocked at this new addition to the story. "He told you that?"

Mira clasped her hand to her mouth, her eyes wide. "Oh my god, did you not know?"

"No, no, I knew." I hadn't known, of course. But what really struck me was the possibility that it could be true. I'd dismissed it when it had occurred to me before. Now, I couldn't dismiss it so easily.

I also couldn't think about it right then. Not when Mira still looked frightened that she'd said something she shouldn't have. I tried to ease her. "It was crazy romantic that he bought the club. I just didn't think he'd tell anyone."

What I said worked. Mira's face relaxed. "It is surprising. He's usually so private about his emotions. You must bring out something in him." She stepped away from me. "And this dress will totally bring something out in him or else he's completely blind. You look incredible!"

She was right—I did look incredible. And when we walked out into the boutique, Hudson did more than merely smile and nod. He hung up his phone and gawked.

"Do you like?" I could already tell the answer from his hungry eyes. That look of his, it never failed to arouse me, never failed to make my panties wet.

He nodded slowly, seemingly speechless, and I marveled that I had brought him to that state. It made me feel more attractive and more powerful than I'd ever felt.

"Wow, Huds is at a loss for words," Mira said, her hands resting on her pregnant belly. "Call Ripley's."

Ignoring his sister, Hudson walked up to me. "I'd take you in my arms," he murmured, "but I wouldn't be able to look at you anymore. You're stunning, Alayna."

"Thank you," I whispered. This moment was for us, not Mira. I was beautiful to him and that made him all the more beautiful to me. It also made my nipples stand at attention, an uncomfortable predicament when a corset already had my breasts in a vise grip.

"Okay guys, I'd tell you to get a room, but I'm afraid you'll use one of the dressing rooms." Mira threatened to break the moment, but the intensity of it lingered. "I don't have to ask if you're buying this one."

"We're taking it." Hudson didn't take his eyes off me, proving the truth in his statement since he couldn't stop looking.

A brief image flashed into my mind of him and me going at it right there on the showroom floor. But since we had spectators—and since, by my own decree it was a sex-free day—I looked away. The lapse in eye contact helped give me the strength to pull away as well. "I'll get changed."

Mira led the way, stopping at the door of the dressing room to glance at her watch. "Aw, crap, is that really the time? I'm totally late! Go on in. I'll send Stacy to help you undress." She hugged me quickly. "And it was so wonderful to finally meet you. I'll see you tomorrow at the fashion show."

I huffed at a strand of hair that had fallen over my face and entered the dressing room, not at all eager to encounter Stacy and her dagger eyes alone. While I waited for her, I reached behind my back to see if I could unlace the corset myself, snagging my fingernail on one of the threads. I was examining the nail, trying to smooth out the rough edge when I felt

Stacy's hands undoing the laces. She had so much hatred for me she hadn't even offered a greeting.

I glanced up from my nail at her in the mirror. But it wasn't Stacy undoing my corset—it was Hudson.

He met my eyes, pinning my reflection with a greedy stare. Slowly, without breaking his gaze, he continued loosening the laces of my bodice.

I didn't stop him. He didn't ask, and I didn't stop him.

When he'd finished loosening my gown, his hands traveled to the spaghetti straps at my shoulders. I watched as he moved the straps over the curve of my bones and down my arms. The dress fell to the floor, leaving me in nothing but black strappy heels and my red thong.

Hudson's eyes widened and my sex clenched.

I wanted him. Whatever I told myself about healthy and unhealthy relationships, it didn't matter. I was already in this with him. If there was a point of attachment that would lead me to obsession, I'd already passed it. And admitting that made me sorry I'd ever tried to be anything different with him.

Hudson's hands ran around my waist, meeting above my navel. Then while one hand traveled up to fondle my breast, the other moved under the band of my thong. I stepped my legs apart, an invitation for him to find my swollen bud. His lip twitched the slightest bit as he slid his fingers through my slick desire, parting the folds of my sex, and releasing the musky aroma of my lust. In that moment he knew how much I longed for him, embarrassingly wet as I was.

He continued to plump my breast that was suddenly heavy and tender as he flicked his thumb across my raised nipple. The attention he gave to my bosom magnified the action below, his pad returning to tease my clit, and I let out a breathy moan. He stretched his arm over my torso, supporting me as I weakened from pleasure and I closed my eyes to relish in the nearness of climax.

"Alayna, watch." Hudson's thick voice at my ear startled my eyes open. "See how beautiful you are when you come."

My sexual history had not been comprehensive. Dark rooms with half-drunk partners and clumsy fumbling hands. Keeping my eyes open during only ever happened on accident. Mirrors and public places were never on my fantasy list. But I watched his hand moving at my core, his thumb circling my sensitive nub, his finger dipping into my wet center. He was right—it was beautiful. It was beautiful how he stroked me, how he knew what to do to make me feel the way I wanted to feel, how my skin flushed and my back arched. It was beautiful how he held me when I jolted in his arms, my orgasm moving through me in one long eruption.

"Put your palms on the mirror." His husky command and the anticipation of knowing what he was about to do sparked a new wave of arousal, even more intense than before.

Still shaking, I reached my hands out in front of me, his arms leaving me as soon as I had managed to support myself. Behind me, I heard his zipper, the sound raising my level of excitement, knowing his cock was released and seconds away from being inside of me. The four-inch heels I still wore put me right at his level, and he pushed easily into my moist channel with a groan. "Fuck, Alayna!"

Our eyes met in the mirror, the connection between us frighteningly intense, and a panic rushed through me. He saw it, or sensed it, and he coaxed me through it, telling me he was with me, assuring me he'd take care of me, promising me he felt it too.

I bit my lip to suppress the moans that threatened to escape, aware that only a door stood between us and Stacy—Stacy who likely rehung and folded the discarded outfits I'd tried on earlier as I was gloriously fucked by the man she lusted after. But when I came this time I didn't hold back my cry, desperate to let Hudson know what he'd done to me.

I was still whimpering when his own orgasm took him, his weight heavy on my back as he leaned into his release.

And if I wondered that the whole act was a display for his sister's assistant, his whisper in my ear said otherwise. "*This*, precious. This is for real."

— CHAPTER —
ELEVEN

Hudson let me choose the majority of clothes and shoes he purchased for me. In the end, it was a generous pile. I purposefully didn't listen to the total cost as Stacy read it off for him, afraid that I'd feel like I had a sugar daddy or, worse, that I was his whore.

We ate a nice dinner in an Italian restaurant in the Village then Hudson drove me to the club. Unusually lucky to find a curbside parking spot on the block, he took advantage and parked, letting the car idle.

"My mother's charity fashion show starts at one tomorrow. I'll need to pick you up at twelve-fifteen. I'm sorry you won't get more sleep. You're off at three this morning?"

"Yeah. I can handle it."

"Jordan will be here to pick you up. I'll make sure he has all your packages and that he helps you up to your apartment." A sly grin crept onto his face. "Unless you'd rather I picked you up."

Hudson take me home? Yes, I'd rather, but I needed to keep some boundaries. I'd already let him have me when I explicitly said I wouldn't. "I'm afraid I'd get even less sleep that way."

"Right. Probably not a good idea."

We sat for several seconds, the sexual tension sparking in the silence. Should I kiss him goodbye? Would he kiss me goodbye? Did we have time to sneak into the coatroom for a quickie? I had cleaned up as well as I could in the restroom of the restaurant, but the smell of sex still hung in the air and it had me thinking dirty thoughts. I didn't want to leave.

"Is everything okay with work?" It was an excuse to linger, but I also was genuinely interested in his series of texts and calls at the store.

"I can handle it," he said repeating my earlier words.

I'd hoped he'd tell me more, but he hadn't shared any business with me since I'd known him. There was no reason to believe he would now. I gazed at him for a bit, until it made me feel funny, my stomach flip-flopping as if I were descending on a Ferris wheel. Then I looked out the front window. Liesl strolled down the street, her purple hair making her easy to spot. It gave me an idea. Another excuse, actually. This time to get the physical contact I longed for.

"Since the ruse is on, we'd better make it official." I gestured toward Liesl, and Hudson nodded in understanding.

"Excellent idea." He paused, waiting for Liesl to get a little closer, ensuring she got a good show. Then he got out of the car and crossed to my door, opening it to let me out. He brushed his thumb down my cheek. "Ready?"

I was never ready, but I tilted my chin up so my mouth could meet his. Our lips joined, our tongues flitting around each other. My knees buckled, but his hands were around my back, supporting me. I gripped his shirt, wanting desperately to tangle my fingers in his hair, knowing that would only fuel my lust. Seriously, it had only been a couple of hours since our adventure in the dressing room, and yet it felt like I hadn't gotten any in months.

He pulled away and stole a glance at Liesl. "She saw," he said softly.

"Oh." I'd already forgotten our PDA had been meant for her. "Good." I swallowed. "Thank you," I whispered, still breathless. "For today." For buying me pretty clothes, for ignoring my request to keep the day sex-free, for taking the air out of my lungs with a kiss on Columbus Circle.

"Tomorrow, Alayna."

I managed to pull myself away from him, only looking back once as he got in the car. Liesl folded her arms across her chest, leaning against the door, holding it open for me. "Time for details," she said as I passed her.

And I delivered, telling her all about Hudson and Alayna, the happy couple, interweaving truth with fiction. I told her we'd met at Stern and that he'd bought the club to be near me, but not to tell that to David. I told her we spent all our free time together, that we couldn't keep our hands off each other, that we were madly in love.

The lies came easily and they felt good. They felt believable. Not because I knew Liesl believed them, which she did, but because I almost could too.

It was nearly four when Jordan and I had finished unloading all my packages into my apartment, but I wasn't tired yet. For a moment I had a pang of regret, wishing I'd let Hudson take me home instead. Thoughts of him had clung to me all night—I couldn't count the number of times I'd started and deleted a text to him—and my sex felt swollen and aching with want of him.

I'd been strong in the car, recognizing the unhealthiness of filling all my time with the man. Now, alone and needy, I weakened. Instead of heading straight to bed, as I should have done, I turned on my computer and allowed myself to do the one thing I'd tried so hard not to do: I cyber-stalked.

I told myself I needed to find information about Hudson so I'd be prepared. What if his mother made a comment about his college background? I'd want to know he studied at Harvard. Or what if someone asked me about my thoughts on Hudson's philanthropic investments? It benefitted me to know he was a major benefactor of the Lincoln Center and that he funded a private scholarship at Julliard.

And his exes. I needed to know about them, too. Though, I didn't find much in that department. Mostly pictures of Hudson with a variety of women. I gasped when I recognized one of the women as Stacy from Mirabelle's shop. She'd been on at least one date with Hudson. No wonder she had animosity toward me.

Not one face repeated except for Celia Werner's, the thin, pretty blonde his family wanted him to marry. They never actually appeared "together" together, but she did have a look of adoration in her eyes that caused me to doubt that she would be completely unhappy with an arranged marriage with him. But, then again, I couldn't believe anyone would be unhappy with Hudson.

I found out a great deal about my supposed boyfriend in those hours, but, truthfully, my Internet search had little to do with being prepared for Hudson's family and friends. I searched because I felt compelled to understand the man who affected me so completely. I read article after article because I wanted to know the silly little trivia that only a true fan or intimate friend knew. I sat behind my computer until my eyes were blurry, soaking up every bit of Hudson Pierce enlightenment I could find, because I couldn't *not* do it.

If I was obsessing, I didn't care. Hudson drew me to him with magnetic force. And while I knew that my behavior could only be allowed as a one-time lapse, I relished the high of fixating on the man who had already clearly stated he would never be mine.

I FIDDLED WITH the beads on the bodice of my purplish gray Valentino dress as the limousine pulled up to the Manhattan Center at a quarter to one the next day. I was nervous, yes, but also, I felt confined in the corset I wore underneath my dress as a surprise for Hudson—the one he'd chastised me for wearing in public.

"Stop fidgeting," he said. "You're beautiful."

I took a deep breath as Jordan opened the limo door. Hudson was closest to the curb, and began to step out when I stopped him. "Wait."

He raised a cautious brow. "Another request for a sex-free afternoon?"

I blushed. "No. I've given up on that."

He smirked, not at all bothering to hide his pleasure in my declaration.

"Anyway..." I peeked up at him under my heavily mascaraed lashes. "I just wanted to say...you look hot." And whoa, did he. The charity fashion show called for semi-formal attire, and Hudson rocked the look wearing a fitted John Varvatos gray suit with a muted purple dress shirt that coordinated perfectly with my outfit. He'd decided to go sans tie, leaving the top buttons undone, exposing only enough skin to drive me crazy. "Really hot."

He eyed me for a moment then shook his head before stepping out of the car. He reached back to help me out, his face still plagued with a curious expression.

"What?" I asked, wondering if I'd said something wrong.

"Alayna," he sighed. "There's so many things I want to do to you right now. But we're on-duty, and so I'll have to settle for this." He pulled me in for a kiss that, while not chaste, felt restrained, lacking the usual passion he poured into his kisses. This kiss was for the onlookers, the handful of photographers that surrounded the doors of the Hammerstein Ballroom.

When he broke our embrace, he took my hand, his fingers lightly crossing the rubber band I wore at my wrist. "What's this?" he asked as he led me inside the double doors of the venue.

"It's to remind me to buy coffee," I lied. Actually, I'd worn it to remind me to not think about him. I'd learned the technique in counseling. Whenever an unwelcome or unhealthy thought entered my head I was supposed to snap it and the sting would help curb the behavior.

Yeah, right. Like the snap of an elastic band could stop the thoughts that Hudson elicited—thoughts of us together, naked, all night long. And those weren't even the thoughts that worried me. Fantasies that we could be together beyond our little sham, beyond the bedroom—those were the ones that worried me, and I hadn't had them. Yet. But after my Internet adventure earlier that morning, I felt the need for a safety net. The elastic band was all I could come up with.

"You must really need to buy coffee."

"You haven't seen me go...." My words trailed off when I recognized more than a few of the people chatting in the lobby as celebrities. I don't know why it surprised me. The Pierce Annual Autism Awareness Fashion Show was a huge event and always drew the rich and famous. Really, I hadn't thought about it.

Hudson grinned at my stunned expression as he guided me past the ushers—the ushers who didn't even ask him for a ticket like the couple next to us who, I'm pretty sure, were the mayor and his wife. Um, yeah, Hudson was a lot cooler than I had comprehended.

We passed the bar and walked into the main doors of the ballroom. "If you'd like a drink, you can get something inside. My mother will be anxious to meet you." We stopped near the doorway, Hudson scanning the room.

I took in our surroundings. The place was extravagant—an old century opera house that had been infused with modern technology. The central focus was the runway, which extended from a low stage. A complex lighting system that seemed more appropriate for a rock concert than a fashion show hung above. Chairs lined the runway on both sides, and, beyond that, white clothed tables circled the room. Three levels of ornate balconies climbed the walls to the seventy-plus foot ceilings.

"Hudson! Laynie!" I turned to the sound of the familiar voice and saw Mira moving toward us as quickly as her round belly would allow. "Wow, you look incredible!" she said to me. "This dress looks so great paired with those shoes. And Huds matches you! How sweet!"

Hudson's arm tightened at my waist, the only indication he gave that his sister annoyed him. "You aren't the only one in the family who has fashion sense, Mirabelle."

"Of course not. Chandler's also very savvy. You, though, are generally too stiff to be considered anything at all creative."

"Ouch." But he grinned. Hudson was nothing if not proud of who he was.

Mira smiled, too. Then, her face tensed abruptly. "Excuse me, I know this is totally rude, but…" She pulled her brother's ear down to her mouth to whisper something I couldn't hear.

Hudson's jaw stiffened. He straightened, pulling away from Mira. "She knows about Alayna."

Mira nodded her head toward me. "Does she know about…?" She trailed off.

"She does." His words relaxed Mira, if only slightly.

I wanted to remain unaffected, but I knew my puzzlement read all over my face. They were talking about me and someone else, and I apparently knew about something or someone, which, of course, I doubted because Hudson never told me anything about anyone. My curiosity won out. "What?"

Mira looked to Hudson as if asking permission to fill me in. He remained expressionless. She took that as a go ahead. "Celia's here." Her mouth twitched. "I didn't know if that would be a problem."

Celia Werner. He'd said I knew about her, but I really didn't. I knew his family wanted them to marry. I knew her family owned majority stocks in television and media. I knew she was pretty. Very pretty. And she adored the man who currently rubbed his thumb back and forth across the back of my hand. The man who did not currently adore her. Or me, for that matter.

If my hand had been free, I would have snapped the elastic band. That had not been a healthy thought.

I swallowed then put on a cheerful smile. "No, Celia's no problem. Right, H?"

He grimaced at the nickname. "None at all."

"Where is she?" If the bitch was on the premises, I figured I'd better face her head on.

"There." Mira pointed discreetly.

I followed her gesture. There she was, the woman from the pictures, wearing a red, one-shoulder crinkle dress that accentuated her model thin figure.

"You look better than her," Mira said. I didn't, but I appreciated the comment. I didn't look better than her at all.

Snap. Another unhealthy thought.

"Mirabelle, must you be so catty?" Hudson squeezed my hand. "Anyway, Alayna looks better than most people."

I kissed him. Not only because it seemed a good time for a girlfriend to reward her boyfriend for a compliment, but because I wanted to. I wanted to remind myself that no matter what Hudson and I did or didn't have together, I was the one kissing him—I was the one convincing people that he shouldn't be with *her.*

He kissed me back in that reserved way of his that I had learned was for the public, his tongue sliding barely inside my lips.

"Oh, hell, no. Huds making out is not something I want to see," an unfamiliar voice interrupted our embrace. Hudson stepped aside revealing a blonde haired, blue eyed teenage boy wearing a suit jacket over a t-shirt and jeans. "But, wow." The boy scanned me up and down with a lusty stare. "Anytime you feel like moving up the social ladder, you can lay those lips on me."

"Chandler," Mira scolded. "Be polite."

Chandler. The youngest Pierce sibling. I'd read some gossip blogs that speculated the reason for the large gap between Mira and Chandler was because the three children didn't share the same father. Indeed, staring at Chandler now, I saw very little resemblance to his older siblings.

"Alayna's nine years your senior," Hudson said, a stern look on his face.

"I'll be eighteen next month." Chandler's eyes remained pinned on me.

I'd never told Hudson I was twenty-six. I shouldn't have been shocked that he knew—the man who had uncovered my restraining order had obviously done his research on me, too. Well, we were on equal ground now. As if there was equal ground with Hudson.

Hudson facilitated a half-hearted introduction. "Alayna, this is our brother, Chandler." Hudson smacked his brother on the shoulder in a gesture that almost appeared playful. "Chandler, stop undressing Alayna with your eyes. That's inappropriate."

Chandler crossed his arms with a look of challenge and superiority that could only be delivered by a teenager. "Because we're in public or because she came with you?"

"Because that's not how you treat women." Hudson's tone was clipped but even.

"And you're who's going to teach me how to treat women?" He stared at his elder brother, an unspoken conversation passing between them in those few seconds. And then Chandler dropped it. "Mom sent me to summon you. She wants to meet your arm candy." He turned on his heels, peeking once nonchalantly to see if we were following him.

Mira followed, grabbing him at the elbow to whisper in his ear. Correcting his impudence, I suspected.

Hudson sighed. "Ignore him. He's a horny teenager."

"He takes after his horny older brother," I whispered.

"Behave." He took my hand in his. I shuddered at his commanding tone and the feel of his skin against mine.

We followed the younger Pierce siblings across the ballroom, weaving around tables and the increasing crowd of people until we approached one of the tables closest to the stage.

"This is our table," Chandler said. He gestured with his chin to a group of people talking a few feet away. "Mom's over there."

I stared at the back of the woman I knew to be Sophia Walden Pierce from Internet pictures. Her dark blonde hair was swept up in a tight bun showing off her long graceful neck. Even from behind, it was evident that Hudson's mother was a beautiful, commanding woman.

As if she sensed our presence, she peered over her shoulder at us, offering a smile to her acquaintances as she did so.

A wave of unexplainable nervous energy rolled through me. What if she didn't buy our act? What if I screwed it all up?

Hudson must have sensed my anxiety because he tightened his grip on my hand and leaned in to whisper, "You're going to be great. I have no doubt." He kissed my hair.

His distraction worked. I was no longer worrying about impressing his mother, focused now on wondering whether his tender kiss had been for me or for anyone who might be watching us.

And why did it even matter? We weren't a couple, this was pretend. Tender kisses were romantic and we were not involved romantically. Sexually, yes. Romantically, no. I visualized another snap of the elastic band. Obviously I hadn't counted on holding Hudson's hand all day when I'd put the dang thing around my wrist.

By the time I'd thoroughly reminded myself that everything Hudson did was pretend, Sophia had wrapped up her conversation and approached us. As I had suspected, she was quite beautiful. Her body was lean and trim, and her complexion perfect. She'd had Botox, her forehead smooth and unexpressive. Or else she wasn't an expressive person, which was highly possible considering she was related to Mr. Show-No-Real-Emotion at my side.

"Hudson." The slight nod of her head matched the stiffness of her greeting.

Hudson responded in kind. "Mother." Her eyes flickered to me briefly. "I'd like you to meet Alayna Withers. Alayna, this is my mother, Sophia Pierce."

"Glad to meet you, uh..." I suddenly didn't know what to call her—Sophia? Mrs. Pierce? If I had inflected my voice differently, I could have ended at "Glad to meet you" but I'd left the sentence hanging and I had to finish. I settled on the safe bet. "Mrs. Pierce." I let go of Hudson's hand and thrust mine out to shake hers, hoping my palm wasn't noticeably sweaty.

My worry was unfounded. Sophia Pierce made no effort to take my hand. Instead she scrutinized me with narrowed eyes, circling around me like a hawk. "She's pretty enough."

I lowered my hand to my side and made a conscious effort to close my jaw.

Before I could decide if I was supposed to say thank you, she'd moved on. "Where did you find her again?"

I was flabbergasted. She spoke about me like I wasn't there—like I was a puppy Hudson had found on the side of the road.

Mira tried to save me. "Mom—"

Sophia waved her away, and I caught Mira's unspoken apology in her eyes.

I looked to Hudson, but his gaze was locked on his mother's. "I told you. We met at a function at Stern."

Sophia chortled. "What the hell were you doing at NYU? Slumming?"

I flushed with anger, my hands balled into fists at my side.

Hudson stiffened as well. "Mother, don't be a bitch."

Chandler smirked openly at his brother's choice of words.

Sophia, on the other hand, made no indication that she even heard. "Tell me, Alayna—were you first attracted to my son because of his money or his name?"

Pissed didn't even begin to describe how I felt. I was seething, but still in control. Without skipping a beat, I wrapped my arm around Hudson's and answered. "Neither. I was attracted to him because he's hot. Though, I stayed with him because he's fucking awesome in bed."

Sophia's mouth fell open. I had a feeling she was a woman that was rarely thrown off guard and seeing her taken aback gave me a thrill.

Hudson raised a brow, but he didn't appear displeased. In fact, the gleam in his eyes seemed amused. It empowered me to continue. "Look, Sophia Pierce. I may not have graduated from Harvard like your son and your husband—" Admittedly, I paused to note Hudson's reaction to the fact that I knew details about his family even though he hadn't told me a single thing. Again, I saw the gleam. "But I'm proud of my NYU degree. And I didn't come here today to have my education insulted by a woman who dropped out of law school."

Sophia took a threatening step toward me. I was taller than her by a couple of inches in my heels, but she carried her stature with authority. "Why *did* you come here today?"

It occurred to me that as bitchy as Sophia Pierce was being to me, she wasn't *my* mother. And though my parents were dead, they had been kind and loving and would never have treated anyone—let alone someone I supposedly cared about—with the judgmental malice that Hudson's mother had imparted on me.

And now I understood why Hudson didn't have any qualms about lying to his mother about a relationship. If I had to deal with her, I'd do anything to get her out of my life.

So instead of backing away, I straightened, my arm still wrapped around the man at my side. "I came here because Hudson wanted me to meet his mother. He seems to care about your opinion, for some reason. And since I care about him—a great deal, I might add—I agreed to come."

Hudson wrapped his arm around my waist, drawing me in closer. I felt his grin as he kissed my temple.

Sophia's lip raised into a slight smile.

"Oh," Mira gasped. Chandler appeared to be equally shocked.

As before, Sophia ignored the reactions of her family. "We're going to our Hampton house later this week. I expect you and Hudson will join us."

I opened my mouth to say, *thanks, but no thanks.* Okay, maybe I really meant to say, *fuck off, bitch.*

But Hudson spoke before I could. "We can manage a long weekend."

Sophia appeared to want to interject, which was nothing compared to what I wanted to do.

"That's all I can promise, Mother. Some of us work for a living."

She sighed. "Fine. Now I have important people I need to speak with. Excuse me, please." She waved her hand in greeting. "Richard! Annette!"

I watched her saunter away, amazed by her suddenly pleasant and friendly tone of voice. I guessed pretending ran in the family. When I turned my attention back on the Pierce offspring, I saw they were all looking at me. "What?"

Mira and Chandler exchanged a glance and then burst out laughing.

I furrowed my brow, still confused.

Hudson pulled me into his arms, a grin playing on his lips. "Alayna. You're amazing."

I started to melt into him, but remembered he'd told his mother we'd join her in the Hamptons. I punched him lightly on the shoulder. "I'm working this weekend."

"Get out of it." It wasn't a request, it was a command.

I couldn't tell him that "getting out of work" was impossible, because, well, he owned the place. It would be awkward though. I had a meeting scheduled with David for the next day—hopefully to officially give me a promotion. What was I supposed to say? *Thanks for the raise, now I need Friday and Saturday off?* I'd have to tell him I was seeing Hudson, though the thought made me cringe.

Beyond that, I didn't want to go to the Hamptons with Sophia Pierce. I pulled back from Hudson's embrace. "H, I'm sorry to say this since she's your mother and all, but I can't handle spending time with her. She's not nice."

He laughed. Then he locked eyes with mine, sweeping his thumb down my cheek so softly it made me shudder. "We won't spend every minute with her. And, anyway, you seemed to handle her just fine."

I couldn't help it. His boyish grin and gray eyes had a power over me. And, he'd said we wouldn't spend every minute with Sophia, sending my imagination into overdrive with images of what we'd be doing instead. My nipples tightened at the thought. How could I resist him? "Okay, but I can't be responsible for my actions if she's like that again."

He leaned in to kiss me, whispering as he did. "That's what I'm counting on."

— CHAPTER —
TWELVE

Lunch passed quickly. Sophia was too busy greeting high-paying donors and socializing to eat with us, thank god. Adam, Mira's husband, joined us after our salads had been served. He was a surgeon and had an emergency case that morning. He looked good with her despite their differences in height—Adam tall and lanky, Mira petite and small. For half a second I tried to picture them having sex before I realized that once I thought it, I wouldn't be able to unthink it.

Though nothing eventful happened during the course of the meal, I enjoyed myself. I watched the friendly banter between the siblings, joining in the laughter when one had a particular good burn on another. The conversation directed toward me was easy and unencumbered. I often feared it wouldn't be with new people who wanted to know all about me and my family. When something got too private, I noticed that Hudson deflected for me. Was it because he knew the sadness of my past? Or was he politely keeping my job light and carefree? Either way, the luncheon was more intimate than anything I had experienced in a long time.

When I sent a casual look toward him midway through the meal, his smile made my chest tighten. It may have been for show, but my reaction was genuine. I realized that no amount of elastic band snapping would stop whatever I was beginning to feel for him.

After dessert and coffee, the ballroom became a bustle again with people visiting with other tables and more guests arriving who'd only purchased tickets to the fashion show. Chandler found a group of younger girls to hit on, and Mira roped Adam into assisting with her backstage where she was managing the models and designers.

Though I'd liked getting to know Mira and Adam, and while Chandler never failed to entertain, I was glad to have a minute alone with my date. I trailed my hand across his shoulders and down his back, drawing his gaze to me. I saw longing, the few flecks of copper blazing in his eyes. He grabbed my thigh and leaned in, but the anticipated kiss never came.

"Oh, you don't need to be all PDA on my account," a silky voice purred behind us. "Remember, I know."

Hudson stiffened under my hand and my eyes followed his, landing on the leggy blonde taking a seat next to me. She was intimidating, not because of her attitude, but because she was drop-dead gorgeous. I tucked my hands into my lap, though Hudson's hand remained secure on my leg under the table.

"I'm Celia." She smiled, showing white perfect teeth. "I thought we should probably meet. Though, it doesn't look like Hudson's too keen on it."

I glanced at Hudson who indeed appeared uncomfortable.

"No, you're right. You should meet," he said, his hand stroking my thigh. I felt purpose behind his touching me, but wasn't sure if he meant it to claim me, calm me, or calm himself. "Now you've met."

"You aren't getting rid of me that easily, you oaf." She smirked at Hudson then delivered another smile to me. "Believe it or not, we're actually friends."

I believed it. She felt comfortable around him, and he didn't even flinch when she'd called him an oaf. It made my stomach wrench unexplainably. Then, when I wondered if they'd had sex, a sharp stabbing began in my chest. I didn't need to flick the elastic band, already associating the thought with pain, but I did anyway since my hands were finally free under the table to do so.

Hudson sighed. "What do you want, Ceeley?"

Someone Hudson actually called by a nickname? The stabbing deepened.

"I wanted to personally thank Alayna for this whole charade."

So, she really did know. Which really put me at a disadvantage since I knew almost nothing about her.

Celia leaned into me as if confiding a secret, but loud enough that Hudson could still hear her. "You can't know how dreadful the idea of marrying that pain in the ass has been." A teasing grin appeared on her lips.

"Um, I can imagine." The stabby pains in my chest made me want to stab Hudson, too. "He's not the settling down type."

Hudson removed his hand from my leg, and I instantly regretted my words, even though they hadn't been *that* mean, had they?

Celia giggled. "Wow. You already know him so well." She giggled again.

Ugh, she was a giggler. I wanted to puke. Or hate her. But something about her also drew me in. "It's nice to talk to someone else who knows."

"But isn't Hudson amazingly good at pretending?" She narrowed her eyes at him, and I caught the daggers he shot her in return.

"He is." I thought about our time together, the touches, the kisses in public. Some of them had been confusing, and I had blamed that on my own tendencies to create more when there wasn't more. But maybe it hadn't been my overactive imagination. "Quite good."

"I'd love to continue this wonderfully entertaining conversation, but I see someone I need to talk some business with." Hudson stood and reached his hand out for me. "Alayna?"

I had the strange feeling he didn't want to leave me alone with his almost-but-not-really-fiancé. The last time I'd felt that way, I'd received rather interesting tidbits of info from his little sis. "Go ahead, H. I'll hang with Celia."

"We'll be fine," Celia assured him. "And we'll end our conversation with a pretend catfight if you want to up the charade."

Hudson's jaw tightened. "No catfight. In my script, you're friendly toward each other."

"Then she and I should sit and chat, since we're supposed to be friends." Celia winked at me. "Right, Alayna?"

"Right." I winked back. I couldn't help it. She was sort of adorable. "And since we're friends, you should call me Laynie."

"Friendly, not friends." He took a deep breath, but his voice was still tight when he spoke again. "Fine. I'll be back shortly."

I watched him stroll off, the tight muscles of his butt hidden by his jacket, but his backside attractive all the same. Suddenly, I remembered I had a witness to my ogling, and I turned my attention back to Celia only to find she was ogling as well. Plus she had the adoration look that I'd spotted in the pics of her with him.

"You like him," I said before I could help it. I wasn't sure I wanted to know.

She shrugged then cocked a brow. "Seriously? I'm probably your one opportunity to get any real information about Hudson and his life and that's what you want to know?"

I laughed. "You're right, I'd like some info." The list of questions I could attack Celia with was so long I didn't know where to begin. Since I wasn't sure how much time we had, I needed to make it good. "Okay, Mira seemed to think I should be jealous of you. Should I be? I mean, should I be pretending I am?"

Celia pursed her perfectly plump lips. "Well, isn't that a clever way to ask the same question? No. Hudson and I have never been anything but friends. If he were a boyfriend who spilled his guts to his girlfriend, he'd tell you that I liked him, but that he's never felt anything for me but friendship. So unless you're the shallow type who's jealous of all girls her guy's friends with, then don't play jealous."

I was a bit shallow like that, and definitely the jealous type when in the throes of obsession. But I was playing a part, so why not make my character void of my own imperfections? "No jealousy then. What about his family? Is he close to them or is he as withdrawn with them as with everyone? I can't quite tell."

"He loves them all, deeply. As deeply as Hudson can love anyone, I mean. But it takes quite a lot of perception to get that." She leaned back in her chair and eyed me. "I think someone he was in love with would know that."

I nodded, taking it in. Then I dove into the question that had plagued me since I'd first heard about his predicament. "Why doesn't Hudson's mother believe that he'd be in love? Other than that she's a cold-hearted bitch herself." This elicited a grin from Celia. "Has he never dated anyone before?"

"Sort of. I mean, he's dated women. Not women he ever brought to meet his mother, but, yeah he dated."

The stabbing pain returned. Simultaneously, I noted a flash of agony darken Celia's bright face. It occurred to me that this conversation must be even more difficult for her, considering she actually had feelings for the guy and I had...well, not feelings, but something.

"You know, date is not the right word. He'd sleep with them. And then he'd mess with them. It got him in all sorts of trouble. More than once."

I stilled. "What do you mean messed with them?"

"I shouldn't tell you. He doesn't want you to know. But I really think you should. Otherwise you might be caught off guard if Sophia says something."

My voice was a whisper. "How did he mess with them?"

She sighed. "It's hard to explain. Like, he'd say he only wanted to be friends or friends with benefits, but then he'd manipulate them in that way of his, you know, how he always gets what he wants?"

Boy, did I. I could only manage to nod.

"He'd manipulate these women into falling in love with him. Which isn't really hard, I mean, he is Hudson. But he'd really play them. Lead them on, get them really hooked on him. It was like a game for him—one of the crappy things spoiled rich kids do just because they can." She paused. "I can say that because I love Hudson dearly. Also, I'm a spoiled rich kid, too."

The world felt like it had fallen out from underneath me. Was that what Hudson was doing with me? My throat felt tight. "Does he, um, still do that?"

"I honestly don't know. He's had a ton of therapy so I'd like to say he's 'better' now, but who knows? Of course, because of it, his mother got the idea that if he married someone like me, I could keep him in line. And my parents want me married to the Pierce name and bank account—they're disgustingly greedy. But I could never deal with those head trips—even though I am very fond of him. And I'd love to get in that beautiful man's pants. Can you imagine how gorgeous our children would be? Sigh."

She said the word sigh instead of actually sighing. That was what I clung to from her monologue because I didn't want to think about the rest. Therapy helped people—it did, I couldn't deny it—but I had doubts that it had fixed me. And knowing what I knew about patterns of past behavior, I recognized that Hudson should not be having just sex with anyone if he were seriously "better."

Exactly like I shouldn't be in an emotionless relationship if I were "better" since a lack of affection from a person I desired was one of my triggers.

I put a hand on my knees under the table to stop their knocking. I had to get out of there.

Celia continued, unaware of my torment. "But this plan of Hudson's is brilliant. As soon as Sophia relaxes enough to believe he's fallen for you, she's going to be ecstatic. She wants him to be normal. She wants him to be happy and in love. *I* want him to be happy and in love. Too bad it's not real."

Yeah, too bad.

She frowned, concern etched in her brow. "Are you okay? You seem really pale."

No, I wasn't fucking okay! I'd just been informed that the man I shouldn't have been fucking in the first place was probably trying to fuck with my head as well as my body. "I'm not feeling well all of a sudden." Not a lie. I seriously thought I might throw up. "Excuse me, I have to..." I couldn't think of any excuse to leave. I only knew I had to..."Go."

I snaked quickly through the crowd toward the doors, pushing my way into the packed lobby. The show was starting in fifteen minutes and I was going against traffic. I ducked and headed for a different door when I saw Sophia by the bar, hoping she didn't see me. Not because I cared anymore about Hudson's stupid scam but because I didn't want to deal with her.

Focusing on avoiding Sophia, however, made me completely miss that I was walking right past Hudson.

"Where are you going?" He reached a gentle arm out to stop me, and familiar tingles shot straight to my womb.

Accompanying the tingles, my stomach churned in disgust. I threw his arm off mine. "Don't touch me!"

Hudson's brow knit in confusion. "Whoa." He put his hands out in front of him, showing he wouldn't touch me but blocking my route of escape. "What's wrong with you?"

I scanned the lobby for a way to sneak past. "What's wrong with you would be the more appropriate question."

"Alayna." He stepped toward me, his voice low and stern. "I don't know what you're talking about, but you're making a scene. You need to calm down and save whatever this is for later."

He moved to grip my elbow, but I pulled away before he could. "There isn't going to be a later—I quit." I darted past him and out the main doors to the sidewalk.

"Alayna!" He followed me.

Anger surged through me, tears forming in my eyes. I was vulnerable and floundering and he had taken advantage. I turned on him, hot tears streaking my cheeks. "Tell me, Hudson, did you pick me because you thought my obsession issues would make your game more fun? Because really, where's the challenge in that?"

Hudson's jaw tightened, realization setting in. "Fuck Celia and her big mouth." He took a step toward me, his hand reaching for me. I stepped away. He softened, but his glare was insistent. "Let's talk about this in the limo."

"I don't want—"

He cut me off. "Alayna. It's not fair of you to listen to a stranger tell her story and not give me a chance to explain." His eye twitched, but, other than that, his features and composure were controlled. "I'm telling you we will talk about this in the limo which is parked in the lot next door. First, because my mother is watching, I'm going to bend down and kiss your forehead. Then I'm going to walk over and tell her that you aren't feeling well. I will meet you in the car."

I peeked over his shoulder and saw Sophia inside the doors, a smug grin on her face. I'd already told him I was quitting. I'd get a job at whatever loser place Brian wanted me to work at, because I obviously couldn't work anywhere that Hudson Pierce would be. But I knew he wouldn't let me walk away unless I agreed to his plan. Then, when I got to the limo, I'd tell Jordan to take off before Hudson joined us.

I gave him a tight nod. He approached cautiously and kissed me softly on the forehead. I crossed my arms over my chest to hide my nipples that had pebbled traitorously.

"The limo, Alayna. I'll meet you there."

I wiped the tears roughly from my face as I walked toward the lot he'd pointed to, picking up my pace as soon as I was out of his view. There were several limos parked, but I spotted Jordan leaning against the hood, playing with his phone. When he saw me walking toward him he opened the door without a word.

"Take me home, please, Jordan," I choked as I slipped in.

Jordan shut the door and I heard him get into the driver's seat. He hadn't said anything, hadn't agreed or disagreed to my direction, and, for a moment, I feared he'd only take his orders from Hudson.

Relief swept over me when the car started...

...and then immediately left when he pulled up next to the ballroom and Hudson climbed in, the doors automatically locking after he'd closed the door.

Shit! Hudson had probably texted Jordan that I was coming out, to pick him up after, and to not take me anywhere without him. Unreasonably, I felt betrayed by my driver.

As the car pulled into traffic, I pressed into the opposite corner, as far away as I could from the man sharing the car with me.

Hudson pressed a button and spoke. "Jordan, drive around until I say otherwise. Or find someplace to park for a while."

Normally I'd blush, afraid of what Jordan would think we were doing in the backseat. But I was too pissed and hurt to care.

We sat a few minutes, not speaking. I couldn't imagine that the always-in-control Hudson Pierce was at a loss for words, so I assumed his silence was meant to calm me down. Or unnerve me. Some sort of expert manipulative tactic.

It didn't calm me. Instead, the silence gave me time to review every moment of the past few days, allowing me to recognize his domineering hand in all of his actions. It gave me fuel to hate him for his control over me. And myself for falling in with the prick in the first place.

Finally he spoke, quietly. "What exactly did Celia tell you?"

I couldn't remain silent. "Oh, just how you fuck with vulnerable women's emotions. Is it true?"

"Alayna—" He moved across the seat, placing his hand on my knee.

"Don't touch me!" He removed his hand. "And stop saying my name. Is it true?"

"Will you calm down so I can explain?"

His soft tone felt patronizing, emboldening my fury. I needed him to admit it. I had to hear him say it. "Is. It. True?"

His answer came in a burst. "Yes, it's true!" He took a deep breath, regaining his control. "In the past, it was true."

I froze, my eyes riveted on him. I hadn't expected a confession. Hadn't expected him to tell me anything—he never did—and I feared if I moved he'd stop talking. So I remained still.

He took his time, not looking at me as he made his admission. "I did… things…that I'm not proud of. I manipulated people. I hurt them and often it was deliberate." He turned to me, piercing me with his intense gray eyes and the grit in his voice. "But not now. I don't do that now. Not with you."

His delivery affected me, but I bit past the emotion, knowing I had proof that betrayed his words. "Really? Because it seems completely obvious that you did exactly that with me. The way you picked me out at the symposium and you tracked me down and gave me a spa vacation and Jesus, you bought the club!"

He shook his head. "It's not like that. I explained the gift and I was looking at the club anyway. When I found out you worked there, yes, it helped me make my decision—"

I cut him off. "And you 'hired' me and seduced me. And when I told you I needed to not have sex with you, you somehow got me to do exactly that. You *are* manipulative. You're a bully, Hudson." I wrapped my arms around myself, hoping to stop the new onslaught of tears that threatened.

"No, Alayna. I didn't want that with you." The anguish in his tone set my tears into motion. He leaned forward and I sensed he wanted to touch me. Instead, he put his hand on the seat next to me, putting himself as close to me as I'd let him. "I don't *want* to be like that with you."

I swiped at the tears, unable to keep up with their pace. "Then what do you want to be with me, Hudson?"

"Honestly? I'm not sure." He sat back against the seat. His expression confused, torn.

Suddenly, he looked much younger than I'd ever seen him. He no longer seemed the confident, commanding alpha male that I knew him to be, but like a group member in one of my therapy sessions, exposed and accessible.

He let out a brief laugh, as if he recognized his own vulnerability and it amused him or confounded him. "I'm drawn to you, Alayna. Not because I want to hurt you or make you feel a certain way, but because you're beautiful and sexy and smart and, yes, a little crazy, maybe, but you're not broken. And that makes me hopeful. *For me.*"

I let out a shaky breath. God help me, I wanted to reach out to him. I wanted to comfort him, knowing his words about me said more about himself than any he'd ever spoken.

I didn't move, though, still not willing to break the moment. Even my tears had stilled, as if they'd interrupt.

"And maybe I've been a bully. But I'm a dominant person. I can try to change things about me, but the fundamentals of my personality are never going away." His voice lowered further. "You of all people should be able to understand that."

He had me earlier. Probably back when he'd insisted he didn't want to be whatever with me, but for sure when he'd inferred he was broken, and that I was not. And if none of that had reached me, his last statement would have. I *did* understand him. More than I had ever thought possible. What it felt like to be a certain way and to loathe myself for it. How difficult it was to change and learn to accept the parts of me that were fundamentally never going to change. And what it did to me to believe I was incapable of falling in love the way normal people do.

I knew what it felt like to be that person.

"I'm sorry." It came out as a choked whisper so I repeated it. "I'm sorry. You didn't judge me and I judged you."

He nodded once and I knew that was his way of accepting my apology.

"And I exaggerated when I called you a bully. I haven't done anything I didn't want to. And your whole confident, domineering thing is actually kinda hot."

He almost smiled, but squeezed his eyes shut as if trying to reign in his emotions. When he opened them again, they were pleading. "Alayna, don't quit. Don't quit me."

I looked away, knowing how easy it would be to give in if I kept staring into those gray eyes. "Hudson, I have to. Not because of this, well, not only because of this, but because of my past. I'm not well enough to be with someone who has his own issues."

Truthfully, I didn't know if I was well enough to be with anyone.

"You are, Alayna. You only tell that to yourself because you're scared."

That drew me to face him. "I should be scared. It's not safe. For either of us. You should be scared, too."

He let out a heavy breath. When he spoke again, he was resigned, as if he didn't expect his words to make a difference yet he spoke them anyway. "I don't believe that. I think spending time with another person who has similar compulsive tendencies can provide insight and healing."

I leaned my head back against the seat and stared at the car's ceiling. I wanted to believe like he did—that we could make each other better. But I couldn't. All I'd witnessed and experienced in my life around addicts told me otherwise. Besides, if he'd wanted me around him to confide in and give some understanding, he should have told me his secrets from the beginning. And he hadn't.

As much as it pained me, I had to break things off. I had to do the right thing once and for all.

But there were my own financial woes. As irrelevant as money might have seemed at the moment, being able to keep my job at the club had an enormous impact on my own mental well-being.

"I won't quit." I turned to face him. "But I can't have a relationship with you, Hudson." My throat felt tight, but I kept on. "All I can give you is the fake. I have to protect myself here." I should have ended all of it, but I didn't have the strength for that. This had to enough.

Hudson's shoulders lowered slightly. "I understand." He nodded as if to reaffirm that he understood, making me suspect that he didn't understand at all but was accepting my decision anyway. "Thank you." He straightened, his poise returning, and I knew that he was back to his regular confident self.

I had one more thing to say, though. I leaned toward him, placing my hand firmly on his knee. "Hudson, you're not broken."

His expression faltered briefly, his eyes cast downward. When they rose again I saw them pass my exposed cleavage. His brow rose. "What are you…? Is that…?"

I looked down to see what he saw. The corset. Damn, I'd forgotten. A familiar tug of desire formed low in my belly, followed by a more painful ache in my chest. "Yes. I'd worn it for you."

He sighed. "Wow. That was…that was very thoughtful of you."

We still wanted each other, and it would be so easy to let that want rule us.

But I was stronger than that. I could be stronger than that. "I'm sorry."

"I know. I am, too." His eyes lingered on mine for a moment, before he shifted gears entirely. "This may be poor timing, but I need to get back to my mother's show."

"Sure."

"And since you're supposed to be sick, you will need to go home."

I listened as he ordered Jordan to drive toward my apartment.

"When is our next show, boss?" I asked, half praying the answer was soon, knowing that the more time before I saw him again, the better.

"I'm not sure. I have to fly to Cincinnati tonight." He pursed his lips. "And I am not your boss."

"Cincinnati? Tonight?"

"Yes, tonight. I have a meeting first thing in the morning. My jet's leaving early evening." A private jet. Of course. "I'll text you later to arrange the Hamptons. We'll leave Friday afternoon."

"So you'll be gone all week?" I don't know why I asked. It shouldn't have mattered.

"I'm not sure yet."

"Oh." He already felt distant, like he'd already gone. I turned my head to hide the tears that were filling my eyes.

The car pulled over to the side of the road. I looked out the tinted window and saw we were in front of my apartment. Jordan got out of the car, and shortly after, my door opened.

I didn't want to get out. It felt awkward and awful—my second sort-of-not-at-all break-up in a week. Why did this one hurt so dang much?

Without looking back at Hudson, I stepped out of the car.

"Alayna." He called me just as I stood fully. I pasted on a fake smile and ducked my head back in. "Thank you for today. I think you've truly made an impression on my mother. Good work."

I stayed at the curb until Jordan had shut the door and gotten back into the car. A shiver ran through me, despite the hot summer day. Wrapping my arms around myself, I headed up to the small studio apartment that felt big for all the loneliness it held.

At my door I found a bag of gourmet coffee and I dissolved into tears, completely melted by his gesture. *My elastic band lie.* Hudson never missed a beat. I wracked my brain trying to figure out when he had arranged to have it delivered, and realized it had to be before the limo conversation. It was a sweet gesture. I wondered if he wished he hadn't done it now.

Whether he regretted it or not, it gave me an excuse to reach out to him once more. I pulled out my phone and typed a carefully thought out text. "*Thanks for the coffee. And for everything else.*"

It was a goodbye to the great whatever it was we'd had, fleeting as it was. I needed the closure. Maybe he did, too.

I pushed send and had a moment of panic, wondering if I'd done the right thing by ending our relationship, wondering if I could undo it, praying that his response would show me he was having the same doubts as I was.

But Hudson didn't respond at all.

— CHAPTER —
THIRTEEN

I stalked Hudson online again that night.

Not because I felt I needed to learn more about him, but because the distance between us felt so overwhelmingly vast. It was a familiar feeling, one I'd felt with guys I'd dated only to discover later, in therapy, that I'd been overreacting. But this was different. We were apart for real, not only in my psycho head. And I couldn't bear it. I had to get closer to him in whatever way I could, even if it was only via the Internet.

There were already new blog posts and news feeds from the fashion show. The event had great reviews, and more money had been raised than projected. I flicked through the pictures of models, a little wistful that I had missed that part of the day. And there were pictures of me with Hudson, kissing outside the limo when we were on our way in. I stared at those the longest, saving one particularly close shot as my wallpaper desktop.

Most of my stalking, however, was on Pierce Industries and its business ties in Cincinnati. I searched way longer than I should have, trying to deduce if Hudson really was going there, and finding nothing helpful. Did he really have business or did he just want distance?

It shouldn't have mattered. Our next assignment wasn't until Friday. But the need to know ate at me, consuming my mind until I'd spent hours exhausting every avenue of research I could think of.

At least I stopped myself at online stalking and checking my phone over and over for a response from him. I didn't call the airport to see if a Pierce Industries jet had taken off—that wouldn't have been healthy behavior.

Besides, I had no idea what airport.

I AWOKE THE next afternoon with a knot in my chest. My muscles felt jittery even before I'd had any coffee. They were my usual anxiety symptoms, but I couldn't say for sure what had caused the attack. Worry about my meeting with David? Or stress about Hudson?

In an attempt to relax, I popped in a yoga DVD before I had to get ready to leave. The narrowed focus and rhythmic breathing loosened me for the most part, but the edge still lingered.

I spent longer than usual prettying up for my meeting at the club. Not for David, but for myself. Sometimes looking good made me feel good, and I was willing to try every trick in the book to get rid of the tension. But no matter what I did, the anxiety remained, buzzing through my veins with a steady electric current.

It was simply nerves about the promotion, I told myself. I'd feel better after meeting with David.

As I was on my way out the door, I got an incoming text. I checked it eagerly. But it wasn't from Hudson. It was from David.

"*Something's come up,*" it said. "*Reschedule for Wednesday at 7.*"

Then I knew. That the stressing had nothing to do with David, because moving our meeting did nothing to change the way I felt. I should have felt relief, or a spike in the tension since it would have to be dragged out two more days. Also, I should have wondered about what had come up. David and I were close enough that he'd tell me. But I had no desire to ask.

Hudson. It was Hudson that kept coming to mind. Where was he? What was he doing? Was he thinking of me?

I texted back a confirmation to David and paced my apartment, trying to decide the best way to get my ex-lover off the brain. I needed to catch a group. Checking online, I made sure there was still an Addicts Anonymous session scheduled on Monday afternoons. There was, but I had plenty of time before the session started.

I could run. With Jordan driving me around so much, a bit of aerobic activity would be good for me. I changed into shorts and a tank top, put on my running shoes and started out.

The run helped clear my head, the endorphins flowing through my body making me feel better and more confident. And invincible. Which was why when I found my route had led me to the Pierce Industries building, I convinced myself it didn't mean anything. It wasn't a big deal to be there. Especially since I only went inside to use the bathroom in the lobby before resuming my run.

I felt so good from the exercise that I decided to skip therapy all together and keep on with my run for a while longer, continuing to the Lincoln tunnel before turning around. I passed the Pierce Industries building again on my way back. And since I knew there was a drinking fountain inside, I went in again, this time lingering a bit in the lobby, scoping out the elevators looking for some sign of Hudson in the building. I managed to make myself leave before I slipped into a car and pushed the button for the top floor.

The next day I didn't possess as much strength.

Not only did I return to the building three times, but each time I rode the elevator. I told myself it couldn't be called stalking exactly, because Hudson was out of town—though I had yet to accept that as truth—and because I never actually pushed the button for Hudson's floor. Instead, I let fate take me wherever, journeying with whoever stepped on to whatever floor they were going to, then forcing myself to return back to the lobby. It felt like elevator roulette—if the car took me to the top floor, then I was meant to stop by Hudson's office. But each time, I missed the bullet, the other passengers never choosing his floor.

Until Wednesday.

Even though my shift the night before had gotten me home at almost six in the morning, I was awake and back at the Pierce building before one that afternoon. My first ride took me only to the fifth floor. When the passenger stepped out and the doors closed, I leaned against the back of the car and sighed, knowing the car would return to the lobby if I didn't push a button.

But instead of going down, the car went up. Someone must have summoned it from a floor above. I held my breath as I watched the needle rise higher and higher. Then it stopped on the top floor. Not the secret top floor that required a code and would take me to the loft, but to the floor that Hudson's office was located on. I braced myself for what I'd see when the doors opened, hoping I'd learn something by peeking around whoever stepped into the car with me.

But I wasn't prepared for the sight that met me. Three men in suits were laughing and joking as the doors parted. And with them was Hudson.

"Alayna." His voice was even as always, with only a hint of surprise in his tone.

I froze, my body unable to move, my mouth unable to speak. A wave of jumbled emotions ran through me: I was happy to see him, yet petrified. Enraged to find he was in town after all and somewhat satisfied that my suspicions had been right.

Hudson held a hand out to me. Automatically my arm moved to take it, and he pulled me out to stand next to him. He turned to the men with him. "Gentlemen, my girlfriend has decided to surprise me with a visit to my office."

I managed to smile before pinning my stare to my gray running shoes.

"That can never be good," one of the other men said and they all laughed. "Well, we'll leave you to her then. Thank you again for meeting with us."

I barely heard the goodbyes the men exchanged with Hudson before they took my place in the car, and how I made it the short distance to his office was beyond me. I was numb, my mind consumed with the fact that I was someplace that I shouldn't be.

The office doors clicked closed behind us. Hudson must have held my hand the whole way there, but I didn't notice until he dropped it and walked away from me. "What are you doing here, Alayna?"

I couldn't bring myself to look at him, but the absence of anger in his tone brought me out of my haze. I could get myself through this. I'd been good at talking my way through things in my obsessive days. I'd explain and he'd believe me and all would be fine.

But I didn't want to be that girl anymore.

It was right then that I'd realized the severity of what I'd been doing: I'd been stalking. For the first time in years. I'd fallen off the wagon with probably the worst person I could fall off the wagon with. If I'd thought restraining orders and lawsuits had been a nightmare when they were filed by Ian, my last object of obsession, imagine what it would be like with a powerful man like Hudson.

But even more than that—recovering from my addiction to Ian had been hard, but possible. Hudson, though…I couldn't even bear to think about not being around him in some way or another, no matter what the context.

Hudson was waiting for my answer. I could feel him studying me. I hugged my arms around myself and took a deep breath. "I, uh, I wanted to see if you were back."

I nearly sobbed with the honesty of my statement, but if Hudson noticed, he didn't let on. "I got back late last night. You could have called. Or texted."

My mind reached for the steps of talking through unhealthy behaviors. I'd learned them many times in therapy. *Communicate your fears openly and honestly.* Closing my eyes to stymie my tears, I said, "You don't answer my texts."

"I didn't answer one text."

I opened my eyes and found him staring at me intently as he leaned against his desk. I brushed away the one tear that had escaped down my cheek and met his gaze. "It was my only text."

I heard how it sounded. Ridiculous, an overreaction. We weren't together. Why should he answer my texts? He had to be regretting his choice for a pretend girlfriend now. Now that he saw the extent of my crazy.

Our eyes remained locked, but I could read nothing in his expression. It seemed like forever before his face softened and he said, "I didn't realize it was important to you. I'll make a better effort to respond in the future."

My mouth fell open.

He straightened to a standing position. "But you can't just come here like this. How do you think it looks to have my girlfriend wandering around the lobby, riding the elevators when I'm not even in town?"

"How did you…?"

"I pay people to know things, Alayna."

He knew. Of course, he knew. I'd decided to communicate honestly, but had hoped I didn't have to be that honest. That he knew I'd been by his office several times, that I'd roamed the building…I was humiliated.

More tears fell. "I…I'm sorry. I couldn't help myself."

"Please, don't do it again." He was stern, but did I detect a note of compassion?

His reaction was all wrong. He should have been more pissed, more freaked out. "Why are you being like this?"

His brow wrinkled. "Like what?"

"I've fucked things up, Hudson! You should be calling your security to escort me out. I'm a mess and you're taking it all in stride." The tears fell fast now. There was no stopping them.

His face eased and he stepped toward me. "No," he said softly, his tone embracing me even though his arms didn't. "That's what I meant about being around someone who understood. I know about compulsion. I know about having to do things you know you shouldn't."

He wiped a tear from my cheek with his thumb, his hand resting there longer than necessary. "When you feel you can't help yourself, talk to me first."

The anxious knot I'd felt for days dissolved under his words. Had he been right? Could we help each other through our pains? Could we fix each other?

I looked into his eyes and wanted again to believe as he did, this time much closer to saying that I did.

But before I could say anything, his secretary's voice boomed through the office. "Mr. Pierce, your one-thirty is here."

Hudson sighed, dropping his hand from my face. "I apologize for cutting this short, Alayna, but I have another meeting now. And I'm leaving again this evening."

My spirits sank. I didn't know if I believed him, but I did know I didn't want distance between us. That was what had spurred my obsessive episode this week. Well, he'd asked for me to share…"I hate that you're leaving. It makes me feel a little distraught." A lot distraught, actually.

His eyes lit up. "I'll be back tomorrow." He took my hand and squeezed. "Join me tomorrow night for the symphony."

My heart flip-flopped. "Yes."

"I'll pick you up at six. Wear the dress."

I MADE IT to group that afternoon before meeting with David. I'd made a mistake, but Hudson was willing to look past it. More than willing. And that made it so much easier to believe that I wasn't doomed to be totally freaky with him. I had to make an effort to stay well.

Not comfortable telling my situation to everyone, not when people might know about my connection with Hudson, I was vague on my turn to share. "I'm…I've slipped a bit."

It was an accurate enough statement. My behavior hadn't been as bad as it could have been. But every journey starts with a single step—even the journeys we shouldn't be taking, and at the rate I'd been going that week, I'd be well on my way down the obsession road before I had a grip.

Lauren nodded sympathetically. "When you get home, I'd like you to write out a list of your recent negative behaviors, including behaviors you only thought about engaging in. Then come up with a list of healthy behaviors you can substitute whenever you feel compelled to engage in an unhealthy one. Do you need any help?"

"No." I'd done this before. More than once. I still had all the substitute behaviors memorized from the last time I'd gone off the wagon: *Run, do yoga, take an extra shift at work, concentrate on school, visit Brian.* Obviously my list needed updating.

"Good. You know your patterns. Are you still journaling?"

"I haven't in a while." A long while.

Lauren smiled. "I recommend you start again." She was always good for a swift kick in the butt.

"Okay." And I would. But something told me that of all the suggestions I'd received that day, the best one had been from Hudson himself: *When you can't help yourself, talk to me.*

I was quiet the rest of the session, replaying an old favorite quote over and over in my head, committing myself to modifying my actions. *If there is no struggle, there is no progress. If there is no struggle, there is no progress.*

I felt better after group, stronger and my head clear. As Jordan drove me to work later, I added to my substitute behaviors list, including making it a goal to watch every title on the AFI's 100 Greatest Movies list and continue reading the top one hundred books on GreatestBooks.org.

My good mood and healthy attitude gave me courage to send a text to Hudson before I walked into my meeting with David that evening. *"Do you really have to leave town again?"*

This time I got a response instantly. *"I'm afraid so."*

He'd listened—had adjusted his behavior knowing how it affected me to not get a response. Before I could decide how to answer, he sent another. *"But I'm glad to know you're thinking of me."*

A tingle spread through my body. *"Always,"* I told him before I could stop myself. What was I doing? What were *we* doing? We weren't lovers anymore—were we becoming something else? Something more like friends? Friends who flirted by text?

Whatever we were doing, it felt good. So good that I followed my last text with another more dangerous message. *"Are you thinking of me?"*

David opened his office door, interrupting my feel-good moment before Hudson had a chance to reply. "Laynie, come in." David was stiff and his voice tight.

His serious demeanor made me stuff my phone in my bra. "Is everything okay?" I thought back to his message from Monday. "What came up the other day?" I asked as I took a seat in front of his desk.

"This." David threw a folded newspaper down on the desk before sitting in his chair across from me.

Puzzled, I picked up the newspaper and scanned for what might have put him in such a foul mood. And there it was, in full color on the top of Monday's society section, the picture of Hudson and me kissing.

"Oh. That." David had been the one person I'd been scared of telling. I feared he'd jump to conclusions. The wrong conclusions.

And he did. "You want to explain this, Laynie?" He stood and began pacing, not pausing long enough for me to answer. "'Cause I'll tell you what it looks like. It looks like you were so eager to get your precious promotion that, when you couldn't get it by playing me, you chose to go after the next guy who could get you what you wanted."

I put a hand out in front of me as if to stop him from saying what he was saying. "It's not like that, David. It was never like that." How could he think that I'd liked him for a promotion? That I'd been insincere when I'd been with him?

"It wasn't?" He stopped pacing and leaned toward me, his palms on his desk. "Then tell me what it was like, Laynie."

"It's…I can't…" My floundering was exacerbated by the buzz of my phone against my breast. I knew it was a reply from Hudson, and I longed to read it. But there was no way I could right then. Not with David raging in front of me.

"Yeah, that's what I thought." He straightened, a look of utter disgust joining the scowl on his face. "Now I'm forced to move you up, implement your ideas, never mind that I was going to anyway, or fear for my own job." He laughed dryly. "I'm probably grooming you to take my place."

"David, no." This was worse than I had imagined. I didn't want him to think I ever wanted to take his job from him. I had imagined us running The Sky Launch together. Though the romantic part of that duo was no longer appealing to me, I still very much wanted the business duo.

"Does Pierce have any idea about me?"

"David, don't."

His eyes narrowed. "Does he know that you're The Sky Launch slut?"

That was the turning point. Instead of feeling bad, I got pissed. And when I got pissed, I used all the weapons in my arsenal. "If you really believe what you're saying, David, that I have some power over Hudson, then maybe you should be a little more careful how you talk to me."

His eyebrows lifted, surprised by my steady tone and pointed words.

"Now, sit down," I continued, "and we can talk about this in a civilized manner." I waited while he plopped down in his chair. "Good. Let me see if I have this right—you think I'm dating Hudson so that I could get a promotion at the club. A promotion that you've basically promised me because of my hard work here over the past few years. A promotion I earned before you and I even kissed."

"Why else would you be dating him?" His words were challenging, but the fight had left.

"Not that it's any of your business, but I'm dating Hudson because..." I was on-duty in that moment, but my reason was honest. "Because I like him. And he likes me. We connect. And, even before our first date, he spelled out to me that he would have nothing to do with helping me move up here. And I accepted it because I knew I could get the manager title on my merit alone. Tell me, did Hudson instruct you to promote me?"

His shoulders slumped. "No."

"And were you going to offer me the position before you saw our picture in the paper?"

"Yes."

"Then what are we even talking about?"

He shook his head and shrugged. "Laynie...I...I don't know what to say. I guess I jumped to conclusions. I said things that were uncalled for."

"I get it. I knew it would look that way." I let out a silent breath, relieved that he'd calmed so easily. "Maybe I should have said something earlier."

David shook his head. Then he met my eyes directly. "No, I was acting jealous. And I didn't have any right to. I'm the one who ended things."

"It's okay." I looked away. His jealous remark hung in the air between us. Once upon a time I would have jumped all over it. Now, it felt weird to have him feeling things about me.

So I changed the subject. "Um, about the promotion…did you say you were giving it to me?"

He smiled. "Yes. Of course I am. Pierce didn't tell you?"

Up until recently, Hudson and I didn't talk much when we were together. But I wasn't telling that to David. "He really didn't."

"Good. I'm glad to be the first to tell you. Congratulations." He outstretched his hand to shake mine then took it back. "What am I doing? Come here." We both stood and met at the side of his desk for a hug.

I pulled away first.

He noticed, covering by jumping into work mode. "And we're taking your suggestions. We'll extend the club hours starting in August. Which means you have a lot of work to do to get the place ready. Plan on lots of marketing and promotional meetings."

I put a hand on his arm. "Thank you, David."

"You deserve it."

We spent the hours until the club opened working on a business plan. It was distracting and exhilarating and exactly what my obsessive mind needed. Work would automatically make it to my list of substitute behaviors. I now had a salaried position and many of my shifts would take place during daylight hours. Wouldn't Brian be proud?

When the club opened, I shadowed David, learning more managerial duties. By the time we closed, I was exhausted and grateful that I didn't have to walk home.

It wasn't until Jordan was helping me into the backseat of the car after my shift was over that I remembered to read my text from Hudson. "*Always,*" it said.

My heart stopped. I reread my text to him to be sure I correctly remembered what I'd sent. I did. I had asked him if he was thinking of me, and his answer was *Always.*

— CHAPTER —

FOURTEEN

Jordan was waiting for me with the Maybach at six outside my apartment, but I saw before he even opened the door for me that the backseat was empty.

"Mr. Pierce is late getting back in town," Jordan explained. "He'll meet you at Lincoln Center. I have your ticket."

Having felt anxious all day about seeing Hudson, not sure what the context of our evening would be, I didn't want to be alone. "Do you mind if I ride up front with you?" I asked.

"I'm sure Mr. Pierce would rather you sat in the back."

I pulled the back door from Jordan's grasp and shut it without getting in. "Then we won't tell him, will we?"

Jordan shook his head at me and crossed around to the driver's seat. I opened the front door myself and climbed in next to him.

We rode in silence for a bit, and I read the ticket that Jordan had given me. The New York Philharmonic playing Brahms's Symphonies Two and Three. *Nice.* I loved the arts and it had been forever since I had treated myself to an event of any sort.

Luckily, I didn't have to be at work until one a.m. since I was staying after close to learn how to do monthly inventory. Leisl had come to my apartment that afternoon to help me tie the back of my dress and had taken some of my clothes to work with her so I could change when I got there. It meant Hudson and I had all evening for...for what? Were we on show tonight? Was this a date? Were we going out as friends? I had no idea.

Glancing over at Jordan, I felt inspired to get answers to some of my questions. "Jordan? What has Hudson told you about me?" Jordan had been in the office when we were negotiating the terms of our arrangement. What did he think about us?

Jordan didn't answer.

"You're not supposed to chat with me, are you?" His expression gave me my answer. "Oh, come on. He probably also said to keep me happy. And right now some validation is what would make me happy."

He sighed as if not believing what he was about to do. "He said you're the lady in his life."

"He did?" Of course, he would have. That was my role, after all—to play the lady in his life. But had there been others? "How many ladies has he had in his life?"

"I haven't been hired to drive any others, Ms. Withers. I've only always driven him. Occasionally he might have a date, but not very often."

I frowned, not wanting to think about Hudson on dates.

"Certainly none of them held his interest like you do."

I rolled my eyes, not wanting to be patronized. "You don't have to say that."

"I don't. But it's true."

What did that mean, exactly? That I was special to him? Or that I was the only one he'd hired to show off?

But I couldn't ask Jordan those questions. So instead I asked, "What do you think about Hudson?"

"Me?" Jordan's eyebrows rose in surprise. "Well, he's a good boss. Very clear with his expectations. He demands a lot but the benefits are proportional."

That was nice to know—that he was a decent employer. But it wasn't what I was looking for. "I mean as a person."

Jordan laughed. "I don't know him as anything but a business man." He glanced at me. "You may be one of the only people I've ever met who knows him as just a man."

"I doubt that." Not only because I didn't know him but because I suspected Hudson didn't let anyone know him.

"I wouldn't be so sure."

I wanted to continue the conversation, but we'd arrived at Lincoln Center. It felt strange to arrive by myself, but Jordan directed me to Avery Fisher Hall and gave me all the information I needed. "Tonight is a donor's event. So there's a light buffet in the lobby. Mr. Pierce insisted you enjoy yourself."

I smiled as I pictured Hudson giving the orders to Jordan. Had it been by phone? By text? Either way, I recognized that a great deal of care had gone into the evening. "Do you know when he'll be here?"

Jordan shook his head. "A late meeting of the day delayed his take-off. But he assures he'll arrive as soon as he can." He paused before stepping back behind the driver seat. "Ms. Withers? If I may say, you look quite lovely."

I blushed as I thanked him, but his compliment gave me the courage to make my way into the hall by myself. Finely dressed patrons crowded in with me, the richest in the city, the people who had money to donate to such trivial things as the arts. I'd always been into nice clothes, but had never cared about designer names until that moment when the only thing camouflaging me in the sea of expensive clothes was my own designer gown. I was out of my element. I needed a cocktail.

As Jordan had said, buffet tables lined the lobby and caterers wandered around with trays filled with delicious appetizers and glasses of champagne. I wasn't very hungry, but I grabbed a crab puff as it passed so I'd have something in my stomach when I drank the champagne that I acquired soon after. I spent the next forty-five minutes nursing my drink and nibbling on veggies, my eyes pinned on the front doors searching for my date.

When the crowd thinned, I reluctantly made my way to the seat listed on my ticket. Box seats, of course. My spirits perked up as I noticed patrons entering the box ahead of me. Perhaps Hudson had managed to sneak past me.

But when the usher showed me to my seat, I found the seats on either side of mine empty. Three other seats in our box were taken by a middle-aged couple and a woman my age—a woman I knew. It was Celia.

"Laynie!" Celia said as she sat down. "I'm so glad you came. Where's that handsome man of yours?" Her voice wasn't exactly quiet, and I realized she wanted her companions to hear.

My chest constricted. Definitely not a date, then.

"I wouldn't have missed tonight. I've been looking forward to seeing you again." I did my best to pretend I knew that Celia would be there as she had seemed to know I would be in attendance. "Hudson's late flying in. He's been out-of-town most of this week." I'll admit I hoped the mention of him being out of town would be news to Celia. I felt I needed the upper hand somehow and knowing things about my supposed love that Celia didn't was the only trick I could play.

"Oh, yes. He told me he was leaving again when I talked to him yesterday." So much for insider knowledge. "Let me introduce you to my parents, Warren and Madge Werner. This is Alayna Withers, Hudson's girlfriend."

Mr. and Mrs. Werner exchanged glances before they leaned over their seats to shake my hand.

"It's nice to finally meet you," Madge said. "Sophia has told me so much about you."

Huh, yeah. Whatever Sophia Pierce had to say to her best friend about me couldn't be anything I'd want to know. My stomach knotted at the thought. Where the hell was Hudson? How could he leave me alone with these people?

"Sophia's a delight," I said with as much pleasantry as I could muster. It actually wasn't hard to smile as I said it, as if I had told a private joke about Hudson's monster of a mother.

"Isn't she?" Celia muttered so only I could hear.

Her dig made me feel more comfortable.

Until Madge started to grill me. "Where did you meet Hudson again?"

I repeated the story, embellishing as many romantic moments as I could without going too far overboard, all the while checking over my shoulder, wishing Hudson would appear.

"Withers," Warren said when there was a lull. "Any relation to Joel and Patty?"

"No, sorry." If he was trying to discover the depths of my breeding, I'm afraid he was going to be sorely disappointed.

Relief flooded over me when the lights lowered, ending our conversation. Simultaneously, my resentment toward Hudson grew. I quickly shot him a text, something I should have done an hour earlier. *"Where are you?"*

The response to my text came as a whisper in my ear as the conductor walked on stage and the audience began clapping. "Right beside you."

Chills spread through my body and I looked up to see Hudson had slipped into the seat next to me. *He was there.* Even in the dim theater, I knew he looked gorgeous, wearing a classic tuxedo. His hair was mussed as if he'd dressed quickly, and his face scruffy, increasing the sexy factor.

He nodded to Mr. and Mrs. Werner then took my hand.

His hand in mine—the warmth of it, the strength—it didn't matter if it was for show, I had needed it, and I clung to it until intermission, only letting go so we could applaud.

While the audience was still clapping, he leaned toward me. "What did you think?"

"I loved it." I'd never heard the New York Philharmonic, and Brahms had never been my favorite composer, but the performance had been breathtaking. That I had experienced it with the hottest man on the planet sitting next to me didn't hurt.

"I knew you would." As the lights came up, he pushed a strand of hair behind my ear, and whispered, sending a fresh set of shivers down my spine. "Showtime."

He stood and took my hand to help me up, then turned to face the Werners. "Madge, Warren. I wish I'd been here to make introductions. I take it you've all met now."

"We have," Madge said. "Celia introduced us."

"Good. I wanted the most important people in my life to know each other." Then, with all eyes on us, he wrapped me in his arms, turning my knees to jelly. "I'm sorry I was late, darling. You look stunning. The most beautiful woman here tonight."

He'd said I was stunning when we'd bought the dress, and just as I'd known he'd been saying it for my benefit then, tonight I knew it was for the Werners. He'd never call me "darling" otherwise.

I stared into his eyes, not needing to fake my adoring gaze. "You don't know that. You've barely looked at anyone else."

He rubbed his nose against mine. "Because I can't take my eyes off of you."

God, we could write sappy romance novels. We were that good. *He* was that good.

"You were out of town this week?" Warren asked, not seeming to care if he interrupted fake Alayna and Hudson's moment. "Celia said you were away on business."

I hid a grimace. Celia hadn't said that. *I* had said that.

Hudson kissed my forehead lightly before letting me go and directing his attention to Warren. "Yes. A development with Plexis."

Warren shook his head. "That's been a thorn in your side for some time."

"Excuse us," Madge interrupted. "While you men talk about all your boring business, us girls will freshen up."

I wasn't sure if Madge meant to include me as one of "us girls," but I planned on staying. I wanted to hear the boring business talk. I didn't want to leave Hudson.

But Celia took my arm, obligating me to accompany them, and Hudson appeared to be waiting until we left to continue. Besides I did need to pee.

I didn't miss Hudson's warning glare to Celia. Even I, who hadn't been lifelong friends with the man, knew that look told her to be careful what she said to me.

He didn't need to worry. The conversation on the way to the restroom and while we waited in line was banal and trivial. Mostly Madge made snide comments about what other people were wearing and tried to discern what and how much Hudson had bought for me.

It was after I'd peed that the talk became interesting. Madge and Celia were powdering their noses in the side mirror, and didn't see me come out of my stall. I moved to the sink to wash my hands, and found I could hear their conversation perfectly.

"She's pretty," Madge said. "I'm sorry she's so pretty."

"Mom," Celia groaned. "Stop."

"I'm sure it's only a fling, honey. This is Hudson's first real girlfriend. You never settle down with your first."

I washed my hands for a long time, listening.

"Mother, I don't feel that way about him anymore. I've told you. He's psycho, anyway. You wouldn't want our kids to have those genes."

"He's got better genes than most. And I know you say you're over him, Ceeley, but you don't have to pretend with me. Just make sure he gets thoroughly tested when you get him back."

"Mom!"

An immense wave of rage swept through me. Not only because Madge had insinuated pretty shitty things about me and my sex life, though that did sting. But also because Celia, the woman who was probably Hudson's closest friend, had called him a psycho. No wonder Hudson kept himself so guarded and shut off from the world. Even the people who were supposed to care most for him seemed to have no understanding or empathy for the inner demons that he likely fought on a daily basis.

No wonder he'd come looking for me.

I spritzed cool water on my face, attempting to fan my fury. Then I dried my hands and rejoined the Werner women. Even though I'd just been with him, I suddenly couldn't wait to be with Hudson again. I regretted that I'd pushed him away. He needed me, I realized now, in a very profound way that I couldn't put into words. And I needed him. I practically ran to the box.

Hudson put his arm around my waist when I came to him, though he continued his banter with Mr. Werner and I melted. Wanting even more contact with him, to share physically the epiphany I'd had in the bathroom, I slid my hand under his jacket, desperate to touch him more, gliding my fingers along his lower back.

He stiffened.

I withdrew my hand and he relaxed.

I had to concentrate to not let the sting of his rejection show on my face. Maybe he didn't realize what I was trying to tell him. So I tried again in the dark when the symphony started again, placing my hand on his knee. Then I trailed it higher along his thigh.

He stopped me, taking my hand in his. He held it there for the remainder of the show, and though it still held warmth and strength, it felt like a restraint rather than a comfort.

Disappointment wrapped around me with a cold chill. I was too late. I'd pushed him away and now the invitation was gone. I was grateful for the dark. He wouldn't notice my eyes filling.

After the concert was over, we walked out with the Werners toward the parking garage rather than the pickup area.

"I drove," Hudson said, answering my brow raise.

He kept his arm around me as we walked. His touch was constant, but it was all pretend. The pressure and passion he'd shown me in private was missing.

Also gone were his eyes. Before, whenever I was with him, his eyes never left my body, my face. Now he didn't make eye contact once and he barely talked to me at all. Instead, he chatted comfortably with Celia, sharing inside jokes. With each step we took, I felt more and more distraught. Sobs built up in in my throat and I concentrated on forcing them back down, keeping them at bay.

We parted with our companions at the Mercedes. Celia gave me a quick hug while Hudson shook Warren's hand and kissed Madge on the cheek. I nodded to the Werners then Hudson held the door open for me as I climbed into the passenger seat.

Before getting in himself, Hudson said goodbye to Celia. I watched through the window, my stomach curling. He hugged her and whispered something in her ear that made her laugh. I wiped away the stray tear that slipped past my defenses.

Besides destroying me, watching them made me mad—mad as in crazy and mad as in angry as hell. Wasn't Hudson supposed to be proving that he and Celia *shouldn't* be together? And after I'd learned her true thoughts about him, I knew they shouldn't be together. She was all wrong for him.

Envy spread through my veins like liquid ice. Celia might not have romance with Hudson, but neither did I. And she had friendship with him. At the moment, it appeared I had nothing.

We didn't speak while we maneuvered through the long line out of the garage, Hudson humming fragments of the Brahms symphony as he drove. Was I the only one feeling the thick and heavy tension? A tension that seemed to grow thicker by the minute.

By the time we were on the road I couldn't hold in my feelings of frustration and heartbreak any longer. "So you knew Celia would be there tonight." It wasn't a question. I already knew the answer, but I wanted him to say it.

His eyes widened, as if surprised at my harsh tone. "I knew Celia would be there with her parents, yes." He glanced at me sideways. "Her parents, whom are friends with my parents, remember."

Right. Fooling them was as essential as fooling Sophia Pierce.

What was my problem? I wrapped my arms around my chest and banged my head against the window once, twice, three times. I shouldn't have been angry—he'd told me he'd be fake with me. I shouldn't have been jealous—Celia had him as a friend way before I came along. And she didn't have more than that.

And neither did I. Not since I'd ended things four days before. Funny how I'd been afraid that being with Hudson would make me fall into bad patterns. Instead, not being with him had been what triggered my anxiety that week and what made me feel so rotten at the moment.

Another tear slipped down my cheek. I dabbed at it with my knuckle.

"What's wrong?" Hudson asked, concern in his voice. Or maybe it was simply puzzlement.

I considered what to say. I could keep the barrier up between us and evade the question. Or lie. Or confess my envy. Or I could be honest.

Unable to go another minute with the loneliness that had settled in my chest, honesty won over. "I want you," I whispered, my face pressed against the glass, too embarrassed to look at him.

"Alayna?" I felt his eyes on me.

"I know what I said." I wiped my eyes, determined to keep the rest of my tears in my eyes. "But maybe I was wrong. I mean, I don't know if you're right—if spending time with you can make me better. But I know that since we've been apart, I've been worse." Taking a ragged breath, I braved a look at him. "I miss you." A nervous giggle escaped from my throat. "Told you I get attached."

A trace of a smile crossed his lips. "Where do you think I'm taking you?"

I glanced out the window, having not been paying attention to our destination. Lincoln. Headed East. We were blocks away from Pierce Industries. The loft.

I straightened, a blush crawling on my cheeks. "Oh," I said, the lonely ache inside burning away with the spark of desire. Then irritation took over. "I told you no more sex, and you were taking me to the loft without asking?"

"Alayna," he sighed with frustration. "You are a bundle of mixed signals. At the symphony you seemed to indicate—"

"And you totally blew me off," I interrupted. "Don't talk to me about mixed signals!"

He put his hand on my knee. "I was trying to avoid mixing business with pleasure. A difficult task with you, precious." His voice grew low. "Especially with your wandering hands and how hot you look in that dress."

I blinked. "Oh," I said again. How did he do that? How did he compartmentalize, dividing the pretend from the real, never the two to cross while I tied myself up in knots?

"If you want me to ask, I will, though you know it's not my style." He took my silent stare as a "yes" even though it was simply me processing. "May I take you to my bed, Alayna?"

His request came out in a rumble that had my passion buttons going off like fireworks. "Yes," I half moaned as he pulled up to a red light.

His hand moved to my head, pulling me to him. His mouth was greedy and full of need, his tongue tasting of deep lust and the Amaretto coffee he'd had at intermission. My panties felt slick, and the corset binding of my dress felt tight against my breasts.

The honk of a horn pulled him back to the steering wheel. He shifted in his seat and my eyes shot to the bulge straining his pants. My mouth watered, wanting it inside me.

Hudson shifted again. "Those hungry eyes are not helping the situation."

And then we were there. Pulling in at the valet station of Pierce Industries. I was oblivious to the motions Hudson went through, greeting the valet, handing over his keys, moving to walk behind me toward the elevators, his hand firmly on my ass.

In the elevator we were alone. Hudson entered the code for the penthouse and, as soon as the doors closed, he pressed me against the sheer metal wall of the car. Pausing inches from my lips, his breath mingled with mine. "You're so beautiful, Alayna."

"Then kiss me."

One side of his mouth curled up seductively. "I think I'll take my time." Slowly, he traced his nose against my jawline, and down my neck. I moved my mouth to try to capture his, but he was quicker, always a step ahead of me. His merciless seduction turned me on to no end, creating a pool of moisture between my legs.

His slow pace was killing me. "I think I'll urge you to move faster." I slid my hand down to fondle the bulge in his pants.

"Fuck me, Alayna!" he hissed as I continued to knead his erection through the material.

"You'll get no protest from me." I felt him growing stiffer under my palm. "Actually, I'd like to fuck you with my mouth."

His eyes widened, but before I could act on my statement, the elevator stopped at the top floor. He pulled me out of the car, letting go of me to fumble for his keys. I rubbed his back while he unlocked the door, unable to stop touching him. "Get in," he growled as he held the door open for me.

We'd only made it over the threshold, the door slamming behind us before he'd pushed me to the wall. He flipped on one light, then he took my face in his hands and my mouth in his, thrusting his tongue inside to battle with mine, his stubble chaffing against my tender skin. I loved his aggressiveness, as if he couldn't get enough of my taste. I certainly couldn't get enough of his.

But I'd been serious about wanting my mouth elsewhere on his body, and though Hudson liked to dominate our time together, I wanted to please him. While he still cradled my face, controlling the intensity of our kiss, my hands unzipped his fly and slipped inside to stroke him. Even through the material of his briefs, Hudson groaned against my lips at my caress.

His sounds ignited my desire. I pulled away from his grip and turned him to the wall. He was going to need support for what I had planned. Then I wrestled his pants and briefs down his legs enough to release his cock. "There's the big boy," I purred as I swirled my hand across his head. Catching a bead of pre-cum, I circled my fingers around his shaft and let the moisture glide my hand down his erection.

He moaned again, and I sank to my knees. Holding his cock at the base with one hand, I curled my lips around his crown, and sucked him gently. He gasped, gripping my hair in between his fingers, pulling it to the point of a delicious sting. "God, Alayna. That's so…ah…so good."

His praise encouraged me. I stroked my fist up and down his shaft, quickly developing a steady pace, while I licked and sucked his head into my hollowed cheeks. I gave him the full treatment, trailing my tongue along his thick ridge and softly grazing my teeth across his crown. He grew thicker under my attention, and my own arousal spiked.

I hadn't thought whether or not I intended to suck him to orgasm, but suddenly I was desperate for it. I needed his climax, maybe as much as he did, and my mouth greedily portrayed that need.

"Alayna, stop." Before I could react, his hands pulled my head away, his cock falling from my mouth with a pop.

Shocked and confused, I let him help me up. "Did I do something wrong?"

"No, precious. Your mouth is amazing." He reclaimed my lips for a deep kiss. "But I need to come inside your cunt. I've been thinking about it for days." He wrapped his arms around my back and began working on the ties of my corset. "And you need to be naked."

I groaned, knowing it would take forever to get me out of my dress. "That will take too long," I murmured into his neck.

"It has to be." He pulled me tighter so he could see what he was doing over my shoulder. "I have to have access to your breasts. I love your breasts."

I sighed and began working the buttons of his shirt. "Then you have to be naked, too."

He shook his head against mine. "That will take longer."

"But I love the feel of my breasts against your bare chest."

His chuckle turned into a groan of frustration. "I don't even want to know how you got into this dress. Turn around." I did so, lifting my hair so he could work better. His fingers moved deftly and soon he had loosened it enough for me to take over.

I felt his fingers leave me and heard him fumbling with his own clothing. With my back still toward him, I slipped the gown off the rest of the way, and climbed out. Then I removed my panties. I left my shoes on, knowing he liked to do me in heels. Before I turned around, I took a deep breath, knowing that when I saw him naked, he would take it away.

And, boy, was I right. I'd only really gotten to look at him naked the one time in the shower, but I hadn't forgotten how the sight affected me. His stomach was washboard tight, and his thigh muscles strong. And in between his legs, his erection stood proudly, even more virile and beautiful without his clothing to hinder the view.

Finally my gaze made it to his face, and I noticed he was leering at me with the same amount of intense desire I felt for him. Our eyes met. Then I was in his arms—his strong, beautiful arms—as he kissed me with deep hunger, my breasts smashed against his torso. Soon, he tucked his hands under my ass and lifted me. I wrapped my legs around his waist and my arms around his neck, as he adjusted my hips over his cock.

He paused at my entrance. "I haven't gotten you ready."

"I'm close enough. Come on in, Hudson."

He smirked as he rammed into me in one fierce drive. His cock burned inside my not yet fully wet pussy, but it also felt so wonderfully good. So deep and so hard.

He wasted no time establishing a steady rhythm, powering into me with each stroke. The strength it must have taken to hold me in that position and to fuck me with such force amazed me. I'd known he was fit, but hadn't realized the extent. The awareness heightened my arousal and slickened my sex, allowing him to slide in and out with ease. My breasts bounced with our movement, and shocks of delight shot through my body as my sensitive nipples brushed against his chest. "Hudson, yes. God, yes."

Our eyes remained locked and I could see the strain and the pleasure etched in his forehead as he continued to pound us toward climax. "So… damn…good," he panted. "You feel…so…damn…good."

His encouragement and the sound of our thighs slapping drove me insane, so close to orgasm. With each thrust of his hips, my sex tightened around his steel erection. He turned me to the wall for added support, adjusting his stance so he could pummel me with greater impetus. The new position freed his hand, and he rubbed my clit as his crown found a tender spot. "Come with me, Alayna," he commanded. "Come."

His authoritative tone and circling thumb were my undoing. I threw my head back into the wall, my cunt trembling as my orgasm crashed through me. He followed, groaning my name while he released into me in long, hot spurts.

I unwrapped my legs from his waist and felt numbly for the floor with my foot, knowing that he couldn't possibly continue to carry me after that violent of a release. Though he no longer held my weight, he didn't let go of me.

"Can we do that again?" I panted, before our bodies had even cooled.

His brow furrowed as he released his grasp on me to look at his watch. "You have to be to work at one? I think we can manage to do that again twice."

— CHAPTER —
FIFTEEN

"Okay, H, we need to have a heart to heart." We'd been on the road to the Hamptons for less than ten minutes, but I was too anxious to postpone this conversation. I swiveled in the front seat of the Mercedes and pushed my sunglasses to my head so I could see Hudson clearly.

He glanced sideways at me, his own eyes hidden behind his dark Ray Bans. "Sounds intriguing."

I took a deep breath. "I have some grievances about last night."

His brow rose skeptically over his sunglasses, but he kept his eyes on the road.

"Not that part of last night." I hit his arm playfully. "The earlier part of the night. The later part was fine."

He frowned. "Only fine?"

"More than fine," I laughed. "It was spectacular. Incredibly spectacular." My thighs tensed just thinking about the sensual delight we'd experienced the night before at the loft. A kernel of insecurity crept in under my praise, causing me to wonder if he felt the same. Bracing myself, I asked, "How did you think it was?"

"Fine." His smirk let me know that he was teasing, but I lightly pinched his thigh anyway. Another excuse to touch him.

He took one hand off the wheel and grabbed the hand that had pinched him. "Careful! I'm driving." He brought my hand to his mouth and nipped at my finger before letting it go. "But you have grievances?"

I pushed away thoughts that his mouth on my skin had elicited. "Yes. I do. I was not prepared for the situation you put me in. I need to know more going forward. I knew nothing about the Werners being at the symphony last night. Couldn't you have at least given me a heads up?"

Hudson took off his sunglasses and studied me, as if trying to gauge my seriousness.

I was very serious. I was tired of always being in the dark about him and the world that he weaved me in and out of so flippantly.

He tucked his sunglasses into the compartment above his mirror, not needing them anymore with the sun setting and us directed east. "Except for your predilection for putting your hands all over me—"

"Oh, don't exaggerate."

"—you were magnificent." He was serious as well, which shocked me. I felt anything but magnificent. "How would any information I could have given you have changed how you performed?"

I opened my mouth but found I didn't have a specific answer. "I would have been more at ease because I was prepared." That was the best I could come up with. "The same goes for the day at the fashion show. I could have handled your mother, Celia—" I paused, wanting to indicate what I'd found out about his past without actually saying it. "You know, the whole day would have been better if I'd been prepared."

"Again, I thought you were brilliant."

"Not on the inside. And it's the inside stuff that makes me do crazy things. Like stalk office buildings." I winced as I mentioned the embarrassing behavior that I wished I could forget. But if I wanted to be well, I needed to address my insecurities, and not knowing much about Hudson led to many of mine. "Anyway, I have you trapped in a car for over two hours—"

"Are you sure I don't have you trapped?"

"You're driving. I'm providing the entertainment." Though, I found his uncharacteristic playfulness extremely entertaining as well.

"I like the sound of that." He grinned, sneaking a look at my bare legs.

I resisted the urge to tug at my black skort, one of my prizes from shopping at Mirabelle's. I enjoyed that he liked looking at me, but his gaze turned me on to the *n*th degree and I wanted to keep focused. "Stop interrupting. We are playing a get-to-know-each-other game." I put my hand up as if to shush him. "Don't even say whatever it is you're about to say. If we have any hope of fooling your family when we're with them twenty-four/seven then we need to know more about each other."

"I already know plenty about you." This time his gaze went to the bosom of my super tight tee.

"No, you don't." I snapped my fingers by my face to get his attention to move upward. "Have you ever gotten to know a woman—nonsexually? Besides from a background check?"

"Not on purpose."

His answer was quick and honest. And it pissed me off. "Hudson, you're kind of an asshole."

"So I've been told." He met my glowering eyes. "Fine. How do we play this game of yours?"

The triumph wiped out my irritation. "We'll take turns. On your turn you can either ask a question or tell a fact about yourself. Your choice. Nothing too heavy. Basic stuff. I'll go first. I don't like mushrooms."

His eyes widened. "You don't like mushrooms? What is wrong with you?"

"They're gross. They taste like rotten olives."

"They taste nothing like olives."

"They taste like rotten olives. I can't stand them." I made a face to show my disgust, but inside I was ecstatic that he was taking an interest in what I had shared. I hadn't been sure he would. Especially with such a benign subject as food tastes.

Hudson shook his head, seemingly bewildered by my confession. "That's a terrible inconvenience. That has to hinder your fine dining experiences."

"Tell me about it." For some reason, mushrooms seemed to be in a great deal of fancy recipes. "Imagine my horror when my senior prom date made dinner for me and it was chicken Marsala."

His eye twitched, almost unnoticeably. "Your senior prom date? Was this a serious relationship?" His voice had also tensed slightly.

I narrowed my eyes. Was he jealous? "Are you asking that question for your turn?"

"Uh, yes, I suppose I am."

He *was* jealous. Of a high school prom date. I was flattered. "It was a serious relationship for me. Not for Joe."

"Joe sounds terrible." But his smile returned.

"Thank you. He was." Hudson pulled onto the Interstate, and I put my sunglasses in my purse. "My turn." I sat back, chewing my lip. I'd eased us into the game, but now I wanted some answers. Something good. "Why do you never call people by their nicknames?"

He groaned. "Because nicknames are so gaudy. Call a person by their given name. That's why they have it."

I rolled my eyes. He was so formal. Sometimes I wasn't sure I even liked the guy. That was part of the reason I had wanted to play this game. I had to know if my attraction went beyond the physical.

And I really wanted him to call me by my nickname. "But nicknames show a degree of familiarity."

"You tell everyone to call you Laynie. Even people you've just met."

Because answering to Alayna was weird. The only people who had really called me Alayna were my parents. "Maybe I feel familiar with everyone I meet." I made an effort to say my next words casually, as if the fact didn't really bother me. "And you call Celia by a nickname."

"Really?" He knew it bothered me. I hadn't covered well enough. "She's the only person on earth, Alayna. I've known her my whole life. I didn't even know her name was really Celia until I was almost ten."

I crossed my legs, pleased when he glanced as I did so, and swung my foot with irritation. "If you are trying to convince people you care more about me than Celia, then you should have a nickname for me. It will establish endearment." And I really wanted his endearment.

"Calling me 'H' shows endearment?"

My phone vibrated in my pocket. I lifted my hips so I could pull it out, and Hudson eyed me as I did so. "It does. I don't go for the real lovey-dovey words like sweetie and honey. But Hudson is way too formal."

"I like formal."

"I like cherry-flavored blow pops. It doesn't make them appropriate for every situation."

"Blow pops?"

"Yeah…blow pops." I planned to respond with a sexy comeback, but was distracted by reading the text on my phone. It was from Brian asking me to call him. I'd ignored all of the texts he'd sent over the last week, and wasn't about to start answering now. I threw my phone into my lap, frustrated. He didn't know I'd found a solution to my money issues and still expected me to give in to his terms. Not happening.

"You didn't like 'baby'?" Hudson's question pulled me back to the car.

My answer held the tension I meant for Brian. "Not so much." Only because it was unoriginal and insincere. It wasn't a name Hudson had picked specifically for me.

"I'm sticking with Alayna."

I turned to him and glared. "Come on. You could call me 'precious' every now and then in front of other people."

"No way," he murmured.

"Why? You call me that sometimes already."

His voice rumbled low and quiet and serious. "That's private."

I shivered. Even if his tone hadn't indicated the matter was settled, I would have dropped it. His answer was perfect—sensual and even a little romantic. Not like I was getting my hopes up romantic, just sort of sweet.

Hmm. Hudson never failed to surprise me. I shook my head. "It's your turn."

My phone buzzed again. Another text from Brian. This time saying he was coming to see me first thing the next day. And I wouldn't be there. Guess the laugh was on him. I grinned as I turned off my phone and stuffed it back into my pocket.

When my focus returned to Hudson, he was eyeing me, his brow cocked. "Who keeps texting you?"

Something about his jealousy made me want to purr. "Is that your question?"

"It is."

I considered making something up, something that would really provoke envy from the man, but the game was meant to be about honest answers. "My brother. He's an asshole."

"Like I'm an asshole?" he asked, recalling what I'd said to him minutes before.

"Worse. He's an asshole who doesn't know it."

Hudson grinned. "And you're ignoring Brian?"

He knew Brian's name. It made me realize that he already knew I had a brother. I wondered what else Hudson knew about Brian. And my parents. My whole life.

Well, if he wanted to know anything more about Brian he'd have to wait until his turn. "You already asked your question. It's my turn. I lost my virginity when I was sixteen."

I meant it to be a shocker, still irritated about Brian's constant texts and Hudson's knowledge of things he shouldn't know about me until I told him. "Sixteen? Fuck, Alayna. I don't think I want to know that."

"Sorry." I smiled.

He shook his head, his eyes narrow. "I seriously doubt this is going to come up in conversation with my family."

"You never know."

"Who was the guy?"

His jealousy was seriously hot. "Is that your turn?"

"No."

I cocked my head, questioning his sincerity.

He changed his mind. He couldn't help himself. "Yes."

I didn't even try to hide my elation. "He was a random guy I met at a party. I thought that having sex would help me forget that my parents had died. It did not."

"No, I suppose it wouldn't."

He sounded sympathetic and I was glad he didn't press. It had been an awful time in my life. My parents' fatal car accident had pushed me to behave in ways I wasn't proud. Random sex, excessive drinking, drug experimentation. And then the addiction that had stuck—obsessive love, which shouldn't be called love at all, but rather obsessive wanna-be-loved. If I was really with Hudson, I mean really his girlfriend, then he should know all the details, and I liked to think I'd tell him. But for a strange moment I was exceptionally glad that I wasn't really with Hudson so I wouldn't have to tell him.

Whoa. Did that mean that there were other moments when I wanted to be really with him? When had that started?

I shot a glance at Hudson who seemed to be heavy in his own thoughts. What would it take to get in there? I tried to guess what he could be so absorbed with. "What were you doing in Cincinnati?"

"Business."

I pinched the bridge of my nose. It was so much easier to have sex with the man than to get him to share anything real. "That's not very much of an answer."

"I wouldn't talk to my girlfriend about business."

"You wouldn't be my boyfriend if you didn't." Despite finally believing that Hudson was indeed out-of-town that week, insecurity nagged at me still.

I pushed for more information. "Didn't your mom and dad talk about business with each other?"

"My parents don't talk about anything. If Dad's at the house when we get there, he will not sleep in the same room with Mother. Loveless marriage, remember?"

"Not a good example then." I tried a different tactic. "Look. I'm a business major. I like to know about these things." I licked my lips purposefully. "Doesn't my smart mind turn you on?"

"*Your* smart mind, not mine." But he was hiding a smile.

I slipped my hand down his thigh. "Come on. I've shown you mine. Show me yours."

He couldn't resist me in full flirtation mode. He sighed. "There's been some outside interest in Plexis, one of my smaller companies. But I'm not keen to sell to this particular buyer. The other members of the board feel differently."

Hudson furrowed his brow and I thought he'd finished, but he went on. "Actually it's been quite stressful, fighting to keep Plexis together when so many are opposed. Many stand to gain a sizable profit from a sale. I know that this buyer would run the place to the ground. The company would be torn apart. People would lose their jobs."

I sat mesmerized. In his brief divulgence, I saw something besides his passion for his companies and the people that worked for them. I saw him relax and maybe even enjoy telling me about something that weighed heavily on him. Did he have anyone he shared these things with? It didn't seem likely.

He noticed me staring and he shifted.

I was sure he'd be disturbed to discover how much I'd discerned from such a brief conversation. So I deflected and lightened the mood. "Thank you! Was that really so terrible?"

His mouth tightened into a straight line, but I saw the gleam in his eyes. "I'm not answering that. It's not your turn." He only paused a second before he said, "Fine. It wasn't that terrible. That's what I'm offering for my turn."

"Hudson?" I asked softly, hoping he didn't see the full extent of my adoration in just the speaking of his name.

"Yes, precious?"

"You aren't really an asshole."

He brought one finger to his mouth. "*Shh.* You'll ruin my reputation."

We continued the game through dinner at a clam bar in Sayville, covering a variety of topics from favorite movies to worst dates to first kisses. Hudson and I had very few things in common, but that only intrigued me more, and I had the distinct impression he felt the same. Most of our differences seemed to come from our backgrounds rather than our tastes. I didn't know if I loved the opera—I'd never been. And my favorite pastime—buying one movie ticket and sneaking into several movies after—was born of a lack of funds that Hudson had never experienced.

Underneath it all, we both knew we shared one very vital commonality—our destructive pasts. Though we seldom spoke of it, it shadowed many of our confessions. But unlike with other men when I went through the routine of talking about myself, I didn't feel like I was holding back the truth. I wasn't lying, like I had to so many others. We didn't talk about it, but it didn't lie in the deep recesses of ourselves, threatening to be revealed. It made the simple exchanges between us easier and more poignant.

After dinner when we returned to the road, we played the game at a relaxed pace, letting long moments of comfortable silence fill the spaces between turns. Finally, Hudson turned off Old Montauk Highway onto a private drive. At the gate midway down the entry, he entered a code that opened the wooden doors and allowed us to continue past the high hedge to the circle driveway. He stopped the car in front of a traditional two-story estate.

"We're here," he said in a sing-song voice not typical of Hudson Pierce.

My mouth fell open as I stared up at the mansion, clearly lit with bright torchlights like the fountain in the center of the circle drive. I'd tried not to think too much about Hudson's money, not wanting that to be the focus of my attraction to him, but if there was ever a time to be appreciative of his wealth, this was it. The stone house was breathtaking and extravagant, the kind of thing I'd only seen in movies.

"It's…wow."

Hudson laughed. "Come on. You'll love the inside."

I opened the car door, immediately overwhelmed with the smell of the ocean air mingled with a variety of early summer blooming flowers. The front doors opened and an older balding man in a light gray suit approached us.

"Good evening, Martin," Hudson said, slipping his arm around my waist. "This is my girlfriend, Alayna Withers. Martin is our household assistant."

"A pleasure, Ms. Withers," Martin said, taking my hand. After he released it, he spoke to Hudson. "Mr. Pierce, I'll set your bags in the guest suite in the west wing."

Hudson frowned as he handed Martin the keys to the car. "Is everyone in the west wing?"

"Yes, sir."

"Then set us up in the master of the east wing."

With his hand still at the small of my back, Hudson escorted me through the double doors into the entryway of the house. The entry was bare except for an ornate table set into the curve of the wide staircase.

"Hudson, we're in the kitchen," Mirabelle's voice called from the back of the house.

"I know it's late," Hudson said to me, his tone full of apology, "but we should at least say hello. Do you mind?"

I wasn't tired in the least. This was my time of day. If we hadn't left town, I'd just be starting my shift at the club. "It's not late for me."

For some reason, this made Hudson smile. "Good."

The sensual promise in his tone made my thighs tense. God, with his endless flirting in the car and the intimacy of our get-to-know you game, I was more than seduced. All I needed was a bed and Hudson alone. And the bed was optional.

Hudson directed me through the back hallway of the entry toward the back of the house, his fingers at my hip not providing nearly enough contact. At the kitchen, he dropped his hand, and I sighed at the loss.

Fortunately, I was able to disguise the sigh as one of awe at the room we'd entered. The kitchen was larger than my apartment. Hell, the entryway had been larger than my apartment. The walls were a light yellow cream, and the counter tops a brown and white flecked granite. All the appliances were stainless steel, a striking comparison to the hardwood floors. Even as someone with no interest in kitchens, I admired its beauty.

We found Adam and Mira leaning over the center island, scraping out what seemed to be the final crumbs in a pie dish.

"I'm pregnant," Mira said before anyone could ask. "I don't know what Adam's excuse is."

"Was that one of Millie's pies?" Hudson asked.

Mira nodded.

"Then there's his excuse right there. No one makes better pies than Millie. I can't believe you didn't save any for us."

"There's more for tomorrow," Adam piped up. "We were strictly forbidden to touch them. Millie's our cook," he said for my benefit. "She's amazing."

"Now that the little one's been fed," Mira said, rubbing her belly, "I can give a proper greeting. Laynie!" She wrapped her arms around me. "I'm so glad you came!"

"Thank you," I said, stunned by her exuberance.

"How was the trip? Did you get anything to eat?"

"Are you offering to fix them something?" Adam put his hand near his mouth and mock-whispered, "Mira doesn't cook."

She narrowed her eyes at him, playfully. "I know how to use the microwave, though."

"No need to prove anything. We stopped in Sayville," Hudson said.

"The clam bar? Ooh, I'm jealous." Mira moved to her brother and hugged him, giving him a light peck on the cheek. "I'm still glad you're here. It's been ages since you've come out."

Hudson slipped out of her grasp, but smiled. "I am too. Did Dad come?"

Mira took the empty pie plate to the sink and filled it with water before leaving it to soak. "Yeah, he's already gone to bed for the night. Or he's hiding from Mom. He's in the guest house."

I exchanged glances with Hudson, remembering our earlier conversation about his parents' loveless marriage.

"Where is Mother? And Chandler?"

"I'm here." I looked behind me to see Sophia Pierce leaning against the arched doorway. She wore a dressing robe and had a glass of something light brown on ice. "Chandler's out with the Gardiner girl. I don't expect him until late."

"Hello, Mother." Hudson walked over to her and kissed each of her cheeks.

"You made it." Sophia glanced at me. "Both of you."

"Alayna and I are seldom apart," Hudson lied, pulling me to him.

"Good evening, Mrs. Pierce." I had been dreading seeing her again, but I made my greeting as warm as possible. Hudson's arm around me helped. "Thank you for the invite. Your house is lovely."

She nodded. "I'm sure you want to get settled. I chose a room for you in the west wing."

Hudson straightened. "I told Martin to set up the master suite in the east wing."

Electric tingles spread from my lower belly throughout the rest of my body. Hudson and I sharing a master suite…the thought made me squirm. I'd tried not to dwell on how we'd spend our nights in the Hamptons—whether they'd be filled with sex or considered on-duty hours, I didn't know. But now that the idea had been firmly planted, I couldn't stop thinking of the carnal possibilities.

Sophia obviously didn't feel the same way about her son and me sharing a bed. "Hudson, that's so far away from the rest of us." Her ire was evident. Like Hudson, I had a feeling she rarely had anyone oppose her. I imagined the shared trait made for some pretty uncomfortable family meals.

And I was about to share several of them before the trip was over. Lucky me.

Hudson knew how to handle his mother. "We need the distance, Mother." His tone was final.

"Why? We don't bite."

"Alayna does," he grinned wickedly. "And she can be quite loud."

I turned ten shades of scarlet. Did he actually believe every pretend girlfriend wanted their sex life discussed with the mother? Though, I really could be quite loud.

It was Sophia's shocked look that Hudson responded to, her expression likely the intended outcome of his scandalous remark. "Oh, Mother, don't look at me like that. Neither Alayna and I have been virgins since we were sixteen."

Sophia pursed her lips and walked past us, finishing her beverage before placing it in the sink.

Hudson leaned into whisper in my ear, the warmth of his breath sending a shiver down my spine. "Well, what do you know? That virginity fact did come in handy."

I elbowed him in the ribs, exasperated at being the victim in his poke at his mother.

"Don't get pissy, Alayna." He pulled me in front of him and wrapped his arms around me, my backside to his chest. "Trust me—we want a room away from them."

I sighed into his touch, aware that we were on show, but enjoying the contact nonetheless.

And maybe he enjoyed the contact, too. Or he simply wanted to get away from his mother because he excused us then. “We’ll see you in the morning. It’s late and we’d like to get to bed.”

Or maybe he really did just want to get to bed. God knew I did.

— CHAPTER —
SIXTEEN

As we climbed the stairs and turned toward the east wing, nervousness set in. I had learned that Hudson was very intent on separating the fake from the real, and that left me to wonder what would happen between the two of us at night when we were alone. It stood to reason we'd have sex, and he had made sure our room was away from the others. But did he want privacy so we could be intimate or so that his family wouldn't know we weren't being intimate?

It was so confusing. He so easily compartmentalized, but for me it was impossible. Everything I knew and felt about him wrapped itself tightly around me at all times. There was no separation of the pretend and the real except for how he reacted to me.

Silently as I worried about the impending situation, I followed him through double doors into a beautiful master suite. The room had two ornate mahogany dressers and a matching four-poster queen bed. Our luggage sat at the foot of the bed, opposite a small sitting area with two armchairs and a mahogany table. A fireplace lined the inner wall and the floors were hardwood covered almost entirely by a plush rug. Though it was traditionally decorated, a flat screen TV centered the wall across from the bed.

As I stood taking the room in, worrying out our situation, Hudson removed his suit jacket, humming as he did, obviously unaware of my anxiety. Next he loosened his tie and flung it over one of the chairs. He turned back to me as he unbuttoned his shirt and paused, noticing I hadn't moved since entering the room.

Before he could ask, I blurted out what had me fretting. "Am I off-duty or on-duty?"

A small smile crossed his lips. "My family's not around." Yes, he'd made sure of that. "Off-duty. Besides, I told you I'd never use sex as part of the sham and I intend to have sex with you now."

The shiver that passed through me caused every hair on my body to stand on end. "Really?"

"Of course." He continued to pin me with his stare as he resumed his unbuttoning, moving slower than he had before.

I took in a shallow breath. "We've never spent the night together."

"So we haven't." He took a step toward me, his sly grin growing wider. "Are you nervous?"

Yes. "No."

His brow rose as if he sensed my lie. "You should be. You'll be within my reach all night long. I expect you'll be sore tomorrow."

My nervousness melted away, replaced by intense arousal. "Hmm. Sounds lovely."

"Good. Go get ready for bed." He nodded toward the en suite bathroom door. "Don't take too long. I'm eager to lick you senseless."

I didn't hesitate, grabbing the small bag that held my toiletries as I scurried into the bathroom. After I shut the door behind me, my finger lingered at the handle while I considered locking it. But why would I do that? Any invasion Hudson planned I would welcome.

After washing my face and brushing my teeth I paused again. What should I wear? I had packed a sexy nightie, not sure if I would use it or not. Nighties seemed to suggest a romantic tone. Didn't they? It didn't matter, because I'd left my suitcase in the bedroom. Should I go out clothed? Naked?

I decided to strip to my underwear, thankful that I'd worn a pretty black lace bra and matching lace boy shorts under my outfit. I folded my clothes and left them on the counter then stepped quietly out of the bathroom.

Hudson had turned off the overhead lights and switched on the nightstand lamps. His back was to me, and I could see he'd lost his dress shirt and belt and his feet were bare and sexy. God, feet had no right being sexy, but his were.

He turned and my breath caught. Our sexual relationship was still so new. Seeing his naked chest still thrilled me to no end. His hard angles, the way his pants hung low enunciating his hips, his abs of steel—I didn't think I could ever get tired of looking at him.

Eventually my gaze fluttered to his face where I found his dark eyes, devouring me where I stood. "Nice choice." He nodded at my attire, and my skin tingled with his approval. "Come here." His low growl pulled me to him as effectively as if he had me on a rope. I stopped within his reach, but he didn't touch me. He circled around me instead, standing so close I could feel the body heat radiating off of him, increasing my own already rising body temperature.

He stopped behind me, and I felt him at my neck, his breath grazing my skin. "So beautiful," he murmured before his lips nipped at my ear. "I need to make you come." I jumped as his hands skimmed down the length of my arms. "Over and over." He licked along my lobe. "Do you think you can handle it?"

Words failed me. I answered with an incoherent moan, leaning my body into him, letting his heat envelop me.

He let out a wicked laugh then spun me around to face him, his mouth stopping centimeters above my own. "You don't know if you can handle it, do you, precious? Let's find out."

He took me with his mouth, consuming my breath with his ravaging kiss, urging me to succumb to his control. I didn't fight it, giving myself over to him in every way he demanded. And with each demand, I lost more of myself to him as he taught my body how to be adored and worshipped. How to be taken and dominated. Like I was made simply for his pleasure, but by the same token, that he was made for mine.

He did lick me until I was senseless, and he did make me come over and over. And in several moments I feared I couldn't handle it. But he pushed me through each climax—both those that rolled slowly and those that ripped violently through me—with the experience and confidence of a lover that had known me intimately for far longer than he had.

After several orgasms passed between us, he lay heavily on the bed next to me, his shoulder touching mine, either spent for the night or taking a break, I wasn't sure. My own body was boneless, every muscle lax. Sleep threatened at the edges of my consciousness, but I pushed it away, unwilling to put our evening to bed yet.

I turned my head toward him and caught him watching me, a satisfied smile on his face. Returning his grin, I sighed. "That was…incredible."

In a flash he was on top of me, his body covering the length of mine. He laced his hands in mine and lifted them over my head. "What was your favorite part?"

All of it. Every minute of it. But that answer seemed lame and I knew he wanted something more concrete. Several amazing moments came to mind, each making me blush simply from thinking of them—like when he'd crawled up my body and straddled my neck, silently ordering me to take his cock in my mouth. That had been pretty hot.

And when he'd commanded me to play with myself while he sucked and tugged at my breast. Again, pretty hot. Also, a bit awkward. But only until I warmed up to it.

Unable to voice the memories, I turned the table on him. "What was *your* favorite part?"

He trailed his nose along my jaw. "The way you respond to anything… everything…I do to you." He licked along my lower lip and I opened to kiss him, but he pulled out of reach. "Your turn."

His mood was unusually playful and inspired me to join him. "I'll never tell." I grinned.

"Tell me." He moved my hands together and pinned them with one of his. His other hand he lowered to rest lightly at my hip.

My exposed ribcage made me feel vulnerable. He could tickle me mercilessly. I tempted him anyway. "Make me."

"I can't make you do anything." His hand flickered across my sensitive side and I flinched.

"I think you could." I braced myself for his assault. "I hear you're quite good at making women do things."

And suddenly I wasn't playing anymore, but hinting at deeper meanings. I hadn't meant to go there, but his confession of manipulating women for sport always hung right below the surface of our time together. Lying nude beneath him now, completely stripped of senses from multiple orgasms, it bubbled to the top and escaped my lips.

His eye twitched, the only indication he gave that my true implication affected him. "I *am* good at making women do things."

I couldn't help myself. I nudged the conversation on. "But not me."

"No." His voice lowered, the playfulness gone. "Not you."

"Am I not..." I searched for the question I wanted to ask, needing the answer even though I couldn't yet form the words. "...intriguing...enough to play that game with?"

My hands still pinned above me, he propped himself up with his other arm so he could glare down at me. "God, Alayna, do you want me to do that to you? Possess you? I would crush you. I would destroy you." His tone was dark, but also honestly inquisitive. "Is that what you want?"

My eyes filled. I hated the truth of my answer. "No, but a little bit yes too. That's how my stupid brain works. If you don't do with me what you normally do with other girls, there must be something wrong with me."

He laughed as he lowered himself to the bed beside me. "Oh, it's all you, huh? It's not that there's something wrong with me? How self-centered of you."

Free to move, I rolled to my side toward him. "I'm very self-centered. I want to be special. I'm afraid that I'm not."

"You are." His words were emphatic. "Even more than you could imagine you are." He turned his body so he could face me. "Because I don't want to destroy you more than I need to possess you. That's progress for me."

We were both vulnerable now. Two damaged souls spilling our brokenness in a private therapy session. Was this what he had wanted between us? Sharing like this, without judgment, without shame? It was...nice.

I stopped worrying about being exposed and spoke from the gut. "Then I'll try not to fixate on what it means that I'm different for you. That will be progress for me."

He nodded, the weight of my words sinking in. "Do you know why you do it?"

"Why I become obsessive about guys?"

"Yeah."

"My counselors have said it's probably about not feeling loved as a child. Aggravated by the early death of my parents. So I'm constantly seeking affection and doubting it when I receive it because I don't know what it really feels like."

"How did you get over that?"

It wasn't at all what I thought he'd ask, and I sensed he was asking as much for himself as he was about me. I'd gotten this far into the depths of candidness, might as well dive right in. "I haven't. It's a constant battle. Lots of self-affirmation. Lots of silly little tricks, like wearing elastic bands to remind me."

He nodded, understanding about my elastic band settling in. "You still fall into old habits."

"Yes."

"With me?"

"You know the answer to that." My voice came out a whisper. I wanted to look away, but our eyes were locked and in the softness of his gaze I found the courage to tell more. "I didn't believe you were away on business. I thought you didn't want to see me. That's why I came by your building."

His face fell, as though my honesty crushed him. He closed his eyes briefly. When he opened them, they were dark and intense. He reached his hand out to cup my nape, insuring that my face was fixed on his. "Alayna, I will never lie to you." His voice was gruff. "Not when we're off-duty. I will always tell you the truth. I swear it."

His grip loosened, and his thumb stroked across my bare cheek. "Do you understand?"

I nodded and covered his hand with mine. "Hudson, *this*," I choked, my throat tight with emotion. "*This* was my favorite part."

For a split second I worried I'd scared him with my intensity, that he'd pull away. But he didn't. Instead he put his hand on my ass and pulled me closer. He stroked down my thigh, urging it forward to rest around his waist. Then he slid inside me, my pussy already wet from earlier orgasms. He was slow and steady with his pace, less rough than he often tended to be, his usual sex talk absent. But, because of the things we'd shared, his measured thrusts felt raw, more intent on connecting than on gratifying.

Climax came quickly for both of us, mine crashing through me in waves that tightened my belly and curled my toes and caused fireworks to cross my vision, his spurting hot and prolonged as he groaned my name. His eyes never left mine, though they narrowed as he came, and it deepened the intimacy. I knew he'd told the truth, I trusted him. In his words, in his actions, I felt fixed. I'd fallen into something that had nothing to do with love. Into healing.

And it was love too. If I could stand to admit it to myself, love was exactly what it was.

— CHAPTER —

SEVENTEEN

Streams of sunlight poured through the windows, warming and waking me up earlier than I would have on my usual sleep schedule. Before looking, I sensed I was alone. When I turned, I squinted at the clock on the nightstand next to where Hudson should have been sleeping. Nine-twenty-seven.

I blinked several times, adjusting my eyes, while I considered whether I wanted to get up and search for my lover or roll over and go back to sleep. I still hadn't made a decision when the doors opened to the bedroom and Hudson appeared wearing nothing but black silk pajama bottoms and carrying a breakfast tray.

"Good, you're awake," he said as I sat up, the smell of coffee luring me further out of sleep. "I'm showing my family what an awesome boyfriend I am by bringing you breakfast in bed. Omelets. Sans mushrooms, of course. No cherry-flavored blow pops." He winked as he set the tray on the table in the sitting area.

"This is one of those inappropriate moments for a blow pop anyway. And you should have said amazingly awesome boyfriend. Breakfast in bed is the best." Though the thing making my mouth water was the never tiresome sight of Hudson barefoot and shirtless.

"I'm not that awesome." He left the tray and untied the string of his PJs, letting them fall to the ground, exposing his beautifully erect penis. He slid under the covers and climbed over me. "I'm going to make you eat it cold."

Before his kiss prevented me from speech or thought I mumbled, "Cold breakfast sounds perfect."

It was almost noon before we were ready to dress for the day. Hudson had offered to draw me a bath to soak my sex sore limbs, but I opted for a shared shower, wanting to extend our intimacy as long as possible before we were on-duty again.

After we'd dried and dressed—Hudson in khaki pants and polo, me in a cream sundress—he left me to take our dirty dishes down while I finished primping. I chose to sweep my hair into a ponytail, an easy and quick option, so I could follow him shortly, though the idea of hiding out in the bedroom as long as I could, had crossed my mind. Truth was, as much as I didn't want to face Sophia, I wanted to be with Hudson more.

Not knowing my way around the house yet, I headed first to the kitchen, hopeful that he'd still be there. I paused outside the swinging kitchen door when I heard voices—Hudson's and Sophia's.

"—didn't invite you so you could stay in your room all day and fuck like bunnies," Sophia was saying.

Yeah, I wasn't walking in yet. I pressed my ear to the door, listening.

"Then why did you invite us?" Hudson's voice was calm, his ability to smoothly wield his mother impressing me. Was Sophia the first woman he'd mastered? Had he practiced his skills of manipulation on her? Was our elaborate scheme to fool her now a substitute for the games he'd played on other women?

I wasn't judging him for any of it. Just curious.

"I invited you because I think she—any woman you involve yourself with, for that matter—has a right to be protected. Has a right to know."

"Her name is Alayna, Mother." He surprised me with the sharpness of his tone. "And she already knows." He laughed gruffly. "I love how you believe no one could possibly feel something for me because of who I was in the past."

My chest tightened, ached for what I knew Hudson must be feeling. Brian had held my mistakes over me as well, always doubting that I could ever be better. The lack of familial support made healing all the more difficult.

Maybe Hudson and I could be strength for each other. It was a dangerous thought, putting too much importance into our solely physical relationship, but whom was I kidding? I'd long passed the moment when my emotions had entered into the picture. What was the point of fighting it longer?

Maybe we could be...more.

I'd missed some of the conversation, lost in my own head, but Sophia's raised voice drew me back. "—can't understand how you could tell her? What if she exposes you? Exposes us? Our family doesn't need that kind of scandal."

"My life is more than a scandal waiting to happen, Mother."

"Your life is a series of scandals. Scandals that your father and I are continuously cleaning up. Your bartender whore is just the next scandal."

Even though I'd promised myself to not let her get to me, Sophia's insult was a punch in the gut. My eyes stung, but before tears could form, Hudson's defense softened the blow.

"Don't you dare talk about Alayna like that again. If you do, I—"

"Finding out anything good?"

I jumped away from the door, the unfamiliar male's voice behind me both startling and shaming me for being caught eavesdropping. I forced my eyes to his and blushed even deeper. The chiseled face was more attractive in person than in the pictures I'd seen on the Internet, and the resemblance to his son so striking it was almost eerie, as if I were viewing Hudson thirty years in the future. He looked younger than the sixty years I knew him to be, his frame trim with only a slight paunch, and his features striking against his goatee and long salt and peppered hair.

Hudson's father cocked his head and stroked his goatee, a gesture that seemed so natural I imagined he frequently employed it. "I'm judging by the look on your face that you already know who I am."

"Yes. You're Jonathan Pierce."

"And you...hmm...don't tell me..." He looked me over in such a way that I knew he appreciated what he saw, yet I didn't feel ogled. "You're a little old for Chandler, and Mira doesn't ever pick friends who are prettier than her. That leaves Hudson. I'd heard a rumor he was dating someone, but I never imagined it was true."

His tone was charming and easy, a hint of a drawl revealing his Texas roots. His manner relaxed me even though I'd been caught in an embarrassing situation. "I'm Hudson's girlfriend, Alayna Withers." I held my hand out to him. "But please call me Laynie, Mr. Pierce."

He took my hand with both of his and held it as he spoke. "My friends call me Jack, and I have a feeling we're going to be great friends." He patted my hand, the action managing to stay just on the right side of the okay/creepy line. When he let go, he nodded his head toward the kitchen. "Who's in there anyway?"

A guilty smile lined my lips. "Hudson and your wife."

Jack rolled his head dramatically. "Please refrain from reminding me I'm married to that woman." His eye twinkled mischievously. "We obviously don't want to go in there. Have you been given a tour of Mabel Shores?"

"Mabel Shores?"

"If Hudson hasn't told you the name of this house, he's certainly not given you a tour. How lucky that I'm available to do the honor." He offered me his arm. "Shall we?"

I hesitated only a second, Jack's charismatic demeanor impossible to turn down. Besides, Hudson had said our sham was meant to convince both his parents. Spending time with his father could only be beneficial to the cause. And the truth was, though I knew Hudson expected me, postponing my next face-to-face with Sophia sounded like an excellent idea.

Jack leisurely led me through the house, providing historical and architectural trivia spattered with the occasional humorous anecdote. The main floor featured a spacious living room, library, gym, and a media room as well as two guestrooms. The décor remained traditional throughout, but very up-to-date and stylish.

He ignored showing me the upstairs, stating that there wasn't much to see besides the bedrooms. We also avoided the dining room and kitchen, slipping out the French doors in the office on the opposite side of the house to explore the grounds instead.

We talked easily throughout the tour, Jack's charm never faltering. Though he was more than twice my age and the father of my lover, I adored him and his shameless flirting. He was harmless and fun and much more pleasant than I'd ever imagined a renowned businessman could be. I began to piece together the Pierce family, understanding Mira's welcoming personality now that I'd met Jack. I could even spot what Hudson had inherited, recognizing his magnetism and sexual prowess came from his father. And the playfulness that Hudson occasionally adopted—that was his dad.

When we'd circled most of the east gardens and were headed back toward the house, Jack grew somewhat serious. "So you and Hudson…that's a pleasant surprise."

"I'm not sure that I want to know what's surprising about us."

"Nothing bad. Hudson doesn't date much. I'm glad to see that the girl he finally brought home is someone as delightful as you. I hope it sticks."

I smiled. "Thank you." I savored my next words as I said them, relishing the sweetness of their honesty. "I'm quite stuck on the man. I've fallen for him pretty hard."

Jack stared at me, reading my face. "Yes, I believe you have. That's wonderful. Truly."

His sincerity was touching, and a rush of emotion surged in my chest. It felt good to have someone rooting for our fake relationship. It validated my growing belief in the possibility of more.

My confidence was short-lived, however, Jack's next words reminding me of the barriers lying between Hudson and myself. "What was Sophia saying about you? I've been dying to ask."

"When? Oh." I turned away, pretending to admire the purple grapelike flowers lining the cobblestone path.

He pushed gently, understanding lacing his words. "It had to be not very nice. You were ashen when I found you."

I sighed, thinking how best to sum up what I'd overheard and how it made me feel. "She doesn't like me."

Jack shrugged. "Sophia doesn't like anyone." He didn't bother to hide his own disdain for the woman, and I wondered how he had ended up with her in the first place. "But I imagine she especially doesn't like you. Which is why it's so delicious that I do."

Shaking my head, I ignored his teasing. "Is it because of me or because of Hudson?"

"The reasons I like you have absolutely nothing to do with Hudson."

I leveled a stern look in Jack's direction. "I was talking about Sophia—your wife. Why does she especially not like me?"

Jack stroked his goatee and resumed walking toward the house. "It isn't you."

Bartender whore. I followed him, Sophia's earlier remarks resounding again in my head. "Really? I bet she'd welcome Celia into Hudson's arms."

"Because she adores Celia. Always has."

We'd reached the veranda at the back of the house where Jack gestured to sit. I sank into a cushy loveseat and curled my feet up underneath me. "Doesn't she want Hudson to be happy?"

Jack took the chair across from me, a small wooden table separating us. It was his turn to sigh. "She doesn't want anyone to be happy. Particularly Hudson. They've had many battles in a lifelong war, and she's not a forgiving woman."

Again I thought of my relationship with Brian. As much of a pain in the ass that he'd been lately, I couldn't say I didn't understand why. He and I had suffered our own battles and the wounds ran deep. And I wasn't Brian's child. I imagined the dynamic between us would be so much worse if I were. Also, though my brother could be domineering, neither he nor I could compare to the battle of wills demonstrated by Hudson and Sophia.

I rested my head back against the loveseat and stared at the rough textured concrete ceiling. "Then there's no way to win her over?"

"No." His answer was firm, final.

If that were true, then the job I'd been paid to do was doomed to fail from the start. "Your son seems to think there is."

Jack shook his head sadly, taking a long moment before responding. "That's too bad. I thought he was long past caring." His expression was raw, and I could see that though he hid it well, he'd been deeply affected by the bad blood between his wife and son.

Then the mask went back up, the pain on his face replaced with his earlier easy-going character. "Now, I on the other hand, am very easy to win over. I can give you some ideas if you need them." He winked.

I laughed, letting go of the serious thoughts and emotions weighing on me. "I've already won you over."

He feigned disappointment. "Damn. I've never had a good poker face."

"But I bet you still win plenty of hands."

"Shall we play later and find out?" He leaned toward me, his eyebrows raised suggestively. "Alone? In the guest house? Strip?"

I laughed again. "I'll play in the main house, you dirty old man. With others present and all our clothing on."

"You just killed all the fun."

We were both laughing when Hudson appeared in the doorway of the house, his features appearing anxious at the sight of his father. "There you are." He came behind me, and laid a firm hand on my shoulder. "I was worried and now I see I should have been."

"I'm fine." I placed my hand over his and craned my neck up to meet his eyes. "Jack's been showing me around Mabel Shores. I've had an amazing time."

Hudson's tone was skeptical. "Then he hasn't tried to come on to you?"

"No, he has." I smiled over at Jack. "But we're all good."

Hudson moved around to sit next to me on the loveseat, resting his hand possessively on my knee.

As if challenged by his son's marking of his territory, Jack said, "I'm telling you, Laynie, with age comes experience. If you really want an amazing time..."

Hudson's grip tensed. "I don't like this."

Jack laughed, confirming my suspicion that he enjoyed toying with his son. "Relax, Hudson. It's all in fun."

I uncurled my legs and leaned into Hudson's side, secretly thrilled with Hudson's jealous show. "We're fine, H. He knows I'm hopelessly devoted to you. Don't you, Jack?"

"I do." He paused, eyeing Hudson. "I wonder if my son does."

Hudson didn't respond, not with words anyway. But he gazed at me for several long seconds, perhaps attempting to discern exactly what had transpired between Jack and me. Or maybe he sensed that his father knew something he didn't—that my emotions were genuinely growing deeper. That my fondness for him was real.

Whatever he decided, he pulled me closer into him and nuzzled his cheek against my head. He'd promised his actions in public would all be for the benefit of our audience, but this one felt different. Almost like he wanted to believe our relationship was real, too.

— CHAPTER —
EIGHTEEN

"Lunch is ready. Should I serve it out here?"

I twisted in Hudson's arms to see who had spoken and saw an older woman in the doorway of the house. Her hair was completely gray, and her face had more wrinkles than Jack or Sophia, but I suspected she was near their age. She wiped her hands on the white apron she wore over her plain navy dress.

"Millie, you're an angel," Jack said. "Out here is a terrific idea."

"I'll let Adam and Chandler know they should join you." It wasn't quite a question, but I understood her statement gave the Pierce men a chance to object, which they didn't.

A short time later, Adam and Chandler sat with us on the veranda enjoying a lunch of cold meat sandwiches, fruit salad, and lemonade. Even though it was simple, it was one of the best lunches I'd had in ages.

I waited until my curiosity couldn't be contained any longer to ask why Sophia and Mira weren't eating with us. Not that I wanted Sophia's company, but I would have loved to spend time with Hudson's sister.

"They're out shopping for baby stuff," Adam said in between bites of ham sandwich. He took a swallow of his lemonade. "Mira wanted to invite you. She looked for you before she left, but she couldn't find you."

"Darn. That must have been when we were touring the grounds. Sorry, Laynie." Jack didn't look at all remorseful.

My own response to the idea fell out unfiltered. "Fuck that. Like I'd go anywhere with Sophia, let alone shopping." I covered my mouth with my hand. "Sorry!"

Chandler was the first to burst into laughter, joined a moment later by Jack and Adam. Even Hudson let out a chuckle.

"I'm totally with you there," Adam said when he could speak.

"I think Mom feels the same way about you," Chandler said, putting his feet up on the edge of the table. "She seemed to be glad when Mira couldn't find you."

"Chandler." Hudson's tone was a warning.

"It's okay, H." I put a hand on his thigh, careful not to let on everyone see how much I enjoyed feeling his tight muscles through the material of his slacks. "Your mother and I are a long way from friendly. It's not a secret."

Hudson nodded, but his brow furrowed. Did he really care that much about his mother's opinion? Jack was right—that was too bad.

After lunch, Adam and Chandler corralled me into playing X-Box 360 with them in the media room. Hudson spread out on the couch near us, his thick reports and folders taking up most of the sofa while he worked on his laptop. Eventually Jack brought out a deck of cards and we played poker using pistachios for chips. As I'd suspected, Jack won a great deal of the time, though Chandler also had a surprising knack for the game.

After losing all of my pistachios in a bluff that Chandler called me on, I stretched and looked over at Hudson. Even though he hadn't participated in our games, I never forgot he was near, his presence invading every part of my body like a constant electric pulse. Occasionally when I glanced over at him, which happened often, I saw he was already staring. It was our own game of secret foreplay—looking at each other, undressing each other with our eyes. Later, I knew, he'd make good on the promises in his sexy stare.

This time, his eyes were glued to his screen, his glasses resting low on his nose while his fingers moved on the keyboard at a pace that suggested he was thinking as he typed. I crossed behind him and leaned down to rest my chin in the crook of his neck, wrapping my arms around him.

At my touch, Hudson lifted a hand from his computer and patted my arm. "Game over?"

"For me." I pulled to a standing position and rubbed my hands along his shoulders. "Wow, H. You're tense." He sighed as I massaged my fingers into the knots of his back. "What's getting you stressed out?" I hoped it wasn't our girlfriend/boyfriend show, though his tight muscles could have been attributed to the activities of the night before. The man had performed some moves that had to have required a great deal of strength.

"This situation with Plexis." He paused and I knew he was deciding whether to say more or not. It wasn't in his nature to share, but I'd thought I convinced him that he could talk business with me. I continued working his back as I waited, giving him a chance to continue.

My patience was rewarded. "The board is moving to sell. I need to come up with an attractive proposal to convince them it's more profitable to keep the company."

Even though he couldn't see me, I nodded. I studied the screen over his head, enjoying the quiet moans that escaped from his throat as I massaged his tension away. "You're redistributing production?" I asked. But I didn't need his answer. I could see from what he'd entered that he was. "You'd make a whole lot more if you moved those North America lines to your Indonesia plant. You're far from capacity there."

"Oh, you're one of those types who resort to taking jobs away from American people to cut costs."

"Not usually," I said, balling my hand into a fist to push into the rock under Hudson's shoulder blade. "But you're going to lose all your USA jobs if you don't do something, right? Losing a few is better than losing them all."

"Yes," he admitted.

I smiled as he changed his data to implement my suggestion, giddy that I'd offered an idea that he'd accepted. Throwing a bit more back into my hands, I felt Hudson's tight muscle close to releasing. "Take a deep breath." He did and I pushed once more into his knot, feeling it loosen as I did.

"Thanks," he said, slightly awed, rolling his shoulders.

I shook my hands out. "You're welcome."

Returning my focus to Hudson's work I noticed the technical specifications sheet of a new product on the pile next to him. "Besides," I said, reaching to grab the piece of paper, "if you start producing this energy efficient bulb in the American plant in its place, you'll maintain those jobs and save money with that new tax law. Plus you'll get a tax break for employing Americans."

Hudson shook his head. "That law only benefits new companies."

"No, it benefits any product that hasn't been produced in the U.S. before, new company or not."

"I don't think that's correct."

I'd led an entire seminar on the new tax code my last semester at Stern. I knew what I was talking about. His opposition was a challenge. "Do you have a copy of the current tax code?"

"On my Kindle. Under there somewhere." Hudson nodded his head at the stacks of reports sitting next to him.

I moved around the couch and started to dig through his piles in search of the device. "Wouldn't you be more comfortable at a table?"

Without looking at me his lips curved slightly as he said, "I wanted to be near you."

His answer surprised me. The other men in the room weren't paying attention to us. He hadn't said it for them. He'd meant it.

"I like being near you, too," I said, when I recovered enough to speak. I didn't look at him, hiding the blush from my admission while searching for the Kindle. After I found it, I quickly looked up the law I was referring to and handed the proof to Hudson.

"Well, well," he said after he read it. "Looks like you're onto something here."

He started to hand the Kindle back to me, but paused, studying me.

I couldn't interpret the meaning, but the intensity of his gaze made my chest tight and my thighs warm. "What?"

He shook his head. "Nothing." Passing the Kindle to me, he asked, "Would you mind sharing your thoughts on the rest of my proposal?"

My heart sped up, delighted at the invitation. From what I'd learned about Hudson, inviting his girlfriend—or woman he was sleeping with, anyway—to work on a business project with him was not his typical mode of operation. It was new territory for him, which made it exactly the territory I enjoyed charting most.

We spent the rest of the afternoon working together, Hudson bouncing ideas off of me as I researched further information when he needed it. While I'd always enjoyed the world of business, I hadn't thought it could be so fun, hence the reason I'd chosen to manage a nightclub rather than to pursue an office job. But now an office job seemed rather appealing. Especially if that job included working side by side with Hudson Pierce. Though, with all the accidental brushes and searing looks we exchanged, I doubted we could manage working together for a prolonged period of time without losing most of our clothing.

But, really, that only made the job sound more appealing.

The savory aroma of a roast wafting from the kitchen wing caused my stomach to growl. I stretched. "Is it close to dinnertime?"

Behind me, Mira answered. "I was just coming to tell you dinner is served."

"I didn't realize you were home. When did you get back?"

"A few minutes ago. Mom has a headache but everyone else is already waiting in the dining room."

"A headache, huh?" I eyed Hudson. I was beginning to suspect Sophia was avoiding me. How had the conversation in the kitchen ended that morning? Had Hudson won the battle, giving me reprieve of his mother's nastiness?

"She's known to get them from time to time." His expression was tight, giving nothing away. Which told me everything I needed to know. I'd have to repay him later for the kindness.

After supper, Chandler left to meet friends and the rest of us headed back to the media room. Hudson got back on his laptop and I assumed he was diving back into work. Instead he handed his laptop to me. "All right, Alayna. Tell me something you need to see off your list and we'll download it from iTunes."

Puzzled, I took his laptop and found he'd loaded up the AFI list of best movies. I tried not to grin too wide, not wanting to seem too surprised because he remembered my goal to watch all the titles on the list. He was my "boyfriend," after all. He should have remembered.

But he really wasn't my boyfriend, and I found the gesture oddly touching.

"Are you going to watch it, too?" I asked, suddenly worried he meant to keep working on his Plexis dilemma without me.

"I am." He'd already begun packing away his reports into his briefcase as he spoke.

I chose *Midnight Cowboy* after discovering Hudson hadn't seen it either. Adam took care of setting up the movie then settled into one side of the couch with Mira. After Hudson cleaned up his area, he patted the seat next to him, his arm outstretched and inviting. Gladly, I sank into the sofa next to him, cuddling into his warm embrace.

The American Film Institute named *Midnight Cowboy* as number forty-three on their Top One Hundred. But watching it snuggled with Hudson—it was my new number one.

When it was over we all went our separate ways for the night. In our bedroom, Hudson sat on the bed, fully dressed, and pulled out his laptop again.

Though he'd relinquished his computer during the movie, content to hold me and to snack on microwave popcorn, he'd worked most of the day. I studied him, his intense features appearing tired. We'd stayed up late the night before, and I didn't know what time he woke before bringing up breakfast. I wouldn't be surprised to find he'd been buried in work then too. "H, you're a workaholic. Are you going to be at it all night?"

He grinned though his eyes never left the screen. "Oh, precious, work is not what I'll be at all night. But I need a few minutes to send this new proposal to the board before I can devote my attention to you. Do you mind?"

"Take your time. I'll get ready for bed." I lowered the lights as he had the night before, then took advantage of his distraction and retrieved the sexy nightie I'd brought with me before slipping into the bathroom.

I didn't hurry as I undressed, taking the opportunity to shave and apply lotion before slipping on the red lace halter baby-doll I'd purchased on Friday afternoon. The halter-top accentuated my breasts, an area of my body that Hudson appreciated. I removed the ponytail holder from my hair and let it spill around my shoulders in a seductive mess. I brushed my teeth and applied a thin layer of strawberry lip gloss.

When I was satisfied with my appearance, I opened the door to the bedroom and posed in the doorway, waiting for Hudson's reaction.

I was met with quiet snoring.

With his hands still propped on his open laptop, Hudson had fallen asleep, fully dressed. I sighed, debating how to address the situation. Of course I wanted him awake, but he wouldn't have fallen asleep like that if he wasn't truly worn out. Plus, I had to remind myself, night was my time of day—not his.

Gently, I slipped the computer from his grasp and placed it on the nightstand. The movement didn't disturb him in the least—he was out. I decided to let him sleep, but as for myself, I wasn't in the least bit tired. I wondered if Jack was still awake—maybe we could play another round of poker, though being alone with the man wasn't entirely a great idea. I peered out the window and saw the guesthouse was dark. Probably for the best.

The pool sprawled below my window though, and suddenly a midnight swim sounded heavenly. I traded my lingerie for a string bikini, threw on my robe, and grabbed a towel. Then I slipped on my flip-flops and turned off all the lights before venturing down to the grounds.

The pool was heated and felt amazing—exactly what I'd needed. I hadn't been for a swim in months, since I'd let my gym membership expire earlier in the year. And I had the place to myself—perfection.

I pushed myself through thirty serious laps before relaxing into a dozen or so at a leisurely pace. Then I sat on the step in the shallow end of the pool, letting my heart rate return to normal while lazing in the warm water.

"Where's Hudson?" Sophia's voice startled me from my reverie.

I shifted in my spot and found her standing behind me, dressed in the same robe she'd worn the night before, and, again, a glass of amber liquid in her hand. I wondered if she was a heavy drinker or if my being in her home brought it on.

"He's...he fell asleep." I climbed out of the pool and reached for my towel, feeling small in her presence. She had that effect on me in general, but also I hadn't asked anyone if I could use the pool and I worried I'd taken advantage of my host's hospitality. Although, Sophia hadn't been hospitable in the least, so perhaps it was a moot concern.

I faced away from her as I toweled off, but I heard her take a seat in a deck chair behind me. "He doesn't love you, you know?"

I'd heard her, but didn't trust my ears. I turned to meet her narrow eyes. "Pardon me?"

"He can't." She swirled the liquid in her glass as she spoke, her tone laced with pain. "He's incapable."

Incapable. That was exactly what Hudson had said. Had it been his mother who had forced him to embrace such an idiotic idea about himself? The earlier hostility I'd felt toward her when I'd listened at the kitchen door returned and spilled like poison from my lips. "Maybe you're projecting your own incapability of emotion."

Her voice grew colder, but remained steady, in control. "Your words can't touch me, Ms. Withers. This is *my* house, Hudson is *my* son. I'm the one in power here."

"Fuck you."

She smiled. "He's had years of therapy. Extensive therapy."

So have I. I threw my towel down and wrapped my robe around me, taking the time to make sure my tone was as level as hers when I spoke again. "He's told me."

"Has he? But he hasn't shared the details." She leaned forward, her eyes catching one of the outdoor lights, causing them to glow red. She couldn't have looked nastier if she'd tried. "If he had, you'd know he can't love anyone. He's sociopathic. Diagnosed at age twenty."

She surprised me, the lack of strength in my response telling her as much. "Hudson's not a sociopath." Was he?

"He's deceitful and manipulative, egocentric, grandiose, glib and superficial. Incapable of remorse. He engages in casual and impersonal sexual relationships." She ticked off traits easily, as if they always bubbled right there at the surface of her consciousness. "Look it up—he fits the definition to a tee. He has no concern for others' feelings. He can't love anyone."

"I don't believe that." But my voice cracked.

"You're extremely naïve."

"You're an extreme bitch." I gathered my towel in my arms and slipped on my flip-flops, needing to be away from her and her horrible accusations. But her words had already done their job. I doubted, and she knew it.

"He's only with you for the sex." She stood, blocking me from the path to the house. "You're attractive." Her eyes skidded down to my bosom. "And clearly his type. He seems to like fucking buxom brunettes the most."

I had nothing to say in my defense. He'd told me our relationship was only sex. I was aware enough of my obligations to my on-duty job, though, and I spoke as if we were a real couple. "If it was just sex, he'd never bring me to meet you."

Her smile widened. "That's an added bonus for him. He can rile me up and get his kicks with you all at once. It really has nothing to do with you. It's about me and my son." She took a step toward me, and it took all my strength not to cower. "You, Ms. Withers, are insignificant."

I wanted to believe that I would have slapped her or pushed her into the pool—she deserved either, both really. But our confrontation was interrupted by Chandler and four other teenage boys boisterously entering the pool area, dressed in swim trunks and carrying towels.

"Mom?" Chandler said upon seeing his mother's back. Sophia stepped aside and he met my eyes. "Laynie," he said, surprised to see me or perhaps recognizing the stricken look that I must have worn. "I didn't know anyone else was out here."

"Alayna and I were getting to know each other." Sophia switched gears as easily as Hudson.

Chandler cocked a brow skeptically.

I used the boys' intrusion to escape. "The pool's all yours. I'm done here." Without looking back, I hurried into the house through the kitchen and up to the east wing, not stopping until I was outside our bedroom doors.

Then the tears fell, thick and heavy. I leaned against the wall, and slid down to a sitting position, unable to stand in the weight of my grief. So many emotions and thoughts warred for top billing. Sophia's insults had hurt, but what pained me most was the possibility that she was right.

What had I seen to show me differently? We'd had instances—Hudson and I—where I believed he truly cared, that he felt more for me than physical attraction, but had I imagined them? I had my own history of making meaningless moments carry heavier weight than they were meant to.

And her description of a sociopath did fit Hudson. I didn't need to look up the definition—I'd been in enough group therapy sessions to be familiar with the signs. But I'd never associated Hudson with the definition until Sophia had pointed it out. Had I purposefully ignored the connection?

Or was Sophia wrong?

I'd had therapists misdiagnose me early on in my therapy. And Brian's understanding of my problems was way off base. What if Hudson believed the worst about himself because Sophia had believed it? Maybe he'd never had a chance to prove her wrong.

Maybe that's what I was—a chance.

The possibility calmed me, though I was smart enough to realize its improbability.

I wiped my face with my damp towel and pushed myself up from the ground. Taking a deep breath I pushed open the door as quietly as I could.

"Alayna?" I heard Hudson reach to switch on the bedside lamp. "Is that you?"

"Yeah." I turned toward the door as I closed it, giving myself a minute to compose myself. "I wasn't tired, so I went for a swim." I took a deep breath then plastered a smile on my face before facing him.

"Good, I'm glad you…" He leaned forward, his body tense. "Hey, what's wrong?"

"Nothing." Was I that transparent? I couldn't talk to him—not now.

"Your eyes are red. You've been crying."

"No, no. The chlorine. Bothers my eyes." I rubbed at my puffy eyes hoping to accentuate my point.

He tilted his head, as if deciding whether I was being honest with him.

I couldn't take his scrutiny. If he pressed, I'd break, and I needed to settle my emotions about him and his mother's claims before I spoke with him about them. What would he say anyway? He'd either deny it or he wouldn't. If he denied it, could I trust him? If he didn't deny it, could I trust that?

Searching for an escape, I said, "Um, I'm going to jump in the shower."

"I'll join you."

I didn't argue. But we didn't speak as we entered the bathroom and undressed, Hudson helping me untie the back of my bikini top before he worked to remove his own clothing. I hung my wet suit on the edge of the tub and climbed into the shower, adjusting the temperature until it was near scalding.

When Hudson joined me, his penis already semi-erect, longing overcame me. I didn't know all the truth about Hudson, and I did know many damning truths about myself. But faced with his naked hard body and the awareness that—whether or not he could love me—he could make me feel better, at least for the moment, I pulled him toward me urgently, claiming his mouth with a hunger I'd never experienced.

"Alayna?" He pulled away, his hands firmly grasped on my shoulders. "Something's wrong. Tell me."

"I'm fine. I just…" I loved him. That was why I was torn up over everything Sophia had said. I loved him and I wanted—needed—to believe Hudson could love me too.

Not able to say those words—not yet—I settled for another version of the truth. "I need you."

He knew I was hiding something, but he nodded. "I'm here, precious." Then he took over, fulfilling me in ways only he could, satisfying me as deeply as he was able.

I lost myself to it, letting myself forget that he might never be able to love me in any way but this—with his mouth and tongue and cock.

Maybe it could be enough.

— CHAPTER —

NINETEEN

I woke early, aware of Hudson working behind me in the bed, again on his laptop. But I didn't let on that I was awake, allowing myself to process the events of the night before.

Maybe because it was a fresh day, or perhaps because I wasn't face-to-face with Sophia, the facts didn't seem as overwhelming as they had. The truth was, whatever the reality of our relationship, it didn't change the fact that I was in love with Hudson Pierce. And being in love with Hudson Pierce put me on his side, whether he was capable of returning my feelings or not. His side meant proving to Sophia that her son was not the unfeeling sociopath that she believed he was, a task that might very well be impossible, but I resolved to give it my best shot. After all, that was the job I'd been hired to do.

And, if I played it right, the work might even be enjoyable.

Determined, I stretched, sat up against the bed frame, and leaned into Hudson. I needed to get him out of his computer and on board.

"Good morning, precious." He glanced over, his eyes pausing on my bare breasts before he returned his focus to the screen, a twinkle in his eyes. "Did you get enough sleep?"

"I did." The alarm clock on the nightstand read a few minutes past eight. It was early for me, but I felt rested, adapting somewhat to his traditional sleep schedule.

Hudson still in bed at that time of morning was what was surprising, even awake and working. I'd learned during our get-to-know you game that he usually got up around six. I suspected that this morning he lingered because of my behavior the evening before. He'd sensed my distress and he cared that I felt that way. Didn't that show capability of love?

Now wasn't the time to analyze. I filed it away to ponder later.

I skimmed his shoulder with my lips, running my fingers through the soft hair at the base of his neck. "Hudson? Are you going to work all day?"

He stopped typing and rubbed his rough chin against the side of my forehead. "Does my working bother you?"

"Not really. But I was thinking..." I took a deep breath then plunged in. "I didn't really see your mother yesterday. Shouldn't we try to spend some time with her today?"

He tensed. "I don't know if that's necessary."

I had guessed he was keeping his mother and I apart on purpose, that he meant to control the animosity between us. While I appreciated the gesture, it was counterproductive. We'd come to the Hamptons because of her. "Isn't she the person we need to be impressing with our fabulous relationship sham?"

"Being here together is enough." He straightened his head and returned to his screen, the matter settled in his mind.

But it wasn't settled for me. I moved to kneel in front of him, demanding his attention. "No, it's not enough." He lifted his eyes to meet mine. "I think we should go at her gangbusters. Throw ourselves in her face. You need to ignore your work to make it really convincing, though. Show her that you're so in love you can't even concentrate on business. You can only think of me."

Hudson rubbed a hand over his stubbly face and shook his head.

"What? Not a good idea?"

He shrugged. "It could be a good idea." He closed the lid of his laptop and placed it on the nightstand. "But do you really want to spend time with my mother? She can be..."

"A total bitch?"

"I was going to say abrasive, but your words fit as well."

Of course I didn't want to spend time with Sophia. But I'd realized that she hated me even more than I hated her. Spending time with her would bring more misery to her than to me. "It's only two more days. I can handle it."

Hudson reached a hand out to cup my cheek. "You're pretty incredible, you know?" His eyes wandered down. "Actually, I'm finding it hard to concentrate on anything but your beautiful naked breasts."

He pulled me in for a kiss, licking his tongue greedily into my mouth.

When his hand circled around my breast, I pulled away. "No, no, no. We can't stay locked up in here all morning. We have to be downstairs, in the public eye. Or the Sophia eye, anyway. What time is breakfast?"

He sighed. "Eight-thirty."

"Damn, I'll have to shower afterward then." I hopped out of bed and began rummaging for clothes in my suitcase. "Hope no one minds me smelling like sweat and sex."

Hudson crossed to his own suitcase. "I'm not going to complain."

As I pulled out an outfit, I remembered the night at the symphony, how Hudson reacted to my hand on his thigh. "I'm warning you right now—I'm playing this full out." I slipped on some pink panties. "Expect lots of fondling and touching and kissing and such." A pair of tan shorts followed.

Hudson dressed quickly too, pulling on a pair of jeans, not bothering with underwear. "Thank you for the warning. Though it should probably be me that initiates most of the fondling and touching and kissing and such." He paused to pull a plain dark t-shirt over his head. "Since it's my emotions we're trying to convince her of, not yours."

I stilled. Did he know my emotions ran deeper? Was he trying to hint that he knew?

No, I was reading too much into his words. I reached behind my back to clasp my bra. "Good point." I turned to face him. "But can you bring it?"

"Are you challenging me?"

"If it helps." I pulled a blue sleeveless blouse over my head.

"I don't need a challenge. I can totally bring it."

I slipped my feet into flip-flops and swallowed back a laugh, his words sounding so out of character. When I'd composed myself, I met his eyes. "Game on, then?"

"Game on."

God, he was adorable.

Arriving to an empty dining room, we sauntered into the kitchen where Millie promptly pointed us to the veranda before hustling to get together plates and utensils for us. Hudson took my hand, lacing his fingers through mine and squeezed, a silent reassurance before we stepped onto the battlefield. Then he pulled me outside through the open French doors where we found Mira, Adam, Jack and Sophia already dining on eggs, potato casserole, ham and fruit cups. Chandler, I guessed, was sleeping in after his late night adventure. He was a teenager, hardly expected to be out of bed before noon.

Sophia noticed us first. "Well, well. They managed to leave the bedroom."

Mira's expression turned puzzled then embarrassed when she saw us. "Mom!"

Adam mumbled a half-hearted greeting, consumed with whatever he was reading on his phone. Jack nodded at us, adding a wink, then sat back in his chair as if about to watch something entertaining.

Sophia set her fork down and dabbed at her lips with a napkin. "It's a fair observation. I didn't expect them down this early." Her eyes bore into me. "Especially when Alayna was up so late swimming." It was meant to be a reminder. *I'm in control. You're insignificant.*

I fidgeted as Hudson stole a glance at me, probably piecing together that my mood the night before had been because of Sophia. She knew I hadn't told him about our conversation—if I had, Hudson and I would have likely been out the door first thing that morning. She had gambled, and had won the hand. But I still had cards to play.

I kept my features even and lifted my chin slightly. "Hudson and I wanted to make sure we got to spend some time with you." My words spread like honey, but underneath they were hot pepper. "Are you feeling up to it? I mean, you were up late, too. And you had that nasty headache."

"You'd have fewer of those if you'd lay off the sauce," Jack jabbed.

Sophia ignored her husband. "I am feeling better. Thank you." Her stiff tone belied her insincerity. "And I never turn down time with my son. Please, join us."

On cue, Millie set two more place settings and Hudson pulled two chairs closer to the table, Mira and Adam already occupying the loveseat. By the time I sat, spread a napkin on my lap, and accepted a mug of coffee from Hudson, a plate of hot breakfast had been placed in front of me.

We ate in silence for several minutes, the usual noises of dining the only sound. Hudson and I exchanged several looks, both of us eager to demonstrate our supposed romance, neither of us knowing how. Under the table, my knee bounced with anxiety until he stilled it with a firm hand. He kept his hand there, resting while we continued eating, my skin tingling under his touch.

I closed my eyes and drew in a breath. The smell of summer flowers wafted through the air, the breeze warm and pleasant. It was a gorgeous day in a beautiful setting, and the atmosphere relaxed me enough to break the quiet. "So." I waited until all eyes were on me to continue. "What's on the agenda for the day?"

Mira beamed as if grateful for conversation. "Adam and I want to hit the beach. Don't we, sweetie?"

"Uh huh," Adam mumbled without looking up from his phone. What was with the men around here? Always sucked into their electronics.

If Mira minded Adam's distraction, she didn't show it. "It's perfect weather for it. We can relax and soak up some rays. Millie could pack us a lunch. Want to come with us?"

I'd been in the Pierce estate for more than a day and still hadn't ventured down to the ocean at the edge of the Hampton property. The beach sounded wonderful. "I'm up for it. Hudson?"

Hudson grinned a little too wide, but I was probably the only one who noticed. "Wherever you are, baby, I'm there."

I surprised myself by not cringing at his choice of endearment.

"Hudson, you'll get sand in your computer," Sophia said. "And we don't get great Wi-Fi down there. Wouldn't you rather work up here?" Her assumption that Hudson would spend the day working fit right into my scheme. Now, would he follow through with his part? He'd never quite agreed.

He set his fork down and looked directly at Sophia. "Actually, I'm not doing any work today, Mother." He moved his hand from under the table to my neck, stroking gently under my hair. "I promised Laynie I'd give her my full attention for the rest of our trip."

I would have preferred that he'd played it like he couldn't even concentrate on work because of me, but, besides his version being much more believable, his use of my nickname was perfect. Even Adam looked up long enough to exchange a surprised look with his wife.

Sophia's reaction, though, was priceless. She gaped.

As much as I would have liked to take in every second of Sophia's shock, I slid my focus to Hudson. "Thank you, H." My gratitude extended deeper than the superficial show we were performing. I appreciated that he'd listened to my suggestions, that he heard me and then acted on it.

Hudson's deep gray eyes erased our spectators from my view. "It's nothing," he murmured. "You're worth it." Was his response as genuine as my thanks? Or was he just an excellent actor?

"Mom? Join us at the beach?" Mira practically bounced in her seat, the idea of a family outing right up her alley.

Sophia's expression was unchanging, her voice level. "Sure. Why not?"

Jack guffawed. "Sophia spending the day in the sand? This I have to see."

Again Sophia ignored her husband, but Jack seemed pleased all the same.

"Adam," Mira elbowed her husband in the ribs. "Go wake up Chandler. We can take the Jet Ski out."

"Uh, okay." Adam stuffed his phone into the pocket of his khaki carpenter pants, crumpled his napkin into a ball, and stood, appearing grateful for the excuse to leave. It occurred to me that I'd never seen him around Sophia. Perhaps he had buried himself in his phone to avoid interacting with her. Smart.

Mira turned her attention to Jack. "And Dad, if you wear a thong again, I swear to God..."

"Fine." He leaned back in his chair. "I'll dress like an old man. But only for you, ladybug."

While her family conversed around her, Sophia sat solemnly, her eyes calculating. At least, that's how I interpreted her narrow gaze, fixed at nothing in particular on the table in front of her, her hands laced together.

"Hudson," she said finally. "The Werners are arriving at their Hampton house this evening."

"That's nice." He poked at what was left of his ham with his fork, his features even. "Why are you telling me this?"

I put my hand on Hudson's knee, bracing myself for where this conversation was going.

"Celia's coming, too." And there it was—Sophia's bombshell. "I know how long it's been since you've gotten to spend time together so I invited her for brunch tomorrow."

Hudson's face was steel, his jaw tight as he set his fork down with a noisy clink.

I imagined my heart plummeting through my chest, landing in my stomach with the same clink. Celia was a weak spot for me. She fueled my jealousy in ways that were absurd and unreasonable but real nonetheless. To keep from betraying my emotions, I bit my lip. Hard.

Mira's face went red. "Mom! Why would you do that?"

Jack, who had rolled his eyes at Sophia's announcement, now leaned toward his daughter, his arm resting on his knee. "Honestly, Mira, does this type of behavior from your mother surprise you?"

Sophia's eyebrows raised in mock innocence. "What did I do?"

Mira groaned in response. Hudson remained silent, anger rolling off his body in waves.

Sophia either delighted in her son's rage or didn't recognize it. "Anyway, we've been talking about redecorating the main rooms. I figured this was a great opportunity for her to show us some ideas while catching up with her dear friend." She turned up her sickening sweet smile. "Alayna, you've met Celia. Did you know that she did all the decorating for Hudson's offices and penthouse?"

I glanced at Hudson who was barely containing his fury. "I did."

I took a sip of coffee, preparing my next words. The loft above his office wasn't where Hudson lived. I'd never been to his penthouse, but, of course, Sophia assumed I had. Anything I said I'd have to phrase carefully. "Celia's got excellent taste. I think she managed to capture Hudson's style quite well in both his living and working space." It was true of his office and the loft, anyway. Hopefully it held about his penthouse.

"Which is your favorite room?"

"Sophia." Jack's tone was a warning.

Hudson tensed beside me, and I shoveled a mouthful of eggs into my mouth to stall. He'd hinted that he never took women to his penthouse, which had seemed like a good safety net for me—I couldn't stalk a man's house if I didn't know where it was. But did Sophia know he didn't take women there? Was she trying to trap me or was I being paranoid?

And underneath the concern of responding correctly was the punch of jealousy: Celia had been in Hudson's private home. She had to have been if she had done the interior design.

I swallowed the bitter sting with my eggs and gave Sophia the only answer I could, lame as it was. "Oh, I love all of it. I could never pick one room."

Hudson took my hand that still rested on his knee and laced it in his. "Didn't you tell me you liked the library the best?"

Thank god. He'd cooled himself enough to throw me a line.

"Only because it has books." Of course I'd love the library, being an avid reader.

Sophia's smile was smug. "He barely has any books at all."

Leave it to Hudson to have a library with no books.

He cleared his throat. "Actually, we're working on improving that." I exchanged a glance with him that I hoped expressed my thanks. "Alayna loves books so I've purchased quite a few since we've met. You haven't been there in a while, Mother."

"I haven't been invited."

"Since when has that stopped you?" This time Jack's comment earned a scowl from his wife. He answered it with an innocent shrug.

Sophia turned her attention back to me. "Are you officially living together then?"

"No," I said as Hudson said, "Yes."

I met his eyes, one brow raised. Saying I lived with him was a pretty big lie not to discuss with me first. Talk about bringing it on.

His eyes pierced into mine. "But you practically are. Once your lease is up, next month. Or have you changed your mind?"

A bubble of uncontrolled excitement rose in my chest. For a moment, it felt real, like he was asking me to be that in his life.

It wasn't real, though. What it was instead was an excellent move on Hudson's part, one sure to rile up his mother. I couldn't wreck it.

I swallowed then smiled shyly. "No, I haven't changed my mind. I just didn't realize we were telling your family, yet."

"Hell, I'm telling everyone." He practically beamed. God, he was good. "It's the best thing to ever happen to me."

Jack nodded, a twinkle in his eye. "I think it's terrific."

Sophia turned to her spouse and frowned. "Why are you here anyway, Jack? You haven't vacationed with us in years."

"Mira invited me."

"Hudson was coming and it's been so long since we've had the whole family together." Mira's intentions were the best. How had she lived in this family all her life without realizing it could never be the Brady Bunch she longed for? I'd known them all for only a minute and recognized dysfunction like a big neon sign.

Then, speaking of dysfunction, Mira asked, "What's your family like, Laynie? Are you close?"

I took a deep breath. "Actually, no. My parents passed away in a drunk driving accident when I was sixteen. My brother looked after me, but now we're…" I hadn't said the word aloud to anyone yet, but it was honest and it needed to be said. "Estranged."

"Oh, no!" Mira clasped her hand to her mouth.

Hudson stayed silent, but he raised a brow as he unlaced his hand from mine and rubbed it soothingly across my back. He knew Brian had been trying to contact me, probably realized the estrangement was a recent thing.

Jack shook his head slowly and *tsk*ed. "I hope that drunk was held accountable, at least." I swear he looked at Sophia when he said the word "drunk."

It was an opportunity to lie. I had before when people had asked, but I wanted to say it now, whether to shock or gain sympathy, I didn't know. "You could say so. The drunk was my father. He was a full-time alcoholic, actually."

"I'm sorry," Jack said softly. "I didn't realize."

My eyes glistened. "It was years ago. I've learned to accept it."

I couldn't look at Hudson. I hadn't told him anything about my parents, but if he had looked hard enough to find my restraining orders, he likely already knew. I couldn't bear to see him look at me with pity.

"Less than ideal pasts," Hudson said, loud enough for everyone to hear, but gentle all the same, his fingers continuing their sweeping pattern across my back. "It's something Alayna and I have in common."

I turned to him and found his gaze absent of pity. Instead it held understanding. More and more I realized that I was special to him because of this unique recognition he saw in me. Were we really that alike?

"I don't like what you're implying," Sophia snarled.

"I'm not implying anything, Mother. I'm stating an unattractive fact."

"Keep your unattractive facts to yourself for the rest of the day, will you?" The fury in her tone was unmasked. She scooted her chair out and stood from the table. "Now, if you'll excuse me, I'm going to prepare for our beach outing."

With every card we'd played throughout the meal, Hudson had wounded her with one brief comment, the evidence plain in her expression.

I snuck a victory smile at Hudson, which he returned with equal delight shining in his eyes. This round had gone to us.

— CHAPTER —
TWENTY

Round two began almost two hours later on the sands of the private beach below Mabel Shores. It took over an hour to change and load up the beach chairs and Jet Skis from the storage shed into the back of the Ford Raptor the family used to drive the half mile down the hill to the beach. Millie also made a lunch for later and packed a cooler with beverages.

Sophia was mellow when we arrived at the beach, choosing to doze while the rest of us finished setting up our chairs and other items. By the time I was lounging next to Hudson under a big rainbow colored umbrella, I'd convinced myself that I could relax and enjoy the warm breeze and rhythmic sound of the waves rolling on the sand.

The idea of quiet serenity disappeared when Adam and Chandler suggested a game of beach volleyball.

"Alayna?" Hudson looked up from his Kindle. "We could be a team."

"You play?" I'd been about ready to move my lounge chair into the sun and try to get a cancer-causing tan, but I could be talked into some friendly competition.

He scowled at me, a challenge glinting in his eyes. "Don't act so surprised. I'm very skilled."

I could tell from his tone that he was, and as competitive as I knew a man of his success had to be, I imagined he was quite good.

"He rarely loses," Jack confirmed, returning from an ocean swim. He shook his long wet hair before taking a seat. "He takes after his old man."

Hudson shook his head almost imperceptibly, not seeming to want to credit his father with any of his ability.

"Fantastic." Sophia shifted in her seat, reminding everyone of her presence. "I'm trying to relax and you all are going to be noisy and wild and disturb the peace."

"That's what beaches are for," Jack said over his shoulder, not bothering to look directly at his wife. "You could go back to the house if you don't like it."

Sophia's opposition made my decision. "I'm in." I pulled off my cover-up and began slathering sunscreen on the newly exposed areas of my body while Adam and Chandler attached the net to the permanent poles anchored in the sand.

"That's your swimsuit?" Hudson grumbled beside me. "You're practically naked. It's going to distract the men playing."

"Think of it as your secret weapon."

"Except one of those men will be me." He casually adjusted himself in his long navy swim shorts.

I shot him a smile, my insides melting at his obvious arousal. "Later, big boy." And that was a promise. "Meanwhile, would you mind getting my back?"

I leaned forward and hugged my knees. Hudson took the lotion and sat in the space behind me, straddling me. I suppressed a moan as his hands applied the lotion, his fingers kneading longer and deeper into my skin than necessary.

"I love touching your skin," he murmured near my ear, then nipped at my lobe, soothing it afterward with a smooth swipe of his tongue. It was an awfully sexual gesture, one I didn't expect from him in the company of others. Either he'd upped his game or he was no longer finding it as easy to compartmentalize as he usually did.

I turned my head into him to see if I could read his face but stopped when I spotted his mother watching us, her eyes narrow slits of anger. So that was the reason behind his display. Satisfaction rose in my chest, but simultaneously I felt a wave of disappointment. Though I thoroughly enjoyed Sophia's misery, our job had been to sway her to acceptance, not alienation. The task was impossible, I'd embraced that. But I knew Hudson hadn't, and I hurt for the distress that his mother caused him.

"Net's ready," Adam declared, kicking a pile of sand toward us to make sure he had our attention.

Hudson stood and reached his hand out to help me up beside him. Once I was up, he didn't let go, even as I pulled at my swimsuit bottoms with my other hand, relieving myself of the wedgie I'd gotten from sitting. All the while, I felt Sophia's stare, knew I was on her radar. Soon, she'd fire. I sensed it.

"Dammit. I want to play," Mira whined. "You know I'd be MVP."

"Yes, baby, you would." Adam bent down to rub her full belly protruding over the top of her bikini bottoms. "But you play rough, and that wouldn't be good for little jellybean."

"Yeah, you gotta protect my first grandchild," Jack said proudly.

Sophia peered at her husband. "But she isn't technically having the first grandchild, Jack." She paused to ensure all ears were tuned to her. "Celia and Hudson's baby claims that title."

A whooshing sound filled my ears and I felt dizzy, as if on a tilt-o-whirl. *Celia and Hudson's baby.* Why...what...?

My shock was magnified by Hudson's reaction. He didn't deny it. Instead, he tried to pull me closer. "Alayna," he whispered.

"Sophia!" I heard Jack hiss. "How *dare* you compare that to Mira's baby?"

Vaguely I was aware of Mira saying something, but I couldn't make sense of anything except the cold disappointment that rattled in my bones. I had to get away, had to think, had to breathe. I pulled my hand from Hudson's grasp and left, walking quickly down the beach, away from the Pierce family.

"Fuck you, Mother," Hudson said behind me before I was out of earshot.

A baby. Hudson had a baby. With Celia. I couldn't even grapple with trying to figure out where the baby was or what happened to it, too pained by the conception of a baby in the first place. It was ridiculous. He wasn't mine, he never was. But a baby...merely another way he belonged to Celia. Belonged *with* Celia.

I kept walking when Hudson called after me. But I didn't run from him when he jogged to catch up.

"I'm fine," I said, forcing a smile. "I'm playing the part of a wounded girlfriend."

He matched my stride, but didn't try to touch me. "Then why are you crying?"

I'd hoped we didn't have to acknowledge the tears spilling down my cheeks. I swiped at them with my palm, still holding my smile in place. "I'm just surprised." My voice was tight despite the cheer I tried to inject in it. "I didn't know you had slept with her."

"I didn't."

"You obviously did."

"No, my mother thinks I got Celia pregnant. I did not."

His words stopped me, a bubble of hope forming inside. "And why is that?"

He ran his hand over his face before he answered. "Because when Celia got pregnant I told our parents I was the father."

I folded my arms over my chest waiting for more, but he gave nothing. "Are you going to explain?"

"No." He mirrored my stance. "It's not relevant."

I spun on my heels, walking faster this time. How did he expect me to be in this fucking fake relationship when I didn't have all the information? Maybe I was only a pawn in his mind games. It was the only thing that made sense.

"Alayna, stop."

He followed after, reaching for me. This time I pulled away.

"Stop!" He caught up to me and grabbed me firmly at the shoulders. He turned me to him. "I said, 'stop!'"

"Why can't you tell me?" My tears had turned to sobs.

"Why can't you trust me?"

I let out a single laugh, maddened by the insanity of his request. "That's funny—you asking me to trust you when you trust me with absolutely nothing." I mean, what did I know about him? Besides his expertise in bed and a few random tidbits that I'd learned in one long car ride, he'd shared nothing.

His voice tightened. "You know more about me than most people."

It felt like an accusation. That I knew that thing—the one thing he didn't want anyone to know. But he hadn't even been the one to tell me that. And it was only one detail of the complex makeup of Hudson Pierce.

"No," I said, sticking my chin out defiantly. "I know one thing about you that most people don't. It's different."

"It's the only thing that matters."

"Bullshit." If he truly believed that...how could he be so blind to think that all that mattered about him were the mistakes of his past? It broke my heart and my voice cracked as I spoke. "There's so much more to you than that."

I wanted to touch him, to caress his face, to make him see. I stretched my hand tentatively toward him, but he stepped back.

"Obviously you do know me," he spit out, "if you feel comfortable making that kind of statement." His tone was nasty, sarcastic. He didn't believe it. He was spinning my words, my meaning.

I turned away from him, processing. I did know things about him—things I'd discovered from spending time with him. I did believe there was more to him than the guy who manipulated women for sport. I saw it in him, felt it when he kissed me, and when he lay between my legs.

And if I really believed his sincerity in those moments, then I had to say I trusted him.

Which meant he was telling the truth now—he hadn't fathered a baby with Celia. But then why would he tell his parents that he had?

The realization punched my stomach like a ton of bricks. "It's because you love her, isn't it?" Voicing it made the weight even heavier. "That's why you told your parents it was your baby."

"No!"

His defiant protest spun me back to face him. "There's no other logical reason." To assume such a huge responsibility for another person—that required an emotional connection. It was proof he wasn't a sociopath—that he could care for someone at that level—but that was hardly comfort to me in that moment.

"Stop this, Alayna." It was a command, a low even tone that I guessed few people argued with.

But I was determined to hear him confirm the truth that would kill me. "You're in love with her."

He threw his arms out emphatically. "For the love of God! If I am even capable of that emotion, Celia's not the one I'd be..." He stopped himself, his jaw snapping shut.

*Celia's not the one...*His words echoed in my ears like a song I loved to hear.

He stepped toward me. Cupping his hands at the sides of my face, he lifted my chin roughly toward him. "I'm not in love with Celia. I promised I'd be honest with you, Alayna, but it does no good if you don't trust me."

I was still reeling from his slip. Celia wasn't the one he'd…what? Be in love with? Then who—with me?

But he wasn't giving that away. For now, his almost statement was enough—it calmed my nerves and steadied my heart.

He smoothed the hair down behind my ear, and I stared into his gray eyes, noting a tenderness that I hadn't seen earlier. "I've never slept with Celia." His tone was soft but urgent. "I'm not in love with her. I didn't get her pregnant. Trust me." Even softer, even more urgent. "Please."

"Okay."

His brow creased in surprise. "Okay?"

"Okay, I trust you."

"You do?"

I thought of how eager I'd been to have Brian's trust, how disappointed I'd been when I realized I still didn't. Hudson needed someone, needed me to believe in him. I should have been telling him every second. If I loved him, like I believed I did, then I'd have to do better at building him up.

I smiled at him. "I do."

His body relaxed like a huge weight had been removed from his shoulders. "Thank you." He kissed my forehead. "Thank you."

I was absorbed with him in that space of time, but not so much as to not observe its oddity. We were holding each other close, exchanging assurances that portrayed us as more than casual lovers. *What are we doing?* I almost asked him; I felt the shape of the words on my tongue, but couldn't locate the air to push them past my lips. Did he sense it too?

If he recognized it, he hid it from me, pulling my head down to his shoulder where I couldn't look for it in his eyes. And that was fine. I enjoyed his embrace, the warmth and security it gave me, whatever it meant for us.

After the possibility of addressing the moment had passed, he said, "Look. My mother's leaving."

I pulled away to glance at the group we'd left behind. Sure enough, Sophia with her oversized sunhat was walking alone up the pathway toward the house. With her gone, it made the idea of rejoining the group more tolerable. "We should get back."

"We should." A hint of reluctance laced his tone and his eyes shifted to my lips. "We should kiss and make up first." He'd already begun lowering his face to mine. "In case anyone's watching."

I didn't have time to agree before one hand wrapped around the back of my neck and his tongue swept into my mouth. Unlike the majority of our kisses that were generally reserved for sex, this one was sweet and easy. That didn't mean it lacked passion. Hudson sucked and licked and nibbled first at my top lip and then gave equal treatment to the bottom. Then his tongue was inside my mouth again, reaching and searching, circling mine in a lazy spiral.

He labeled it as a kiss for our distant spectators, but it was completely ours—a harmonic blending of him and me, so thoroughly fused I could no longer remember where he began, where I ended, whose taste belonged to who. And it was more—a love song without words, a promise without fear. It was a spark, a beginning of something new.

We parted hesitantly, both of us afraid to break the spell. Then, I slipped my hand in his and we returned to our roles as girlfriend and boyfriend.

Hudson changed after that, perhaps because Sophia had left, but I chose to believe it had more to do with the faith I had placed in him. He became playful and lighthearted. I witnessed it first in the volleyball match against Adam and Chandler. He skillfully dominated the game, as I was sure he dominated a boardroom. But in between plays he surprised me—giving me high fives and patting me lightly on the behind. It didn't feel like he was putting on a show—there wasn't any need to convince Adam and Chandler of our relationship.

I welcomed the development, embracing it perhaps too readily, the line between real and pretend blurring.

After we'd won two sets of volleyball, we took a spin on the Jet Skis—Hudson driving, me clutching to him tightly from behind. He rode confidently across the choppy water, and I thrilled at the speed and the closeness and how easy it was to just be with him.

And when we lost our balance and fell into the ocean, he clutched me to him and laughed then kissed me mercilessly before righting the Jet Ski and pulling me up behind him. "Again, precious?" he yelled over the motor.

"Again."

Later, after we'd packed up and returned from the beach, we changed our clothes and went down for a BBQ on the veranda that included brats and dogs cooked by Jack. Sophia claimed another insufferable headache and only showed herself momentarily to say goodnight, though I suspected she really came down to fill her glass.

We finished the evening with several rounds of poker where Jack cleaned everyone out. Then Hudson and I headed to our bedroom, our eyes wandering along the landscapes of each other's bodies as we climbed the stairs.

The door had barely shut behind us before Hudson had me caged to the wall, his body pressed against me as he took my lips in a hungry desperate kiss, probing and demanding with his tongue until I was gasping in his mouth. My head swam, my panties instantly drenched with arousal, but I summoned strength to push my palms firmly against his chest. "Hold on, Hudson," I said, breathless.

"Dammit, Alayna, I have to be inside you. I can't wait any longer."

He moved in again, but I turned my head and his mouth found my jawline instead. "Soon, H." I darted out under his arm. "Lower the lights like you did the other night." I walked backward as I spoke until I hit the closet where we'd stowed our suitcases. Hudson had hung several items of clothing and put others into the dresser drawers, but I still hadn't bothered to unpack. "Get settled in bed. Naked." I winked.

"Oh, you're taking charge," he said, leaning on the wall with an outstretched arm. "How adorable."

"Don't patronize me." I bent inside the closet to rifle for the red baby doll halter nightie he'd missed seeing me wear the night before. When I found it, I wadded it up in a tight ball so he couldn't see it yet and took off for the bathroom.

"I'm not. I'm excited." He rubbed along the crotch of his pants. "I'm already hard."

My lip curled into a wicked grin. "Good. Now do as you were told." I stopped in the doorframe of the bathroom. "And don't fall asleep!"

"Then don't take forever in the bathroom."

Grinning, I shut the door. Charged with nervous anticipation, I changed at lightning speed. The day had been beyond wonderful and real. It had been so long since I felt anything more than contentment, and with Hudson, I did. I was certain he did, too. We'd been falling together. And now I wanted to celebrate those feelings with my lover, acknowledging the depths of my emotions with my body even if I couldn't yet express them in words.

I positioned my hair to fall around my shoulders, turned off the bathroom light then opened the door. The lights were low so I took a step forward where he could see me.

Hudson sat naked on top of the bed covers. His breath caught when he saw me. "Jesus, Alayna. You're so goddamn beautiful." He moved to a kneeling position. "I might have to let you wear that while I fuck you."

I was used to his forward sex talk, but I blushed anyway.

"Come here," he growled.

I started toward him then stopped. "Wait, I'm in control, remember?"

He sat back on his haunches and tilted his head. "Then take charge."

Tingles spread from my belly throughout my body, turned on by the commanding way he relinquished his authority. He'd always dominated our sex, yet he was letting me take over, a choice that might even diminish the experience for him, though I hoped not. It added an element of pressure that I hadn't expected, but also thrilled me.

"Sit back against the headboard." My demand sounded stronger than I had expected.

Hudson grinned then did as I'd ordered.

Throwing my shoulders back to assume more confidence than I had—and, also to showcase my haltered bosom—I sauntered to the foot of the bed. Facing him, I climbed up and crawled toward him.

I kept my gaze on his face watching as his eyes flitted back and forth from my eyes to my breasts as I crept toward him. My hands trailed along his calves as I moved up him then swept past his knees to his firm thighs. I stopped at the base of his rock hard penis and dipped my head down, licking along the length with one swipe of my tongue.

Hudson's pupils were hot coals of desire. "Do it again."

It would have been natural for me to give in to his command, but I wasn't ready to relinquish my dominance. "Maybe I will."

His grin widened. He had been testing the hold on my control and I'd passed.

I dipped again, this time kissing along his head, my eyes never leaving his. I licked across the crown one more time, savoring the salty taste of him before I fed his erection past my lips into the warmth of my mouth.

He let out a groan. "Oh, precious, you suck me so good."

I teased him, fondling and caressing his balls in one hand while I licked and sucked and cherished his dick with my mouth, never taking up a steady pace. Soon, he threaded his fingers through my hair and began to take over, holding my head still over his penis, as he bucked into my mouth, establishing the rhythm he craved.

I let him keep control for only a moment, treasuring the grunts and groans that accompanied his thrusts. Then I pulled at his arm to release his grip on my head, and raised my body, letting his cock fall from my mouth.

He moaned.

"You want more?" I teased. "You'll have to wait." I climbed further up his body and spread my legs to straddle his waist and felt his firm ridge knocking against my ass.

His eyes widened in curiosity.

I spread my palms across his bare torso and leaned down to take his mouth. His kiss was greedy and eager, his tongue working inside my mouth. He moved his hands to the sides of my face, holding me in our lip-locked position, but I shook my head free.

"What do you want?" he asked, breathlessly.

It put him on edge, to let me dictate. But he was willing to try, and it gratified me immensely. Though he hadn't given me his trust in other areas, he was giving it to me here. That was a big step for him and, though a huge part of me wanted to let him take me in the way he wanted, I remained committed to the role reversal because of how much it meant for both of us to try.

But in answer to his question, I was at a loss. What did I want? "Touch my breasts," I said, finally.

Hudson slipped his hands inside the silk of my halter-top. With a flick of his thumbs, my nipples became stone, my breasts heavy and sensitive as he squeezed them in his firm hands.

I bent down to lick at his lips, but he ducked his head to my bosom instead. Pulling down the material of my nightie, he took the tip of my breast into his mouth. He sucked and tugged at my nipple causing a shallow cry to escape from my throat. "Hudson, oh, god."

A hand slipped under the thin lace of my panties and grazed my clit on the way to the hot opening of my pussy. Releasing my nipple from his mouth he said, "You're already so wet, precious." He licked lightly across the tip and I shuddered. "Shall I put my fingers inside you? Tell me."

Hudson was so good at turning my mind to mush, my body pliable under his hands. I gave into the pleasure he could give me, but on my terms.

"I want your cock inside me." I spoke softly, not quite at ease with saying the words.

He smiled, but didn't move to take me up on my request. Instead he suckled on my other breast eliciting an involuntary moan from me. Then he said, "But you aren't ready for me, precious."

"I'm ready enough." I was more forceful this time. "I want to ride you."

A flash of desire crossed his face. In one swift move, he ripped the sides of my panties open, pulled the torn material out from under me and threw it aside. I shivered at his primal act, lust rushing through my veins like wildfire. Desperate to have him, to possess him, I scooted back to balance myself over him. I took his gorgeous thick penis in my hand and lifted the head to my wet entrance, my arousal fueled further when his cock throbbed in my grasp.

"I can't imagine why I deserve this," Hudson said hoarsely, splaying his hands over my breasts. "I should be rewarding you for your very believable girlfriend act today."

I stilled. His comment stung, but I wasn't sure if it should. Was he reminding me the day had been pretend? Or was he trying to elicit a reaction from me? Was he putting his guard up, refusing to let any emotions into our relationship?

Or maybe he felt nothing of what I thought he felt, and his words were simply a statement of what he saw as an accurate representation of our day.

No, it wasn't true. I believed with all my heart that something more had developed between both of us. He may not be able to admit it to me, or even to himself, but I knew. I *knew*.

I slid down onto his pulsing cock, taking him in with a gasp. He was right—I wasn't fully prepared, and he felt full and big inside. I squirmed, trying to ease the bite of discomfort as I worked him in deeper. Hudson placed his hand flat along the middle of my torso and pushed me to lean back. The angle opened me and I glided down to his root.

"Fuck," he groaned. "You're so tight, Alayna. So good."

I lifted my hips, raising myself up his length before lowering again.

Hudson shifted beneath me, churning his hips, eager to direct the pace, but I kept my steady speed as I slid smoothly up and down his steely erection. His hands moved on me restlessly, wandering from my breasts to my thighs to my hips before he finally settled one flat on my stomach and circled his thumb on my clit with a delicious firm pressure.

"God, oh, god," I cried, squeezing and clenching around him. The exquisite feeling of his cock skimming against my vaginal walls combined with the expert attention he was giving my tender bud drove me mad. I was on the edge, near orgasm, though not quite able to get the release I longed for. Tears formed in my eyes and sweat beaded on my skin.

"I'm happy, Hudson. You've made me happy." I couldn't stop myself from telling him, my words mixed with throaty moans.

Under heavy lids, his eyes pierced mine, glowing with the intense need to fuck. They widened at my declaration, a new spark lighting the dark desire already held there.

"And I've made you happy too." It spilled from my mouth like I wished my elusive orgasm would. I sensed the warning in Hudson's face, but I couldn't stop myself from saying more. "We're falling in love. This is us, falling in love."

"Enough." In a flash, he flipped me underneath him, maintaining our connection at the groin. He bent my legs at the knees and pushed them back while he plunged into me, pummeling me with a drive that fought to tear me apart. In that position he struck me deep, deeper than he'd ever been. He meant to punish me for my words—for knowing he'd connected with me. But the punishment only acknowledged I was right.

And in that finding, combined with his maddening thrusts, I lost everything to him, coming so violently that my body seized, quivering uncontrollably beneath him.

Hudson continued to ram into me, hitting the very end of me with each stroke until I came again. This time he joined me, burying his cock even deeper as he released, my core milking him while he spurted long and hot.

When we'd both stilled, he rolled off of me and fell hard into the bed at my side. Without words, he pulled me into the crook of his arm, closed his eyes, and went to sleep.

I tightened into his embrace. Usually he cuddled longer, and stroked and caressed me before falling asleep. But I'd challenged him in more ways than one that night. He needed time to process. At least he was still holding me at all. That had to be a good sign.

It took longer before I was taken by sleep, but when it finally came, I slept deep and peacefully.

In the morning, I awoke alone, but despite remembering that Celia would visit today, I felt happy. Until I went to the closet to get an outfit and found my belongings the only occupants.

Hudson's clothes and suitcase were gone.

— CHAPTER —
TWENTY-ONE

I swallowed the acid rising in my throat and dressed in a flurry, not bothering with my hair or my face or shoes. Just because his things were gone didn't mean he was, I told myself as I descended the stairs, trying to squelch the growing unease. There had to be an explanation.

I followed the sound of voices and found Mira and Sophia leaning over the dining room table, examining several large poster boards spread in front of them. Mira lifted her head as I approached and smiled. "Good mor—"

"Where's Hudson?" I cut her off, my arms folded over my chest.

Sophia glowered at me over her reading glasses. "He left with Celia." An undercurrent of pleasure laced her statement.

Mira rolled her eyes and turned her body to give me her full attention. "He had a business thing come up. Some sort of emergency. He had to fly immediately to Cincinnati."

"Celia drove him."

"Mother, honestly! Stop it!" I'd never seen Mira irritated and it looked unnatural on her usually smooth, unruffled features. It worked to silence Sophia. "Celia was already here to show us the designs when Hudson discovered he needed to leave. She offered to drive him to the airport so that he could leave the car for you to get back to the city whenever you wanted."

He was gone. He'd left. With Celia.

Suddenly, the air in the house seemed stifling and thick. Breathing became difficult. Had Hudson really had a business emergency? Or was he running from our emotional connection the day before? He'd told me he wouldn't lie to me, but this time he hadn't said anything to me at all. He'd just vanished.

And the thing that I hadn't ever wanted to face—when he said he'd always tell the truth—that could have been a lie itself.

It was too painful to address, especially in the presence of others, namely Sophia. Getting back home became priority number one. He'd left the car for me. "But I don't drive."

Mira shrugged. "Hudson said you might not want to. Martin can drive you then."

"I'm not giving up my hired help to—"

Mira threw her hands up in the air and shot a piercing glare at her mother. "Then I'll take her! Or Adam or Chandler."

"I'll drive you."

I turned to find Jack behind me. Gratitude boiled inside so intensely, tears formed in the corners of my eyes. "Thank you. Give me ten minutes to pack."

I rushed out before anyone could say another word. Taking the stairs two at a time, I sped to our bedroom. *Our* bedroom. The thought pained me in the absence of Hudson. After dragging my suitcase out of the closet, I scrambled around the room picking up random items that I'd left lying around the past few days—my swimsuit, my robe. The red nightie.

When I'd returned from the bathroom with my toothbrush and other toiletries, Mira was standing in the doorframe. "Laynie, you don't have to leave yet."

I walked past her and dropped my things into my luggage.

"Stay until tomorrow. We can go do something girly, get mani-pedis if you want."

There really were great people in the Pierce household. I adored Mirabelle. And Jack had become a fast friend. Even Chandler and Adam for all their boyish personality had taken a piece of my affection.

But the goodness of all of them was outweighed by the horror of Sophia.

And no one meant anything to me in comparison to what I felt for her son. "Thank you, Mira, sincerely. But I can't stay here without Hudson."

"I understand."

I zipped up my bag and stood to face Mira, searching to see if she really did understand. From the softness in her eyes, I believed she did.

Maybe she understood more than I knew. I took a deep breath and asked, "Did he say...anything about me?" I bit my lip, embarrassed to let her see my insecurity. "Or leave any message for me?"

She seemed unsurprised by my question. "I think he was going to call you or something. Have you checked your phone?"

My phone—I hadn't looked at it since I stuffed it in my purse on the drive up. I returned to the closet and found the purse hanging on a hook inside the door. Rifling around inside, I quickly located the phone. "It's dead," I said. "I forgot to bring a charger."

"Is it a standard USB? You can take my car charger."

I wanted to hug her. "Thank you, Mira."

"No problem." She watched while I set my suitcase in the rolling position. "Martin can get that."

"I got it." I didn't want to wait to call someone up to carry a suitcase I could manage myself. I scanned the room one more time then started toward the door.

"Laynie." Mira stopped me before I'd crossed the threshold.

It was difficult to give her my attention when every fiber of my body wanted to go. I fidgeted as I met her eyes.

She took a step toward me, her face soft and compassionate. "I know he loves you," she said firmly. "I know he does. But he's been through... things...that's made it hard for him to open up, so please don't take that as, well, as evidence of anything if he can't tell you how he feels."

My eyes felt misty. Maybe Mira was as snowed as I was, but it felt good to hear. I swallowed hard. "I know."

"Good."

"But..." I might never get the chance to have this conversation again. "Why do you believe that? I mean, what makes you think that he loves me, or that he even can?"

Surely Mira knew the things Sophia claimed about her brother. That he was a sociopath, that he couldn't feel anything for others. Unless all of that had been her mother's way of riling me up. But I suspected there was more to her claims than that—they were rooted in truth somewhere, a therapist's opinion, a doctor's diagnosis.

Mira closed her eyes briefly and blew out a steady stream of air. "I don't know, Laynie. He's different around you. I've never seen him like he is with you."

"Maybe you see what you want to believe."

"Maybe." She stuck her chin out. "But I'm not giving up on him. I hope you don't either."

"I won't." But Hudson might have already given up on me.

And, if not me, himself.

Back downstairs, Mira left me in the foyer to grab her phone charger from her car. Jack had gone to the garage to bring the Mercedes up to the circle drive. I paced, waiting for him to pull up.

I sensed Sophia behind me without seeing her. Hoping she'd go away if I didn't acknowledge her, I kept my eyes focused on the front driveway. I was wrong.

"You shouldn't be surprised that he left you."

I still didn't look at her, but I pictured the satisfied grin she likely wore, imagined myself slapping it off her face. Violence never hurt as much as a good verbal argument, though. Problem was, if I reacted to her bait, she could very well win. Again.

"I told, you he doesn't feel anything." She was a warrior. Good at the game. I had no doubt she'd been the one who taught Hudson to be so good at his own games. "For anyone," she added.

"That's a lie." I had no chance against her. She drew the reaction she desired. But if I had to spar, I'd put my best fight into it. "I've seen proof to the contrary."

"Because of how he seems to love you? He's a good actor."

I spun to face her. "No, because of how he seems to love you." I spit the words like venom. "When there's no reason he should. When you've alienated him and betrayed him and destroyed him and made him the confused man he is by your lack of affection and support and faith. If he can continue to care about a piece of shit like you, after all you've done to him, then I have no doubt of his capability of love." *You fucking bitch.*

And then I opened the front door and walked out, rolling my suitcase behind me, relieved to see Jack pulling up as I did. Sophia didn't follow.

Mira had given Jack the charger in the garage. He handed it to me in exchange for my luggage. While he stowed my suitcase in the trunk of the running car, I climbed in the front passenger seat and plugged in the charger and my phone before securing my seatbelt.

We were on the road before my phone had enough charge to turn on. I had twelve texts and four voice messages. I opened the texts and skipped the eleven from Brian, going immediately to the one from Hudson. "Plexis crisis. I'll call as soon as I can."

My heart sunk. I should have been grateful that he'd left a message at all, but didn't I deserve more? He had led me to believe that I did.

I accessed my voicemail with only faint hope. He'd never called me, and I doubted any of the messages were from him. I listened long enough to the first one to hear Brian's voice then immediately deleted it and skipped to the next one. All were from my brother. All were deleted without a full listen.

Jack was more considerate company than I could possibly ask for. After asking me to enter my address into the GPS, he offered enough small talk for me to understand he was there if I needed him. Then he allowed me to wallow in silence.

For the better part of an hour, I flipped my phone around in my hands, opening the text slider and closing it again without using it. The old me—the crazy, obsessed me—would have already sent a series of messages to Hudson, each heightening in tone and accusations. It took everything in me not to physically do so, but in my head I let myself compose them.

"Why did you go? Are you really on a business trip?"

"I can't do the on-duty anymore. I quit."

"Why won't you let me in?"

"I love you."

Finally I dropped my phone in my purse, leaned my head against the window of the car, and closed my eyes. I'd allow myself one well thought-out text when I got home. Then I'd go to a group meeting. I just had to make it until then without doing anything stupid.

I must have fallen asleep because when I opened my eyes again, we were outside my apartment building. There were no spots available along the street, so Jack had turned on the emergency blinkers and pulled up next to the line of parked cars.

Standing at the driver's door, Jack leaned across the top of the car. "If you wait here, I can find a spot somewhere and help you up to your apartment."

As harmless as Jack was, having him in my apartment did not sound like a good idea. And I didn't need the help or the company. "I can get it. Thanks, though." Standing on the curb with my bag, I felt moved to say more, to express my overwhelming gratitude. "And thank you for driving me here and for...well, for..." *For not treating me like Sophia treats me.* "For being so kind."

Dammit. I was choking up again.

He chuckled. "I'm not really that kind. I just appear so in comparison."

I didn't have to ask whom he meant to compare himself with. "Jack." I shouldn't keep him when he was parked illegally, but suddenly I had to know. "Why are you still married to her?"

"I wish I could say it's because I remember the sweet woman she once was, but she was never a sweet woman." He looked off at the traffic behind him, not seeming to be bothered by the cars honking as they passed in the next lane. "Sophia came to the marriage with a couple of businesses given to us by her father. I took control when her father retired and have spent my life making them successful. Now Hudson runs them. If I divorced Sophia, the controlling interest would go to her. As long as we're married, she doesn't care what we do with them. And she'd never ask for a divorce—it would be too embarrassing."

He turned back to face me. "I wonder sometimes—if I'd let go of the businesses, divorced her when the kids were still young, could I have changed how they are now? But she would have gotten joint custody at the very least. And she may have messed them up even more, retaliating against me. It's not an ideal situation, but it is what it is."

Not an ideal situation—it was similar to what Hudson had said. No, it wasn't ideal, but it was life.

In my small studio apartment, I left my suitcase standing by the door and collapsed on my bed. Tears came, long and steady. I couldn't even say what I was crying for exactly. All I knew was that I hurt. I hurt from Hudson's departure, for his unwillingness to open up to me. I hurt because the lines of our pretend and real relationship had become so blurred that I couldn't tell the difference anymore. I hurt from Sophia's words and hatred. I hurt for the mother she'd been to her son and for the brother Brian had been to me. I hurt for the things I'd done to Brian, for the things Hudson had probably done to his family.

Most of all I hurt because I was alone and in love. And that was the worst combination of things to be.

An hour had passed before I'd calmed enough to send the one text I'd promised myself I could. It was as harmless as I could come up with—a message that said all I dared to say, afraid more would scare him further away. *"I'll be here when you return."*

Not even thirty seconds had gone by after I pushed "SEND" when there was a knock on my door. We had a doorman in the lobby—only building occupants were allowed in without prior approval. But Hudson could pull strings, couldn't he? He was the only person I knew with such power.

The hope that it was him, as weak of a hope that it was, propelled me to my feet and to the peephole.

The man in the hall wore a crisp black suit with a yellow tie. But the face didn't belong to Hudson—it belonged to Brian.

I should have known it was Brian. His name was on the lease, he'd be allowed up. I pressed my face against the door and debated whether or not to let him in.

"Open up, Laynie." Heavy banging on the other side of the door jolted my face from its resting position. "I know you're in there. The doorman told me you came up."

Fuck. He must have been staying in town—at the Waldorf, most likely. What the fuck was so important that he had to see me? Maybe I should have listened to his messages.

Reluctantly, I opened the door partway.

He pushed past me forcefully. He was angry. Probably because I'd been ignoring him.

"What are you doing here, Brian? Are you stalking me?" The joke made me smile even though Brian's eyes only glowed hotter.

"You haven't returned any of my calls." I watched as Brian's fists clenched and unclenched at his sides. I knew he'd never hit me—at least, I hoped he'd never hit me—but I'd seen him rage enough to punch holes in walls. Maybe it was a good thing his name was the primary on the lease instead of mine. He'd have to pay for any damage.

I shut the door and turned to face Brian with a fake smile. "Oh, did you call?" Innocent wasn't usually the best tactic with Brian, but I was too exhausted for anything else. "My phone's been dead and I've been out of town."

"Yeah, I got that from your boss at the club."

God, he'd even called David. What the fuck?

Brian ran a hand through his hair then took a step toward me. "You were with him, weren't you?"

"Him, who?" But I knew he must have been referring to Hudson. That was the who I'd been with after all, and David had known that. But why Brian cared was beyond me.

Brian slammed his fist down on the top of my dresser. "Dammit, Laynie, don't play games. This is serious." He took a step toward me, his eyes narrow slits. "Hudson Pierce. Were you with Hudson Pierce?"

"Yes." I crossed my hands over my chest. "And Jonathon Pierce, for that matter. And Sophia Pierce and Mirabelle Pierce and Chandler Pierce. At their Hampton house. Brian, what is your problem?"

His brows rose almost as high as his voice. "What is my problem? *You* are my problem. Always. Alayna, I saw you in the society pages—you're dating him?"

Well, no. But I kept that to myself.

"You can't date Hudson fucking Pierce. Do you know who he is? Do you know *what* he is?"

For the briefest of moments, my chest felt like it might burst. I had no idea how, but Brian knew about Hudson's games with women somehow and was worried about me. I hadn't felt concern from him in years. I didn't realize how much I'd craved it.

Brian continued. "He's a goddamn giant, is what he is, Alayna. If you fuck with him—*when* you fuck with him—I won't be able to get you out of it. The Pierces are so big, they'll squash you like a bug."

"Wait a minute, wait a minute." I swallowed, processing what Brian had said. "You're not concerned for me, you're worried about...Hudson?"

"Why should I be concerned for you?" He pointed his index finger toward me. "You're the one with the history of going mental over guys."

"Get out." I could only manage a whisper.

"Harassment, drive-bys, breaking and entering, stalking—" He held up a finger for each item he ticked off.

"Get out," I said, stronger. There were no words for the depths of betrayal I felt, no reason to even defend myself against his accusations because he'd already marked me as guilty without even giving me a trial.

"Were you even *invited* to the Hamptons?"

"Get the fuck out!" I screamed. "Get out! Get out! Get. Out!"

He didn't move. "My name's on the lease, not yours."

"Then I'll get the lease changed. Or I'll move." I crossed to the door and opened it for him. "But now I'm telling you, so help me god, if you don't leave I'll call the cops and, even if it gets me nowhere, it will at least occupy your life with yet another embarrassing sister incident. So I'm telling you, get the fuck out, now."

"I'm done, Alayna." He raised his hands up in a surrender position. Still he didn't move.

"Get out!"

This time he stepped toward the door. "I'm leaving, but I'm telling you, I'm done. Do not even think about coming crawling back to me." He turned back to face me after crossing the threshold. "You're on your own with this mess."

I slammed the door in his face.

Brian was out of my life. Out of my life for good.

Maybe because I'd already cried all those tears earlier, or maybe because I'd simply had enough of family members who constantly kept their loved ones down when they needed compassion and support most, but the sigh I let out wasn't in frustration—it was in relief.

— CHAPTER —

TWENTY-TWO

David leaned against his desk and stared at the new brown leather sofa across the room. "Should we move it to the other wall?" It was the fourth time he'd asked since I'd arrived.

Truthfully, I couldn't care less where the sofa was. The only reason I'd come into the club so early was to have something to occupy my mind. It had been thirty-three hours since I'd left the Hamptons, longer since I'd seen Hudson, and all I wanted to do was buy a plane ticket to Cincinnati and find him, whatever it took.

But another part of me—a very small, but surprisingly solid bud of calm at the center of my being—believed that Hudson would be back. That he'd be back for me. He felt something for me. I knew he did. And maybe that emotion, even if he couldn't acknowledge it, would be enough to bring him to me. Eventually.

Hopefully.

If I didn't cling on to that small sliver of hope, I'd fall apart. It was the only thing keeping me from giving into the crazy. That and trying to concentrate on my job.

"It's fine, David. Leave it."

"Are you sure? This is your vision, Laynie. Make it work."

"It works perfectly as is."

I suspected David's anxiousness had more to do with me and my mood than couch placement. He crossed to the sofa and sat down. "It's pretty comfy, too. Check it out."

Sighing, I tossed my inventory report on the desk and joined him. "Hmm," I said, settling into the corner. "Not bad."

But really I was thinking about how the new couch reminded me of the one at the apartment above Hudson's office. It had been my initial attraction to it when I'd seen it in the catalog. I loved the way it felt masculine with its rich dark color, yet also warm and soft with its curved back and arms.

Now I wondered if every glance at the piece of furniture would bring to mind thoughts of the man who hadn't called or texted me since his vanishing act.

My thoughts traveled to the email I'd received that morning from his bank—the one that owned my student loans—stating my debt had been adjusted off in full. And the credit card that I'd kept secret from him had also shown up with a zero balance. Having them both paid for made the whole deal feel done.

And I wanted so much not to be done with Hudson Pierce.

"So what's going on in your pretty little head, Laynie?"

I'd gotten lost in my mind again. Boy, was I bad company.

"Stuff," I said, feeling bad about the brush off, but not bad enough to expound upon my answer.

He nodded and rested his ankle on his other leg. "Pierce okay with that Plexis deal?"

I twisted my head toward him. "What do you mean?"

David's brows rose. "I figured you knew. It was in the paper this morning." He stood and moved toward his desk.

I hadn't looked at the news that morning. Knowing I'd be tempted to stalk Hudson online, I hadn't even gotten on my computer except to check my email after Brian had left the day before. It had been hard to fight the compulsion, but after kicking my brother out, I'd felt a renewed sense of self-strength. So I turned off my computer and spent the night watching some of the movies from the AFI list that I hadn't seen yet while I ate a pint of mint chocolate chip ice cream. And I cried some more. Overall, a very productive evening.

David rifled through some papers in the recycling bin. "Here it is."

He returned to the couch and handed me a folded section of the newspaper. I scanned my eyes over the article he'd pointed to. The headline read *Plexis sold to DWO.* Skimming, I quickly got the gist of the story. DWO, a rival corporation of Pierce Industries, had convinced the other shareholders to sell, even though management, and lone hold-out shareholder Hudson Pierce, fought to prevent the acquisition.

My stomach sank. Hudson had really cared about Plexis and the people that worked there. He had to be devastated over the loss. No wonder he'd run off to Cincinnati the day before—he must have been making one last ditch effort to save his company.

Which also meant he'd been telling me the truth. He hadn't run from me. Why was I so self-centered to believe everything had to do with me?

I closed my eyes and felt the couch sink next to me as David sat back down.

"You like him more than you let on."

"I do. I love him." I peeked over at him, remembering how David had reacted the last time we'd talked about Hudson and me. "I didn't mean to fall in love. I just did."

David smiled but kept his eyes downcast. "That's how it usually occurs."

I threw the newspaper on the ground, put my elbows on my knees and covered my hands with my face. Awkward—that's what this was. Totally awkward.

David leaned back on the couch. "And he feels…?"

I peeked over my shoulder toward him. Did he really want to talk about this? Well, he was there, and he did ask. "I'm not sure."

"That's a real bummer." David leaned forward. He was so close to me I could smell the faint aroma of his body wash and feel the warmth of his breath. "For what it's worth, I'll tell you how I feel: Stupid."

"Stupid?" I folded my arms across my chest, feeling strangely vulnerable so near to a guy I'd once been gaga over.

"Yeah." He lowered his voice. "How did I let you slip through my fingers?"

"David…" I didn't want that, not now. My heart, my mind, my body had tuned to Hudson. He was the only guy I could think of anymore. It scared me a bit. Singular thoughts of someone—that could be the beginnings of an obsession.

But also, and I wasn't sure because I didn't know from experience, but couldn't those kind of thoughts be attributed to being in love? Lauren had said as much. As long as I remained in control of my behavior, as long as my affection was welcomed, then wasn't it perfectly okay to think of Hudson, to *choose* him over anyone else? I thought maybe so. I *hoped* so.

I opened my mouth to speak, to tell David that there was no chance for us, but he seemed to understand without me having to say anything.

He sighed and nodded. Then he shrugged. "I just thought you should know."

"Thank you," I said, because I didn't know what else to say. And because I was grateful that he'd taken my rejection so well.

He stood up and held his hand out to me. "Back to work."

I took his hand and let him help me to my feet.

David held onto my hand after I stood. "But if you ever find yourself on the market again…"

Even without Hudson, David and I couldn't be together. He'd been a safe option, someone who wouldn't drive me to obsessive behaviors. But safety had come at the price of no sincere emotional investment. Maybe I risked more with Hudson, but there was also something real to be gained.

But I smiled and said, "I'll keep you in mind. For sure."

"Can we hug it out?"

I nodded and David pulled me into his arms. His embrace felt…good. Stronger than I'd remembered, but it didn't make my heart beat faster. And it comforted me, but didn't warm me to the bone the way Hudson's arms did. Still, it was nice, and I let myself relax into its goodness.

David broke away first. Abruptly. Bringing his closed fist to his mouth, he coughed, his eyes darting from me to a spot behind me.

I furrowed my brow, confused by his strange actions then twisted to see what was behind me.

"Hey, Pierce," David said as I came eye-to-eye with Hudson.

The blood drained from my face. The hug had been innocent, but I knew what it must have looked like. And it didn't feel exactly innocent, not when David wanted more, and not when we'd sort of been together in the past. Especially since I'd never told Hudson about it.

Hudson's expression was stoic, his eyes piercing into mine. He gave nothing away and that terrified me. Not only because I couldn't read his reaction to what he'd witnessed, but because it meant he'd withdrawn further. With the way he'd left me, the circumstances of the last time we saw each other, he may have had the same blank expression if he hadn't just walked in on me hugging my boss.

"I'll, uh, let you guys have some privacy." Out of the corner of my eye, I saw David leave the office, shutting the door behind him. My focus never left the man in front of me.

Alone with Hudson, the tension became thicker. He looked as painfully beautiful as ever in a dark gray suit and a solid blue tie that made his eyes seem more blue than gray. He didn't speak, didn't move. Just stared into me. Stared through me.

I swallowed hard, afraid I might cry. For more than a day I had longed to see him, had ached for him. Now that he was here, everything was all wrong.

"Hudson," I began, not knowing what to say next. Then I remembered the article. "I read about Plexis." I reached my hand out and took a step toward him. "I'm so sor—"

He cut me off. "What's going on with you and him?" His tone was even, controlled, but his right eye twitched.

"Nothing," I said on a heavy exhale. "David was, um,..." Yeah, where was I going with that? David was trying to get with me and I turned him down so we were hugging it out? "It was a friendly hug, that's all."

Hudson's jaw tensed. "The expression on his face was much more than friendly." He took a measured step toward me. "Have you fucked him?"

"No!"

His eyes narrowed, studying me. "But almost."

"No." Except that wasn't quite true. We had come pretty close to screwing in the past. Right there in that office, in fact. It didn't seem like a good time to bring that up, though. And all of that had been before Hudson.

"Why don't I believe you?"

"Because you have some serious trust issues." I felt a twinge of guilt knowing that his distrust might very well be because he sensed I was holding something back. Still, I didn't appreciate being drilled. And Hudson did have trust issues. "What is your fucking deal, anyway?"

He stepped toward me again. "I told you before," he growled. "I don't share."

A surge of euphoria pulsed through me. He still thought of me as his. I remembered when he'd said those words to me the first time, how it had turned me on to no end. The rawness of it, the primitive way he claimed me as his own.

Now, though, despite that it indicated I still had something to fight for with Hudson, the statement struck a nerve. "But I have to share you with Celia?"

"Goddammit, Alayna. How many times do I have to say it? There is nothing going on with me and Celia."

I felt uneasy about insinuating otherwise. I'd accused past lovers of cheating on me—many times—but it had always been paranoia on my part, doubtful that anyone could ever really love me. My accusations had ended relationships, and my stomach lurched at that possibility with Hudson.

Yet, he had secrets where Celia was concerned. That wasn't my mind playing tricks on me, he'd confirmed that much. He'd asked me to believe that those secrets weren't relevant to us, but if he wanted my trust, he had to give me his. "And there's nothing going on with me and David."

"Really?" His tone was icy. "That's not how it looked when I walked in here."

My vision blurred with tears. "Just like that's not how it looked when you left with Celia while I was still naked in your bed?"

Anger flashed in Hudson's eyes. He grabbed my upper arms and yanked me toward him until my face was only inches from his. "Leaving you that morning was the hardest fucking thing I've done in a long time," he hissed. "Don't treat it lightly."

Then his mouth crushed mine, before I could digest what he'd said, before I could let the sweetness of his words sink in. He nipped and tore at the tender skin of my lips with his teeth, his kiss abrasive and impatient.

My body begged to give into his demanding passion, his mouth and tongue coaxing me to bend to him, but my brain still held onto our disagreement and our whereabouts. Jesus, we were in the goddamn office of the nightclub!

I broke away from his lips. "Hudson, stop."

But he didn't stop. He continued kissing down my neck and his hand found my breast, which he squeezed and fondled roughly over the fabric of my dress. His cock pressed into me at my thigh, and I felt it stiffen.

"Stop!" I said again, pushing at his chest with both my hands.

"No," he rumbled in my ear. "I have to fuck you. Now."

"Why? Are you marking your territory?" I'd only been half serious with the comment, but he pulled back and the look in his eyes said that was exactly what he was doing.

I wriggled out of his grip, the nausea returning in painful waves. "You don't own me, Hudson! Stop messing with me like I'm one of your other women. *Not with me*, remember?"

"Don't you think I know that? Every minute of every day I remind myself that I can't conquer you. That I can't do that to you." His jaw twitched. "But it doesn't mean that I don't want to."

He might as well have struck me. Even though I'd told myself that it was possible that I was merely another on his list of women he'd played, I'd truly believed that I was different. The tears that had threatened earlier spilled freely. "So I am just like the others."

"No. You're not." His voice tightened. "I told you before. I don't want to hurt you more than I need to win you."

Sobbing now, I choked out, "You've already done both."

"Fuck!" His features were overcome with horror, as if I'd told him I'd killed his mother. Or maybe not his mother, but someone he was fond of.

He took a step backward, away from me. It was devastating, to be hurting so deeply, to see my pain echoed on his face through the torrents of my tears. I couldn't stand to feel like that, like I was losing him. I needed his comfort and to comfort him the only way I was sure that he would let me—I lunged for him, seizing his lips with mine.

It took only seconds for him to give in to me, and then he was the way I liked him most, dominating and in command. And I took the reverse role and gave myself over to him.

"Alayna," he growled. His hand found my breast again, and he kneaded the ache away as he devoured my mouth. He wrapped his other arm around me, drawing me to him so tightly I felt consumed from all sides. Even inside, the flames of lust licked intensely, my arousal immediately kindled by the welcome assault on my body.

"Hudson," I cried against his lips, not caring this time that we were in the middle of a fight or that the office door might not be locked. "I need you, too."

He'd known we'd needed this before when I'd pushed him away. He was such a perfect lover, understanding my body and its demands even better than I did. Submitting to him, everything became easy. I could forget for a moment what barriers lay in between us while he took me in the way where no barriers separated us at all.

Hudson moved my body backward until the couch bumped against the back of my calf, and a fleeting thought of, "Oh, yay; we're going to christen the couch!" passed through my mind when he let go of me to reach under my short A-line dress and pull my panties down below my knees. He pushed me back on the couch, spread my legs open and gathered the material of my dress up around my stomach, completely exposing my most private parts for him.

I felt beautiful like that—lying in wait for my lover who I knew would give and take as he pleased.

He gazed down at me, desire clouding his eyes as he undid his belt and lowered his pants only far enough to release his bulging cock from its prison. As fast as he moved, it seemed forever before he lowered himself on top of me, urging my legs further apart with his knees. Then he shoved into me with such force I gasped.

He pounded into me with driving thrusts, focused on his own need, his own desire for orgasm. But even through the fog of his own lust, he attended to me, his thumb pressing expertly on my clit, massaging me toward my own climax.

The act may have been primarily physical, but a deeper connection resulted from the joining of our bodies. Each stroke eased the sting of his earlier words, and I was certain that the motivation behind each deep lunge was to chase away his own torment, to release himself from the guilt of wounding me.

He didn't shower me with his usual sex words, but we were hardly quiet as I whimpered under him and he repeated my name over and over like a mantra, like a prayer. And then the sound turned guttural as he flexed into me, coming in me with such violent eruption that it spurred me to release with him on my own shaky cry, "Hudson!"

He collapsed onto me, his head buried in my neck where his warm breath against my skin felt soothing. I loved it there, buried beneath him, his cock still buried inside me, our precious bond so fragile it required this carnal connection. Hudson's breathing becoming even, and his body became lax until his weight pressed into me with sweet agony.

Just as I began to wonder if he'd fallen asleep he whispered, "I wanted to win you. But I didn't want to hurt you." His arm tightened around me. "That's the last thing I wanted."

I understood him completely. After destroying so many people, after ruining my relationship with my only living relative, it was hell to imagine hurting even one more person. It had kept me from becoming close to anyone for so long. But now, I was ready to move past that fear so that I could earn the reward of intimacy.

I stroked Hudson's hair. "That's part of relationships, H. People get hurt." I kissed his head. "But you can make it better, too."

He lifted his head to meet my eyes. "Tell me how."

Cupping his face in my hands, I rubbed my thumbs across his skin, rough from five o'clock shadow. "Let me in," I pleaded.

"Don't you see I already have?"

I closed my eyes, hoping to stop a fresh stream of tears. He had opened up, but only enough for me to slip the tip of my toes past the threshold of the door he kept so tightly closed. It was a big step for him. But it wasn't really letting me in. Everything he shared with me I had to pry from his lips. He hadn't given me his trust. It wasn't enough to build upon and if that was as far as the door was opening, we had no hope for a future.

I swallowed hard and opened my eyes, letting one teardrop escape. Wiping it away, I rolled out from underneath him and pulled my panties up as I stood.

Hudson sighed. Then I heard the sound of his zipper and, to my ears, it was a metaphor—putting himself away, shutting himself off. Again.

But when he stood, he wrapped his arms around me from behind. His voice rasped in my ear. "Why do you act like I'm running?"

"Because you shut me out. Isn't that the same as running?"

"What about you? What about how you showed up in our bedroom crying and couldn't even tell me why?"

"That was different." But maybe it wasn't. I hadn't told him what his mother said because it hurt too much. Because I was embarrassed.

He spun me around to look at him. "What did she say to you, Alayna?"

He'd thrown down the gauntlet. If I wanted him to be open, I'd have to be too. "That I was insignificant. She called me a whore." I looked at a chip of paint on the wall, not able to meet his eyes.

He cursed under his breath. "My mother's heartless and cruel." Putting two fingers under my chin, he turned my face to him. "You're not a whore, Alayna. Not even close. And the magnitude of your importance in my life can't be put into words."

"She also said that you can't ever love me."

He froze. Then his hand dropped from my face. "I've told you that before."

The pain of his statement hit me hard in the gut. I pulled out of his arms. "Well, she told me again." I swung back toward him. "So there, I opened up. Are you happy?"

"Alayna…"

I ached in the center of my being. This was why I hadn't told him—because despite what he and Sophia had said, I'd believed that he could love. That he could love me.

Tears flooded my eyes and splashed down my face. "How could you not think I'd fall in love with you, Hudson? Even if you didn't mean for it to happen, how could I not?" I wiped at my damp cheek with the back of my hand. "Does that mean anything to you at all?"

He drew back as if I'd slapped him. "How can you ask that? Of course, it does. But, Alayna, you don't know that you'd still say that if you knew me."

"I *do* know you."

"Not everything."

"Only because you haven't let me in!" We were spinning in circles, getting nowhere.

He spread his arms out to the sides. "What is it you want to know? About what I did to other women? About Celia? I'm the reason she got pregnant, Alayna. Because I spent an entire summer making her fall in love with me when I felt nothing for her. For fun. For something to do. And then, when I'd completely broken her, she became destructive—sleeping around, partying, drugs. You name it, she did it. She didn't even know who the father was."

I heaved a breath, wiping the lingering tears from my face. "So you claimed it was yours."

"Yes."

"Because you felt responsible."

"Yes. She lost the baby at three months. Likely from the drinking and drugs she'd consumed early on. She was devastated."

"That's awful." I could sense he felt as responsible for the death of Celia's unborn baby as for its conception in the first place. It was a lot of weight to carry, a lot of blame.

But even though I could concede Hudson had a role in the situation, it didn't scare me away. "It's awful," I repeated, "but I don't understand. You thought this would make me not love you…why?"

He perched on the arm of the sofa and pierced me with an incredulous stare. "Because it changes everything. I did that. That's who I am. It's my past and it's very ugly."

A sob threatened, but I choked it back with a hard swallow. The ugly things—there were so many ugly things about myself that always lay beneath the surface of every conversation, every moment. They poisoned and destroyed. I was well versed in the ugly.

It broke my heart that the same darkness haunted Hudson. That he believed his history to be so horrible that it could change things between us. It couldn't. It didn't.

I moved in front of him and rested my hands on his shoulders. "Do you think your ugly is any different than mine?"

"This isn't like following someone around or calling too many times, Alayna."

"It was an unforeseen tragedy, Hudson. A game that got out of hand. You didn't set out for Celia to get pregnant and have a miscarriage. And you can't diminish the things I've done to a simple statement like that either. I hurt people. Deeply. But that was before. Less than ideal pasts, remember? It doesn't mean it defines our future. Or even our now."

He blew out a warm breath as his thumb brushed at a lingering tear in the corner of my eye. "When I'm with you, I almost believe that."

"That just means you need to spend more time with me."

He chuckled softly. "Is that what that means?" He trailed his thumb down my face to caress my cheek. "Yesterday morning, when I got the phone call that required me to be in Cincinatti—I couldn't even let myself look at you, sleeping in that bed. If I did, I wouldn't have been able to leave."

My chest swelled with his confession. "I thought you left because you were freaking out." His puzzled look drove me to clarify. "Because of the love stuff."

"I wasn't freaking out. I was surprised, that's all."

"Surprised?"

"That that's what we were feeling." His gaze was soft. "That it was love."

I could barely breathe, afraid that if I did I'd disturb the path of our conversation. "It was." I swallowed. "It is."

"Hmm." He smiled. "I never felt this before. I didn't know." His swept his hands down the sides of my torso. "But, Alayna, I've never had a healthy romantic relationship. Every woman who's loved me..." His voice tightened. "I don't want to break you, too."

"You're not going to break me, Hudson. I thought you might, at first. Turns out you make me better. And I think I do the same for you."

"You do."

"If you decide to not..." I searched for how to say what I meant. "Follow through...with whatever this is that we have, it will hurt. But I won't be broken."

"But it would hurt?"

"Like a motherfucker."

"Then we better follow through." He drew me closer, wrapping his arms around my waist. "Alayna, you're fired. You can't be my pretend girlfriend anymore." His face grew serious. "Be my real girlfriend instead."

Joy swept through me in a dizzying rush. "I kind of think I already am."

"You are."

"Can I still call you H?"

"Absolutely not." He turned his mouth to meet mine and kissed me with lips sweet and tender, but passionate all the same.

I don't know how long we stayed there like that—on the arm of the chair, his body wrapped around me, kissing and cuddling. Time was irrelevant in that moment we were sharing.

Finally though, when I remembered that the club would be opening soon and that I still had a shift to work, I pulled my lips from his and asked the question that I knew was burning in both our minds. "What now?"

One side of Hudson's mouth curled up in a sexy smile. "Come to my place after you finish here."

Yes. Of course, yes! "I'm not off until three."

"I don't care. I want you in my bed."

"Then, yes."

With great reluctance, I pulled myself away. I offered my hand to help him up, and he took it, rising in the graceful way of his. He let go of my hand and tugged the back of his jacket down and adjusted his tie, transforming back into the man most people knew: Hudson Pierce, ruler of the business world.

I watched, mesmerized, still in shock that this man was mine. *Mine.* It was the first time I'd said it to myself, and it sounded so wonderful I thought I could never get tired of saying it—*mine, mine, mine.*

His eyes swept behind him as he buttoned his jacket. "Nice couch," he said, as if noticing it for the first time.

"Thanks," I laughed.

He studied me with amusement before fixing my hair and straightening the collar of my dress. Then he took my hands in his. "Tell Jordan to take you to the Bowery. He knows where it is."

"Not the fuck pad?" My voice seemed unusually high, laced with surprise and excitement.

"No. My home. I'll leave a key with the doorman."

I hadn't been anywhere but the loft with him and didn't even know where he lived. I'd thought it was a good thing before. But now that he'd invited me, there was no other place I'd rather be.

And, besides, I was ready—ready to stop being afraid of making mistakes, ready to let myself be truly healed of my past, ready to start again without fear of regret.

Lacing my fingers through his, I giggled. Since when did I giggle? "We're really doing this, aren't we? Moving forward."

"We are."

He pulled me in for another embrace, seemingly as unable to let go of me as I was unable to let go of him. As fixed on me as I was on him.

"I'm going to rock your world," I said at his ear before sucking on the lobe.

He nipped at my neck, kindling my desire yet again. "I can't wait," he said.

"Neither can I."

FOUND IN YOU

BOOK TWO

— CHAPTER —
ONE

I paused at the doorway to the Park Avenue high-rise and stared at the building's name engraved on the stone. *The Bowery.* Jordan had already pulled away from the curb behind me. He probably felt I was safe enough to be left with the doorman who held the door for me while I stood frozen in thought.

This was real, a big step—a giant step—moving deeper into Hudson's life than anyone had ever been before. I was excited, of course. I loved the man. But did I really even know him? Could I truly love him based on the little I knew about him? His address had been a mystery to me until two minutes ago when his driver had dropped me off. And what would I find inside the building? What was inside Hudson Pierce, behind the mask he wore so well?

I felt like I'd seen the true Hudson, like I was probably the only person in the world who truly had, but I'd barely scratched the surface. There was still so much left to uncover and learn about the young business mogul who had captured my heart.

I also knew that Hudson held secrets. He'd abandoned his mind games and predilection for manipulating women before meeting me, but the possibility of his past habits returning was very real. As real as the possibility of mine returning.

And that was the fear that overwhelmed me most—that I might be driven to my old habits of obsession. Of all the relationships I'd destroyed with my stalking and unfounded jealousy, I knew that fucking this one up would destroy me. Thankfully, so far, I had felt fixed with Hudson. Only time would tell if that would last.

The doorman looked at me, an anxious expression on his face—should he continue holding the door open for the crazy indecisive woman, or should he let it go?

I eased him with a smile. "I'll be just a minute."

He returned the smile with a nod and closed the door.

Taking a deep breath, I looked toward the top floor where Hudson's apartment was surely located—I didn't even know his unit number. Was he awake up there? Was he looking for me from his window? Could he see me down here, hesitating?

He said he'd be sleeping, but it was that last idea that gave me the courage to move. I wouldn't put it past him to wait up for me and I didn't want him to suspect I felt any doubt at all. Because I didn't have doubts. Not about him. My doubts were about me, about whether I could handle us. And truly, if I let my hopes take root—hopes that I could finally have a real relationship with another person without losing myself to the fears and unhealthy habits of my obsessive past—then even those doubts were superficial.

The doorman smiled again as I stepped toward him, opening the door for me. Inside, another man sat at the security desk in front of the elevators.

"Ms. Withers?" he asked before I had a chance to give him my name.

I shouldn't have been surprised. Hudson said he'd leave a key for me at the desk and it was three-thirty in the morning. Who else would I be?

I nodded.

"Mr. Pierce left you this key. Both elevators on the left will take you to the penthouse. Simply insert the key into the panel when you get inside."

"Thank you."

The doors opened the minute I pushed the call button. Inside the elevator car, my hand shook as I inserted the key in the panel, and I was grateful to no longer be in sight of the security guard. The ride to the penthouse was fast, but not fast enough. As soon as I'd squashed down my trepidation, the emotion had been replaced with eagerness. I wanted to be in Hudson's space, in his arms. I wanted to be with him and even the minute that it took to arrive at the top floor was too long to be away from him.

The doors of the elevator opened into a small vestibule. I stepped out and turned the only direction I could, finding myself in a foyer. The space was quiet, but I could hear the sound of a clock ticking somewhere nearby, and there were very few lights on. I suspected the bedrooms were to my left, because my right opened up to a large living room with floor-to-ceiling windows.

As anxious as I was to find Hudson, I turned instead into the living room, attracted by the gorgeous view. Before I made it to the windows, though, a lamp flipped on and I saw him sitting in an armchair.

Startled, my mouth fell open and then stayed open as I ogled the gorgeous man dressed only in boxer shorts. The definition of his sculpted chest quickened my heart before my gaze caught his gray eyes through the flop of his brown hair in the dim light. I'd never seen him in boxer shorts, and damn, had I been missing out. It struck me again how little I knew him, but this time the thought didn't scare me—it excited me. How much more there was to discover about this man, and I was ready to dive in and explore.

Yet, the excitement didn't ease the awkwardness, the anxiety. This was new territory, and I didn't know how to proceed. Certainly, Hudson felt the same.

My hand held tight to my purse while the other absentmindedly clutched at the blue fabric of my dress, a short A-line that hedged the border of professional and sexy. It was the type of outfit I always wore at The Sky Launch, the night club where I worked as an assistant manager. The night club Hudson owned. The place I'd met him.

A memory flashed through my mind of the first time I'd seen him sitting at the end of the club's bar, of how he took my breath away. I'd known then I should've run. But I didn't. And now, I couldn't be more grateful.

He took my breath away now like he did then. With a meek smile, I braved breaking the silence. "You're awake."

"I thought it would be best to be waiting for you when you got here so that you wouldn't be disoriented."

"But you should be sleeping." As president of Pierce Industries, a multi-billion dollar company, his hours conflicted with mine at the club. Coming over in the middle of the night, when his daily wake-up time was six in the morning—what was I doing? How could our two very separate lives ever be compatible?

No, I wouldn't think that way. That was an excuse to deny myself happiness. And Hudson and I both deserved some happiness, for once in our lives.

The object of my desire stood and crossed to me, lifting the hand that held my purse. "I slept. Now I'm awake." That simple touch quieted my trepidation to a dull buzz, easy to ignore under the thud of my heart. That's what Hudson did to me, overwhelmed and astounded me in such a beautifully delicious way.

He took my purse from me and moved to set it on the end table.

Without his contact, my nerves returned and mindless small talk slipped from my lips. "I've never been in a penthouse before. Unless you count the loft." The loft above his office, the place where he'd fucked me to oblivion. Thank god the dark room hid my blush. "This is beautiful, H."

"You've barely seen any of it." He didn't cringe at my absurd nickname for him. Perhaps he was getting used to it.

"But what I *can* see..." My eyes scanned the expansive living room, noting the ornate detail of the architecture and the simplicity of the styling. "It's incredible."

"I'm glad you like it."

"It's much different than I expected. Not like the loft. That's what I thought it would be like." The loft was black and leather, masculine and strong. This place was white and light—I could tell that even in the low glow of the lamp and the moon.

"Alayna."

My name on his tongue sent goose bumps to the surface of my skin. How could he still do that to me? Turn me on with only a word? Turn me into knots so easily?

"The furniture is so different, too." Nervousness drove me to talk, avoiding the connection we'd make the minute I gave in. I stepped toward the white sofa and ran my hand across the expensive upholstery. "But Celia decorated this place too, right?"

His voice tightened. "She did."

Celia Werner, his childhood friend and ex-fiancée. Well, not really, but practically. Why had I brought her up? Was I trying to destroy us? Celia had been a constant source of tension in our relationship since Hudson had hired me to convince his mother that we were together. Sophia Pierce, believing her son was incapable of love, thought a pairing with the daughter of her good friends the Werners was a perfect match for Hudson. Even if he couldn't feel anything for her, Celia could at least keep him in line—keep him from getting in trouble with his addictions.

Except it turned out Hudson *could* love. And during our ruse, he'd fallen in love with me.

Still, Hudson had something with Celia, a bond that fueled my jealousy. Deflecting, I moved to the windows. "The view here…"

"Alayna."

I pressed my face against the glass and looked down to the world far below. "It's gorgeous."

Hudson came up behind me, his warmth emanating against my back even though he hadn't yet touched me. "Alayna, look at me."

Slowly, I turned to him.

He lifted my chin up, forcing me to meet his eyes. "You're nervous. Don't be. I want you here."

His words were the consolation I needed, sending calm over every part of my worry like a blanket smothering a fire. "Are you sure?" I'd been eased, but I wanted more where that came from. "You've never brought a woman here before, have you? It's weird, isn't it?"

His thumb stroked my cheek, my skin awakening under his caress. "It's different, because I haven't brought a woman here, but it's not weird. And I am completely sure that I want you to be here."

I thrilled at the confirmation that I was the first woman he'd allowed in, the first woman he'd make love to in this house. "Me, too. I mean, I'm sure that I want to be here." His gaze burned into me. I could get lost there forever and that scared me just enough.

Looking for a way to keep myself, for only a moment longer, I glanced over at the room connected to the living room. "What's over there? Is that the dining room?"

"I'll give you a tour in the morning." He brought his other hand up to cradle my face, capturing my eyes again with his.

"A tour in the morning," I repeated. And there I went—lost to him. "But not now."

"No, not now. Now I want to welcome you to my home." His mouth crashed into mine, taking me to dizzying heights that put the view behind me to shame. His lips sucked my own before his tongue slid inside my mouth with delicious strokes that threw me off balance, provoking me to throw my arms around his neck and hold on for dear life.

He moved a hand from my face to wrap around my waist and pulled me into him where I could feel his erection against my thigh through the thin material of his boxers. His other hand reached behind my head to tangle in my hair. I pressed my breasts into him, needing to feel him with every part of my body.

A moan caught in the back of Hudson's throat, vibrating underneath our kiss and kindling the desire in my belly. I shifted, trying to get closer, my leg antsy to hook around him.

His lips still wrapped around mine, he said, "I do have one room I want to show you tonight."

"I hope it's the bedroom."

"It is." In a blur of motion, he lifted me in his arms and headed back to the foyer I'd come from. Just like that he carried me away, the movement imitating the effect he had on me in general—with him, I was a branch in a roaring river, rushing toward the sea. And Hudson, he was the current, pulling me whichever way he wanted to take me. I was at his mercy.

He'd promised me that he wouldn't play his manipulative games with me, that he'd never try to control me. But it was a promise he couldn't keep. He swept me away with him whether he intended to or not. And that was perfectly fine with me.

He carried me through the foyer, kissing me as he did until we reached the end of the hallway where he turned into what had to be the master bedroom. My attention still entirely on him, I only registered that he was laying me on a king-size bed, the light gray sheets disheveled on one side, the left side. His side. The intimacy of being in the place that Hudson slept, had slept in earlier that evening, shot a pang of need to my already aching core. I wanted him on me and in me, not standing above me gazing down with hooded eyes.

He'd take his time with me though, and there was no use disputing his tempo. There was no reason to dispute. Though a dominant lover, he always focused his attention on my needs, always attended to me in the ways he knew best. And god, did he know me best, knew how to turn my body boneless and sated, knew how to arouse and love me, even when I didn't.

His hand lagged down the length of my leg to my ankle where he removed my strappy sandal with a gentleness that had me writhing. He repeated the action with my other shoe, then knelt over me to deliver a brief kiss. I reached up to pull him in for more, but he resisted.

"Last time we went quickly. This time I need to savor you." Last time had been fast and fraught, a reprieve mid-argument, on the new couch in the manager's office at The Sky Launch, and he hadn't left me with any complaints. But being savored sounded pretty damn awesome, too.

With a trail of wet kisses, he made his way down my body to the hem of my dress. With a wicked gleam in his eyes, he shoved the material up around my waist, placing a kiss on the center of my want.

A moan escaped my lips and he chuckled softly. His fingers slipped under the band of my panties, pulling them off and tossing them aside. He hooked my leg over his shoulder and then his mouth was back on me, licking and sucking greedily at the bundle of nerves between my thighs.

I was already delirious from pleasure when he slipped two fingers inside me, probing and twisting until he pulled my orgasm from me with ease. I shuddered and quaked while he climbed up to reclaim my mouth where he kissed me with deep hunger.

The soft sounds he made as he devoured me, the taste of me on his tongue, the jab of his cock in my thigh—it was only half a minute before the tightness built again in my belly, ready for another ride up the hill to ecstasy. Drawn to touch him, my hand found his cock and rubbed it through his underwear.

His mouth broke from mine with a groan. I nudged at him to roll to his side while I continued to stroke him. "Boxers? Do you wear these often?"

"To bed."

"I like them. I've never seen you in them." My hand slipped inside the opening of his shorts, marveling as I always did at the softness of his thick shaft in my hand, at the heat rolling off his skin.

"Because when I go to bed with you—" His voice broke as I ran my hand across his crown. "I wear nothing."

"Oh, yeah. I like that even better." It was my turn to slip my hand into the band of his underwear and pull them down his strong legs, my eyes pinned on the gorgeous sight of his erection as I did.

As soon as his boxers hit the floor, he drew me to him again. "I like it when you're wearing nothing." His fingers were already tugging my dress up over my belly. "You need to be wearing nothing right now."

"I won't argue." I sat up to help him pull the outfit over my head. He tossed the dress aside and his hands circled around me to unhook my bra, freeing my breasts. Then he was stretched out over me, his penis hot at my entrance for only a second before he plunged inside of me, penetrating me, stretching me, filling me the way only he could.

He turned to his side, taking me with him, and I wrapped a leg around him, urging him deeper. He'd wanted to savor me, but either he changed his mind or he couldn't contain himself, unleashing his passion with rapid thrusts. Each time he drove in, he hit a tender spot that made me crazy, drawing another climax to surface, starting in my core, tightening my thighs, traveling down to curl my toes as it rolled through my body.

Hudson continued his assault, increasing his speed until he grunted out his own release. He collapsed, still inside me, and gathered me in his arms to spread kisses down my face—an unusually tender gesture from the guarded man I'd grown to love. I delighted in the sweetness of it.

"Did I mention that I'm awfully glad you're here?" he asked, breaking his sentence to continue his trail of kisses.

Hearing those words meant everything. I recognized it as Hudson's version of *I love you.* He hadn't brought himself to say it to me directly—he was too new to the emotion, and I didn't expect it. Though he had accepted it earlier in the evening when I'd informed him that I knew he was in love with me, and he hadn't freaked when I told him I was in love with him.

Still, I didn't fool myself into thinking we'd have instant hearts and roses. Baby steps. Saying how he felt at all was a step in itself. That it included how he felt about me equaled two steps in my book.

I ran my hand through his hair as his mouth lowered to my neck. "You did say it. And if you hadn't, I think I figured it out." I waggled my eyebrows to make sure he knew I was referring to what had just occurred physically. "But you can tell me as many times as you'd like." *In as many different ways as you'd like*, I added silently.

He shifted over me and sucked further down my body, heading toward my breasts. Obviously, we were already headed for round two. "I'm glad you're here, precious." He tugged my nipple between his teeth then eased the sting with a swirl of his tongue.

I drew in a deep breath, delighting in the mix of pleasure and pain as he showered my other breast with the same attention. His nickname for me, *precious,* floated through my mind as his mouth licked at my skin. He'd called me that since our first sexual encounter, nearly two weeks before. Had it only been that long? And had it only been another week before that when I'd first met him at the club, when I didn't yet know he was *the* Hudson Pierce? It already seemed like a lifetime. The term of endearment he used for me had held weight from the first moment he'd said it. But we'd only just met then. Maybe it didn't have as much meaning as I attributed to it.

Curiosity overtook me even though my body was already vibrating under his ardor. "Why do you call me that, anyway?"

He answered without looking up from my bosom. "Because you are."

"You started calling me precious before you could ever possibly know."

"Not true." He propped his elbow up on the bed and leaned his head on his hand. "I knew the minute I first saw you."

For a brief second I thought he meant at the bar—the first night *I* had seen *him*. Then I remembered he'd seen me nearly two weeks before that when I was still working on my MBA and he'd been in the audience during my graduate symposium. I hadn't found out about that until later, and he'd barely told me anything about it.

I propped my torso up on my elbows and eagerly waited for him to continue.

"You were on that stage at Stern," he said, his hand stroking along the dip and curve of my waist to my hip. "When you started your presentation, you were nervous. It took you a few minutes to fall into the rhythm of your speech. But when you hit your stride, you were magnificent. Yet you had no idea. It was completely obvious that it never crossed your mind that the room was full of people who would have hired you had you spoken to any of them. Thank god, you didn't. Because I watched them watch you and I knew. I knew that they saw you were smart. They saw you had business savvy. But none of them recognized the rare jewel that stood before them. Precious."

Tears stung at the corners of my eyes. No one had ever seen me like that, no had ever even looked. Not my parents before they died or my brother, Brian, or any of the men I'd ever dated or obsessed over. No one.

"I love you, Hudson." It was out before I could think not to say it, before I could worry about him freaking like he had the first time I'd voiced my feelings for him. I wouldn't have been able to keep the words inside if I'd wanted to—they were always at the surface now, at risk of tumbling off my tongue at any given moment. If we were going to make a relationship work, we'd both have to get comfortable with it.

My eyes never left his while he processed my declaration.

Then, in a flash, he covered his body with mine. Bracing one hand under my neck, he circled my nose with his. "You can tell me that as many times as you like," he said, repeating my earlier words.

"I plan on it." But it came out mumbled, lost inside his mouth as his lips overtook mine, and we expressed our emotions with our tongues and hands and bodies and a slew of other ways that didn't require talking.

— CHAPTER —
TWO

Awareness of movement in the room woke me the next morning. I opened my eyes and saw Hudson adjusting his tie in front of the dresser mirror, his back to me. He had yet to put on his jacket so I had a full view of his tight behind. God, that man could wear a suit. He could wear nothing as easily. I wasn't choosy.

He met my eyes in the mirror and a slight smile graced his lips. "Good morning."

"Morning. I'm enjoying the view."

"So am I."

I blushed and pulled the sheet up over my naked body. The room seemed awfully light for as early as it had to be. "What time is it?" I glanced around for a clock and found none.

"Almost eleven." He finished with his tie—a silver patterned one that brought out his eyes—and opened a drawer, retrieving a pair of dress socks.

Eleven? Hudson was usually at work before eight. "Why are you still here? Shouldn't you have made half a million dollars by now?"

"Half a billion," he said, straight-faced, as he sat on the bed next to me. "But they don't need me for that. I canceled my morning."

"When did you do that?" I was mesmerized with watching him put on his socks. It shouldn't be so sexy to watch a man get dressed, yet my belly tightened and my girl parts started humming.

"Last night. Before you got here."

"Smart thinking." His invitation to spend the night in his penthouse had come at the beginning of my shift at The Sky Launch. I'd obsessed about it the entire evening, but being at work, there was nothing I could do to prepare for it. I didn't even have a change of clothing or a toothbrush. It hadn't occurred to me that Hudson would have used the time to get ready for my arrival. But of course he did. He was a very organized man, a planner with a fine attention to detail.

And since two rounds of lovemaking had transpired, we hadn't gone to sleep until nearly six in the morning. Canceling his morning was good planning indeed.

I yawned and stretched my arms over my head, the sheet falling below my breasts as I did.

Socks on, Hudson stood and peered down at me, his eyes clouding as he perused my naked body. "Fuck, Alayna, you're making me want to cancel my afternoon, too. And I can't cancel my afternoon."

I grinned. "Sorry." But I wasn't. Hudson could make me wet from across a crowded room. It was nice to think I had some of the same power over him. "Um, I need to get up. Is that going to be too…distracting?"

He narrowed his eyes at me then turned and disappeared into a closet returning with a cream robe. "Here."

I took the robe from him, not bothering to put it on until I was standing.

"You're a wicked, wicked woman," he said as he watched me pull the garment around myself.

"And you love it."

Without acknowledging my statement, he nodded toward a closed door. "The bathroom's there. There should be brand new toothbrushes in one of the drawers. Look around until you find what you need."

"Thank you." I crossed to him and gave him a peck on the cheek before making my way to the bathroom to pee.

It hadn't been a cuddly afterglow morning like we'd spent together at Mabel Shores, his family's summer house in the Hamptons. But this was Hudson—aloof and compartmentalized. He was focused on getting to work, and, to his credit, he'd been pretty hospitable considering.

I found the toothbrush easily; as he'd said, there was a drawer full of them. While I brushed, I wondered about that. What was with the surplus? Did he simply want to always be prepared, in case he needed a new one? Maybe he believed toothbrushes should be disposable. He certainly could afford that attitude.

Or *did* he have them for overnight guests? Female overnight guests, to be precise.

I might have decided I was being paranoid, except it wasn't only the toothbrushes. Now that I looked around, there was floral scented deodorant by one of the sinks with a bottle of women's face cream and another bottle of moisturizer next to it.

And the robe—the woman's robe that I was wearing at that very moment—where had that come from?

A chill ran down my spine. I tightened the sash around myself, despite my growing concern that I was wearing clothing that belonged to someone else. To another woman. Another woman in Hudson's life.

Okay, okay. No need to panic. Maybe there had been other women before me at the penthouse. That was fine. Not wonderful, but fine. I just wished he hadn't lied about it. And *why* had he lied about it?

I opened the moisturizer and brought the bottle to my nose. It smelled fresh and familiar—was that the scent Celia wore?

Now I was being ridiculous. Paranoid, even. Knowing that didn't change the sick, angry emotion rooting through my gut. It was a feeling I'd once been very intimate with. The driving force of most of the unhealthy behaviors I'd acted upon in the past. Behaviors I did not want to relive.

I had to get calm, handle the situation constructively. I forced myself to count to ten. In between each number I repeated the mantra I'd learned in counseling: when in doubt, talk it out. *One, when in doubt, talk it out. Two, when in doubt, talk it out.*

Yeah, easier said than done.

By the time I reached four, the mantra had turned into *when in fucking doubt* and still I was very much doubting.

But that was my tendency, my go-to in all of my relationships. I jumped to conclusions—conclusions that very often were way off-base and unfounded. Late nights at work meant another girlfriend. Mysterious phone calls meant cheating. With my previous boyfriends, I never asked. I assumed. I accused.

Not this time. This time I would be different. Even though the evidence suggested that Hudson had lied to me, I couldn't accept that as fact. I would have to ask him about it.

I scrubbed my face clean with the facial cream, hoping that stalling before I talked to Hudson would relieve the simmer of fury. After patting my face dry with a hand towel, I convinced myself that I was together enough to address him and started out of the bathroom, grabbing the cream and moisturizer to take with me as evidence.

So, maybe collecting evidence was more of an attack than a discussion tactic. As long as I didn't end up throwing them, I considered it an improvement on my past.

Hudson wasn't in the bedroom when I came out, so I made my way out through the apartment until I found him in the kitchen. He'd donned his suit jacket now, and he stood at the kitchen table, reading the paper as he drank from a mug.

He looked up when I appeared. "I made you some—"

"Why do you have all this stuff?" Though I'd cut him off, I was pretty sure my question sounded more curious than accusatory. Hopefully.

"What stuff?"

"This stuff." I set the bottles on the table in front of him. All right, maybe it was closer to a slam. "And you have a plethora of toothbrushes and this woman's robe. Why do you have a woman's robe?"

His eyes narrowed and he took a sip from his beverage before answering. "I have more than the robe. I have several pieces of women's clothing in the extra closet in my bedroom."

"That's not helping." The panic I thought I had smothered deep inside worked its way up my throat, tightening my voice. "You told me you never had a woman here before."

"Do I detect a hint of jealousy?"

The gleam in his eye unleashed me. "You detect more than a fucking hint. Also, a whole lot of suspicion. Come on, H, this isn't any way to start a relationship. If you've had a woman here—if this is someone else's clothing I'm wearing—I need to know." My eyes burned, but I managed to keep them pinned on him.

Hudson set his mug down and turned his whole body toward me.

I kept my hand on the table, bracing myself for whatever excuse he'd give. What he said—if he chose to speak the truth, if I chose to believe him—it could make or break us.

"They're yours, Alayna."

"What?" That, I wasn't expecting.

"I purchased them for you. Except the toothbrushes. My housekeeper buys me those so I have plenty for when I travel. The clothing and cosmetics are yours."

Mine?

No, it wasn't possible.

I swallowed. "When did you get them?" Had he been planning for me to be there before he invited me? Or was this part of the scam we'd tried to pull on his mother, a piece of proof that we were a couple should anyone look in his closet?

"Last night after I left the club."

Last night. "But that was almost eight." He'd left me at the start of my shift. That couldn't have possibly been enough time to arrange anything. "How did—"

"I understand what it looks like," he cut me off. "There's likely still a tag on the robe if you…" He reached his hand inside my collar and tugged. "Yes, see?" He held up a tag, the price—an extravagant price for a robe—listed boldly under the size.

I glanced over at the cosmetic bottles again. They were completely full, seemingly unused. I hadn't realized that in my heated emotion. But, still, I had questions. "Why? How…?"

"Why? Because I knew you'd have nothing to wear today and I didn't want you to have to do the so-called walk of shame through my lobby. Plus I figured you'd want to wash that club makeup off your face and freshen up a bit. As for how…I have people."

I ran my hands through my hair. "You have people." The tension in my shoulders relaxed slightly as I processed what he'd said. He'd left me at work and then he'd prepared. As he always prepared. He'd canceled his morning. He'd arranged to have clothing for me. Even at that late hour, Hudson managed to make arrangements. Because he had *people.*

"Mirabelle?" I asked. Hudson's sister, Mira, owned her own boutique. She knew my size, knew what I'd look good in.

"Yes." He cocked his head. "And others."

Others like the same people he had launder and deliver my undies within a couple of hours when I'd left them at his office one time. Like Jordan who was always available to drive me to and fro at the drop of a hat. I'd known he had *others.*

"Oh." A medley of emotions washed over me as I let the pieces settle into place. I was relieved to find my jealousy was unfounded and delighted to realize how much thought Hudson had put into my arrival at his apartment.

I was also touched to know he was serious about wanting our relationship to work, because didn't this type of preparation show sincerity?

But then I also felt embarrassed. And ashamed. I'd overreacted, and even though I hadn't gone crazy like I would have in the past, I felt the seed of it inside. It scared me. Scared me to know Hudson saw it too.

I lowered my eyes to my hands where I wrung the sash of the robe anxiously. "It must be nice to have people," I mumbled. "I want people." Silly, senseless words, but they were all I had.

Hudson lifted my chin to meet his stare. "I want you."

The look on his face—he wasn't upset by my outburst at all. Other men had been scared away by similar unfounded accusations. But Hudson—not only did his expression show an absence of fear, it showed hunger, desire. Almost as though my paranoia was a turn-on.

"You have me," I whispered.

He took the sash from my hands and pulled the knot free. "I want you right now." His hand wrapped around my breast, squeezing as his thumb flicked across my nipple.

"Oh, you *want me,* want me."

"Uh-huh." He shifted me so my backside was against the table. Flattening his palm between my breasts, he pushed me down; the surface of the table met hard with my backside and a brief flash of worry about spilling his coffee and breaking the cosmetic bottles entered my mind.

"And I want you now."

Fuck the coffee. Let it spill.

Hudson nudged me back so that my bottom met up with the edge of the table, scooting the bottles out of the way with his arm as he did. I was laid out before him now, my robe open to expose the most intimate parts of me.

His eyes darkened as he rubbed his hands in long strokes from my belly up to my breasts and back again. Then they went lower, to the center of my desire.

"I could stare at your pussy all day long." His fingers slid through my folds and circled my hole.

"Don't you have to be somewhere?" My voice didn't sound like mine, breathy and needy and desperate.

And what the hell was I doing? I didn't want him to leave. I didn't want him to stop. *Please, god, don't let him stop.*

"I do have someplace to be. We'll have to be quick." His hands left me to work on opening his pants. "But I'm not leaving here without fucking you good morning."

I may have sighed out loud in anticipation.

Leaning up on my elbows, I watched as Hudson adjusted his pants and briefs enough to free his stiff cock. A sight I'd never tire of. And it was all mine, only mine.

Another random worry crossed my mind. "Your housekeeper isn't going to walk in on us, is she?"

"She comes on Tuesday and Friday. If I'm not mistaken, it's Wednesday." He grabbed my ankles and bent my legs up. "And if she did walk in, would you care?"

He thrust in.

"No," I gasped. Right then I didn't care about anything but the man in front of me. The man inside me. The man who wanted me, wanted me in his house, wanted me in his bed. Wanted me in his life despite my shortcomings.

Hudson pulled out and pressed back in, again and again, the sturdy table rocking with the force of his jabs. He adopted a rapid tempo, apparently serious about the *have to be quick*. At this rate, he'd be there soon.

He adjusted his grip on my ankles and folded my knees into my chest, the new position bringing him deeper inside me. "Touch yourself, precious." His voice was tight with effort to hold on. "Let's come together."

Without hesitation, I moved my hand to rub my clit, swirling the bud at a speed that matched his. I'd done this before—played with myself for his viewing pleasure. It was a turn-on for him, based on how quickly it always brought him to release.

It was a turn on for me, too. To see the pleasure in his face, to feel his drive increase as I writhed and moaned at my own touch—there was nothing hotter. Already, I was tightening, clenching around him.

"That's it, Alayna." His face contorted. "Fuck, that's…it…" His voice broke as he came, shoving deeper into me as his climax erupted.

My hand fell to the table, my body numb.

He smiled as he pulled out. "How was that?"

He knew the answer. The perv wanted to hear me say it.

I grinned. "You can fuck me good morning anytime you want."

"I wouldn't mind fucking you good morning every morning." He reached behind him to grab a paper towel off the kitchen counter while I pretended not to read a million things into his statement. I continued to pretend while he cleaned himself up and did up his pants.

He raised his brows and gestured toward me. For a moment I thought he might know what I was thinking—how being with him every morning implied living with him, how that was too soon, how I never thought anything was too soon because I was an obsessive freak who wanted to cling, how I was ultimately unable to handle such a proposition with my history.

Then I realized he was simply asking if I needed the paper towels, too. "I'm jumping in the shower." Shit, he hadn't said I could stay. "If that's okay, I mean." Was it totally inappropriate for me to ask if I could lounge around his place while he went to work? Because until that very second, that's exactly what I had planned.

Hudson reached his hand out to help me down from my perch. Reaching around me, he grabbed the ends of my sash and tied it at my waist. "It's more than okay. I want you to stay. I planned that you would stay." Which meant I would likely find women's shampoo and conditioner in the shower, too.

Hudson's phone buzzed and he pulled it out of his suit pocket to read his text message. "My driver's here. Seems I used up the time I meant to spend giving you the penthouse tour."

I shrugged. "Whoops."

"You'll have to explore on your own." He walked to the kitchen sink and washed his hands.

"Are you giving me permission to snoop? Because it sounds like you are and you don't understand—I'm a snooper."

He chuckled. "I don't doubt it. I have nothing to hide. Snoop away. Use the gym. Take a nap. There's food in the fridge. Do and take whatever you like. You work at eight tonight?"

"Yes." I'd stopped being surprised by Hudson's omniscient way of knowing my schedule. It was the sort of thing I'd usually do—memorize a guy's schedule, find out all the details of his life. It was kind of nice to be on the other side of that for once.

"Good. I'll make sure I'm home by six." *Home.* He said it like it was our place, not his. Another ping of anxiety stabbed at my chest. "We'll have dinner together before you leave."

"I hope you aren't expecting me to cook." *Or to not latch on.*

"Don't be silly. I'll arrange for the cook to come."

I nodded, my insides turned into knots by Hudson's easiness about our relationship.

"Oh, and the books for the library should be here today. There's an intercom there." He pointed to the wall by the light switch. "And one in the hallway by the elevators and a third one in the bedroom. When security buzzes up, you can approve the delivery and the guard will let them up."

"Sure thing." Trusting me with intercoms and security…this was getting bigger by the minute. "Wait, books?"

"Yes, I ordered a few books. Since you said it was your favorite part of the library."

"Right." It had been part of our charade for his mother. She didn't believe I had ever been to Hudson's penthouse and, of course, I hadn't. Meaning to trick me, she'd asked me what my favorite room was. I had said the library. An avid reader, the library was a natural room for me to choose, and I mentioned my love of books to Sophia. Apparently, though, Hudson's library didn't have any books.

Not at the time, anyway. "I still feel somehow tricked about that whole thing, by the way. But when did you have a chance to order them?"

The conversation had only taken place on Sunday when we'd been at his parent's place in the Hamptons. The day I voiced for the first time that I was falling in love. The day before he'd left me alone with his family while he went to try to save one of his companies, Plexis, from being sold.

"I ordered them Monday night from my hotel. After the deal with Plexis." His voice held the slightest hint of disappointment when he said the name of his company. His disappointment mirrored how I was suddenly feeling. "What is it?"

I considered saying nothing, but the *talk it out* mantra replayed in my head. "It's silly, but I'd convinced myself you hadn't called me or anything because you didn't have time. But it seems you did." Hudson had left me without anything but a brief text. He didn't call or contact me until more than a day later. I had believed we were over then. I'd been devastated and heartbroken. Now I found he was ordering books when he could have been calling me? "Like I said, it's silly."

Hudson tugged me into his arms. "I was trying to not be with you at the time, Alayna. But I couldn't sleep that night. Because I couldn't stop thinking about you." He kissed me on the forehead as I furrowed my brow. "Tell me—what's going on in there?"

"It's just..." How could I express the myriad of emotions that I'd been through that morning? Especially this growing fear tugging at my gut—this fear that anything that seemed too good to be true usually was.

I took a shaky breath. "You've made a complete one-eighty, Hudson. About you and me. You were so intent to be only sex only half a day ago. And now...who are you?" It scared me. It made me doubt what he felt. It made me wonder if he was playing games with me.

Hudson cupped my face in his hands and pierced me with his deep gray eyes. "Don't do that. I mean it."

He widened his eyes, making sure I was with him.

I was.

"I'm the same man, Alayna. A man who commits to whichever plan he's chosen. I had told myself I couldn't have you. So I didn't let myself even try."

"And now you've let yourself." I said it like a statement, but it was really a question. A question that I absolutely needed answered.

"Yes. And I will commit to this new plan as fiercely as the other. Even more fiercely. Because that plan was a compromise." He pressed his forehead against mine. "This plan is the one I should have pursued to begin with. It's the better plan."

My throat tightened. "The plan with the greater potential of profit."

"Unfathomable potential." He parted his lips and bent in for a kiss, sucking gently as he moved his mouth over mine. It was a sweet and tender kiss and it ended too quickly. "I have to go. Save more of that for later."

"Always."

I walked with him to the foyer. He retrieved his briefcase from the closet then kissed my forehead once more before stepping into the elevator. We stood, eyes latched until the doors closed.

As soon as he was gone, I fell against the foyer wall. Oh my god, was this really happening? Was I really making myself at home in the penthouse of my billionaire boyfriend? I felt like Cinderella. Or Julia Roberts in *Pretty Woman*. Did Hudson really want me in his life like this or was I completely insane?

I *was* insane. Insanely happy.

With a squeal, I ran to the living room and threw myself on the sofa. I closed my eyes and replayed the morning in my mind—waking up in Hudson's bed, the hot sex on the kitchen table. But what I focused on the most were his words.

I'd like to fuck you good morning every morning.

I'll be home *by six.*

I couldn't stop thinking about you.

Unfathomable potential.

After several minutes of grinning so widely my cheeks hurt, the doubts started to creep in again, as they always did. Was it truly possible for Hudson to change so completely, seemingly overnight? Or was I merely a game he was playing? Maybe he wasn't even conscious of what he was doing and he was manipulating me and my emotions out of habit.

Or maybe, like I, he didn't know how to do this relationship thing and he was simply acting the way he thought he should, even if that meant rushing.

Possibly it was all completely genuine. I felt those things for him after all. I wanted to be with him every day, all the time. I was ready for that commitment level, even though I wouldn't have said so two days before.

But I jumped into things, clung too quickly. That was my way.

Maybe it was Hudson's way too.

I sat up and glanced around the room. I had been serious when I'd said I was a snooper and usually I'd jump right on that. But I didn't feel the need to at the moment. I did feel the need to get in the shower and clean up. I was still sticky from the evening before, not to mention our morning activities.

I went back to the master bedroom, noting on the way a closed door that most likely led to the library as well as another bedroom. In the master, I stepped into the closet Hudson had retrieved my robe from. It was a walk-in and was mostly empty except for one rack of clothes. There were a few dresses most likely meant for the club, several pairs of shorts, jeans and sweat pants, and a rack of tops. One dresser drawer was partially opened so I pulled it out the rest of the way and found panties and bras. There was also a negligee. I guess I knew what Hudson wanted me to wear to bed that night.

I let out a happy sigh and headed to the bathroom, this time noticing a closed door on my way. I peeked in and discovered it was a second walk-in closet, this one full of Hudson's clothing. I walked through, running my hands along the rows of suits. Was it ridiculous how much I adored seeing his clothes like this? It felt so personal, so intimate. As if by being in the center of his closet, I was in the center of his life. I twirled around slowly, basking in the metaphor. It felt warm and completely right.

My shower was long and hot. If I'd been in my studio apartment, I'd have run out of hot water long before the time I finally stepped out from the luxuriating pulse of Hudson's deluxe showerhead. I wrapped a towel around my body and put my hair in a turban, then left the bathroom to pick out some clothes from my closet.

My closet.

But once I was in the bedroom, I heard voices coming from the main part of the apartment and a click of heels on the marble floor in the foyer.

It couldn't be the housekeeper—not only was she not due in that day, but she would have been alone. And surely she wouldn't be wearing heels. Maybe Hudson had forgotten to tell me something. Like, that his mother was visiting. God, wouldn't that just be the way to ruin my day?

I bit my lip. My phone was in my purse, which was still in the living room, so I couldn't call or text Hudson to ask who could be in his house. I glanced at the intercom. Should I call down to security? But whoever was there had gotten past security without a problem. Whoever it was had a key.

And from the sound of her heels and soprano voice, it was a woman.

Pressing my body tight against the wall, I peered around the door frame and down the hall. Her back toward me, I saw a woman dressed in a light blue sundress, directing men with boxes toward the library. Her hair, wrapped into a loose yellow bun at her nape, was what gave her away.

It was the woman Hudson grew up with. The woman Hudson had falsely claimed he'd gotten pregnant. The woman Hudson's mother had wanted him to marry.

It was Celia Werner.

— CHAPTER —

THREE

One of the delivery men spotted me and nodded his head in my direction. Panic bubbled in my chest as Celia turned to see what he was gesturing at. I ducked back around the corner, but not before she saw me.

"Laynie?"

Shit, shit, shit. I didn't want to see her, didn't want her to see me.

Her heels clicked as she walked down the hall toward the bedroom. "Alayna, is that you?" She peeked into the room and found me pressed against the wall, still dressed only in a towel.

"Hi."

"Wow." Her smile brightened as her eyes moved up and down my body, taking in my lack of clothing. "I didn't expect you to be here."

This was ridiculous. I was acting like I'd been caught doing something wrong, but I hadn't. I had every right to be there and, as far as I knew, Celia did not.

I straightened my back and stepped away from the wall. "I didn't expect you either. Hudson didn't say you were delivering the books."

Celia shook her head. "He didn't know. He ordered them through my office and my schedule was open today, so I thought I'd make sure they got here okay and help unpack them if need be."

"You have a key." It was honestly the only thing going through my mind at that point, and I hated how pathetic I sounded mentioning it. I had a key too, after all.

She leaned her shoulder against the door jam. "I do. Since I did the interior decorating. We're always updating, and we thought it was easiest for me to keep a key." Her eyes glanced over to the unmade bed, sheets in disarray from my night with Hudson. When she looked back at me, her smile seemed wider. "I did buzz though before I came up and there was no answer."

"I was in the shower."

"I see that." She winked, and I knew she was saying that she was seeing more than me wrapped in a towel. She was getting the whole picture.

Well, good. I was glad. Then I wouldn't have to feel like a jerk when I spelled it out for her. Hudson and I were together now. Whatever anyone else had ever planned for Celia and Hudson, it was moot. I was the one he'd chosen. End of discussion.

Except that discussion had only occurred in my head. Some things probably still had to be said out loud.

Celia seemed to be thinking the same thing. "Look, let me get finished with the delivery guys and you can get dressed. Then we can chat or whatever. It seems we have some catching up to do."

She shut the door behind her, and I let out a deep breath. I wasn't sure why Celia's presence was giving me so much anxiety. She wasn't a threat to me. She felt like one, though. I'd been jealous of her since I'd met her. As Hudson's oldest friend, she knew him better than anyone. He told her things. He kept her secrets. She'd been the only one who knew about Hudson and me pretending to be a couple. It was an intimate friendship they had.

Hudson had insisted that friendship was the only thing between them. I had to trust that or the envy would tear me apart. The whole charade had started in the first place so that Celia and Hudson's parents would stop trying to pair up the two. If there really had been something between them, then why would I have been brought into the middle?

I'd only discovered the day before that the reason the Werners and Sophia Pierce were so keen on playing matchmaker was because they thought Hudson and Celia had been together in the past. They thought Hudson was the father of the baby Celia had miscarried. But he wasn't, and they had never been together. The truth was worse—Hudson had played Celia, had tricked her into falling for him, had sent her spiraling into depression and wild partying. So when she'd ended up pregnant, he felt responsible and claimed parentage.

In a way, Hudson *had* been responsible. But he wasn't the man of his youth anymore. He wasn't so responsible that his games had to follow him for the rest of his life. I couldn't believe that. Otherwise I would have to believe the same about the things I'd done to others. Certainly even people like us—people who had been so broken that we destroyed others around us—deserved happiness of our own. We didn't have to spend our entire existence making up for our mistakes. Did we?

I brushed the guilty thoughts out of my mind and quickly changed into a dress I could wear to the club later. I threw my wet hair into a bun and took a deep breath before opening the door.

The delivery men had already left, and I found Celia straightening a row of boxes into an orderly line. There were dozens of boxes, many more than I had anticipated. "Damn. He went all out, didn't he?"

Celia looked up from her task. "He always does. But as I'm sure you've noticed, he has lots of shelves to fill."

I scanned the room for the first time. A large mahogany desk sat at the far end surrounded by a curved wall of windows. Two armchairs and a long sofa created a sitting area in the middle of the room. A beautiful marble fireplace graced the center of one wall with a large flat-screen television set centered above it. The rest of the wall space was filled with shelves. Shelves and shelves—a booklover's dream. Except that only one small section near the desk had any books on it.

"Uh, yeah. These boxes are barely going to put a dent in that shelf space."

"He ordered more, but this is what was already in stock. The rest should come in the next few days or so. And, yes, he'll still have a lot of empty space. Maybe you can help him fill the rest."

Was that supposed to be a leading statement? Was she trying to get me to open up about Hudson?

If she wanted to know, she'd have to come out and ask. I responded to her statement with a simple, "Maybe." I joined her in pushing the boxes into a line against the wall, doing a count of them as I did. Twenty-seven in total. Guess I knew how I was spending my afternoon. Unpacking books—the thought had me more excited than it should.

I nudged the last box into line with the others and turned to find Celia staring at me, arms crossed over her chest, one light brow cocked. "So. You and Hudson."

"Yeah. Crazy, right?" Celia had only ever been nice to me. Why was this so awkward?

"It's real then? You're *really* together?"

"We are. No more pretending. It's the real deal now." It felt strange to say that. With other relationships my declarations were most likely exaggerations. Was I exaggerating now?

No. I wasn't. This was real.

"Since when?" The question didn't sound disbelieving, but curious. Excited, even. "I was with him Monday and he didn't say anything had changed between you, though he did seem awfully lovesick. I thought he was being moody about his business-whatever that was going on. But now that I see you here, I'm thinking it was about you."

Celia had driven Hudson from his parents' house in the Hamptons to the airport for his business emergency with Plexis. "Just since yesterday. When he came back from Cincinnati, we sort of had it out and then—" I suddenly realized the source of the awkwardness. Though Celia and Hudson hadn't ever been together for real, she had thought she loved him. I had no reason to be jealous of her, but she had plenty reason to be jealous of me. "Is this weird for me to talk about?"

"Weird? Why?" Her face relaxed with understanding. "Oh, he told you."

"He did." I wasn't sure how she'd feel knowing I knew such intimate details of her life. "I'm sorry if that makes you uncomfortable."

"No, not at all. It surprises me. He's never talked about it with anyone. I'm not even sure he told his therapist." She chewed on her bottom lip for a moment. "What exactly did he say? Do you mind me asking?"

"Of course not, it's only fair I tell you. But can we sit down first?" Maybe sitting would get rid of the confrontational feeling between us.

She nodded and we made our way to the sofa. I sat facing her, my legs curled up underneath me. "Well. He, um, explained about how he, uh, made you fall for him and then slept with your best friend. He said it was all a game. Which makes sense now, how you knew that he did that to women." Celia had been the one who'd filled me in on Hudson's mind games.

"Yep. I spoke from experience." Her voice had lost some of its usual cheerfulness, but nothing seemed to indicate that talking to me was painful or unpleasant.

Her ease helped me go on. "And he told me about the baby."

I watched her chest rise and fall before she responded. "What did he say about that?"

"That you didn't know who the father was, so he said it was his. So you wouldn't be disowned or disgraced or whatever. Since he felt responsible for the situation." Even though none of the information was new to Celia—she'd lived it, after all—a part of me felt guilty for sharing things Hudson had told me in confidence.

Another part of me, a bigger part, wanted to know more about his rocky past and getting anything out of him was difficult, to say the least. Celia's unexpected arrival brought an opportunity to learn, and I wasn't throwing that away.

"Hmm. Well, that about covers all of it." She tapped a long peach-painted nail on her knee as she processed. "Silly Hudson. He shouldn't feel responsible for anything. I was a grown woman. I can own up to my actions. He doesn't still feel that way, does he?"

"Yeah. I think he still does." I didn't *think* he did, I knew it. It was the reason he kept himself so closed off, the reason it had been so hard for him to let me in. Because of his mother or his therapist or for whatever reason, he'd been conditioned to believe that he was incapable of caring for anyone, and the horrible things he'd done to people such as Celia was his proof. That he could take his friend and manipulate her life, cause her to act so recklessly that she got pregnant from a stranger and then lost her child—that was evidence to Hudson that he was a despicable person. Because no decent person would do that in his mind.

But to me, the fact that he was so traumatized by the things he'd put Celia through was evidence of the contrary—he could feel. He cared enough to regret his actions. That didn't show heartlessness. That showed humanity.

Celia rolled her eyes. "That's ridiculous. He really needs to get over himself. That was practically a decade ago now. It's old news."

I agreed on that count. Maybe by finally having love in his life, Hudson would learn to move on.

As for Celia, I wasn't sure she had yet. "So you don't still have feelings for Hudson?" It wasn't hard for me to imagine harboring an unrequited love for ten years because I obsessed. The only reason I'd gotten over some of my past obsessions was because I'd had therapy. Not that Celia suffered from the obsessive disorder I did, but it wasn't unheard of to be in love with your friend for years and nothing ever coming of it. It was the material of great books.

What did that make me? In Celia's story, was I the villain?

Possibly I was over-dramatizing. As always.

Celia leaned forward and put her hand over mine, taking me off-guard. "I totally have feelings for him, Laynie. He's my best friend. I've loved him since I met him which was before I could even talk. But I'm not *in* love with him. I don't think I ever was. He played me and I thought…well, anyway, I'm not now. My mother will tell you differently, but she believes what she wants. If I was in love with him, I would have let that arranged marriage thing work out instead of supporting a sham to throw our parents off."

"Yeah, that makes sense." I took my hand away from hers before it felt creepy. It already felt creepy—I wasn't much of a touchy-feely person. "Then it doesn't bother you that we're together?"

"Bother me? I'm happy for him! For both of you, actually. Truthfully, I was beginning to think Sophia was right, that he couldn't possibly love anyone because he'd never shown any inclination toward anyone. Except to mess with them, of course. It was really very sad. This is definitely a change for the better."

I wanted to be happy with her. Except when she'd brought up Hudson's past, it reawakened one of my greatest fears.

"What did I say?" Celia asked.

She must have seen the worry in my expression. I never did have a good poker face. "Nothing." It was probably best that I didn't say anything. Only, Celia might be the one person I could talk to about it. The one person who would understand and give me insight.

I shifted, bringing my knees up to my chest. "It's just, I've been worrying it was too good to be true, and I keep wondering if maybe I'm…if he's…"

"If he's playing you, too?"

My brown eyes met her blues. "Yes."

She nodded once and frowned. "That is something I'd worry about."

Well, that wasn't the consolation I was hoping for.

"I'm not saying you should be worried," she added. "It would just cross my mind as a possibility. Especially knowing his past, and since this arrangement or relationship he has with you is so entirely different than anything he's ever had before."

"You know him, what do you think?" Jesus, my lip quivered when I spoke. How pathetic was I?

She tapped her finger on her knee again. "I don't think he's playing that game anymore. Really, I don't. He's had counseling, and it's been a good two years since he's had any...incidents."

I made a mental note to ask what she meant about incidents at another time. Right now, though, it wasn't enough of a priority to interrupt.

"I guess he could be having a relapse, but..." Her words trailed off. "What has he said to you?"

"That he wants to be with me. That's he's committed to making a relationship work." Or similar things that I didn't want to share. They were my words and not meant to be given away to just anyone.

Celia scooted an inch closer to me as if we were in a room full of people and she was about to divulge a secret. "Let me tell you something about Hudson and the way he plays women. He doesn't lie. Ever. That's the brilliant part of his manipulative skills. He never says anything that you can throw back at him later. It's all truth spun to make you read more into what he's saying. He makes you think he's offering more than what he's really offering without ever saying the words. You know what I mean?"

"I think so." Now that I thought about it, I knew exactly what she meant. Hudson chose his words so precisely and handled himself with such care that I could see how he'd be able to spin any situation so that he'd have the upper hand. It was what made him a good businessman, I imagined.

"So if he's said those things to you, I'd believe them," Celia reassured. "And he's never, ever brought a woman to his penthouse before. That's common knowledge. Even Sophia knows that. He's never wanted anyone to be able to find him after he, you know, broke their heart."

That made total sense. If you were a guy playing people, you wouldn't want them to have access to your private life. I'd felt almost the same when I'd feared my ability to remain aloof from him—I hadn't wanted to know where he lived so that I wouldn't latch on.

Funny how we both were now in exactly the positions we hadn't ever thought we'd be in.

Celia was watching me, gauging my reactions. I could sense she wanted to say more, but perhaps didn't know how. "Has he said...how he feels about you?"

"Yes." *Well...*"No." But he had implied it. Now I couldn't even quite remember what he *had* said and the ball of worry in my stomach began to tighten. "I mean, he's said some things, but he hasn't actually said he loved me."

But I knew he meant it. Right?

Celia smiled. "I don't think he's ever told anyone he loved them. Not even his mother. So that might be a while, if ever. Don't take that omission as a sign of anything." She straightened. "No, I think you're good. I think this is good. I think it's real." She clapped her hands together. "Yay! Hudson Pierce has a girlfriend! How exciting!"

"Yeah, it is exciting." The warmth of it spread through my body. "Totally exciting." Because none of this had happened to me before. I'd never had a relationship with someone who returned my feelings. Every guy I'd found to be *the one* never had a chance to see if they felt the same before I ruined it by clinging and suffocating. And the times I'd thought I'd been in love I'd really been more in love with the idea of someone being in love with me. I'd learned that through group therapy. That was why I held on to any slim nugget of interest a guy threw my way—because I so desperately yearned to be loved.

But this time, I wasn't being desperate and I wasn't clinging and I wasn't obsessing. Not more than reasonably, anyway. It was definite cause for celebrating.

I beamed at Celia. "I can't tell you how good it feels to talk to someone about him. Thank you so much."

"I bet. And no problem. Any time." She paused. "How are things going with Sophia?"

"I don't know." More like I didn't care. Hudson's mother and I were never going to be friends. Not when she'd belittled me and called me a slut. Not when she was so against Hudson finding anything good in life. "I told her off the last time I saw her. I'm hoping I don't have to deal with her anytime soon."

"Oh. You don't have plans to see her then? Like, to show her your coupledom and everything?" She seemed surprised by that, and perhaps it *was* surprising after the lengths Hudson had gone to show me off to his mother when we weren't actually a couple.

"No, thank god. I think Hudson's given up on convincing her of anything. Which is fine by me."

"Totally. Who needs Sophia?"

I didn't, that was for sure. But Celia, on the other hand..."You're chummy with her." We'd addressed everything else, might as well address Sophia too.

"Well, I live by that friends close, enemies closer philosophy. It works for me."

"Yeah it does. She adores you." I may have sounded a little bit jealous. Which was ridiculous since I hated Sophia Pierce.

"She adores me because she adores my mother. Besides, she thinks that if I'm with Hudson, she'll have complete access to his life. Like I'd share anything personal with her. I have her snowed, that's all."

"Then all I have to do to get her on my side is to snow her too?"

"Maybe." Celia's eyes narrowed as she considered. Then she shook her head. "Seriously, forget her. She's not worth it. Have you heard about the time that Hudson told her—" The grandfather clock in the foyer chimed once. "Oh, my, is it really one o'clock already?" Celia checked her watch. "It really is. I have a full afternoon. I've got to get going." She stood and smoothed down her dress. "I'm sorry to rush off like this. It was great talking to you."

"Yeah, this was nice." I hated to admit it, but I was disappointed to see her go. Especially when she was about to tell me a story about Hudson. She had so much to offer in terms of understanding him. She'd already made me feel better and there was so much more to be gained from speaking with her.

"We should totally get together again," Celia exclaimed, almost at the exact moment I was thinking it. "Here." She pulled a card out of her purse and handed it to me. "My cell is on here. Call me and we can do coffee. Tomorrow, maybe?"

"I'd like that." I took the card from her, glancing at the print. *Celia Werner, Corporate and Private Interior Design.*

"Awesome. Give me a call in the morning then." She paused. "Oh, and if I don't answer, keep calling. I have a nasty habit of leaving my phone in random places and if you call over and over then I will get to you. And I'll find my phone! It's a total win-win."

I laughed at her method of phone control. "Perfect."

"Great! Tomorrow then. Give Hudson my love." She started toward the library door and then stopped and turned back to me, her hand clutched against her chest. "You know, it really is about time Hudson had someone in his life, and I'm so glad it's someone who loves and understands him as it seems you do." Her words and actions would seem overly dramatic for most people, yet she was just classy enough to get away with it.

"Thanks. I do. I get him." Probably more than either he or I knew yet.

"I know you do." Her face grew serious. "He's told me things about you, too. I hope that doesn't bother you."

She could only be referring to my crazy stalker past. Some of it was quite embarrassing. I'd violated a restraining order once. For that, I had a police record. It was buried now, by Hudson and my lawyer brother, but that didn't change that it had happened. That I had done that. It was only one of a long list of many shitty things I'd done.

Normally I would have been humiliated to find that someone knew about my history. But right then, with all the good that was going on with Hudson, I didn't. "No, it doesn't bother me. Surprisingly."

"Good." She smiled. "I won't tell anyone, of course. I'm glad that I know though. I can see how perfect you are for him because of what you've been through yourself. I'm on your side."

"Thank you. I'm very grateful."

She winked. "Okay, well, I'm off. Good luck!"

I stood in the library thinking over Celia's visit long after she had gone and I had programmed her number into my phone. I was looking forward to having coffee with her, and, the truth was, that made me feel twitchy. As sure as I was that she could be a vital source of Hudson insider knowledge, I was also sure he'd be none too happy about it. And rightly so. If I wanted to learn about his past, I should go through him.

Still, could it really hurt to have coffee?

I decided to put my decision off until the morning.

Scanning the dozens of boxes once again, I decided to open some up and start unpacking them on the shelves. Hudson had said to make myself at home, and it would keep me from snooping. Even though I'd gotten permission, it wasn't the healthiest behavior.

I found a letter opener in one of Hudson's drawers and, kneeling beside one of the boxes, I used the opener to cut through the packaging tape. Molière was on top, along with a copy of Shakespeare. Underneath, I found several other classics from Dante to Dickens. I sat back on my heels and looked at the shelves, formulating a plan to organize the library.

My library.

Hudson hadn't said it was mine, but I couldn't help but think of it as such. I loved books—not only the stories they contained, but the feel of them in my hands, the silk of the pages, the words all collected in one place. Hudson didn't have any interest in physical books. Obviously. His bare shelves were proof of that. He read everything on his e-reader. These were my books. I'd already adopted them and was sure Hudson wouldn't protest. He'd only ordered them to fool his mother, even though I doubted Sophia visited his penthouse very often.

Also in the stack of lies told to Sophia, Hudson had declared I was moving in with him. How long before that became a reality?

No, I couldn't plan for that. Like I'd told myself earlier, it was too soon, and we weren't ready.

But would it really hurt to fantasize about it for a few minutes? To imagine living with him in the penthouse? And more? Me running the nightclub with Hudson at my side. Engagement rings and bridal parties flashed through my daydream. Was it really so bad to hope for?

Yes. It was. I had to stop now because daydreaming could very easily lead to fixation. I needed a substitute obsession. Something else to occupy my mind.

I tried to return my focus to the books, but again my mind wandered to the future—weddings and the club and parties.

That was when the idea hit me. I abandoned my task and found my phone to call Jordan. I needed a ride.

"BACHELORETTE PARTIES?" David Lindt leaned back in the desk chair and swiveled from side to side.

I hadn't been sure David would be at The Sky Launch so early in the day, but I'd lucked out. He was the general manager of the nightclub, and since Hudson had relinquished the running of the business to him, he was the one I needed to approach with any ideas for improvement.

Which was why I'd come in more than six hours before my shift started to share my stroke of genius. "Yes. Bachelorette parties."

"Seriously? That's your big idea?"

"Come on, it's perfect!" I threw my hands up for emphasis. This was a good idea, and talking about it calmly had not seemed to have done the trick of convincing David. "It's wedding season and the bubble rooms are the perfect place for privacy while still being surrounded by the club scene. You know as well as I do the stuff that goes on in those rooms."

The bubble rooms were, in my opinion, the highlight of The Sky Launch. The ten circular rooms ran the circumference of the second floor. Each room had its own entrance and was completely enclosed to ensure privacy. Or rather, a sense of privacy. It was an illusion since each of the rooms also had a window that overlooked the dance floor below and if you looked across, you could see everything that happened on the other side. Plenty of times, the things that went on in those rooms were rated R and, more often, rated X.

The bubbles, however, had been neglected in promotion for as long as I'd been an employee of the club. I'd gotten my promotion partly on the promise to find ways to better use the unique feature. Promoting them for bachelorette parties—that plan was gold.

David didn't seem to have the vision I did. "We've had bachelorette parties in here before. Not many, but a few."

"And they always go well, don't they?"

"The customers are always pleased." He twisted his lips as he considered.

With his constant fidgeting and weird faces, I wondered briefly how I'd ever thought I was attracted to the man.

The answer was that I hadn't been. Not truly. David had been a nice option when I'd been too afraid to go after any men who really turned me on. I'd thought I could have a future with him. I'd figured that being with a man like David was the cure to my obsession—not actually caring for him kept me from the outrageous behavior of my past.

And he'd been cute enough. We'd never gone all the way, but we'd come pretty close, and becoming aroused had never been a problem.

All thoughts of David had disappeared when Hudson entered my life. I gave up the safe bet for the real thing, and, even with the ups and downs of loving Hudson, I didn't regret it one bit.

David regretted it, however. He wanted something more between us and had told me so just the day before. But he knew where my feelings lay. He knew whom my heart belonged to.

Now he brought his pen up to his mouth and bit on the already chewed end. Pen between his teeth, he asked, "How do you expect to draw people to book the rooms for that?"

"Marketing." Obviously. That had been my emphasis area of my newly acquired MBA, and I was anxious to use it. It was what I had to offer the nightclub—my expertise. "We've never advertised those rooms to any specific market. They're underutilized and wasted space compared to what they could be used for. And if we bundled the rooms in packages designed specifically for soon-to-be-married brides, I think we could really attract some attention."

"Yeah, I see some potential." *Finally.* "What's your strategy?"

"I need some time to put it all together into a formal plan, but I'm thinking I could book some meetings with wedding planners. If I can offer a good deal, they'd tell their clients. Maybe we can give them referral bonuses or offer them a certain percentage of our booking fee as a kickback. But first we need to design some packages. Include some party trays and a certain dollar amount from the bar and we've got something to sell."

Behind me, my phone beeped with an incoming text. It had died on my way to the club right after I texted Hudson my plans for the afternoon. Luckily I had a spare charger I kept in the office by the file cabinets and I'd plugged it in as soon as I arrived. "So what do you think?" I asked as I crossed to my phone.

"I think you're onto something. Let's do it."

I grinned triumphantly before glancing down at my message.

"I've arranged the cook. Will you still be home for dinner?"

"I wouldn't miss it for the world," I responded, his use of the word *home* making me as giddy as it had that morning.

"Pierce?"

David's question broke through my euphoria. "Yeah, it's Hudson."

"Something good?"

I hadn't realized I'd been smiling until then. "Everything good."

Leaving the phone to continue charging, I returned to the chair I'd been sitting in. "I'm meeting him for dinner. Don't worry, I'll be back by the time my shift starts."

"Actually, I wanted to talk to you about changing your schedule." David stood and came around the front of the desk, leaning on the corner. "I promoted you so that you could do this kind of stuff. We have enough managerial coverage. If we need someone else—which I'm sure we will if your plans work out like I know they will—Sasha's ready to be a manager. Your gift, what you bring to The Sky Launch, is your business ideas. I need you to go work magic. That's not my department."

"So," I furrowed my brow, "what are you saying?"

"I'm saying make your own schedule. I need you on the clock forty hours a week—not a problem for you, you work addict—but you can put it in whenever you need it. Set up those meetings with the wedding planners. And I'd like to go forward with your idea of expanding hours and our services. That's going to take a lot of daytime planning as well. You'll need to meet with cooks and additional staff. It's going to be a lot of work."

It felt like my eyes were going to pop out of my head. "Seriously? I mean, seriously do all that amazing stuff *and* make my own hours?" This was my dream job coming to fruition. All the hours of fighting with my brother Brian about wasting my education and the job opportunities I'd turned down with Fortune 500 companies—this made every doubt and heartache worth it.

"Yes, seriously. I wouldn't joke about this shit. Start with taking tonight off."

"Don't be ridiculous. You can't run the upstairs bar with one person."

"Liesl's coming in. It's already covered."

Of course Liesl would agree to work a shift for me. She was pretty much my one and only friend in the city. Half space cadet, half genius, she was everything I wasn't—free and laid-back and flirtatious without having to worry about becoming attached. Even though we were complete opposites, she understood me like no one else and was much more generous to me than I often deserved. "She worked for me the whole time I was in the Hamptons. I can't make her do that."

"She volunteered. We hired that new waitress, and Liesl's determined she be *trained right*—her words, not mine. And if you're going to set up some meetings for tomorrow, you'll need to adjust to being awake during the day. Right now you're sort of a vampire." He moved his eyes down my legs. "A tan vampire, but a vamp nonetheless."

I laughed, hiding my unease at the obvious lust in his stare. I stood to put us on the same level. Otherwise it felt like he was looking down at nothing but tits. "Thank you, David. Thank you, thank you, thank you. I'm..." There weren't words for how grateful I was for this opportunity. "Just thank you."

"You deserve it." He straightened from his leaning position and threw his arms out to his sides. "Hug it out?"

"That got me in trouble last time." Hudson had walked in on that and been pretty pissed. He wasn't a man who shared. I'd managed to talk him down, convinced him my hug with David had been innocent, which it had been, as far as I was concerned. Still, Hudson suspected there was something more between me and David. And, like a chicken-shit, I hadn't been able to bring myself to admit he was right. David and I did have a history. But compared to what I felt for Hudson, it seemed like an insignificant detail.

I stuck my hand out toward David. "Settle for a handshake?"

He nodded as he took my hand. He held it much longer than he should have, his thumb caressing along my skin, sending unwanted goose bumps down my arms.

I pulled away, hoping he hadn't noticed. Though I felt nothing for David, my body still reacted to his. He was plain but attractive—his eyes a dull blue, his hair dark blond and curly. He worked out but had a stocky frame. He'd never been my type, and my reaction was likely only out of habit. But it was enough to make me feel a weight of sudden guilt—I shouldn't hide my past with David from Hudson. I'd been quick to accuse him of keeping secrets in our relationship, and here I was doing exactly that. It was wrong, and I knew it.

I also knew I wouldn't tell him. I doubted he'd let me continue working with David if he knew we'd had a past, and if he found out on his own, my silence might help in my defense. I'd explain to Hudson that I didn't say anything because there was nothing to say. He'd understand.

Maybe if I kept telling myself that, I'd eventually believe it.

— CHAPTER —

FOUR

Hudson was already home, jacket discarded, when I got back to the penthouse that evening. He met me as I stepped out of the elevator, greeting me with a lush kiss that swept me off my feet.

"Well, hello to you, too."

"You're late," he said against my lips.

"And?"

"I worried." His mouth swept across my cheek and down toward my earlobe.

My eyes widened both in surprise and at the yummy thing he was doing to that sensitive spot below my ear. "That something had happened to me?"

"That you weren't coming."

I pushed him back to meet his eyes. "Why Hudson Alexander Pierce, did you worry I'd stand you up?" It was silly to even think about. "Don't you realize I'm the kinda girl that sticks?"

He leaned back in to rub his nose against mine. "If you acted as smart as you are, you would have stood me up weeks ago."

"Good thing I don't act smart."

"Good thing for me, yes." He released me and took my purse off my shoulder, which he stowed in the coat closet. Then, weaving his fingers through mine, he tugged me after him through the foyer toward the living room.

"Guess what." I admired his back as I followed him, his taut muscles visible through his dress shirt.

"You don't have to work tonight."

I stopped short, my hand slipping from his grasp. "How do you always know everything?"

"I don't." He turned back to face me, a smile toying on his perfect lips. "But where you're concerned I make an effort. David called me this afternoon and asked if I approved of you making your own hours."

"And you said, 'Yes, because then I can conform my schedule to Alayna's so we can fuck as much as possible.'" I laughed at my horrible imitation of Hudson's voice.

"I said I thought it was a good idea." Instantly, I was back in his arms. "But I was thinking what you said." His mouth circled above mine, teasing.

"I love you."

He moved tighter into me. "I hope that my ability to change your working hours is not the sole basis of your fondness for me."

"It is not. Trust me." This time I kissed him, licking along his upper lip.

When he pulled away, his eyes were clouded with desire. "Dinner's ready, precious."

He led me to the dining room where the table was set with a bouquet of white orchids, two lit candlesticks, an opened bottle of wine, and two place settings at one end.

He waved his hands toward the candles. "These would have a more dramatic effect if it weren't so light in here."

"Yes, it's terrible that your penthouse has floor-to-ceiling windows that let in so much sun," I teased. "Honestly, it's lovely." Our eyes locked for a moment, caught up in each other.

Jesus, if we kept looking at each other like that, food would have to wait. I was already feeling moist in my panties.

Noticing the aroma of fresh herbs, I broke our gaze and looked toward the quiet kitchen. "Where's the cook? Did she abandon you?"

"She did not. She cooked and then she left. Our plates are waiting under the warmer." He pulled a chair out, gesturing for me to sit. "I presume I can manage the service without her."

I kept my eye on him as I sat. "Honey, you don't need anyone's help with service."

"Hey now." He tapped my nose with his finger as he delivered his reprimand. "Food first. I need my energy to keep up with you. But if we get through dinner, perhaps there will be dessert."

"A naughty dessert, I hope."

"No hoping necessary."

Hudson poured white wine into my glass before filling his own. Then he disappeared into the kitchen returning a few minutes later with two plates of food. He set a plate in front of each of us and then sat down. Together we dined catty-corner from each other, tangling our legs under the table. We chatted about our day and when I told him about my bachelorette party ideas for the club, he was both supportive and impressed.

"Do you want me to get you in touch with my company event planners? Not that they'd be helpful in the pre-wedding party arena."

"Nah, I got some things set up already."

He took a swallow of his wine, and I guessed it was difficult for him to let me keep the reins on my project. But when he set down his glass, he seemed resigned. "Let me know if you change your mind."

The meal was delicious—chicken breast stuffed with sundried tomatoes and artichokes. Sautéed zucchini and jasmine rice accompanied the chicken. I'd stayed at work all afternoon, arranging meetings for the week, and had skipped lunch. It wasn't until I was eating that I realized how hungry I'd been.

"This is so good, Hudson," I said when my plate was half-clean. "Wherever did you find this cook?"

"She used to be sous-chef at one of my restaurants. Things didn't work out with her and another staff member, so she works privately for me now."

I thought for a moment about what I knew from Hudson's portfolio of businesses. "Fierce?"

"That's the one."

Fierce was one of the hottest restaurants in the city. The head chef had a reputation for being a complete hard-ass. I didn't have to ask if that was the reason she'd left.

My work-oriented mindset of earlier lingered into the conversation. "Would she consider working at The Sky Launch?"

"Then who would cook for us?"

I ignored the rush I had from the way Hudson referred to us as an "us," and pressed on. "For private events then. It doesn't have to be a full-time gig."

"I like the way your business brain works, Alayna. But why don't we put the job away for the night? I'd like to spend time with the other sexy parts of my girlfriend."

That shut me up. It was the first time he'd called me that—girlfriend—and holy wow, what it did to me. My chest warmed with what felt like a radioactive level of heat, spreading down my limbs and up into my cheeks. *Girlfriend.* I was Hudson Pierce's girlfriend.

Pretending he didn't know what his statement had done to me—he knew, he so knew—he continued with the common conversation that boyfriends and girlfriends exchanged after a day apart. "Other than work, how was your afternoon? I noticed the books came. Did the delivery go okay?"

I nodded as I swallowed my food, following it with a sip of wine before answering. "They did, and yes, it went fine. Celia accompanied the delivery."

Though his face stayed even, he stopped chewing for half a second. "Oh?"

I had guessed that Hudson wouldn't be that happy about Celia stopping by. Ever since she'd spilled the beans about his manipulative past, he seemed to fear what she'd say to me. No matter what I said, he didn't understand that nothing she could say to me about him would ever change how I felt for him. Perhaps I shouldn't have told him about her visit, but that didn't feel right. I was already keeping my history with David on the down low. I didn't want another secret.

The only thing to do was convince him Celia and I could be trusted together. "She surprised me. I guess I was in the shower when she buzzed up so she let herself in."

His brows furrowed. "I need to take away her key."

"Yes, you do." I didn't like worrying that she could stop by any time she wanted. "But it wasn't bad. In fact, we had a nice chat."

Hudson's entire upper body tensed. "I don't like that. At all."

I'd only seen that possessiveness of his a couple of times before. It was frightening and thrilling, sending bolts of hormones to my lower regions and raising my arousal levels to full alert.

It was also unnecessary. "Don't get all panicked. It was fine."

"I don't want you two to spend time together. Remember, in my script you aren't friends." He stabbed at the air with his fork, enunciating his point.

I clucked my tongue. "Come on, that's not fair. I only want to feel close to you and she's your best friend."

He shook his head once. "She's my only friend. It's different."

I stroked my foot up his calf, hoping to lighten his mood on the subject. "She didn't give away any deep dark Hudson secrets."

"Says you."

"She only said she was happy that you'd found me." I paused to let that sink in. "She thinks you deserve someone."

Instead of softening, his expression hardened. "That's a deep dark Hudson secret right there." He leaned closer to me, speaking low. "So deep and dark, it's a lie. I don't deserve you and I never will."

"Shut up." I rolled my eyes then placed my hand over his. "You deserve much better than me. You're out of my league and everyone knows it."

"Alayna—" His tone was a warning.

I narrowed my eyes. "How about instead of arguing over who deserves whom, we agree that we fit pretty damn well together and leave it at that."

"I don't want you spending time with Celia."

Damn, he was serious. So much for getting insider knowledge over coffee. On the other hand, who was he to tell me that I couldn't spend time with someone?

But we were trying to make a relationship work. If it was important to him then…"All right, I won't spend time with her. And I don't want you spending time with her either."

"I can live with that compromise."

"You can?" I tried not to sound surprised.

"Yes. I barely see her anyway. From now on, if I have to see her, it will be with you."

"Agreed." It wasn't as much of a sacrifice for me as it was for him. She wasn't my friend.

"Good." Then a wicked gleam filled his eyes. "We do fit pretty damn well together."

"Now who's getting naughty?"

He set down his fork and looked at our nearly empty plates. "It is time for dessert."

"Hold that thought. I'll be right back." I wiped my mouth with my napkin and got up from the table. The hall bathroom wasn't visible from the dining room so I hoped that's where Hudson assumed I had gone. Instead, I went to the master bedroom, to my closet. I grabbed the lingerie set from its drawer and changed as quickly as I could.

I stopped in front of the bedroom mirror to fluff my hair into as close of a sexy tousle as my straight strands would allow and noticed, damn, I looked good. The teddy was a coral baby-doll flyaway that pushed my already perky boobs up to soaring heights. The middle opened to expose my flat belly and the matching lace thong. Hell, I'd do me.

I slunk back to the dining room and found the table cleared and Hudson at the bar making a drink, his back to me. Awkwardly, I tried to come up with some stripper pose, but when he turned toward me, I'd only managed to cock my hip and put a hand at my waist.

He nearly dropped his glass, his eyes wide. "Holy, fuck, Alayna. You look so goddamned hot, you've surpassed naughty and gone straight to sinful."

"Why, thank you." I swayed toward him, his lustful gaze never leaving my body. When I was close enough, I pulled on his tie, beckoning him forward. His brow arched in surprise, but he let me lead him back to his chair and push him to a sitting position.

Leaning forward so his view was all tits, I ran my hands up his thighs to his waist where I undid his belt and began working on his fly.

"What are you doing?" His voice was hoarse, his eyes pinned on my cleavage.

"You served dinner. I figured I should serve dessert." I wasn't sure he'd let me take the lead. He rarely did where sex was concerned—where anything was concerned. But instead of waiting for his permission, I simply took charge.

I tugged at his waistband and waited to see if he'd play along. After a moment's hesitation, he submitted, lifting his hips for me to pull down his pants and underwear. I lowered them just enough to expose his already rock hard cock.

"Holy, fuck, Hudson," I repeated his earlier words as I took his dick in my hand. "Talk about sinful." Still gripping him in my hand, I knelt before him, nudging his legs wider for me to fit in between them.

Leaning forward, I rubbed my breasts along his bare cock.

He let out a heavy breath, and I did it again, running my fingernails along his chest, digging through his shirt. His eyes were pinned to my tits as I stroked his penis between them.

"You're so fucking beautiful, Alayna." His voice grated, like he was losing control. "So fucking beautiful."

"So are you." This time I maneuvered my hands under his shirt to claw at his skin as I rubbed my tits along his throbbing cock. "Do you like fucking my tits?"

"I love anything you do to me."

"Is that so?" I sat back on my haunches and leaned down to run my tongue up the length of his shaft.

He growled—actually growled—and I shivered at the sound.

But despite how his sounds and reactions made me completely weak and dizzy, I suddenly felt powerful. There was nothing in the world that I could imagine that would be strong enough to cause Hudson Pierce to relinquish his authority—nothing in the universe that could make him yield to anyone.

Yet here he was giving in to me.

Yes, I felt very powerful.

I licked again up the other side of him then swirled my tongue across his head as I pumped him once with my hand.

He jerked in the chair, his fingers gripping the arms. "Jesus, yes."

I wanted his hands on me, him grasping my hair. But I knew, as he did, that if he touched me, he'd take over. He'd run the show. His lack of contact was a gift, and I took it graciously. Greedily.

Moving one hand to fondle his balls, I placed my lips over his crown and slid my mouth over his soft, stone cock, my hand grasping the length of him I couldn't fit inside. Up and down I pumped him, sucking him off with an insatiable passion.

I felt his thighs tense around me and I knew he was close.

"Alayna, slow down," he pleaded through gritted teeth.

I ignored his request, continuing to stroke and suck him toward his orgasm.

"Alayna!" His hands flew to my shoulders.

Next thing I knew, I was on the floor, Hudson hovering over me as he tore at my thong, ripping the flimsy thing off of me. Then he was inside me, filling me, stretching me, thrusting into me with such force I thought he might rip me apart.

And, god, he felt good. So goddamn good.

"You feel amazing, Alayna," he said as he drove into me, his face sweaty and pinched with the effort. "I was about to come in your mouth."

"That would have been fine." I would have sucked him dry and licked him clean.

"But I much prefer coming in your tight cunt." His jabs slowed as I clenched around him, constricting his movement. "Fuck, I'm coming now."

I groaned with him as his climax pressed him deeper into me, as my own heightened arousal took me to a gentle release behind him. It wasn't the earth-shattering variety of orgasm that I'd grown accustomed to having with Hudson, and somehow that made it even sweeter, more savory.

When he'd emptied himself completely, Hudson fell to his back beside me and took in several deep, ragged breaths. "I apologize for that."

I sat up on my elbows and cast him a questioning glance. I could recall very few times he'd apologized to anyone for anything. Certainly not for sex.

"I got carried away. I didn't give you the attention you deserved."

Laughing, I rolled to lie across his chest. "I love it when you get carried away. You rarely let yourself go. It's a nice change. Not to mention, it's hot."

Hudson's chest rose as he chortled—another sound I heard infrequently from him—and he draped an arm over my back.

I propped myself up on my arm. "Someday, though, you're going to let me suck you off until you finish."

"You know I love to come buried inside you."

"God, I do, too." I smiled, dreamily. "But I'd also love to have you come in my mouth. I'm craving it, actually."

His arm tightened around me. "Stay tonight."

It wasn't a question or even an invitation. It was a declaration that I would stay, and of course I would. But I responded anyway. "Okay."

Where else would I want to be?

HUDSON HAD MISSED his usual morning workout since we'd slept in that morning. Though I was convinced we'd worked out enough in the bedroom—and the kitchen and the dining room—he decided to hit the penthouse gym. Wanting to be near, I joined him.

The gym was in the back of the apartment, next to the master bedroom, and was equipped with a treadmill, elliptical trainer, rowing machine and a weight system. I changed into a sports bra and shorts from my closet and claimed the treadmill. Hudson started out on the elliptical and moved to the weights for the bulk of his workout.

I'd always been a fairly good runner, usually pounding Central Park or the blocks from the club to my apartment, but running with the sight of Hudson's calves and arms flexing as he worked the elliptical was quite a feat, even for me. Admittedly, I tripped a couple of times.

After exercising, we showered and settled in the bedroom, Hudson donning a pair of boxers while I snagged one of his t-shirts to wear with a pair of panties. Hudson brought in his laptop to sort through some business emails, and I curled up with a book from the day's delivery. There were several Hudson had got that I hadn't read yet but were on the list of greatest books of all time that I was working through.

When I'd been reading long enough to get lost in the first few chapters of my book, I suddenly became aware of stillness next to me. Hudson was no longer typing. I looked up and found he was watching me.

Goose bumps marched down my arms. "What?"

"You look good in my t-shirt."

"I know."

His lips curled into a sexy smile. "You look better without it."

I laughed.

He lifted his chin toward my book. "What did you choose to read?"

I held the book up for him to see the cover.

"*The Talented Mr. Ripley.* Interesting. A book about a true sociopath."

An unexpected chill ran through me. Hudson's mother had told me that he was a sociopath—unable to feel empathy or love, detached and self-absorbed. I disagreed vehemently. I'd seen otherwise. Hudson loved and cared for me like no one in my life had.

But, though I hadn't told him about the conversation, I was certain *sociopath* was a term Sophia had used openly with him. I wondered if he thought it was an accurate description of himself. It was hard to bring it up and debate it with him when I knew so little about the things he'd actually done in the past. I only knew the general idea—that he manipulated people. Played them.

If I was being honest with myself, I could see where sociopath might be mentioned by a therapist treating someone with those types of habits.

I didn't know enough. Though I believed in Hudson and his feelings for me, there were still so many unknowns.

Propping the book open on the nightstand, I turned my body to face him. "Hudson, can I ask you something?"

He shut his laptop, set it on the nightstand on his side of the bed and switched on the table lamp. "Yes, I will do wicked things to your body, but only if you promise to do wicked things to mine."

I giggled. "I'm being serious."

"So am I." His eyes blazed as he ran them down my bare legs and back to meet mine. "But wickedness can wait. Ask me."

"I was thinking..." I ran my teeth over my lower lip as I figured how to broach the subject. "Celia had said that you manipulated women, as if it was more than her. What does that mean exactly? Like, what did you do?"

His jaw set. "I thought you said you just chatted today."

"We did." I rushed to correct his impression. "She didn't mention that today at all. Or anything like it. I swear." I took a deep breath. "It was before, at the charity fashion event of your mother's and I've been thinking about it. I should know, don't you think? If we're going to be open and honest with each other, I need to know."

"No, you don't." He stood, and for a moment, I thought he was leaving the room, but he merely turned off the overhead light and started back to the bed.

"I do need to know."

"No way." He said it with finality. Case closed.

But I wasn't willing to accept that. I pulled my legs under me to a kneeling position. "Hudson, I get it. I do. You want to ignore it and leave things in the past. But you're always going to be scared that I can't love you through anything if you don't give me the chance to prove that I will."

He stood at the edge of the bed, his eyes narrowed. "But what if you don't? Have you considered that? Has it crossed your mind that I might have done things you could never forgive?"

"There's nothing—"

He cut me off. "You don't know that."

I switched tactics. "Is there anything I could have done to make you...?" *Stop loving me* is what I thought. But it felt weird to say it out loud like that when he hadn't ever said it himself. "To change the way you feel about me?"

"It's not the same."

"You don't know that either." To be fair, he knew very little about the things I'd done before. I hadn't wanted to tell him, hadn't wanted him to know the awful ways I'd invaded people's lives. I completely understood about wanting to let the past lie.

"Then tell me."

I swallowed but didn't let the trepidation show on my face. "Anything?"

He sat on the bed, facing me. "The restraining order against you was filed by Paul Kresh. Who was he?"

I closed my eyes for half a second. Hudson had read my police files. Of course he would remember the details.

My hesitation spurred him. "See? You can't tell me."

"He was a guy," I blurted out. I wasn't stupid. If I wanted him to share, I'd have to do the same. "Just a guy who picked me up once when I was clubbing."

"You fucked him."

Another deep breath. "Yes."

Hudson's eye twitched. "Go on." His voice was tight.

"He took me to his place. And after...well, after, he wanted me to leave. But I played drunk and stayed the whole night."

"Then what?"

"Then I went through his things while he was sleeping and discovered wedding invitations. He had a fiancée. She was out of town for the weekend or something and I was a girl he'd picked up. But he didn't realize that I'd been crushing on him for weeks. I'd seen him with her, and I didn't care. When I saw him alone that night, I made myself available."

My hands were sweaty—I'd been holding them in a ball. I wiped them on the bed next to me as I went on. "Of course, he wanted me gone, to pretend it never happened. Wanted me to forget his address. He never gave me his number, but I'd gotten that when he was sleeping, too. Sent myself a text from his phone so I'd have it."

I paused, trying to remember how I'd felt, how desperate I'd been for Paul to be in my life. "I couldn't let him go. I thought..." My voice trailed off at the memory. "I don't know what I thought."

Hudson turned so that his back was against the headboard. "Yes, you do. Tell me."

I sat back next to him, stretching my legs out in front of me. "I thought he was my soul mate. That I was meant to be with him or something. Before I even actually talked to him. I know. Crazy. It was crazy." I stared at my toes. "I was crazy."

"No, you weren't. You only wanted to be loved."

Hudson's rich brandy tone pulled my eyes to his. "Yes," I said, meaning so much more than *yes, I wanted to be loved.* Meaning *yes, we understand each other, yes, we get it.*

Yes, we weren't crazy or sociopaths or horrible people. We only wanted to be loved.

"Anyway," I smoothed my hair behind my ear, "I didn't have a job. I was living off my inheritance, which is gone now, and so I had plenty of time to wait outside his apartment and follow him to work. Every day. For months. Two? Three? I don't remember exactly. One day, I told the security guard he was my boyfriend. I convinced him to let me in his office during lunch. When Paul came back, I was waiting for him." I lowered my lids. "Naked."

Hudson's eye twitched again.

"He turned me away, H. Called security before I had a chance to even throw some clothes on." My throat closed at the humiliating memory. "He filed the restraining order after that."

I studied his face, trying to pick up on the slightest change in his expression, hoping to pick up on his thoughts. But I came up with nothing. His features were stone.

Would he ever let me in?

Hudson brought his index finger up to his face and rubbed the tip along his chin. "But that's not all, is it? Your record says you violated the order."

I felt my face flush. "I, um, I did." God, talking about it was embarrassing. Even thinking it made me want to crawl in a hole. Of the stupid, idiotic, insane things I'd done, this had been one of the worst. "I became friends with Melissa."

He nodded once, immediately understanding. "His fiancée."

"Yeah. I joined her Pilates class and became buddy-buddy with her. So she started inviting me out with her and her friends. Eventually I ended up at a party that Paul was at too. He was livid. And he had to decide if he wanted to ignore it or report me. If he reported me, Melissa would find out about the one-night. I wouldn't leave things alone, so he reported it. And she broke things off."

"He deserved that."

"Maybe." I wasn't so sure. Yes, he'd cheated on his fiancée, but that didn't make up for my role in things.

"He deserved worse in my book." Though Hudson was guarding his reaction to my story, his casual crumbs of support in my favor helped put me at ease. "And Paul's the only one this happened with?"

No. Not even close. "He was the only one who went to the police."

"I see." Hudson was quiet for a handful of seconds, absorbing. Finally, he furrowed his brow, and looked me eye-to-eye. "Why would you think that this would change how I feel about you?"

"Are you kidding? Aren't you worried I'll become that hung up on you?"

"I'm *hoping* you become that hung up on me." He draped his arm around my shoulder. "Paul was a fucking asshole who didn't realize what he had in front of him. I do. Get hung up on me."

"I am hung up on you!" I turned to kiss his shoulder. "But careful what you wish for. If I go crazy on you, you'll want me gone."

He turned his cheek to nuzzle against the top of my head. "I'd never drive you away. Not on purpose."

It was sweet—being held and told that I was wanted. I couldn't ask for anything more.

Yet, I still felt Hudson didn't understand the severity of the things I'd done.

I sat forward and turned my entire body to face him, pulling my legs underneath me. "But what if I started to doubt you? That's happened before, too. Where I didn't trust anything my boyfriend said to me, no matter how innocent they were. And then I snooped and invaded privacy and people got hurt."

"Then I simply have to make sure that you never have any reason to doubt me." He swept his hand out in front of him. "Snoop away. I have nothing to hide from you here."

And there was my ticket back to where we'd started the conversation. "You're hiding your past."

He groaned. "I'm not hiding my past. There's simply nothing worth talking about. It's ugly. Why would you want to focus on the bad things?"

"It's not focusing; it's sharing and then moving on."

He shook his head.

"I told you mine. That's not fair."

This time I got a steady glare.

"Come on. Anything. One thing." I felt desperate. Opening up had been hard, and I wasn't even getting the reward that I'd counted on.

I stared at him with wide, pleading eyes.

"One thing and you'll leave it alone?"

I nodded enthusiastically.

"Okay, one thing." He sighed. "It was a game. Always a game. And my favorite was the same one I played on Celia. Make a woman fall for me, and when she did, I was done." He paused, and for half a second I feared that was all he was going to say.

But then he went on, his eyes glossy with memory. "There was one time, though, I wanted to see if I could make someone fall for someone else, someone they had no interest in. I knew this guy, Owen, who was a real ass. A complete man-whore. And this woman, Andrea—a girl, really. She was in my tennis club my second year of college. Very shy, simple, homely. I discovered she had a thing for me. Having a thing for me was very dangerous." He stared pointedly at me. "Still is."

I rolled my eyes. "No, it's not. Go on."

"I set her up with Owen. Not just on a date, more. I played silent matchmaker. Got them together. I convinced Owen he was doing me a favor by taking her out a few times. Meanwhile, I'd fill him with all these stories of how amazing Andrea was, how her true beauty was inside. And it happened—they fell for each other. Completely. Sincerely."

I blinked. Twice. "That's a beautiful story."

"Then I fucked her and showed Owen the pictures."

"Oh, my god." My hand flew instinctively to my mouth. I hadn't been prepared for that and immediately felt ashamed. I'd been trying to be supportive. He'd tried to shock me. He won.

Hudson carried on as if I hadn't reacted. "Andrea tried to tell Owen it was a mistake, that I'd tricked her, which I had. I didn't rape her—I never raped anyone. But he wouldn't listen to her. They were both…broken, is the best way to describe it. Andrea left school in the middle of the semester. I never heard anything about her again."

"And Owen?" My voice sounded much feebler than I would have liked.

"He went back to sleeping with anyone with two legs. Last I heard he'd gotten HIV. I don't know. I lost track of him."

He studied me, the same way I'd studied him a moment before, and I knew he read me. Saw what I was feeling. I couldn't be stoic as he'd been. I couldn't hide my emotions.

His features grew dark. "I told you, you didn't want to hear it. I told you—"

"Just give me a second to process," I stuttered, ashamed that I needed the delay. I'd said his past wouldn't change how I felt about him. Did it? I pushed past the horror of the story and focused on Hudson, the man who had committed the horror. Did knowing these things change how I felt for him?

My pause was too long for him. "See, Alayna? See why your past means nothing to me? Compared to me, you were an angel. You hurt people because you loved too much. I hurt people because I could."

I jerked my eyes to his. No, my feelings for him hadn't changed. If anything, they'd grown deeper. How lonely, how sad, how broken did a man have to be to feel compelled to destroy the people around him? And how strong and worthy was that same man to attempt to be someone different in the aftermath?

I was in his lap before a second had passed by, straddling him, my hands resting on the sides of his neck. "No." I aligned my eyes with his and said it again. "No. You hurt people because you didn't have any idea what love really was. You were trying to understand it in the only way you knew how. It's horrible, yes. But it's forgivable. I forgive you. I forgive a thousand worse things you may have done. I can forgive anything."

I caressed his cheek with my palm. "Because I love you. I love you too much, like I always do, but this time I don't regret it and I don't wish I could take it back because you need it. So take it from me, H. Take it all from me."

He buried his head into my neck and sighed, a deep sigh that sounded both haunting and freeing. Wrapping my arms around him, I stroked his hair, whispering his name at his ear.

Soon he found my lips, and we disappeared into the sweetest, most languid kiss that lasted on and on, neither losing momentum nor turning frenzied.

It was a long time later before our clothes were discarded and Hudson slid us to a lying position, stretching me out over the length of his body. And just like the kiss had lasted on and on, we made love slow and leisurely, giving and taking from each other until the wee hours of the night when we were certain that the memory of our bodies together burned stronger and brighter than the horrid memories we'd shared from our past.

— CHAPTER — FIVE

"What do you call these rooms again? They're amazing!" Julia Swaggert, founder of Party Planning Plus, pressed her forehead on the glass of the enclosure and looked out over The Sky Launch's empty dance floor.

"Bubble rooms," I answered behind her, pleased that Julia seemed impressed with The Sky Launch. Our meeting had begun at eleven, and now, forty-five minutes later she was still engaged and interested in my proposals for a partnership.

"And when they're occupied—" I flipped the light switch on that indicated a room was in use.

Julia's face lit up as the room glowed red. "Ha-ha. Awesome. Can people see inside them?"

"Unfortunately, yes. We'd have too many legal issues if we were to install one-way mirrors in them. But when it's dark on the floor, you can't see very much inside them. Mostly silhouettes."

"Hot."

I liked Julia. Instantly. She was fun and enthusiastic but also had a smart head on her shoulders. I could tell why she came highly recommended in the event planning world. She was definitely someone who could boost The Sky Launch's business, and my excitement grew about the possibilities as I showed her around the club.

"This is totally perfect for Bachelorette parties, as you suggested." She wrote a couple notes down on her tablet with her stylus and turned back to face me. "Actually, I can think of a few types of events that might be interested in this venue. If you can come up with some pricing packages—" She tapped her pen across her cheek, leaving her sentence for me to finish.

"Sure thing." Damn, did that sound too eager? I really wanted to make this deal, to prove that I could do all the things I'd said I could when I applied for the promotion. And, to be honest, I wanted Hudson to be proud of me.

I wasn't taking notes on paper, but I was mentally. "Do you have some things you'd like to see in particular as part of the packages?"

She nodded energetically, her dull brown curls sweeping her shoulders as she did. "A dollar amount at the bar is a must. Perhaps a selection of appetizers. Few pre-brides will be expecting dinner when they're clubbing, so light on the food and heavy on the drinks."

That had been pretty much what I'd been thinking. "Would add-ons be of interest? Like male waiters or a penis-shaped cake?"

She laughed. "I think you know what you're doing."

A *bleep bleep* came from Julia's purse. "Ah, that's my partner," she said, digging inside. "He was overseeing arrangements for an event we have later and said he'd join me here if he got free." She retrieved her phone and read the screen. "Yay, he's here. Mind if he comes up?"

"Not at all. The front doors are locked, though, since we're not open during the day. I'll have to walk down and let him in."

"I'll come with you." She followed me as I exited the bubble room. "I want to get his feedback from the moment he enters. See if he loves it as much as I do. I can't believe I had no idea this place existed!"

We walked back down the stairs and through the club, Julia commenting on different features of the club as we passed them.

She nodded to the bar on the lower level as we passed. "I'm so glad there's a bar on each floor."

"There are two bars on this floor: the main one and a smaller side one that we only operate on the weekends. Food is only served upstairs. So the first floor is tailored for drinking and dancing while the upstairs level with the bubble rooms and lounging areas is geared more toward socializing."

"Nice. And you can rent out the entire club for events?"

"Of course."

"Can you put together some packaging for that? I know some corporations that might like this for holiday parties and such." She pointed to a counter near the front of the club. "And what's this? An information desk?"

"That's the coat check." *Or a fabulous place to make out,* I thought, remembering how Hudson and I had spent some time in there one evening before my shift. "Oh, whoops! That's not supposed to be there." I grabbed a serving tray that had been left on the coatroom counter.

"I'll put this away while you let him in."

I skipped back up the ramp to the front bar to deposit the tray behind the counter then headed back.

As I returned, I heard Julia gushing about The Sky Launch to her partner, whose back was to me. "It's an amazing club, baby. A total gem."

Baby, huh? Partner must mean more than just in business.

"Plus we'd be hooked up to Pierce Industries, and that's a major bonus for us. We have to score this deal. I can already think of two couples this place would appeal to." Julia's tone echoed the excitement I felt about our impending venture. "The Fredericks for one."

Julia spotted me walking toward them. "Here she is. Alayna Withers, I'd like you to meet my boyfriend and partner at Party Planners Plus—"

Her partner turned around to face me, and I nearly choked as Julia finished her introduction.

"Paul Kresh."

My heart stopped. Literally stopped for the space of two beats. Paul Kresh, the man I'd stalked and terrorized. God, oh god. He had a restraining order out on me. I couldn't be within one hundred feet of him and there he was, standing a yard in front of me, his features frozen in a state of shock that had to mirror mine.

Fuck.

There went my affiliation with Party Planners Plus.

Julia carried on, unaware of anything odd between her boyfriend—that's what she'd called him, anyway—and me. "Paul, this is Alayna, the...Wait."

She paused and I worried she'd figured it out, that she'd pieced together his expression and my name. If she knew about me, that was.

But when she spoke again, her words were harmless. "I'm sorry. I don't even know your title." She laughed, and I blinked at the oddness of the sound in contrast to the panic that was rushing through my veins.

David and I had come up with my official title only the day before, but I was so stunned by Paul's arrival and Julia's obliviousness that it took me a second to respond. "Um, Events and Promotional Manager."

I didn't know if I should shake his hand or run. If I should act like an old friend or as if we'd never met.

Paul made the decision for me. Smiling stiffly, he held his hand out. "Pleasure to meet you." His tone was steady. Not sure and commanding and unflinching like Hudson's, but unfazed nonetheless.

I took his hand, my fingers wrapping limply around his. "No, the pleasure's mine." That's what you say to new business affiliates when you meet them, right? Because nothing I could think of sounded correct or harmless. Did it sound like I was flirting? Because I was not. Was. Not. There wasn't any interest in my body for him except to be far, far away.

I pulled my hand away first, unwilling to touch him longer than necessary.

"Paul, you've got to see this place. Can we repeat the tour?" She looked at me, wide eyed and expectant.

Hell, no. That's what I wanted to say. What I should say. But I was numb and no response came at all.

Again, Paul came to the rescue. "Actually, honey, we've really got to get going."

She took his wrist in her hand and twisted it to look at his watch. "Yeah, you're right. We have a thing tonight. Last minute details and all. Mind if I use the little girl's room before we take off?"

She blinked at me twice before I realized that the question was for me.

"Not at all, it's back at the top of the ramp, to—"

She cut me off. "I remember."

I watched as Julia climbed the ramp and disappeared around the corner. Then I found my voice. Words fell like the sweat dripping down the back of my neck. "Paul, I had no idea, I swear. I didn't have a clue that Julia was your partner or that you worked at Party Planners Plus or that you'd be here today or ever. I would have canceled if your name was anywhere attached to the business website, and how the hell would I ever know that you'd become an event planner anyway? Because when I knew you, you were an accountant in that stupid firm on Forty-Seventh—"

"Stop, Alayna." He let out a huff of air as he ran his hands through his hair. "I know you didn't plan this. There's no way you would have known." I wasn't sure if he was acknowledging my innocence in our meeting or reassuring himself. "I'm still an unofficial partner. I've been doing Julia's accounting and we only recently decided…"

His hand dropped to his side. "Anyway, that's not important. The important thing is—"

"That we absolutely don't work together. I know." As I said it, my heart sank, the ideas I'd had for teaming up with Julia rupturing like a popped balloon. "The restraining order was for five years, and I think there's two years or so left."

"A little less than two years," he corrected. "But that doesn't matter. We have to work together anyway."

"What?" I think I actually jerked in surprise.

His hand went back to his dark blond hair, brushing through it like he always did when he'd been stressed or exasperated. "I can't ruin this deal for Julia. She's hired new people recently and she's trying to expand the business. It's a good time for her, but she needs connections like this club. Connections with people like Hudson Pierce."

"But I can't be anywhere near you, let alone working with you." Hudson's name in the air made me even more uncomfortable with being alone with Paul Kresh. I didn't like Hudson being connected to my past mistakes. I was in serious violation of a restraining order that I'd already violated once. My hands balled at my sides, my fingernails digging into my skin at the thought of what would happen if the cops found out.

As if reading my mind, Paul said, "I'm not going to report you. You didn't know. And going forward I'm not going to say a damn word." His eyes narrowed. "Unless you fucking show up on my doorstep, or in my office—"

"I'm not!" I clasped my hands together and put them to my lips, calming myself before speaking again. I counted to ten in wicked speed. "I'm not like that anymore. I'm better. I got counseling. I haven't even thought about you since…" Since the night before when I'd told Hudson about him. "Well, I'm better. And I'm with someone."

I was so much better. There was a time where I would have been dizzy and heartsick over even the slightest thought of Paul Kresh. Now he was nothing but a mistake. A problem I couldn't wait to go away.

"Good. That's good to hear. I'm glad you're better." Paul looked me over. "And I believe you. You look better. I don't know…healthy or something."

"Thank you." Getting emotionally and physically better had improved my physical being. I'd gained weight—mostly muscle—and my skin tone had improved.

Paul seemed to be taking those changes in and my stomach clenched with the urge to throw up.

He must have caught himself, because he suddenly turned away, gazing up the ramp where Julia had gone. "Look, Julia knows nothing about you or Melissa or that I was engaged before."

"Nice. Secretive relationships for the win," I said sarcastically.

He ignored my remark. "We'll simply have to agree to keep all the past under wraps. Not a word that we've ever met before today. We can do that. I know you can." His tone was caustic, as if he had a bad taste in his mouth. "You were always good at acting like things were just fine."

I fought the urge to kick him in the shins. "Paul, this is a bad idea. A really bad idea for me."

He stepped toward me, a finger pointed in my direction. "You owe me. You owe me this at least. Don't you think?"

Fuck. He had me there. Didn't I owe him a whole shit load? Sure he'd been a dick at every opportunity, but that didn't excuse the way I'd invaded his life. And paying him back, cleaning the slate—it sounded awfully appealing.

Against every warning siren blaring in my head, I said the words I hoped I didn't live to regret. "All right." I swallowed and said it again. "All right. I'll pretend we just met."

"Fine. You'll be working mostly with Julia anyway. We won't see each other. It shouldn't be an issue."

I put my hand over my churning stomach and nodded weakly.

"Alayna, hey!" The female voice came from the opposite direction of where Julia had gone.

I squinted toward the sound and found Celia making her way toward us. Really? Could this day get any more complicated? Or filled with people I wasn't supposed to be with?

"What—what are you doing here?" My voice was dazed.

"You never called me for coffee and I didn't have your number so I stopped by."

I hadn't called her because Hudson and I had agreed not to see her without each other. I certainly hadn't expected her to show up out of the blue. And, how had she gotten in anyway? I frowned. The door had been locked and should have stayed locked after Julia let Paul in. Maybe they hadn't shut the door hard enough.

"How did you know I was here?" Was my head muddled or was her appearance as baffling as Paul's?

"Jordan told me."

Of course. Her endless connections to Hudson's life. Why was I even surprised anymore?

"Is something wrong?" Concern laced Celia's question.

"No…I…well." My head hurt, my stomach hurt, my mouth was dry and I felt shaky. "Everything's fine."

I followed Celia's questioning glance to Paul. Oh, yeah. Fucking Paul. "Celia this is a potential business associate, Paul Kresh." I turned to Paul, unable to look him in the eye. "This is a friend of my boyfriend's, Celia Werner."

Paul's brow rose. "As in, Warren Werner?"

"Uh-huh." Celia straightened at the mention of her father's name, ready to be the show pony that she was raised to be.

Paul broke into a smile. "We did an event for your mother once. I didn't actually talk to you, but I saw you around."

"What company did you say you worked for?"

"Party Planners Plus. My girlfriend is the owner and I recently joined on board as her partner." Paul's eyes traveled toward the ramp. "Here she is now." He turned his focus to his girlfriend. "Julia, this is Celia Werner. You remember when we did that event for Madge Werner."

Julia's eyes brightened. "Totally. It was at the MoMA last spring."

"Ah, that was you? How nice to meet you. It turned out lovely, no matter what my mother said."

Julia and Paul exchanged a glance that said there must have been a story behind the matter. Frankly, though I would usually be curious about the gossip regarding Celia's mother, at the moment I couldn't care less. There were too many conflicting pieces of my life trying to meet up in one place—Celia, Paul, trying to land my first great business deal for the club—once again, I felt the urge to throw up.

"I hope you don't mind, but as Paul said, we've got to be running." Julia smiled brightly. "It was so awesome to meet you."

I did my best to recapture the enthusiasm I'd had earlier when it was just Julia and me. "You, too. I'll draw up those packages and get back to you by tomorrow."

"Perfect!"

Paul seemed ready to leave without saying anything to me until Julia cast him a stern look. "Yes, we look forward to working with you. A joint venture would be beneficial to both of us."

I read his subtext, the reminder that I should go along with his ridiculous plan to pretend we were strangers. "I certainly hope so," I said, my face plastered into a businesslike grin.

I held my breath until the door shut behind Julia and the unwelcome ghost of my past. Then I let it out in one slow exhalation.

"What in the hell was that about?"

One stressor gone, the other still stood by me. At least I couldn't get arrested for speaking to Celia.

I headed up the ramp toward the main part of the club, hoping to somehow escape my anxiety attack.

"Laynie?" Celia pressed, following after me.

I shrugged. "I don't know what you're talking about."

"You could cut the tension with a knife."

I opened my mouth to deny it but what was the point? "Was it that obvious?"

"Yeah. It was. Wanna talk about it?"

I stopped walking and paused.

"Ooh, there's hesitation." Her eyes twinkled with the anticipation of gossip. "Let's talk about it. But not here. Over coffee."

I rubbed my fingers over my brows, trying to alleviate the throbbing behind my eyes. "All right." I didn't have the energy to argue or make up an excuse. Besides, I needed a drink, and since it was too early for liquor, coffee would make a fine replacement.

"Great! I'm sure you need to lock up. I'll head to the coffee shop next door and get us a table."

Fifteen minutes later, Celia and I were seated at my favorite cafe in Columbus Circle. I'd already downed a third of my iced double espresso and was realizing that maybe caffeine was exactly the opposite of what I needed because now my shakiness had increased to full-on jitters.

Celia had so far filled the conversation with easy topics that I was able to respond to with only one- or two-word sentences. Meanwhile, my head spun, unable to concentrate on any one thing for any length of time. The one thing I was sure of was that I shouldn't be having coffee with Celia Werner. Should. Not.

"So who was the guy?"

I rocked back and forth in my chair. "No one. A client."

"That's a lie and you know it. There was all that weird vibe stuff going on."

Her eyes bore in to me, but I was unwilling to give anything except a one-shouldered shrug. What would I tell her, anyway? Hudson didn't even want me talking to her, let alone telling her big important things. And if I did explain about Paul, what if she told Hudson?

Shit, shit, shit. Hudson.

I had the distinct feeling that he would not approve of my working with Paul Kresh. And it wasn't like it was something I could necessarily hide. Hudson did own the club, after all. Fuck, fuck, fuck.

Unaware of the turmoil in my mind, Celia tried another method of getting the dirt. "I mean, I get it. He's yummy, as in I wouldn't mind having him in my bed for a night or twelve."

I chortled. "Good luck with that. His business partner is also his girlfriend." Of course, Paul had been engaged when he hooked up with me. "On second thought, you probably still have a chance."

"Obviously you speak from experience."

No shit, Sherlock. I was about as experienced as you could get when it came to Paul Kresh. I knew his habits, his patterns, his workout schedule. Details of his life I'd committed so deeply to memory that they were impossible to forget. Keeping it all bottled up wasn't helping. I'd learned to cope through talking. I needed to talk.

"Tell me. You know you want to."

Celia was right. I did want to tell her. So I did.

Hudson had told Celia a few things about my past, but I wasn't entirely sure what so I told her everything. When I finished she was silent and wide-eyed for several seconds.

"Damn," she said finally.

"Right?"

"Like, ugh. I don't even know what to say." She took a deep breath and straightened from her leaned-in position. "Does Hudson know?"

"He knows about the restraining order, of course. He told you about that, didn't he?"

She nodded. "He mentioned something about it."

I tried not to be embarrassed that he'd shared that with Celia. I'd already guessed she knew that much. It made sense why he'd told her. She was in on the scam we'd tried to pull on Sophia and it was important that Celia knew all the details, I supposed.

Whatever. It didn't matter what Hudson had said or why, because now I'd told it all to Celia myself. "But he doesn't know I met with Paul today. I didn't know I was meeting with him until he showed up. Now I don't know what to do."

I sipped at the straw of my iced espresso that was mostly water by that point. "The obvious answer is to not work with him. That's what I have to do. And Paul can say whatever he wants, but I can't put myself and The Sky Launch in that kind of jeopardy."

"There you go! You got it worked out." Celia's eyes narrowed as if she were considering. "Except…"

I had a whole bunch of "excepts" running through my mind. Except working with Paul would be good for the club. Except I owed him. Except he might get mad and cause me trouble if I didn't go on board with his scheme. Except I really wanted Hudson to think I could do good things with his club.

I wondered what Celia's "except" was. "Except what?"

"Party Planners Plus is getting a really good name around town. It's impossible to please my mother and she was almost happy with what they did at the MoMA. That's saying a lot. They'd do great things for the club." She took a sip of her nonfat latte. "And Hudson would be proud."

"Are you reading my mind?"

She smiled. "I'm just thinking logically." She set her drink down and seemed to go into planning mode. "Would you have to work with Paul hands-on?"

"No, I think I could go strictly through Julia."

"You could make that a stipulation to signing a contract with them."

"But Hudson would freak! My brother would freak!" I said it before I remembered that I'd cut Brian out of my life. "Not that I'm speaking to my brother, but he worked his ass off to get me out of the whole Paul debacle."

Celia didn't bat an eye. "Don't tell him. Don't tell either of them."

"How can I hide Paul from Hudson? He owns the club!"

"Your contact is going to be with the girlfriend, right? If Hudson happens to see the paperwork—which is unlikely—it will say Party Planners Plus. If I remember correctly, Paul's not even really an owner. It's legally all in Julia's name."

"Right, right. That's right." I was impressed. Celia was actually good at this scheming stuff. "But since that's the case, maybe I should tell Hudson."

"You can tell him, but if I know Hudson—and I do—there's no way he'll let you keep that contract. He's too protective of things he considers his. And in this case, that's not only The Sky Launch, it's you."

My feminist side wanted to get pissy at being considered a man's object, but the in love side—the more dominant side, at the moment—blushed in agreement. "I know. It was worth a shot though."

"So you have two options: forget the contract or forget telling Hudson."

I didn't like either choice. But I wanted that contract. Badly. So badly I could taste it. And feeling like it was a way to pay back Paul made the decision all the richer. "I won't tell him. I'll work with Party Planners and Hudson will never be the wiser."

"Then I won't tell him either." She put her hand up and dangled her last finger. "Pinky swear."

Her promise made me feel better. Made me feel like I had someone on my side. Made the lie seem less likely to explode in my face. "Thank you. Talking to you really helps me figure things out."

"Of course it does." She smiled in that way where she knew she was adorable and made no apology for it. "Hey, why didn't you call me this morning anyway?"

I took another sip of my watered-down drink while I decided if I should tell her the truth or make up an excuse. After I'd been honest about everything else, I settled on the truth. "I didn't think it was a good idea to see you. Hudson wasn't happy when he found out we chatted yesterday."

"Hmm. I imagine he didn't." She rubbed her lips together, and I wondered briefly how she kept her gloss looking so fresh all the time. "Well, tell you what," she said after a minute. "We don't have to tell him about this either. I didn't tell Jordan I was going to go find you so I'm sure he wouldn't say anything. You could just not say anything either."

The thought had crossed my mind, but only fleetingly. "I'm not sure if I'm good with keeping it from him." The list of things I wasn't telling Hudson was getting much longer than I felt was acceptable. My past with David, working with Paul, now seeing Celia behind his back. I looked at my watch. It was only a little after one. Was that too early to have a beer?

"Sure, I get that. I'm not trying to encourage keeping secrets or anything, but he's so weird where you're concerned. Protective or something. The last time I talked to you, he was pissed for days. He thinks I'm going to turn you against him or something." She rolled her eyes. "But it's up to you. Just let me know so I'm on the same page."

"Okay." But I planned on telling Hudson about Celia. We were supposed to be working on honesty and the weight from two secrets was heavy enough without adding a third one.

— CHAPTER —

SIX

"Precious."

It was a quarter after two when I answered my phone to Hudson's voice. We hadn't seen each other that morning. He'd slipped out while I was asleep in his bed, but he'd left my phone next to my head and a text message flashed on it telling me to make myself at home and he'd call me later.

Now, hearing him on the other end of the line, I realized how much I'd missed him in the mere handful of hours we'd been apart.

"Hey," I sighed into the receiver. "I'm glad you called."

"I said that I would."

We'd had so few phone conversations that they still took me by surprise, still delighted me to no end. "I'm glad both that you said you would and that you did."

"You are easily pleased." The smile on his face was apparent through the phone. "How has your day been?"

"Dreadful until this very moment." After Celia and I had parted ways, I'd thrown myself into putting together packages for Julia. The work had been fun and had occupied my mind completely. Still, the horror of the morning clung to me like a shadow.

"Oh? Why? What's wrong?" Immediately Hudson was on guard, ready to fight whatever battle I was facing.

His reaction made me eager to tell him about seeing Paul, but I swiftly reminded myself why that would be a bad idea. "Nothing. Nothing's wrong. Just everything is dreadful in comparison to being with you."

"I feel the same."

Just like that, Hudson could make me weak in the knees. "You don't know what that does to me to hear you say that."

"I can imagine." The husky tone of his words suggested he was imagining much naughtier things than he was saying out loud.

"How did your meetings go?" His change of subject was abrupt, and I was sure he'd been thinking naughty things and now he needed a safer topic of discussion.

Though pleased at Hudson's obvious arousal, I felt the chill of a shadow at the mention of my earlier meeting. "I've only met with one company so far. And it went well. I have to follow up, but I'm pretty sure it's a done deal."

"Of course it is. Who wouldn't want to work with you?"

"Should I make a list?" Before that morning, that list would have included Paul Kresh. Funny how quickly things changed.

"Yes, do. And I'll have each and every one of them shot." Something told me he was only half-kidding. Maybe even less than half. "Do you have any plans this evening?"

I switched over to my browser on my computer and loaded up an image of Hudson to stare at while he spoke. "I had planned to be adored by a hot, virile man." I traced my finger along the strong jaw of the picture on my monitor. "But I could cancel with him if you have something better in mind."

"You're teasing."

"Am I?"

"You are, and I don't like it." His jealous growl was a turn-on. "Some people I know are holding an event at the Brooklyn Botanical Gardens and I'd like to be there. With you."

"I'm all yours, H. Every time."

"Good. I'll pick you up at the club around six."

I looked down at my outfit—a dark green flare dress with a cut-out row of crisscrosses across my abdomen. It had a sense of class to it but perhaps was a little too risqué. "No, pick me up at my apartment. I need to change first."

"What you're wearing is perfect."

"How do you know what I'm wearing?" I looked around, half-surprised when I didn't see him standing in the office doorway. "Do you have security cameras in the club or something?" I wouldn't put it past him. I shivered, realizing what else cameras might have recorded. Like my meeting with Paul.

"Of course I have cameras. But I don't monitor their feed. Jordan told me what you were wearing."

"Ah, yes, Jordan." This was the second time my actions had been given away by him. If Hudson had spoken to my driver today, had he learned that Celia had been inquiring after me? How much did Hudson rely on Jordan to fill him in?

I tensed, the stress of carrying my secrets beginning to wear on me and raising my level of paranoia. "Tell me—is Jordan more than just my driver?"

"You didn't want a bodyguard. I had to compromise."

Hudson's matter-of-factness was almost as unnerving as what he was admitting. "So Jordan spies on me for you?"

"Spy is not an accurate description of what he does. He drives you places, makes sure you're safe, and reports back to me."

For a moment I considered arguing about the arrangement. But after I let the idea settle, I realized it wasn't so bad to be cared for by an overly cautious boyfriend.

I exhaled, letting my anxiety go.

"I heard that sigh. Tell me what bothers you about this?"

"Nothing, really. Only I wouldn't have come on to Jordan so unmistakably if I'd known he was reporting back to you." It was an obvious joke, considering Jordan was hired to drive me because he was gay.

"We both know that didn't happen," he scolded. "That's twice you've tried to rile me. What exactly is your motive?"

"No motive. It's just fun to hear you get all possessive alpha male."

"If you want possessive alpha male, I can certainly comply."

I smiled, leaning back into my seat. "I want you to be you. Which is already really possessive alpha male, but if there's more of that you're keeping from me, bring it on."

"I changed my mind. I'll pick you up at five-thirty."

"Okay. Extra stop planned?"

"No. I need time to fuck you on the way over in the limo without worrying about being rushed."

I was glad I was already seated. Otherwise, I may have hit the floor. "You need to mark your territory?"

"I need to be inside you. Otherwise, I'll be uncomfortably hard and unable to concentrate on business."

I closed my eyes and let my mind fill with his dirty plans. "Then I shall be waiting at five-thirty."

"Be ready for me."

"I will be." I had an appointment with another event planner, but it was scheduled for four. Plenty of time. "I should be done with my appointments by five."

"When I said *ready*, I meant that I want you wet."

"Oh. Well, I'm sure that won't be a problem." It never was where Hudson was concerned, especially when he exerted his alpha male persona. "But maybe you can send me some dirty texts on your way to help heighten the mood."

"I'm sure that could be arranged."

"Awesome."

It was ten minutes before Hudson was supposed to arrive when he sent his first text, and honestly, by that time I'd forgotten to expect it. So when my phone buzzed that I'd received it, I read it without preparing myself. Which was a mistake.

"I'm craving the taste of your pussy on my lips."

"Everything okay?" David had arrived a few minutes before and my shock at Hudson's message must have read across my face.

"Yeah. I'm fine. I'm…just…"

A second text buzzed through before I could finish my thought. *"I've been thinking about it all day. Your pussy. How it feels, how it tastes, how it smells."*

Followed by a third. *"And the sounds you make when I'm touching you and eating you."*

My body felt warm. "Uh, Hudson's on his way," I managed. "I didn't realize it was already so late."

"Then better get wrapped up. Don't want to leave the boss waiting."

I internally cringed at David's reference to Hudson as the boss—Hudson hated that—then sent a quick text reply. *"I'm already wet."* Nothing had ever been truer.

I'd only had time to shut my laptop and stand from the couch where I'd been working before his next message came through.

"I'm hard for you, too. So hard it hurts."

I turned away from David, fearful he could guess the gist of my text conversation if I didn't hide my face. *"What will you do to me when you're with me?"*

Hudson's response came quickly, but I waited until I'd packed away my laptop in my computer bag before reading what he had to say.

"First I'll spank you for teasing me with talk of other men."

"Then?"

"Come outside and find out."

"You're here? You came early." Thank god I'd already finished my work. I was suddenly desperate to see Hudson, glad that I could leave immediately.

"Have a good night, David," I said, barely paying attention to his response as I left the office, reading Hudson's next text as I walked.

"No. I'm fucking hard as stone for you, but I won't come early." His next text came before I had a chance to respond. *"Get out here."*

Computer bag on my shoulder, purse tucked away inside it, I was practically running, stopping only to text one quick word. *"Coming."*

I waited until I was about to step out of the club to read his final reply. *"Yes. You will be."*

I shielded my eyes as I walked into the sunlight and saw Jordan standing with the door of the car open. Not just any car—a limo.

I raised a surprised brow as I approached. "Fancy ride." Maybe I should have insisted on going home to change. I was definitely not dressed for black tie.

Jordan nodded but offered no explanation.

I poked my head in the back of the car and shrieked as Hudson's strong arms pulled me, belly down, across his lap. His hand was under my skirt fondling my rump before Jordan had the door shut behind me.

"Well, hello to you, too," I purred under his caress.

He gathered the material of my dress up around my waist, exposing my thong-wearing ass cheeks. "The fancy ride is merely for privacy. No one should witness the things I intend to do to you on the way to our event."

Craning my neck to see his face, I asked, "And what, pray tell, do you intend to do?"

"First, this." His hand came down hard on my bottom, and I gasped. Hudson had swatted me before, but spanking—this was new. And it was hot.

I was vaguely aware that the car hadn't moved yet when his hand came down again even harder this time. "One for each time you teased me about other men today," he said.

It suddenly felt very Dominant/submissive to me—like something I'd read about in a trashy romance novel where the billionaire alpha hero got off on whips and chains. Though Hudson was definitely domineering, and the spanking was a nice treat, I was pretty sure it wasn't a lifestyle either of us planned to explore any deeper. It was too base of a form of control for Hudson—he preferred his domination with a heavy dose of manipulation. At least, according to what I knew about his past.

But role-playing—that was a different thing entirely and likely up Hudson's alley. I decided to test it out. In an affected meek voice, I said, "Thank you, sir. Thank you for the spanking."

Hudson laughed. "Do you need another one for mocking me?"

Either he wasn't getting it or he wasn't into it. I tried my submissive tone again. "I'm not mocking, sir. I enjoy my punishment, if it pleases you."

"Oh, we're playing that game, are we?" *And the light bulb goes on.* "In that case, another one because it pleases me." He spanked me again, the slapping sound such a turn on that I squirmed in his lap. "And another for the secret you've been keeping."

My breath caught. We were playing a game. He couldn't be serious. Still, dread gathered in my belly at the thought of things he might have found out. "What secret is that, sir?"

"That you enjoy being spanked. I can smell how wet you are from here."

A combination of relief and arousal washed over me. "Yes, sir. I do."

His finger slipped past the small triangle of material at my crotch and inside my cunt. "Yes, you certainly do. You're dripping."

His hand retreated and he spanked me once more, rubbing away the sting before sitting me upright next to him. Then he reached over to grab the seatbelt and pull it across me. "I insist you buckle up while we're driving. I have to protect what's mine."

I smiled. It was actually I who insisted on seatbelts whenever we were in the car. The whole parents dying in a car accident thing really sheds light on the importance of safety. It was a good move on his part, though. Quite in character. Not for the first time, I saw flashes of the man who liked to play games more often. Perhaps this little bit of role play could be a way for him to act out the part he'd so long taken with other women.

Since Hudson seemed to be enjoying the fun, I turned up my performance. "But sir, how can I ever please you when I'm held to one spot?"

"Are you challenging my decision?" His eyes twinkled with a wicked gleam. "Because I'm not above putting you back over my knee."

"I'm sure you're not. Sir." He'd enjoyed the spanking as much as I had.

His eyes narrowed, but he left me in my spot. After we were both secured in our seats, Hudson pressed the intercom. "Jordan, we're ready."

As the car lurched into traffic, Hudson looked me over, his eyes heavy-lidded. "Turn in your seat as much as you can to face me."

I did as he commanded, shifting as much as the seatbelt would allow. I had no idea what he had planned, where he would take this game, and the anticipation sent a shiver through my body.

With one hand around my nape, he brought me in for a rough kiss. I heard his other hand working the fly of his pants as he stroked into my mouth with long licks of his tongue. He continued his assault for several minutes, leaving my lips plump and raw when he pulled me away from him with a tug of my hair.

As if by magnetic force, my interest was drawn down to his stunning cock, bare and ready.

He pulled my hair until my gaze returned to his. "Eyes on me."

The smartass part of me wanted to say that my eyes *had been* on him—on a deliciously exciting piece of him. But I knew what he meant, and smartass wasn't part of the role I was playing, so I kept my mouth shut.

"Good girl." His hand was still tangled in my locks. "That kiss was to set the tone. Now you will suck me off. And I want it to feel like that kiss."

"Okay. Now as in now?" God, I was a shitty submissive.

"Yes, now."

I inhaled his unique scent as I bent forward, eager as always to take him into my mouth. My usual cock sucking ritual involved lots of licking and teasing, but if the tone was to mirror the kiss, then I had to assume he wanted me to skip the foreplay. Instead of licking, as I'd normally begin with, I circled both hands around his penis and sucked his crown.

I took his low hiss as a sign of approval.

Fisting him at his base with one hand, I covered my teeth with my lips, hollowed my cheeks and pumped him with my hand and mouth in tandem.

His voice was strained as he encouraged me. "Like that, Alayna. Just... oh, god...just like that."

I loved giving him pleasure, loved pleasing him. He grew thicker as I picked up my tempo, greedily sucking, brushing my tongue across the thick ridge of his shaft as I bobbed up and down.

"Yes, Alayna. You feel so good." He was still in control, though. And I wanted him crazed.

I moved my free hand to cup his balls, rolling them gently in my palm in complete contrast to the frantic way I worked at his shaft with my lips and my tongue.

"Christ...Alayna..." It was then that he took over. He wove his fingers into my hair and directed my head to move at his pace, pushing me down to take him in deeper, deeper, deeper, his hips thrusting up as he fucked my mouth.

I tightened my grip at the root of him, hungry and greedy for his climax. He was so thick and so close and the idea that he might stop me before he reached the goal made me all the more desperate for his release. I was squirming with lust, so turned on by his primal need, by the intense pleasure that I was giving him—I moaned low and deep, the vibration of the tone spinning inside my head and against his shaft.

Hudson's grasp tightened in my hair. "Fuck!" he rasped. "I'm going to come. Take it, Alayna. Take it all."

I moaned again, partly because I couldn't contain how excited I was, partly to push him over the edge.

And it worked.

He poured into me with a long grunt of pleasure as his hips thrust up hard, his cock twitching as it hit the back of my throat. My fist pumped him as he came and came and came. And I took it all. Just like he'd asked, like I'd wanted, though I felt near choking and I could barely breathe. I took every last drop, licking him clean while he shuddered beneath me.

When he was spent, his hand relaxed at my nape and I sat up to face him. Instantly he pulled me in for another kiss, this one sweeter than before, the taste of his mouth mingling with the taste of his semen until all I could recognize was a flavor that was unique and new, yet all Hudson.

"Thank you," I murmured against his lips. He had been playing at lord and master but he'd succeeded in pleasing me. I'd wanted to taste him, had yearned for him to finish in my mouth. Not because I was especially in love with giving blowjobs, but I wanted every experience with Hudson—the good, the bad, and especially the carnal. I recognized it for the gift that it was, and it made the episode all the more wonderful.

He sat back, stroking my hair from my face. "Alayna." I adored how he said my name, how it always felt like he was saying so much more with only those three syllables. Like a prayer, like a touchstone. It made me feel beautiful. Who was I kidding? It was what *made* me beautiful.

His gray eyes searched mine for long seconds. "How does it feel to belong to me?"

I didn't know if he was still playing or not. For me, the game was over. It was with sincerity that I answered. "Perfect."

— CHAPTER — SEVEN

Hudson was not willing to let me go unsatisfied. By the time we'd reached the Brooklyn Botanic Gardens, I was spent and ready for a nap. Hudson, on the other hand, seemed revived, a smug grin on his face as he took my hand, escorting me out of the limo.

An attractive blonde with Eighties pink nail polish stood at the main entrance, checking invitations as guests made their way into the gardens. Hudson was allowed in without flashing any credentials.

"You seem awfully pleased with yourself," I whispered as we entered the grounds.

He dismissed my comment. "Everyone knows who I am."

"That's not what you seem pleased about."

He shot me a wicked grin. "I think I deserve to be pleased. A lot was accomplished within a relatively short amount of time."

"If *by a lot was accomplished* you mean I can barely walk, then yes, you're correct." I'd never had sex in a moving vehicle before, and considering my rigid seatbelt safety policy, it hadn't ever occurred to me that it would be something I'd want to do. Hudson, however, made everything seem like something I'd want to do, when it involved him anyway. And the man's skills in the bedroom apparently carried to the backseats of cars as well, his expert techniques and positions making me come without ever having to unbuckle.

We walked along a pathway to the atrium where dinner was being served buffet-style. Around us, the pleasant smells and aromas of the fresh outdoors overcame me, putting me in a relaxed mood that was impossible to achieve in the hustle and bustle of the city. It was amazing that such a place existed so close to the chaos of NYC.

"What is this event for anyway?"

"It's sponsored by CotF," Hudson answered. "Children of the Future. They're a foundation that provides resources for foster children. This event is a thank you for those who have donated."

"And how much have you donated?" It truly interested me the causes Hudson contributed to.

"Not how much, what."

I looked at him questioningly.

"I donated a school."

Holy shit. A whole school. Of course he did.

"And several scholarships on top of that. I came tonight to meet the new principal. I want the foundation's Board of Directors to realize that though I'm not hands-on with their program, I'm still around."

I shivered at his hint at omnipotence. It was the same way he handled all his business, I was finding. He left things in capable hands, yet was never too far away for things to go unnoticed. Hopefully, he trusted me enough to not notice everything going on at The Sky Launch. Like, who I was making deals with for events.

God, I had to stop dwelling on that. Hudson wouldn't find out. It would be fine.

I grabbed a glass of wine off a server's tray as he passed and downed half of it, grateful for the instant buzz.

Hudson kept his arm around me as he greeted people at the buffet. He'd told me once that he never ate at these things and now I understood why. He was too popular to ever pick up any food. I decided to wait to eat with him later, nodding and smiling as he introduced me and made small talk. But, having never been to the Brooklyn Botanic Gardens, I was also eager to explore. So when a new associate came by to say hello, I excused myself politely.

"One moment." Hudson put a finger up to pause the balding man he was speaking with. To me he said, "Alayna, you're welcome to stay."

My heart thumped loud enough I feared he'd hear it. It had been difficult for Hudson to let me in on his business dealings and inviting me to participate was a big step.

"Thank you, but I want to catch the sights before the sun sets." I squeezed his hand. "Unless you need me—"

"No." Though there was a trace of need in his tone. Need like I felt for him every minute of every day—the unquenchable desire to always be near him. "I simply want you to be comfortable. Let me introduce you before you leave. Alayna, this is Aaron Trent. Aaron, this is my girlfriend, Alayna Withers. Perhaps of more interest to you, she's also my promotions manager at The Sky Launch."

I stepped forward to take Aaron's hand.

Aaron's grip was strong, though nothing compared to Hudson's. "Nice to meet you." His greeting was dismissive and he quickly dropped my hand, turning his attention to Hudson. "The Sky Launch? I'd heard you were giving the place a makeover."

"I'm not. Alayna is."

"Great," Aaron said, but his focus stayed on Hudson. "I'd love to chat sometime about what my team could do for you."

Hudson gestured to me. "Alayna's your woman. I'm sure she'd be happy to meet with you. Alayna, Aaron owns an advertising firm. His company is quite excellent. We've used his services many times."

A surge of giddiness shot through me as I understood why Hudson had wanted me to stay. "Ah, Trent Advertising. I didn't realize you were *that* Trent." They were a hard firm to get in with. Hudson introducing me could be a big coup for me. If we were alone, I would have shown Hudson just how much I appreciated the connection.

Finally, Aaron turned to me. "Ms., uh…"

"Withers," Hudson filled in for him.

"Yes, Ms. Withers. Sorry, I've never been good with names."

No, you simply weren't interested in me until you realized I could give you something.

I decided to make it easy for the man. "Mr. Trent, I'd love to meet with you. Should I call your office to set something up?"

"I'd love to stop by the club when it's open, check things out so I can come up with some ideas for a campaign."

"How about tomorrow evening?" Hudson asked.

I deflated momentarily at the thought of spending a Friday evening away from Hudson. But, he was right in his suggestion. Friday was a great night to see the club at its best.

Aaron appeared as if he also regretted giving up a Friday night. But who could say no to Hudson Pierce? "Sure."

"We open at nine, but if you can come by around, say eight-thirty, we could talk a bit before it gets crazy." Good thing I had my business plan already outlined. Otherwise I'd have to pull an all-nighter to be prepared.

Aaron agreed to the time and then began discussing campaign ideas with Hudson. Feeling like a third wheel, I excused myself again, and left to wander.

I made my way first to the Shakespeare Garden with a second glass of champagne in hand, stopping here and there to admire the unusual plants, their fragrances mixing and lying heavily in the sweltering June air. From there, I journeyed through the Japanese Hill-and-Pond Garden. Astounded by the tranquil beauty in the rolling landscape, I found a bench to sit on and enjoy the view as dusk fell as I sipped on my beverage.

Now and then, other guests passed, and eventually a man in a navy suit showed up accompanied by an older gentleman with salt-and-pepper hair that matched his silver three-piece. They lingered over the pond and in the quiet gardens, their conversation drifting over to me.

"The deal closed Monday?" the navy suit asked. "Unfucking believable. You're a lucky son-of-a-bitch, you know that?"

I closed my eyes, hoping to close out the conversation that was in stark contrast to the serenity of the environment. But then, a familiar word caused my ears to perk.

"...Plexis wasn't something he wanted to let go. Had to fight him tooth and nail." It was the older guy speaking now, speaking about Hudson's beloved company that he'd fought to keep from being sold by his shareholders, but lost. "Fortunately, the rest of the board was not on Pierce's side."

This guy must work for the corporation that bought Plexis out from under Hudson.

"So what are your plans now?" the younger guy echoed my internal questions.

"With Plexis? Well, there's a lot of money in it if we break it up and sell off the pieces."

My stomach fell with the salt-and-pepper's admission. It was exactly what Hudson had been afraid would happen. It would mean a lot of jobs lost.

"But we're not discounting the idea of reselling it as a whole." The older man turned toward the younger, eyebrow raised. "If we had a good offer."

"Oh, are you expecting me to offer?" Navy suit guy took a step back. "Don't get me wrong, I'd love to get my hands on Plexis, but I don't have that sort of money right now."

"Just thought I'd put the bug in your ear. In case."

The men resumed walking the path, the older one smiling at me as he passed.

I waited until they were several feet away before I shot up from the bench and headed off in the opposite direction, back toward Hudson. This was his chance to get Plexis back, to turn it into the company he'd envisioned it could be. I'd even helped him work out some preliminary ideas on how to make it profitable. I was as excited as I hoped Hudson would be, *knew* he would be.

It took a bit of searching before I spotted Hudson in the Cherry Esplanade. He was conversing with a striking auburn-haired woman, maybe a little older than me. An unexpected knot of jealousy formed in my gut, and I had to keep myself from running to his side.

He saw me as I approached, his eyes beaming with a fondness that made the knot loosen. "Alayna."

The way my name slid off his tongue—it never failed to make me dizzy.

Hudson turned to the woman who I could now see was definitely older than me, perhaps by ten years. "Please meet my girlfriend, Alayna Withers. She's running the promotional division of one of my nightclubs."

The woman introduced herself before Hudson had a chance. "Hi. Norma Anders." Her focus went right back to Hudson. "I hadn't realized you were seeing anyone, Hudson."

"We've been private. Her wishes, not mine." Hudson's lie tickled me. "But I've finally convinced her we should tell everyone."

Norma's mouth tightened as her eyes swept me from head to toe. "Congratulations, then. Honestly, I'm glad you're done with the Werner girl. She was entirely too bubbly for you, if you ask me. Plus, I never trusted her. She was up to something, Hudson."

I tensed. Never mind that the woman obviously felt familiar enough with my man to give him dating advice, she had thought Celia and Hudson were together. I'd thought that had only been the perception of their parents. Was there something I was missing?

Hudson straightened at the mention of Celia as well, and I felt his eagerness to get away from Norma—to get *me* away from Norma.

"It was nice to see you here tonight, Norma. Those reports—"

She touched his arm as if it was second nature. "I'll get them to you on Monday."

"Thank you, Norma."

It was a good thing Hudson pulled me into his side and led me away or I may have socked the woman in her hazel eye. Or punched him. "First name basis, huh? That's…different." Hudson rarely called anyone by first name unless they were important to him.

He was nonplussed by my aggravation. "We've known each other for years. First name basis becomes inevitable after so much time."

"Why does she think you were seeing Celia?" It felt like the Celia/Hudson conversation was a dead horse, yet new information kept popping up, and there I went beating it again.

"Celia often accompanied me to charity events and functions where Norma saw me socially. You know that."

A blush crept up the back of my neck. I'd never told him that I'd internet-stalked him. That's where I'd seen the dozens of pictures of him with Celia. He knew me too well.

His hand loosened at my hip. "Norma must have assumed we were a couple. It never occurred to me to correct her."

My mouth tasted bitter. "Because you liked that people thought you were with Celia."

"Because I liked that Norma thought I was off-limits."

"Oh." Maybe I could let the Celia horse rest for a while. But now I had a whole other slew of questions about Norma.

But before I could ask, he offered. "Norma manages the financial division of one of my companies."

"Then you're co-workers." I wondered how she'd gotten such an elite position. Had she slept her way to the top? The familiarity she had with him was unnerving.

His mouth twitched, fighting a smile. "Why, Alayna, this shade of jealousy is becoming on you."

I clenched my jaw. "That's not a comforting response."

"Not co-workers. Boss and employee."

Though I appreciated that he'd taken my mood seriously, his answer irked me. Hudson was technically my boss, after all. "That's a familiar scenario."

He stopped suddenly and turned to face me full on, his eyes blazing with determined insistence. "I've never been your boss, Alayna. If anything, you're the one who owns me."

Well, wow.

Whatever Norma had with Hudson, she didn't have what I had. The realization was moving.

Unable to maintain the intense eye contact, I turned my gaze to the Esplanade that I hadn't quite taken in as of yet. The lush grassy spread was lined with large cherry trees, full and green.

Hudson followed my stare. "Have you seen pictures of the cherry blossoms when they're in bloom?"

"No." I'd seen pictures of the Washington D.C. Cherry Blossom Festival and imagined the Esplanade must be nearly as beautiful.

"It's breathtaking. All the trees filled with pink popcorn. The fragrance is absolutely incredible." He swept his thumb across my cheek. "We'll come here in the spring."

"That sounds lovely." I meant it. At the same time, my stomach twisted at both the prospect of still being with Hudson in the spring and the idea that I owned him. Both notions were so completely wonderful and also entirely too rushed. Could I maintain a relationship with him that long? Could I live up to the woman he obviously saw me as to him?

Rather than dwell on it, I refocused my mind on the bit of news that had set me searching for him in the first place. "Hey, I have something to tell you that you might be interested in."

Placing his arm at the small of my back, Hudson directed me out of the Esplanade.

"It doesn't have to be now," I said, realizing his intention to take me up on my information at that very moment. "You can finish your mingling first."

His mouth was hot at my ear. "The only mingling that interests me at the moment is the mingling of our genitalia."

"You're insatiable. You had me in the car." But his suggestion caused my skin to tingle with want and anticipation.

"It wasn't enough." He pulled me off the path through a hole in the hedges—somewhere we certainly weren't allowed to be—and pushed me up against a tall tree, his hip anchoring me in place. "I can never have enough of you."

My breath caught in a moment of complete adoration for the man in front of me. This man who had worked through his own demons to let me in his life, had ignored every natural inclination to stay closed off and instead was trying his damndest to be with me in the way we both wanted.

I buried my gaze in his eyes. "I love you."

He bent closer, his nose grazing the skin of my cheek. "Is that what you pulled me away to tell me? I'm not complaining if it is."

I giggled. "*You* pulled me away, not the other way around, silly. And it's not what I had to tell you. But I'm glad every time I get to say it."

Hudson's mouth curled into a slow smile, but movement on the path nearby caught my attention. I turned my head toward the small group walking up and spotted the salt-and-pepper man walking past. "Actually, you picked the perfect location. You see that man over there?"

Hudson followed my eyes. "The one in the tan?"

"The man next to him." I gave him a minute to make sure he got a good look. "Do you know him?"

"Not that I recall. Should I?"

I shrugged. "Not necessarily. But I overheard him talking with another guy—" I swiveled my neck around, looking for the other man. "—that I can't see right now. Anyway, not important. The salt-and-pepper man works for the company that purchased—wait for it—Plexis."

Hudson relaxed his hold on me and studied the man one more time before he walked past. "How do you know this?"

"I heard him. When I was wandering earlier. He was boasting about how he was lucky to snatch such an amazing company from the likes of Hudson Pierce."

Hudson's posture stiffened. "Go on."

I bit my lip. "You were right. They're planning to dismantle the company."

"Damn it." It wasn't often that Hudson showed any emotion where business was concerned—or showed any emotion period—yet I'd guessed he'd felt passionately about the company he'd lost. Now I knew for sure.

It made my next bit of news so much sweeter to deliver. "But he mentioned that they might be interested in selling if they got a good offer first." I waited until I saw the wheels spinning behind his eyes. "You know what that means? It means all you need to do is get in there with a good offer."

In a flash, he had me pinned again, pushing his body heavily against mine. "How about I get in you with a good offer?"

"Hudson!" I pushed lightly at his chest. "I'm serious."

"So am I." He nibbled along my jawline.

Unable to ever resist his advances, my body was already yielding, melting underneath him, throbbing with need to be closer. Still my brain continued to pursue answers. "I thought Plexis meant something to you."

"It does." He smiled as he bent in toward my lips.

I swerved my head to the side and met his eyes. "Then how come all you can think about is sexing me up? Is that all I am to you?" I knew that wasn't all I was to him, and my words were more playful than anything, but I was disappointed that I'd been wrong about Hudson's commitment to Plexis.

Adjusting his grip on me, he pressed tight to me again, and moved his lips near my ear. "No, it's not. You know that your business mind turns me on to no end, especially when your business mind is looking out for my interests. And because I'm not skilled at expressing how I feel in words, I'm wishing I could show you exactly how into you I am at the moment."

I melted. Completely.

Still my brain struggled for more validation, my voice sounding soft and full of need. "So you're grateful for the information?"

"Very." He thrust against me, his hard bulge showing me exactly how grateful.

I squirmed, trying to touch as much of him with as much of me as possible. "And you're attracted to me beyond the physical?" My words were thick.

But I must have been coherent enough to be understood, because he responded between kissing and licking at my neck. "I'm attracted to everything about you—your body, your mind, your sass. Even your 'crazy,' as you call it."

"You're crazy, too, if you're serious about that last one."

His head jerked up so I could see the sincerity in his eyes. "I've never been more serious, Alayna. You're the first person I've ever met who makes me believe I might *not* be crazy. It's the best thing that's ever happened to me. *You're* the best thing that's ever happened to me."

The world stood still around me, and all I could see and hear and feel was Hudson in front of me, on me, in my skin, in my bones. "You need to rethink that whole I'm-not-good-with-words angle, because those words were perfect."

His nose brushed mine as he nodded once. "Now stop talking and let me occupy your mouth in other ways."

"What happened to that good offer you had?" I bucked my hips forward, searching for something to rub against, to ease the ache growing between my legs.

"Patience, precious. Patience." His lips took mine, caressing against them lightly at first then crushing forcefully, as his tongue lapped hungrily inside my mouth. Cupping his hands on each side of my face, he controlled our movements, pulling sweet sighs from my throat that he swallowed with his deep kiss. My own hands pressed into the tree, the bark stinging against my skin in stark contrast to the sweet ecstasy of Hudson's mouth on mine.

I was lost to everything but him and his all-consuming kiss.

"Excuse me. Excuse me." I vaguely heard the woman speaking, barely registered her clearing her throat. "Excuse me!"

We broke apart as it finally clicked that someone was speaking to us.

"Excuse me, but the lawn is off limits except for in—" The woman's voice broke off. "Oh, Mr. Pierce. I didn't realize that...Alayna?"

Still half-dazed, I turned toward the voice. "Julia? What are you—" Julia had said that she had an event later in the day. "Is your company in charge tonight?"

"Yeah."

The good feelings that had spread from head to toe during Hudson's dominating kiss vanished with a whoosh. This was Julia's event. Julia was standing right here. And if Julia was here, Paul had to be here as well.

With effort, I swallowed. "Ha, wow. What a coincidence." Did I sound flakey? Nervous? Scared out of my mind?

I gestured toward Julia. "Hudson, this is Julia Swaggert. She's the owner of Party Planners Plus. I met with her today." *And my ex-subject of stalking, Paul Kresh, who better not be anywhere nearby or I'm going to shit a brick.* "Julia, this is Hudson Pierce."

The normally confident and assured Julia seemed flustered. "I'm…Mr. Pierce, it's an honor to meet you. I'm really excited about the potential our companies have working together." Her face was lit with delight, and I realized just how much this deal meant to her. Understood why Paul was so willing to risk having me around.

As he had done earlier with Aaron, Hudson deferred the attention to me. "You're in good hands with Alayna. She takes care of all business with the club. I'm merely a name on the deed." He touched my arm lightly. "If you'll both pardon me, I see someone I need to speak with."

There was no one anywhere near our hideout, and I recognized Hudson's words as a line to leave me to my work. I'd never been more grateful. Not only for letting me own my business deals in full, but because with him gone, the chance of Paul coming up in conversation—or in real life—wasn't as threatening.

Julia stared after Hudson as he walked away. I didn't blame her. He was hot coming and going.

"So you and Hudson Pierce?" She waggled her eyebrows. "Is it simply a getting frisky in the moonlight thing or the whole enchilada?"

"It's, well, both. We're together, if that's what the whole enchilada means." But I didn't want to talk about my boyfriend. I wanted to know about hers. "Speaking of 'together,' where's Paul?"

She pursed her lips. "He's about somewhere. He usually stays behind the scenes at these things."

"Ah, of course." He was there, though. Which meant I needed to not be. "Well, I think Hudson was about ready to call it a night—"

"Yeah, it certainly appeared as such. Lucky you."

Her sigh made me wonder how long it had been since she and Paul got frisky. I didn't wonder too hard. Thinking about Paul and his relationships was the last thing I wanted to do. A polar opposite to the way I'd been when I'd known him before.

"Well, I should get back as well," she said, sounding reluctant.

But I'd already slipped through the space in the hedge. I spun around to give her a final wave. "Nice to see you at work! You're good."

"Thanks."

I was teeming with anxiety as I searched for Hudson. Paul Kresh was nearby. We had to leave. We had to leave before Hudson discovered my worst mistake had reentered my life.

I'd only made it a few feet along the pathway when Hudson stepped out from a nearby bush and took my hand, pulling me back toward the garden entrance.

"We need to leave. Now." His tone was forceful, urgent.

Fuck. He knew. Had he overheard us talking? Would he assume that any Paul mentioned would be Paul Kresh?

I played innocent, in case I was wrong—*hoping* I was wrong. "Why? What's the problem?" My heart stopped while I waited for his response.

Instead of answering, he took my hand and placed it over his still hard cock.

"Oh, my." I hoped my exhalation sounded like awe rather than relief. Especially since some of it *was* awe. I was always impressed by Hudson's penis. Even in the middle of a personal crisis.

I turned my flirt on full force, knowing that it was my easy ticket out of there. "Or you could take me here in the gardens."

"Don't tempt me. I'm near throwing you on that bench over there, but that might not be in the best of taste. And I wouldn't want to tarnish your reputation." His eyes darted toward me. "Besides, what I have in store for you will take most of the night and I'm sure the Brooklyn Botanic Society would prefer to close before I'm anywhere near finished."

Instantly, I needed a change of panties. "Um, okay."

"Is that a problem?"

"Not at all."

We were almost at the park entrance when Hudson cursed.

"What is it?"

"I see someone I should talk to. Do you mind?"

I was hot and needy and desperate to be jumped, so yes, I minded. But a glance at Hudson said he minded more. "Considering how you're walking, I think you'll be the miserable one."

He gave me a pained glare and began leading me toward a group of gentleman talking nearby.

Then I saw him, out of the corner of my eye. I turned my head to be sure it was him. It was. Paul Kresh in the flesh. Twice in one day, what were the chances? He wasn't with the men that Hudson needed to speak to, thank god, but standing near the Visitor Center talking to a server balancing a tray of empty champagne glasses.

I started to look away but not in time. Our eyes met across the sidewalk. "Hudson, I'll let you talk with your peeps. I'm going to look for the girl's room."

He pulled me closer. "Maybe I'll have to come find you there when I'm done here," he whispered before kissing me on the forehead.

I felt the blush spread down my neck, even though his words were rather innocent compared to how he usually talked. But I was so aroused already that anything he did or said was a trigger. It was also inconvenient. I didn't want to be flustered and horny when I spoke to Paul. He'd surely assume it was for him.

I took deep breaths as I walked toward Paul, calming myself. He waited until I was only a couple of feet away before he spoke. "Should I be worried that you're stalking me? Again?"

I rolled my eyes.

"Don't bother explaining." He nodded toward the man I'd left. "That was Hudson Pierce, wasn't it? If you're with him, I get why you're here."

I tried not to let it bother me that he knew so much personal info about me. Julia would have told him eventually anyway. "Yes, that's Hudson. We're seeing each other."

"Huh."

I watched the gears spin behind his eyes. I didn't spend months memorizing every detail about him to not realize what he was thinking. "Hey, there's nothing to gain from this information, Paul. He knows about you and my past, knows about the restraining order, and if you have any intention—"

"What the fuck intention would I have? You're acting like I'd blackmail you or something. Which is pretty ballsy coming from someone who handcuffed herself to my desk naked."

"I'd say it's a damn fair assumption since you pretty much blackmailed me just this afternoon."

"That...wasn't blackmail. Exactly." He rubbed at his nose, like Pinocchio disguising his lie. "It was heavy-handed persuasion."

"Whatever it was, it was pressure, and I didn't like it."

"Look, Laynie—"

"I know, I know." I didn't need him to try to persuade or pressure or whatever the hell he wanted to call it. I got it already. "You want this deal for Julia, and because I really want to work with her, I'm agreeing to it. But

I don't want any interaction with you. Zip. Nada. I don't want to bump into you at events or have you showing up at my club or calling me—none of it. I want the restraining order restrictions to be adhered to. This can't come back to bite me in the ass, okay?"

"Fine. Whatever." But the victory gleamed in his eyes. "It won't come back to bite you. It's only me and you this affects."

"Tell that to Hudson. He would not like it if he found out that I signed a deal that even remotely involved you." And suddenly I realized that if I didn't want Hudson to find out about Paul, I couldn't tell him about meeting with Celia either. It would open the door for him to find out the things she and I had talked about. Like Paul. And there was no way Hudson would take that lying down.

"Why would he care? As long as we keep it professional and at a distance like you said, this doesn't have anything to do with him."

"Because, while you and I both know that most everything that happened between us was my fault—"

"Most everything? Try everything."

I gave him a stern look. "You did cheat on your fiancé."

Paul shrugged.

What an ass. "Anyway, Hudson doesn't see you as innocent. And it's not because I said anything to point you out, it's simply because..." I couldn't finish the statement. I didn't have the answer. "I don't know why. He sees the good in me for some reason." Good that I was beginning to doubt existed.

Paul chortled. "I didn't know from his reputation that he was a psycho."

I stepped forward, closing in on his personal space. "You know what? You need to shut the fuck up. He is not a psycho. I am not a psycho. You, however, are an asshole. I can still back out of this shit. Go ahead and throw whatever you want to throw at me, I have Hudson Pierce on my side."

"And wouldn't he love it if the whole world knew about his girlfriend's criminal past? He'd be a laughing stock. Especially when I tell everyone how you sought out Party Planners Plus so you could work with me again."

My heart felt like I'd been dropped three stories. "But that's not true."

He shrugged again, that carefree shrug of someone holding all the cards. "People don't care if it's true. They love gossip, particularly when it's about the elite."

My mouth tasted sour. "I thought this wasn't blackmail."

"Not yet, it isn't." He leveled his gaze at me. "Does it need to be?"

A chill ran down my spine. I was trapped, as I'd known I was earlier, and I knew it even more definitively now. "Fine, Paul. I'll do the deal but on the terms I listed." Over his shoulder I saw Hudson striding our way. "I'm walking away now. Smile and head the other direction."

I didn't know if he did what I said because I left him, striding to meet Hudson before he came any nearer. "Hey." I felt breathy and lightheaded and not in a good way.

"Did you find the restroom?"

"Um, no." Thank god I hadn't really needed to go. "It's okay. I can wait until we get home."

I tried to turn him toward the exit, but Hudson looked questionably back toward where Paul was retreating.

Thinking fast, I filled him in with a story before he had a chance to ask. "That was one of the event workers. I was trying to get the dirt on Party Planners from him."

He raised a brow. "It seemed to be a rather animated discussion."

"Yeah, he was passionate about what he was saying." Then I realized it was probably me who had seemed animated. "I guess it got me riled up too. He says they're a great company all around. I'm more excited than ever to work with them." The lie felt heavy on my tongue, my gut twisting with the acid of it. It made me wonder how I'd spent so many years lying and manipulating people so I could be close to men who didn't want me. It had been so easy then. Now, with the man who did want me, it felt gross and disgusting.

Hudson bought my act, which made me feel all the worse for it. "That's excellent." He drew me into his side. "Want to know what I'm more excited than ever about? Getting home. More specifically, getting *you* home. Or, at least to the car."

"Me, too." Whatever he planned to do to me would take me away from everything else in the world. It would distract me from my secrets and the blackmail and the promises I'd broken. At least, I hoped it would.

— CHAPTER —

EIGHT

We were still curled up together when Hudson's alarm woke us the next morning. He kissed me breathless before pulling me with him out of the bed.

"You start the shower," he ordered. "I'll start the coffee."

Grinning, I did as instructed, traipsing to the bathroom to pee first. Then I turned on the shower, waiting until the water was nice and hot before stepping in.

This. Was. Awesome.

Not only the double oversized nozzles that sprayed down on me, relaxing my sex-sore muscles, but the entire routine. Making love in the middle of the night, waking with my lover, preparing the shower for him, for us—I could do this every day.

I sighed softly at the idea, letting the too-soon fantasy of living with Hudson take me away for the briefest of moments.

"Well, the look on your face says you might not need me anymore for pleasure." Hudson stepped into the stall, immediately tugging me into his arms, as if he wanted to be in constant contact the way I did.

"This shower is amazeballs," I said, my eyes drawn immediately to the semi-erection pressed between us. Could I never get enough of seeing him naked?

"Amazeballs?"

"But it can never compare to what you do to me." My hand closed around his divine penis, my mouth watering as always at the size and shape of him.

He moaned, turning harder in my hand. "What if I did amazeballs things to you while we're in the amazeballs shower?"

It was hard not to giggle at his use of urban vernacular. It was so foreign, so unlike him. So absolutely irresistible. "There's not even a word for how amazeballs that would be."

AFTER OUR SHOWER, we went about getting ready for our day. Hudson named one of the sinks as mine, and side-by-side he shaved and I powdered, each of us wearing only a towel. Again, I thought how easy it would be to fall into this life. How natural.

He finished in the bathroom first and by the time I came out, he was dressed in a two-piece black suit that made my thighs twitch. God, the man was the yummiest thing on the planet.

"Hungry?"

Could he read my mind? "Oh, for breakfast?"

"Yes, for breakfast. Get your mind out of the gutter, precious. I've already spent more time than I allotted on you this morning."

I shivered at the memory of being pressed against the shower wall, his dick inside me. "Well, I'm glad to know there was an allotment."

"There was." He walked past me toward the bedroom door and I caught the scent of his aftershave. "Toast and grapefruit okay?"

"Perfect," I said, inhaling his amazing smell. "Meet you out there."

I threw on the only dress left hanging in the spare closet, wishing I had something a little more businesslike for my meetings that day. Which made me face the issue I'd been avoiding—my apartment. I needed to stop by there. I also needed to figure out what I was going to do about a place to live. My lease was ending and since my brother was no longer paying my rent, I'd have to find something more affordable.

It would certainly be easier to move in with Hudson.

But it would be a bad idea, I reminded myself. *Too soon, too soon, too soon.* Plus, he hadn't even made the offer.

Once dressed, my hair tied in a knot at my nape, I joined Hudson at the kitchen table. He'd already set out my breakfast with a travel mug of coffee.

"I didn't know what time you were planning to be out of here so I gave you that." He nodded at the travel mug.

"Soon. I have an appointment at ten-thirty with a graphic designer to go over new menus, and I want to make sure I have my presentation for tonight's meeting with Aaron Trent ready before that, because I have a crap load of other things to do this afternoon." I was rambling, a bit nervous about my day's to-do list.

Hudson raised a brow. "A crap load of things?"

"Yeah. I'm sure Trent will want a formal marketing plan, and I need to set up some interviews for an additional cook." I took a swallow of my coffee. "And I really should go home."

"Home." It wasn't a question, merely a repeat of my word, but his tone was darker, surprised. Disappointed maybe.

"My apartment."

"I understood the reference. Why?"

I stabbed at my grapefruit with my spoon. "I don't know. I need to pick up my mail and check on things. Make sure the place is okay. You know, all my stuff is there."

I'd known the conversation would be awkward when I began it. Though it was necessary to go to my place, I didn't want Hudson to think I didn't want to be with him, that I didn't want to be invited back. The best way to get that across was to be straightforward about it. "I should get another change of clothes if you're inviting me to stay the night again."

Hudson dropped his own spoon with a noisy clank. "Inviting you to stay the night? What are you talking about? I gave you a key. You can come and go as you please."

I leaned forward, a big grin on my face. "So, then I definitely need a change of clothes. Because it pleases me to spend the night with you."

"It pleases me for you to spend the night with me, too." He wiped his mouth with his napkin and set it over his plate. "And as long as we're talking about it, it would please me if you would spend all your nights here and if all your things were here as well."

I froze. There it was. At least, I thought that there it was. I needed clarification before I freaked. "What are you…I don't know what you're saying."

"Yes, you do. But I'll spell it out if that makes you feel better." He stood and took his dish to the sink as he spoke. When he returned, he remained standing, leaning against the breakfast bar behind him. He probably didn't realize the impact of his towering presence. Or perhaps he did. Perhaps it was purposeful. He did know how to mold a situation to his favor.

"Yes, spell it out." My voice squeaked, unsure whether to be excited or terrified.

"Why do you need your apartment? Your lease is almost up. Move in here."

I didn't even bother asking how he knew about my lease. If I thought about it too hard, I'd worry about the safety of my other secrets. Besides, I was too stunned by his statement to be able to think about anything but those three words: *Move in here.*

"I love that I can still shock you." Hudson tilted his head, looking at me from a new angle. "But I'd prefer that this wasn't one of the times that I did. What about that plan is shocking to you?"

Shaking, I set my spoon down. Even though I'd only eaten half of my fruit, there was no way I was eating more. I could barely formulate thought let alone think about chewing and swallowing. "Well, um, it's just, it's awfully soon."

He frowned. "It is. It's unfortunate that a lengthy time span is regarded as such an important element to appropriate landmarks in relationships. It shouldn't be a factor."

"But shouldn't it?" I shifted on my chair to face him head-on.

"Not for me. As I said before, when I have a plan, I commit. I plan to be with you as much as possible. And not only in the carnal sense. Moving in is a logical way to make that happen."

I stood, gathering my dishes to take to the sink. I had to clutch them against my body so he didn't hear them rattle in my unsteady hands. "And that's another reason it might not be a good idea. It seems a little like a business plan. Like this is the next step on a list. Not very romantic or anything."

His voice tightened. "I didn't realize you were in need of romance. You know that's not in my nature."

"Hey." I waited until he turned to face me, the breakfast bar between us. "That's bullshit. You say you aren't romantic, but you really are very much so." The things he'd said the night before, for example. "I wasn't complaining about your romantic overtures."

"Then what are you complaining about?" He seemed genuinely confused.

"Nothing! I'm complaining about nothing."

"You were complaining about the way I asked you to move in with me."

"No, I'm not." I shifted my eyes. "Okay, yes, I was. A little, but that's not why I'm saying no."

This took him aback. "You're saying no?"

"No." *Wait.* "I mean, yes." Except, I didn't really want to say no. I wanted to be with Hudson all the time, like how he'd said he wanted to be with me. Still, the length of time we'd been together…"I mean, I don't know."

Hudson came around the bar and put a hand on each of my upper arms. "Alayna, do you know how you feel about me?"

"Yes. I love you. You know that."

"Then move in with me."

I bit my lip and tugged on his lavender tie. "I have to think."

He put a finger under my chin and lifted my face so I was forced to meet his eyes. "Why?"

"I just do." I pulled away, unable to concentrate with his hands on me. Unable to stand my ground with the electricity surging between us as it always did when we touched.

Turning back to the sink for distraction, I dumped the grapefruit shells into the garbage and ran water over our dishes. "This is big, and yes, it would make things easier and I can't deny that I want to—"

"Then do it."

"—but I don't know if it's the right thing to do." I turned off the water and flicked my wet hands over the sink. Without facing him, I admitted the heart of my hesitation. "I'm falling for you too hard, Hudson. Too fast and that scares me."

"Falling? Or fallen?"

Both. Every time I was certain I'd met my max capacity of love for him, that I'd fallen as far as I possibly could, he'd go and do or say something spectacular and I'd find I loved him even more. "Either way, does it matter?"

"If you've already fallen, then why are you worried anymore about whether it's too hard or too fast? It's already done. That's how I'm approaching it."

There it was again—an allusion to the way he felt about me without an actual declaration. That was a problem right there, wasn't it? How could I live with a man who couldn't even say he loved me?

I took a deep breath and turned to him once again. "Can I just have a little time to think about it? When I'm away from you?"

He stiffened. "Are you suggesting that I'm pressuring you?"

"I'm suggesting that you're distracting. And yes, it's pressure, whether you mean for it to be or not. And honestly, a tiny bit manipulative. And with your past, it does cross my mind that maybe you want to control me, and that this is the easiest way for you to do so."

His expression hardened and I ran to him, wrapping my arms around his neck. "Now, don't, don't be upset, H. I'm not saying you are manipulating me or that you want to control me, I'm saying I need time to think. To be sure. Give it to me. Please?"

"If that's what you need." His tone was chilly, his arms remaining at his sides, even as I held him.

I curled my fingers into the hair at the back of his neck. "Hudson!"

"What?"

"Don't be like this."

He remained stiff. "I'm not being like anything."

"Then are we okay?" I pressed kisses underneath his jaw, wanting—no, *needing*—him to yield to me, to give in to my embrace.

He exhaled, finally wrapping his arms around me. "Of course we are." He kissed the top of my head. "Always."

HUDSON'S DRIVER PICKED him up at the same time Jordan arrived for me. The minute I was alone in the backseat of the Maybach, I pulled out my phone to call Liesl. I had to talk to someone about Hudson's move-in proposition, and she was the person I turned to when things got rough. I stopped before I dialed, however. Liesl had worked for me the night before. She'd likely still be sleeping. Besides, even though she knew me, she didn't know Hudson. Not truly. Knowing Hudson was a vital part of helping me make a sound decision.

But there was someone who did know Hudson—knew Hudson very well. And I had her number.

When Celia didn't answer, I hung up and redialed as she'd instructed. It took until the third call before I got through to her. I considered telling her my news on the phone but decided we might need something more personal. At least, *I* needed something more personal, so we arranged to meet for lunch at one.

Celia was already seated when I arrived at A Voce. I waited until after the waitress had taken my order for an iced tea and chicken and watercress salad before diving into conversation.

Though I'd planned to lead with Hudson's invitation to move in, it was something else entirely that came out of my mouth. "What do you know about Norma Anders?" She'd invaded my thoughts several times since she'd put her hand on Hudson's and he'd called her by her first name.

Celia's brows rose. "Ah, you heard about the slut."

"You mean, Hudson and—" My stomach churned. Maybe I shouldn't have asked.

"Honestly, I don't know for sure. It's not like Hudson discusses his conquests with me. And if I had to guess, I'd say no because if he had fucked her—sorry, that was a bit coarse, but you know what I mean—if he had, then he'd be done with her and she certainly wouldn't still be working with him."

I wanted to grab on to Celia's words like a lifeline and believe there was no way Hudson had been...*intimate*...with Norma Anders. But there were holes in her theory. "That's if he slept with her when he was still, you know, messing with women. He hasn't done any of that for a while, right? Like not in the last two years."

Her forehead creased. "Uh, yeah. Of course."

"So Hudson could have slept with her after he'd started therapy and then it wouldn't have been such a big deal for him to keep her employed."

Celia nodded. "I get you. But I still don't think so. Here's the thing. Norma's always been after him. From way before he ever had therapy. And I can't tell you how many functions I went to where I watched her try to seduce him, hence the reason I refer to her as *the slut*. Yet despite all her attempts, he never made any move to play her."

"Which makes it all more likely that he'd go to her *after* therapy. Trust me, I know." It made perfect sense. The people I'd dated since therapy had been the safe ones, the men I didn't feel intensely about. If Hudson had never been interested in playing Norma, then she was similarly safe.

On the other hand, Hudson had told me more than once that he'd never wanted to play me either. Did he refrain from playing Norma for similar reasons? Because he felt something for her?

The idea made me sick with jealousy.

And it didn't give me any answers as to whether or not she was special to him now or in the past. If I really wanted to know, I'd have to look closer at Norma. I made a mental note to do a Google search in my free time.

Then I deleted the mental note.

What the hell was I thinking? Internet-stalking was for the old Alayna Withers. I would not stoop to that level. Hudson wanted me with him. Always. What other proof did I need to know I was the important woman in his life?

We halted the conversation to let the waitress serve us. When we were alone again, I started up as if we'd never stopped. "You're probably right. I don't know why I'm worrying about it, really. I'm the one he asked to move in with him, not her."

"Exactly." Her smile vanished. "Wait, what? He asked you to move in? That's awesome!"

It was awesome. Utterly awesome, and for the first time, I let myself truly feel the awesomeness of it rather than just the fear. I played it casually though, shrugging it off as no big deal. "I don't know. It's too soon. Isn't it too soon?"

"Whatever. Are there rules about these things?" Celia talked around a forkful of salad. "When Hudson knows what he wants, he doesn't hesitate."

I tried not to let it bother me that Celia knew Hudson cold. "He told me pretty much the same thing." I swallowed. "When I told him no."

"You didn't!" She gasped and her expression matched her surprised exclamation.

"I did. Well, I said I'd think about it."

Celia was beyond excited. "And now you've thought about it and you're going to say yes. You have to say yes. How can you not say yes? This is Hudson Pierce!"

"I don't love him for that reason." Not because he was world renowned billionaire business mogul Hudson Pierce, anyway. But because he was who he was—unique and special in so many ways.

"All the more reason you have to say yes. And that's exactly why you're the one he wants. You aren't caught up in the show that surrounds him. You can't imagine how few people are." She pulled her loose blonde hair to one side of her head. "Jesus, Alayna, you're perfect for him. You have to move in. You'll break his heart if you don't. He so obviously loves you."

Was it really that obvious? "He still hasn't said it."

"But didn't he? Asking you to move in with him…that seems like saying it to me. In the only way Hudson can."

Just like how he'd needed to show me the night before how he felt about me with his body since he couldn't say it with words.

Okay. Maybe Celia had a point.

Or she simply understood my lover way better than I did.

"Damn it." I had wanted to be responsible this time. Wanted to ride this relationship with caution, to not fuck any of it up like I usually did, and here both Hudson and Celia had compelling reasons to throw all caution to the wind. "I do need a new place to live."

"Get out! This is perfect then. Like, fated or whatever."

It had been convenient that I'd found Hudson just when Brian had decided to stop supporting me. I hadn't ever bought into the idea of fate or destiny, but maybe there was something about being meant for each other that deserved to be credited. Or else Hudson merely had impeccable timing. Whatever the reason, we'd found each other, and thinking about the immensity of that made me choke up. "Ah, I can't talk about this anymore. It's making me all twitchy and emotional."

Celia smiled with equally watery eyes. "But you're going to say yes, right?"

I gave an almost imperceptible nod.

"You are!" Celia clapped her hands together. "I feel like I should hug you. I'm a hugger. But we're eating and in a restaurant so maybe that would be weird. This will have to do." She placed her hand over mine and squeezed.

I was beyond grateful that we were at a restaurant because I was not a hugger. The hand squeeze was a good compromise and actually sort of nice. It was good to have a friend that really understood the things I was going through. That's what Celia was now to me—a friend.

She was still beaming when she took her hand off mine. "When are you going to tell him? Tonight?"

"No. I don't think so. I have a meeting at eight-thirty so he's taking me to an early dinner at six and I don't want to tell him when we're rushed."

She frowned. "You have a meeting? Tonight?"

"Yeah. Why do you think that's weird?" Or was I misreading her expression?

"Not weird. Just horrible that you have to work on a Friday evening. Doesn't the fact that you're sleeping with the boss award you certain privileges?"

I laughed. "You would think. It was Hudson that set it up for me, and I don't want to look a gift horse in the mouth."

"Oh. Interesting." She smoothed her eyebrows with her index finger, as if they would have gotten out of place. "Who's the meeting with anyway?"

"Aaron Trent."

"Wow. Major score, Laynie." For a minute I thought she might give me a high five. "I guess you can't complain about landing a meeting with Aaron Trent. Even if it occupies your Friday night."

"And that's the privilege I get for sleeping with the boss. Good contacts. I owe Hudson big time." I thought about what I'd said. "Except he hates being referred to as my boss."

"Why doesn't that surprise me?"

"So I'll tell him I'll move in tomorrow. No big deal. Then I can plan some way special to tell him." Or at least make sure that there would be time for celebrating after, because there was no way I'd make it through that conversation without being mauled. Not that I was complaining.

"Hey, can I borrow your phone a minute?" Celia held her hand out expectantly.

"Uh, yeah." I unlocked my screen and handed it over, curiosity lacing my tone.

"Thanks. Mine is acting so stupid. It doesn't ring half the time, which I figure is part of the reason I never get to the phone." She dialed some numbers on my phone and waited. "See? Not ringing." She hit redial and tried again. "Nothing. I guess I need to take my phone in. Thanks."

"No problem." I took my phone back and stuck it in my bra. "Oh, I, um, I didn't end up telling Hudson I saw you yesterday."

"Decided it was too tricky of a convo?"

"It never came up. And then after today—"

"You aren't going to tell him," she finished for me. "I wouldn't either. I mean, I really don't want to encourage secrets, but this is really no big deal. And Hudson would make it a big deal."

"A huge deal." Especially considering the subject matter of our discussion. "So we're good keeping it on the down low?"

"I won't say a word. Pinky swear."

"Pinky swear." I waved my little finger in the air, mimicking her.

Hopefully pinky swears actually counted for something in the rich, exotic world of Celia Werner and Hudson Pierce. Because things were going so well in my life, and that meant I had so much to lose. All it would take is a little slip of the tongue from one of us to knock down my beautiful house of cards.

— CHAPTER —

NINE

The rest of the afternoon flew by as I finished up my marketing plan for my meeting with Aaron Trent. Then, an email from Julia with suggestions for package changes occupied me long enough that I had to put off going to my apartment for another time. All in all, it was a productive day, and by the time Hudson texted that he was on his way, I was famished and eager to see my man.

I stopped at the upstairs bar when I saw purple hair dancing behind the counter. "Liesl!" It hadn't occurred to me how much I'd miss my co-worker when I changed my schedule to work days.

"Hey, girlfriend!" Liesl knew me well enough to know I preferred to keep my personal space. Instead of a hug, she offered a high five. "You're looking hot." She chomped her gum as she looked me up and down. "Things must still be good with Houston Piers."

"Hudson Pierce," I corrected. "Say it with me."

She blew a big bubble and let it pop. "I know his name. Now. I just like dickin' with you." She grinned. "Tell me all about you and the psychotically hot one. And start with the sex."

"That would take a while." I suddenly wished I wasn't on my way out, that I had time to sit and chat with my friend. I'd lied to her like I'd lied to everyone when the Hudson/Alayna coupledom was pretend, even though I'd ached to tell her the truth. And at the sight of her, I ached again to tell her how amazing things were going, but I'd have to give her the backstory to explain why things were different than the last time I'd said things were amazing. Given the chance, I'd tell her everything. But I didn't have that chance at the moment, and a sadness settled over me at the realization of how far apart we'd grown over the last couple of weeks.

She pinned me with a penetrating stare. "But things are good?"

I knew what she was really asking—was I still in control of my obsessing? Was I still sane? "Things are very good, actually. Wanna do lunch some time and catch up?"

Her eyes went wide. "Definitely. I miss you!"

"I miss you, too!" Having Celia as a friend didn't take the place of Liesl. I'd have to make a better effort to stay in touch.

"You have your purse on your shoulder. Does that mean you're leaving?" She leaned her elbows on the bar and rested her chin in her hands.

"I am. But I'll be back. Hudson's taking me to dinner."

"Yeah, dinner. That's what it's called." She winked. "But David said you'd been here all day, so why are you coming back? We got your night shifts covered."

"I know, and thanks so much for that. But I have a meeting later."

"Oh." She tugged at her purple strands that I noticed now had blue highlights added. "Wait, does that meeting of yours happen to be with some Trent guy?"

"Yes—" *How did she...* "Liesl, is there something you forgot to tell me?"

She popped another bubble, the watermelon scent wafting to me. "Yeah, his secretary called a while ago and said he needs to reschedule." She shrugged.

I clapped my hand to my forehead.

"Sorry. Guess I forgot to mention it."

"No, it's fine. It's actually awesome news. Okay, maybe not exactly awesome since I spent all flipping day preparing to meet with the guy, but now I have Friday night off."

"And now you're not coming back." Liesl put on her best pout.

"Nope. My turn to say sorry." My phone buzzed with a text from Hudson saying he was outside. "That's Hudson. Gotta go."

"You're choosing him over me?" Liesl loved to play up the drama.

"You don't have the goods that Hudson does." I pushed my purse strap higher on my shoulder.

"I have different goods. Still good goods, though. You just need to give them a chance!"

I laughed as I walked away, waving over my shoulder. Liesl was bi-curious and often pretended to flirt with me. At least, I thought she was pretending. Didn't matter, I had no interest in women sexually. No interest in anyone but the man waiting for me outside.

I stepped out of the club and shielded my eyes against the sun, expecting to see the Maybach. Instead, a black limousine was at the curb. Upon seeing me, Jordan climbed out of the car and circled to open the back door.

"Hey," I said, to Jordan, ogling him as discreetly as I could. He was too yummy not to.

"Good evening, Ms. Withers."

I stepped in the car, my heart immediately picking up its pace at the sight of Hudson waiting inside. "A limousine two nights in a row? What's the occasion this time?"

"I thought we had a nice drive yesterday."

The door shut behind me, and I was already scooting toward Hudson as he reached for me, pulling me into his lap.

"A nice drive or a nice ride?" I was already slippery down below remembering our trip to the Botanic Gardens. I would not be opposed to a repeat performance.

"If I remember correctly, you rode. I drove." His mouth found mine, one hand cradling my face as the other wrapped around my waist. He sucked at my bottom lip before slipping in to lick along my teeth. I stroked my tongue under the bottom of his until he accepted the invitation to dance, wrapping around mine as our lips shifted and molded against each other.

The lurch of the car pulling into traffic pulled me out of our embrace. I maneuvered to the seat next to Hudson and latched my belt. A part of me was surprised that he hadn't brought up moving in again or that he wasn't tense waiting for my answer. Now that my night was free, I could go ahead and tell him over dinner. Or screw dinner and tell him in the car. But I'd wanted the moment to be right. "So…how was your day?"

He put his arm around my shoulder, holding me as close as safety would allow. His fingers played with the loose tendrils of hair at my neck. "You were there for the only part of today that mattered. And that part was fantastic."

He took my hand in his, caressing it, and the way he moved his fingers across my skin lit my whole body on fire. "How about your day?"

"Ditto." I'd been eager to share the details of what I was working on in the club. But now that I was with him, business could wait. Now my only interest was us. Us together. Us in love. "Though, I do have a surprise for you."

His lips curled into a devilish grin. "Are you not wearing underwear?" His hand slid between my thighs as if he was determined to discover the answer for himself.

I smacked his hand away even though I burned to have his fingers go further, to rub against my clit in that expert way of his. We'd get there soon enough. I had time to tease. We had all night now that my meeting had been canceled. "I'm wearing underwear, you perv. If you'd wanted me to go without, you shouldn't have stocked me with panties."

"The panties were for when you were in the company of others. And right now we're alone."

I nodded toward the direction of the front seat, knowing full well that Jordan couldn't see or hear us behind the dark divider. "Somewhat."

"Somewhat enough." He let go of my hand and placed it high on my thigh instead. The gleam in his eyes said he was planning to ravage me right there in the back of his limo on the way to dinner. Again. "Tell me your surprise."

"I spent most of my day preparing for my meeting with Aaron Trent. And I just found out he canceled."

"He canceled?" Hudson was instantly furious. He pulled out his phone and scrolled through his contacts. "Let me call him. If he can't bother to show up tonight then he doesn't need to bother working on my other accounts with him."

I put my hand over his, stilling his phone search. "He must have had a good reason to cancel. I'll call him in the morning. It's not a biggie. I had a long day anyway and I'm happy to postpone."

"Then I'll call to reschedule."

"No, let me. Please." I hadn't realized how important this was to me until right then. Yes, I'd landed the connection because of Hudson and I'd likely get a good deal because of him as well. But I needed a chance to prove what I could do. "I'd like to handle this on my own."

Hudson sighed, pocketing his phone. "If that's what you want. But tell me if he doesn't give you the respect you deserve."

"Because my rich, powerful boyfriend stepping in to fight my battles will earn his esteem."

"Isn't that what boyfriends are supposed to do?"

"Um, not my boyfriend." Leaning into the crook of his arm, I traced my finger along the curve of his jaw. "I'll let you know when I need you, H. For now, though, let me do this myself?"

"Of course." He captured my finger between his teeth and chewed on the pad. I was wet instantly.

My eyes never left his mouth, riveted to the things he was doing to my finger—promises for later that evening. Or sooner, the way things were progressing. "And, the awesome thing about him canceling is that now you've got me all night. Whatcha gonna do with me?"

He removed my finger from his mouth. "You're not going back tonight?"

"Nope. I'm all yours. You can take me out, and then I can take you in." I waggled my brows suggestively. I hadn't had that many opportunities to play with Hudson, and I was enjoying myself. Our relationship before had been confined to "show" and "sex." This in between stuff was still new. And awfully fun.

Hudson sat up straighter, his arm moving from my shoulder to the back of the seat instead. "Actually, I can't." He didn't meet my eyes. "I arranged dinner with you, but then I have other plans."

"Oh." I swallowed. "Yeah, of course. I shouldn't have assumed." Just because we had a relationship now didn't mean that he didn't have a life of his own. Hudson was a busy man—he had business deals and charity events and all sorts of things that didn't involve me. Why did it feel so much like a rejection, then?

Hudson sighed. "Alayna."

"Nope, my bad." My throat felt tight, but I forced a smile. "I'll watch one of my movies or catch up on my reading. Not a biggie."

"But we still have dinner."

"Yep." I nodded too long. As if nodding could erase all the suspicions that were entering my mind. Like, what were his other plans? Who had plans at eight on a Friday night? Why wasn't he telling me what they were so that I wouldn't assume the worst? Because I *was* assuming the worst. Big time. Assuming dates with other women and…and…well, mostly that—dates with other women. Women like Norma Anders.

I could ask him. But I knew if I asked, it would sound like an accusation. Or I was afraid it would sound like an accusation. Because it would totally be an accusation.

So I didn't ask. I wouldn't.

We sat in silence for about thirty seconds.

Then I couldn't handle it any longer. "So, um, what exactly are your other plans?" I squeezed his leg, hoping that would lighten any tension I might have created.

"It's…" He shook his head. "It's nothing."

So much for lightening the tension. "Seriously? You can't say it's nothing and expect me to let that drop." I added an awkward laugh to cover any shrillness that might be hiding in my tone. Inside, the paranoia built in my chest—paranoia that absolutely drove me insane and, like the most determined weed, was almost impossible to kill once it took root. I had to fight it, I couldn't let it win.

Hudson's jaw twitched. He was considering. Or trying to make up a good lie. Finally he spoke. "I'm going to a dinner with my mother."

Sophia. Just thinking about her made my spirits sink. No wonder Hudson didn't want to bring it up.

"Oh." I pinched the bridge of my nose, trying to sort the situation out. "But we're going to dinner now."

He didn't bat an eye. "I was planning to eat light."

"You were planning to eat twice? We can skip dinner. Eat with her. I can catch a bite later." That sounded like an understanding girlfriend, right? Because that's how I needed to sound, despite the fact that I felt anything but understanding.

"I'd rather eat with you and skip dinner with her."

"Then do that."

"I can't. It's her birthday. She expects me there."

And there it was. The rest of the story. "Today's your mother's birthday and you weren't going to mention it?"

He removed his arm from behind me and dropped it into his lap. "It's not like you two are close."

"But you are!" I swiveled as much as the seatbelt would allow so I could face him. "She's your mother. Your family is important to you, whether you want to admit it or not. If I'm important to you, too, then shouldn't you share what's up with them?"

He met my eyes, piercing me in such a way I had to brace for his words. "You are important to me, Alayna, and me not telling you about this has no reflection on that." He relaxed his stare. "You were going to be at work, there was no reason to even mention it."

"But now I'm not working..."

"And now you know."

I knew because I'd dragged it from him. I knew because my circumstances changed and forced him to have to tell me. And the only reason I'd planned to be at work in the first place was because Hudson had conveniently arranged for me to be. He'd worked to keep this dinner from me. Did he really think that he could pick and choose the things he chose to share in a relationship?

Maybe he did. To his credit, he hadn't had a real relationship before.

And wasn't I picking and choosing what I shared with him?

I didn't want to think about that. My secrets had no bearing on the conversation at hand. My secrets were still safe. His was not. And finding out he'd kept something from me didn't feel right, it didn't feel good. He should have told me. Hell, he should have invited me!

I blinked back a tear that was threatening to fall. "Is it just going to be you and her?"

"No. The rest of my family will be there, too."

My lip quivered. "And you're still not going to invite me?"

"No, I'm not."

I didn't say anything. Tears were falling now and I didn't think I could talk. God, since I'd been with Hudson, I'd turned into a total crier. How embarrassing.

Hudson moved to wipe away a tear, but I pulled away, not wanting his touch.

"It's family only, Alayna. Not a big deal."

"Family only. Yep, I get it." I tried not to let that sting. Of course I wasn't family, but I'd been welcomed by most of them—by Mira, her husband Adam, by Hudson's father Jack. And now Hudson wanted me to live with him. Didn't that automatically earn me invites to family events?

"Family only. And you don't get along with Sophia. Why would you want to be there?"

"Because you're going to be there." I wiped my wet face with my palm. "And we're a couple, Hudson. When we were pretending to be a couple, you wanted her to see me with you all the time. Now that we're really a couple, you don't. That doesn't make any sense."

"Now I care more about you than her, and I'm not going to subject you to an evening with my mother." His voice was steady. In another situation, I might have admired his continued calm, cool, collected bit, but right now all I could think was, *how is he not affected by this? By me?*

"Can't you understand that you not letting me go feels like you're leaving me out of your life?" My voice cracked. "It hurts."

"I'm not leaving you out of my life. I'm leaving *her* out of *your* life."

"It doesn't work like that. You can't protect me. Besides, it feels like an excuse. It feels like you're ashamed of me or like I'm not good enough to be with your family." I was beginning to doubt my decision to move in. Gratefully, I hadn't said anything yet. If he was setting up barriers between us, was cohabitating really a good idea?

"Don't be ridiculous. You've been with my family many times."

"Then why not tonight?" That was exactly my point. If I was good enough for them before, why not now?

His silence told me he wasn't willing to explain.

If he needed to be alone with his family, then all right. But I couldn't help how I felt. Crushed, that's how I felt. Absolutely crushed.

I needed to be alone before I got awful with him. I didn't trust myself not to.

Scanning the backseat, I spotted an intercom on each door. I undid my seatbelt and scooted to the door away from Hudson. I depressed the button. "Jordan, can you drop me off at my apartment?"

With lightning speed, Hudson hit his own button. "Ignore that, Jordan."

"I want to go home, Hudson. I can't be with you right now." I could barely see through my tears, but I heard him unbuckle his seatbelt and then felt him slide across the seat to me. "I don't want to be touched right now. Please."

He ignored me, pulling me into his arms. I resisted, which was senseless, really. He could overpower me in a heartbeat.

Still, I leaned into the door, pushing him away.

"Stop it. Stop fighting me." He caught each of my arms in his and held them, his hands circling my forearms with strength I couldn't hope to defeat. "Stop fighting."

"Then stop hurting me," I sobbed.

He knew I didn't mean physically. He wasn't gripping me that tightly.

"All right." He let go of me, his voice full of resignation. "You can come. If you really want to be part of this awful night, then you are welcome to join me."

My tears had frozen, surprised that I'd won. I'd never won these battles. They usually ended in me groveling, and then, when the guy refused to take me back, I would resort to crazy behavior. Like stalking. And stealing mail. And showing up at places where I knew the guy would be.

It never ended with me still with the guy.

Maybe because I was so relieved or because I was in shock, or more likely because I suddenly felt overwhelmingly guilty about the whole conversation, I burst into a new set of tears.

"Now what?"

My crying continued, but this time I let him pull me into his arms. "I'm such a bitch," I said into his shoulder.

"What?"

I lifted my mouth from the material of his jacket. "I'm a total bitch. I didn't mean to pressure you into an invite, and I did. I won't go, I'll stay home." He'd asked me out of duress. It felt shitty.

Hudson pulled me tighter against him, kissing the top of my head. "You're not a bitch. And you didn't pressure me into anything. You're coming with me. It will be awful, but at least it will be awful together."

Wiping the tears from my face, I raised my eyes to his. "Are you sure?"

"I'm completely sure it will be awful."

I chuckled. "Are you sure I can come?"

He leaned his head against mine, placing a hand on my cheek. "I am. I want you there. I always wanted you there." He trailed his hand down my neck. "But my mother is mean and terrible and she wants to hurt me. And she knows the easiest way to hurt me is to hurt you." His hand at my waist gripped me tighter, his fingers digging through my dress into my skin. "I can't bear to watch you go through that."

It was my turn to assure him. I reached up, placing my hands on the sides of his face, forcing him to look at me. "Nothing she says or does means anything to me. Do you hear me? I already won. I have you."

His eyes clouded—not simply with the lust that often darkened his gray hue when he looked at me—but with emotion that I could only name as love.

He pulled me even closer, as if he could pull me into him if he tried hard enough. "You do have me. Completely."

I don't know if I moved to him or he moved to me, just that our mouths were together, shifting in such a way that it was much more than kissing. It was a declaration—a statement of a union between the two of us that we couldn't yet express in any way besides with our bodies.

When he pulled away, I was breathless and flushed.

His eyes lowered to my outfit. "You'll need a dress. We should have time to stop by the boutique." He reached across me and pushed the intercom. "Jordan, change of plans. Take us to Mirabelle's."

— CHAPTER —
TEN

Mirabelle owned one of the hottest boutiques in New York City. Despite never needing to work a day in her life, the middle Pierce child had an eye for clothing design and she put it to good use. Her shop was by appointment only, and I'd nearly lost myself in fashionista heaven when Hudson had taken me to purchase racks of clothing almost two weeks before.

After directing Jordan to Greenwich Village where Mira's was located, Hudson pulled out his phone and called his sister. I listened half-heartedly to their short conversation. "Thanks, we're on our way," he said before hanging up.

"She won't be there," he said to me as he pocketed his phone. "She's getting ready for the party. But Stacy will take care of you."

I groaned inwardly at the thought of dealing with Stacy, Mira's too-thin blonde assistant. She had a thing for Hudson, had even gone out with him on at least one occasion. Needless to say, she wasn't fond of me. The daggers she shot with her eyes were poisonous enough to kill an army.

Plus, she made me jealous. Mira insisted that Stacy wasn't even a blip on Hudson's radar. But one night, when I'd cyber-stalked him, I'd seen a picture of Hudson and Stacy together. They looked good. And I bet she didn't have a history of crazy like I did.

If I could avoid seeing Stacy, I'd be a much happier person. "If Mira's not going to be there, maybe we shouldn't bother with the boutique. We could go back to my place and get something that we bought last time."

"No, we need something new. I'll want to show you off."

I wasn't sure if that made me happy or irritated. On the one hand, he liked the way I looked enough to feel like he could parade me. On the other hand, was that all I was? A show pony? Was this left over from our convince-everyone-we're-together scheme?

It was likely none of the above, simply a complimentary statement from a man to his woman. My emotions were still too muddled from the last fifteen minutes—from the last twenty-four hours—and now everything had a twinge of heaviness. It didn't seem like I could simply take anything at face value. There were layers to every gesture, every comment, every moment, and I was having a hard time getting my head around it all.

The nearly forty-five minute drive from Uptown to the Village didn't help. I cuddled into Hudson and closed my eyes trying to nap, unsuccessfully. When Jordan finally pulled up in front of the boutique, it felt like a lifetime had passed.

Hudson didn't wait for our driver to open the door. He climbed out and extended his hand. He continued to hold my hand as we walked to the shop, and I couldn't help but remember the last time we'd been there, how he'd held my hand then. How it had been pretend then and this time was real. It was real, wasn't it?

As if he could read my mind, Hudson squeezed my hand as we waited for Stacy to answer the bell. I turned to him and his lip curled into a half-smile.

It occurred to me that I'd seen him smile more in the last twenty-four hours than I had the entire three weeks I'd known him. Yeah, this was real.

Behind him, I saw construction workers at the shop next door, clearing up for the day.

"I wonder what's going on over there."

Hudson followed my glance. "Mirabelle's expanding. I believe they've almost finished. We'll come to the open house. She'll want you there."

"Wow. More clothes for me to choose from. Can your wallet handle it?" It was hilarious considering his bank account could clothe a small country. A large one, even.

We were both laughing when the door opened. Stacy barely glanced at us as she stood aside to let us in. "I have a client I'm finishing up with, but I already picked out some options for you. They're in the big dressing room."

So much for hellos.

She returned to her customer, and I glanced at Hudson to gauge his reaction to the lack of greeting. His face was stone. Whatever he thought about Stacy, he didn't show it. Perhaps she really did mean absolutely nothing to him. But if that was the case, why had he ever gone out with her to begin with? Even if it was only the one date, wouldn't he have had at least an ounce of attraction to her?

After my mini-tantrum in the limo, it didn't seem like such a good time to bring up his relationship with Stacy, if it even qualified to be called that. But I made a mental note to ask about it in the future. And not just about Stacy, but about all of Hudson's past women. Because I needed to know.

As she had said, Stacy had left several dresses in the dressing room, and despite my fear that she'd spitefully only pick hideous items for me to try on, they most definitely were anything but. Not that Mirabelle's even had anything remotely ugly on its racks. These dresses, though, were particularly exquisite. With all her scowling about, Stacy must have paid attention to what I chose the last time I'd been there, noticed what looked good on me, because these seemed almost tailor-made to my style. My eyes widened at the selection, too many called my name, and I was eager to try them all on.

Hudson, on the other hand, immediately fixated on one specific dress—a magenta satin Jersey. It was pretty enough, but awfully simple and brighter in color than something I'd wear at a family function.

He fingered the convertible straps. "This one." There was finality in his voice.

"I haven't tried it on. You don't even know how it—"

"I do know." He took the dress by the hanger and, after turning me to face the mirror, held it in front of me as he stood behind. "It's perfect."

I looked in the mirror, trying to picture the dress on my body, but all I could think of was the last time I'd been in that dressing room with Hudson, standing in front of that very mirror. He'd done incredible things to my body then, made me watch as I came undone from the ministrations of his hands on my breasts and between my thighs. Then, he'd entered me and took me with such force and desire that I'd come undone again.

My face heated from the memory, and I met his eyes in our reflection.

Hudson leaned into whisper at my ear. "I know what you're thinking. Stop it." He unbuttoned his jacket and pressed up against me so I could feel the thick ridge of his hard-on against my rear. "I'm thinking about it, too. And we don't have time to deal with those thoughts as I would like."

"Are you sure?" I reached my hand behind me to fondle his erection.

He took a deep breath. "You're certainly a different woman than the one I brought in here last time. The one who wanted to keep things sex-free." His voice was tight, the only indication of what my half-assed hand-job was doing to him.

"I never *wanted* to keep things sex-free. I just thought it would be best for me if we did." That was back when I thought for half a second that I had a chance of staying away from him. When I thought I might become obsessed with him if I didn't keep my distance. When I didn't realize how complete of a hold he already had on me.

He placed his hand over mine, controlling the pressure of my touch. "Is that still what would be best for you?"

Together, we stroked the length of his cock through his pants, and I longed to touch his bare skin, to slide my fingers across his crown, to pump him with my fist. He did this to me, completely turned me on, made me wet and interested in nothing but satisfying his need for me while he satisfied my need for him.

"You're best for me." My words were full of the ache I felt for him. "In every way—beside me, inside me…"

"Fuck, Alayna. You get me so hot, I—"

There was a single rap at the door followed by barely enough time for us to separate before Stacy walked in.

Her eyes flitted from my face to his then back to mine. "I should have waited for an invitation to come in."

"Yes, you should have." It was the first time I'd seen Hudson address Stacy in any way, and it was short and clipped. He turned to hang the dress back on the rack and buttoned his suit jacket before turning back to us. "I'll step out while you change, Alayna." He nodded back to the magenta dress. "That one."

Stacy's face was even, but her eyes flickered with the rejection. I almost felt sorry for her. I'd been her—dejected by men I thought I was into. Part of me wanted to reach out to comfort her.

But then the spite returned to her gaze. "Is that the dress you'd like to start with?" Her voice was cold as she took the magenta Jersey from the hanger without waiting for my response.

I reached behind and unzipped my clothing myself and let it fall to the floor. "Yes. It's the one Hudson wants." I used his name as a weapon, claiming him as mine. "He thinks it will be perfect."

Actually, it was. I could tell as soon as the dress was over my head. The color lit up my skin, highlighting my natural olive tone. It was low-cut enough that it showed off my boobs, an asset I was proud of. Hudson had always been quite fond of my bosom, surely one of the reasons he'd chosen it. The length was short enough to show some leg, but the flowing shape would only hint at my curves rather than hug them like many of my dresses did, leaving more to the imagination. It was a different style for me and that might have been what had prevented me from the same vision Hudson had. But he knew my body well, better than I did.

"He's right. It's perfect for you." I'd been so mesmerized by my reflection, Stacy's voice startled me.

I turned to her and found her expression had softened. It occurred to me that she was comparing herself to me as much as I compared myself to Celia, that she was measuring her flaws against mine. It was enough to send a person into dark depression. At least, that's what that kind of thinking could do to me. Again, I felt sorry for her. Or maybe it wasn't pity, it was something else—solidarity, maybe.

Stacy reached up to adjust a strap. "He has good taste."

Her tone suggested she wasn't talking about the dress. It hinted at more. The connection I felt with her, odd though it may be, led me to prod. "But…?"

Her forehead creased. "But what?"

"I sense there was more to your statement."

She looked away, busying herself with adjusting the breast cups of the dress. "It's not my place."

"Go ahead. Whatever you have to say, I can take it." Did I sound too eager? What I was hoping to gain from the conversation, I couldn't say. Maybe I was simply curious.

That was a lie. I was obsessed. No matter how "well" I was, no matter how healthy, I'd always be drawn to dig deeper, to find out as much as I could about the people I was attracted to. This was no different. Stacy had something to say regarding Hudson—something that might give me insight into the man I loved. I had to keep digging.

When she didn't offer more, I nudged her. "I know you've dated Hudson before."

She let out a sharp laugh. "Is that what he told you?"

I took a deep breath, hoping the words I chose to speak would keep her talking. "He hasn't told me anything about you. I've seen a picture of the two of you together at an event or something."

"Right." She nodded as if she knew exactly what picture I was talking about. "I was his escort for the night. We never dated."

"Escort?" My mind immediately went to hookers and high-priced call girls.

"Not that kind of escort. I never slept with him."

A huge weight lifted off my chest at her admission. I knew Hudson had slept with other women. Of course he had, but I didn't want to think about it. Because if I did, that's all I'd think about—him and whomever, sharing the intimacies that he and I shared now. So knowing that Hudson and Stacy never had that—it was a relief.

With that worry abated, I could concentrate on the other thing niggling at the edge of my brain. If they hadn't dated, if they hadn't slept with each other, yet Stacy emanated such scorn—

Then I got it. "Oh. I think I understand." She'd been one of his victims. One of the women whom he'd played—made her love him with whatever he said or did, then discarded her. It made me sick, and I hated that about me. I didn't want to feel sick about the things Hudson had done. I wanted to love him enough to look past anything.

But I was human. And even though I did love him past anything, it wasn't pleasant to focus on the things he'd done that had hurt people.

That thought was the one I clung to—if it made me feel this way to realize the brokenness of his past actions, then Hudson must ache inside, carrying the weight of these mistakes. I surely ached from the damage I'd inflicted on others—my strained relationship with my brother, how I'd hurt the men in my past. *Paul...*

I dismissed the name of my past lover and refocused on Stacy.

"Maybe you do understand," she was saying. "And maybe Hudson's changed. But I should warn you—"

"I don't need to be warned." It was absolutely schizo how I went back and forth from encouraging to defensive. I bit my lip and when I spoke again, I tried to assume the calm and inviting posture I had before. "I mean, he's already told me everything." *I hope.*

Giving voice to my fear, Stacy raised a brow and asked point blank, "Has he?" She let it sink in for a moment, letting me wonder.

She gathered the dress I'd been wearing off the floor. "Believe whatever. All I'm saying is he's not what he says he is." She hung it as she talked. "No matter what he tells you, it's a lie."

I'd been around this before: He tells me he won't lie and if I believe that, then I can believe everything he says. But if that is in itself a lie…"But it's not just what he said," I thought out loud. "He's shown me who he is. And Celia said—"

Stacy froze. "Celia Werner?"

I nodded.

Her face grew serious. "Don't believe anything she says either. They're together."

"They're friends." I meant for my tone to be insistent, but it came out weak and, again, defensive.

"They're together." Her tone succeeded at insistent. "Or they were. I can prove it too, if—"

The door opened, cutting her off. Unlike Stacy, Hudson didn't knock. He simply took his place in the world. I loved that about him.

"Gorgeous." He wanted me and it showed in every part of him from his posture to the gleam in his eyes, to the thickness of his voice.

And everything Stacy and I had been talking about vanished from my mind. My knees went weak with desire, and whatever doubts I had disappeared. He was there fixed on me. How could I be anything but sure? Sure about him, about me. About us.

"Thank you." I glowed; I could feel the warmth in every part of my body, reaching toward him. "It is gorgeous. You chose well."

"I did. I chose you."

How was I possibly still standing upright when it felt like every part of me had fallen into delight?

He saw what he did to me, his lips curving into a knowing smile. "She'll wear it out." His eyes never left me even though he spoke to Stacy.

Stacy.

Our conversation came rushing back to me, and the sweet feelings Hudson had brought became jaded. I should drop it, let myself stay lost in that happy, warm place.

But she'd said she could prove it…

"Hudson, I'll be a minute. I need to freshen up my face."

He nodded, and I realized he meant to wait while I reapplied my makeup. But I wanted him out of there, bad idea as it was.

I caught sight of the shoes that I'd worn earlier, sticking out from under the rack where I'd flung them. "Would you mind picking out some other shoes for me, H? Those ones don't quite go."

He followed my gaze to the discarded shoes. "No, they don't. I saw some silver heels that would look stunning."

Like me, Hudson had an appreciation for shoes. It was another one of the things I adored about him.

"Grab them for me?" I didn't have to tell him I'd let him fuck me in them later. He knew. He'd be the one to decide that anyway. He could dominate me all he wanted. Fine by me.

"Sure thing, baby." He winked and I smiled at his endearment. He was so unused to any terms of affection that they all sounded strained and forced on his tongue. Except for when he called me precious. That one came out with complete sincerity.

He opened the door and left to hunt for shoes. Stacy began to follow him, but I reached out and grabbed her forearm.

"You said you could prove it." I hoped my whisper wasn't as shaky as it sounded to my own ears. Was I actually doing this? Giving in to my doubts about Celia and Hudson? This was not a healthy move. It could very well be the beginning of spiraling into a loss of control. Or maybe I'd already lost control, because against my better judgment, I couldn't keep myself from asking. "Can you really?"

"Yes. Not here, but—"

"Give me your phone."

She pulled her phone from her pocket, and I entered my number in before handing it back to her. "You can text me." It was a bad idea—inviting doubts with whatever so-called evidence Stacy had to share.

But on the other hand, my mind could make up a pretty hefty dose of horrible things that Stacy might produce to prove a more-than-friends relationship between Celia and Hudson. The real proof was probably much less malignant.

At least, that's what I kept telling myself.

We arrived at the restaurant a few minutes after eight. This time Hudson waited for Jordan to let us out of the limo, for appearances perhaps. I'd never been to this restaurant and knew nothing about it, hadn't even caught the name. I only knew we were back Uptown. We rode the elevator hand-in-hand to the top floor in silence. I was quiet because I was nervous—nervous to interact with Sophia again, especially if she wasn't aware I was crashing her birthday party.

I couldn't say why Hudson was quiet. Perhaps he was nervous too.

"Mr. Pierce," the host said, recognizing Hudson. "Your party is already seated. Right this way."

We followed him into the restaurant toward windows that overlooked the city, the tree cover of Central Park the highlight of the view. The Pierce family was spread over two tables pressed together. I scanned the faces as the host set up an extra place setting for me, the unexpected guest. Chandler, Hudson's teenage brother, and Sophia, her face expressionless. Next was Jack, Hudson's father, a real charmer. It surprised me that he was sitting next to his wife since he openly detested her. Across from them were Mira and Adam.

That should have been everyone, but near me, their backs toward me so I hadn't spotted them at first, were Warren and Madge Werner. And Celia.

I tensed, so many warring thoughts in my head, emotions so strong that they spread through my body. Hudson hadn't invited me, hadn't wanted me at this social function, but Celia had been on the guest list all along. Was that the true reason he hadn't told me about Sophia's birthday? Both of us had agreed not to see her. Yeah, I had gone back on that deal, but at least there wasn't a chance that I was going to jump her. At least I hadn't almost been engaged to the woman. Had he not invited me to this dinner because of that silly agreement, or was it because he wanted to be alone with her? Well, alone as in without me, anyway.

And Celia, whom I had confided in and bonded with just that afternoon, hadn't mentioned the dinner either.

My eyes flew from the blonde to the man standing next to me. His face was even. This was why he'd been quiet. He knew I'd be upset.

I was.

I couldn't take it. I had to bolt. Through gritted teeth, I hissed, "I thought you said this was family only."

Then I turned and walked away.

— CHAPTER —

ELEVEN

Before I was out of earshot, I heard Hudson defending my departure. "She left something in the car. Excuse us a moment."

Fuck, he was coming after me.

The sure way to lose him was to head for the bathroom, not that I put it past Hudson to follow me in, but I didn't know where it was located, and I'd already made it past the host's desk. My eyes scanned the hallway. There were the elevators, which would require waiting for a car, and a door to the stairs.

I took the stairs, and, realizing fifty flights down in heels was maybe not a good idea, I went up.

The breeze hit my face as I stepped onto the roof, the heavy door slamming behind me. I kept walking.

The roof was practically abandoned, so I knew the sound of the door shutting behind me was Hudson. Still I kept on, rushing through the gardens and leisure seating arranged across the building top, trying to find a spot where I could be alone, where I could breathe, where I could sort out my paranoia from the legitimacy of the situation.

At the corner wall, I stopped. I leaned over the edge of the cement enclosure, gulping in huge lungfuls of air. Deep breathing was the only thing keeping me from breaking down into sobs.

His footsteps were quiet behind me, but I still heard them, as if I was hyper-attuned to his movements. He stopped before he got to me, reaching out to me with speech instead of his body. "The Werners are practically family."

At least he was smart enough to know why I'd run. And brave enough to not pretend otherwise. He deserved credit for that.

But I couldn't give him anything but disbelief. "Right. Uh-huh." I didn't turn toward him. I didn't want to see his face as he explained. If his expression said I was being ridiculous—it would break me.

"What, do you think I didn't tell you on purpose?" His voice was calm despite his words.

I spit out a harsh laugh. "You don't want to know what I'm thinking."

"Actually, I do."

I spun around. "No, you don't." I backed up until the high corner wall met my back. He didn't get it. Chances were that my feelings were magnified—I had no way to judge their validity when I was this upset. Experience and counseling taught me to not deal with these situations until I calmed down. I needed time to get calm.

"Trust me when I tell you I do."

"Hudson, you can't say that when you don't know what I want to say. It's not good. In fact, you need to leave me alone. Or I'm going to blame you for things. Things I'm probably overreacting about and you're going to be offended. And I'm going to lose you."

That was the only thing I knew for sure. That whatever I said, whatever I felt, it would drive him away. My intense emotions had never failed to scare off the men in my life. Even my own brother had grown tired of dealing.

"You aren't going to lose me." He took one step toward me. Not cautious, but completely sure. As if to say he had complete control of the situation. As if to say, *just try to back me down.*

I pressed harder against the cement behind me, wishing I could disappear inside it. I didn't want him to witness me like this. "You haven't seen this side of me, Hudson. You don't know."

"Then I need to stay. I need to see every side of you."

He was so calm. I shook my head and bit my lip, fighting off the tears that threatened. Fuck, I couldn't cry. Eventually I'd have to go back to that restaurant and I didn't want to be tear-stained.

But if Hudson stayed, if he pressed me, I didn't think I could keep it together.

Or maybe I *could* tell him. If we were going to share things, then shouldn't this be one of them? Shouldn't he be the one person whom I could go to about anything? He'd always brought me peace in the past, when I'd explained what was going on in my head.

"Go ahead. Ask me."

"It won't be asking; it will be accusing." I continued to fight, but my defense was weaker.

And underneath all the accusations rolling in my mind, one thought kept repeating: It wasn't fair. Not fucking fair. None of it—my parent's dying, my father's drinking, my past obsessions, whatever led to now when my history of crazy made it impossible to determine whether or not what I was feeling at the moment was valid. Whether I should be laying into Hudson over his deceit or whether I should be apologizing for running out.

"Do it. I want to hear it. I need to know what you're thinking. Trust me."

Trust me. It always came to that. I either trusted him, or I didn't.

And the simple fact was that I did. Trust him.

I swallowed. "You didn't invite me tonight because you knew she'd be here." It was barely a whisper, but he heard me.

He nodded once, saying he understood. "That's not true. I told you why I didn't invite you. And I did invite you in the end. You're here."

"But you didn't want to at first." I stared at my shoes, but my voice strengthened as I fell into the accusations waiting on my tongue. "That's probably why you had to doll me up. To show up Celia, whatever your game with her is. It wasn't about your mother at all."

"You're right."

My head whipped up.

"You're right that it wasn't about my mother. It was about you. I wanted everyone to see how beautiful you are. How beautiful the woman who loves me is."

His statement stirred up my fury. Was he turning my love into a trophy? Into a weapon against her?

It sure felt as such.

"Celia," I spit her name. "You wanted to show Celia, you mean."

He shook his head again.

"She's here, Hudson!" I didn't care that I was shouting. The few people on the roof could enjoy the scene. I didn't even notice if anyone's head turned, I was so wrapped up in my anger. "She's here with free rein and I had to beg to be here. And you told me you wouldn't see her without me. What is she to you?"

"Nothing. An old friend."

"Bullshit." My voice cracked, but, so far, the tears were staying in my eyes. "Otherwise you would have told me about this dinner from the beginning. You were hiding it from me." I pointed a shaky finger at him. "Because you knew she would be here too."

"I didn't know." His lids closed in a long blink as he took a breath. "I suspected," he conceded. "But she's not here because of me. Her mother is my mother's best friend. You know that."

"Fuck that. She's twenty-eight years old. She's old enough to not go to every goddamn function with her mother. She's here for you."

"And I'm here with you." His tone was solid, unwavering. Such a contrast to mine.

"She's still in love with you."

"And I'm with you."

He closed the gap between us, and I secretly sighed in relief, placing my palms against the wall for support. He braced his arms on either side of me, caging me in. "I'm with you."

My fingers curled inward, trying to hold onto something. Having no success against the cement, they flew forward and gripped onto his jacket instead.

He took that as an invitation to move closer. Or he just moved closer, not caring if he was invited or not. He pressed his body against mine, and I couldn't help but press back into him, soaking in his warmth. I'd feared my words would scare him off, and even though my doubts hadn't yet been stilled, he hadn't gone anywhere. He was there.

There and wanting.

His erection pressed against my belly.

My eyes flew to his, surprised. He was turned on? How did...why was... did my doubts do that? Did my messed up anxiety make him want me more?

"I'm hard for you and only you." He spoke low, his words gritty with desire. "It's you that I adore." He lowered his mouth to kiss along my neck, and I let my head fall to the side, granting him access. I moaned as his lips met my skin.

Then, with simply his touch, I relaxed, melting into him. This was all I needed—his mouth on me, his body against me. Who cared about the why? I only cared that he was there.

I threw my arms around his neck, and his mouth crushed into mine, hard. His tongue plunged inside, stroking and caressing—I went wet wanting him inside me in the same way.

He pulled my lower lip between his teeth then let it go. "I'm with you," he said again as his hands gathered the material of my dress up around my waist, tucking it in to the band of my underwear. And again, as his fingers slipped inside my panties.

His fingers circled against my nub, and I bucked forward with a moan.

"That's it." He continued his expert caressing, kissing me and encouraging me. "Relax. Let me be with you."

I whimpered as fingers slid along the length of my slit and found the center of my heat. But instead of entering me as I so desired—so needed—Hudson dropped to his knees and pulled my panties down to my ankles.

Before I could protest the loss of his hands on my core, he licked along the lips of my vagina. "It's you that I'm about to go down on." He spoke between long strokes with his tongue. "It's you I'm going to make come with my mouth so that when we go back down there and you start to feel insecure, you will still be wet and you'll remember my lips were on you and no one else."

I was about to come from his words alone, so turned on by his possessiveness, by his demand for me to know that I was his.

He lifted one foot out of my panties and threw my leg over his shoulder. Then he returned full force, sucking my clit into his mouth. His fingers jabbed into my hole—I have no idea how many he used—but he bent them and stroked me until I was writhing. I clutched my hands into his hair for support as my orgasm exploded through me, rocking me against his hand, against his mouth.

Hudson didn't wait for me to calm before he stood, pressing his pelvis against me, urging me to give his cock attention. I cupped his length—God, he was so hard.

"Take it out," he commanded.

Laughter drew my eyes across the roof to a group of people lounging in the sitting area. How long had they been there? "We're not alone."

"Take it out. I don't care about anyone or anything but being inside you right now. I have to be inside you."

And really, I didn't care either. Not in the least.

I undid his belt and unzipped his pants. He lowered his clothing enough to release his cock. Immediately I circled my hands around it. He was so hard that his veins protruded from the soft skin of his shaft.

He didn't let me fondle him as long as I would have liked. Instead, he lifted me, my back still against the wall, and pushed into me, hard.

"Goddamn, your pussy is so good." He drove into me with rapid, staccato thrusts. "Do you hear me? Your pussy makes me this hard. No one else's."

I admired his ability to talk, to be able to speak to me with such coherence while I was a puddle beneath him. And his words—his amazing words—they melted me even more. I soaked them up as I clutched onto him, as he undid me again and again.

His voice strained as he neared his climax, but still he spoke. "When we go back down to dinner, I will smell like you and you will smell like me. And you'll remember that we are together. I am with you."

We came together, me biting into his shoulder to suppress the scream that threatened to escape my lips, him grunting, "No one but you."

No one but you.

I wrapped the sentiment around me like a child's favorite blanket. If I could stay like that, stay embraced in the knowledge that I was there for him, then I could dismiss all the doubts that crept into my heart. I could forget about Stacy and her wild claims of proof. I could believe that Celia was merely a friend.

If I could believe that one statement, Hudson and I would be just fine.

— CHAPTER —
TWELVE

Amazingly, the calm Hudson gave me on the rooftop continued as we made our way back to the restaurant. Even Sophia's peeved glare didn't fluster me as the waiter pulled out my chair for me.

Sophia took a sip of the brown liquid in her hand. "It's about time you returned."

I remembered what Hudson had said as we'd left—that I'd forgotten something in the car—and I started to apologize, using that as the basis of my excuse.

But Hudson beat me to answering. "We got distracted." He squeezed my hand before relinquishing his hold on me, letting me sit in my chair. As soon as I sat, he took my hand again under the table. I couldn't think of another time that I'd been so publicly claimed. And after his private appropriation of my body minutes before, relaxing into a comfortable doubt-free place with Hudson seemed like a real possibility.

Not just a possibility but a reality.

"Laynie!" Mira seemed about to burst out of her chair. "I'm so glad you made it!"

The last time I'd seen her, she'd been worried I was done with her brother. My presence was a declaration otherwise.

"Me, too." I smiled back at her and passed the same grin on to the others at the table, including Chandler's head that was bent over his iPhone and the Werners. But I didn't look Celia in the eye as I did. I could feel her trying to catch my gaze, but I wasn't interested. She hadn't told me about the dinner either and that made me suspicious. Perhaps wrongly so but suspicious all the same.

"Me, three," Jack said, winking at me.

Maybe it was my imagination, but Hudson seemed to snarl at his father's statement. His protectiveness of me was silly at times, yet it also warmed me.

Sophia finished off her glass and set it on the table with an attention getting *thunk*. "Well, we already ordered."

"That's fine. We'll catch up." Hudson signaled the waiter, who hastened over. He ordered for us both, in beautiful French that made me slick between my thighs. Or, rather, slicker.

"And while you're here, I'll have another of these." Sophia held up her empty glass to the waiter, and I saw Mira and Hudson exchange a glance. I could relate all too well to what they were feeling—the dread of having an alcoholic parent, the questions and worries that occupied every moment. *Would she drink too much tonight? Would she make a fool of herself? Of us?*

Except in my life the *she*'s were replaced by *he*'s. It was my father who had been the alcoholic, the one who had caused me anxiety. Was that where I had first learned to worry? Maybe something I should talk to a therapist about sometime. Or, since I wasn't seeing a therapist anymore, then maybe my counselor at the group I attended on a somewhat regular basis.

The thought was interrupted by Hudson leaning in to whisper in my ear. "I hope you don't mind that I ordered for you." The feel of his breath on my earlobe caused my hair to stand on end.

I didn't. It saved me the trouble of having to decipher the menu. And listening to him speak in a foreign language....I sighed as the smooth lilt of his words lingered in my memory. "As long as my dish doesn't have mushrooms, I'm happy."

"No," he chuckled, the sound sending an electric spark through my body. "I wouldn't want you gagging at my mother's birthday dinner."

"Quite the opposite." I leaned toward his ear now, so that only he could hear me. "The way you ordered, I'm salivating. I didn't know you could speak French."

"Fluently."

My eyes widened. "Say something else?" We were flirting, something we didn't do often in front of others, and it came so naturally that I let myself be carried where it took us.

"*Oui. Plus tard, quand tu es enveloppé dans mes bras, je vais parler jusqu'à ce que tu es éclatement avec passion.*"

His husky tone combined with the return of the accent drove me mad. "What did you say?" I was breathless.

He moved his arm around me, pulling me closer before speaking again. "I said, 'Yes. Later, when you're wrapped around me, I'll speak it until you shudder with delight.'"

My face blazed with heat.

"You know there are other people at this table, Hudson," Sophia chided.

I hoped those other people didn't understand French better than I did. And that his translation had truly been quiet enough for only me to hear. But the darting eyes of Madge Werner across the table from me made me think Hudson had been heard.

Oh, well.

Mira rolled her eyes. "Mother, leave them alone." Usually Mirabelle had endless patience for Sophia. Perhaps she was becoming more short-tempered as her pregnancy proceeded. "Can't you see they're in love?"

Hudson turned his head to smile at me. We were still so unused to the word—it felt odd hearing it being said about us. And it also felt apropos. Obvious, even. Like, duh. How could anyone not see it?

Sophia couldn't. "Or they're working awfully hard to make me believe that." She smoothed her hair, which was so stiff that the movement did nothing.

Mira leaned back in her chair and rested her hands on her baby bump. "Why on earth would they want to fake a relationship?"

I kept my eyes on my plate, worried my expression would give something away. Why would Sophia jump to that conclusion? We had indeed tried to fake our relationship. I even had the feeling that Mirabelle suspected as much. But she also knew I loved her brother, and she'd never tell that to her mother. Mira was the type of person that hung everything on love. An any-obstacle-could-be-overcome-if-there-was-love type of person.

For the first time ever, I didn't want to laugh at that idea.

Sophia took her refill from the waiter, not even bothering to let him set it down before indulging in a long sip. "Beats me. Why does Hudson like to do any of the shitty things he does to people? I long ago gave up trying to figure it out."

Celia shifted uncomfortably in her seat, but her parents showed no reaction. Which confirmed that Hudson's past was common knowledge to everyone at the table. No wonder he'd referred to the Werners as family. If they knew his dark secrets, then they practically were.

Then again, how could they not know his secrets? Their own daughter had been his victim, even though it wasn't to the extent that they thought. He hadn't knocked her up, anyway. Whatever he'd done to her head—well, we'd all had people that shaped us for better or worse. Blaming another person for our own actions was selfish. We had to be responsible for our own actions. I'd learned that the hard way.

Sophia was responsible for her bitchy comments now, no matter what hard-knock story formed her. Her cattiness was disgusting and unforgivable.

But Jack was the only one who seemed to think her behavior needed to be reined in. Or the only one to say something, at least. "Just because it's your birthday doesn't mean you have the right to ditch being polite."

Mira snorted. "No, she believes that merely breathing gives her that right."

All eyes turned to the perky brunette, her face growing bright red. Mira never said anything the least bit snarky. It was surprising.

Adam coughed at her side, whether signaling her to say something else or trying to alleviate the tension, I wasn't sure.

She looked down, sheepishly. "I'm sorry. I shouldn't have said that."

"Thank you for the apology. You're hormonal. I don't know what Jack's excuse is for speaking to me so rudely." Sophia cast a sideways glare at her husband and I wondered if it ever crossed her mind to apologize as well. Instead, even.

No, it didn't cross her mind at all. Her expression remained unaltered, not even a flicker of remorse passing over her face.

She peered around the table, as if challenging someone to call her on it. No one did.

"Chandler," she said as her eyes grazed the top of his head. "Put down your damn phone and be present. I want to enjoy the evening with us together. All of us."

But her glance skidded right past me. *All of us* clearly meant everyone except me.

Chitchat replaced the heavier conversation after that, the attention moving away from Hudson and myself. I enjoyed my salad while Hudson talked business with Warren, and Celia bantered with Mira and Sophia.

Sophia even relaxed enough that I saw hints of the carefree fun person she must have been once upon a time. So long ago now that only the smallest remnant graced her current being, hidden from anyone that didn't bother to look hard enough.

How I could see it…well, maybe I was looking. Searching for the person that Hudson wanted to please so much, the reasons that he still kept her in his life instead of separating from her once and for all the way I had from Brian.

Hell, that wasn't necessarily a better option. Cutting Brian from my life hurt. It was a reality I'd been ignoring for the past several days, and I shoved away the impulse to think about it now. I was at a family get-together. Of course I'd think of him. It didn't mean I had to dwell.

Things continued with an air of banality through most of our main course. The dish Hudson had ordered for me was delicious and like nothing I'd ever tasted. Minced lobster and fish dumplings covered with a dill cream sauce. It made me want to lick my plate clean.

Hudson had ordered some sort of duck crepes. He fed me a corner of the pastry that wasn't drenched in the mushroom sauce that accompanied it, the poultry melting in my mouth as my lips slid along his fork. "Divine."

He watched me greedily. "I could say the same thing."

Madge had gotten the brunt of our romantic display that evening since she sat across from us. Now she cleared her throat.

I smiled with what I hoped was an apologetic grin, though I was anything but sorry. I was well aware that Madge believed that Hudson was merely slumming with me, that he'd eventually dump me for her darling Celia. I wanted her to see me with him, knew it irked her, but I wasn't performing for her benefit. I was simply enjoying the evening with my lover. It was genuine.

Madge returned my smile with a sour one of her own. Then she turned in her seat toward Mirabelle on the other side of her.

Pretending I wasn't there was one way to handle me, I supposed.

"Mira," she exclaimed, peering over Celia who sat between her and Mirabelle. "Only four more months until the newest Pierce is introduced to the world. You must be so excited!"

Mira's hands flew instinctively to her belly. "I am!" She frowned. "But when you say four more months, I want to puke a little."

Sophia cleared her throat with disapproval. God, correcting a full-grown woman's language was beyond ridiculous. I wanted to puke a little myself.

Mira was used to Sophia though. "Sorry, not great dinner conversation. I wish it were sooner, that's all. I'm anxious to have her in the world instead of sitting on my bladder."

"It will be here soon enough. Trust me." Unlike his wife, Adam sounded happy that he still had months to prepare.

Warren shook his head, triggered by Adam speaking. He elbowed his wife. "That's not right, Madge. Mira's not a Pierce anymore. It will be baby Sitkin."

Mira's eyes went straight to her mother. "Or Sitkin-Pierce, if we decide to hyphenate." The look on Mira's face said this was a conversation she'd had before. Mirabelle had kept the name Pierce for business endeavors, but the hyphenating was new. I'd bet my entire bank account that it was an attempt to please Sophia.

But nothing pleased Sophia. "It's not the same. Sitkin-Pierce is not Pierce." She sighed dramatically. "So the bloodline continues, but not the name."

It was funny how concerned the woman was with a name that she'd only earned through a loveless marriage. It showed how materialistic she was, how tied she was to appearances. It was the Pierce name that held weight in the world. Any deviation lost the power that the Pierce Industry carried. In her eyes, anyway.

Adam sat forward as if about to go to battle. "Mira's not the only Pierce offspring. Chandler could have children."

And Hudson, I thought to myself.

"Then it will be the name but not the bloodline," Jack said nonchalantly.

My hand flew to my mouth, stifling a gasp. There were rumors that Chandler wasn't Jack's child, but I didn't know it was something the Pierce family discussed openly.

"What?" Chandler looked up from his lap where he'd been trying to hide that he was texting or whatever it was he was doing on his phone.

"Nothing," Mira called down the table. "Go back to whatever you were doing."

So maybe it was common knowledge to everyone but Chandler.

Sophia took another swallow of her drink—her third of the evening. "Hudson and Celia's baby could have been both."

I tensed. Hudson and Celia's fictitious baby caused a fair amount of contention in the family. It had happened years ago, yet the weight of it had been so heavy that it refused to disappear. Why Celia didn't own up and explain the baby wasn't Hudson's was beyond me. It pissed me off that she let him continue to save her from humiliation no matter what it cost him. I couldn't help but throw her a glare.

Celia missed my scowl as her own eyes darted toward Hudson. Or maybe Jack. They were sitting next to each other and it was difficult to tell, but Hudson made more sense.

Jack dropped his fork to his plate, the noise clattering loudly in the quiet restaurant. "Not this again, Sophia. Really? Goddammit, I won't listen to this." He wiped his mouth and threw his napkin over his half-eaten food. Then he stood. "Thank you everyone, I wish I could say it has been a lovely evening, but, well, I'll leave it at that. I'll take care of the bill on my way out. The rest of you stay and enjoy. Order dessert. As for my wife, I'm not going to invite her to rot in hell as I probably should because I think she already lives there. At least hell is where anyone who spends time with her feels like they've been sent."

He deserved a standing ovation. But he simply got open-mouthed stares as he walked away from the table.

Sophia was the first to speak. "What a drama queen." She took a bite of her chicken. "I was merely pointing out that we had a chance at a Pierce grandchild and now it's gone."

"Talk about drama queen..." Though his head was bowed, Adam said it loud enough that the whole table heard it.

Sophia glared at her son-in-law, but it was Hudson who drew the attention of the table. "I could have a child with Alayna."

I nearly choked on the bite of food in my mouth. Sure, I'd been thinking that Hudson could have a kid, but it hadn't for a moment crossed my mind he would have one with me.

Okay, maybe it had crossed my mind for a moment. But a small one. Certainly it wasn't a thought I'd ever share out loud.

But when Hudson had said it, had said it out loud like that to everyone, a strange warmth spread through my chest. It wasn't the low, deep burn of desire, but something different. Something related to the love that I felt for the man, mixed with a dash of hope.

I wanted to share that feeling with him, let him know what it did to me that he'd said it, and I tried to catch his eye. But he was focused on the plate in front of him, taking another bite of his crepes as if talking about having children—*children with me*—was every day and unremarkable.

Maybe he didn't mean anything by it. I felt the bubble of warmth dissipate as I recognized the possibility that he merely meant it as a line to rile his mother up. In which case, it worked.

Sophia set down her fork and turned in her chair, ire blazing through the cool mask she usually wore. "Are you talking marriage and children already? It's early for that Hudson. Incredibly early."

"Oh, Mother, don't be so old-fashioned. You don't need to be married to have children." Hudson took a swallow of his wine, continuing the nonchalant façade. But when he set down his glass again, I caught the twitch of his jaw, the only betrayal that inside he was boiling. "And what Alayna and I are discussing is frankly none of your business."

Sophia's eyes narrowed. "You brought it up."

"I was stating that *I* could father a child and that would continue both your precious bloodline and your precious name." His voice was oddly calm and strong all at once. I imagined it was the tone he took in the boardroom. It was powerful. Controlled. Sexy as hell.

Then he delivered his punch line. "And the only person I could ever imagine wanting to have a child with is Alayna."

The impact wasn't any less having heard him pronounce the possibility a moment before. It rang through the air as if every other sound had been muted, as if it were the lead violin in a string concerto. A lonely piercing sound that made people notice.

At once, all three Werners shifted in their seats, and even though Celia and Hudson were never a couple, were never meant to be together, the tension his statement created was as extreme as if the violinist's bow had crossed against a too-taught string. It was so much. Too much.

"Hudson, I..." My voice trailed off. I had no idea what I planned to say. I just wanted the tension to end, to get rid of the general air of hatred I felt rushing at me from so many eyes.

He picked up on my cue. Placing a reassuring hand on my leg, he gave me an apologetic glance before turning back to Sophia. "The point is that you need to let the past go, Mother." His tone was softer, but still held weight. "There is still a future to look forward to. For all of us."

He turned back to me, our eyes locking, and then, instead of *me* telling *him* how it felt to hear him talk about a future with me, *he* told *me.* He told me with that long silent stare, his hand stroking up and down my thigh in a way that was more comforting than sexual. With that look, he said everything—how much he believed in us, how good we were. How much he loved me, even though he couldn't yet say the words.

Then the tears that I'd managed to keep at bay earlier filled my eyes.

"If you'll excuse me," I said, breaking our stare. "I need to use the powder room."

I made it to the bathroom and took a stall before the tears spilled. There weren't many—a few, each of them happy and sweet and filled with promise. With love.

I heard the bathroom door swing open and shut a handful of times before I'd finished my brief cry. I peed and flushed, then, after washing my hands, made my way to the vanity to freshen up my face.

Fortunately, happy crying didn't muss up my face as much as ugly crying. I continued to grin like an idiot as I leaned toward the mirror to dab at the small smudge of mascara under my left eye.

"You look perfect," someone said behind me.

I glanced sideways, meeting Celia's reflection in the mirror.

Immediately my smile disappeared.

"You just need a touch of gloss. I have some if you want to borrow." She opened her tiny purse and pulled out a lipstick wand.

"No, I don't want to borrow anything from you." I pushed past her, headed for the exit.

But she grabbed me by the forearm. "Hey, wait!"

I pulled my arm away from her grasp but stopped my retreat. I might as well hear what she had to say, whatever grandiose excuse she had about keeping Sophia's birthday dinner a secret from me.

Folding my arms in a dramatically bored stance, I nodded for her to speak.

Naturally poised Celia for once looked awkward, fidgeting from foot to foot.

"I'm not waiting all night. Speak."

Her forehead creased in confusion. "Why are you angry with me? I could feel the tension all through dinner. You wouldn't even look at me. Which is why I followed you in here. Why are you mad?"

"Don't play dumb, Celia. It doesn't suit you."

"I'm not playing. Spell it out for me." Her arms were at her sides, her body in a totally open position, as though she had nothing to hide. "Please."

"Celia..." Was I being ridiculous? Again? Maybe I was letting myself be influenced by Stacy's cryptic warning about the blonde beauty.

I sighed, deciding to put it out there. "I saw you today and you didn't mention anything about this dinner tonight. And you know that I didn't know because I told you that I had no plans to see Sophia and that I had a meeting tonight. All the while, you're saying you're rooting for me." My voice was calm, straightforward, less accusatory than I felt. Maybe I was learning from Hudson.

Celia echoed my sigh. "You're right, you're right." She looked at her shoes, mumbling. "I thought that might be it." Her gaze met mine again. "I didn't say anything, you're right, and I should have. But you were happy and beaming and things were going good, and when I realized that Hudson hadn't told you about the dinner, I didn't want to stir things up between the two of you."

"Or you wanted him for yourself tonight."

"No! I told you, I'm not after Hudson." She ran her hand across her forehead, delicately, as though not wanting to mess up her foundation but so used to the cautious movement she didn't have to think about it. She was a thoroughbred through and through. So out of my league.

I dismissed the flash of envy and focused on her words.

"Look, Laynie, I'm on your side. I am. Can't you see what would have happened if I'd brought it up? You would have cornered Hudson about it and then you'd have to tell him how you found out and that would mean you'd have to tell him about us chatting about him behind his back. And he brought you anyway! So it all worked out. Everything's good!"

"Yeah, everything's great." I reacted before I'd truly digested her words. Once I did, I saw the truth in what she'd said. Honestly, if our roles had been reversed, I would have probably done the same.

I bit my lip. "God, I'm sorry. I just…I don't know who to trust. It feels like so many people are against us."

Her face eased, her worry replaced with a comforting smile. "That's so not true. Sophia is against you. She's the only one. And my parents, but they're only trying to do what they think is best for me. It's a silly parent thing. They don't understand. Obviously."

She meant they didn't understand that she'd never been with Hudson. They didn't realize that her baby had not been his. "Why won't you tell them? It's been years, you said so yourself. Why don't you or Hudson admit the truth about the baby?" I'd been wondering about it since I found out. It would solve so many problems. "If you really cared about his happiness, you'd tell the truth and set him free."

"It seems like that would be the right thing to do, doesn't it?" Her eyes glazed over as she was thinking, remembering perhaps. When her focus returned, her expression was apologetic. "It's…it's complicated. I can't say more than that. I'm sorry, I wish I could. But it involves more than just me. You have to trust me, this is best for everyone. Hudson included."

It bothered me that there might be something about the situation that I didn't know, that Hudson hadn't chosen to share. But maybe Celia was simply making up excuses, not ready to let her parents know the truth. "Like I said, I don't know what I trust."

"Alayna—"

I cringed at her use of my name. No one called me Alayna but Hudson. It wasn't hers to use. It was his.

The door swung open behind us and someone walked in. We were both quiet until the woman took an empty stall.

"This is a bad time. But you have my number. Call me if you need anything. To sort things out or just to talk."

I hesitated. The evening had shown me many things, one of which was how easily keeping secrets could tear Hudson and me apart. I didn't want to keep lying to him. Perhaps this was a good opportunity to end my friendship with Celia. Maybe even come clean about our lunch dates thus far.

Seeming to sense my reluctance to "kiss and make up," Celia put her hand over mine. "I want things to work out for Hudson more than you can imagine. Believe me."

Celia gave one more sparkling white smile before exiting the restroom.

I pulled my phone out from my bra and considered deleting her contact info. It was certainly the safest. But, on the other hand, she'd been helpful to me providing insight that I lacked. And she was important to Hudson. I didn't want to cause problems by being a divide between them.

Funny. The old me would have done just that. The old me, the one before therapy—that me would have made Hudson choose. Her or me. Now, as nice as it sounded to be free of the Werners, I had no desire to force an ultimatum.

And besides being incredibly unrealistic and unhealthy, I was pretty sure Hudson would never go for it.

— CHAPTER — THIRTEEN

It was only seconds after Celia walked out and I had stowed my phone back in my bra when Mira stepped into the vanity from the stall area. Since no toilets had flushed recently and I hadn't heard any running water, I realized she must have been standing around the corner for a while. Her face was more serious than I'd ever seen, and something about her expression made me feel unexplainably guilty.

"Hey," I said, trying to shake the strange feeling.

She pierced me with her brown eyes. "You were talking to Celia."

"Yeah." I put my hand on the vanity counter for support even though I hadn't done anything wrong. We were at a family get-together, eight of us in total. Should I really not be expected to talk to one of the other guests? To my boyfriend's only friend?

"I don't think you should do that anymore." Mira's voice was even and absent of any chiding.

"Why?"

She softened as she stepped toward me, her regular bubbly persona returning. "She's your competition, Laynie! I mean, Hudson is totally into you and no one but you, but Celia is after him. She's pictured herself married to him for so long, it's a done deal in her head."

"I know, I know." A strange pang of pity washed over me. Maybe Celia really didn't want Hudson, and everyone just kept saying that she did, accusing her of something that she'd long past outgrown. I knew how that felt. To be thought still crazy long after I'd gotten better.

Swallowing, I voiced the defense that surprised even me. "She says she doesn't, though. Want him, I mean. She really seems like she might be over him. She's been really supportive, actually."

Mirabelle fluffed the back of her bobbed hair. "Okay. Maybe that's true. I might be overreacting. But I've known her my whole life, and she hasn't always been the best person."

I could imagine what it looked like to Mira, when Hudson had left Celia heartbroken and devastated. To the young impressionable teenager that Mira must have been, it would be easy to blame Celia for the awfulness that had surrounded Hudson. Especially with her as devoted to her brother as she was.

But she was a grown-up now. She had to see the story was bigger than she'd once thought, even if she didn't know the details. "Hudson hasn't always been the best person either," I reminded her.

Disappointment flashed across her eyes.

"I'm not saying that I'm not for Hudson. I don't care what he's done or who he's been. Truly." I would stand by him no matter what shit he'd gone through, just like he stood by me and all the shit I'd done. "It's only that we've all been worse people." Except probably Mira. "At least, a lot of us have been worse people," I amended.

"I'm sure that's true." She stepped toward me, placing her hand lightly on my arm. "But, don't feel like Celia's your only resource, okay? If you need to talk, Laynie, call me. Or better yet, talk to Hudson."

My head was throbbing with all the back and forth—accuse Celia, defend Celia, trust Celia, don't trust Celia. Truth was, the only person I really needed to defend was Hudson. The only person I needed to trust was him.

Yes, he was the one I should turn to when I needed someone to talk to. He was the only one who mattered. The only one who knew how to calm me down. "I'll talk to Hudson. Good idea."

She grinned. "Sometimes I have them. Good ideas. Pregnancy brain and all."

Suddenly, I felt like I'd been away from Hudson for entirely too long and I ached to see him. The ache dissipated the moment we came out of the bathroom, and I found Hudson waiting, his posture strong and one hundred percent male, his eyes blazing at the sight of me. It never failed to make me weak in the knees.

With a wave, Mira headed toward our table on the heels of Celia. She must have lingered after leaving the bathroom. I had to guess she talked to

Hudson. Which was fine. Totally fine. Expected, even. It wasn't her he was waiting for. It was me. Always.

Hudson took my hand when I approached him. "Are you ready to go?"

Despite not having finished my meal, leaving sounded heavenly. "I thought you'd never ask."

"Then let's get going." He seemed distracted as he pulled me toward the front of the restaurant, but who wouldn't be after the evening we'd had.

We'd nearly made it past the host's desk when Sophia stepped in front of us. "Were you planning on sneaking out without a proper goodbye?"

I rolled my eyes. But Hudson, level and controlled as always, merely raised a brow. "Were you waiting here to attack me in case I was?"

Sophia frowned, her Botox'd forehead barely moving. "Of course not. I stepped away to call for my car. It's impolite to do such things at the table." Her tone was chiding. As if it had been Hudson wrapped into his phone all evening instead of her other son.

Hudson's grip tightened on my hand. "I already said goodbye to you, Mother."

"You did." She nodded at me. "She didn't. In fact, I don't remember her saying hello."

My stomach tightened and a thousand harsh responses crossed my mind in the matter of half a second. Taking my lead from Hudson, I chose to remain cool. "Neither did you."

"No, I didn't." Her smile was tight, but her eyes brightened. Suddenly I understood that she enjoyed sparring with me. If I were smart, then I wouldn't react. That would take away her reward.

But perhaps I liked the banter as well, the challenge similar to a good game of chess. "Actually, I thought that was very clever of you, Sophia. The evening went fairly well when we were pretending each other didn't exist. Don't you think?"

"Thank you. It was purely unplanned, seeing as how I didn't know you were coming until an hour before when Hudson called to tell me." Sophia was teasing me, trying to rile me up by letting me know I hadn't been on the guest list. It would have been a brilliant play if I hadn't already known.

I played it smooth. "Oh, you did call, H? I thought you were leaving it as a surprise."

"Yes, I called while you were dressing. I decided that Sophia might be better behaved if she was prepared." Hudson fell right into my game. Though he preferred to keep me sheltered from his mother's antics, he was generally amused by the way I handled her.

Her back straightened, a direct contradiction to the way she must have felt, her move having been countered so effortlessly. "Yes, it did work out well. I'll remember the ignoring tactic for next time."

My turn. "Then you've finally accepted there will be a next time?" *Check.*

Her smile widened as if I'd walked into a trap. "I'm nothing if not realistic, Alayna Withers. The question remains how many next times there will be. I'm in Hudson's life permanently. Are you?"

My composure faltered, my shoulders tensing, my body preparing for a fight.

Hudson stepped in. "Mother, stop it. It's your birthday. Happy day to you. If you're miserable, it's only because you won't let yourself enjoy anything." He let go of me and hugged Sophia awkwardly, giving her a dry peck on the cheek.

For the millionth time, I wondered at the relationship between mother and son. It had taken far less for me to cut off my brother. Of course, that had only been two days before. I couldn't speak for what would happen next between us. And I could only guess at Hudson and Sophia's past. The details were hidden from me, much like most everything in Hudson's life.

Time, I reminded myself. I'd learn about him in time.

Hudson broke the embrace, his hands pushing gently on Sophia's shoulders.

"You smell like sex," she said when he stepped away.

I couldn't help but take that as a compliment.

"I'm surprised you recognize the smell." Without moving his eyes from his mother, Hudson reached for my hand again.

I slipped my palm against his and absorbed the electric spark that always shot through my body at his touch.

Sophia's gaze drifted to our connected limbs and back to her son's face. "I'm not a prude."

Hudson shook his head once, bored with the conversation. "No, no one's accusing you of that. I'm simply shocked you could smell anything over the aroma of bourbon." *And checkmate.*

"Go home, Hudson. "

"Gladly."

We rode the elevator in silence and the limo as well. There was too much to think about—Jack and Sophia, Celia then Mira. So many aspects of the evening to dwell on, reasons to be confused and muddled. The one thing I wasn't confused about was Hudson. Not anymore. Not since the roof when he'd done some sort of magic sex trick that alleviated all my fears about him. He'd fucked away my doubts, said the right words, and for the first time in, well, ever, I thought that maybe I could be a normal girl in a normal relationship with a normal guy.

Okay, I'd never be a normal girl and Hudson would never be a normal guy, but perhaps we'd found the closest thing to normal that we'd ever be capable of achieving. And it was pretty damn good.

As I absentmindedly watched the buildings passing through the limo window, it didn't even cross my mind to wonder if we were going to The Bowery or if I was being taken home. Hudson hadn't given any instruction to our driver. I simply took it for granted that I'd spend the night with my lover. Hudson must have taken it for granted too, because Jordan pulled up to the curb in front of his high-rise without a word to me.

It was when we were in the penthouse and the quiet between us persisted that I realized it wasn't only me lost in my head. Hudson had disappeared inside his head too. It wasn't unusual for him to be quiet and within himself—that was the man I'd first met and been drawn to. But even when I'd seen him consumed with his work, he always had a sliver of his attention pinned to me. Though subtle, it was unmistakable.

Tonight was different. We exited the elevator and without a word, Hudson immediately headed to the library. I trailed after him, unsure. Though he hadn't been home since the arrival of the books, he didn't even give them a glance. He beelined to his desk, threw his jacket across the back of his chair and sat down.

Without looking at me, he said, "I have some work to do. It will likely be a late night. I don't expect you to wait up."

"Oh. All right." There was more shock to my tone than hurt. We'd never been alone and not all over each other. It was...strange.

For several seconds, I stood frozen, not knowing what I should do. Then common sense kicked in. "Do you need anything? A nightcap, perhaps?"

He sifted through some papers on his desk, furrowing his brow at one of them. "I may make myself a Scotch later." Then he turned to his computer and was gone from me.

I could make him a Scotch. I wanted to, actually, because then I'd feel needed, wanted. Like I had a purpose in being there.

But Hudson's tone was definitive. He didn't want me to serve him, for whatever reason, and even if I ignored him and got him his drink, I knew already that he wouldn't acknowledge it. Probably wouldn't even notice.

I made him the drink anyway, leaving it on the corner of his desk. He saw me, I knew he did. But like I suspected, he didn't respond.

He'd gone somewhere, somewhere far away. Somewhere he was unwilling to take me.

I slipped away to the bedroom and sat on the edge of the bed, still unmade from the night before. Hudson Pierce, obscenely rich and powerful, and he didn't even have someone who came in to make his bed daily.

Trivial thought, but it was what crossed my mind first.

Then the questions swept in, the constant examination that my mind never seemed to tire of. What had triggered this distant mood of Hudson's? Had it been the last conversation with his mother? The night in general?

Maybe he simply had work to do. He'd expected me to be at The Sky Launch all night. He hadn't planned to entertain me. And I shouldn't have expected that he should. We'd found each other, but that didn't mean the rest of our lives stopped. We still had things to do, responsibilities. Especially a man such as him.

I was sure it wasn't me, it wasn't us. He'd claimed me, the last time only two short hours before. I was his. His mood wasn't because of me.

As further proof, if I needed it, he'd brought me to his place when he could have easily taken me to my own. He wanted me there, even if he couldn't let himself be with me entirely. I knew that. *Knew.*

I took a deep breath, letting my tense muscles relax as I exhaled.

Then I let go.

Let go of all of it—the thoughts, the worries, the doubts. I wasn't doing psycho. Not anymore. No more obsessing. No more examining. Just let go.

Clarity settled in. People got moody. I was still practically a stranger to Hudson's life, relationships were new to both of us—I couldn't expect either of us to be perfect at communicating with each other. We had to learn, and that took time.

We had time.

I stared at the empty doorway, considering what to do with myself. Watch TV? Or read a book? There were plenty to choose from. I could join Hudson in the library, work on unpacking the books.

But my gut said he needed his space. Though he'd ignored me when I asked him to leave me alone on the roof, that tactic wouldn't work in reverse. Hudson didn't like to be handled like I did. I loved to be handled by him. Adored it. Craved it.

Hudson, though—his walls weren't as easy to overcome. They were mountains. I had to scale them cautiously with stealth and firm handholds. Sometimes I had to chill on a ledge and wait until the weather was better before I began my upward climb again. And sometimes, I'd reach the top of one, and he'd be there, waiting and exposed, and together we'd enjoy the breathtaking view.

Right now I was at a ledge. Chilling.

I laughed to myself. Whoever thought I'd be able to chill about a man? Yet, here I was, not acting crazy, no matter where my head wanted to go.

I stood and looked at myself in the dresser mirror. Did I look different? Paul had said I did. Did my eyes shine brighter? Were the ever-present dark circles under my eyes lighter than usual? Was this what it looked like to be mentally healthy? Because, even if my reflection showed nothing had changed, this me was completely new and amazing.

So even though Hudson's current temperament was baffling and mysterious, I felt good. Strong.

And I'd move in. If he was going to have bouts of isolation, I'd rather still be near him physically, even if I was apart from him emotionally. Besides, that night had proven we could weather stress, and we always seemed to weather it best together.

It was after ten, but I decided to run. I changed and slipped into the penthouse gym, spending forty minutes on the treadmill, followed by a quick shower. Then, after debating over a nightie or a t-shirt or simply my panties, I settled on staying nude and climbed in bed alone. I meant it to be a message to Hudson: *I'm naked for you. Bare for you. No more walls, no more guarded emotions.*

When he joined me later, he'd see. He'd get what I wasn't able to speak to him at the moment, an echo of the words that he had repeated to me over and over earlier. *I'm with you. I'm with you.*

I awoke sometime later in the dark room, lying on my side, with Hudson's arm around me, his hand fondling my breast. Silently, he kissed along my shoulder and up my neck.

I sighed into him, even half-asleep my body was instantly attuned to him, ready, wanting. Slipping my hand between my thighs, I rubbed at my clit, and he thrust into me with ease. It was only moments before we'd found our rhythm, our heavy breathing the lone sound as we moved together toward the same goal.

As my climax approached, my fingers yearned to be wandering up and down the landscape of Hudson's chest. Reaching behind to grab his ass wasn't enough. My hands felt empty and a vague thought drifted through my mind that our position mirrored the current state of our relationship. Both of us looking forward, working together toward a singular outcome, but with Hudson still not completely within my reach. My hands reaching for something I couldn't quite grasp.

We finished near together, and we laid there for several movements without moving or speaking. When our breathing had calmed to normal, I broke the silence. "Where did you go? Earlier."

He nuzzled his nose into my hair. "Does it matter? I'm here now."

I'd told Mira I'd talk to Hudson. But what was I supposed to do when he closed himself off? Even now, in the midst of intimacy, he left part of himself closed.

And maybe that was for the best. Because the parts of him that he opened were bright and blinding, like a beacon in the darkness. So I let my questions roll away, evaporating into nothing as he turned me toward him, lining me up underneath his form. Maybe conversation wasn't needed now. We would speak as we spoke best, with physical touch, our bodies rocking in simultaneous waves. Together.

"*Mon amour. Mon précieux*," he said against my ear. "*Mon chéri. Mon bien-aimé*."

He was speaking French. He said he would later, with my legs wrapped around him. So I threw my lower limbs around his hips, tilting into him.

Though the words were unnecessary, he muttered them over and over as we made love again. Between the kisses he placed on my neck and on my mouth, as he rolled in and out of me in rhythm with the beautiful poetry on his tongue. "*Je suis avec vous.* Always. I'm with you, *mon précieux*."

— CHAPTER —
FOURTEEN

The sun was still low and streaming through a gap in the curtains when Hudson released a hand from my breast to look at his watch. "I know it's Saturday," he said, kissing along my shoulder, "and it's early, but I have some business I have to take care of before it gets any later. Then I'll ravage you nonstop the rest of the weekend."

"All right. If you must." I was still recovering from two good-morning orgasms, barely able to form sentences, let alone do anything that required thought. But I did have an important task to attend to myself. One that I'd been avoiding. "I have a few things to do as well so it works out. Lucky for you."

"Lucky for me, indeed."

Hudson hit the shower first, while I got in a run on the treadmill. When I'd finished my workout, Hudson had withdrawn into the library. I took a shower of my own then sat on the edge of the bed, towel wrapped around me, phone in hand and contemplating the call I needed to make. It took four attempts of hitting *Dial* quickly followed by *End Call* before I got brave enough to let the call go through. Then I heard the ring on the other end of the line, and, knowing my number would be recognized, I couldn't hang up. He probably wouldn't answer anyway, so why was I being such a chicken shit?

It seemed like forever but finally my brother answered. "Oh my god, Laynie, are you okay?"

His concern irritated me. Either it wasn't genuine or it was too little too late. "Of course I am. Why wouldn't I be?" I hadn't been answering his calls, but that shouldn't have been cause for alarm.

"Because you haven't been at the club all week."

"What are you talking about? I've been there every day."

He sounded exasperated. "I called and asked for you every night this week and you were never there. At first I thought you'd told the staff you weren't taking my calls but then I gave a different name and called from a different phone."

"Jesus, Brian, I didn't realize that stalking was genetic."

"Ha ha." His tone was not amused. He'd never liked it when I joked about my disorder. Which was exactly why I did it.

"I wasn't at the club because I'm not working at night anymore, you moron." As if it was any of his business. Yet, something in me couldn't help but tell him. To brag, to seek for approval. "I got a promotion. I'm working marketing and promotional planning. Day hours. Just like you wanted."

"Oh. Wow. Congratulations, Laynie. I'm proud of you."

For half a second I felt warm and fuzzy. Then I remembered what a shit he'd been to me, how he'd cut me off financially, how he'd feared for my relationship with Hudson because of my obsessive history. Yeah, warm and fuzzy wasn't there to stay. "Whatever, Brian. I don't want to hear it."

"I mean it."

"Only because you're happy that I'm now following the plan you'd laid out for me." Brian had thought that night shifts and the club environment were not appropriate for someone with my condition, despite the fact that working at the club was what had helped me chill out in the first place. If he'd had his way, I'd be doing marketing for a Fortune 500 company during daylight hours, making a shit ton of money doing respectable work. But had I gone that route, I'd have been so bored and stifled I was sure I'd have shot myself within the first week of employment.

"That's not true." He almost sounded remorseful.

I almost felt bad.

"Wait, did you get this promotion because of Hudson Pierce?"

So much for feeling bad. "No. I did not. And fuck you very much for asking."

"What do you expect me to assume, Laynie? You want me to change my entire experience with you because you say things are different?"

"I don't know what I expect, Brian." As much as I wanted to, I couldn't really blame him for being spiteful. I'd been a burden, and, to his credit, he'd been there when I needed him most. Financially, if not emotionally. Truthfully, he was probably as broken as I was.

But understanding him didn't make it better. It simply meant I couldn't hate him.

I lay back on the bed and rubbed my hand over my eyes. "What was so important that you needed to reach me, anyway?" He'd said he was done with me. I figured that would have ended all communication.

He cleared his throat. "The lease on the apartment expires this month."

Of course. Tying up loose ends. "That's actually why I was calling you. I'm moving out. So whatever you need to do to end the lease, go ahead and do it."

"Where are you going to live?"

If I told him I was moving in with Hudson, he'd freak with a capital F. "That's none of your business." Besides, why did he even care?

"Fine, be a bitch. I'm sure you think I deserve it."

I ignored his blatant try to guilt me. "What do you want me to do with the keys?"

"You can give them to me personally when I come there. When are you planning to be out?"

"In the next week or so." Knowing Hudson, he'd have me completely moved out within a day of telling him. It would be an easy move anyway. The furniture belonged with the apartment.

But I didn't want to see Brian. There was no reason that I needed to. "Why do you need to come here?"

"To make sure the place is in good shape before I turn it over. I want to get my deposit back."

I sat back up. "You were there Monday, Brian. You saw what shape it was in. I didn't destroy the apartment after you left, if that's what you're suggesting. Do you think I'd do that just because I'm pissed at you?"

"I don't know what you would do." Brian's voice was raised. "I'm not surprised by anything anymore where you're concerned."

"This conversation is pointless. Text me when you're in town and I'll get you your fucking keys. Other than that, we're done." I clicked *End Call* and threw my phone on the bed.

What had happened to drive us so far apart? I would have thought that the tragic loss of our parents would make us more devoted to each other, more committed. We certainly loved each other. There was no question about that. But loving a person didn't necessarily make you right for them—didn't make them a good person to be in your world. That was definitely a common theme in therapy.

I ignored what that might mean about Hudson and me. That wasn't territory I was willing to broach. Besides, he'd been my salvation in ways that had nothing to do with money and everything to do with real support.

It was Brian who needed to be out of my life. It pained me to think about it in depth, so I didn't. So what if Brian was my only living relative? It didn't matter. I wouldn't let it.

I sat up, about to get dressed, when my phone bleeped that I had an email. I rarely received emails, but since my work email hadn't been set up yet, I'd had to resort to using my personal account when I sent my official proposal to Julia. Picking up my phone, I tried not to get my hopes up. I pressed the email icon and held my breath as I read. By the time I got through the first paragraph, I was nearly dancing. The email *was* from Party Planners Plus. And it was good news.

Hurriedly, I dressed into a pair of shorts and black and white sleeveless top, skipping the underwear entirely, then headed to the kitchen to grab something to eat before I ran to tell Hudson my good news. On the counter I found half a bagel and a banana waiting for me next to a mug of coffee. I smiled at Hudson's never-ending attentiveness. Yeah, moving in was a good decision.

Now I just had to tell him.

But, first, I'd share my news.

After eating three quick bites of the bagel, I peeled the banana, grabbed the coffee and headed for the library.

Hudson was on the phone when I entered the room, his back to me as he faced out over the city. His tone was direct and in charge as he spoke in a combination of English and Japanese. Wow—Hudson knew Japanese, too? He would never fail to surprise me and I loved that.

Not wanting to disturb him, I walked in quietly and perched on the edge of his desk behind him. I must not have been quiet enough, because he spun to look at me, not once halting his conversation. Wearing jeans and a tight blue polo that accentuated his firm abs, he looked hot—fuck, he was always hot, but his casual look was one I still wasn't used to. It made me squirmy and aware. Especially as I listened to him conducting his business. He always said my brain turned him on. I wondered if he had any idea that his turned me on as well.

He was equally enraptured by me, his eyes never leaving me as he continued his call. Perhaps the way I ate my banana was a bit sultry. I couldn't help myself. Could I ever when Hudson was in the room?

When he'd finished his call, he set the receiver in the cradle on the desk and swept his glance down my body, as he often did, like he was already fucking me in his head.

His gaze roused me instantly. My body was humming with electricity, my legs swinging with restless energy. "Am I interrupting?"

"Not at all. I'm done for the day." He hissed as I moved my lips slowly over my final bite of banana. "Done with work."

"Sounds like your phone call was a lot more productive than mine was then." I sucked at the tip of my thumb, pretending to clean off banana remnants when there weren't any there.

When I began to move on to my index finger, Hudson grabbed it and sucked it instead. "It's amazing I could even concentrate with your gorgeous mouth wrapped around your fruit. But that was your intention."

I gave a one-shoulder shrug. "I have no idea what you're talking about."

His mouth lifted up into a smile. "Such a wicked, wicked tease." He sat in his desk chair and rolled to face me square on. "Who was your conversation with?"

"My brother. It was painful."

"Want to talk about it?" His hands slid along my calves, sending electric sparks through my body.

"Nope." Not yet anyway. "I'm not letting him ruin my day and this day is fabulous. You know why?"

"Because I'm about to pounce on you?"

"That too." *God, that too.* My heart quickened with the anticipation. "But also because the event planners I met with agreed to make a deal."

"Of course they did. You're brilliant, remember?" His hands slid past my knees to my bare thighs, his fingers dancing lightly over my skin. "This is with Party Planners Plus?"

I tensed unwittingly. "Wow. Good memory." I'd hoped he would forget the details. The fact that he paid attention made it harder to believe he wouldn't discover Paul Kresh's involvement.

"Only where you're concerned."

That's what I'm afraid of. But I smiled, letting him believe I enjoyed his attention, which I did in general. Just not where Party Planners was concerned.

"Congratulations. I can't wait to see what you do with them." He leaned forward to place a kiss on the top of my thigh, so close and so far away from places that wanted his mouth more thoroughly.

"Me neither." My breath caught as he kissed me again, this time on my inner thigh. "It's a start. I'm excited about it." I wasn't certain I was talking about business anymore.

Hudson took my hand and tugged me forward to straddle him in his chair. "Then we both have good news today."

"Tell me yours." My hands wandered over his shirt, enjoying the feel of the firm landscape underneath.

His eyes closed in a long blink, and I knew he was enjoying my touch as well. Mirroring my movement, his palms fondled my braless breasts through my top. "I was on the phone with a contact in Japan. I've asked him to arrange for me to make a trip there in the next few days."

My hands stilled. "What? Why?" Japan was so far away. The thought of him going there for even a short time made my chest ache.

"To make a bid for Plexis."

"Really? Oh, Hudson, that's so great!"

"I approached that gentleman you heard talking. His name is Mitch Larson." Hudson continued to knead my breasts as he spoke, my body arching into his touch. "Turns out he doesn't have any selling power in his company, but he arranged for me to bid directly to his boss in Japan. I wouldn't have gotten the meeting if I hadn't gone through Mitch." I moaned as he pinched my nipples to two proud peaks. "And I wouldn't have known to approach Mitch if it weren't for you."

I squirmed, trying to get pressure where I needed it, low in my crotch. "I wouldn't have even been at that party if it weren't for you."

"You could easily have tuned the conversation out. Or not bothered to tell me. You did. For which I'm grateful."

His hands, still on my breasts, felt too far away. I needed them on my bare skin, ached for him to touch me without a barrier. Soon. He'd have to take me soon.

I bent to whisper in his ear. "How grateful are you?"

"I think you know." He bucked up and I could feel his erection—finally—meeting me at my core.

His mouth lifted to meet mine, but he took his time, brushing my lips with his nose, licking along the curve of my chin. His teeth nipped at my bottom lip and I couldn't take it anymore. Putting my hands on each side of his face, I held him steady as I crushed my lips to his. My tongue stayed shallow, teasing along his lower teeth until he plunged his tongue into my mouth. Then I claimed his mouth fully, sucking his tongue like it was his cock, reveling in the moan at the back of his throat as I did.

His hands stroked up and down my back but still hadn't gone under my shirt. I pulled on the bottom, hinting what I wanted, what I needed.

Instead of following my lead, he placed his hands gently on my shoulders and pushed me back. We were both breathless, and I, more than a bit confused, and so utterly aroused I couldn't sit still.

"Alayna, there's something I need to say." Hudson moved his hands to my hips to stop my fidgeting. "About yesterday. About moving in."

Fuck, was he taking it back? In the middle of a really hot make-out session? "Yes?"

"I don't want you here..."

He paused, and I got nervous that he'd reached the end of his statement.

But then he continued. "...so I can *control* you. I want you here because I can't bear it when you're not. I want you here because I want you with me—always."

It was perfect, absolutely perfect.

I let out a shaky breath. "Okay."

His body relaxed, his shoulders lowering. "Good. I needed you to understand."

"No, not okay, I understand. Well," I conceded, "that too. But I meant okay, I'll move in with you."

Hudson's brow arched in astonishment. "You will?"

Warmth spread through my body. "Why are you so surprised? I'd think you'd be used to getting your way. I bet you get everything you want."

"Most everything. But I often have to fight first. And I was prepared to fight for this. For you. It was much easier than I'd planned."

"Probably because I'd already decided to say yes. But even if I hadn't, you would have won me over with that." I placed my hands on the sides of his face. "Hudson, I want to be with you always, too. And who the hell cares if people say it's insane or too soon because I'm already crazy and I'm already madly in love with you."

"Alayna." His voice was gruff and heavy, as if the utterance of my name carried much more weight than it should have. Like it held so many meanings that Hudson wasn't able to express. With that one word, I was elevated to a state of emotion that I hadn't felt before, one that was deep and rooted and at the same time high and euphoric. It was falling in love all over again with someone I already loved to the bone.

He moved quickly, pulling my shirt off me in one swift motion, then lifting us up from the chair enough to work free his cock. I wrapped my hands around his hard length, stroking him with a mad sort of desperation while he kissed me senseless. His face still focused on me, he attacked my shorts with his hands, clawing at them as if he could tear them away. After a few frenzied minutes, he reached in the top drawer of the desk behind me and fumbled around blindly until he found what he was searching for—a pair of scissors.

Then he cut off my shorts.

I'd never imagined it would be so outrageously sexy to have my clothes cut off of me, or that anyone would actually do it. It was one thing when he'd ripped off flimsy thongs, but taking scissors, cutting so near my skin—I was wetter and hotter than I'd ever been, driven by his rabid need to have me naked and bared for him.

Once he'd tossed aside the torn material, he shifted his hands under my ass and lifted me on top of him. I was so wet; I slid down on him easily, sheathing him entirely.

"Oh, god, Hudson!" I could feel him so completely at that angle, his throbbing cock hitting against the wall of my vagina, making me writhe on top of him. I sat forward on my knees so that I could push off of him again, lifting and lowering at a frenetic speed that was more reminiscent of the way Hudson rode me, not the way *I* rode *him*.

My orgasm came without warning, ripping through me out of nowhere, slowing my pace. I fought to keep the momentum as the waves overtook me, shaking me and shattering me until I gave up with a long cry of pleasure.

I was barely aware of the chair rolling until the desk pressed into my back and Hudson took over the driving. He thrust into me with skill and precision, my legs wrapping around his waist as he shifted our position, the seat behind him serving as a place for him to fall rather than actual support.

When my vision cleared, I noticed the windows behind me. Though we were on the penthouse level of the building and it was highly unlikely that anyone was looking in, it was still possible and the realization added a profound level of eroticism. The delicious tension had just begun building again, intensifying exponentially when Hudson spilled inside me with a deep primal groan.

He gave himself no time to recover before he laid me across the desk. Pushing aside the chair, he knelt between my thighs, propping my ankles on the edge of the desk. I was naked and spread wide in front of the windows, in front of my lover—I was near my second climax before Hudson's tongue ever touched me.

He didn't tease or go slow like he often did when he ate me out, but sucked and licked at my clit with urgent strokes of his tongue. I came instantly and still he continued. It was too much—too intense for my heightened senses and my hips bucked away.

"Once more," Hudson said before renewing his attack.

"No!" I writhed but his hands held firm to my ankles. "I can't take it."

"Once more." He was insistent, not to be swayed, but he did redirect his approach, moving away from the singing ball of nerves and plunging his tongue into my hole instead.

My hands flew to his head, clutching fistfuls of hair as he worked me toward yet another high, his tongue licking up my slit back to my clit then down to plunge in again at my core.

Somewhere in the part of my brain that could still formulate thought, I knew what he was doing—he was thanking me, showing me how happy I'd made him by deciding to live with him. His own climax had come quickly, but he could get hard again. I knew this from experience. He probably already was hard again as it turned him on to no end to go down on me. Yet, instead of burying himself inside me, he was giving me all the pleasure. It was a message, and I got it loud and clear.

His endeavor slowed, but his ardor remained. The next orgasm came more reluctantly and he pulled it out of me with sweet, drawn-out dedication until I went over the edge, shivering as the warmth spread outward to my limbs, curling my toes.

Hudson stayed between my legs until I'd calmed, licking me and lavishing me with soft praise while my heart rate returned to normal.

Then he stood and carried me to the couch, laying me down.

He gazed at me, his eyes still half-closed with desire as he stripped naked. I was right—he was hard again, hard and throbbing. He lay beside me, wrapping his arms around me. Smoothing my hair with sensuous strokes, he spoke low at my ear. "I know it's scary and our situation hasn't been ideal, but you are everything good for me. Nothing in this world is important to me beyond you. I can be the same for you. I know it. And I'm so grateful you've given me the chance to prove it."

I shifted to face him. "You have nothing to prove. You're already everything good for me, too."

"Shh." He kissed my forehead. "Not yet. I haven't been able to give you everything you need yet."

My mind scrambled to figure out what he possibly thought I needed that he hadn't given me. The three words. That was the only thing I could settle on. But I knew them even if he didn't say them. I knew them with every fiber of my being.

"It's okay, Hudson. It's—"

He cut me off. "It's not. But I need you to know that I'm trying and I'm not going to stop trying until I get there. Do you hear me? Don't give up on me." He was vehement, his expression frantic.

"I'm not giving up on you." I reached my palm up to caress his face and he leaned into my touch. "Why would I do that? I love you, Hudson. So much."

His eyes closed tight, almost as if my statement were painful to him. "I don't deserve your love. I don't think I ever will."

"You deserve more than I can ever give you."

"We have a difference of opinion on that. We'll have to agree to disagree. Again." He pushed at my shoulder. "Turn," he ordered.

I shifted to face the back of the couch and immediately felt Hudson's thick erection pressing behind me. Lifting my leg up and back around him, he slid into me again. "This time," he whispered between kisses at my neck, "we're going to take it slow."

— CHAPTER —
FIFTEEN

As I imagined would be the case, Hudson was eager for my moving in to commence immediately. Correction—immediately after another round of lovemaking. Bursting with an excitement I'd never seen from him before, he made arrangements with "his people," and by the end of Saturday, the relatively few things I owned had been boxed and brought over to The Bowery. It happened so fast that the anxiety of it didn't even have time to overwhelm me, and whenever I felt it creeping up, I simply promised to deal with it at my Addicts Anonymous session on Monday.

It was easy to unpack. Almost all my belongings fit in the extra closet in the bedroom—*our* bedroom. Only one item, a hope chest that had belonged to my mother, found its way to the extra room. I was completely settled by Sunday evening, and the sore muscles I boasted were not from carrying boxes but from other physical activity.

Monday came too soon, yet wasn't dreadful since I adored our wake-up routine. Our cell alarms going off in tandem, a quickie in the shower, getting ready side by side at the twin sinks, sharing a fast bite at the kitchen table—all of it rocked. The still thrilling newness of it combined with the security of knowing the situation wasn't temporary sent me to the club with a spring in my step, a rarity for me since I had never been anything near a morning person.

Since I was in such a good mood, I began my workday by tackling what felt like the most daunting of my tasks: rescheduling with Aaron Trent. I had suspected that the only reason he'd agreed to meet with me in the first place was because of Hudson. When he'd canceled on Friday night, my suspicions were confirmed. All it would take was one call from my boyfriend and I knew the meeting would be back on. But I wanted to do it myself.

Since I didn't have a direct phone number to Trent's office, and I didn't want to ask Hudson, I had to use the agency number listed on his website. It took two transfers before I reached Trent's assistant. "I need to make an appointment with Aaron Trent. Is that something you can help me with?"

The voice on the other end was bubbly and professional. "I can take your information, but I'll have to check with him before any meeting time is approved."

"That makes sense." I ran my hand over my face. Why on earth did I ever think I'd be able to get to talk to the man myself? Despite the futility of it, I delivered my information. "This is Alayna Withers from The Sky—"

"Ms. Withers," Bubbly Professional cut me off. "I didn't realize it was you. Mr. Trent said if you called that we could go ahead and reschedule for whenever would be most convenient for you."

"Oh. Okay." So maybe he hadn't been planning to bail on me after all. I was pleasantly surprised. Not that I was fooled that his eagerness to meet had anything to do with me and nothing to do with whom I was sleeping with, but I also knew if I had him in front of me, I could impress the balls off the guy.

We made arrangements for an evening later in the week, but before I hung up, I asked the question itching on my tongue. "Hey, do you have any idea why Mr. Trent canceled to begin with? I know it's none of my business. Just curious."

Bubbly Professional seemed surprised. "Mr. Trent didn't cancel. Some woman from your club called Friday afternoon and said something had come up. I'd assumed it was you."

That was impossible. No one even knew I had the meeting that night except for David and Hudson. And last I checked, neither of them were women. "It wasn't me. Are you sure?"

"Yep. I took the call myself."

Either someone had canceled my meeting on Friday without my permission or I was seriously being pranked. Whichever it was, Bubbly Professional didn't need to hang on the line while I figured it out. "My mistake. Thank you and please apologize to Mr. Trent for any inconvenience it may have caused him."

"Honestly," her voice lowered as if she were sharing a secret, "this worked out better for him. He would have had to miss out on a daddy daughter dance if you'd kept the Friday appointment, and Rachel's the type of girl that doesn't take disappointment well. So you kind of did him a favor by canceling."

Ah, so it was probably Rachel Trent who canceled. I'd never been close to my father, but I could appreciate her wanting to be with her dad. I'd definitely done things equally as manipulative as a teen.

I thanked Bubbly Professional for the information, hung up the phone, and moved on to the other items on my day's agenda.

It was nearly three when the bell rang at the service entrance. I checked the camera feed since we weren't expecting any deliveries. It was Liesl.

"Be right there," I told her through the intercom then ran down to let her in.

I opened the door and opened my arms for Liesl to give me a bear hug. She was one of the only people I allowed to touch me so intimately and only on my terms.

"What are you doing here so early?" I asked into her hair. "Do you work tonight?"

"Nope. Off tonight." She let me go to give me a high five. "We could hang out later, if you want."

"I do want. I have group at five-thirty. Maybe after that?"

"Groovy. I just had coffee with some friends next door. They want me to go to a concert with them so I came by to check out next week's schedule. Is it up yet?"

"Yeah, I think I saw it. Come on up."

We climbed the back stairs to the office. I found the schedule on David's mess of a desk and turned around to hand it to her and jumped when I saw a figure in the doorway. Another half second and I realized it was Hudson. I'd almost forgotten he had his own set of keys.

"Hi! What are you doing here?" It was a nice surprise to see him unannounced in the middle of the day, though also odd.

His expression was even. "You need to come with me."

"Why? What's up?" I took a step toward him before I recognized the tension in his body, the firm set of his jaw, the light missing from his eyes. "Hey, are you mad at me?" He'd never truly been upset with me before.

Not like this, where the anger rolled off him in waves so thick it was almost palpable.

"Get your things and come." He spit out the words, as if it was difficult to speak civilly.

"That bossy thing is so hot." Liesl didn't even bother whispering.

Admittedly there were times I thought the bossy thing was definitely so hot. This was not one of them. His tone and body language scared me. I didn't believe he'd ever hurt me—not physically, and not on purpose—but his agitated state suggested he didn't have control of himself.

I crossed my hands over my chest defiantly. "Hudson, I'm not leaving just because you say so. I need more information."

"Alayna, I'm not doing this here." He was shaking. I'd never seen him so upset. "You will get your things and come. Now." It wasn't a suggestion. It wasn't an invitation. It wasn't even an order. It was fact. It was what I would do, as expected as my next breath.

He had to know.

The certainty rushed through me at lightning speed, leaving me dizzy and weak.

I couldn't say how or which of my secrets he'd discovered, but there was no doubt in my mind that he had found *something* out, and I understood with irrefutable conviction that if I had any real interest in our relationship then I needed to do as he said. Hudson had reasons to be mad at me—very real, very valid reasons. And if I wanted to salvage what we had, I'd have to take his wrath. I deserved it. I owed it to him.

I started toward my purse, ready to leave at his side when I remembered Liesl. "I, I have an employee here and I'm the only other person here. David's not due in until five."

"It's fine, Laynie." Liesl flashed me the palm of her hand and I could see pen marks that I guessed were her schedule. "I got what I needed. I'll leave with you."

It was almost comical that Liesl didn't understand the gravity of Hudson's mood, that she took it for granted that his behavior was commonplace and that I welcomed it. But I was too mortified to laugh. Too deeply disgraced.

I swallowed down the thick ball in my throat and looked to Hudson, not meeting his eyes. "I need to close everything up. I unlocked the bar when I got a soft drink earlier and the computers are still up—"

Hudson's hands were balled into fists at his sides. His patience was wearing. "Text David and tell him I required you to leave on short notice. Alarm the main door. It'll be fine." Tersely, he added, "I doubt David will care."

Was it David, then? Was that what this was about? Or was I reading into things?

I was in a daze as we walked out, my feet moving automatically while Liesl chatted nonstop about the new bartender. I'm sure that I nodded and said, "Uh-huh," at the appropriate times because she didn't call me out on my lack of attention.

At the door, it took me three tries before my unsteady hands entered the alarm code correctly. We stepped outside into the daylight, the sun blinding after the dark of the club. Liesl squeezed my hand in goodbye. "I'll take a rain check on that girls' night out. Have fun with Mr. Dominant." She wiggled her eyebrows before she took off toward the subway station.

I looked to the curb and realized there were no familiar cars waiting for us. When I turned back to Hudson, he was walking toward the other shops, already several feet away. I jogged to catch up with him but slowed my speed before I got to his side. It was easier to avoid his gaze if I were a step behind him.

We walked in silence and my mind struggled to get a grip on the situation. We were headed to Central Parking. He must have driven himself, probably parked in one of the club's designated parking spots. He usually only drove himself for sport, and he didn't really seem in the "for sport" mood. He must be driverless for another reason. Like, he'd been so worked up he couldn't even wait for a ride to be arranged. He simply took off, in a rage. I tried to imagine it—him at his office, immersed in working when—what? What had happened to make him drop everything and drive himself to find me? But wasn't that the million dollar question? Well, we were talking about Hudson Pierce—100 million dollar question was more like it.

At the garage, Hudson clicked the security button on his key ring, and the Maybach announced its presence, parked, as I'd guessed, in one of the club's two VIP spots that were rarely taken. Despite his chilly attitude, he opened the passenger door for me and reminded me to text David before walking around to the driver's side.

I punched a quick message into my phone that I prayed made sense without sounding like I was in trouble. But wasn't I? In big trouble?

No, why should I be? Just because I was in love with the man, because we had some unspoken commitment to each other that I had broken with my secrets—none of that meant that I had to sit by like a wayward child waiting for her punishment. I was a big girl. Sure, I had to take responsibility for my actions, but I didn't deserve to be in the dark, handled with hostility and rage.

We'd just pulled out of the garage when I decided to take a stand. "What's going on?" I was met with silence. "Hudson?"

"I'm not ready to talk about this yet." The vein in his neck twitched. I'd never seen him like that. Not even when he'd accused me of being involved with David.

David. If I had to make a guess, I was betting that was the source of his ire. Still, I played it cautiously, giving nothing away, even though a part of me wanted to spill everything, tell Hudson every little moment of betrayal. But I was too frightened that I'd lose him, so instead I delivered a generic plea. "Whatever it is I did, I'm sorry. I'm sorry and I'll do whatever I have to do to fix it."

A cabbie honked as Hudson switched lanes, pulling out in front of him. "Alayna, I can't talk about this while I'm driving."

He accelerated through a yellow light and I braced myself against the console. "Yeah, good idea. Focus on the road because you're scaring me."

The look he shot me was pure fury. "Good. Maybe you should be scared."

I didn't try to talk after that. His driving didn't improve, even in the silence, and I was grateful it was a short distance to The Bowery. I hadn't even been aware the underground parking existed until we'd entered the tunnel and parked next to his Mercedes. *Huh, I'd wondered where he kept that when he wasn't using it.*

Being with Hudson, I'd gotten used to doors being opened for me, but I hopped out the minute the car stopped. He might be mad, and I might deserve it, but I didn't have to take it like a pussy.

We rode the elevator in sharp silence. In the penthouse, Hudson headed straight for the bar. I followed, my arms folded over my chest, and waited for him to decide that he was *ready to talk*.

He'd poured and drank half of his Scotch before facing me. "Tell me one thing. One thing and think carefully before you answer because I want to believe what you tell me." His voice was even, measured.

I leaned against the back of the couch, bracing myself.

"Are you still in love with him?"

So it was David. How Hudson had found out was beyond me. I couldn't imagine David sidling up to his boss and sharing the sexual adventures he'd had with me. Especially when David had ended things specifically so Hudson would never find out.

However he'd figured it out, it didn't matter. What mattered was setting the record straight now. "No, I'm not. I was never in love with him."

Hudson closed his eyes briefly, almost as though he were relieved. But when he opened them again, the stone coldness remained from before. "Then whatever it was—attraction, obsession. Do you still feel that for him?"

"I never felt any of that for him. He was safe. We messed around a few times." I winced at Hudson's hurt expression. "That's really the extent of it. Really and truly. He was just a guy I had chemistry with but not enough to drive me crazy." *Not like you. Never like you.*

"Then why did he file a restraining order?"

A whoosh of air swept through my ears, leaving me lightheaded. Dizzy. "Wait, who are you talking about?" The only restraining order I'd had was with Paul. And the secret that I was working with Paul was much heavier than the David thing.

My fingers curled into the sofa behind me as I waited for him to say the name I knew he'd say.

"Paul Kresh."

"Oh." I nodded slowly for several seconds. "Oh." There was nothing else to say. I had no reaction, I had no defense. "You found out about Paul."

His teeth gritted. I could hear as he ground them together. "Since you know I'm already aware of your past with Paul, you must be referring to the fact that he's a partner in Party Planners Plus."

I shook my head.

"You didn't know?" There was hope in his tone. He wanted me to not know.

But I couldn't lie. It was one thing to keep it from him, quite another to lie outright. "Well, he's not technically a partner, so that's not a fair question."

"Dammit, Alayna. Don't hedge around the facts. Because I'd like to think that you would never do something so stupid as to sign a deal that would put you in close working proximity with someone that you are legally not supposed to be anywhere near. The Alayna I know would never do something so brainless."

But I *had* signed the deal. That morning, in fact. "Guess you don't really know me."

He slammed his empty glass on the bar. "This is not a fucking game!"

"Don't you think I know that?" I raised my voice to match his. "I'm the one who has the restraining order. I get the seriousness of the situation." I pointed my finger into my chest at each mention of the word *I* so forcefully, I knew it would bruise.

"Then why?" His eyes were pleading. "You can't have been that desperate to sign a deal. I had thought—I'd *hoped*—that you didn't realize that Kresh was engaged to Julie Swaggert—"

"Engaged? I thought they were just dating."

The look on his face said that wasn't the thing to say.

I quickly corrected. "Which doesn't matter, I know. I didn't mean to seem interested, because I'm not. I'm not, Hudson. I don't care what or whom he's with. It's only that he didn't say they were engaged when we talked."

"You talked to him?"

I hadn't thought he could be more enraged. Turned out I was wrong.

"So help me god, Alayna, you better say it was on the phone."

Lie, lie, lie. It was a song in my head, repeating the same refrain. I willed myself to ignore it. "It wasn't. It was in person."

He stepped toward me, his hands poised like he wanted to wring my neck. "Dammit, Alayna! What the fuck were you thinking?"

"Stop yelling at me and I'll explain." Even though I knew he wouldn't hit me, his rage wasn't productive. And as mad as he was, I was afraid he wouldn't get past his anger. That he'd end things for sure. I needed a hint that there was a chance we weren't over.

"I'm waiting." His volume was lower, but his demeanor hadn't changed in the least.

"I'm not saying anything until you calm down. You're scaring me."

He looked as though I'd slapped him. "That's fair." He ran a hand through his hair. "But this is as calm as I'm going to get."

I swallowed. "I, um, had the meeting with Julia. On Thursday. And I didn't know she was involved with Paul. But then at the end he showed up and I was totally unprepared." A chill ran through me at the memory of seeing him in the club, at the shock I'd felt. "He acted like he didn't know me so I followed his lead. And then when Julia went off to the bathroom, Paul told me he didn't want to ruin the deal for her and so we had to pretend we'd never met."

I stepped toward Hudson, hating the look on his face, wanting him to be comforted. "I told him I couldn't work with him, Hudson, and he said I had to. He said Julia was dying to work with Pierce Industries and this was her *in* and if I screwed it up…" I bit my lip and tasted blood. "He said I owed him."

"Alayna, you don't fucking owe him anything." His voice was still harsh, but less so.

My eyes stung. "I do! I ruined his life."

"He cheated on his fiancée. He ruined his own life."

"But there's more to it than that, and you know it."

"You still don't owe him shit. You were sick. You weren't responsible for what you were doing."

I took that in. I had been sick. I hadn't been in control of my actions. I knew this. I'd accepted this in therapy.

But that didn't change anything. "It doesn't matter. Even if I don't owe him, he has this over my head. He could say that I set up the meeting simply to get to him. I mean, I didn't, but it could look that way." I chuckled harshly. "Even you thought that I did. And then he was there again that night at the Botanic Gardens. It looks like I could have been following him. Who's going to believe me over him?"

I'd been avoiding his eyes, but I met them now. "If I violate that order again, I could see jail time." Not to mention what could happen to Hudson in the media. He'd be the joke of the town.

"Alayna." He closed the short distance between us in two quick steps and wrapped his arms around me.

I hadn't realized how close my tears were to the surface until I was safe and in his arms. I cried softly into his shoulder, not only because of what I'd done or because of the pressure I'd been under keeping it in, but because he was holding me. They were tears of relief.

Hudson pulled me in even tighter. "Why didn't you come to me? I would never let anything bad happen to you. Never. You have to know that, don't you?"

I turned my face so my words wouldn't get lost in the material of his suit jacket. "I got scared. Of what he could do to me. Of what he could do to you." The long strokes he ran along my back made it easy to keep talking, easy to confess. "And I wanted you to be proud of me. Of the deal I made."

He pushed me away suddenly and gripped my upper arms. Bending to catch my gaze, he said, "I'm always proud of you, Alayna. Always."

It broke me. Again.

I clutched on to his shirt inside his open jacket. "I should have told you. I'm so sorry. I didn't know what to do and I wanted to tell you. Please, don't be mad at me."

Softly, he shushed me. "Don't. Don't cry, precious." He held me as I cried. When I was calmer, he said, "I'm only mad because you put yourself in danger. You scared me. You can't imagine what I felt when the background report came across my desk and I realized the situation. Don't you know I couldn't stand it if anything bad happened to you?" His voice cracked.

"Yes, I know." It was exactly how I'd feel if something happened to him.

"And I'm mad because you didn't come to me."

"I wanted to. I did. But Ce—" I almost mentioned Celia, stopping myself right before I did. I didn't think it was a good time to add that secret to the mix. "But I didn't want you to have to get in the middle of my mess."

I pulled away, looking aimlessly for a tissue.

Hudson pulled a handkerchief from his pocket. Who the hell carried handkerchiefs? There was still so much to learn about this man.

"Don't be silly," he said, dabbing at my eyes. "First of all, I own The Sky Launch so I'm legally responsible for anything that goes on in regards to employees and the people they interact with."

I hadn't thought of that.

He ran his thumb gently down the side of my face. "But more importantly, if you're in a mess of any sort, then so am I. Not legally. But because you're mine. And I'm yours. And that means I'm tied to you in every way. Good and bad. If you can't see that, then we have no chance."

Oh, god. The enormity of it hit me. I'd put all we had in jeopardy, put *us* at risk. "I really fucked everything up." I felt the color leave my face. "Oh, god, Hudson."

He tilted my chin up with one finger and kissed my nose. "You didn't fuck everything up. I can fix it. Now that I know."

"What will you do?" I had a brief flash of men in trench coats meeting up with Paul in a dark alley. Sad that the thought brought a smile to my face.

"I wouldn't do anything illegal, if that's what you're thinking."

Damn, he could read me so well.

"I'll offer Party Planners Plus a deal with Fierce in exchange for terminating the contract with The Sky Launch. Fierce is a bigger name and can offer a better payout. They'll still be working with the Pierce name. Kresh will have nothing to complain about."

"Good plan. Thank you." If I'd only come to Hudson in the first place, he would have arranged a deal like this and I wouldn't have put anyone—myself—in a precarious position. My stomach churned with self-loathing. "I'm sorry, Hudson. I'm sorry you have to clean up my mess. I'm such an idiot."

"Shush up." His arms were around me again, holding me, comforting me when it was the last thing I deserved. "Stop feeling guilty. It's our mess, remember? And I want to clean it up. It's one of the things I'm capable of. Let me."

"All right." I took a deep breath, letting all my worry and regret out as I exhaled. "All right, I'll let you."

— CHAPTER —
SIXTEEN

Hudson pocketed his damp handkerchief, and I could feel his disposition change, could feel him moving away. "Now, Alayna. What else do you need to tell me?"

"What—what do you mean?" I was still recovering from the last horrific confession. What other information did I need to disclose? At this point, I was ready to spill everything.

Hudson took his jacket off, folding it and setting it on the back of the sofa. "When we started this conversation, you thought I was talking about something else. Some*one* else." His eyes pierced me. "Who did you think I was talking about?"

Honesty. I owed him honesty. "I thought you were talking about David."

"David Lindt?"

"Yes."

He backed up until he was leaning against the wall. I hated that he needed the support. "You told me there was nothing between you and David."

"There's not. Anymore."

"But there was."

"Yes."

I could see the pain across his face. It killed me. It was exactly how I'd feel if I found out there had been something with him and Celia. I wanted to go to him, to hold him like he'd held me, to make it better.

I stepped toward him, but he put a hand out to stop me.

"It was nothing, Hudson. We were sort of together. But not really. We didn't go on dates or anything or tell anyone about us. Just, when we worked late, alone…things happened." The words tasted awful in my mouth.

"Did you sleep with him?"

"No. Things never went that far." This hadn't been the first time the subject had been broached. "You've asked me this before and I told you *no* then as well. I wasn't lying."

He shot me a challenging glance. "I also asked if you had wanted to and I never got a straight answer."

"I don't know the answer." I considered leaving it at that. But I knew it would always hang over us unless I let it all out. "Yes. I suppose I did. Once upon a time. But not now." Again, I wanted to move toward him. This time I stopped myself before he did. "There's nothing now, Hudson. You have to believe me."

It was after several long seconds that he spoke. "I do."

"You do?" I couldn't hide the shock from my voice.

"Yes. You don't look at him the way you look at me."

"Of course, I don't."

"But he looks at you the way I look at you. The way I imagine I look at you."

"No, he doesn't." Yes, David had feelings for me, but they didn't compare to the way Hudson felt about me. "You're exaggerating."

Hudson straightened and began pacing. "I'm not. It's a problem and I can't have it continuing."

"What does that mean?" I knew the answer without having to ask, the dread washing over me in a thick wave.

"It means he's going to have to leave The Sky Launch."

"Don't even joke." As if Hudson was the type to kid.

"Does it seem like I'm joking?"

"Hudson, no. You can't do that." My voice was louder than I would have liked it. I'd prefer to be stoic and cold like him, but that wasn't me. "You can't fire David because of a stupid fling we had before I even met you. He's the responsible one at the club. He's the one who said we needed to end it."

His glare was heart-stopping. "You aren't helping your case."

"But you can't fire David because we messed around once upon a time. It's over. It's not fair. It's not fair to David." I felt very near to throwing a tantrum. I may have even stomped my foot once.

Hudson returned to the bar to refill his Scotch. "It was going to happen anyway. Regardless of what you and he…" He took a deep breath and I knew from the awful pain in his eyes that he was thinking about David and me together. They were horrible thoughts. Things I never wanted him to have to imagine. But there wasn't anything I could do. I'd certainly thought of him and Celia in the same terrible ways. It was painful and heartbreaking, but endurable.

Hudson would endure as well.

Despite his misery, I had to ask, "What do you mean by *it was going to happen anyway*?"

He shook his head, took a gulp of his drink and set it down. "This isn't how I wanted to tell you. It was meant to be a surprise at an appropriate time. But the truth is that I've wanted to make a management change since I bought the place."

I leaned against the sofa back, not wanting to hear anymore, unable to stop the inevitable words.

"Alayna, I want you to run the club."

"Hudson…no."

"I bought the club for you."

A shudder ran through me. "What are you talking about? You didn't know me when you bought the club."

"The symposium—"

I cut him off. "You told me you were already looking at the club. The fact that I worked there influenced you. Never did you say anything about buying it for me." In my head, I replayed everything I knew about our strange meeting. He'd seen me at the symposium, but I hadn't known that until later. He came into the bar, once. We'd flirted and he'd given me a big fat tip and a trip to his spa, behavior that in itself was psycho-aggressive. None of it warranted the purchase of a business. If that was the real reason he'd bought the club—well, then he was crazier than me.

"I didn't tell you because I didn't want to seem too forward."

"Well, too fucking late for that."

He continued with an annoying degree of impassivity. "It wasn't as insane as it sounds, Alayna. It was business. I saw you at the symposium and knew I needed you working for me. Since you weren't taking any interviews with companies, I had to buy the company you were already at. Yes, I was attracted to you. Yes, it influenced my decision to pursue your talent, but wanting you working for me was the driving force of that pursuit."

It wasn't an uncommon scenario. Smart-minded business players often made large company purchases simply to get control of a talented workforce. "Then you got what you wanted. I *am* working for you. I don't have to run The Sky Launch to be working for you." I ran my hands up and down my arms, trying to get warm. "I have an important role, and I don't need anything more right now."

He stepped toward me, his impassivity replaced with vehemence. "Alayna, you have so much potential!"

"Stop it! You sound like my brother. Don't decide that I'm wasting my potential. I'm building up to it at my own speed. I'm not ready to run a club, Hudson." My hands flew expressively as I spoke—pointing at him, then at myself, then flinging madly at my sides.

Hudson chortled. "You're going to have to be ready. Otherwise someone else will have to step into that role when David's gone."

"Then this isn't about me at all! It *is* about David. You can't fire him. You can't!"

"It's about you, Alayna. No one but you." The calm exterior he'd adopted after the Paul Kresh situation was completely abandoned now. "I told you I don't share. I won't share you. Not with him. Not with anyone. I will bend over backwards to give you everything you need and want, but this is the one thing I have to have in return. Fidelity."

"I am faithful. I've never been anything but faithful. I have no desire to cheat on you with David or anyone. I'm yours, like you said."

"Yes. You are. Mine. And I should have gotten rid of him the minute I suspected there had been anything between you."

The truth of what he was saying hit me in the gut. "In other words, you don't trust me."

"I don't trust *him*!"

"It doesn't matter if you trust him as long as you trust me!"

His face transformed into a bitter expression I'd never seen before. "Today I discovered you kept both your relationship with David and your recent interaction with Paul Kresh from me and you're talking about trust? Good timing, Alayna."

Ouch. But I deserved that. David, however, did not. "I told you why I didn't tell you about Paul. And this is why I didn't tell you about David.

Because I was afraid you'd overreact, and wow, here you are trying to fire the best employee The Sky Launch has!"

"*You're* the best employee The Sky Launch has."

Under different circumstances, his faith in me would be flattering. "I beg to differ. I wouldn't be worth shit without David, and I don't want his job."

Hudson leaned forward, his eyes dark. "It's not an option. You want to work at the club, you'll work in the position that I choose."

Rage boiled through me. "Then I quit! Because I can't work for someone who's so obviously jealous and controlling. And you're seriously making me reconsider my living situation as well."

"Don't!" He stepped forward, his face in mine. "Don't throw our relationship on the line because of a good business decision."

I wanted to push him back, push him away. At the same time, I wanted to pull him in and kiss away all the jealousy and angst between us, wanted to end the awful tension. I'd threatened our relationship, but I didn't mean it. I wouldn't throw it away. I'd do whatever I had to in order to keep him mine.

But I wasn't letting my cards show yet. I didn't touch him at all. I stayed rigid as I spoke. "You aren't making this decision because it's good business. You're trying to punish me."

His eyes widened. "I'm punishing you by giving you a promotion?"

"A promotion I don't want!"

He spun away from me, as though he were too afraid of what he'd do if he stayed in such close proximity. When he'd taken a few steps, he turned back to face me. "You want me to take everything from you, but you won't take from me? How am I supposed to feel about that?"

"This isn't the same." He was twisting my words, taking something I'd said in a time of beauty and bringing it into a war zone. It hurt. Deep, in my bones. I wanted it to stop. "I don't want this, Hudson. I don't want it!"

I turned to run away. Where, I didn't know. Just away from him and the terrible situation he was putting me in.

But I'd only made it a few steps when he came after me, his arms circling around my waist from behind.

I squirmed, kicking and hitting at him. "Let go of me!"

"No. I'll never let you go." He must not have meant physically, because he did let me go. He threw me on the couch and began undoing his pants.

Immediately my sex felt on fire. The thought of him fucking me with all that rage and passion was a big turn-on. And, honestly, we probably needed the contact—to reconnect before we grew too far apart.

But I was headstrong, not willing to give in. I slipped under him to the floor, crawling toward the elevators as fast as I could.

His strong hand grabbed my ankle, drawing me back to him. I clawed at the floor, but I already knew it was hopeless. Not because he was stronger than me, but because he knew what I really wanted—that I wanted him to overpower me.

He stretched out over me, holding me to the floor, both my hands pinned above my head with one of his. He nipped at my ear. "God, you are so maddening. How can I want you so much when you drive me so insane?"

Using his whole body, he turned me underneath him and crushed his mouth to mine in a fierce kiss—a kiss that was forceful and dominating and full of so much emotion.

I resisted at first, turning my head away from him. But he was relentless and his unusual display of emotion disarmed me. My head was overruled by my body—by my heart—and I surrendered to him, giving in to his demanding mouth and the masterful hands that had already freed his rock-hard cock.

He reached down under my dress, moving the flimsy thong material out of the way to stick a long finger inside me. If he didn't understand my need before, he did now. I was wet and swollen for him.

He groaned in satisfaction.

"It doesn't mean I'm not mad." It was my last attempt to state my case before he replaced his finger with his cock.

I cried out at the exquisite bite of pleasure, the incredible feeling of fullness, almost too much yet also not enough. I needed him to move, to thrust, to ride me.

"Fine," he said, jabbing deeper into me, still not moving the way I ached for him to. "Be mad. Take it out on me. I'm planning to take out my emotions on you."

And he did. He drew himself out almost to the tip. It must have taken more control than I could imagine, his contorted expression showing the strain of the slow retreat. Then he let go, pounding into me with thick, insistent stabs. My hips bucked at each deep plunge in rhythm with his primal grunts. Even the sound of his loose belt buckle slapping against the floor added to the animalistic way he took me, as if it were a whip driving the beast, urging him on.

I moaned and tightened around him within minutes, surprised to feel the build of orgasm so quickly with only vaginal stimulation. It was the whole scene, the depravity of it, the utter baseness. It was wild and feral and uncontrolled. I hated that I loved it—loved it so entirely.

He wrapped his loose hand in my hair, yanking at it with just the right amount of pleasure and pain. My eyes began to close.

"Look at me," he snapped.

My eyes flew open, meeting his.

"Can't you see?" I was surprised he could speak through his exertion. "Can't you see what you do to me? Can't you see how you make me feel?"

He shifted, and I gasped as he hit a particularly tender spot. "Do you feel how hard you make me?"

I didn't know if he wanted an answer, didn't think I could speak if he did.

But he tugged again at my hair. "Do you?"

"Yes," I cried out.

He picked up his speed, reaching a frenzied pace that threw me over the edge. "You do this to me, Alayna."

I struggled to keep my eyes on him, to focus on his words through the rapturous haze that enveloped me. His words were important, and I wanted to hear what he said as much as I wanted to lose myself in the ecstasy he'd bestowed on me.

He was on the brink, too—I could read his body like it was my own—but still he kept his gaze connected to mine. "Even when you're petulant and contrary, I still want you. Always, I want you. I want to give you everything. All of me. Why can't you take it? Take it."

He delivered one more elongated thrust, burying himself deeply as he poured into me with a low groan. "Take it!"

I whimpered as his release shuddered through me, extending my own into a second wave of euphoria that sent chills down my spine. Lost in the fog of post-orgasm, my ears still thrumming with the pulse of my heartbeat, I had a brief moment of clarity—what if it wasn't Hudson that was incapable of being loved fiercely, but me?

The thought was fleeting, gone as soon as it had come. Of course, I could take his love. It was he who didn't know how to show it.

He'd rolled off me by then and was sitting with his back braced against the sofa. Only traces of the wild passion he'd displayed a moment ago were present in his features, his shortness of breath one of the only indicators that he'd ever lost control.

Suddenly I was angry. Angry with him for resorting to fucking as a way to end our disagreement like he always did. Angry that he expected it would change anything. Angry at myself for being seduced.

I propped myself up on my elbows and glared.

"Now, come on, Alayna." His eyes narrowed. "You can't tell me you didn't enjoy it."

His condescending tone irked me even more. "Sex isn't the only way to show a person how you feel."

"I know. I tried to give you a nightclub."

His words stung though I couldn't quite grasp why.

I was still figuring it out when he stood and zipped himself up. "If you want to continue fighting about this, which I'm sure you do, it will have to be later. I have work to do."

My scowl remained long after he'd left. It was almost funny that I felt so enraged. I'd thought he'd fall to pieces if he'd known I wasn't telling him things about my past with David, that I'd withheld my interaction with Paul Kresh. And if he'd gone crazy because I'd hidden things, I would have taken it. I'd kept things from him, and I deserved whatever distrust and hurt feelings that came from that.

But it hadn't been my keeping secrets that put us on opposite sides. It had been his jealousy and my refusal to take over the club. Either he'd always truly meant to give me The Sky Launch, or he was manipulating the situation with David to make me believe that. Both were possible. I'd probably never know for sure which one. Maybe he didn't know himself.

One thing was certain, I wasn't letting David get fired, whatever the reason. One day, perhaps, I'd be ready and want to take over the management of The Sky Launch, but not now. Not so soon. Not only a month after graduating with my MBA.

And I wouldn't do that to a manager as good as David. It wasn't right.

I brought myself to my feet and stretched. The discussion wasn't over, but I could put it on pause for the night if Hudson could. And I didn't intend to mope around about it. It was unhealthy and could quickly turn to obsession if I wasn't careful. Which meant I had to find something to occupy myself.

I looked at my watch and was surprised to find it was after six. Guess I was skipping group therapy since I'd already missed it. I didn't have the energy for exercise, so that was out. There was a TV in the living room, but I preferred movies to shows and I hadn't yet come across any DVDs. Hudson probably had everything on a movie drive somewhere. I wasn't about to ask where. I'd already finished *The Talented Mr. Ripley.*

Actually, what I should do was work on the library. Another slew of packages had arrived on Friday and the room was crammed with unopened boxes. I should have unpacked them over the weekend, but I'd been too content to lie around naked with Hudson, doing nothing but each other. I'd put it off too long. So what if Hudson was already working in there at his desk. We were grown-ups. We could share the space.

Though the library was big, the room felt confined with the tension still lingering between us. Hudson sat at his desk, focused intently on his computer screen. It was as if he didn't even know I was in the room. But he did. Of course, he did. He could seem so single-minded, so compartmentalized, but he was always aware of me in every way, as I was always aware of him. I simply wasn't as good at hiding it as he was.

I took a deep breath and knelt at the stack of boxes furthest from him. Soon, I was wrapped up in the task of unloading and alphabetizing, enjoying the thrill of each newly discovered book title. He'd purchased so many great ones. Classics and contemporaries. Many I'd read, many I wanted to read, many I wanted to reread.

It was after I opened the box with the DVDs that I realized it. Not right away. At first, I was surprised to find the contents were movies rather than books, but I simply started on another section of the shelves and began unloading, not paying too much attention to the titles until I pulled out *Midnight Cowboy*—the movie Hudson and I had watched while we were in the Hamptons. He'd pulled up the list of AFI's Greatest Movies, a list I was slowly working my way through, and he'd told me to choose one I hadn't seen. I chose *Midnight Cowboy.*

Seeing it in the box, it hit me. I looked over the titles I'd shelved to be sure, and yep, it was true. Each and every movie was on the AFI list. And the books—I ran to look over the books, paying more attention this time. *The Brothers Karamazov, Anna Karenina, Catch-22, Beloved*—they were all titles from The Greatest Books list. I'd told Hudson I wanted to read them all before I died. And here he'd bought them for me. Each and every one.

I was suddenly overcome with emotion. It was a strange thing to move me, but it did. Before he'd decided to commit to me, before he'd asked me to come to his penthouse, let alone move in with him, he'd purchased a library full of books and movies tailored specifically to my interests.

He hadn't said I loved you. Maybe he never would. But was there anything this man did that didn't show me how much he did love me?

I was halfway to his desk before I'd even thought about what I was doing. He must have heard me coming, because even though he didn't look at me, he swiveled in his chair, opening toward me a bit. Maybe it had been subconscious, that he aligned himself with me as I often did with him. It was nice to think so.

I fell at his feet, placing my head on his thigh.

He shifted and I could tell that I'd surprised him.

"Make love to me," I said, my face nuzzling against his leg. "Please. Make love to me."

I held my breath as I waited for him to respond. I heard him click his mouse a few times and then set his glasses on the desk—the glasses he only wore when he read or worked on his computer because he was slightly far-sighted. There were some things I knew about him.

Then he bent down and lifted me with him to a standing position in one fluid movement.

Cradling me in his arms, he carried me to the bedroom—*our* bedroom—not a word spoken between us. He laid me on the bed. Silently, with such tenderness, he undressed me, then himself.

He stretched over me and kissed me—every inch of me from head to toe. He lingered in new areas, cherishing my belly button and the spot behind my knee and the sensitive area at my tailbone. Every part of my skin, he lavished with attention, adoring me as he'd never adored me before, yet each touch, each caress felt familiar. Like home.

When at last he settled himself between my thighs, he entered me with slow precision. And it was with sweet, languid strokes that he took me to orgasm, not once, not twice, but three times.

He met my eyes the last time, and we maintained the contact as I rode the wave of euphoria. Then he joined me, moaning low as his climax spiraled into mine, our gazes still fixed on each other. And even when my vision glazed over with fireworks, all I could see was him and love. So much love.

— CHAPTER —

SEVENTEEN

Hudson was already dressed and bustling around when I awoke the next morning. I peered at him with one eye closed then ventured a look at my watch. It wasn't even quite six yet.

He either saw me stirring or was so in tune with me that he recognized my breathing had left sleep mode. "Do you mind sharing, or do you want your own suitcase?"

I yawned, my brain still fuzzy. "Um, suitcase for what?"

"For Japan."

I wiped the sleep out of my eyes. "Japan? Why would I go to Japan?"

"Because I'm going to make that play for Plexis. And I want you to come with me."

I sat up, realizing I should be concentrating harder on the conversation. Hudson was putting his toiletries into a suitcase propped on a folding luggage rack. A travel bag for suits was already zipped up and hanging on the bedroom door. "When exactly is this happening?"

Hudson stopped packing and flashed his heart-stopping smile—the widest one he had that he used so rarely and which always got the butterflies fluttering in my tummy. He was obviously in a good mood. "The plane's set to take off late tonight. It's a long flight. Might as well sleep. Or, we could *not* sleep." His eyes gleamed wickedly. "It would be easier to adjust to the time difference if we stayed awake the entire flight." His gaze wandered to my naked breasts. "I'm sure we could think of something to occupy our time."

With a frown, I flung the sheet off my legs, rose and headed toward the bathroom. "I can't go to Japan tonight."

"Why not?"

"Because I have work," I called over my shoulder. Thinking of work, I suddenly remembered the whole evening before—Paul and David, and Hudson wanting me to run the club. Then the spectacular lovemaking. I wasn't sure where that left everything.

"So what about work?"

Where were we in our conversation? Oh, yes, Japan. "I have work. You know? That thing you do where you go someplace and make lots of money? Even those of us who don't make lots of money still do the work part. In fact, it's even more necessary for us."

"Anything you need, I can provide. I expect to provide."

I'd left the door open while I peed so I could still hear him clearly. It felt nice having that level of comfort with a guy, but I wasn't so sure about the provide thing he was talking about. "Hey, we just moved in together. Can we step back and keep this on the topic at hand?"

"Fine. But that discussion will come eventually. Sometime soon."

My stomach twisted with both panic and anticipation. Dammit, what was this man doing to me?

"You make your own schedule." His voice seemed close. I looked up to see him leaning in the doorway.

My brow knitted, still hung up on his last statement. I really needed coffee before embarking on such mind-spiraling discussions. "Because I make my own schedule doesn't mean I can leave on a moment's notice."

"Sure you can. I own the club."

"Funny how you pretend you don't until it's convenient for you to remind me."

He grinned but didn't dispute.

"And don't think we're done talking about the club management." I wiped, flushed and washed my hands, flinging droplets of water on him as I pushed past him back to the bedroom.

He followed me as I went to my closet. "I didn't think that for a minute. But right now we're talking about Japan."

"I have a meeting set up with Aaron Trent tomorrow. I can't miss that."

"Reschedule. He'll make time for you."

"That's so tacky." I pulled out a pair of plain cotton underwear. I hadn't showered yet and didn't feel like wasting a pair of nice ones. "He already thinks I rescheduled once."

"Why? I thought it had been he who canceled?"

"Long story." Hudson's eyes stayed glued to me as I pulled on a sports bra. "And you're distracting me from my point."

"I think *you're* the one distracting me."

"They're put away, you sex fiend. You can surely find my eyes now."

He laughed. Yes, he definitely was in a good mood. "Tell Trent something came up and reschedule." He handed me a pair of running shorts. "He'll understand. I'll make him if I have to."

"You know I want to handle him myself." I stepped into the shorts and found a tank to pair with them.

I grabbed some socks and turned to face him. He was staring at me—not my body—at my face, waiting for me to continue. I sighed. He was serious about the trip. And I was not. I gave it sincere thought for about for fifteen seconds.

The idea still seemed ludicrous. "It's not only him, Hudson. I have other things I'm working on. And I don't even have a passport."

"I already have that arranged."

"I don't even want to know how you pulled that off." I pushed past him again and headed for the bed. I sat on the edge and put on my socks.

Hudson appeared from my closet carrying my running shoes.

"Thank you." He was always so considerate, but I knew his attentiveness this morning had motive. It occurred to me that I could just give in. But I could be stubborn too.

I picked up right where I'd left off with a new excuse. "Also, my brother's coming out from Boston sometime this week. I need to get him the key to my apartment and let him harass me for some reason."

Hudson bent to put on my left shoe while I worked on the other. "I can arrange for someone to meet him, you know. It doesn't have to be you."

Now that sounded like a good plan, even if I didn't go to Japan. *Even if I didn't go to Japan*? Dammit, he had me considering it.

I shook my head. "You seriously have a solution for any protest I make, don't you?"

"I guarantee that I do. So why are you still protesting?"

"Because I have a life that involves more than you."

"I hate that."

I looked up from my tied shoe to see him giving me a pretty effective pout. "Don't be cute."

"I want you with me. I'll use any tactic I can to make that happen."

He held out his hand to help me up. I took it and was immediately pulled into his arms.

Yeah, that felt good. How had I gone all that time since waking without touching him? He'd become so necessary to my life, to my routine. Was it even possible to spend time away from him? And how much time were we talking about?

Always in tune with me, he spoke directly to my unvoiced thoughts, nuzzling his cheek against mine. "I may be gone for several days. I can't bear to be apart from you that long. It kills me that you think you can."

They were the kinds of words I'd always dreamed of being told. *I* was the clingy one. *I* was the get-too-fucking-attached chick. What was it about Hudson that kept my obsessiveness at bay? Did it mean I didn't feel as deeply about him as I thought I did? That I didn't truly love him?

No, I did love him. Truly. There was no doubt. It was because I felt secure about his feelings for me, god only knew why, that I was able to remain sensible.

But I also understood that look in his eyes, that yearning to be with someone who didn't necessarily reciprocate. I'd been passed up and thrown away so many times. It hurt.

Even though Hudson was only going for a short trip and not forever, I got his need and I couldn't stand the idea of making him feel that misery.

I also couldn't imagine putting everything on hold and flying off to Japan at the drop of a hat. "I don't want to be apart from you either, Hudson. I…can I think about it?" I bit my lower lip, waiting for his response, hoping he wasn't too disappointed with my maybe.

He pressed his forehead against mine. "I suppose."

Well, he took it better than I'd thought he would. "When do you need a decision?"

"Any time before the plane leaves the runway. Say, ten-ish."

"Okay. I'll think about it and let you know by this evening. Does that work?"

"It does." He stuck his hands down the back of my running shorts and pulled me closer. "You know, every time you say you need to think about something, you end up coming around to my way in the end. When are you going to learn to just say yes to begin with?"

I laughed. "Not today."

"It was worth a try."

We held each other in silence for several long seconds. He was out of sorts—in a good way—his mood playful and easy, his touch soft and tender. It seemed every emotional scene we shared was followed by a reunion that brought us closer than we had been before. Our evening before had been one of our worst. But this, like the lovemaking that followed the fighting, was oh, so close.

Thinking about it brought warmth to my chest. "Thank you for last night. It was beautiful."

"That it was." He circled my nose with his. "Very much so." It seemed he wanted to say more, but he didn't. Instead, he kissed me sweetly.

When he was finished, he pulled away reluctantly. "That's enough." He swatted my behind, as if I were the one who'd started the embrace. Then he eyed my outfit as if taking it in for the first time. "So I'm guessing you aren't going straight to the club."

I scooped my hair into a ponytail and threw a scrunchie from the nightstand around it. "I thought I'd get a run in first. A real run, outdoors. Before it gets too hot."

"Good idea." He looked in the mirror, straightening his tie. "I have an early meeting myself."

"I figured. You aren't usually dressed this early." He had yet to don his jacket and looked positively scrumptious in his fitted maroon dress shirt and skinny black tie. I may have even licked my lips.

"Trust me, precious, if I didn't have other plans, I would definitely not be dressed." He did that thing where he scanned my body with his eyes, lighting my skin on fire. "And you wouldn't need to get your exercise with a run."

"So sure you'd score, huh?"

He raised a brow. "Wouldn't I?"

"You would." He always would. He always did. Fortunately, when Hudson scored, I scored, so it was worth letting him be a winner.

Hudson grabbed his suit jacket, and we left the bedroom together. I snagged my key to the penthouse from my purse and slipped it into the cup of my bra.

His mouth curled into a half smile. "Do you hide everything there?"

I shrugged with one shoulder. "It's pretty handy if you ask me. They should build pockets into bras. I guarantee they'd sell."

"That can be our next business venture together."

I rolled my eyes. Hudson was way more ambitious than I was. Probably part of the reason he was a multi-billionaire and I was living paycheck to paycheck.

"I'm ready to go down. Are you?"

He raised an eyebrow.

"Go down to the lobby, you pervert."

"No, I need to answer a few emails first. Go on ahead." He turned toward the library then changed his mind, swiveling back to me. "Hold on."

He reached for my hand and pulled me in for another kiss, this one deeper yet still more tender than sexual. It was me who pulled away first and only because I knew if I didn't that I might drown in him. He insisted on one more peck after that.

"What?" he asked when he'd finally let me go.

"You're so…I don't know…sweet this morning. What's up with you?"

"I suppose I'm simply happy."

"I'm glad. Really glad." I pushed the button to the elevator then had a horrible thought. What if his unusual demeanor was meant to distract me from the David situation? "Hey, I meant it when I said we're not finished with the discussion about management at The Sky Launch."

"Persistent little vixen, aren't you? We'll have plenty of time to discuss it on our flight to Japan."

I scowled. "Now who's being persistent?" I stepped in the elevator. "We'll talk later. About all of it."

The door was closing when his hand stopped it. "Alayna."

I pushed the *Door Open* button and looked at him questioningly. He continued to lean against the elevator door, his brows knit. "Why did you… come to me last night?"

His wording was tentative, and I suspected he was tiptoeing around the words I had used. He seemed to avoid the L word with quiet precision, I noticed.

Regardless, he wanted to know what had spurred my need for him the night before. It made sense—it must have seemed odd when I'd been so mad and then so desperate for affection. "It's sort of hard to explain."

"Would you try?"

I pursed my lips, wondering if I could put into words the strange epiphany that I'd experienced. "I was unpacking. And I don't know why I hadn't noticed it before, but I realized the books you ordered—and the DVDs—that they were for me."

His brow furrowed even further. "I told you they were yours. You know I prefer to read on my Kindle."

"No, I mean, that they were the books I wanted to read. That you'd thought very specifically about what I wanted. It made me feel good. Made me feel loved. Made me feel loved by you."

"Oh." He cleared his throat, and I swear his cheeks seemed pink. "Well, yes. Good, then." He backed out of the doorway, stumbling and catching himself as he stepped.

"Wow. I had no idea I had the power to fluster you."

His smile returned though his face still appeared flushed. "Don't get used to it."

My grin remained all the way to the lobby.

MY SMILE WAS long gone by the time I'd returned to the empty penthouse.

Instead of bringing me into a calm, meditative state, my run only jumbled up my thoughts. There was so much to sort out, so many conflicting emotions to wade through. Hudson had handled the Paul situation fairly well, and he was going to fix it for me. He deserved me to give something in return. What compromise could I make regarding David? I didn't want him gone, and I didn't want to run The Sky Launch. If I went to Japan, would that show him the extent of my love and gratitude? It would be a real sacrifice for me—I really wanted to stay in town, set up an advertising plan with Aaron Trent, and start over with another event planner.

I had come to no conclusions by the time I'd showered and dressed. Then, as Jordan dropped me off at the club a little after eight, I received a text from Brian.

"I'm headed into the city. I'll be at the Waldorf. What time can we meet?"

"What's wrong?"

I jumped at David's question. I'd known he still must be in the club—the alarm hadn't been set as I walked in—but I hadn't expected him to be standing at the top of the entry ramp.

Taking a deep breath, I tried to shake off the bulk of the weight hanging on my shoulders. "Nothing. Just overwhelmed with…stuff."

He reached to take my laptop bag from me, his expression inquisitive.

I handed him my computer, deciding what, if anything, I wanted to share with him, because obviously *stuff* wasn't going to cut it. Hell, maybe talking would help me put some things in perspective. "I moved out of my apartment this past weekend," I said as we made our way toward the offices. "And my brother wants to meet with me to get my key. But we're not getting along. Not since I started dating Hudson."

"Hmm." His shoulders tightened, his face contorted in…what? Jealousy?

Okay, perhaps David did like me more than I realized. He was so much easier to read than Hudson. How had I missed how deep his affection ran?

He held the door to the back hallway open for me. "So you moved in with Pierce?"

I brushed past him and led the way up the stairs. "I did." Well, better that he knew the truth. He had to come to terms with my relationship with Hudson if I had any hope of helping him keep his job. "I know. It was fast."

"That's not what I was thinking."

"What were you thinking?"

"I was thinking I should have been faster."

His words stopped me mid-step. I turned back to see if he was serious.

He was. He did look at me like Hudson did. I'd never recognized the intensity because it was completely absent of the electricity and heat that Hudson's stare always contained.

The color drained from my cheeks.

David cleared his throat. "Sorry. That was uncalled for." He brushed past me, continuing on to the office. "Anyway, congratulations. I'm happy for you."

I fell into step behind him. "I'm happy for me, too." My voice had lost its earlier enthusiasm, still shocked from David's proclamation. Maybe we couldn't work together.

I couldn't stand thinking about it. I changed the subject. "And I'm stressed. Hudson wants me to go to Japan with him tonight."

David pulled out his keys and unlocked the office door. The room was dark, the computers off—he must have been on his way out when he met me at the entrance.

"Why are you here so late, anyway?" Usually closing managers were out by six-thirty, tops.

He shrugged. "Waiting for you. And, yeah, Hudson told me about Japan."

I flicked the office light on. "What? When?" I'd only found out about Japan that morning. I didn't even want to acknowledge the first part of his statement.

"About an hour or so ago. He wanted to make sure we'd be covered without you."

Hudson had already talked to David that morning? This day was getting more interesting as it progressed. "I haven't said yes yet."

"But you will." He didn't bother to hide the ache in his voice.

I sank on the couch and rubbed at my forehead. "Is that the only reason Hudson called you?"

David sat on the front of his desk. "Actually, he didn't call. He stopped by."

"To tell you he's taking me to Japan?" Hudson had said he had an early meeting. Why hadn't he mentioned it was with David? Or was his encounter with David coincidental?

"No, to discuss some other things."

Dread dripped into my veins. "Oh, really? Like what things?" I pretended to examine my nails, going for an aloof demeanor while really I was anything but. Which was silly, because there was no way Hudson would have talked to him when he'd promised me we could still discuss it first. Besides, David wouldn't still be there if he'd been fired.

Still, I couldn't help feeling anxious for David's response.

He shrugged, and it felt as equal of a show of calm as the one I was giving. "He said he's transferring the Party Planners deal to Fierce. Something about a conflict of interest."

The knot in my stomach loosened, if only slightly. Of course. Hudson had to deal with Paul.

"He took all the copies of the contract." David eyed me, searching for my reaction. "But he said you already knew all that."

"Yeah, I did." Boy, did I.

"Sorry, you lost your deal."

I sensed David was testing me, making sure Hudson wasn't jerking around with my business just because he could. It was sweet, actually.

Also, totally unnecessary. "Nah, it's fine. The more I got to know about the company, the more I realized it wasn't a good fit after all."

David's shoulders should have relaxed, if I was reading him right, but they didn't.

"And that's all you and Hudson talked about?" I studied his expression carefully. "There's more, I can tell from your face." The ball of dread returned.

David came over to the couch and sat on the arm, facing me, with one foot on a cushion. "Well, I'm not supposed to tell you this until you get back from Japan, but I don't feel good keeping a secret from you. Plus, I'm really excited and have to tell someone."

"What is it?" My voice was barely a whisper, my hands white as I wrung them in my lap.

"He offered me a promotion." His eyes twinkled, his excitement evident. "General Manager at Adora, his club in Atlantic City."

My vision went black for half a second, and I had to lean back into the couch for support. "What did you tell him?" There was no way he couldn't see me shaking, couldn't hear it in my voice.

"I said, hell yes. Adora? That place is world famous."

Or maybe he actually was oblivious to my devastation. And I was oh, so devastated. Not just because the thought of losing David was terrible, but because of what Hudson had done, when he'd specifically told me nothing had been decided yet. I wanted to throw up.

I focused on the more immediate situation at hand—convincing David to stay. "But we're only getting started here. The Sky Launch could be the next Adora. With you and me—"

"I'm sure it will be the next Adora. Bigger even, with Pierce's money and your ideas. But I'm not a guy who builds things. I'm a guy who runs things someone else has built. Adora is the biggest career move I could ever hope for." He looked down at me sheepishly. "I'm supposed to start in two weeks."

"That's so soon. And you'll have to move to Atlantic City." My throat clogged with tears.

"If I didn't know any better, I'd say you're going to miss me." His tone was hopeful.

"Of course, I'll miss you, you dope." I had enough control of myself to tack on a platonic addendum. "You've been such a great manager. It was really you who inspired me to want to stay in the nightclub business."

"Really? I had no idea." He moved to sit beside me. "I'll miss you, Laynie. And not just because I have a big crush on you, but because you're a good friend."

His unabashed flirtation made sense now. He was laying everything on the line. Why not? He would be gone soon. Gone because of Hudson.

God, my head hurt. I sighed and threw a glance at David. "You don't have a big crush on me."

"You're right. I'm totally in love with you."

The wind left my lungs. I had to stand up and walk away, putting distance between us. The man I'd moved in with hadn't even told me he loved me. And he'd gone and betrayed me so deeply. What was I even doing with Hudson? Was I crazy? Should I be running away with David?

The answer was, of course, no. No matter how much David felt for me, it didn't make up for how much I felt for Hudson. Even after what he'd done.

Thank god, I didn't have to say it out loud.

"I get it," David said. "I just really needed you to know how I feel before I go."

I turned back to face him.

"And now you realize that I really have to do this. I can't stay here with you. And Adora..."

I nodded. I got it, too.

"But I'm only a phone call away. You can dial me up anytime you need anything. Like, if you have questions about The Sky Launch, or if you want to hear my voice."

I leaned against the desk, my hands gripping the edging. "Did he tell you who was taking your place?"

"He hinted. We both know it's you." He leveled his stare at me. "Come on, we knew it was coming the minute you started seeing him."

"No, I didn't know it was coming. I really didn't." My relationship with Hudson had been complicated from the beginning, surprising at every turn. Still, in my wildest dreams, I had never imagined his intention was to put the club in my hands. I would have been far less shocked if he'd wanted me stowed away in his penthouse, barefoot and pregnant. And that was a pretty shocking idea in itself.

"I'm not saying it's unwarranted. You deserve to run the club. Truly."

David's sincerity was touching. It also made me all the more pissed at Hudson. Even though David was happy about the promotion, even though it probably was for the best that he moved on elsewhere, away from me—it still wasn't right how the situation had been handled. I'd been lied to and misled.

I had to go confront him. I straightened, tugging my dress into place. "Hey, I just remembered that I need to stop and pick up the new sample menu design."

"I thought Graphic Front was emailing it."

My mind was so unsettled I couldn't get my excuses right. "They are. I mean, they did." I paused, gathering my thoughts. "I want to see it printed. Feel the weight and all that. Anyway, I'm not sure when I'll be back."

David smiled. "I'm really not the one you report to anymore."

I looked away, hiding my wince.

"Hug it out?"

This time I didn't decline. I stepped into his embrace, finding it warmer than I remembered. "Thank you, David. For everything." I buried my head in his shoulder. I wasn't going to cry—I was too mad for that—but I did feel a burst of affection.

I stepped back before he took it the wrong way, before I got swept away with the need to be comforted. "And congratulations. I'm glad things are working out for you."

I texted Jordan to pick me up. Then I grabbed my bag and pulled all my rage and heartache inside myself, holding the emotions in the pit of my stomach. Saving them for Hudson.

— CHAPTER —
EIGHTEEN

When I stepped out of the elevator at Pierce Industries, I didn't even stop to check in with Trish, Hudson's secretary, before I rushed into his office.

"Ms. Withers!" Trish followed after me.

Hudson sat behind his sleek black desk, the phone cradled between his cheek and his shoulder with his fingers perched on his keyboard. He glanced first at me then behind me at Trish. "Hold on a moment, Landon," he said into the receiver.

He pushed the hold button. "It's okay, Patricia."

I didn't wait for the click of the door to shut behind Trish as she left. "Finish your phone call and meet me in the loft." I was heading for the elevator at the back of the office. "And so you know, we're gonna fight."

The private elevator went to Hudson's loft—the bachelor pad where he and I had spent many of our first sexual encounters. I hadn't been back there since he'd invited me to the penthouse, and while I would have expected a rush of nostalgia, I felt nothing but betrayal and rage.

In the loft, I only had time to throw my bag on the couch before the elevator returned with Hudson. He stepped into the loft, located me pacing, and took a seat in an armchair, his attention completely focused on me.

I'd composed a hundred different things to say to him on the way to his office, but now that I was in front of him, my anger had me tongue-tied.

But Hudson was as calm and cool as ever. "He wasn't supposed to tell you until we got back from Japan."

He. Hudson wouldn't even say David's name. At least he wasn't pretending he didn't know what I was pissed about.

It didn't make me any calmer. "Lucky for me, he's a good friend. Also, I never agreed to go to Japan."

"Touché."

"What the fuck, Hudson?" My emotions were boiling inside of me, threatening to explode.

He crossed one leg over the other, resting his ankle on his knee. "I offered David an opportunity, and he took it."

"You agreed we could discuss it further."

"I agreed we could discuss the future management of The Sky Launch further, and we certainly will."

He was so even, so in control—it only fueled my rage. "This was part of that!"

"You should have been more specific." He didn't even blink.

God, I wanted to throw something—anything. Instead I threw my words at him. "You knew what I meant. You knew how I felt and you went ahead and ignored everything I said. I thought you cared about me, but you obviously don't, because that's not how you treat someone that you're in a relationship with."

He put his leg on the floor and leaned forward, finally animated. "Yes, I did know how you felt. And *you* knew how *I* felt. You wanted me not to fire him, I wanted him gone. Offering him a job elsewhere—a promotion, mind you at my biggest club in the country—was, I thought, a pretty damn good compromise."

There was logic to his words, and his offer had certainly made David happy. But that didn't change that Hudson had made the offer without my knowledge, behind my back. "Compromises are supposed to involve both parties. You alone can't arbitrarily decide what the compromise is."

"I didn't, really." He leaned back again, resuming his composed exterior. "David did when he accepted the job. I had no idea that he'd agree when I asked him, and if he hadn't, then I would have come back to you to find a suitable solution to our problem."

"You should have talked to me before you even offered the job to him!"

"I took the opportunity when I saw it. You weren't around to confer with."

"Don't even pretend you didn't go to David today with every intention of making him that offer." Hudson's giddy mood that morning, his need to understand my change of heart the night before—he was feeling out the situation. I could see it clearly now. "I can't believe you don't see why this isn't okay!"

I was yelling. I wished I wasn't, wished I could be as controlled as he was. It definitely had a chilling effect. But that wasn't me, I was emotional and riled up and all the turmoil I had inside was spewing all over the loft.

Hudson stood and stepped toward me, one brow raised. "Are you upset because you assume I want you to take David's place?"

It was part of it, yes, but so much more than that. I turned my back to him, not knowing how to answer.

"I do want you to, of course, and I have full confidence that you would do an excellent job. But if you are unwilling, then I hope you will be instrumental in deciding who will take his place instead." His hand settled on the nape of my neck.

I spun toward him, hitting his hand away. "Dammit, Hudson. I don't want anyone to take his place. I want to work with David. David Lindt, that's all."

"You're defending him with the passion of a lover, Alayna. You're making it hard for me to believe there really is nothing between you."

This new insult was the lowest. It stung so badly I went numb, no longer able to feel anything but cold, cold, cold.

"This is so manipulative, Hudson." My voice was strained, but low and quiet. "Everything you've done and said to me today is a total mind game. I thought you were done with that. I don't even know how to react. Which is probably exactly what you were going for, so guess what—mission fucking accomplished."

He advanced toward me. "It is not fair for you to throw my past behaviors in my face every time you disagree with my actions. I am in no way trying to manipulate you to do or feel anything. I'm merely staying committed to my plan—to you, Alayna. Everything I've done has been to protect our relationship and our future. That is all."

"Really? Because right now the future of our relationship feels pretty vulnerable, if you ask me." It was downright cold—as cold as I felt at the moment, but even seeing his face fall as if I'd struck him, I didn't wish I could take it back. I only wished it not to be true.

He reached for me again, but I sidestepped him, putting my hands out in front of me as a barrier. "Don't even come near me. You try to solve all our problems with sex, and this time is not going to be one of them."

He ran his hands through his hair. "I do not try to solve our problems with sex. I simply recognize that when we're fighting, the physical connection puts us back in tune with each other."

"You mean it makes me easier to manage." He opened his mouth—to protest, most likely—but I spoke on before he could say anything. "I can't deal with this right now. I have to go."

I nabbed my bag off the sofa and headed to the main door. He tried to catch me as I walked past him, but I slipped from his grasp.

He didn't try again. "Alayna, do not leave things like this."

"Right now the last thing I want to hear is you telling me what to do."

"Alayna, please—" The ache, the pleading in his voice—it wrecked me.

But I needed time.

I paused, my hand on the doorknob, not looking at him. If I looked at him, I was afraid I'd fall into his arms. I needed to be in a place where I could think clearly. And his arms was not that place. "I'll be at the penthouse later. That's all I can give you. Right now, I need some space."

The ball in his throat was so tight, I heard him swallow. "Fair enough."

Then I was gone.

I KNEW BEFORE the elevator doors closed that I wanted to talk to Celia. I'd been blindsided, Hudson's behavior baffling me so completely, twisting me in knots. I didn't have the experience with him to sort it out. I desperately needed insight.

She didn't answer on her first ring so I did the hang-up and return call thing several times. In the midst of my fourth redial, my phone buzzed.

"Did you get my text? I'll be at the Waldorf this afternoon. Need to see you."

Goddamn Brian. I hadn't responded to his earlier message. How fitting was it that I had to deal with him today of all days?

"Text me when you're in. I'll come by."

I pushed *Send* then tried Celia again. This time she answered right away. "Hey, it's Laynie. Are you busy?"

"Uh, sort of. What's up?"

"I, um, need to talk." My voice cracked.

"Oh, no! What's wrong? You sound like you've been crying."

I hadn't *been* crying—I *was* crying. "I'd rather talk in person. Are you free to meet up?"

The elevator doors opened in the lobby of Pierce Industries. Dammit. Now I was surrounded by people. I hid my hair over my face, wishing I had my sunglasses, and hurried to the main doors.

"I could do later. Like, this afternoon. Would that work?"

"I don't know." I couldn't comprehend the next fifteen minutes, let alone hours ahead of now. "Let me think. I have to see my brother. Sometime this afternoon. Even though I don't want to. I don't know." I was repeating myself, my mind a fog.

I stepped out onto the street and walked until the glass doors turned into wall. I slumped against the brick. "I'm not really able to make any decisions right now."

"Okay, I get it. You're upset." Celia seemed distracted as she spoke. "You said your brother's in town? Brian? Is he staying with you at the penthouse?"

"God, no. The Waldorf. It's Brian's favorite place in the world."

"I'm doing a design install in the foyer at Fit Nation on Fifty-First. There's a coffee shop next door. How about we meet there around two? You'll be close to the Waldorf, as well."

Even though it was hours away, I felt better. Not great, but better. "Perfect. Thank you, Celia."

"Anytime."

I glanced at the digital clock before pocketing my phone. It was a little after nine. It felt like I'd packed a whole day into a short morning. Whatever I would do for the next few hours was beyond me.

"Ms. Withers?"

I looked up to find Jordan standing at the curb with the Maybach.

"Mr. Pierce suggested I drive you somewhere. To the penthouse or the club, perhaps?"

That was Hudson. Always looking out for me, even when I wanted nothing of the sort. It was actually a relief to have Jordan there. I'd been so muddled that I hadn't thought to text him for a ride.

With a reluctant gratefulness, I climbed into the back seat. "I don't want to be at the penthouse. The club, I suppose."

I spent the rest of the morning shuffling papers around in the office and staring at the blinking cursor on my laptop. I couldn't seem to get my mind to concentrate on anything. In the past when I felt stressed and unsettled, I resorted to old habits, fell into obsessive behaviors. Those patterns calmed and relaxed me with their compulsive nature. But instead of feeling the need to act, I felt the need to shut down—curl up in a ball and sleep until I felt nothing.

Fuck, I was screwed up. Still. I'd felt cured with Hudson, but I still didn't know how to handle emotions. I didn't know what normal people did when they hurt. I regretted missing my group session the day before. I needed it now.

Or at least I needed Lauren—my favorite group leader.

In the evenings, Lauren volunteered to lead Addicts Anonymous and some other groups at a Unitarian church nearby. I'd attended faithfully for years, only recently slipping into a part-time goer. But I hadn't found Lauren at Addicts Anonymous. I'd originally met her at Stanton Addiction Center, a rehab facility where she worked as a counselor during the day. I'd been a patient for a short time after I'd violated my restraining order with Paul. Brian, decent lawyer that he was, had been able to negotiate that instead of jail time.

It was a quarter to noon. If I hurried, I could probably catch her on her lunch break.

I texted Jordan and within twenty minutes I'd made it to the center.

I checked in at the front desk and got a pass to the staff wing. After finding Lauren's office dark, I went to the lunchroom for employees and spotted her with a group of orderlies laughing around the pop vending machine.

"Hey, girl." She stepped away from her friends when she saw me to give me a hug. "I was disappointed when I didn't see you yesterday at group."

I smiled tensely, eager to get her alone. "Sorry about that. Stuff came up."

"The fact that you sought me out here leads me to believe that it wasn't good stuff."

"Some of it was. Very good stuff. And some of it definitely not good stuff." I glanced toward an empty table in the back of the room. "Do you have time to talk?"

She held up the brown paper bag she'd been clutching. "As long as you don't mind me chowing down while you do."

"Chow away."

I didn't talk until we were seated at the table. Then, I filled Lauren in on the highlights of the past week—the shift in my relationship with Hudson, moving into the penthouse, seeing Paul again, the secrets I'd kept, and finally, what Hudson had done regarding David. I was quick about it, knowing that Lauren's lunch was only an hour. When I was done, I felt worn out, like I'd been throwing up for the last thirty-five minutes.

Lauren took a napkin and wiped her mouth, her lunch long finished now. "Well, that's quite a week of events. What have you learned by saying all of that out loud?"

This was one of her favorite therapy techniques—turning a venting session into an opportunity for self-examination. "I don't know." I was out of practice at this. I took a deep breath and thought a moment. "I see my culpability in Hudson's betrayal. I kept secrets from him first." It was difficult to admit, but crucial. How could I expect him to think that being honest and upfront was a must for me? I certainly hadn't demonstrated the same to him.

"Very good. What else?"

God, wasn't that one enough? I searched for more. "I've realized I don't know how to handle my feelings. I used to cling and obsess when I felt off. What am I supposed to do instead?"

"Exactly what you're doing. You deal with them constructively." Lauren sat forward, her hands clasped on the table in front of her. "Listen, honey, being healthy doesn't mean you don't feel things anymore. You will always feel things—good and bad, depending on the day, depending on the minute. That's called life. Being healthy is talking your emotions out, writing them down, realizing that you don't have to *do* anything to change them. Sometimes you just have to ride them out."

"Well, that sucks."

"Doesn't it?" She sat back in her chair. "There's something else I want to point out that I don't know if you're seeing."

Lauren usually avoided highlighting issues that her clients hadn't stumbled onto themselves. She believed that if someone couldn't yet see the forest, then they weren't ready to deal with it. If she was pointing it out to me, it had to be vital. I wrung my hands in my lap. "What's that?"

"Hudson—I don't know him personally, but his behavior sounds familiar."

For a minute I wondered if she'd encountered him at some point in therapy of his own. I knew barely anything about his treatment programs. I guessed it was possible.

But then I realized what Lauren was getting at. I felt the blood rush from my face. "You mean, he sounds like me. Like me in the past."

"Jealous, manipulative, deceitful." She ticked them off on her fingers, one horrible adjective per digit.

Hearing the words on her lips made my gut clench. "He's really not like that. You're making him sound worse than he is." Reducing Hudson to such vile behavior was wrong. He was so much more.

"I'm not making him sound like anything. Those are attributes you used to use to describe yourself in therapy." Lauren cocked her head. "Why do you think you were that way?"

A wave of memories cloaked me, things I'd rather not remember about myself, emotions I'd felt, motives for my behaviors. I always hated wading through the remembering to get to the learning. It made me nauseous and light-headed.

I closed my eyes to ground myself. "Because I felt unloved. Because I was desperate to get the guy I wanted. Because I didn't think there was any other way to get noticed."

"Do you think those might be the same reasons Hudson's done what he's done?"

I opened my eyes. His words from earlier replayed in my head. *I'm merely staying committed to my plan—to you, Alayna. Everything I've done has been to protect our relationship and our future.*

I had no doubt that he'd meant it. That he honestly believed he was doing what was best for us. It wasn't the right action, but his intent was decent. Moving, in fact. Was that a good enough excuse for what he'd done?

Lauren read my thoughts. "Look, I'm not validating his behavior. Or yours. It sounds like you both have a lot of work to do before you know how to function together. I'm simply giving you some perspective. It seems you've been able to connect with each other because you both come from similar places. Maybe you should use that experience to understand where he's coming from. It's a start, anyway."

My lips drew into a frown. "So what—do I just forgive him?"

"No. You could walk away." She said it so easily, as if the task would be no big deal.

Leaving Hudson—I couldn't even entertain the idea. It would destroy me.

Lauren studied me. "You probably *should* walk away. But I'm sensing that's not in your plans."

"No, I don't want to leave him. And it kills me that right now he probably thinks I'm doing exactly that."

She smiled. "Then there's going to have to be forgiveness. It doesn't have to be unconditional, though. Tell him you understand him. Thank him for his good intentions. Then explain to him what will happen if he does anything like that again."

"That doesn't sound too horrible." Actually, it sounded like heaven compared to losing him altogether.

"Understand, though, that you'll have to be able to back up anything you say. If you say you'll leave him if he does it again, then you need to leave him."

"I don't want to think about that."

She winked at me. "I'm sure you don't. Also, he could put conditions on you. If he finds out you're keeping more secrets, for example. He could walk."

"Guess I better come clean on everything to him before any conditions are delivered." I had to tell him I'd been meeting with Celia behind his back. Honestly, it was the lightest of the secrets I had carried and I had little doubt that he'd forgive me for it. Still, the air needed to be cleared completely.

Lauren's brows rose. "You have more you aren't telling him?"

"I know, I know. Don't look at me like that." I rolled my eyes, knowing how bad my situation looked. "You think we're both fifty shades of fucked up, don't you?"

"Nah, not that bad. Maybe twenty-five shades."

I laughed, and she joined me. Damn, that felt good—to laugh and relax. I needed to find a way to do it more often.

Lauren stood, and I knew it was time to part. I hugged her and thanked her and promised her I'd be at group the following Monday. Then I left.

After talking to Lauren, I no longer felt the need to see Celia. I tried to call her to cancel, but even after several attempts, she didn't answer. That was fine. I'd use our coffee date to tell her that I was going to come clean to Hudson. I might as well give her a heads up.

I got to the coffee shop ten minutes early, but half an hour later, Celia hadn't shown up. I called her several times, texted her, but got no response. I waited another thirty minutes then decided to pop my head in at Fit Nation. She'd said she was working there—maybe she'd gotten caught up.

Inside, I headed straight to the welcome desk. "Hi, I'm looking for Celia Werner. She's supposed to be doing some design work here. Have you seen her?"

The man who greeted me was about my age and built like a weight lifter. "I know Celia." His eyes brightened as if he had a bit of a crush. Hell, she was a knockout. Probably all men reacted that way to her. "She hasn't been by at all today, though."

"Are you sure?" She'd specifically told me she'd be working there that day.

"Positive."

"Huh." A chill ran through me. Considering how little I really knew Celia, I didn't have any reason to jump to worrisome conclusions. Maybe she did this often—flaked out on her jobs and her appointments. Maybe something had come up. I didn't know anything about her personal life. But something about the situation was unsettling. Something I couldn't quite put my finger on.

I left my number at the desk in case she stopped by later. Then I shook off thoughts of Celia and prepared myself for cleaning up my shit storm.

When Jordan picked me up, this time I was ready. "Take me to The Bowery." It was almost three. I could send someone to take my key to Brian whenever he texted. I'd have plenty of time to pack my bags for Japan and gather my thoughts before Hudson came home. Then we'd talk, heart-to-heart, everything on the line. If he said the wrong things, I could still back out of the trip. But he needed to know that I was committed to our relationship too. He needed to know I was all in.

Except when I got there, the penthouse wasn't empty like I'd expected. Heated conversation hit my ears the minute I stepped into the vestibule. My stomach twisted as I recognized who the voices belonged to—Hudson. And Celia.

— CHAPTER —

NINETEEN

I found them in the living room, standing so close to each other they would only have to lean in a little to kiss. I could only see Hudson's face clearly from my angle, and he didn't look about to make-out—he looked about to strangle.

A fireball mixed of jealousy, hurt and confusion sparked through my body. And betrayal. We'd vowed to not see Celia without one another. I'd betrayed him too in that department. Served me right to get a taste of what that felt like. It felt like shit.

"Why would Celia make it up?"

I'd been too wrapped up in the scene in front of me to realize Celia and Hudson weren't alone. The voice that pulled my attention belonged to Sophia. Sitting next to her on the couch was Brian—shit! My And Jack was at the window, his back to the room.

What. The. Fuck.

"Because that's what she does." Jack turned from the window. "Ah, and many of these questions can now be settled because the subject at hand has arrived."

All eyes in the room turned toward me.

I addressed my question to Hudson alone. "What's going on?"

"Alayna—" His voice was as tense as his body, but a flicker of light passed through his eyes at seeing me.

Celia stepped in my sight line, her expression hard. "I've told them. They know."

"Celia, stop it," Jack said.

"Know what?" The hairs on my arms stood on end, the electricity in the air prickling all around us.

No one answered.

Jack looked around incredulously. "Are you going to tell her, Celia? It's only fair for her to hear it from the horse's mouth."

Sophia's jaw dropped. "Are you calling Celia a horse?"

"Dammit, Laynie. I knew this was going to happen. I knew it." Brian stood and began pacing.

"Shut up, Brian." I took a step into the room. "What is going on?"

Celia exchanged glances with Sophia. "You need help, Laynie." Celia took Sophia's outstretched hand for support. "I want you to know, I'm not mad at you and I don't blame you for anything—"

"What the fuck are you talking about?" While I still did not understand the situation, there was one thing that was suddenly clear—this was an intervention. An intervention for me.

"Fine." Jack crossed the room to me. "Since you aren't going to explain, then I'll do it. Laynie, you know I love seeing you. I'm sorry it's under these ludicrous circumstances." He put his hands on my upper arms and even across the room, I felt Hudson bristle.

"Celia showed up at our house this morning throwing a hissy fit with these outrageous claims about you. Then she called Hudson and your brother here," Jack paused to glance toward Brian, "and arranged for this whole extravaganza. Good thing I was around so I could come along and try to pound some sense into these people who are listening to her." At the end of his speech he turned to the others, his voice and body animated.

"What is she saying about me?" In my bones I knew the answer without hearing it, but I held my breath, hoping to hell that I was wrong.

"That you've been harassing her."

My knees buckled and Jack helped me into the armchair. "Oh my god." My mouth tasted sour as I swallowed down bile. "Oh my god."

Celia held up her cell phone. "I have the proof. She's called several times and hung up. It's on my call log."

Click. Now it made sense—the reason she'd told me to call repeatedly, why she'd played with my phone at A Voce. She'd wanted the phone record. She'd played me. My head throbbed with the realization.

"Laynie?"

I looked to Brian, who had his arms crossed, waiting for an explanation.

Oh, how many times had I seen that look on my brother's face? How many times did I promise that I would never hurt him like that again? Though I'd kept my vow, here he was with that same expression. It was unbearable.

I swallowed past the lump in my throat. "I did. But only because she told me to call her over and over."

"That's ridiculous," Celia scoffed. "Why would I ask her to do that?"

"She said her phone wasn't working." It sounded ridiculous even to my own ears. "She said that if I wanted to get a hold of her I should keep calling until she answered."

Celia didn't let anyone have a chance to acknowledge my excuse. "She also followed me around town, to jobs I've been working. I've been working at Fit Nation and my bodyguard saw her at the coffee shop there today, alone, for nearly an hour. And when I called to check in, she'd left a message for me."

"She set me up." I said it to myself more than anyone else. "Stupid, stupid, stupid." Mira had warned me about her. And Stacy from the boutique. Even Hudson had said I shouldn't hang around with Celia. I hadn't listened. *So stupid.*

"And the staff at A Voce can confirm that Alayna just walked up and joined me when I was about to have lunch the other day."

"What, did you pay them off?" I spit the words out.

"I didn't have to. It's the truth."

Our lunch that day had been uneventful. If she hadn't paid them, then she'd probably told the hostess she was dining alone. Then when I showed up, it looked like I was invading her lunch. And I'd left before her—she could have cornered the waitress and complained about me, setting the scene for them another way.

Jack perched on the arm of my chair. "And what did you do, Celia? Did you notify security?"

"I didn't want to be rude." Her blue eyes sparkled. She was enjoying this game of hers. Was this whole thing a ploy to get Hudson by getting rid of me? Or was it revenge for the con he'd pulled on her years ago?

Or—the worst thought of all—had she learned manipulation from him? Had they played these games together?

I looked to Hudson. He'd said nothing since he called my name when I first arrived, his face steel, no emotion showing. I couldn't tell whose side he was on. And that worried me—he should be on my side, shouldn't he? Automatically?

"It's bullshit." I spoke to Hudson alone, not caring who else believed me. "She's lying. We were having lunch together. She invited me."

"She also harassed me in the restroom," Celia said. "On your birthday, Sophia."

"I did not!"

Celia put a hand on Hudson's arm. "I told you that night, remember?"

"I don't need a reminder." He pulled his arm away from Celia's grasp and my heart buoyed with the small victory.

She pretended his rejection didn't faze her, turning to Sophia, her ally. "He refused to believe me then too."

"He's blinded by the sex," Sophia said. "It's not real."

I ignored Sophia. "She told you I harassed her?" I tried to meet Hudson's eyes, but he kept them fixed on the floor.

I thought back to the night of Sophia's birthday, how Celia had been talking to Hudson when I left the bathroom. He'd been withdrawn afterward. Was this the reason why? Because she'd accused me of harassment? "Why didn't you say anything to me, Hudson?"

He didn't answer, but I could think of a reason he hadn't told me—because *I* hadn't said anything to *him*. God, the secrets we'd kept. Now they could undo us.

My stomach flipped as if I was going to throw up. "*She* approached *me* in the bathroom. I went in first, remember? And there was no harassing." I snapped my fingers, suddenly remembering I had proof of the real conversation we'd had. "Mira was in a stall at the time! She'll back me up."

Celia's face faltered for only half a second. "Mira's always hated me. She'd lie to get me out of the picture."

Jack chortled. "God, Celia, now you're dragging Mira into this? How low will you go?"

Sophia scowled at her husband. "Stop attacking the victim."

"Oh, Celia is anything but a victim." Jack's tone held a wealth of subtext. He obviously had his own issues with the Werner girl. On another occasion, I'd be itching to know what that was about.

Celia sighed—the kind of sigh that was for nothing but attention. "Please, don't think of me as a victim, Sophia. I'm not complaining. I'm really not. I'm just…scared." She wrung her hands in front of her. "I suppose it's my fault. I stopped by the club one day—I was in the neighborhood and thought I'd be friendly. She asked me to coffee. I went, but I regret it now. That seems to have been the trigger point. She begged me not to tell you we'd met up." She turned again to Hudson. "I should have told you immediately. I'm sorry."

My only consolation at the moment was that Hudson refused to meet her eyes as well.

"This is ridiculous. You're the one who suggested I didn't tell Hudson." Why was I even giving Celia the satisfaction of addressing her? "She's twisting everything!"

Hudson stepped away, looking out across the room toward the windows.

Celia followed after him, putting a hand on his shoulder. Again he flinched away.

She straightened her spine. "I don't know if you know this, Hudson, but when I talked to her that day, she was obsessing over some guy from the past—Paul something or other. She was trying to set up a deal with his company so she could be close to him."

Rage spread through me like wildfire. "You fucking bitch."

Jack put his hand over mine, trying to calm me.

Celia stepped closer to Hudson. "I'm only here because I'm worried Laynie won't get the help she needs. You have to help her, Huds."

All I could see was red. "The only help I need is a cleanup crew for after I destroy your pretty face." I lurched from my chair. Immediately Jack and Brian were at my sides, holding me back.

"Laynie!" Brian admonished.

Jack was more soothing. "Stay calm. Getting violent isn't going to fix anything, even though it might feel good."

"Do you hear her, Hudson?" Sophia stood and faced her son's back. "She threatened Celia. In front of everyone."

"Mother, stay out of this."

I held on to Hudson's words like a lifeline.

"Hudson, you have to get rid of her. She's dangerous. Celia tells me she has a record. Why on earth would you let her into your life when you knew these things about her?"

"Shut up, Mother." Hudson spun, brushing past both women. He stopped in the center of the room, finally looking at me.

I clung to his eyes with mine, trying to get my balance as the world tilted around me. I couldn't read everything in his expression, but I could see definitively the one thing he'd told me so many times—*I'm with you.*

Sophia's voice sounded muffled and far away as I remained in the safety of Hudson's gaze. "It makes sense why she'd be obsessed with Celia. She knows you belong together, Hudson, and she's jealous. Celia was pregnant with your baby. She can't compete with that, no matter—"

Jack let go of my arm. "Aw, shut the fuck up, Sophia. It wasn't even Hudson's baby. It was mine, you ignorant bitch."

Then my connection with Hudson was lost as all hell broke loose.

Celia's skin went ashen.

Hudson's face blazed with anger. "Goddammit, Jack."

If I hadn't been so dizzy from the accusations that had occurred before, then I would have been more of a participant in the scene. Instead, I was frozen, watching in horror as the secret unfolded at lightning speed.

"It's my business to tell," Jack said, "and I'm tired of this lingering lie."

"It wasn't a lie we told for you," Hudson said.

"I never thought it was. It was to protect Celia's ass. And I'm sure some of it was you protecting your mother's feelings. Heaven knows why you care about how she feels when she obviously cares nothing for how you feel."

"I don't understand." Sophia sank into the sofa.

It was Celia's turn to be comforter. She sat next to Hudson's mother. "Sophia, I'm so sorry. It was a mistake. I was drunk. It was a long time ago."

Jack laughed. "You weren't *that* drunk. And I know what you're all thinking, but she seduced me, not the other way around."

"Your baby wasn't Hudson's?" Sophia didn't want to believe it. I could hear it in her tone.

Celia continued to plead for forgiveness.

Jack headed to the bar and began making a drink as he spoke to no one in particular. "Hudson stepped up because he knew her father would freak about the age difference, though Warren's had some pretty young little mistresses himself. Granted, it's different when it's your daughter. Anyway, Hudson said he felt responsible for some reason or another. Never could figure that one out."

He turned to face the room, glass in one hand, decanter in the other. "But I'll tell you what, and I can't prove any of this, but I'd bet my life that the whole thing was a set-up. She knew Hudson would claim that baby. That's the only reason she came knocking on my door to begin with. To trap him."

"That's low, Jack," Celia seethed.

"You're one to talk." I said it under my breath, not wanting to draw attention to myself.

She caught my words anyway. "Let's not forget why we're here. Not to discuss the past but to discuss Laynie's future."

"I think that topic is on hold for the moment." Jack brought the glass of amber liquid to his wife.

Sophia took it from him, her hand shaking. "You and…Celia?"

"Don't act so surprised. We haven't been faithful to each other for years."

Sophia took a long swallow of her drink. Then she stood and threw the rest of it in Jack's face. "You coldhearted asshole. I've always been faithful."

Jack wiped bourbon from his eyes. "One word for you sweetheart—Chandler."

"Chandler is yours. I don't know why he doesn't look like you. I'll get a blood test to prove it if you want me to. And despite the myriad of affairs you've had over the years, I would never have thought you'd stoop so low to sleep with your son's girlfriend."

"She was never my girlfriend!" Hudson said at the same time his father said, "She was never his girlfriend!"

The scene had moved from shocking to uncomfortable.

Brian sidled up next to me. "Wow. This family is fucked up."

It was strangely comical, those words coming from my brother's lips. Our own family with our alcoholic father and distant mother and me—the sister with a mental disorder—had always seemed the definition of fucked up. The Pierces, though, made us look like the Brady Bunch.

I gave Brian a wry smile. "Tell me about it."

Totally fucked up. And why I was still there was beyond me.

So I left.

My hands shook the entire ride down the elevator. I didn't know where I was going, only that I had to go. Hudson and I could work things out later when it was only the two of us. There was so much to sort through, but I knew in my heart of hearts that we were okay, that we were as connected as our eyes had been when we stood in the living room with chaos surrounding us.

I paused in the middle of the lobby, wondering if I should call Jordan for a ride. But where would I even go?

"Alayna!" Hudson called after me. He must have taken the other elevator down.

He'd noticed I was gone. It warmed some of the chill that had settled over me.

"Why did you leave?" he asked when he reached me.

"Isn't it obvious? That was a madhouse and I didn't want to be there anymore."

"Yes, that it was."

"I, um…" There was so much to say, but only one thing important to me—to us. "Why didn't you defend me up there? Are you that mad about the David situation? It's me supposed to be mad at you, remember?"

He met me with silence.

"Wait—" The truth burned into me with sickening certainty. "You believe her."

His jaw twitched.

"Hudson?"

I'd thought—when our eyes had met, when we'd connected—I'd thought it had meant he was on my side. I'd been wrong. And it was like a knife to the gut.

Hudson put his hands on my arms, echoing the way his father had grasped me not fifteen minutes before. His touch felt…wrong. Cold where it was usually warm.

"I believe in you." His voice was soft. "And whatever you need, I want to give it to you. If you need help—"

"Oh, my god, I can't believe this." I backed out of his grip. "I can't fucking believe this."

Hudson clenched and unclenched his fists. "Tell me that you didn't do it. Tell me you didn't call her. Tell me you didn't see her."

But I couldn't say that. I had called her. I had seen her. Even when I promised I wouldn't. It was only my motive that was debatable and I couldn't prove it.

I shook my head. "It's not how it looks, Hudson. I didn't stalk her or harass her or whatever she's claiming." I could go into details, explain everything. But it came down to the simple fact that either he believed me or he didn't. "Are you on her side or mine?"

"I'm on your side. Always, your side."

"Then you believe me?"

He stuck his hands in the pockets of his suit pants. "Did you call her?"

"Yes! I said I did upstairs!" I didn't care that I was loud, didn't care that the doorman was watching us. I pulled my phone from my bra and held it out toward him. "Here, you want to see? Take it! You'll see all the times I called her since that's what you seem to be concerned with."

He ignored my outstretched hand. "I don't want proof. I want to help you."

"I don't fucking need any help!" I threw my phone across the lobby floor. It shattered against the wall.

For three seconds, I stared at the mess. It occurred to me that was happening inside me. My heart was shattering into a dozen pieces. So much for being able to let go of my past. It would always come back to haunt me.

I turned and ran—ran across the lobby and out the front door.

Hudson was right behind me. "Alayna, come back here."

I kept running but I was no match for him, especially when I was wearing heels. He reached me before I'd passed the edge of the building, grabbing me at my wrist. "I'll cancel my trip. We'll find the best treatment—"

"I'm not sick." I yanked my arm from his hold. "Go to Japan, Hudson. I don't want to see you."

"I'm not going to Japan now." He was smooth, in control. Like always.

I began walking away. "Go to Japan," I called over my shoulder. "I don't want to see you for a while, if not ever. Got it? If you're at the penthouse when I get home, I'll find somewhere else to sleep and I don't mean for just one night."

He didn't follow me. I couldn't decide if that made things better or worse.

Better, probably. Because every part of me was in deep pain. And that kind of ache can only be suffered alone.

I RODE THE subway for a long time. I was lucky to get a seat before the rush hour crowd hit, and I stayed planted there on the E line all the way down to the World Trade Center. After a while, I switched to the A line and eventually ended up at Columbus Circle out of habit. I didn't go to The Sky Launch though. I wandered over to the Walter Reade Theater at Lincoln Center and caught a foreign film. When it was over, I snuck into the next showing. Still, after having viewed it twice, I had no idea what I'd seen. My head—and heart—were too muddled for the subtitles.

I didn't get back to The Bowery until after midnight. With my phone broken, I was out of touch. There was no way of knowing what I'd find there. Part of me hoped Hudson ignored me, that he'd be there waiting for me. But then I remembered what Lauren said about being willing to stand behind my conditions. If he was there, I'd have to leave, and as twisted and broken as I feared our relationship was, I wasn't able to do that.

The penthouse was dark, the place quiet except for the sound of the grandfather clock. It felt so much like the first time I'd come in there in the middle of the night, except then things were new and the trepidation I had was fused with excitement. Now, I felt numb and empty. I knew without looking around that Hudson wasn't there.

I made it halfway down the hall to the master bedroom when a light flipped on in the guest room.

"Laynie, is that you?"

It took several seconds to recover from the minor heart attack Brian had given me. "Yeah, it's me."

My brother came to the guest bedroom doorway wearing a white t-shirt and striped pajama bottoms. "Awesome. Are you okay?"

That was the question of the year. "I guess so." I slumped against the wall and tilted my head. "What are you doing here?"

"Hudson said he had to go on some business trip, but he didn't want to leave you alone. So he had some guy pick up my stuff from the Waldorf and moved me in." He leaned his shoulder on the doorframe. "I hope you don't mind that I'm here."

"I'm actually kind of glad." The words were out of my mouth before I realized I meant them. Having someone else around helped lessen the emptiness. And it warmed me that it had been Hudson who'd arranged it. Even with everything that had gone down I was still on his radar.

Brian crossed his arms over his chest. "Personally, I think he should have canceled his trip."

"He probably should have. But I told him not to." I slid down to the floor, too exhausted to stand anymore, but needing to get more information from my brother. "Anything interesting happen after I left?"

Brian moved out of the doorway and sat down on the floor across from me. "Not really. More of the same. Accusations and liquor. You know, a typical family party."

He said it all tongue-in-cheek, but that was exactly what our family parties had been like growing up. At least, the liquor part. There was always lots of liquor.

"Hudson's mother's an alcoholic." I wasn't sure Brian had figured that out.

"Yeah, I picked up on that. She has that weird yellow skin thing that Dad had. And she was shaky when I first met her. Does she acknowledge it?"

"No. No one does. She's a different drunk than Dad was, though." Our dad had been a happy drunk. He'd talk too loud and laugh a lot. When we'd been little, we'd thought it was fun. It took growing older to realize what his antics did to our mother.

"How so?"

"She's mean. Hateful. Vindictive. Bitter." I paused. "Did I say mean?" I rubbed my hand over my eyes. "God, this baby thing is probably killing her."

"Right? What a way to find out your husband cheated on you."

"Not even because of that. Jack's infidelity is old news. That he was with Celia is a surprise. I thought he had better taste than that." Maybe that was why Hudson hated it when his father touched me. He was afraid Jack was after me, too. If Hudson had only told me the truth about Celia and his father, I could have tried harder to…

I let the thought die. It was no good thinking about the things Hudson hid from me. It only led back to the things I'd hidden from him. If we'd both been honest from the beginning, maybe we wouldn't be in the mess we were in now.

"Anyway, I meant because Sophia was so set on that pregnancy being evidence of why Celia and Hudson should be together. Like, she brings it up all the time. Nearly ten years later, she's still pining over this miscarriage. For this match that didn't happen."

Brian chewed on his lip, something he always did when he was concentrating. "You know what I think? I think she knew all the time that there'd been something between Celia and Jack. You know how you just know things like that sometimes. She probably thought if Celia was with Hudson, then maybe somehow that would punish Jack or maybe even help her win him back or something. It's obvious she loves the guy."

I leaned my head back against the wall. "That's very insightful. You actually make me feel kind of sorry for the lady." I scowled. "Stop it. I prefer hating her."

Brian laughed and I felt lighter with the sound. It was good to hear him be something besides angry. He was like Sophia in so many ways. Hardened because of the things life had dealt him. He was the one I felt bad for. "I'm really sorry you got dragged into all of this."

He nodded in acceptance of my apology. "I'm really sorry I haven't been here for you." He kept his eyes on his hands, his fingers playing with the drawstring to his PJs. "I guess I was wrong to cut you off like I did. It didn't help you like I thought it would."

"I hate to say this, but it was probably the best thing you could have ever done for me." Funny thing about 20/20 hindsight. "Despite how it looks at the moment, I've been doing pretty well."

"That's exactly how it looks. Good job, good boyfriend..." He met my eyes. "I know you didn't do those things that Celia says you did."

My brows rose. "You do? How?"

Brian gave me a no-nonsense look. "First of all, calling and hanging up? That's so not your style. You're much more creative than that."

I smiled genuinely at the strange compliment.

"Second, you've never messed with women. And, third, no matter what shit you've pulled, you've never denied it. That was one reliable thing about you—you were always willing to admit your mistakes. Plus, you look...good. You've never looked this good before. Not since they died, anyway."

It was the look of feeling loved. That was the change in me. I wondered how long it would last. "Thank you, Brian. It means a lot to hear you say that." More than he could possibly know.

But just because Brian believed me didn't mean I was out of trouble. "So what do I do now, Mr. Lawyer?"

"About Celia Werner? Nothing. She doesn't have anything to press charges for and she says she's not pursuing a restraining order."

"Because a restraining order would keep her from Hudson too." I frowned. "As long as he's with me, that is."

"Is that why she's saying all this stuff about you? Is she in love with him?" His question was tentative, as if he were afraid the subject would hurt me.

"Maybe. I'm not sure if she's in love with him or if she wants to mess with him. People warned me not to trust her. It makes me wonder if she has a rep for doing shit like this. I'm not sure."

"All I can suggest is to stay away from her now."

"No kidding." Actually, Celia's scam had me wondering about her and Hudson in a different way. It couldn't be entirely coincidental that they were friends and both of them had instances of manipulating people. More and more I believed they'd played their games together—as partners or as competitors, I didn't know. And I wasn't sure I wanted to find out.

"Oh." Out of the blue I remembered what Brian was in town for to begin with. I dug into the purse still hanging loosely on my shoulder and found my old apartment key. "I need to give you this." I held it up for him.

He leaned forward but stopped before he took it from me. "You sure you don't want to keep it? I could sign another year lease. In case things don't work out here."

"Which is very possible at this point." I flipped the key along its ring. It felt heavier than it should, and I wanted it out of my hands. At the same time, I had to be smart.

Brian studied me. "I told him, you know. Hudson. That I knew you didn't stalk that girl."

My eyes met his. "What did he say?"

"Nothing. He's a very hard man to read."

I let out the breath I'd been holding. "Yes, he is." What had I expected? For Brian to convince Hudson of the truth and that everything would now be hunky-dory? Even if Brian had changed Hudson's mind, would I be able to forgive Hudson for not believing me when I said I didn't do it? Lauren had said that if I wanted to stay with him, there would have to be forgiveness. How much could I forgive?

In that painful moment, when I wanted Hudson back so bad that every fiber of my being ached with longing, I would have forgiven anything and everything. And that wasn't necessarily the best thing for me.

Good thing he was out of the country. Hopefully I'd be stronger by the time he returned.

I leaned forward and dropped the key in Brian's palm. "No. I don't want another lease. I don't want you taking care of me anymore. It's time for me to do it myself. If things don't work out here—" My voice caught and I had to swallow before I could go on. "I'll have to get something cheaper. Which is fine. I could find some place closer to the subway. Maybe I'll get a roommate or something."

Brian nodded. He could tell that moving wasn't what I wanted, but there wasn't any point discussing it. What mattered was that I had options. I'd be okay.

We sat in comfortable silence for several minutes, before I got the strength to try to make it to bed. "I'm gonna go collapse now."

Brian stood first and held his hand out to help me up.

"Goodnight, Bri."

I was at the end of the hall when Brian called after me.

"Yeah?" I turned to look at him.

"Let's not be like them, okay?"

He didn't have to specify for me to know exactly what he meant. "You mean the hateful, spiteful, backstabbing family thing isn't appealing to you?"

"Not really."

I stared at him in the dim light. He seemed younger than usual, more boyish than I tended to think of him. A week before, I thought he was out of my life. Now he was asking not to be.

My smile was weak but sincere. "Then it's settled. We won't be like them."

Without even undressing, I fell onto the much too large, much too lonely bed. Burying my sobs in the pillow that smelled the most like Hudson, I cried until dawn when sleep finally swallowed me in its welcome black void.

— CHAPTER —
TWENTY

When I stumbled out of bed the next morning, I felt hungover. Emotionally hung over, I guess, since I hadn't been drinking. I stripped out of the dress I'd slept in and replaced it with my robe. I found a pot of lukewarm coffee in the kitchen, and after heating up a mug in the microwave, I set out to find Brian.

He turned up on the balcony. He was sitting at the patio table flipping through a stack of papers. Something for a case, I supposed. Brian was the take-work-with-him-everywhere type of guy.

"Good morning." He looked at his watch. "Or should I say good afternoon?"

"Sorry. I didn't get much sleep last night." I pulled my robe tighter around me and sat in the seat across from him.

"You look like shit."

"Thanks." I took a swallow from my mug, wincing when I burned my tongue.

"Are you supposed to be at work today?"

"Tonight." I was meeting with Aaron Trent at eight that evening. Good thing I'd prepared earlier because I certainly wasn't in the shape to do it now. "Thanks for asking, *Dad*."

"Got to start practicing."

Jesus, I was a lousy sister. I'd forgotten that his wife was pregnant. I hadn't even asked him anything about it. "How far along is Monica, anyway?"

He smiled in a way I'd never seen him smile before, all proud and happy. "Four months. We find out the sex in a few weeks."

"That's pretty cool. And a little bit scary too."

"Tell me about it."

Brian as a dad. Wow. So exciting and weird and that meant I was going to be an aunt. That hadn't clicked yet. God, I wasn't ready to be an aunt. How could Brian be ready to be a father?

I took another sip of my coffee, this time blowing on it first. Yeah, I needed the caffeine to calm me down. That sounded about right.

Brian went back to shuffling through the papers in front of him and I caught the logo of a phone company at the top of one. "What are you looking at?"

"Celia's cell log. She left a printout here." He rifled back a page. "I was looking at the calls she made. She called The Sky Launch once. Last Friday. Here it is." He put the paper on the table and turned it toward me, pointing to a familiar one. "Isn't that the club's number?"

"Yeah, it is. But she never called me at the club. Wait, I know that number, too." I pointed to the one above it. "That's Aaron Trent's office." Things clicked into place. "That bitch. She's the one who canceled my meeting with him."

"What are you talking about?"

Celia had known about the meeting with Trent and about Sophia's birthday dinner. She had to have guessed that if Trent rescheduled that I'd end up at the party. She had caused a scene. How good was she?

Brian was still looking at me expectantly.

"Oh, it's nothing now. I had a meeting and when it got canceled it stirred up a lot of crap between me and Hudson. Long story." My eyes trailed down the list, spotting a number I knew by heart. It was all over the page. "That's Hudson's number."

"She has quite a few calls to him."

"I see that." I swallowed. "I don't know what to think about that."

"None of them are very long. And she always called him."

"Hmm." That was comforting, wasn't it? Except what did Celia Werner call Hudson about? Why so often? I didn't like the unanswered questions.

I sat back and pulled my knee to my chest, resting my foot on the chair.

"So what now? Between you and Hudson Pierce?" Brian echoed my thoughts.

And wasn't that the question—*What now?*

"I'm not sure." I rubbed my cheek against the silk fabric draped over my knee. "I guess I'll wait until he comes back and we'll see how that goes. The time apart might be good for us. Give us some time to think." Time to decide where I fit in Hudson's life, where Celia fit in Hudson's life. Where Hudson fit in *my* life.

"Good plan." He paused. "You know, just because he doesn't believe you doesn't mean he doesn't love you. Trust me. I speak from experience."

I met his eyes. "Yeah, I guess you do." I'd always known Brian loved me, even when he was a total shithead. And I'd always understood his motives. Why was it so hard for me to grasp that about Hudson? Because he'd never said he loved me? Because the idea was too good to be true? I wasn't sure. Yes, there were definitely things to think about.

Brian tossed the cell phone papers down. "Anyway, speaking of phones, do you want me to go with you to get a replacement today?"

This was the one thing I'd already thought about. "No. I'm afraid if I have it I'll call Hudson." The tug of fixation already threatened whenever I thought about my laptop sitting in my bag in the bedroom. How I could internet-stalk him. How I could try to figure out where he was, what he was doing. I'd been so strong. The last thing I wanted was Celia's fake accusation to find truth.

I peered at Brian, seeing if he understood. "I need to be completely cut off from him to get my head around everything, you know?"

"Not really. But if you say so."

"Yeah. I say so."

BRIAN LEFT THURSDAY morning and the days after that became a blur. Without him around to pull me out of myself and put time in context, I lost track of the minutes and the hours that Hudson had been gone. All I knew was that every passing second felt like a decade, every night alone in our bed felt like a century.

David, thinking I was only out of sorts because I was missing Hudson, suggested I take some time off, but the club gave me a sense of purpose. After meeting with Trent, I continued working nights instead of days. At least then I could stand behind the bar and go on autopilot. I worked myself long and hard and when I got back to the penthouse in the early hours of the morning, I hit the treadmill until I couldn't stand anymore. That was the only way to fall asleep—to get myself so exhausted that I slipped easily into a coma.

Without my phone, Hudson tried to contact me in creative ways—at the club, leaving messages with the doorman, calling the penthouse phone, which I never answered. I stayed true to my self-proclaimed edict that time apart would be good for us. Except, as the days stretched by, I hadn't managed to figure anything out. I'd hoped to gain clarity in his absence. Instead, I just felt lost.

It was after one of the longer nights that Mira showed up, when I'd stayed so long closing the club that the sun was already planted in the sky. I'd changed into workout clothes and ran from the club to The Bowery. The traffic seemed light. It was Sunday morning, I guessed.

Mira was waiting in the lobby, sitting on a couch in the foyer with her hands resting on her swollen belly. At the sight of her, I felt warmth for the first time in days.

She stood when I approached her.

"He sent you to check up on me?" I was beaming. I missed Hudson so horribly and his attempt to reach out through his sister was a nice touch.

Unless he'd sent her to break up with me.

The smile left my face instantly at the thought.

"You're not taking any of his calls, Laynie. What else was he supposed to do?"

"He already left notes with the doorman."

"Did you read them?"

"Not so much. I was afraid of what they'd say." Like that I needed to be out of the penthouse by the time he came home.

"Did you think he was breaking up with you?" She laughed. "No. Way. Even if he wanted to, I wouldn't let him. And he doesn't want to. Trust me."

I hadn't realized how worried I'd been about the prospect until Mira had relieved the tension with those few simple words. My shoulders relaxed, and my jaw didn't feel so tight. Now I wished I hadn't thrown away his messages.

But here was a message in the flesh.

I tilted my head toward the elevator. "Want to come up?"

"I was counting on it."

We didn't talk as we rode up to the penthouse, and all I could think about was how much I probably stunk from my run and how I hoped that Mira was really there to tell me Hudson would be home soon.

"Can I get you something?" I asked as we stepped into the vestibule.

"Um, mind if I raid your fridge? I just ate breakfast and I'm still starving."

I dropped my purse and key on the floor. "Go for it."

She knew her way around and I followed her into the kitchen. While she poked about in the fridge, I grabbed a couple of glasses from the cupboard. "Want anything to drink?"

"Water's good." She stepped away from the fridge, carrying a veggie tray and a block of cheese.

Before the door shut behind her, I reached in and snagged a bottle of water then poured half in each of the glasses. When I'd turned back, Mira had made herself comfy at the breakfast table. I grabbed a knife and plate for the cheese and joined her.

"So," she said, chomping down on a piece of celery. "Lots of crazy went down here last week."

"We're jumping right into it then? No small talk first?" Personally, I was glad. I hadn't wanted to be the one to seem eager for the dirt.

"Are you kidding me? I've been dying to talk about this with you. Do you not know I'm a gossip fiend?" Mira reached for the knife and began working at the block of cheese.

"You hadn't known about Celia's baby either?"

"Nope. No clue. I was always sure it wasn't Hudson's. I don't know why—I was barely fourteen when it all happened, but he never seemed to be into her. They never even kissed or anything that I saw. And, trust me; I was the type of sister that saw a lot."

I could picture Mira as a perky young teen, spying on her brother whenever she had the chance. "Somehow I don't doubt that."

"I didn't ever think it was Dad's though." She took a piece of the cheddar and layered it on top of another celery piece. "I still can't think about that. It's gross." She shuddered then bit into her celery/cheese sandwich.

Talk about gross.

I moved my eyes from her snack of questionable taste and pretended to study my nails. "How is your mother dealing with the news?"

Mira shrugged. "Who knows? Every time she starts to feel something other than bitterness she simply refills her bourbon."

I nodded, surprised by her openness. "Good times."

I hadn't actually spent much time alone with Hudson's sister. I'd assumed she was as closed-off as Hudson, hiding her true thoughts and feelings behind a veil of happiness where he hid his behind cold stone walls. Perhaps I'd been wrong.

"Mom will get over it. Or she won't. Whatever." She paused to finish chewing her celery. Then she frowned. "I don't know why she was so attached to Celia to begin with. I'm sorry about that."

"Whatever. You aren't responsible for your mother's bad taste."

She giggled. "I know, but it's embarrassing. Celia's such a bitch." Mira leaned back in her chair. "She's always been…I don't know…fake. I've never trusted her, but I still can't believe she did this to you."

It was my turn to shrug. "It was my own fault. Not because I stalked her, but because I didn't listen to the warnings not to get mixed up with her."

"I know you didn't stalk her." Mira rolled her eyes. "Please. Do you think I don't? Why would you do that? It's not like you at all."

Her confidence in me was startling. As well as completely off base. I'd figured my obsessive days were out in the open now for the whole Pierce family. It was nice to know it wasn't the case.

But I was tired of secrets and bitter about my predicament. "Joke's on you, I guess. That's exactly like me. I used to do that crap all the time. Stalk people, I mean. I have a record."

Mira narrowed her eyes and studied me. "No wonder you and Hudson are so good for each other."

My mouth curled up at her unexpected comment. It was exactly the reason I'd thought I *wasn't* good for Hudson. Interesting that she had a different perspective.

"Anyway, you don't do that stuff now, do you?"

"No."

"See? And you *now* is who I know, so don't correct me again." She grinned as she snagged another piece of cheese, this time sans celery, thank god. "Plus, I was in that bathroom. You didn't harass her in the least. I told Hudson that, by the way."

She was the second person to have defended me to Hudson. While I was glad for the support, I wished I didn't need it.

Still, I was dying to know. "Did he believe you?"

"Of course, he did." Her brown eyes widened. "Is that what this is about? You don't think he knows you didn't do that stuff? He totally does."

"Because of what you told him?"

"Yeah."

"That's what I thought."

Her face flushed. "I mean, maybe it wasn't me. He probably believed you without…" Her sentence trailed away. "Shit." She ran her hand through her short hair. "He would have figured it out if you weren't avoiding his calls."

"My phone's broken."

"And the times he's called at the club?"

"Okay, I'm avoiding those." I folded my arms over my chest, suddenly feeling defensive. "It's not because I don't want to talk to him. It's…it's complicated." I chewed the inside of my lip. Was it really that complicated? I loved Hudson, and Hudson…well, I knew he loved me, too. Was that enough? There was no way of knowing without talking to him.

And I'd been avoiding that like the plague.

I sighed. "There's more than this. I did some things that I shouldn't have done. And he did some things that he shouldn't have done. There's a lot of fixing and stuff to be said and I think the things we need to say need to be in person."

"So go to him."

I arched a brow. "To Japan?"

"Why not? What you're saying makes sense. Big things need to be face-to-face. It's easier to be honest. Harder to run away. Yeah, you should go to him." Mira's whole face transformed with her enthusiasm.

Though adorable, her notion was insane.

"Isn't he going to come back soon?"

"It doesn't sound like it. The people he's dealing with are dragging their feet."

"Oh." My heart dropped into my stomach. If it truly was Sunday, it had now been five days since Hudson had left. I didn't think I could stand many more.

But the alternative was crazy. "I can't go to Japan. I don't have that kind of money."

"I'd foot the bill."

"Oh, no. I'm not letting you pay for me to go to Japan. Get real."

Mira scowled and put a fist on what was probably once her waistline. "I have about as much money as my brother, you know. A trip to Japan is a drop in a very large bucket, and I'm not trying to brag. I'm trying to be clear."

I opened my mouth to continue my protest.

"But if that's really an issue," she said before I had a chance, "then charge it to The Sky Launch. Hudson's money. He wanted you out there to begin with."

It wasn't a bad idea necessarily. Not the best, but not bad.

Except what if he didn't want me there?

Or maybe that's why he'd sent his sister. I eyed Mira suspiciously. "Did he send you to convince me to go to Japan?"

"No!" She seemed appalled. "Uh-uh. Do not give him credit for my idea."

But I'd wanted to give him credit. It would make it less scary to show up unannounced.

"Think about it," Mira said, her eyes all dreamy. "Wouldn't that be an awesome surprise?"

I imagined the roles reversed, if he showed up and surprised me. "Yeah. It kind of would be." *More than kind of.* "I miss him."

That was all Mira had to hear. "Laynie, he's dying without you! I can hear it in his voice. He's a basket case. He can't eat, he can't sleep—"

"He told you this?"

"I can tell!"

I popped a piece of cheddar in my mouth to keep from laughing. "Has anyone ever told you that you're a hopeless romantic?"

"It doesn't mean I'm wrong about Hudson."

"Maybe not." Though I couldn't imagine the calm, collected Hudson ever being anything close to a basket case.

Mira sighed. Then her eyes brightened. "You know, he told Celia he doesn't want her in his life anymore." She said it nonchalantly, but she was an easy read—she knew this was big news.

"What?" It was hard to hear myself talk over the pounding of my heart. "Are you serious?"

She nodded.

"Why didn't you lead with that?"

"I guess I probably should have."

Holy shit! This changed everything. *Everything.* "What else? Tell me all the details."

"I don't know what else. I wasn't there. It was here, that day that everything else happened. Dad told me about it. Said she was crestfallen."

"So this was before he believed that I was innocent?"

"Yeah."

"Then why did he tell her he didn't want her around?"

Mira leaned in—as far as she could anyway, with the round ball at her belly—her expression animated. "This is so third-hand gossip, but Dad said that Hudson told Celia that she was obviously not good for you and so he expected her to stay out of your life from now on. No phone calls, no stopping by the club, no stopping by the penthouse, no family functions. Completely out of your life." She tapped her finger on the table enunciating *completely, out* and *life.* "And he said that since your life was *his* life, that meant he couldn't be around her either."

"No. Way." She totally had me captivated. The girl certainly did have a flare for dishing out the dirt.

"Yes, way. Of course way. Why would you even doubt way? I keep telling you he loves you. You hang the moon for him. He'll do anything to keep you. Can't you see that?" Her hands flew as she talked, but I stayed glued to her face.

I blinked. Several times. "He chose me over Celia. Even when he thought that I'd gone all crazy again. That's…that's big."

"Yes! It's big! It's huge!" She hit the table so hard the knife went flying to the floor. Ignoring it. she pinned me with her eyes. "Now what are you going to do to match that?"

I stood, needing to pace the room. "Okay." I ran my hands threw the hair that had fallen from my ponytail. "I'll go to Japan."

A sound somewhere between a shriek and a gasp filled the room. The startling part was that it came from me. *Did I really just say I'd go to Japan to surprise Hudson?* Oh my god I did and I didn't even want to take it back.

Mira jumped up with a squeal. "Yes!"

"It's Sunday, right?" In my mind I was already packing, making a mental list of preparations. "I can't leave until tonight. Someone's renting out the club and I'm scheduled to get them set up. I could leave right after that though. Like eight or so."

"That's perfect."

I stopped pacing. "This is going to sound ridiculous, but I don't even know how to travel out of the country. I've been to Canada once. That's the extent of my foreign travel."

"I'll take care of everything," Mira said, laughing. "Do you have a passport?"

I nodded. "Hudson got me one. He left it on the nightstand. Do you need it?"

"No, *you* need it. Make sure you bring it with you." Her eyes were moving like she was making her own mental list. "Do you have a credit card for The Sky Launch?"

"Yep." I ran—actually ran—to the foyer where I'd dropped my purse.

"Here you go," I said when I returned, handing her the American Express I carried for business expenses related to the club.

"Yay!" Mira pulled me in for a hug that I actually didn't mind. "This is so exciting! I always wanted a sister! You guys will make the most beautiful babies."

"Hey, slow down." That made the hug come to a quick end. "No one said anything about..." I put my palms to my face. "I can't even finish that sentence."

"Sorry. I'm an optimist."

I dropped my hands and pointed a finger at her. "Keep your optimism to yourself from now on, okay?"

She rolled her eyes. "Okay." But she was twitching like she had more to say. "I mean, not okay. I have to know because I'm ultra nosy—do you want that stuff? You know, kids, marriage. The whole package." She bit her lip. "With Hudson."

I didn't know what to say. The answer was tricky and the conversation already had me breaking out in a sweat. "Here's the thing, Mira." I still didn't know what I was going to say. Then the truth spilled out. "I used to want it so bad that I thought every guy was the whole package, that every guy was

The One. And I'd do everything to make them believe the same about me. I mean everything. Not so good things."

A breath shuddered through my lungs. "So now I can't even let myself think about it, not even to daydream for a few seconds or to test it out and see how it feels. So the answer is *don't ask me that*. I can't." My voice cracked so I said it again. "I just can't."

Mira didn't even blink. "Then don't. I daydream about it enough for both of us."

"Thank you," I said.

"You're welcome." She smiled. Then she shooed me with her hands. "Now get packing, girl! We've got to get you to Japan!"

— CHAPTER —
TWENTY-ONE

"Should I change or stay in this?" It was the third time I'd asked Liesl this question in the last fifteen minutes. She'd answered each and every time, but I couldn't remember what she'd said—my mind was a mess of exhaustion and nervousness. I'd managed to nab a short nap in between packing and figured I'd catch up on the rest during the long flight. Until then, I had espresso.

Liesl spun on her barstool and grabbed my shoulders, looking me directly in the eye. "Laynie, chill the fuck out. You're making me insane."

"Okay." A thumping noise drew our eyes downward. It was the heel of my shoe, bouncing with the twitching of my leg. I put my hand on my thigh to still the movement. "Okay. Chilling."

"Thank god." She ran her eyes again over my short wraparound skirt and white button down blouse. "You look smokin'. But you should change into sweats for the flight so you can be all comfy and drool while you sleep and all that. Then change back into this in the airport bathroom."

"Okay." *That's right. That was the plan.* I would have been in sweats already except that I was waiting for the club renter to show up.

Though I had plans to change the hours of The Sky Launch, we currently weren't open on Sundays or Mondays. Occasionally a private party would rent the place for various functions. I didn't know much about this particular rental situation. David had set it up. He would have handled the exchange too, except he'd left for Atlantic City after we'd closed that morning to check out Adora on the sly. I hated to admit it, but Hudson had made David's life by giving him that job. It had been a good move.

Liesl turned back to the bar where she was creating some sort of counter artwork with olive spears. "Do you know where you're going when you land?"

"Mira arranged for a car to pick me up and take me to his hotel." Anxiousness pulsed through me again and I started pacing. "But what if he's not there? What if I have to wait or what if I miss him? Or what if...." my stomach lurched at this thought, "what if he's with someone?"

"He won't be with anyone. He's with you."

"But how do you know?"

"I..." She paused as if she were going to say something and then changed to something else. "Just do."

I scowled. That answer wasn't satisfying.

"What? Are we in grade school?" She sighed. "I can tell by the way he looks at you. Everyone can. Come on, Laynie, he asked you to move in with him. After what? A week? He's into you, girl."

"All right, all right. You're right." I glanced at the clock above the bar. "The renters are supposed to be here in twenty. We should go down in case they get here early."

"Um, okay." Liesl suddenly looked as nervous as I felt. "Hold on a minute." She shuffled the spears around then rearranged them in the same design.

Jesus, now she was the one making me crazy. "Leisl! They could be waiting at the door—"

"I'm coming, I'm coming." She jumped from her stool. "Wait; one more thing." She took her phone from her shorts pocket and typed a message to someone. "Okay. Let's go."

Internally, I rolled my eyes. "You didn't have to come in tonight. I could have handled this myself." I headed to the stairs at a fast pace but had to slow down to wait for Liesl, who was walking at turtle speed.

"I know. But I thought you could use the company. It's not a good idea to be in the club alone."

As if I wasn't in the club alone all the time. Strange that she suddenly cared about that. "It was very thoughtful of you."

"Uh-huh." She bit her lip. "Um, are your bags packed?"

"Yep. Jordan will have them when he picks me up." We continued the descent of the second flight of stairs and the main dance floor came into view. And my heart stopped. "What the..."

The floor was covered—absolutely covered—in red and white rose petals. The main lights had been turned off and candles were set on the tables surrounding the floor, illuminating the space with an ethereal white-yellow glow. It was beautiful and romantic.

Liesl made a small gasping sound. "Wowzers."

It hadn't been like that when I'd arrived only an hour before. Liesl had been with me the whole time, so it couldn't have been her.

A figure stepped out of the shadows, his hands tucked casually in his pockets.

"Hudson?" Just like that, I forgot how to breathe. The sight of him… even in his rumpled attire, his suit jacket missing, his dress shirt untucked—he was stunning. "You did this?"

He nodded. His focus went to my friend. "Thank you, Liesl, for keeping her occupied."

I turned to her, eyes wide. "You knew about this?" I still hadn't fully grasped that he was the renter, that this whole arrangement was for *me*.

"Hey, he kept calling and you wouldn't talk to him and then he trapped me into this whole surprise you thingamabob. He asked me to keep you busy upstairs while he did—" Liesl gestured at the room. "All this." Her expression said she felt guilty about the betrayal. "He's my boss, what was I supposed to say?"

"He's not your boss," I said, remembering his frequent claim to me.

At the same time, Hudson said, "I'm not your boss."

My eyes flew to his at the dual mention of our inside joke. Then they were locked there, as if there were nothing else in the world to look at but him. As if the only things worth meaning could be found there.

And he gazed back at me with the same intensity.

Distantly, Liesl's voice penetrated through the haze. "I'm going to slip out the back. 'K, thanks."

I'm not sure I even addressed Liesl. She was already gone—I was already alone. With Hudson.

Part of me wanted to run to him. But I couldn't let myself. Even though I was ready to forget every bad thing that had transpired between us, I understood that if we didn't fix things first, we could never last. So I walked to him instead, my legs shaking as I stepped down to the dance floor, and this time it wasn't because of the espresso.

Though there were many things waiting on the tip of my tongue, he spoke first. "'Bags packed'?" He stepped toward me, one brow raised. "Are you going somewhere?"

I could hear the tension in his voice. He thought I was leaving him. It made it that much sweeter to be able to say my next words. "Oh, nowhere special. Just Japan."

"Because...I was in Japan?" His expression was so hopeful and adorable, I melted a little. Or a lot.

"Yeah." I circled him, taking in the details of his setup. The tables draped with white cloths, the candlesticks letting off a vanilla fragrance. "I thought I could put my stalking skills to use to find you."

"I would have liked to have been found by you."

I turned back to face him, playing cool and flirty though my subtext was hot and needy. "Would you? I wasn't sure."

"Then you're an idiot."

"Thank you."

"A beautiful idiot that I can't take my eyes off of."

I couldn't stop looking at him either. Less than a week apart, it felt like I hadn't seen him in a lifetime. We were still several feet apart. I took a step toward him, but the distance between us felt just as wide. There was no way I could get to him without...without saying everything.

"Hudson, I saw Celia behind your back."

His eyes closed for half a second. "I've figured that out."

"I should have told you." I bit my lip, trying to come up with the right explanation of why I'd done what I'd done. "She was welcoming and supportive and I needed someone to talk to. It's no excuse."

His mouth straightened. "You could have talked to me."

"We don't always talk that well."

"We need to work on that, then."

My throat tightened. He still thought we had a chance. That made all the difference.

Yet there was still hard stuff to say. "You hurt me, Hudson."

He took a breath so shaky I heard it shudder through him. "I know."

"Do you?"

"Yes. I transferred David without talking to you."

"Well." There were other issues between us. I could let him off the hook on this one. "It turns out that's probably for the best. It was a good compromise."

"And I didn't believe you." He shook his head, looking down at the floor. "I should have believed you." His eyes came back to mine. "I'm sorry."

"Why didn't you?"

He sighed. "I was more concerned with being the guy who would stand by you. I wanted you to know I'd help you, get you treatment."

"I didn't need treatment. I needed you to believe me and you didn't."

"We hadn't had a good track record in being honest with each other. It was instinctual to doubt."

My back stiffened. "Then it's my fault that you took her word over mine?"

"I didn't take her word over yours. I took the evidence and put it into a plausible scenario."

It was my turn to look at the floor. "Right." There was nothing wrong with what he said, yet it didn't ease the ache in my chest.

"The thing you aren't hearing, Alayna, is that I don't care."

My eyes raced back to his.

"I don't care if you did stalk Celia or call her a million times or leave a dead chicken in her bed—I don't care. I just want you. I want to be with you. If you were sick, then there was a chance that I would lose you. And I can't. Whatever it takes to make that happen. Whatever I have to do. Whatever I have to say. I have to have you in my life."

Goosebumps rushed across my skin. Hudson's words were both freeing and binding. They relieved me of so many of the doubts that constantly pulled at me. His reluctance to believe me hadn't been about trust, though I certainly hadn't deserved his trust. It had been his way to hold on to me. Even at my most crazy, he would still be there for me. That was almost unbelievable. After years of thinking no one could ever want me past my mistakes, his declaration was more of a dream come true than any other aspect of our relationship.

At the same time, I now realized the extent of my failures in our commitment to each other. While he would stand by me through anything, I had pushed him away with secrets and lies. And when I had believed that he had resorted to his past behaviors, when I believed he had manipulated me—I'd only gotten high pissed. He'd been sick in the past, just as I had, yet I'd blamed him instead of offering understanding.

I fell to my knees with the weight of it all. Tears stung at my eyes. "I don't know how to do this."

"Do what?" He collapsed in front of me an arm's length away. So near but, without his touch, so far.

"Have a relationship." I swiped at the tears falling down my cheeks. "I keep fucking it up. I kept things from you. I accused you of manipulating me. I didn't try to compromise about David."

"I don't care about any of that." He nudged an inch closer, his expression desperate. "Just don't give up on us. Please, don't give up. I'm a shell without you, Alayna. I can barely breathe when you aren't near me, when I'm not touching you. Right now, it's all I can do to hold myself back from taking you in my arms."

"Why are you holding back?" My need for him was astounding.

"Because I don't want to resort to sex to solve this."

"You listened. You always listen." I choked back a sob.

"Alayna."

Like always, the sound of my name on his tongue ignited me, and coupled with the distance between us, it increased my want, increased my anguish. "I need you, Hudson. I need you to touch me and bring me back into sync. I'm so far out of tune with you and it hurts—like part of me is missing."

A weak smile crossed his lips. "You get it then."

"I do." I finally did understand it—how the physical connection between us was vital. It brought us closer, united us at a level so deep that our words and actions became meaningless in comparison.

His hand reached out, but he dropped it before touching me. "Are we… okay?"

"I'm not giving up, if that's what you're asking. I'm so lost without you. Find me, Hudson."

"I already have."

Then we were in each other's arms, our lips crushing in a kiss that tasted of hope and love and salty tears. His hands on my back lit my body on fire. I needed my shirt off, knowing the feel of skin-on-skin would be my only salve.

Hudson recognized my urgency. Or perhaps it was his own desire that moved his hands to my buttons as I worked to undo his. Our kiss remained unbroken as we shed our shirts, then my bra. Then, with great reluctance, I let his mouth go so he could blaze a trail to my breasts. He cupped them both, first nuzzling and licking in the spot between them before moving his attention to one nipple. He tugged and sucked for long minutes until I was writhing and gasping. By the time he'd moved to the other nipple, I was aroused and near climax.

I'd been so immersed in Hudson's adoration that I'd missed when he'd unwrapped my skirt until I felt his fingers on my clit through my panties, pushing at the bundle of nerves like it was a *release now* button. And it was—I was already on a hair-trigger. One simple swirl of his thumb and I was tumbling over.

Hudson held me upright as I spiraled into my release, his other hand ripping at my underwear so that by the time I began my descent, I was completely naked.

As my vision returned, I saw him fixated on the moisture between my legs. His eyes were scarred with lust, his expression wild. So hot. It was so hot. No one had ever looked at me like that before him. No gaze had ever come close.

It was too much in every good way. Too much and not enough. I needed him inside me. Craved his cock pushing into me, filling me. Completing me.

I clawed at the waistband of his pants, too insane with desire to productively work on their removal. Hudson took over and in a flash had lowered his pants enough to expose his hard, thick beautiful shaft.

I was already climbing on top of him when he stopped me with a curse. "Hold on."

He stood and kicked his clothes off, the ache of his absence made dull with the sight of him stripped. That's how I loved us best—completely naked, no barriers between us.

He fell back on his knees in front of me. My hands immediately grabbed for his pulsing cock. A trickle of pre-cum glistened on his crown, and I spread it down the length of him.

He groaned. "Come here." Hudson kneeled up slightly and urged me to wrap my legs around him, my feet braced on the floor on each side of him in a squat. Thankfully, my sandals were platform. They gave better support.

His tip throbbed at my core and I clenched in anticipation, all thoughts of shoes flying from my mind. With gentle expertise, he pushed up and in. I slid down him, taking the length of his cock inside my wet core.

God, oh, god, there weren't words—the ecstasy, the intensity, the absolute feeling of wholeness, of completion—it was perfectly indescribable. Perfectly perfect.

He bucked into me, and I threw my head back with a gasp.

"Watch, Alayna."

His command drew my focus back to him. I followed his gaze down to the place where we were joined. He pulled out of me to his crown, his cock covered in my juices, then pushed back in, his rhythm steady and mesmerizing.

"Watch my cock pushing in and out of you."

"It's so hot." *Unbelievably hot.*

He sped up and the sound of our slapping thighs increased the level of eroticism by ten. Already I was tightening again, nearing the edge.

"Alayna, are you with me?"

His question called my attention back to his face. His expression, still lusty and primal, was now highlighted with affection.

"Always," I said. "I'm always with you."

He reclaimed my mouth, plunging his tongue with a ferocity that echoed his movements below. I was breathless and panting when he released me.

"Our pasts will always threaten to come between us. But nothing can come between us unless we let it. Feel this?" He drove his cock deeper into me. "Feel me inside you?"

"It's so good, Hudson. You make me feel so good."

"I know, precious, I know." He tightened his grip, pulling me closer to him so that his breath tickled my ear as he spoke to me.

My vision glazed, I was close.

"Look at me." Again, his command pulled my eyes to him. "This is how connected we are, Alayna. Even when I'm not inside you, we are always this connected."

His stark declaration was the final straw. "Fuck, Hudson, I'm going to come." My legs were quivering from the effort of supporting myself on top of him. Now they tightened with my oncoming orgasm.

"Yes, let go," Hudson coaxed. "I want to watch you give it all to me."

I did let go, squeezing him with my cunt as my orgasm ripped through me with seismic force. My body jelly, Hudson eased us to the floor then pounded to his finish, burying himself to his balls while his climax erupted hot and long.

When he collapsed, he stayed inside me, stroking my hair and whispering. "You're so beautiful, Alayna. Absolutely beautiful. I missed you. So much."

I brushed my fingers along his cheek, scruffy with a five o'clock shadow. "Did you really?"

"Yes, really."

"I missed you too. So much." I kissed along his throat before sucking lightly on his Adam's apple. Still in a euphoric, post-orgasmic stage, it was surprising that I suddenly remembered where I was supposed to be. "Shit! I need to call Mira and tell her to cancel my trip."

Hudson smiled. "Already taken care of."

"She told you? It was supposed to be a surprise!"

"Mirabelle didn't tell me. Jordan. All he said was that he'd rearrange your evening plans. It would have been a surprise." He circled my nose with his. "If I hadn't surprised you first."

"And what a happy surprise it was."

"I'm lucky you didn't kick me to the curb. You know, I've fantasized about taking you in this club since the first time I saw you here."

For whatever reason, this made me blush. "I can't say I haven't had the same fantasy."

He grinned and kissed me chastely, probably knowing as well as I did that anything deeper would likely lead to another round of sex. This suspicion was confirmed with his next words. "As nice as it is having the fantasy fulfilled, I'd much rather take you back to The Bowery and have you in our bed."

"That sounds awesome. Because as beautiful as this all is, I'm sticky and I have rose petals stuck to my ass and thighs."

Hudson laughed, his dick twitching inside me with the motion. "The side effects of romantic gestures."

"You better get out before you get hard again."

"Already halfway there." He pulled out of me, and, sure enough, he was already sporting another semi.

He stood then helped me up after him, brushing petals off my backside. After we'd finished dressing, Hudson turned on the club lights so I could blow out the candles.

"Ready to go home?"

I shivered at the sweet sound of the word *home. Our* home. It had become such a lonesome cave in the days he'd been gone. Now it could be restored to its former glory. "As long as you're there, then there's no place else I'd rather be."

Brushing a lingering rose petal from my arm, I looked around the room. "What about the mess?" Then before he answered, I said, "Let me guess—you have people."

He shrugged. "*We* have people."

I actually didn't freak about his overt suggestion that we were tied even more deeply than we were. I'd told the truth to Mira when I said I couldn't think about those things, but maybe I could be okay when other people thought about it.

Hudson retrieved his jacket from the dance floor railing. He pulled out his phone from one of the pockets and typed something in—a text for our ride, I guessed.

"Oh," he said, digging in another of his jacket pockets. "I almost forgot. This is for you." He handed me a phone, nearly identical to the one I'd broken.

"So sure I haven't already replaced it, are you?" I asked with a laugh.

He winked. "You weren't answering any of my calls or texts. I'd hoped it was because you were still phoneless."

"I was phoneless so that I wouldn't break down and call you."

"Should I ask for an explanation?"

"No. It's just me. Thank you for the phone. It was very thoughtful." I wrapped my arm around his and together we walked toward the club entrance. "Hey, did you get Plexis back?"

"I did. But it wouldn't have mattered if I hadn't gotten you back."

Damn, the stuff he said was sweet. Only two weeks before, he'd been completely cut off from me, sharing very few of his true feelings. To think I could have missed out on all the beauty he had to offer if I'd let him slip away. Thank god, I'd stuck around for the good stuff.

I gazed up at his profile. "You never lost me, remember?"

"That's right. I didn't." We'd reached the door and he turned to look at me. Those startling grey eyes—I could stay in them forever. Not lost, exactly, but more like found.

"I love you, Hudson Pierce."

He breathed it in, physically breathed in my words—I could see exactly how they affected him. He needed them like I needed his touch. They changed him in some way that wasn't quite tangible but real all the same. It made up for the fact that he still hadn't been able to return the declaration.

He shook himself. "Go on out. Jordan should be waiting. I'll set the alarm and lock up."

He needed a minute to himself. I got that. He had the same effect on me.

I walked out, finding Jordan waiting with the Maybach.

"Good evening, Ms. Withers. I'm sorry to say that you missed your flight."

I winked. "Another time, I suppose."

I slid in the car, crossing to the opposite window to leave space for Hudson. While I waited, I turned on the new phone Hudson had given me. I smiled at the front screen wallpaper—it was a publicity picture of us kissing from the fashion show I'd attended with him. Scrolling through my contacts, I could tell that he'd managed to transfer my number and all my personal data to the new phone.

After a minute, the phone buzzed to notify me of incoming texts. I had seventeen in all. I scrolled through them, finding most were from Hudson, one from Brian—probably from before he'd found out my phone had broken.

My brow furrowed as I saw two texts from an unknown number. I opened the first one. *"The video file is too big for text. Text me if you want to see it in person."*

Confused, I scrolled to the next text from that number. *"Btw, this is Stacy from Mirabelle's."*

Ah, Stacy. She'd told me she had some proof about Hudson and Celia. Some reason not to trust her.

I laughed to myself. Too little, too late. Whatever proof Stacy had that Celia was a bitch was completely unnecessary. I'd learned the hard way.

Though it did pique my curiosity.

"Everything okay?" Hudson asked as he slipped in the backseat next to me.

"Everything's perfect." I dimmed my phone and stuck it in my bra. The outside world didn't hold a spark of interest to me when I had Hudson beside me. I was beginning to see that he might be there for a long time. He was right—we were connected. Nothing could break us apart. I was convinced of that now.

I buckled my seatbelt then settled into the crook of his arm thinking perfect was something I could get used to.

FOREVER WITH YOU

BOOK THREE

— CHAPTER —
ONE

I took a deep breath and stared at the door of apartment three-twelve. Whether or not I wanted to go any further, I hadn't decided. Actually, I couldn't remember deciding to come this far. But here I was—my heart pounding and hands sweating, debating the pros and cons of raising my fist to the wood and knocking.

God, why was I so nervous?

Maybe more deep breaths were in order. I took several—*in, out, in, out*—and examined my surroundings. The hall was long and empty. Gold-framed abstract art lined the walls. Though the building was nice and in a good part of town, the carpet was old and threadbare. Rose petals were strewn across the floor in front of the threshold a few doors down. Must have been left over from someone's romantic gesture. *Sweet.*

To the other side of me, the elevator opened. I looked over and saw a couple walking in the opposite direction. The man, dressed in a nice suit, held his hand to the small of the woman's back. Her blonde hair was tied up in a perfect bun. Even from behind, they were beautiful to look at. It was obvious they were in love.

Funny how I was seeing romance everywhere. Perhaps it was my state of mind.

I turned back to the door in front of me. It was plain and ordinary, but something about it felt ominous.

Well, might as well get this over with.

I pulled my bag higher on my shoulder and knocked.

Nearly a minute went by and no one answered. I leaned my ear against the door and listened. It was quiet. Maybe I had the wrong unit. I checked my hand where I'd scribbled the address in red pen, but it had rubbed off from my sweat.

It didn't matter. I knew I was in the right place.

"Try the buzzer," a man said from down the hall.

"The buzzer?" I asked, but he had already gone into his own apartment.

I hadn't noticed a buzzer, but I searched the wall by the doorframe anyway. There I found a small circular button. Strange I hadn't seen it before. I brought a trembling finger up and pushed.

A loud bark ripped through the air, and I nearly jumped out of my shoes, my heart pounding in my chest. I wasn't usually afraid of dogs, but I was already so anxious that it took very little to set me off. Movement sounded from inside and a voice talking sternly to the animal. Seconds later, the door opened.

Stacy stood in the entryway, her face more welcoming than she normally was with me. Her overly bright smile sent a chill down my spine. She was dressed casually in a faded t-shirt and jeans—not at all the attire I was used to seeing her in when she worked at Mirabelle's boutique. She was barefoot and her toes were painted with a pale pink polish. She looked relaxed. Comfortable.

I felt just the opposite.

Her grin widened. "You came."

"I guess I did."

She didn't move to let me in, so I stood where I was, awkwardly shifting my weight from one foot to the other. Did she hear my knees knocking? I was sure she must.

"Oh, sorry! Come on in." She stepped aside and let me move past her.

I took a tentative step inside, scanning her apartment. It was nice. Not nice like Hudson's apartment—Hudson's and *my* apartment, rather—but nicer than the studio that I used to reside in on Lexington Avenue. The space was sterile and cold, though completely immaculate except for the kitchen table to my left. It was covered with stacks and stacks of papers, reminding me of the top of the file cabinets in David's office back at The Sky Launch.

"This way." Stacy gestured to a couch in her living room. It was a twin to the sofa in Hudson's office—brown leather with oversized arms. I'd admired the design so much that I'd ordered a similar, less expensive one for the office at the club. Hudson and I had christened that couch, actually, with a round of heated sex. Stacy's version was not the cheaper variety, and with as prudish as the woman seemed, I doubted that she'd christened it with anyone.

Weird, though, that we all had similar taste.

Actually, what was weird was that I was there finding out Stacy's taste at all. Why was I there? The tight knot in my gut said this was the wrong decision. I should leave.

Except, I couldn't. Something kept me there with an intense force. Like my shoes were metal and the floor a super magnet. I knew it was all in my head—that I could physically walk out the door anytime I wanted. Yet there I stayed, compelled against my better judgment.

I threw my shoulders back, hoping it would make me feel more confident, and took a seat. I sunk lower than I'd expected, my knees sticking up higher than my thighs. I looked and felt ridiculous. So much for being self-assured.

"So sorry," Stacy apologized. "The springs are broken. Scoot down further and you'll bounce back."

Awkwardly, I lifted myself from the concave spot and moved further down the sofa. I sat slowly, testing for firmness. Thankfully, the springs were indeed intact. My poise, on the other hand, was not.

Stacy settled into the armchair next to me. A large gray cat rubbed against her leg, hissing in my direction. The unfriendliness of the cat reminded me of the barking from earlier. I looked around, but found no sign of a dog. Stacy must have locked it up in another room. It was odd that she'd have both pets in such a small apartment. I'd never figured her for an animal lover.

But I'd never figured her to wear jeans and a t-shirt either. It was all the unexpected that had me on edge, I told myself. That's all.

"Can I get you anything? Water? Iced tea?"

"No, thank you." I crossed my legs. "Actually, I'm sort of on a schedule. Do you mind if we get this over with?" It was a lie. I had nowhere to be. I didn't even have a driver waiting for me. I'd taken the subway instead of asking Jordan to bring me. Jordan reported to Hudson, and I didn't want him to know about this visit.

"Yes. Of course." She stood and crossed to her television. I noticed her computer was plugged into it, and when she turned on the set, her desktop showed on the large flat screen.

Having lost its leg to rub against, the gray cat moved over to my leg.

Great. Now I'd have gray fur all over my black pants. How would I explain that to Hudson? Maybe I could change before he noticed.

Stacy chatted as she scrolled through files on her computer. "Honestly, I wasn't sure if you'd come. You hadn't seemed interested before. I was surprised to get your text."

"Yeah, I wasn't sure I'd come either. Curiosity won out." Maybe it was because of the animal at my feet but I couldn't stop thinking about the *curiosity killed the cat* adage.

Fuck, what was I doing? Was it too late to change my mind about this?

It wasn't too late until she actually started the video. But I couldn't turn back now, could I? I'd never be able to stop wondering what secrets Stacy held about Hudson.

Maybe I should have asked him about it instead of showing up here.

"Well, I set up in case you did come. I just have to load the file. Hold on. It's here somewhere."

It seemed to take hours for Stacy to search through her computer. Each second that passed felt like agony. Thoughts of what could be on her video nagged at the edges of my mind—Hudson betraying me in various forms. I tried to shake the images away, but they clung, nipping at me, begging for my attention.

I'd chewed half of my nails ragged before I finally sought to relieve the tension. "Perhaps you could tell me what's on it while we wait."

"Oh, I couldn't do that." She gave me another warm smile. "You won't believe it until you see it. But trust me. It will change everything you know about Hudson. He's a liar, you know." She never smiled this much. It was as if she took pleasure in my discomfort. As if she were delighted to destroy my relationship with Hudson.

"He's not a liar. I trust him." I was the one who'd lied to him. Hudson had done nothing but proven himself over and over.

"You'll see."

Her certainty sent goose bumps down my skin. There was no way she was right. I knew Hudson. He didn't have secrets from me.

"Ah! Found it!" Stacy said in a sing-song voice. "Are you sure you don't want anything before I start this? Water? Iced tea?"

I gritted my teeth, the knot in my belly tightening with every passing second. "I said, no thank you."

"Popcorn?" She laughed. "I always like popcorn when I'm watching TV. Popcorn and M&M's."

"Look, Stacy, this isn't entertainment for me. You say you have something that will make me feel differently about Hudson. Do you think I'm looking forward to this?"

This was ridiculous. What was I doing here, behind Hudson's back no less? I should be talking to him, asking him about this stupid video instead of sneaking off to watch it. I didn't even know if I could trust the woman in front of me. Maybe this whole video thing was a trick.

I stood to leave. "I shouldn't be here. I have to go." I headed toward the door.

"No! Wait! It's already playing."

Again, curiosity got the better of me. I turned back to the TV. The screen was dark, but there was a muffled voice in the background. Little by little, the voice became clearer. It was Hudson.

"I want you, precious. Whatever it takes to make that happen. Whatever I have to do. Whatever I have to say. I have to have you in my life."

The screen was still dark, but I recognized the words. He'd said them to me—earlier. At the club.

"Is this some kind of a sick joke?"

"Just be patient." Stacy giggled.

The screen began to lighten and the picture came into focus. Hudson lay on a bed facing away from the camera, completely naked. I glanced at Stacy, furious that she had seen my boyfriend without clothing, but Hudson's next words drew me back to him. "Whatever I have to say, precious. I have to have you in my life."

They were familiar words, but I'd never seen this scene before. I didn't know that bed or that room. I hadn't been there when this had been filmed. I shook my head—*no, no, no.* Those were *my* words. *Precious* was *my* name. Whom was he sharing my words with?

The camera began to move, zooming around Hudson. I held my breath, waiting to see whom he was speaking to, not wanting the confirmation.

But as the camera zoomed closer, the focus blurred. So much so that it was impossible to make out what was going on or who was on screen. It was like looking through a dirty windshield or a cloudy contact lens. I blinked over and over, hoping to clear the blur, to bring the picture into clarity. I was desperate to see what was going on, desperate to see who was there. Even though I didn't want to, I was compelled.

I went to the TV and slapped my hand on its side, trying to sharpen the image. "Show me, dammit," I screamed at the picture. "Show me what you're hiding!"

I hit the television again and again, my hands red from the force, my breath ragged from the effort. I had to see, had to know. My gut told me the truth—the video held the answers. What I needed, what I was meant to see was here on this screen. Beyond the blur was what I dreaded most, my deepest fears, my darkest imaginings—the thing that could ruin everything.

The thing that could tear me and Hudson apart for good.

— CHAPTER —
TWO

I awoke in a panic, sweat beaded along my brow, my heart racing. I knew it was a dream, but the feeling it left was intense and vivid. Stupid, really. It wasn't real.

But it wasn't the dream video that had me in a panic—it was what might be on Stacy's real life video. She'd said it was some sort of evidence about Hudson and Celia. I'd blown it off earlier in the night, but maybe I shouldn't have because now it was seeping into my subconscious thoughts.

I glanced over at Hudson asleep next to me. Usually we remained in constant contact while we slept. His missing warmth exacerbated the "off" feeling that still clung to me after my nightmare. Not wanting to disturb my lover, I ignored the pull to snuggle into him and instead climbed out of bed, grabbed my robe, and headed to the bathroom.

Splashing cold water on my face, I took deep breaths and tried to calm down. I'd never been prone to nightmares. Even when my parents had died, my dreams had remained sweet and calm. My obsessive mind did enough work during the waking hours—sleep wasn't where I fleshed out my problems.

I wasn't obsessing like I had in the past, though. And there were problems still to be worked out. Yes, I was happy and in love. But the past week had been heartbreaking and stressful with Hudson in Japan and our relationship in limbo. I'd kept secrets that I wasn't sure he could ever completely forgive me for. And he'd betrayed me in his own ways—going behind my back to remove David as the manager of The Sky Launch. Then, the worst, he hadn't defended me. He'd chosen to listen to the lies of his childhood friend who was playing her own game where I was the pawn.

I knew our love outweighed the heaviness of those mistakes. He proved he knew it too when he arrived at the club earlier that evening, surprising me with his declaration of commitment to our relationship. Though he still hadn't said the three words I longed to hear, I didn't *need* them. I felt his love in every fiber of my being. Felt it as he'd made love to me on the dance floor with care and attention that spoke volumes. We were together for the long run, through thick and thin—it was apparent now and with that knowledge there should be a freedom from anxiety.

Except we still hadn't worked out all our trust issues, and that had me feeling edgy. Plus there was this video that Stacy claimed to have. What did it show? Did I want to see it? Was it simply a trick? Or was it actually significant?

It bothered me enough to make me restless and unsure. Make me obsess while I slept.

It's nothing, I told myself. *It won't affect anything with Hudson.*

But the unease that encased me said differently.

"What's wrong?"

Hudson startled me, but the tempo of my already accelerated heartbeat barely registered the shock. I peered over my shoulder at him standing in the bathroom door. He looked as he always looked—sexy and aloof. The sight of his naked body caused my breath to intake—every time—even when thoughts of jumping him weren't on my mind. I bit my lip as my gaze traveled down his body. Well, maybe thoughts of jumping him weren't as far away as I'd assumed.

He came behind me, his gray eyes probing mine in the mirror. "Are you okay?"

It crossed my mind to lie, but I wasn't doing that anymore. I'd gotten a second chance with this man, and if we were going to make things work, I'd have to be better at sharing.

I needed to tell him about Stacy's video.

And I would. But I needed a few minutes to regroup. "I just had a bad dream, and now I can't sleep."

His brow creased with worry. "Want to talk about it?"

I shook my head. Then changed my mind. "Yes. But later."

"Hmm." He wrapped his arms around my waist and kissed my head. "How about I get a hot bath going for you in the meantime?"

"That sounds heavenly."

He let me go and started to the task. I leaned against the shower stall as Hudson bent over the large soaker tub and turned on the faucets. It was impossible not to admire his hard body, not to want to lick along the muscles of his abs, to bite the tight curve of his ass.

He glanced up at me. "Those are naughty thoughts clouding those brown eyes."

My lips curved up into what I hoped was a suggestive grin. "Are you joining me?"

"In the naughty thoughts or in the tub?"

I swatted at his luscious behind. "The tub."

"I'll join you in both." It was three in the morning on a weeknight. He had work in the morning. And the man had jet lag from a week overseas. But he never faltered at caring for me. He was always there. Even when I kicked him away to Japan, he still made sure I was looked after—sending his sister to check in, calling the doorman to deliver messages. When would I stop being surprised by his attention?

Never. That's when.

I undid my robe and hung it on a wall hook, enjoying the lust in Hudson's gaze as I stood naked before him. I stuck a toe in to test the heat. The water was perfect—almost too hot, just like I liked it. I stepped in and leaned forward so that Hudson could slide in behind me. It dawned on me that we'd never bathed together. How could it feel like we'd been through everything yet there was so much we had left to experience? It was a comforting thought—to realize that we were still only in the new, that we could look forward to more.

When he was settled, I leaned back against his chest.

He nuzzled his nose along my cheek. "This is nice."

"The temperature is perfect." My muscles were already loosening in the warmth, the tension of my dream easing.

"I meant holding you." Hudson's voice was soft, as though his words were difficult to admit. "I've missed this."

God, I'd missed it too. That was one of the reasons I felt so uneasy—I was still recovering from the time we'd been apart. My mind was still processing what I'd almost lost—everything.

I'd almost lost everything.

That was surely why I was so worried about Stacy's supposed evidence. The questions that remained between us didn't help my anxiousness. We still had so many things left undeclared.

We soaked in silence for long comfortable minutes. When the water began to cool, Hudson reached for a bottle from the built-in ledge behind the marble tub. He poured a dab of soap into his hand from my cherry blossom body wash—a new favorite scent of mine—and worked it into my skin with deep massaging strokes. When he'd finished with my arms, he nudged me forward to continue the treatment on my back. Then he pulled me against him and bent my legs so he could reach every part of my body.

Last, his fingers splayed along my belly and up my chest. He spent a sweet amount of time on my breasts, kneading them with just the right amount of pressure until my nipples perked up. He nibbled at my earlobe and one hand began its descent to my lower regions. The thickening of his cock against my lower back told me exactly what was on his mind.

But first there were things to say. I didn't believe there was anything worrisome enough to crush our potential future together, but big enough that things had to be said.

I turned to straddle him, the water sloshing at my sudden movement.

Lacing his hands in mine to keep them occupied, I began. "We have stuff to work through."

His eyes stayed pinned on my breasts, as he raised an eyebrow. "We do?"

"We do." I bent my head to catch his gaze. "Who's going to run your club?"

His smile was mischievous. "You."

I smirked but didn't agree. I also didn't disagree. He claimed he wanted me to take over The Sky Launch, but I was convinced it was only an excuse to get rid of David Lindt. Hudson achieved part of his agenda—David was leaving in a little more than a week to take over one of Hudson's clubs in Atlantic City. I'd been pissed, but as the idea had settled over me, I'd realized it had been the right move on Hudson's part. Working every day with my ex wasn't exactly a good idea. I wouldn't want Hudson working with one of his exes, after all.

It didn't mean I was ready to run the club myself.

I also wasn't quite willing to give it to someone else.

Perhaps that would have to be tabled for a time when Hudson's cock wasn't pressing against my core. His cock could make me say *yes* to anything.

His fingers still linked with mine, Hudson began to seduce me with his lips, leaning forward to take my breast in his mouth.

I sighed with pleasure, my body yielding to him. My head, however, was still wrapped up in details. "And what happens next with Celia?"

His lips left my breast. "Really? You want to talk about Celia now?"

"I never *want* to talk about her. But I need to know that she isn't a threat to me." I swallowed the unexpected lump that formed in my throat. "To us." I hadn't realized how scared I still was about her possible influence on my relationship with Hudson.

"Hey." Hudson cupped my face in his hands. "She's not a threat. She has no solid proof of her claims, and she's not pressing charges. Even if she did, I'd still be here with you. You know that."

I nodded weakly. "But what about going forward?"

"Simple. We don't see her. We don't speak to her. We don't answer her emails."

"*We* don't?" Of course *I* wouldn't see her—I hated the bitch. But what about Hudson?

"Yes, *we*. I don't have room in my life for anyone who is against us."

Another wave of tension rolled off of me. "Your mother is against us too, you know." I was pressing my luck. Sophia Pierce, monster that she was to both her son and me, would likely always be a staple in Hudson's life. I would never ask him to cut her off. Though I disliked her, I recognized the importance of family.

"I know." Hudson sighed, his hands leaving my face. "At least she hasn't tried to sabotage us. If she does, I'm done with her. You're the only one that matters."

"Thank you." I kissed him softly. "But I hope it doesn't come to that. It would be nice to believe that there could one day be reconciliation where Sophia is concerned." It had only been a few days since I'd reconciled with my brother Brian. It had relieved a constant knot in my belly that I hadn't even been aware of. The same scenario wasn't likely to happen with Hudson and Sophia, but, hey, what did I know?

My thoughts travelled back to Celia, her reasons for playing me still unclear. "But why did she do it, Hudson? Why was Celia against us?"

"Not *us*. Me." His jaw tightened. "She's mad at me."

"Still? For what you did all those years ago?" My heart panged at his obvious torment. Hudson wasn't proud of his past and how could he be expected to move on when it kept coming back to haunt him?

Then anger took over. "I don't care what you did to her—she's a bitch. It was awful and terrible and horrible to do what she did. Especially when she claims to be your friend. Is she still in love with you? Is that her problem?"

Hudson lowered his eyes. "If she thinks she loves me, hurting you isn't the way to win my affection."

"Well, she certainly acts like a jealous lover."

"Without reason." He brushed his hand across my cheek. "Celia and I have never had anything together. Nothing. Except for…" His voice softened. "Except for what I made her believe I felt for her."

"She knows that wasn't real." I hated that this still tormented him. "And that was forever ago, now. If she's trying to get you back, it seems she already did that when she slept with your father and trapped you into claiming to be the father of her baby instead of Jack. Why didn't you tell me about that, by the way?"

"I should have." His tone was filled with regret.

"Yes, you should have." It would have made things much clearer to me about his relationships with both Celia and his father. And it had been yet another thing that stood as a wall between us—though most of the secrets keeping us apart had been mine. That was my regret.

Hudson released his hands from mine and swept them down my ribs. "It didn't feel like it was my secret to tell."

"Okay, that's fair." I shivered as his fingers kneaded the skin at my hips. He was getting restless, wanting more, wanting me. The time for talking was nearing an end. I had to jump to the meat of my concerns. "But some things have to change between us. We have to be able to share these things with each other. You could have at least told me you had good reasons not to trust her, reasons *I* shouldn't trust her."

"And you could have honored my wishes when I said *don't see her*."

"Yes, I could have." I let out a sigh. "We both have to change. We have to put everything on the line, Hudson, as much as possible. We know now that we're together, thick and thin, right? We have to trust that more than anything. We can't be afraid of our secrets and our pasts. Both of us. Honesty, open doors, transparency."

He cocked a brow. "Nakedness?"

Yep, I was losing him. "You're such a perv."

"I agree." He leaned forward again to lick a bead of water from my nipple. "I am a perv where you're concerned."

I smirked. Which was difficult considering how his tongue on my breast made me crazy. "Hudson, stop. I'm serious."

"I know." He leaned back against the tub. "And I agree with everything else you said. We need to be honest."

"Good." I put my hand up to stop him before he resumed his seduction. "Hold on. I have one more thing."

"Okay, what?"

He was getting impatient but trying not to show it. I almost decided to leave the rest of our conversation for later. But the memory of my nightmare and the cold foreboding feeling that lingered in my chest pushed me forward. "What happened between you and Stacy?"

"Stacy?" He seemed confused. "Mirabelle's Stacy?"

"Yeah."

"Nothing happened." He was bewildered by my question. "What do you mean? Like did I date her? I took her to a charity event a year or so ago. But after that, nothing."

"And I didn't sleep with her," he added before I had to ask.

That was comforting. But that wasn't the reason she concerned me. "Is there a reason she'd have a vendetta against you? Or reason to distrust you?"

He shook his head slowly. "Not that I can think of."

"She wasn't one of your past victims?"

"Victims?" His eyes narrowed. "Is that what you call the people I played with?"

I cringed. "Maybe that wasn't the best choice of words?"

"No. It probably *is* the best choice. That doesn't make it pleasant to hear."

"I'm sorry."

His features darkened. "Don't be. It's my past. I have to live with it. Why are you asking?"

I took a deep breath. We were putting everything on the line, after all. This was part of it. "The last time we were at Mira's, Stacy told me that she had some sort of video. A video that proved something or other about you and Celia. She didn't have it with her, so I gave her my phone number so she could contact me later."

"The last time we were at Mira's together?"

"Yeah. She cornered me while you were finding me shoes. Do you know what she's talking about?" I studied his face, trying to pick up on anything he might be hiding.

"No idea." Either he was really good at acting or he truly had no clue. I'd never seen him so perplexed. "She didn't tell you what the video was of?"

"No. Just that she had it and that it would show me why I couldn't trust you." I bit my lip. "And she texted me again tonight. Or sometime this past week when I didn't have a phone, and I didn't get the message until tonight."

I expected him to ask why I hadn't told him earlier, but he didn't. "What did her text say?"

"That the video was too big to send over the phone but to contact her if I wanted to see it."

He considered. "Do you want to see it?"

"No." But I kind of did. "Yes." Unless I didn't. "I don't know. Should I?"

"Well." He rubbed his hands up my arms. "You know that Celia can't be trusted already. And there is nothing that Stacy could have on me that you don't already know. You know more about my secrets and my past than anyone. You know me, Alayna."

"I do."

"Then unless you don't trust me..."

"I do trust you. If you say there's nothing I should be concerned about..."

His eyes locked on mine. "There isn't."

I paused. The minute I said my next words, I couldn't take them back. I'd have to put the video out of my mind and move on. It went against all my obsessive tendencies—could I do it?

I believed I could. For Hudson. I smiled. "Then I don't need to see it." It was easier to say than I would have imagined. And I meant it. I didn't need the proof of other people to know who Hudson was, what he meant to me.

It was amazing how much better I felt having the subject of the video off my chest. It no longer felt like a weight on me, though there was still some lingering edginess that probably just needed time to distill.

Hudson leaned forward and kissed my chin. "Thank you."

"For what, exactly?"

"For being open with me." He tilted his head. "You didn't have to tell me about that, and you did anyway."

"I'm serious about being more open and honest."

"I see that. I'm serious about it too. The only way we can move on is to decide that we're committed to each other first and foremost." His eyes rose to meet mine. "Are we?"

They were only two short words, but the weight of the question was heavy—heavier than when he'd asked me to be his girlfriend or to move in. And yet it was with ease and certainty that I responded. "I am."

"So am I." He captured my mouth with his, sucking lightly on my bottom lip before his tongue flicked inside, twisting with mine in an erotic dance of foreplay. I threw my hands around his neck, pulling myself closer into him. His cock thickened between us and my pussy clenched in reaction, wanting and needing him as much as his kiss said he needed me.

Without releasing my mouth, Hudson moved a hand to my breast. He was such an expert at handling me in the way I needed, his touch never too gentle, always just the right amount of rough. I cried against his lips as he squeezed my tit, driving me mad. I was so concentrated on his attention to my chest, I didn't notice his other hand traveling lower until his thumb was rubbing against my clit. I jolted at the exquisite pressure, my knees clutching his hips. I was already feeling the tight sensation in my lower belly building toward eruption. So soon, too soon.

I was on top, and wanting to delay my explosion until we could go together, I pushed away his hand from my core. Hudson's eyes closed slightly as I circled my grip around his thick erection. I stroked him once before shifting my weight forward onto my kneecaps. Positioning myself over him, I slid down his hard length, moaning as he filled me.

I sat atop him, sitting still for several seconds as my body adjusted to his size, my walls expanding to make room for him. Damn, he felt good. Just like that, without any movement—he felt made for me, as though his penis had been carved to fit my pussy and mine alone. I shuddered at the carnal thoughts that intensified the heavenly sensation of him inside me.

He shifted beneath me, his impatience evident. So I moved, riding him. Slowly at first, then more determined. My hands braced against his shoulders, pushing me off with the force I knew Hudson desired, the force *I* desired. It wasn't long before his hands were wrapped around my ass, augmenting my movement. And then, he held me still as his hips thrust up and forward in a circular pattern, driving into me with long deliberate strokes.

"Do you always have to take over?" I asked, breathless. Not that I minded. I enjoyed being on the other end of his control.

His lip curled at the edge. "If you want us both to come, then yes."

I laughed, the action causing him to twitch inside me, bringing me to the brink. When I could speak again, I asked, "And who is it that wouldn't come if I stayed in control?"

"You." His fingers tightened at my hips and, as if to prove his point, he pushed deeper into me, brushing against a spot—*that* spot, the one that always did it for me, the one that only he could find and that he found each and every time.

My orgasm came suddenly, taking me by surprise. I gasped, digging my fingernails into his skin as I rode the wave of ecstasy that passed through my every nerve, shooting down my limbs and clouding my vision.

Hudson's tempo didn't abate as I crumpled on top of him. He continued to thrust towards his own climax, driving toward that intangible goal-post. And then he was crossing the finish line, grinding against my clit as he spilled into me, causing another shudder from my already limp body.

While he settled, he kissed along my neck, along my jawline, finally making it to my lips where he sweetly lingered, adoring me with his mouth until our heart rates returned to a more normal pace.

Then he pulled away and met my eyes. His brow furrowed. "Alayna." Hudson cradled my face. "What is it, precious?"

It took me a beat to understand his question. Then I realized that tears were leaking down my face. And then they were more than tears. Uncontrollable sobs broke through me as though a great well of grief had been released.

Embarrassed and unable to explain my outburst, I pushed away and climbed out of the tub.

"Alayna, talk to me." He was behind me, wrapping a towel around my body as he dripped onto the floor.

I shook my head and ran to the bedroom.

Hudson followed. He grabbed my upper arms and turned me toward him. "Talk to me. What is it?"

My body heaved with the anguish. It wasn't a new pain, but one that had been with me for the better part of a week. I just hadn't fully expressed it yet—not to Hudson, not to myself.

"You. Really. Hurt me," I managed. The words were broken and hard to get out between sobs.

"Just now?"

"No." I swallowed and tried to calm myself enough to speak. "You really hurt me. With Celia. When you believed her. Instead of me." The pain was so raw, so fresh. Even though he'd made amends and we were together, the remnants of that betrayal still clung to me. I'd tried to move on before the scar had formed, and now, unexpectedly, the wound reopened.

"Oh, Alayna." He pulled me into his chest. "Tell me. Tell me all of it. I need to hear it."

"It hurts, Hudson. It hurts so much." I took a ragged breath. "Even though you're here. Now. And we're together. There's a hole." My sentences were short and broken. "A deep, deep hole."

His body tensed around me and I felt the degree to which he shared my grief. "I'm sorry. I'm so sorry. If I could take it back, if I could change how I reacted…I would have chosen differently."

"I know. I do. But you didn't choose differently. And you *can't* take that back." My voice strengthened as the ache inside surfaced. Like I was throwing up. Once it started, there was no stopping, and the process was uncomfortable and suffocating.

I pulled away from him, still in his arms, but no longer buried in him. "You can never take that back."

"No. I can't." He pushed my wet hair off my shoulders.

"And that changes things. It changes me."

He paused, worry etching his face. "How?"

"It makes me vulnerable. Exposed." I suddenly became aware that he was wearing nothing. It was fitting. Because, even though I was wrapped in a towel, I'd never been more naked in front of him. "And you know now. That you can hurt me." I choked as my tears returned. "You can hurt me real bad."

"Alayna." He pulled me back into him, his voice thick with emotion. "My precious girl. I never want to hurt you again. Will you ever be able to… forgive me?"

I nodded, unable to respond verbally. Yes, I could forgive him. I already had. But it didn't change how much it hurt. It didn't change how much healing still had to occur.

Hudson rocked me in his arms as I cried, intermittently kissing my head and apologizing. After a while, he swept me into his arms and carried me to the bed. He curled up with me, holding me against him.

When I'd finally finished with the tears, I sat up against the headboard with a hiccup. "Huh. I don't know where that came from."

He sat up next to me, wiping my cheeks. "You needed to let it out. I understand."

"You do?"

"I do." He put a tentative arm around me. "Is it okay that I'm here?"

"Yes! Please, don't leave." I clutched him, afraid that he would go.

"As long as you want me, I'm here."

"Good." I relaxed, letting my heartbeat return to a normal pace. "All that?" I gestured abstractly, referring to my sob scene. "That was just…"

"Healing?"

"Yeah. Cathartic. The last step of all that before stuff. I think I have some closure now." I felt cleansed—inside and out. I smiled as I traced Hudson's lips with my finger.

"I admire your optimism, but old pain has a way of showing up from time to time, even when life is going well." He caught my finger in his hand. "I'm sure we'll both feel this way every now and then."

I took a long breath in. I couldn't stand that I'd hurt him too. It almost pained me as much as his betrayal.

"Don't dwell on it." His voice was soft. "We have the future to make up for the hurts we've caused each other."

Right then, I was ready to dedicate my life to making up. Was I really thinking of us as forever? Well, at least long term.

I twisted my lips at the thought. "This is a new beginning for us, isn't it?"

He leaned forward to brush my nose with his. "No. This is better than a beginning. This is what happens next."

"I like that."

He leaned in and kissed me, sweetly and luxuriously, with promises of all the other things that would happen next. As if there was nothing in the world to do but lavish me with love.

— CHAPTER —
THREE

Hudson called into the office the next morning, deciding to work from home. I'd already made arrangements to be gone from the club for the next several days so I didn't bother going in either. We spent our time in the library, each of us working on our own projects, not talking much, which was fine. Exhausted from jet lag and lack of sleep, Hudson was in a mood. Even grumpy, I was glad for his presence. It was comforting just to be with him.

I did leave the apartment but only to get a wax and attend my group therapy that evening. When I returned, Hudson was passed out in our bed. I let him sleep.

Before I joined him, I got a run in on the treadmill and texted Stacy. *Thanks, but no thanks*, my message said. I probably didn't need to respond at all, but it gave the issue finality. I slept soundlessly the whole night through.

The next day was a holiday—the Fourth of July. Hudson surprised me by taking me to brunch at the Loeb Boathouse in Central Park. Afterward, we walked through the park, holding hands and enjoying each other's company. We were good—it felt right being with him. Easy.

Yet there was a tangible fragility between us. We were cautious with each other, handling one another with kid gloves. Hudson's lingering fatigue didn't help the situation.

Later, getting ready for the evening's fireworks display, Hudson came up behind me as I primped in the bedroom mirror. He wrapped his arms around my waist and kissed along my neckline. "We've been pussy-footing around each other all day," he said at my ear. "I'm warning you now that I'm done. It's time for me to start treating you like what you are: Mine."

My breath caught sharply.

"And yes, that means that you'll be fucked later. Hard."

Just like that, our tentativeness was over. And I needed a change of panties.

EXCEPT FOR A few casual strokes and caresses, Hudson kept his hands to himself during our ride to the Firework Cruise. I had a feeling the minimal contact was purposeful. He was building the anticipation.

And, god, was it working.

The air between us was charged. His sexual promise remained ever present in my thoughts, turning me into a powder keg waiting for that one spark to light me on fire. He, on the other hand, seemed completely unaffected—as though he hadn't uttered those carnal words to me only an hour earlier.

It was late evening, the sun just beginning to set, when we arrived at the pier. Hudson didn't wait for Jordan to open our door. He stepped out of the Maybach and reached for my hand to pull me out behind him. He was striking in his tan pants and dark suit jacket. He'd forgone the tie, leaving his white shirt unbuttoned to expose the top of his chest. The wind blew across the river that shared his name, mussing Hudson's hair into sexy chaos. As always, he took my breath away.

The moment was short lived. Cameras clicking and people shouting Hudson's name interrupted the reverie. Having been to only one other event with him where media was present, I wasn't used to the attention.

But Hudson was.

Like he had the last time when I'd gone with him to his mother's charity fashion event, he put on a show, pulling me into his side to pose for the cameras. He tactfully ignored many of the questions, only answering some with a simple *yes* or *no*.

"Is it true you've bought back your old company, Plexis?"

"Yes."

"Are you planning to break the company apart?"

"No."

"Is this your current girlfriend? Alayna Withers, is it?"

"Yes."

"What about Celia Werner?"

This was one Hudson didn't answer. The only betrayal that he'd even heard the question was a twitch of his eye. The man had stoicism down to a science.

I did not. The mention of Celia's name threw a shiver down my spine. It hadn't only been his mother who thought he and Celia should be together. Even the press had thought they were more than friends. Hudson, not caring what people thought or said about him, never bothered to correct the assumption.

I realized then that the media would never let her out of our life. She'd always be asked about, always be linked to him in the tabloids. I'd have to get used to it if I planned on staying with Hudson long term. And I planned on exactly that.

But just because I had to live with it didn't mean I couldn't fight back.

Forcing a smile, I did something that surprised even me—I spoke to the onlookers. "Don't you think it's rude to ask that when I'm standing right here?" I paused but didn't let the reporter get a word in before continuing. "He's with me now. Bringing up another woman in front of me is completely distasteful. If stirring up gossip is the only way you can write a decent story, I feel quite sorry for you. Don't bother rebutting. We have a party to attend."

Hudson's eyes widened. "You heard the lady." He took my hand and pulled me with him toward the dock where *The Magnolia*, a two hundred and fifty foot yacht, waited for us.

I squeezed his hand. "That wasn't so bad." I needed his reassurance. Needed to know I hadn't pissed him off.

"It was mostly terrible," he hissed.

Immediately I felt guilty for my outburst. "I shouldn't have said anything. I'm sorry."

"Why? You were the only reason it wasn't all terrible."

"Well, then." My smile widened. "Maybe I should talk to the press more often."

"Don't push it." Hudson's smile was brief. He quickly returned to his somber mood. After our pleasant day together, I had hoped that his crabbiness was over. Not the case. It was understandable. Dealing with the press and having to attend a big social event were not Hudson's favorite ways to pass the time.

I, on the other hand, didn't mind parties. Though I would have been just as happy to watch the show on TV from our bedroom. Or skip the viewing altogether. "Why are we going if you hate these things so much?"

He paused, mid-stride. "Good question. Let's not go."

"Hudson…" I tugged at him. Now that I'd gotten all dolled up, we might as well go through with the evening. Besides, even though he didn't want to be there, I sensed he wouldn't abandon the Firework Cruise so easily.

He sighed and let me pull him toward the ship. "I'm here because Pierce Industries sponsors this event. I have to go. If I don't, it reflects poorly on the corporation."

I put on an exaggerated frown. "Poor Hudson Alexander Pierce. Born into responsibility and obligation. Oh, and money and opportunity."

He looked at me, an eyebrow raised. "Really?"

"A little, yeah. If you're going to throw a pity party, H, I'm not planning to attend." Frankly, I was tired of his cranky mood. I wanted fun Hudson for the evening.

The edges of his mouth relaxed ever so slightly. "I'm not throwing a pity party. It's impossible for anyone to feel sorry for me when you're at my side." He pulled me closer to him so his arm could circle my waist.

"Yeah, that's why people envy you."

This got me a smile. "If it's not, it's the reason that they should."

At the end of the dock, a man dressed in naval attire stood waiting by the plank leading to the yacht.

"Good evening, Mr. Pierce. We're ready to cast off whenever you are, sir."

Hudson nodded. "Then let's go." He motioned me ahead of him, but I heard the man, who I assumed was the captain, whispering something else to Hudson behind me.

I stepped off the plank onto the boat deck then looked back to see Hudson's expression had grown grim.

"I'd rather not cause a scene," he said, his voice low. "But have the crew keep an eye out for any trouble."

"Yes, sir."

Hudson climbed aboard, putting his hand at the small of my back when he'd reached me.

"Is everything okay?"

"Fine." His tone was terse.

Dammit. Whatever the captain had said to him seemed to have undone the progress I'd made at ridding Hudson of his bad mood.

I knew from experience that pressing the matter would only make him grumpier. But I couldn't help myself. "Hudson, honesty and transparency… remember?"

He glared at me for three solid seconds before his features softened. "It's nothing. An uninvited guest arrived. That's all."

I suddenly felt guilty for teasing him about his obligations. Even on a holiday night when he should be enjoying himself, he couldn't relax. He'd always have to take care of something, manage someone. No wonder these events were such a pain in the ass.

Making up my mind to try to give him the best night possible, I let the subject of the uninvited guest go, even though I was itching to know more of the details. The last thing Hudson needed was me badgering him.

Instead, I worked again to make him more amiable. I leaned into him and whispered, "By the way, I meant to tell you that I got waxed yesterday." Since he'd been asleep when I got home, I hadn't gotten a chance to show him. Which was probably best since the recommendation was to wait twenty-four hours after waxing before having sex.

"Waxed?" Hudson said too loudly, his brow furrowed in confusion. Then understanding set in. "Oh." Immediately his expression lit with interest.

Behind us, a crew member that was helping the captain draw the plank into the ship looked up, obviously also getting my meaning.

Hudson glared at the man, and ushered me further onto the deck with him. "Tell me more." This time his volume was appropriately quieter.

"I'm talking *waxed*. Like, all the way. Bare." Normally, I kept a little more than a landing strip. This was the first time since I'd been with Hudson that I'd gone clean.

Hudson's eyes narrowed as he adjusted himself. "Are you trying to make this the most uncomfortable night of my life?"

"I was trying to give you something to look forward to, Mr. Grumpy Pants."

"Mr. Strained Pants, I think you mean."

I laughed. "Is that going to be a problem?"

"For you." He pulled me against him so that I could feel his erection against my belly. "It's going to be a long evening. By the time I finally get to be inside you, I'm going to need to be there for a long time. And I don't expect that I'll be able to be gentle."

Okay, wow. "No complaints here."

"Good girl." He stared longingly at my lips, but he didn't kiss me. Finally, he said, "I'll try to improve my mood. Let's go. The sooner the socializing is over, the sooner I can bury my face between your thighs."

Hudson led me up the stairs to the main deck. I'd never been on a yacht before, but I was pretty sure this one was more luxurious than most. I looked up the side of the boat and counted four decks, plus the mini one that we'd entered on. The deck furniture was simple but in good taste. Amazing taste, actually. At least what I could see of it. Most of it was covered by bodies. Dozens and dozens of bodies. There were at least forty people already in full party mode on this deck. Above me, more people leaned on the deck railings. And we hadn't even gotten to the inside yet.

I followed Hudson through the throngs of people and inside to a grand lounge. This area was even more packed then the decks. "How many people are here?" I asked.

He nodded at a server across the room who immediately headed our way. "There were two hundred invited. They were each allowed one guest. We only take this many people out for the annual Macy's fireworks. There are fourteen staterooms, so we'd never actually travel with this many aboard."

Hudson took two champagne glasses from the server and handed one to me. He clinked his glass to mine before taking a swallow. "Except for a few other important people, we'll be the only ones sleeping here tonight."

"Hopefully there won't be much sleeping." The bare skin between my thighs was aching for the attention it had been promised.

"You'll pay for your teasing later."

Just then, the boat launched smoothly into the river. I grabbed Hudson's arm to adjust to the motion as the crowd erupted into cheers. The place was utter chaos. Definitely not my boyfriend's usual type of scene. No wonder he'd been anxious.

We made our way up the grand staircase to an upper level, stopping every so often so that Hudson could greet a guest. He introduced me to all of them, sometimes as his girlfriend, sometimes as the promotions manager of his club. I guessed he chose my title depending on how it would benefit me and my career. Always looking out for me.

The next room we ended up in looked like a large living room. A bar curved around the wall and an abundance of couches and armchairs filled the space. A giant flat-screen TV graced one wall. It was turned onto the telecast of the pre-fireworks show though no one seemed to be paying attention. This room was also crowded, but I heard my name called through the buzz of conversation.

I turned toward the voice and found Hudson's sister sitting on a couch in the corner. She stood as we approached her, and I bent to embrace the petite woman I'd grown to love nearly as much as her brother. It was amazing how tightly she could hug with her pregnant belly between us.

When she released me, I checked out her dark blue maxi maternity dress. "Mira. You look adorable!"

"Ugh, thanks. I feel like a whale." She reached to give Hudson a hug, which he tolerated. "Hello, brother. Glad to see you back in the States, though you ruined all my amazing planning."

Before Hudson had shown up at The Sky Launch on Sunday night, I'd planned to fly to Japan and surprise him. Mira had helped make all the arrangements.

"Not that I'm complaining," she added before Hudson could respond. "You did good. I'm proud of you."

Hudson glowered at his little sister. He wasn't the type to accept praise. And Mira was the type to give it anyway.

I decided to come to Hudson's rescue before Mira could continue. "Did Adam abandon you?" I looked around for her husband.

"Nah, he's finding me something nonalcoholic to drink. It's surprisingly difficult."

"Ah." More like he was probably hiding from the crowd. Adam was another antisocial member of the family. At least Hudson knew how to fake it.

Mira sat back down on the couch, hitting the spot next to her. "Come. Sit. How did you manage to get a holiday off from the club?"

I shrugged as I took the seat next to her. "I'm sleeping with the owner."

"Nice." She shook her head like she was frustrated with herself. "I'm such a dummy! You were supposed to be in Japan. I guess you already got your shifts covered."

"Yes. David and another manager are covering the next few days." I should have felt guilty mentioning David. I didn't. In fact, for some reason I decided to poke at Hudson. "But I won't be able to count on David after this week."

Hudson scowled down at me.

"Why?" Mira asked.

I set my empty glass on the end table next to me. "Hudson transferred him to Adora in Atlantic City."

Mira looked from me to her brother. "Seems like there's a story there."

Hudson perched on the arm of the sofa. "You actually have him for *two* more weeks. I asked him to stay a little longer while we look for his replacement."

Well, that was news. Good news. It gave me longer to figure out my role at the club.

Mira's face twisted in confusion. "Look for his replacement? Why Laynie, of course. Duh."

"Um…" I'd brought it up. I should have been prepared to be put on the spot. I did want the position, and each day I grew more and more comfortable with the idea. But I still wasn't ready to make the commitment.

She must have read the complexity of the situation in my face. "Another story, I'm supposing."

"Yeah. Let's not go there." I patted Hudson's knee. "This guy's cranky as it is. Jet lag and everything."

"Got it. You look gorgeous, by the way. That's not one of mine though." She pursed her lips.

"Whoops." Pretty much my whole wardrobe these days was from Mirabelle's boutique, but wanting to be patriotic, I'd chosen a simple red flare dress with a nearly bare back from my club wardrobe.

She smirked. "You're coming to my Grand Reopening, right?"

I'd only recently found out she was remodeling. I had no idea an event was attached. But this was the social butterfly, Mirabelle. Of course there'd be an event attached. "Sure. When is it?"

"You didn't tell her?" She reached over me to swat Hudson.

"It slipped my mind."

"Hudson, you are such an ass!" To me, she said, "The twenty-second. It's a Saturday."

"I'll have to make sure someone else closes the night before, but that shouldn't be a problem." I was already thinking in terms of being responsible for The Sky Launch. Who was I kidding? I'd totally decided the job was mine.

"Oh!" Her eyes widened. "Will you be one of my models? Please say yes. Please, please, please."

"Um, sure?" It was nearly impossible to say no to the girl, but modeling was not something I had any interest in. Wearing pretty clothes, on the other hand…"What does it involve? Like, do I have to walk a runway?"

"Don't be silly. I didn't remodel that much. Okay, it's a small runway but not like what you're thinking. It's almost nothing. I'm simply showing off a few of my favorite looks for publicity. So I just need you to stand there and look gorgeous in one of my outfits while people take pictures of you."

Except for the pictures part, it sounded fabulous. "Okay. I'm in."

"Awesome! Can you come by sometime to get fitted? Like next Monday? Around one?"

My schedule was up to me and I didn't have any appointments set since I had planned to be overseas. But going to Mira's meant a good chance I'd see Stacy. She hadn't responded to my text, but did that matter?

"Why are you hesitating?" Mira looked offended.

"Sorry. I was running through my schedule in my mind. Yes. I can be there then." What was Stacy going to do anyway? Force me to watch her video? That was ridiculous.

"Yay!" Mira made pom-poms with balled-up fists and shook them in the air.

Beside me, I felt Hudson tense. Then a familiar voice said, "Ah, here's where the party is."

"Jack!" I stood to give Hudson's father a hug, careful not to knock the drinks he held, one in each hand. "I didn't realize you'd be here."

"He wasn't invited." Hudson bit out.

Aha. The uninvited guest from earlier. As if Jack would cause a scene. Or maybe it was Hudson that would disturb the peace. He seemed less than pleased to see his father aboard the yacht.

Jack only smiled at Hudson's displeasure, his eyes gleaming like they often did when he was about to be contrary. "I'm a Pierce. My invitation's standing."

Leaning toward me, Jack said, "Hudson isn't speaking to me."

The last time Jack and Hudson had seen each other was the day that Jack admitted fathering Celia's baby. It had been a secret that Hudson had been determined to keep from his mother. He was not happy that Jack had spilled the beans. "Oh, I suppose he isn't." And while I was thinking of the horrid woman…"Is Sophia with you?"

Jack scratched his temple. "She's not speaking to me either."

"Serves you right." Mira's words were more sassy than chiding. The girl didn't have it in her to be volatile.

Jack nodded toward his daughter. "Can't figure out what I have to do to get this one to stop speaking to me."

"Daddy!"

He winked at Mira. "I'm teasing, pumpkin. You're the light of my life, and you know it. Here, I brought you a virgin daiquiri."

Mira harrumphed but took the drink from her father's outstretched hand. "I'm not exactly happy with you these days myself, you know."

Jack sighed. "I know. Chandler's keeping your mother company tonight so she's not alone. You're a sweet girl to be worried about her. I'll try to make it up to you sometime."

"It's not me you need to make up to," Mira said under her breath.

Either not hearing or decidedly ignoring his daughter, Jack turned his attention back to me. "How are you?"

"I'm good. And I'm so glad to see you. I wanted to thank you. For being my support when all that went down." Jack had been one of the few people on my side when Celia had accused me of harassing her. Bringing it up now, I felt that small pang of betrayal. Hudson was right—it wasn't so easy to forget that kind of pain.

"It was nothing, Laynie. I knew whom we were dealing with. I would have thought others here would have too." He didn't bother to look at Hudson, but his words hit their mark just the same.

I hadn't meant for the conversation to go that direction. Despite the hurt he'd caused, Hudson had valid reasons to think Celia's accusations might be true. "To be fair, you don't know me quite as well as others here do either. But anyway, thank you." I took Jack's hand in mine and squeezed.

"Alayna…" Hudson warned.

I let go of Jack's hand and turned to look at my man who was now standing. His stance was foreboding, even with his hand tucked casually in his pocket. His jaw flexed and his eyes darkened with warning. It was surprisingly hot.

"Jealousy doesn't look good on you, son."

I disagreed. Jealousy *did* look good on Hudson. Quite good indeed.

A low grumble came from the back of his throat.

Jack cocked his head. "Did he just growl?"

Though Jack was clearly not Hudson's competition, I understood his reasons for feeling that way. It wasn't worth it to try to convince him otherwise. "Obviously I'd love to talk more, Jack, but it doesn't seem like it would be a good idea."

He took a sip from the clear drink in his hand as he eyed his son. "No, it doesn't." Again, he addressed me, his free hand on my shoulder. "I'm glad you're still here. In his life, I mean. Even though he's a stubborn oaf that blames me for all the wrongs in my relationship with his mother—"

"Are you saying that you aren't at fault?" Hudson challenged.

Jack's face lit up. "He's speaking to me!"

Hudson wiped his brow. "Ah, Jesus."

"Anyway, I'm glad you're with him, Laynie. He needs you more than he probably realizes. And there's no doubt he recognizes your worth. That boy has real feelings for you." His eyes drifted to Hudson. "Look. He's blushing."

"He is!" Mira exclaimed excitedly. She was a hopeless romantic and never pretended otherwise.

"I am not." But Hudson's protest only darkened the red in his cheeks.

Jack laughed. "See? His love for you is written all over his face."

Hudson stepped forward and put his arm possessively around my waist. "Could you stop pawing my girlfriend?"

Jack rolled his eyes but removed his hand from my shoulder.

The whole scene was amusing, not to mention a big a turn-on. I didn't at all mind when Hudson got all alpha male on me. In fact, I may have even provoked it in him. "I'll have to tell you more how appreciative I am when we get together sometime."

"No, no, no. Not happening," Hudson fumed.

Jack chuckled. "Look at you rile him up on purpose. You're a wicked little woman, Alayna Withers." He looked us over, as if taking in all of who we are and what we meant to each other. "Perfect."

"That's it. We're done here." Hudson turned me away from his family.

"Talk later," I called over my shoulder.

"Monday!" Mira reminded after me.

Yes, Monday. At the boutique. With Stacy.

A knot formed in my gut. The thought crossed my mind without permission—what was on that video? Was there actually something I should be concerned with?

I wouldn't watch it, whatever it was. I'd said I didn't need to.

But wondering about it still—that I couldn't help. I was only human, after all.

— CHAPTER —
FOUR

Hudson escorted me out to the deck and I let thoughts of the video float away in the breeze.

I turned into him and surprised him with a deep kiss.

"What was that for?" he asked when I came up for air.

"No reason." Except that I needed it. He seemed to need it as well. "You know there's no reason to be jealous of me and your father, right?"

"Uh huh." He pushed out of my arms and took my hand, leading me up the deck.

"He's attractive. I won't deny that."

"Not helping."

He was in front of me and couldn't see my smile. I was only teasing him, but he needed to know that I'd never betray him with Jack. "There's nothing between us. No chemistry at all. And if you stopped wanting me, I'd never retaliate against you like that. I'm not Celia."

He spun toward me. "I know you're not Celia. You don't think I fucking know that?"

His heated reaction threw me off guard. "I…didn't…"

He pulled me back into his arms, clutching me tightly. "And don't talk about me not wanting you. Ever. It's not even a breath of a possibility."

I wrapped my arms around him, shocked by his desperate tone. "Okay. I won't."

He kissed my temple. "Thank you." He held me like that for a long beat before he relaxed his grip on me. "The fireworks are getting ready to start. I have a spot reserved for us at the bow."

"The bow?" I was so not a boat person.

"The front of the yacht. We'll have an excellent view." Though his eyes were perusing my body, and I wondered if he wasn't talking about the view of the sky.

"Awesome." I let my own eyes graze his perfect form before shaking myself out of my lustful stare. "I need to use the restroom before the show starts. I'll meet you there?"

He reached in his pocket and pulled out a key. "Use the one in our stateroom. No lines. Number Three. It's just in there." He nodded toward an entry back into the ship. "Oh, and when you come back, I'd like you not to be wearing any panties."

I grinned as I took the key from him. "You got it, H." I knew what that was about. He'd felt threatened by his father and by talk of not being together. Having me at his beck and call was another way for him to feel reassured. Silly man with his insecurities. How did he not know that I completely belonged to him?

It only took a few minutes to find our stateroom. It was beautiful and grand like the rest of the ship and as large as our bedroom back at The Bowery. I didn't linger, eager to get back to the show and, more importantly, Hudson. I used the bathroom, leaving my underwear hanging off the side of the tub, and returned to the deck just as the sky lit up with the first explosion of light.

Hudson was waiting for me at the front—*the bow*—of the ship. He'd acquired a spot at the railing between two small caterer stands where partiers could set empty glasses. Though there were still people everywhere, it gave us a little bit of seclusion, as bodies weren't pressed right up against us like they were around the rest of the yacht.

Not that I minded a body pressed up against mine. As long as it was Hudson's.

His eyes lit up when he saw me. I handed him the stateroom key, which he pocketed, then he held out his hand for mine. "Come here." He tugged me in front of him.

I waited for his arms to circle around me, but instead he grabbed my ass through my dress, squeezing my cheeks. A breeze blew over the river and the feel of the air against my very bare pussy, plus Hudson's massage of my behind, had me feeling aroused.

"Good," he whispered. "You obeyed."

Ah, so the butt rub was simply a panty check. Whatever the reason, I'd take it.

Hudson propped his leg on the lower rail and continued caressing my behind while, overhead, the sky lit up again and again. Each time the sparks caused cheers from the crowd, drowning out the sound of the music blaring from inside the ship. I'd never been so close to the Macy's Annual Fireworks, and I was mesmerized. They shot above the river from at least seven different barges, simultaneously turning the darkness into a flash of color—magical.

Things got even more magical when Hudson's arms wrapped around me. And then his hand made its way under my skirt, hiking the fabric up around my waist, flirting with the skin above my pubic bone.

I was exposed to the night. Though Hudson's propped leg covered the view on one side of us, the crowd on the other side of me only had to move their interest from the sky to us, and they'd see.

I inhaled sharply. "What are you doing?"

"Setting off fireworks." His mouth was at my ear, rumbling with the rockets in the sky.

Fuck, I didn't care who could see—I was turned on.

My eyes burned from the blaze overhead, my nerves lit from Hudson's touch, my lower belly sparking with need.

"Spread," he commanded.

I obeyed, lifting my left foot onto the lower rail, mirroring his stance. It gave more privacy, blocking the view from the other side of us. Yet it wouldn't take a genius to figure out what he was doing to me—all anyone had to do was pay attention.

With full access, Hudson stroked over my pussy, sweetly grazing the newly exposed area. "Ever since you told me you were bare, I've been thinking about touching you." His breath at my neck drove a shiver down my spine.

Then his fingers slid between my lips, finding the sensitive nub, and I thought I might burst—burst with the fireworks above me. He settled his thumb on my clit, circling with expert pressure. "God, precious, I couldn't keep my hands off you if I tried. You're so slick already."

"Hudson." It was barely a word, more of a cry, really. Louder than I'd intended, drawing a glance from a couple not far from us.

Hudson's hand froze. "If you want to come, Alayna, you have to promise me you can be quiet."

"Okay." *Anything.* Anything to make him keep touching me.

He started his movement again, his thumb dancing over my clit as his fingers went lower. "Do you know what it does to me to see you come apart?" he taunted, his touch now spiraling around my hole. "Do you?"

How did he think I could talk? "No," I managed on a breathy exhale.

"It drives me fucking insane." He jabbed two fingers inside. At least, it felt like two fingers. It was difficult to be certain. All I knew for sure was that it felt amazing.

He plunged again as his thumb resumed whirling over my clit. Swirling and plunging, he fucked me with his hand, right there, in the open air, as the crowd around us stared upward in a patriotic daze.

So. Fucking. Hot.

The tension was building, tightening in my womb.

Then his lips were moving at my ear again. "Sometimes it's all I think about. Taking you to the edge. Watching you spill over. It's the most goddamned beautiful thing there is."

I was close. So close. About to explode. I leaned back against him, rubbing his erection with my ass. I felt incredible. Sexy. On fire. Small grunts formed at the back of my throat.

"Bite on your hand to stifle your screams if you need to."

I wanted to challenge him—to say, *oh you're so sure I'll be screaming*—but then he bent his fingers and stroked against a particularly sensitive spot. A moan escaped from my lips.

"Hand," he ordered.

Just in time, I flung my hand to my mouth, biting down on my finger as I came. My orgasm flared through me, erupting in tandem with a spectacular sequence of fireworks. I couldn't tell what parts of my blinded vision were from the display and which were from Hudson. It was glorious.

But I wasn't nearly sated.

I wanted more. Wanted him.

I spun into him, kissing him with frenzy. My hand rubbed his cock through his pants. He was so hard. He wanted me as much as I wanted him. More, maybe.

The fireworks show wasn't over. I didn't care. "Take me to bed," I demanded against his lips.

It was Hudson's turn to groan. I swallowed the sound with another wet kiss, licking into his mouth with deep strokes. God, he tasted good. I couldn't get enough of him, was ready to fuck him right there on the deck.

Somehow Hudson found the strength to untangle from my embrace. "Jesus, woman." His eyes were nearly black with desire. Then he turned toward the entry to the staterooms, pulling me behind him.

The crowd cheered at that moment. For the fireworks, of course, but it drew my gaze up.

That's when I saw her.

On the upper deck, looking down at me was Celia Werner. My mind flashed back to my dream and the terror that accompanied it sparked through me. Her eyes met mine, piercing through me, and I suddenly understood the phrase "shooting daggers." Anger emitted from her cold stare. Hudson had said it was he that she was mad at, and maybe she was mad at him. But she *hated* me. It was evident in her entire posture.

A chill ran down my spine as, again, I realized she'd always be there. She'd always be threatening at the periphery of my life with Hudson.

The realization only fueled my need for Hudson to be inside me.

I pushed Hudson onward, determined to recapture the mood from a moment before, to remind myself that I was the one with him, not her. Me. Only me.

As soon as we were in the hallway leading to the staterooms, we were kissing again. He pushed me against the wall, his hands reaching under my dress to fondle my naked ass.

Desperate to make his groin meet mine, I curled my leg around his thigh. He relaxed his pressure so that I could jump up and wrap my legs around his waist. He sucked and licked along my neck as he carried me to our room. There, he braced me against the other wall so he could fumble with the key and the lock, swearing as he did until we were finally inside with the door shut behind us.

Panting, we both broke into a laugh. Hudson's serious demeanor made outbursts like this rare, and I swam in the sound of his unbridled amusement.

Until our eyes met.

Then we were lip-locked once again.

With me still wrapped around him, he sat—more like *fell*—onto the bed. I didn't hesitate, scrambling down to the floor to my knees so I could undo his belt. He toed his shoes off and lifted his hips so I could pull his pants and briefs down.

As soon as his cock sprang free, my eyes were glued. I wanted to lick it, to take it in my mouth, to feel it filling me, twitching in me. But there were still clothes in the way, and I needed to be naked. Needed *him* naked.

I reached my arms up so Hudson could pull my dress over my head. The backless nature of the outfit hadn't allowed for a bra to be worn. Thank god. One less item to be removed. While he worked on unbuttoning his shirt, I circled my hands around his penis. Damn, it was steel. I only had time to stroke him a couple of times before he was pulling me with him onto the bed.

Both of us naked, we pressed into each other with a frantic need to be skin-on-skin in as many places as possible. Our hands explored like it was the first time, like we might never have the chance again—caressing and touching while we kissed with fevered passion. Hudson's fingers eventually made their way to my lower regions where I wanted him most.

He slid through my wet folds once before tearing abruptly away. "Turn around and kneel above my face. I have to lick you."

I shook as I clambered into the position. Hudson had gone down on me plenty of times, but never with me hovering over him in such a carnal way. It felt dirty and base and so, so sexy.

When I was bent over his face, he put his hands on my thighs and slid my knees further apart so that my cunt was a half an inch above his mouth. I was squirming before his tongue ever touched me. And he took his time before it did, blowing across my clit first, sending delicious little sparks through my limbs.

I peered down at the erotic sight of him between my legs and watched as he buried his nose in my lips and inhaled. "You smell so fucking good," he groaned.

Holy. Fuck. I almost came right there.

Then—*finally*—his tongue flicked across my already excited clit. My body lurched and I cried out, fingernails digging into his hips. *Amazing... so amazing.*

How could it always be so amazing?

As I struggled to hold on, to not go over too quickly, I saw his cock twitch below me. There was no question that I had to have him in my mouth. Immediately. I grasped my hands around the base of his shaft and slid his crown past my lips like I was sucking on a Popsicle. Only Hudson was much yummier.

His whole body shifted underneath me, his grasp on my thighs tightening. “Fuck, yes! Suck it.”

It was what I loved the most about sucking Hudson off—that I could have power over him. I was always the one who fell under his spell. I enjoyed the way he molded me, manipulated my body, bent me to his will—I *craved* it. But when I had his cock in my mouth, I finally understood why he liked being in control. It was quite heady to be the one making him twist and writhe. Making him succumb to me.

And while I bobbed over him, he continued to suckle at my core. The ecstasy warred with my solemn intention to give to the man who was always giving to me. My insides tightened and I felt close to coming, but I held on, focusing on him. He thickened as I hollowed my cheeks and increased my tempo. My free hand ran up and down the inside of his thigh, then moved to cup his balls. He groaned and that was when I knew he was as close as I was. It was a battle—who would get there first? And who would the winner be? The one who came or the one who didn’t?

I considered it my victory when he pushed me away. “That’s enough. On your back. I need to come inside you.”

I swiveled to do as he commanded. I bent my knees, planted my feet on the bed, and spread my legs as Hudson scooted toward me. But instead of covering me with his body, he stayed kneeling. Lifting me under my ass, he urged me up into an arch. One hand moved to support me under my thigh. The other moved to rub my still-throbbing clit.

Talk about a view. I had the perfect vantage point to see his cock knocking against my bare pussy.

“I’m so turned on right now, Alayna. It’s going to be rough.”

He was asking my permission. Crazy, because I trusted him implicitly with my body. Trusted him with all of me.

My eyes met his. “Please.”

He groaned. Then he plunged in, deep and hard, just as he’d promised.

I cried out, fisting the sheets. I had already been on the brink and the minute he entered my channel, my orgasm ripped through me.

Hudson wasn't slowing at all as I clenched around his cock. He drove into me with single-minded fury, over and over. His thighs slapped against mine, the sound driving me mad, stirring up another climax within me. He talked to me—crazy sex talk that I could barely make meaning of in my haze. Each word punctuated as he thrust in, in, in. "You're. So. God. Damn. Hot. You. Make. Me. Come. So. Hard."

And then we were both coming. So hard. He pushed into me with a long groan. My eyes were glued to him, and I watched his entire torso stiffen as his hips bucked against my pelvis. Then my own vision went white, clouding with the intensity of my release. His name was on my tongue, both a curse and a prayer as I surrendered to the convulsions that begged to overtake me.

God, oh, god.

It seemed ages before I recovered enough to speak—to *think*. When I could, Hudson had already fallen on the bed beside me. He was equally affected, I knew. If he weren't, he'd be holding me. Instead, we lay side by side, our shoulders the only parts of our bodies touching, yet the connected feeling was palpable.

I took a final deep breath. "That was incredible." Incredible was an understatement. There weren't words for what it really was. I looked over at the glorious lover beside me. "Seriously. How does sex with you just keep getting better and better?"

Hudson didn't pause in his answer. "We've learned to trust each other."

"Is that what it is?" It meant a lot that he trusted me after the things I'd done. In many ways I didn't deserve it. But I would never betray him again. I'd grown past that.

"Yes. That's what it is." He turned his head toward me, his eyes narrowed. "Did I hurt you?"

"In only the best ways." He had been rougher than usual. But I'd loved every second of it, even though I now felt raw and a bit tender. "I had no idea you were so into a shaved pussy."

He smiled, his shoulder lifting as if in a half-hearted shrug. "I've never really cared. It's you I'm into. Shaved, bushy—I'll take you."

I giggled. "I've never been bushy with you." Bushy had never been my style. But if it was something Hudson wanted…

"But you could be and I'd be turned on." His eyes darkened and I could tell he was imagining it. "Jesus, now I'm hard again."

"Are you kidding me?"

"No. I'm not." He nodded down toward his penis.

I had to look. Sure enough, it was hard. "You're such a horn-dog."

"Perhaps." Except he'd always said it was me that made him crazy, no one else.

Could that be true? Could it really only be me that turned him on to no end, transforming him into a greedy lover?

It had been true for me. Until him, sex had been fun, but that's all. Sometimes it could even begin an unhealthy obsession. But my addictions had never been about the physical. With Hudson it wasn't exactly about the sex, either. It was more about wanting to be as close to him as possible. And, because it was Hudson and he communicated best with his body, being as close to him as possible involved being naked.

He'd never let anyone in before. Maybe sex really had only been for sport in the past. With us, it was speech.

Which might have something to do with why we still had such trouble talking to each other.

We were working on that though. So I brought up the subject that I knew neither of us wanted to broach. "I saw Celia."

Hudson groaned. "And now I'm soft."

My eyes flicked downward. "No, you're not."

"It feels like I should be. Come on—Celia?"

"Sorry. I thought you should know."

"I suppose I should." He sighed. "Did she bother you at all?"

"No. I didn't talk to her. It was as we were coming down here. I think she was watching. On the deck above. When…you know." How come I could do completely nasty things with the man and still be so embarrassed about mentioning them outright?

"When I made you come all over my hand?" Leave it to Hudson to say it bluntly.

It was quite the turn-on, actually.

"Yeah, then."

"Hope she enjoyed the show." His expression was proud.

Like I'd said before—total horn-dog.

I started to tease him back but then I realized he hadn't been surprised by her presence. "It wasn't Jack you were referring to who was the uninvited guest, was it? It was Celia. How did she get here?"

Hudson ran both his hands through his hair. "She came with one of the men in my advertising department. He's always been interested in her and she's never given him a second look. I'm sure she used his crush simply to get on-board tonight."

It was obvious he didn't want to talk about her, but he was willing so I pressed on. "Why does she want to be here so badly?"

"Maybe she wanted to see if we were still together. I don't know. You know more about that kind of obsession than I do." He didn't say it to be hurtful. It was honest. I did know about that kind of obsession. Very well.

I let myself remember the reasons I'd been attracted to the men I'd stalked. "Somehow your attention validates her. Makes her feel alive." I felt my tone get heavy with years of sadness. Recalling those emotions of my past was not pleasant.

Hudson narrowed his eyes, trying to read me. "Do you think I'm being too cruel to her by cutting her out of my life?"

"No." Though if I were right—if she really did feel the way I suspected she did about Hudson—then I understood the pure devastation that she had to be going through at his dismissal. "Does that make me a shitty person?"

"No."

Whether he was right or wrong, I accepted his absolution without debate. Besides, just because I understood how she might feel didn't mean I could soften the blow in any way. Even if she had Hudson, she'd never really think she did. I'd never believed the men who were with me were really with me. Believing Hudson actually cared for me had taken a great deal of healing on my part. Those were steps Celia would have to take on her own.

But if Celia truly were obsessed with Hudson in the ways I used to be…

I shuddered to think of the lengths she might go to in order to win him. I voiced the nagging concern that had been tugging at me the entire night. "She's never really going to be out of our lives, is she? She's always going to try to destroy us."

Hudson rolled to his side to face me. "It doesn't matter." He cupped my face, lining his eyes with mine. "You belong to me, precious. You belong *with* me. I won't let anything come between us. I won't let anything hurt you. Especially not her."

The man couldn't say *I love you*, but somehow he knew how to make declarations that struck right into the core of my heart. And his eyes—they backed up every word he said. I had no doubt that he would fight for me, fight for us. He hadn't before. Now was a different story. Warmth spread from my chest throughout my body and I felt dangerously close to tearing up.

But I didn't want to get emotional. I wanted to tell him how I felt in the way he understood best. With my body. I flashed a suggestive smile. "Now *I'm* turned on again."

Hudson's jaw relaxed and he pulled me flush with him. He leaned in until his mouth was a mere inch from mine. "So we can stop talking about her?"

He smelled of sex and champagne and Hudson, and my desire flamed instantly. "We can stop talking period."

He covered me with his body, teasing me with flicks of his tongue along my jaw. At my neck, he nibbled and sucked, likely leaving a glaring hickey. Which was fine. Perfect, actually. He could mark me in any way he wanted. I was his. I wanted to be *known* as his.

I arched my back and pressed my breasts to his chest. God, I loved the feel of his skin against mine. My hips writhed underneath him, urging him to stop teasing and get on with it already.

He lifted his head to meet my eyes. "Stop rushing me," he chided. He was always very conscientious about varying the moods of our lovemaking. The last time had been driven and furious. This time would be slow and sweet. Always, it was he that decided how it would go.

I didn't prefer one tempo over another. Didn't care if he made it fast or if he took all night. But as it was occurring, whichever way we were fucking, I always thought it was the best.

At his own pace, Hudson took me to where I wanted and needed to go. Loving me thoroughly with his body. Loving me entirely without words. Loving me completely.

And as we spun into the intoxication of our passionate interlude, I said to myself, *this time. This time is the best.*

— CHAPTER —

FIVE

The boat docked while we'd been lost to each other in our stateroom. The drunken crowd had dispersed and *The Magnolia* was quiet—as if we were the only ones on Earth. Enveloped in Hudson's arms with the gentle rocking of the water underneath, I slept better than I had in ages. I guessed he did too, if his mood had anything to say about it. His jet lag seemed to have finally been relieved. Oh, the power of great sex and a good night's sleep.

We left before dawn, slipping off soundlessly. Jordan was waiting at the Maybach when we reached the top of the boardwalk. This time there were no reporters, no flashing bulbs—it was just the two of us and our driver as Hudson and I climbed into the back of the car.

Once on the road, I sidled up to Hudson, or as close as the restraints of the seat belts would allow. With his improved spirits, it was time to talk about the future. "I've been thinking about who's going to manage The Sky Launch."

"You."

My head was tucked under his chin, but I could hear the smile in his voice.

I chuckled. "No pressure."

"Yes, pressure. Lots and lots of pressure." He stroked his hand down my hair. "I want you to run the club. I've always wanted you to run the club. I've told you that."

I sat up to look at him. "I know. And that's what I've been thinking about."

"Go on."

"I want to do it. I do. And I think I have the ideas and the marketing sense to pull it off."

"You do."

I'd only received my MBA a little more than a month before. I'd never been in charge of an entire business by myself. Hudson was being overly optimistic about my qualifications, especially when he intended to have very little to do with the day-to-day operations. "I adore that you think so highly of me, H, but I'm still lacking practical experience. Which was what I was looking forward to learning from David."

Hudson rolled his eyes—an odd gesture on such a solemn face. "David would have held you back. You have more genius in your little pinky than—"

I cut him off with my finger to his lips. "Stop it. Your perception of my abilities is tainted."

He kissed the top of my finger before he covered my hand with his and moved it to his lap. "It's not."

"Anyway." There was no use arguing the subject. It was partly what had kept us at a standstill since he'd first brought up the idea. He believed I could do more than I believed I could do. It was endearing and empowering, but also overwhelming.

Still Hudson's faith in me had worn me down. "I *want* to run the club. And I'm telling you yes to running the club—"

His eyes lit up. "Yes?"

"But on one condition."

"That I also give you my body and soul? If you insist…"

I smiled but otherwise ignored his flirting. "I want to hire another full-time manager to share the load. Someone with the experience I don't have."

He considered. "I don't see a problem with that. But I'd still want you to be the point person. And, hell, I'll still throw in my body and soul."

"Fine. That's what I want." I corrected myself before he could turn my words on me. "I mean I want to be the point person."

"You don't want my body and soul?" He twisted my words anyway. Of course.

"Shut up," I scolded. "I already have that."

"That you do." He wrapped his arm tighter around my waist and kissed me on my forehead. "Go ahead and put an ad out today. Unless you already have someone in mind?"

"That's just it." It was hard for me to ask this. I'd been so insistent about me doing my job without Hudson interfering, but now I needed him to.

"What?"

I pulled away. It felt too odd to be in his embrace while discussing business. Too much like some form of nepotism. "Well, there's no one at the club qualified. No one who knows more than I do. And if I put an ad out and got resumes…I just don't think I'm going to find the type of person I'm looking for. Especially not as quickly as I need them. But maybe you, with your connections and everything…"

"You want me to find someone?"

I bit my lip. "Yes."

"Done."

"I haven't even told you the type of person I'm looking for."

He sighed. "Then tell me."

This was hard for him too. I recognized that. He wanted to assume he knew what was best for me. Maybe he did. But if I was going to be his point person, I needed to have some control. "I'm thinking someone who has a history of managing a club or a restaurant, even. Someone with a resume. Someone who would know the right numbers for what should be incoming and outgoing and could handle the staff. I'd want to do most of the marketing and behind-the-scenes business while he or she would work more of the day-to-day operations. Or night-to-night operations, I guess is a better way to put it. Would you be able to find someone like that?"

"When would you want them to start?"

"Immediately. That way David could help with the training."

"Like I said before, done."

"Really?" I had expected more of an *I'll-see-what-I-can-do* response. Hudson was powerful, but part of his effectiveness came from not making promises he couldn't keep.

"Yes, really. I already have someone in mind. I'll set something up."

There. I'd done it. I'd agreed to run the club and it was happening under my terms. "Perfect."

Hudson traced my cheek with his finger. "You know all you have to do is ask and it's yours."

A sudden wave of anxiety rolled through my belly. I turned to face the back of Jordan's head. "Actually, I don't know that, and honestly, that sort of makes me uncomfortable."

Hudson put his hand on my neck. "Why?"

There were lots of reasons. But I settled on the most obvious. "I don't want to be the floozy manager who only gets things because she's fucking the owner."

My eyes were still on Jordan. He was so good at his job—he didn't even flinch at my crass language.

Hudson, it seemed, preferred that the conversation remain between us. He leaned in to whisper in my ear. "First of all, I love that you're fucking the owner. Please don't stop. Second, that's not why you get things. You get things because you're qualified. If you'd shown up to the interviews after the symposium, you would have had people fighting for you. But third, and most importantly, you get things from me because you're my other half. Everything that is mine is yours. My connections, my money, my influence—it's all half yours."

I shivered. While I adored the sentiment—craved it, in fact—it also made my panic buttons go off. Those were the kinds of words that could make me think things I shouldn't think. That I was more important than I was. That we were closer than we were. They were trigger words for me, and though I'd been healthy with Hudson, it had only come from diligence on my part.

But how I wanted to wrap myself in his declaration…

I swallowed. "I don't know how to respond to that."

Hudson nuzzled his nose against my earlobe. "You aren't ready for that, I know. But I needed to tell you. As for your response, how about you say you'll run our club?"

"I'll run your club."

"Ah—"

I knew my mistake immediately. Funny, how strongly I wanted to correct myself. I turned to meet his eyes. "I'll run *our* club."

"Now kiss me because you've made me a very happy man."

He didn't have to ask me twice. He didn't even really have to ask me once, because his lips were covering mine as I opened my mouth to agree.

His tongue slid in immediately, and he kissed me thoroughly until the car came to a stop in front of The Bowery.

Reluctantly, I released myself from his embrace. "Thank you, Hudson." *For the chance to run the club, for helping me be successful at it, for loving me in the best way you know how, for finding me in the first place.*

He swept my hair away from my shoulder. "No. Thank you."

I SPENT THE rest of the day at the club. After I'd realized I wouldn't be in Japan, I'd arranged to meet with Aaron Trent to discuss an advertising plan. Our meeting was at one-thirty that afternoon and preparations took all morning. Throwing myself into work was energizing. I loved marketing and scheming. For the first time since I'd learned David was leaving, I felt really good about The Sky Launch's future and my part in it.

Because of all my prep, and because Aaron Trent had the best ad team in town, our session went well, and we finished up earlier than I'd expected. It was just after three when our meeting concluded. Suddenly exhausted, I curled up on the couch in David's office to chill out.

"Great meeting," David said, as he entered the office. "I'm bummed I won't get to see the fruit of all your work today."

"Don't worry. I'll keep you updated." I stretched my arms in front of me. With the things Hudson had me doing the night before, it was no wonder I felt tired and sore. The memory brought a smile to my lips.

"What's up with you today?"

I looked up to see David perched on the far arm of the couch, his eyes pinned on me. "What do you mean?"

His brow creased. "I don't know if I can explain it. You're different today. More on fire, if that's possible."

I thought for a moment. I'd always been passionate about my job, but that morning's decision had instilled me with renewed vigor. "Well, I did tell Hudson this morning that I'd take your place when you leave."

He beamed. "Finally! Now I can actually feel good about leaving."

"Whatever. You've been excited about Adora since Hudson gave you the job."

"Mostly because I'd thought Pierce was going to fire me. The promotion instead was a nice surprise."

My smile faded. I'd convinced myself that David was eager to leave The Sky Launch. It made it easier to accept that he'd been pushed out because of my jealous boyfriend. Though I'd rather continue the illusion, the truth was more important.

I shifted my body to face David. "So you only agreed to take Adora because you thought you'd be fired from here if you didn't?"

"Come on, Laynie. Let's be honest. Pierce wasn't going to let me stay here."

David's words may have been true, but I hadn't gotten a chance to fight as hard as I would have liked to for him to stay. If he didn't want to leave, if he really wanted to stay on at The Sky Launch, I'd go back to Hudson and duke it out. "But if he did—if that wasn't the issue—would you have still said yes? Or would you have stayed here?"

David took a deep breath. "I'm not really sure, to be honest. Adora is the pinnacle of nightclubs. I'd never have an opportunity like that on my own. And I think I'll do a good job there. There's a whole team of managers I'll be joining. I'll have flexibility and support that I've never had before. It's sort of my dream job."

I relaxed some.

He moved from the arm to the cushion. "But it's hard to leave the things you love. The move means leaving my home and my friends. This place." He met my eyes. "You."

"David…" I knew he had feelings for me, but now he was alluding to love. Dammit, that was closer than Hudson could get to saying I love you. I didn't want to hear it.

He ignored my warning. "Don't laugh, but I used to have this fantasy that we'd eventually run this place together."

I couldn't help but smile at that. "I used to have that same fantasy." I'd pictured that we'd get married and be this really cool duo who ran the hottest club in town. That dream vanished when I met Hudson.

"Really?"

"Yes, really." Immediately I regretted the confession. David's expression said it meant more than I wanted it to mean.

I swung my legs around so I was no longer facing him. "I mean, seriously. This place needs two managers. It was silly that you did it alone for so long."

"I wasn't really alone. The staff is full of great assistant managers."

I smirked. "That's not the same. Full-time commitment is what you need. I asked Hudson to find a partner for me today." I looked down at my lap. "I don't want to do it alone."

David scooted closer. He lifted my chin with his finger. "Say the word and I'll stay."

"I can't ask you to do that, David." My voice was practically a whisper.

"You could."

"No, I couldn't. And you know why."

He dropped his hand to his lap. "I do. But in answer to your earlier question—if it weren't for Pierce, I'd never leave. You can pretend to interpret that any way you need to, but you know what I'm really saying."

"I…I'm…um." I bit my lip. David had been such a great friend when I'd had very few. And for a while, he'd been more. I was heartbroken that he was leaving. But I in no way returned the feelings he seemed to be declaring.

"You don't have to respond. I get it. You're with him." He wouldn't even say Hudson's name.

"I am with him. Completely."

"And if you're ever not…" David had told me before that he'd be there if I decided things with Hudson weren't working out. It was a ridiculous thing to promise. Especially because I was over him, and, even without Hudson, I wouldn't fall back to David.

But I wouldn't be that blunt about it to his face. He was already leaving. I didn't need to hurt him further. So instead, we sat in awkward silence for several thick seconds while I debated what I could say that would be a gentle letdown.

Fortunately, I was saved by the ringing of my phone. I rushed to pick it up from the side table next to me, not even bothering to look at whom the call was from.

"Laynie!" Mira's voice bubbled through the earpiece. "Are you busy? Can you talk?"

I stood and distanced myself from David. "Of course I can talk. What's up?"

"I was wondering if I could ask a favor."

"On top of being a model at your event?" I was only teasing. I'd do practically anything for the girl. She'd welcomed me into her family even before Hudson had. I owed her.

"A different favor. Man, I'm kind of needy these days, aren't I?"

"How about I refrain from answering that until you tell me what the favor is?" Absentmindedly, I paced the room as we talked.

"Fair enough. Dad wants to have lunch with me tomorrow. And I don't really want to be alone with his sorry ass. And I'd love to see you. So would you consider joining us?"

"I'd love to!" Thinking about Jack put a smile on my face. There was no way Hudson would approve of me seeing him on my own, but what could he say if I was with Mira? I'd be honest about it, tell him upfront and it would be fine. "But why don't you want to be alone with him?"

"He's trying to make up for all the crap with Celia. He doesn't get that I'm not the one he needs to make up with. I don't really give a flying fig what he did or didn't do or should have done. I just want him and Mom to grow up and act like adults for half a second. I mean, wouldn't that be so nice?"

Sophia and Jack grow up? "Keep dreaming."

"I know, I know. Anyway, we're meeting at Perry Street at one. I'll call and add you to the reservation. Yay! You turned something dreadful into something I'm looking forward to!"

"I'm looking forward to it, too."

I hung up and stuffed my phone in my bra then glanced over and saw David working at his desk. Or, rather, pretending to work. He kept sneaking looks at me and I wondered if he wanted to say more than he had. I hoped not.

Instead of waiting to find out, I announced that I had a few errands to run. They weren't pressing, but after his declaration, the office felt stifling.

I stepped out into the summer heat and pulled my sunglasses on. Since I'd left spur of the moment, I didn't have a chance to call Jordan for a ride. The stops I wanted to make were nearby anyway. I could walk everywhere I planned to go. Besides, it was a beautiful day and it was nice to be out in the fresh air.

I didn't notice my follower until I'd nearly reached the first place I needed to go—a graphics shop a few blocks away from Columbus Circle. Perhaps I'd been too preoccupied with thoughts of David and the club. And Hudson—always Hudson. Otherwise, I'm sure I would have spotted her earlier. When I finally did notice her, I knew immediately it wasn't a coincidence that she was walking down Eighth Avenue at the same time I was. I also knew that she meant to be seen. I was an experienced stalker, after all. With a little effort, it's not that hard to remain unnoticed.

Celia wasn't trying to remain hidden at all.

She stopped when I stopped. Started again when I started. All the time her eyes were pinned directly on me. My heart beat furiously, but I remained cool, keeping an even pace to my steps. When I went into the graphics shop, she thankfully didn't follow. But she took her place outside the front window so that I could see she was there.

Celia hadn't exactly done anything to me, hadn't spoken to me, but her presence wrapped me in a blanket of fear. I knew without a doubt she was making a statement—*I'm here. I see you. You can't escape me.* Was this what Paul Kresh had felt when I'd followed him around for weeks at a time? It was an awful feeling and the regret for my past actions had never been so heavy.

There was a line at the counter, so I was able to take a few minutes to collect myself before my turn at the cashier. My thoughts raced to Celia's motive. Maybe she wanted to talk to me. But she could text or email. And if she'd wanted to talk, why hadn't she approached me?

No, she had a different intent with her stalking. First on the boat, now here—would she ever leave me alone? Was this another trick that she meant to somehow turn back on me later? Or did she simply mean to scare me?

If scare was the goal, she'd achieved it. But unlike the last time she'd screwed me over, I was prepared. Now she didn't have my trust. After I texted Jordan telling him where I was and asking him to meet me, I used my phone to click a picture of her—I wanted proof. She saw me take the picture, I was certain, but she didn't leave or seem concerned. Next, I called Hudson's office.

"He's in a meeting," Trish, his secretary, informed me. "I'll have him call you as soon as he's finished."

That wasn't good enough. I knew he'd want me to interrupt him for this, but Trish would never do it herself. Hoping he'd check his cell phone, I shot him a text. *I'm on my way to your office. I need to see you.*

I was calmer when it was my turn at the cashier. I collected the table cards I had ordered, took a deep breath, and headed out of the store. I was terrified to walk out with Celia so near the entrance, but I wouldn't let her see that. Thankfully, just as I put my hand on the door to push it open, Jordan pulled up. Celia took off at a brisk pace down the sidewalk. If all it took to send her away was Jordan, I'd never go anywhere without him again.

I slid in the car before Jordan had a chance to get out and open the door for me. "Up ahead, on the sidewalk," I said pointing toward Celia's back. "Do you see her?" She was walking fast and I wanted someone else to see her before she disappeared in the New York City crowds.

Jordan was quick with a good eye. "I see her. Was she following you?" He didn't seem to be surprised.

"Yes. How did you know?"

"I spotted her this morning when I dropped you off at the club, but I wasn't certain it was her. We need to tell Mr. Pierce."

"I plan to right now. Can you take me to his office?"

He answered with a nod.

I sat back and buckled my seatbelt as he pulled out into traffic. Celia was still in sight and I watched her as we drove closer. She stopped walking when we passed, and even though she couldn't see me through the tinted windows, she smiled and waved.

It was a good thing I was a pacifist, because otherwise I'd have started planning her murder.

— CHAPTER —

SIX

Hudson hadn't responded to my text by the time I'd arrived in the lobby, so I sent another. *I'm getting in the elevator. I'll be in your office in 2.*

I still hadn't received a reply when I stepped onto his floor, but I breezed by Trish as if Hudson were always available for me.

From the way he usually talked, he *was* always available for me.

"Excuse me," Trish called after me. "Mr. Pierce is still with his appointment—"

"He knows I'm coming," I called over my shoulder.

The door opened before I even touched the handle. Hudson stood there, concern etched on his brow. "It's okay, Patricia." He ushered me in.

As soon as the door shut behind me, he cupped his hands around my face and searched my eyes. "I got your text. What's wrong? Are you hurt?"

"No, not hurt." I was shaking, and now that I was with Hudson, I wanted to cry.

"Alayna, what is it?"

I pulled my phone out and began to cue Celia's picture. "I need to show you something. Can I—"

A rustle behind us caught my attention. I peered around Hudson and saw a woman standing by his desk. Her auburn hair was tied loosely at her nape, the color accentuated by the pale cream of her suit.

My back straightened, warning bells sounding in my head. "Oh, I'm sorry. I didn't realize you weren't alone."

Hudson put a hand at my back and gestured toward his guest. "Alayna, you remember Norma."

"Yeah, I do. Norma Anders. We met at the Botanic Gardens event." The same knot of jealousy I'd felt at meeting her formed now. Or rather, her presence tightened the knot that had been in my belly for the past half hour.

Norma had an obvious interest in Hudson. It bothered me. She worked with him daily, touched him casually, used his first name—he rarely let people use his first name, particularly not his employees. And here she was alone with him in his office midday. And he had ignored my texts.

"We did meet then." Norma looked me over, sizing me up. When we'd met before, she'd barely given me a second glance. She'd been too focused on my man. "It's good to see you again, Alayna." Her terse tone said otherwise.

She delivered her next line to Hudson. "If you two need to talk alone, we can step out."

We? My eyes traveled the room and I noticed another woman sitting in the other armchair facing Hudson's desk.

Ah, he wasn't alone with Norma. A wave of relief ran through me, followed by a wave of guilt. I was being ridiculous and paranoid. The events of the day had me off balance. Hudson was simply meeting with two of his employees. No midday trysts. Nothing inappropriate at all.

Still, the knot persisted. I was eager to talk to Hudson about Celia, but it would have to wait. I stuffed my phone back in my bra. "No, no. I apologize for bursting in. It's not like me to interrupt."

Hudson scooted past me toward his desk. "Actually, Alayna, this is perfect timing." He nodded to the woman still sitting and she stood. "This is Norma's sister, Gwen. She's one of the managers at Eighty-Eighth Floor."

"Oh." Not an employee after all. The Eighty-Eighth Floor was a popular nightclub in The Village owned by a rival businessman.

It took a second longer than it should have for me to click things into place. "Oh!"

I kicked myself into gear and approached Gwen, my hand extended toward her. "Alayna Withers," I offered as she shook my hand.

Her grasp was firm. A good first sign for a possible co-manager.

"Nice to meet you."

She had a good smile too. Nice teeth, not too flirty. Her features were very similar to Norma's, except lighter. Her skin tone was pale, her hair either dark blonde or light brown depending on the lighting. Her eyes were gray-blue. She was pretty like Scarlett Johansson—the type of pretty that some people might overlook and other people would over-acknowledge.

I wondered which kind of people Hudson was in this instance.

I quickly chided myself for the thought. What was wrong with me? It had been typical for me to be unnecessarily jealous with past boyfriends, but I'd never been that way with Hudson.

Hudson stepped nearer to introduce me more properly. "Alayna's currently the Promotions Manager at The Sky Launch, but, as I told you, she'll become the General Manager once the current manager leaves."

"Hudson told me you're looking for an Operations Manager." Gwen addressed me confidently and completely. It was refreshing considering her sister's knack for forgetting I existed.

I nodded. "Is that something you might be interested in?"

"Definitely."

A co-manager who worked at Eighty-Eighth. With all the insider information she'd have, plus the experience…I had to admit, Hudson had done good.

And he knew it. Though his face remained businesslike, his eyes twinkled with the pride of a job well done. "She has all the qualifications I believe that you're looking for, Alayna. Perhaps you want to set up an interview for yourself?"

"Yes. Definitely." I pulled my phone from my bra. When I unlocked it, Celia's picture was there, ready to show Hudson. I froze at the sight and another chill ran through me.

"Alayna?" Hudson prompted softly.

"Sorry. Rough day. I'm a bit flustered." I flipped through my schedule for the next day. I had lunch planned with Mira and Jack, but my evening was free. "Would you be able to come into The Sky Launch tomorrow? I think calling it an interview is a little too formal. I could show you around and we could talk then."

"Sounds perfect. I'm off tomorrow so I'm wide open."

It crossed my mind that I should ask why she wanted to leave Eighty-Eighth Floor, but it could wait until we met again. My earlier anxiety was overtaking me and all I cared about was finishing the conversation and getting Hudson to myself. And not for the reasons I usually wanted him alone.

"Great. Then you can come by at eight." I entered the info into my calendar. "You can see the club when it's open."

"I'll be there."

"See, Norma?" Hudson winked at his employee. "The kids didn't need us after all. They worked everything out on their own."

Hudson's playful jab at Norma fueled my angst. Why had she been invited to this meeting anyway? Just because Gwen was her sister, Norma didn't have to be included. And how had Hudson even known that Norma had a sister that managed a club? Were Norma and Hudson closer than he'd led me to believe?

At the height of my obsessive disorder, I suffered greatly from paranoia. Sure, it returned from time to time, but not to any significant extent since I'd met Hudson. Was I being paranoid now or were my questions valid? And if it was just paranoia, why was it returning now?

It was Celia and her fucking mind games getting to me. It had to be that. I couldn't backslide because of her. Otherwise she'd win and I wasn't having that. I had to get a grip.

I stepped out of the way while Hudson ushered the Anders sisters out of his office. Mentally I tried to calm myself, taking deep breaths and reminding myself to communicate rather than jump to conclusions. Perhaps I needed to pencil in another group therapy session for later in the week. Anything to end the rising panic.

When we were alone, I couldn't hold back any longer. "Why exactly was Norma here?" I added a smile and a light tone so that it didn't come off harsh, but how could it sound like anything other than an accusation?

Hudson locked the door before turning toward me. "She arranged to have Gwen meet with me. I'd never met her and Norma wanted to be here to acquaint us. Why do you ask?"

"Just curious." I leaned against his desk, needing the support. "How did you know that Gwen worked at Eighty-Eighth?"

He walked over to me in several easy strides. "Norma's mentioned it."

"Just in casual conversation. Between a boss and his employee?" I folded my arms in front of me. Not the best pose for remaining aloof.

Hudson put his hands on my elbows. "Alayna, you're acting unusually jealous. While it's always a turn-on, I have a feeling it's a symptom of something else today. What's going on?"

I shrugged, not wanting to jump into the Celia issue until I'd cleared up the Norma issue. "It just seems strange that you would know such personal details about one employee when you have hundreds—thousands—of people working for you."

"Hundreds of thousands."

I didn't even crack a smile. "Even stranger then."

Hudson released me and put his hands in his pockets. "What exactly are you asking me, Alayna?"

I already hated myself. The person standing here facing the man I loved was not the person I wanted to be. I didn't want to question or worry or be paranoid.

But my gut was twisting and churning and the words flew out of my mouth like vomit. "I'm asking why you know personal details about Norma Anders' family."

"You're asking what kind of relationship I've had with Norma. The answer is strictly working."

"Have you ever kissed her?" My voice shook and I had a feeling if I uncrossed my arms, my hands would be trembling as well. My mind was already filling with images of them together. It was crazy what I could conjure up—detailed scenes of passion. The only thing that could possibly stop the flood of imagination would be his assurance that it never happened. Even then, there was a chance the images would remain.

"I don't make it a habit to kiss people I have working relationships with."

He'd kissed me when I worked for him. "Yes or no, please?"

"No, Alayna. I've never kissed her. I've never fucked her. I've never anything with her." His tone was smooth but emphatic.

I returned his level expression even though I was an irrational mess inside.

My seeming composure egged him on. Or he sensed that I was a thread away from falling apart. He ran a hand through his hair. "Since she's in the Financial Division, Norma handled the transaction when I purchased The Sky Launch so she knew I had the club. The other day she asked if there were any management positions available there. I told her no, but that I'd keep Gwen in mind. I didn't want to tell you about her because I was afraid if you knew, you'd take that as a reason not to be the manager yourself. It's as simple as that."

"That makes sense." And the slightly manipulative way he kept it from me was totally typical Hudson. In my heart I knew he was telling the truth, but my head—it was in overdrive.

So which did I believe? My heart or my head?

He met my eyes and held my stare for several seconds. "There's nothing with her, Alayna. I'm with you. Always. Okay?"

My heart. I believed my heart. *Always.*

This was Hudson. He loved me, even if he stubbornly couldn't say the words. I trusted him. What had he ever done to tell me otherwise?

I shook my head, ashamed of myself. "I'm sorry. I'm being stupid."

Hudson tugged me into his arms. Finally, I felt calm. I breathed him in—the scent of his soap and aftershave filled me with a soothing balm. There was nowhere that I'd rather be than right there in his embrace.

He ran his hands up and down my back and kissed along my temple. "I know you wouldn't be like this if something hadn't happened. And you came in here upset. What's going on, precious?"

I clung to him, my hands digging into his jacket. Now that he was holding me, I didn't want to let him go. This was where I was safe.

"Alayna, talk to me."

I turned my head so my words wouldn't be muffled in his clothing. "It's Celia."

Hudson pushed me away to meet my face. His eyes were wide with concern. "What did she do?"

"She's following me."

His brows furrowed. "What do you mean, *following you*?"

"Like, showing up where I am and going wherever I go. Following me." I showed him the picture on my phone and explained how I'd spotted her tailing me while I ran errands and added that Jordan had seen her that morning. Plus, she'd been on the boat the night before.

I feared he'd say I was overreacting, that he wouldn't believe me like the time before. I had a picture, but what did that show? Would he think I was the one who'd followed her?

But his response this time made up for his previous doubts. "Fucking bitch!" He spun away from me and ran his hand through his hair. "I swear to god if she does anything to you…"

Tears sprung to my eyes, half from terror, half from relief that he was on my side. "What does she want from us? From me?"

Hudson circled around to the other side of his desk. "It doesn't matter. She can't do this. I'll call my lawyer. We'll get a restraining order." Before I could interject, he'd pushed his intercom. "Patricia, get Gordon Hayes on the phone."

"Yes, Mr. Pierce."

I shook my head and sunk into one of the armchairs. "It's not that simple."

"I don't care if it's simple or not. I'm getting a restraining order."

I'd never seen him so worked up. His calm aloofness had vanished and in its place was a wild passionate man.

It was me who was the voice of reason. "Hudson, you can't get a restraining order for simply being followed. She had a measurable distance, didn't approach me, didn't threaten me or pull any crap at any of the places I stopped. We have nothing on her."

His eyes were pinned on the phone, as if he could make it ring by staring at it. "That's ridiculous. She has you scared. I can see it on your face."

"Yes, she has me scared. But there's nothing you can do about it." Again, I was reminded that I had done this same thing to other people. Paul Kresh had filed a restraining order against me. It had been the first one I'd received. He hadn't been the first person I'd stalked. "Trust me. I'm well-versed in the art of terrorizing someone while evading police involvement."

"Don't talk like that." Hudson's tone echoed the pain I felt.

"It's the truth. I used to do this to people, Hudson! It's horrible. How could I be this horrible to other people?" The tears that had been just at bay broke through.

Hudson rushed to me and pulled me from my seat into his arms. "Hush now, Alayna." He stroked my hair as I sobbed on his shoulder. "This isn't the same. You were searching for love. Celia's actions are quite different."

I pushed him away. Though I wanted and needed his touch, I didn't feel like I deserved it. "Are they? Isn't she doing this because she wants your love? How is that different?"

He sighed and perched on the edge of his desk. "I don't believe that's why she's doing this. She means to keep me unhappy. She knows that hurting you would destroy me. This is payback for my past. This has nothing to do with yours."

I swiped the tears off my cheeks. Dammit, Celia had screwed with both of us so easily. Here we were, regretting our pasts, hating ourselves, undoing years of progress—*fucking bitch* was right.

I sat down again and laid my head against the chair back. "I really don't care why she's doing it. She'll keep on doing it, though, because she's winning. You're down on yourself and I'm a mess. I'm paranoid and anxious and I'm afraid I'm reverting back to my old self." My voice cracked as a new set of tears threatened to fall.

Hudson moved to kneel in front of me. He put his hands on my upper arms as if he meant to shake sense into me. "You aren't. You have valid reasons to feel this way today. She's thrown you off balance, but you'll get ahold of yourself. You're stronger than her."

I wiped at my eye with my knuckle. "I'm strong with you."

"And I'm not leaving you. I'm here. We're in this together. Do you hear me?"

I nodded weakly.

The phone beeped. Hudson stood and reached across the desk to push the intercom. "Did you reach him?"

"No." Trisha's voice filled the room. "I'm sorry but Mr. Hayes has gone home for the evening. It's after five."

Hudson glanced at his watch. "Shit," he muttered. He paused and I suspected he was toying with calling his lawyer's cell. "I want him on the phone first thing tomorrow."

"Yes, sir. Anything else before I leave?"

"No. Thank you, Patricia." He turned the intercom off and turned back to face me. He studied me for long seconds. "She won't win, Alayna. You kept it together in front of her, didn't you?"

"Yes." There was no way in hell I'd have let her see that she got to me.

He beamed with pride. "Of course you did. You're incredible like that. Stronger than you give yourself credit for."

I didn't feel incredible. But his assurance bolstered me.

Hudson leaned against the desk, his expression glazed. I recognized it as his calculating look—the one he got when he was considering a big business deal. "Celia has no idea if she hit her target or not. That puts us at an advantage."

I hated to interrupt whatever he was planning, but I couldn't stop the thought that bubbled to the front of my mind. "What if she doesn't stop at stalking?"

His eyes came back into focus. "Jordan is ex-military. Special ops. He can protect you. You can never go anywhere without him in the future. Promise me."

"I rarely go anywhere without him now. Today was a fluke."

"Just promise me." His tone was insistent.

"I promise." I'd known Jordan was more than a driver but hadn't known the specifics of his background. Knowing it now wasn't what prompted me to agree—I'd have agreed to anyone being charged to me, just to ensure I'd never be alone with Celia again.

"Good. I'll hire another bodyguard for when Jordan's not available. I know you didn't want one—"

I cut him off. "I'll take it."

He nodded a thank you. "I'll bring someone in to check the security cameras at the club and make sure they're sufficient. The penthouse is already monitored. And I'll talk to my lawyer—"

I interjected again. "He can't do anything."

"I'm talking to him anyway. I want to know our rights. If I have to throw money at the situation, I will."

I chuckled. I'd never heard Hudson talk so candidly about what his wealth could buy. It was a foreign concept to me—that solutions to problems could simply be bought. It's why I'd always feared someone else would be more suited for Hudson than me. Someone like the blonde we were currently discussing. "Celia has money, too."

Hudson shook his head dismissively. "Money is only good in the right hands. I have no doubt that my power extends beyond her and the Werner family."

I nodded as I brought the knuckle of my index finger to my mouth and sunk my teeth into the skin. It was either that or let out the scream that had been building the last few minutes. Though Hudson was performing with the take-charge attitude I needed, he couldn't make the promises I wished he could make.

He read my anguish. "Alayna, I'll take care of this."

"I know..."

He leaned forward and pulled my hand from my mouth, lacing my fingers through his instead. "But...?"

"She's never going to be out of our lives, is she?" Even if she were on her best behavior, she'd still be there. Her life was so intertwined with Hudson and his family. I couldn't imagine any scenario that would remove her from being a constant presence.

Hudson rubbed his thumb gently across my skin. "She will. I'll figure something out. Do you trust me?"

"Yes." *With my whole heart.*

"Then believe me—I'll take care of her." He squeezed my hand once more before he let it go. "In the meantime, stay with Jordan. No more outside runs for a while."

Running was one of my favorite ways to calm myself. It was a necessity for my mental health. The treadmill worked, but it wasn't the same as being outside with the sun beating down and the breeze blowing across my sweaty body. "I'll just have Jordan run with me. I'm sure he won't mind. I know he's in good shape, and if he's Special Ops, he must do some running."

"No. Not good enough. He can't be on his best game when he's exerting himself physically."

"I don't know," I mumbled. "You're on your best game when you're exerting yourself physically."

"What was that?"

"Nothing. I just don't want to live in a prison." I hated giving up one of my only sources of solace because of Celia.

"Alayna, please." His eyes were soft but determined. "Just until I get a better plan together."

What was I thinking? Hudson was my true solace. I could give up everything else if I had him. "Okay. Fine. I'll keep my runs to the treadmill. For now."

"Come here." Hudson pulled me out of my seat and into his arms. "I only want you safe. I couldn't bear it if anything happened to you."

I nuzzled into his neck, breathing in his scent and warm words, hoping they'd envelope me in calm.

But as soon as I'd start to relax, a new haunting thought would make its way to the forefront of my mind. I let myself ask the worst. "Do you really think Celia would do something besides scare me?" I'd suggested she might earlier, but I didn't know if I really believed it. I'd never done more than stalk. Well, nothing harmful, anyway.

Hudson's grip tightened around me and he buried his face in my hair. "I don't know what she'd do. I'm not willing to find out."

The edge in his voice coupled with his uncertainty caused another spike in my blood pressure. "Hudson, I'm scared."

He pushed me away enough to cup my face in his hands and meld his gaze with mine. "I'm not, Alayna. Not in the least." It was a one-eighty from his last declaration, and I suspected his words now were only for my benefit, that he was more worried than he was letting on. He couldn't fool me.

But it felt good to hear him try.

"Trust me." He placed a kiss on the tip of my nose. "I'll take care of it." He kissed the side of my mouth. "I'll take care of you."

He licked along the seam of my lips. When I parted my mouth, he eased inside, mesmerizing me with sensual strokes along my teeth and tongue. He kissed me slow and deep and with careful attention. With his lips he did the thing his words had failed to do—he made me feel better. Or he distracted me, at least. Either way, he gave me what I needed.

In fact, I needed more.

I pushed into him, lifting my breasts to meet his chest.

Hudson smiled against my mouth. Then he wrapped up the kiss with a final peck on my lips and pulled away.

My fingers curled into his jacket, drawing him back to me. "Don't stop. I need you." I pressed my body against his, my desire growing with an intense urgency.

"Alayna..." His eyes traveled to the phone on the desk behind him. He wanted to be making calls, setting things in motion. It's what he needed to do to feel better. To feel safe. I got that.

But what I needed to feel safe was much simpler. More tangible. More within reach. "I need you, Hudson." I moved my hand to stroke against the ridge in his pants. "Please. Please make it better."

"Dammit, Alayna," he growled. "You're making it hard for me to do what I should be doing."

I continued rubbing his crotch. "I'm trying to make it harder." God, I'd never had to beg, but if he wanted me to, I would. "Hudson...please!"

"Fuck." In one swift motion, he turned me so that the desk was pressed against my behind. He leaned down, and with the length of his arm, pushed aside the files that lay on top. Then he lifted me so that I sat on the edge of the mahogany surface. "Take off your panties," he commanded, as he undid his buckle.

He didn't have to ask me twice. Hudson had his cock out by the time I'd slid my panties off and kicked them to the floor. I watched as he stroked himself, his shaft thickening with each pump.

I ran my hands along his chest and squirmed, spreading my legs further apart. I ached to have him moving inside me—ached with an intensity that I couldn't recall having ever felt before. I was desperate. Frantic. "Hudson." I couldn't stop pleading. "I need—"

He cut me off. "I know what you need. Trust me to give it to you." With one hand still wrapped around his cock, he placed his other hand between my folds and swirled his thumb across my bud.

I moaned and tilted my hips to increase the pressure.

Hudson leaned his forehead against mine. "You're so eager, precious. It's going to hurt if you don't let me get you ready first." He slid his finger along my lips and back to dance across my clit.

"I don't care if it hurts." It hurt *not* having him inside me. I tugged at his tie. "Come on!"

He swore under his breath. Then he let himself go. Tangling his hand in my hair, he pulled me roughly toward his lips. "It's hard enough to control myself around you as it is. If you give me permission, then you better believe you're going to get fucked."

I wanted to reply, *Thank god*, but his mouth had claimed mine with frenzied passion and speaking was no longer an option. At the same time, he drove his cock into me with a deep, forceful jab. I cried out at the pleasure/pain. I'd been wet, but he'd been right—I hadn't been quite as ready as I could have been.

And it didn't matter. I loved him inside me, and my snug channel let each of his short stabs rub against every wall. I cried into his mouth at each stroke. God, oh god, oh god.

Still it wasn't enough. I wrapped my legs around his waist and bucked against him, meeting his thrusts. I closed my eyes. I was aroused and insane with needing the release I knew would come if I could just get there.

He let go of the lip he'd been sucking on. "Jesus, Alayna. Slow down."

"No. Can't. Want you." I couldn't even speak in complete sentences.

"I know. I know what to give you." He nipped at my jaw. "But if you don't let me take care of you, you aren't going to get where you want to go."

"Need," I corrected. And I couldn't slow down. I was crazed.

Hudson huffed my name in frustration. Wrapping a handful of hair around his fingers, he pulled my head back until I gasped. His strokes slowed to a steady pulse. "Listen to me. Are you listening?"

I nodded.

"Look at me."

I opened my lids and met his gaze. Immediately, his gray eyes soothed me.

"You need to let me take charge, Alayna. You need to trust me. I'm going to take care of you." He wasn't talking about achieving an orgasm. He was speaking about much more. "Okay?"

I did trust him. Implicitly. I'd told him over and over.

But even with my declarations, I was still recovering from his recent abandonment and the pain of it lingered. Saying I trusted him was easier than actually letting myself go to fully act on that trust.

He was calling me out on that now.

And I wouldn't let him down. "Okay," I said.

"Good. Now let's do this." With one hand still pulling my hair, he moved his other to my clit where he rubbed with expert circles. "Hold on to the desk."

I moved my hands to grip the edge of the desk. He picked up the tempo of his thrusts, his tip knocking against the same spot on the inside that his thumb massaged on the outside. The sensation in that one concentrated area built quickly. Soon, I felt the tightening in my lower belly, and my limbs began to tingle.

And Hudson was feeling it too. "God, Alayna. Your pussy feels so good. So tight. You make me so hard. I'm going to come so hard." He quickened the pace again, and the sound of our bodies slapping and his sex words pushed me higher and higher and higher.

When I was about to orgasm, he urged my hips up and drove into me with staccato jabs that sent us over together with a shared moan. He rubbed into me for several long seconds, spilling everything he had, my own fluids mixing with his.

"Better?" he asked before I'd even caught my breath.

"Yes. Much." But even as I was still soaring on the tails of my climax, I recognized that I'd just done the thing I'd always accused him of—used sex to solve a problem. "I, um, I'm sorry about—"

"Shh." He put a finger to my lips and smiled. "It's nice to be on the opposite side for once."

"Well, thank you." I kissed his finger then laced my hands around his neck.

"Anytime you need it, I'm happy to fuck away your woes."

I laughed. After cleaning up and putting my panties back on, I left him to begin the tasks he felt were necessary for our protection.

Celia was nowhere in sight as I climbed into the back of the Maybach, but I shuddered, still feeling her eyes on me from the last time I'd been in the car. Hudson believed he could rid her from our lives. And I had total faith in him.

But I loved the man more than I'd loved anyone. It was totally plausible that my faith was biased.

— CHAPTER —
SEVEN

Instead of going back to the club, I decided to call it a day. Besides, Hudson and I had planned that morning to be home to eat dinner together, and even though the new developments of the afternoon were keeping him at work late, I didn't want to waste the cook's efforts.

At the penthouse, I put our dinner trays in the warmer and sat at the dining room table nibbling on my salad while I tried to concentrate on a new book. I'd picked *Lady Chatterley's Lover* by D.H. Lawrence, hoping it would help me focus on the romantic and sexual aspects of my life rather than the dread Celia had instilled.

But reading required more attention than I was able to devote to the task. Giving up, I tossed the book on the table. A blank business card poked out between the pages at the bottom. I hadn't seen it before—throwing the book must have jostled the card from where it was lodged inside. I flipped the book open to the page the card marked and then turned the card over to see if the other side was also blank.

It wasn't. And the name on the back almost made me drop the card.

With a hand on my chest, I talked myself down from my panic attack. Hudson had ordered the books from Celia and her design company—it was only natural that she'd stick her business card between the pages.

Except the books were new. And the page that the card had marked had a quote highlighted in yellow: *"She was always waiting, it seemed to be her forte."*

Had Celia marked that quote? And had she meant it for me or for Hudson? And whoever the intended target was, what did she mean by it?

"Good book?"

I jumped at Hudson's voice behind me. I'd been too absorbed in the book and Celia's mark on it to hear him come in.

He leaned down to kiss my neck. "Sorry, I didn't mean to sneak up on you."

"It's not that. Look." I showed him the card and held the book up for him. "I found this business card in this book—it's one of the ones you got me. And this quote is highlighted."

I felt Hudson's body heating with rage. He crumpled the card in his hand and threw it across the room. "Goddammit!"

"What does it mean?"

"Who knows?" He took a deep breath and reined in his fury. "You know what? Don't even think about it. That's what she wants. She wants it to mess with you." He grabbed the book from me and took it with him to the kitchen. "Have you eaten?"

"I waited for you. It's in the warmer." I sat quietly until he returned with our dinner plates. "You took her key away, right?"

Hudson set our plates down. "She didn't just leave that in your book now. This has to be from before. When she had the boxes delivered." He disappeared again into the kitchen.

That hadn't been an answer to my question and his avoidance made me nervous. I waited until he came back, this time with a bottle of wine.

"Hudson—her key?"

"Yes. I took away her key." He poured me a glass and then one for himself. He had his half finished before I'd even taken one sip. "The day after she made the delivery."

He hadn't told me about seeing her then. But I'd seen Celia many times without telling him so I supposed it was fair.

Instead of dwelling on why he'd never mentioned it, I thought about what else he'd said—that she must have put the note in the books before they'd been delivered. There were hundreds of books. How had I happened to find the one with the note? Unless there were more. "So there could be secret notes and messages in all of the books."

Hudson took another swallow of his wine—a swallow that finished off the glass. "I'll replace them all."

"You don't need to do that." Truthfully, I was already planning to search them. Curiosity was pretty much my middle name, after all.

Hudson refilled his drink. "I'll do it anyway."

He had made up his mind and when he made up his mind, there was no arguing with him.

I glanced at the clock on my phone. It was after eight. "You got home late. Does that mean you came up with ideas on how to deal with her?"

Hudson didn't look at me as he took a bite of his fish. "I have something in the works," he said when he'd swallowed. "But I'd rather not talk about it, if you don't mind."

"Um, yes, I do mind. This affects me and I want to know what's going on." If he thought he was doing this on his own, he had another think coming.

"You know what you need to know. I've hired security, the new cameras are being installed at the club tomorrow, and I have some preliminary ideas to try to make Celia lose interest in her game." His entire demeanor was dismissive.

And my demeanor was getting pissed off. "Ideas that you aren't going to share?"

"No. I'm not."

I set my fork down, a little more forcefully than I'd intended. Or maybe exactly as forcefully as I'd intended. "Hudson—transparency, honesty—remember? Are you hiding something from me? Is it illegal?"

"No. And no. And you said you trusted me." He raised a brow. "Remember?"

"I do trust you. But we're supposed to be in this together and this is not together. This is you keeping me in the dark while you go play superhero. Or I assume you're playing superhero, because I don't really know."

He sighed and closed his eyes. When he opened them again, he looked at me directly. "We are in this together, Alayna. And I'll tell you. Just not now." He covered my hand with his own. "I'd rather spend my evening with you. Alone."

It hadn't occurred to me that he needed a rest from the subject. It was how he dealt with things—internally and on his own. We both needed to learn to work things out as a couple. But he'd said he'd tell me later. Maybe tonight I could let it go too.

I turned my palm up to lace my fingers through his. "Okay. No more talk of Celia."

We exchanged smiles. Then Hudson let go of my hand to continue his meal.

We sat in silence for several long minutes. Hudson finished most of his plate while I poked at my food, my appetite long gone. I could agree not to talk about Celia, but that didn't mean I could stop thinking about her. She'd penetrated so deeply into our relationship—did she realize that she consumed our thoughts? That our time together was now so intertwined with her that we were practically a threesome?

Hudson swirled his wine in his glass and watched me. "Now you're quiet."

I chuckled. "I don't know what else to talk about."

He ran his hand across his face and I knew he was thinking the same thoughts I'd been thinking—about how we couldn't even have a simple meal without Celia there. He opened his mouth to say something, and for a moment, I thought he was going to go ahead and let her win.

But then his face changed and he became resolved. "Well, let's see. I know how today went. What's on your agenda for tomorrow? You're interviewing Gwenyth, right?"

"Her name's Gwenyth? Hmm." That was the first time I'd heard her full name. And it bothered me. Hudson was not one to use nicknames.

"What's that supposed to mean?"

"Nothing." I was probably making a mountain out of a molehill. But I couldn't help myself from pursuing it. "I've heard you call her Gwen."

He shrugged. "That's what she goes by."

"You never call people by their nicknames." My irritation was showing.

And so was his. "Are you suggesting it means something that I use hers?"

"No." Why did this bother me so much? "I don't know." It was Celia. The mood had been set and now, even as we tried to move past it, we struggled.

It was my turn to sigh. "I'm just tense. I'm sorry."

"I know. I am too." Hudson took another swallow of his wine. "I don't know why I call her Gwen. I knew her as that first. I suppose it's in my brain now."

"You don't need to explain." But I was glad he had.

I took a sip from my own glass, trying to focus on something that wasn't going to piss either of us off. He'd asked about my agenda for the next day…

fuck. I remembered something we needed to talk about. But it was definitely not going to be a pleasant conversation. Might as well get it over with.

"About tomorrow..." I began tentatively. "I do have plans I should tell you about."

"You better not be planning a run in Central Park. Your new bodyguard will tackle you down." His tone was light, but his eyes said he was serious.

"I said I wouldn't run outside. *Trust me* works both ways, you know. Do I get to meet this bodyguard? Is he also very attractive but unavailable because he's gay?"

Hudson smirked. "That's not even a little funny."

I knocked his knee playfully under the table. "It totally is and you know it."

"I'll introduce you on his shift tomorrow. He's not gay. And I trust you so I'm not worried about whether or not he's attractive."

"Good boy."

"Now what do you need to tell me?" He took a bite of his risotto and pinned his attention on me.

I paused, hating to destroy the lighter mood. "I'm, um, having lunch with Mira tomorrow. And Jack."

Hudson froze, his fork mid-air. "What did you say?"

The look on his face said he'd heard me fine. But I played along, trying to sound more confident the second time around. "I'm having lunch with your sister and father."

"Like hell you are." His eyes blazed with fury.

His reaction wasn't a surprise, but I fought not to get immediately defensive. "I'm guessing it's the Jack part that has you upset and not the Mira part."

His jaw twitched. "I'm not upset about any of it because you are not having lunch with my father."

With as much lightheartedness as I could muster, I said, "I'm not sure you can tell me what I am and am not doing."

"Oh, yes, I can."

I groaned, running my hands through my hair. "Hudson, this is ridiculous. I've told you before, I'm not Celia. I'm not going to sleep with your father—even if he comes on to me. Which he won't because your baby sister will be there."

He wiped his mouth with his napkin and tossed it on his plate. "Why do you even need to spend time with him?"

"I don't *need* to. I didn't plan to. Mira didn't want to be alone with him, and so I offered to be a buffer."

"She doesn't need a buffer. Cancel your date and have coffee with her later. Just Mira."

I considered for about half a second. Then I abandoned that and started to get angry. "I don't want to cancel. I want to have lunch with Mira. And Jack. I like him. Not because I'm into him, but because he's your father. And I don't have a father anymore and bonding with Jack makes me feel good." My voice cracked, but I kept on. "Maybe he's not a great replacement, but he's the closest thing I have. Plus, knowing him helps me feel closer to you. And when you keep things from me, H, I need all the access to you I can get."

"Alayna..."

Immediately I felt bad. "That last part was uncalled for. I'm sorry."

Hudson pushed his chair away from the table. Then he reached over and pulled me into his lap.

This was better. The tension that had hung thickly in the air began to dissipate.

He ran his hand up and down my arm. "I'm not keeping things from you, Alayna. Really, I'm not. I just want a night without...her."

"I know," I said, burrowing deeper into his chest.

"And please, don't use my father to get close to me. He's not the road to my heart."

"Where is the road to your heart?"

With one finger, he lifted my chin to meet his eyes. "Don't you know? You're the one who paved it."

I bit back tears, not wanting to spoil the moment with crying. "Don't think I'm going to cancel my lunch because you're being sweet."

He laughed. "Don't worry. I don't think that at all. Have lunch with him if that's what you want. At least I know you'll be safe from Celia with him around. They aren't friendly anymore. And I wouldn't deny you something that makes you feel good."

Desperate to hold on to his lighter mood, I chose to respond playfully. "It's not your right to deny me anyway."

He pretended to sigh. "I hate that."

A rush of emotion swept through me. God, this man…he stopped his whole world to look out for me, to take care of me, and now he'd accepted my decision to meet with his father—a decision that had to be tearing him apart inside. Maybe he wasn't perfect, but he was pretty darn near.

I wrapped my arms around his neck and held on to him tight. "I love you."

"And that's why I'm letting you win this conversation."

I pulled back to meet his eyes, my brow raised. "*Letting* me?"

"Please, indulge me a little."

"How about this—" I shifted so I was straddling him. "How about we cease conversation altogether and indulge in an activity where we can both win?"

"Can we both win twice?"

"Honey, we can win three times if you're up for it."

The growing bulge beneath me told me what he thought about that before he even spoke. "Now that sounds like a plan."

MIRA TAPPED HER pursed lips with a French-manicured finger. "I just don't understand why he wouldn't tell you what he's planning. It makes no sense."

When I joined Mira for lunch the next day, I hadn't meant to tell her about Celia's stalking, but the words poured out the moment I'd seen her. If Jack had been there, I knew I wouldn't have shared as much, but his tardiness had me spilling everything, including Hudson's deflection when I'd asked him his ideas for dealing with the bitch. He'd had a valid reason for not giving me more information, but it continued to nag at me.

Perhaps I was being unfair. "Maybe he really didn't want to talk about it anymore. He just seemed more elusive than that." I opened a packet of pink stuff and stirred it into my iced tea.

Mira frowned. "You're afraid he's keeping something from you on purpose?"

"No." Though, I wasn't quite sure. "I don't know."

She shook her head, her hair bobbing against her shoulders with the movement. "I don't know either. I'm sorry."

Her apology took me by surprise. "Why are you sorry? You have no reason to be sorry."

"He's my brother." When she realized that didn't exactly explain anything, she went on. "I feel like I should understand him better, and I don't."

"No one does." Would anyone, ever? Sometimes I thought maybe I would, but really, could I?

"Are you ladies ready to order?" The waiter's question drew my eyes back to the menu I'd tossed aside. I still hadn't decided on a meal, having been too preoccupied with chatting.

The waiter saw my hesitancy. "Or would you prefer to wait for your other guest?"

Mira glanced at me. She already knew what she wanted to order. "We'll wait."

"Very good." The waiter left us to attend to his other tables.

I picked up my menu and scanned the lunch items. But my mind was still on the conversation at hand. I lowered the menu and leaned toward Mira. "Here's the thing—I'm afraid the real reason he won't tell me what he has planned is that he doesn't have anything planned."

"Wouldn't he just admit that?"

"No." There was no way Hudson would let me believe he didn't have complete control over the situation. "He wants me to feel safe."

Mira beamed. "Of course he does." There was never any doubt that the girl had faith in her brother. "Laynie, he'll come up with something. I know it. And whatever it is, he'll do a good job. He'll be committed and he'll go to great lengths. This is probably a horrible comparison, but look how devoted he was to keeping Celia's secret. All to protect her."

"He wasn't protecting Celia." Jack sat down in the chair between me and Mira. "Sorry, I'm late. Traffic. I didn't realize you were joining us, Laynie. What a nice surprise!"

Mira spoke before I could give my own greeting. "Are you suggesting Hudson was protecting you? Because that makes me sick." She roughly handed him her menu.

"Oh, I know what I want," he said, setting the menu to the side without acknowledging Mira's hostility. "He was protecting your mother. He didn't want her to get hurt from my infidelity."

Mira looked to me. "Still a valid comparison—Hudson will do far more for you than he'd do for Mom." Again, before I had a chance to speak, she turned back to her father. "And you say that as if it were unreasonable that she would be hurt."

"It's unreasonable that he cares." Jack circled his shoulders, probably trying to release the building tension.

Mira's jaw tightened—the same way her brother's tightened when he was upset. "Thank god he didn't inherit heartlessness from you."

"No, he inherited that from Sophia."

Her eyes widened. Leaning forward, she whispered harshly, "Would you just stop?"

My eyes danced from one to the other as they volleyed their attacks. So much for me being a buffer at the meal. Hudson was right—Mira definitely didn't need one.

Jack set his palms on the table and turned to face his daughter. "Mirabelle, I'm not heartless. You think it's cruel that I cheated on your mother. It was. It is. I'm not perfect."

Mira's eyes filled and I suddenly recognized her anger as pain.

"But you have to understand, sweetie, that Sophia is also culpable. She's not an easy woman to love."

Mira dabbed at a stray tear that had spilled over. "And do you love her, Daddy?"

Jack reached over to take Mira's hand in his. "Yes. I do. Of course, I do."

"Do you tell her?"

"Every day."

Mira smiled. But it was brief. She pulled her hand away from his. "Actions speak louder than words, you know."

I'd been silent, letting the father and daughter say the things they needed to say, while I sat feeling like a voyeur. But I couldn't let her last comment go by without reacting. "Sometimes."

Jack and Mira looked at me as if they'd just remembered I was there.

Or maybe they wanted clarification. I wasn't about to turn the meal into a Hudson-hasn't-said-he-loves-me conversation, so I simply said, "Sometimes it would be nice to have both."

The waiter's return saved me from saying more. Since everyone else knew what they wanted, I went last, settling on a Chef Salad.

"And can I get a Manhattan?" Jack asked before the waiter left.

"For lunch, Dad? Seriously?"

"Hey, I'm not the one with the drinking problem."

I braced myself for Mira's reaction. Generally, no one spoke about Sophia's alcoholism. I wasn't even sure if Mira acknowledged it or if she was in denial.

Her dark eyes didn't even flinch. "But you certainly facilitate it." Apparently, she wasn't in denial. "Can't you just have tea? Or water?"

"Oh for the love of Pete. Your mother isn't even here." Jack's eye twitched—another of Hudson's traits when he was upset. "Is it too tempting for you, my dear? Because it doesn't look like you've touched your water. I'm sure you'd rather have something stronger."

Mira folded her arms over her belly and huffed. "I don't care what you drink. I'm not thirsty. I'm saving room for my meal."

There was finally a break in their bickering, and I searched for a new topic to discuss, but before I could think of one, Jack did.

"Now what is this about Celia and Hudson?"

I cringed at the sound of their names together. Like they were a couple.

Mira's eyes lit up. "Can I tell him?"

"Oh my god, no." Though he'd never said so, I had a feeling Hudson preferred to keep his father out of his private life.

Mira had no such barriers. "I'm telling him." Without waiting for my consent, she told a condensed version of the story I'd told her—Celia following me, the notes in the books, Hudson trying to formulate a plan.

When she finished, I realized I was flushed. All the attention focused on me was embarrassing. "It's really not a big deal. I was overreacting to bring it up."

"No, you're not!"

Jack met my eyes, his expression tight. "Mira's right. Celia isn't a threat to take lightly."

"See that guy over there?" I pointed to a man sitting alone a few tables away. "He's my new bodyguard. Believe me, we aren't taking this lightly." Remembering this new addition to my life renewed my anxiety about the situation.

"Good. Hudson's taking her seriously. That makes me feel better."

Jack's concern wasn't helping me. "Why?"

He seemed surprised by the question. "I care about you, Laynie."

I stiffened, afraid of where his declaration was going.

If he noticed, it didn't stop him. "You're family now. You're an important part of Hudson's life and he—and I—would be devastated if anything happened to you."

"Thank you, Jack. I really appreciate that." Of course his affection was innocent. I kicked myself for momentarily thinking otherwise. And his words were an unexpected balm. "I care about you too." I darted my eyes to Mira. "All of you." Maybe not Sophia, but that didn't need to be said aloud.

I swallowed back the lump of emotion in my throat. "What I meant though, is why does Celia worry you? Why does she care so much about hurting me? She acts like a jealous lover. Were she and Hudson together?"

"No way," Mira said at the same time Jack said, "They were never together."

"But Hudson's so secretive. He might not have told either of you. You can't know for sure."

"I know for sure. There's no way he was with her." It wasn't the first time Mira had stated her opinion on the matter.

Jack agreed. "He's been disgusted with her ever since she seduced me."

Mira scowled. "*Seduced you*? As if you weren't part of it."

"Yes, I was part of it." Jack grinned devilishly. "But there are very few men who would turn down a naked woman in their bedroom, no matter what their marital status."

"Oh, I don't know. It's not unheard of." Paul Kresh came to mind. I'd been naked in his office once. All it earned me was an arrest.

The waiter delivered Jack's drink. Mira rolled her eyes but didn't comment on his beverage choice again.

When the waiter left, she asked, "If Hudson's so disgusted with Celia, why are they even friends?"

Her question was one I'd asked myself many times over the past few weeks. It never occurred to me that Jack might be the one with the answer.

He took a swallow of his drink and sat back in his chair. "Hudson blames himself for who she is now. He feels a sort of responsibility for her."

Mira's forehead twisted in confusion. "I don't get it. Why would he be responsible for who she is?"

Apparently Mira didn't know about the true history of Celia and Hudson—how he'd manipulated her into falling for him and then slept with her best friend. It was that betrayal that had driven her to sleep with Jack in the first place. As some sort of revenge.

Jack met my eyes, confirming he knew more than his daughter. "It's a long complicated story. If you want to know more, you're going to have to ask Hudson. Or Celia."

"Yeah, that's not happening." Using her spoon, Mira fished out an ice cube from her still full water glass and stuck it in her mouth. Surprisingly, she didn't pursue the *long complicated story* further.

While hearing from Jack had been insightful, my one haunting question remained unanswered. "Okay, they're friends and he's supported her and he's never been into her and she knows that—so why is she after us?"

Jack sighed. "Beats me. It's probably another one of her games. She's fond of them, you know. And she's good at them. I put nothing past her. She's a calculating, conniving woman, and she hates to lose."

"Great." I rubbed my hand across my forehead, trying to ease the headache that was quickly approaching. "How the hell are you supposed to get out of her grasp?"

"Let her think she's won."

Our meals arrived then, and the conversation turned lighter to talk of Mira's baby and her decision to not find out whether she was having a boy or a girl and what colors she was planning for the nursery. Despite the earlier tension between her and Jack, they settled into an easy groove, and I found myself more relaxed than I'd been in days. Lunch with the two was just what I'd needed.

When we were finished, Mira talked us into crème brûlée and coffee. We lingered over our dessert, enjoying each other's company. Finally, she shoved away her plate. "God, I'm stuffed. And I have to go to the bathroom. Again."

I'd gone with her the first time, but now I chose to stay behind, eager to get a few private words in with Jack. This would probably be my only opportunity, after all.

When Mira was out of earshot, I dove in. "Jack, I have a personal question for you, if you don't mind."

"About six and a half inches. But it's not size that matters; it's what you do with it." Hudson's dirty sense of humor obviously came from his father.

I rolled my eyes. "I'm serious."

He looked as if he might be preparing a comeback, but perhaps the glare on my face changed his mind. "Okay. Shoot."

"Sophia once told me that Hudson was a sociopath. Do you believe that too?" It was blunt perhaps, but I knew Mira would be back soon, and I didn't know how honest Jack would be with her around.

"Sophia's still claiming that bullshit?" Jack shook his head, his expression a combination of disgust and exhaustion. "*One* psychiatrist suggested it *one* time a handful of years ago. Hudson's never been clinically diagnosed as such, and no, I don't believe it. That boy cares. A lot. He just isn't always able to express it. Blame that on Sophia too."

I let out the breath I didn't know I'd been holding. No matter what Jack's answer, I already knew what Hudson was and wasn't. But hearing the details of Sophia's claim—and knowing his father didn't agree—was a relief.

But his words brought up another question, one that had plagued me from the moment I'd met Hudson's mother. "Why do you blame Sophia for his lack of expression? I don't think you mean just her drinking. What did she do to him?"

"Well, if I'm going to explain that then you're going to realize that I'm to blame too."

"I can handle that."

"But can I?" Jack considered a moment. Then he sighed. "Sophia wasn't always hard like she is now. When I married her she was refined and serious, but she could be fun. But then I started building Pierce Industries. I didn't have the money that Sophia came from. Her parents were convinced that she married beneath her. I wanted to prove them wrong, prove that I could be the man she should have married."

"And you did." Though Hudson had taken Pierce Industries to the top, it had been Jack that had built a solid foundation.

"I did. And Sophia wanted that too. But she hadn't expected how lonely it could be, being married to a man who was married to his work. She decided I was cheating long before I ever did."

His eyes glossed with sadness, or perhaps regret. "Not being around—that was my mistake. Her loneliness drove her to drinking. Alcohol made her more closed off. So it became a cycle—I wasn't around because of work and when I was around, I didn't want to be because my wife was a coldhearted bitch. I'd throw myself more into work, just to avoid her."

I hid my smile. If I'd had to live with Sophia, I'd have done the same thing.

Reading my mind, Jack winked, but his somber tone remained. "Eventually, she realized the one person I would come home for was Hudson. He was my son. My firstborn. I made time for him whenever I could." Jack's eyes beamed with a love that only existed between a father and his child.

It made my heart soar—I really did love this man who loved my man as much as I did.

Jack swirled his finger around the rim of his coffee cup. "Sophia used my son to get to me. She dangled him in front of me to get my attention and pulled him from me just as quickly. Hudson was always a smart kid. He learned pretty early on that his mother used him as bait. Poor guy got caught in the middle of so many games. It's no wonder he became good at them himself."

My chest ached, picturing Hudson as a little boy, only wanting to be loved by his parents, instead being used as a pawn. "Was it the same with Mira?"

"No. Hudson had already become Sophia's rival by the time Mira came along. Sometimes I think he fought his mother just to keep his sister out of her focus." This idea seemed to make Jack proud. "Now does that sound like the actions of a sociopath?"

"No. It doesn't. But I already knew he wasn't. He has too much love in him." Or was I just fooling myself? If he really loved me, why couldn't he say it?

I felt a presence come up behind me, and I turned, expecting to see Mira.

"What the fuck are you doing here with her?"

It wasn't Jack's daughter.

It was his wife.

— CHAPTER —

EIGHT

Sophia's fingers clutched the back of my chair. "Celia wasn't enough? Now you have to steal this one from Hudson too?" Her voice was too loud, and people nearby were already starting to murmur.

Jack's face said he was as surprised by his wife's presence as I was. "Sophia. What are you doing here?"

"Spying on you, osbiviously." She meant obviously, but her words were slurred and hard to understand. I'd never seen her that way. Never seen her that intoxicated.

"You're drunk."

"That's illeverant. Irreverant." Sophia slumped into Mira's empty seat. "That doesn't matter."

"How did you even know to come looking for me here?"

Sophia smirked. "Mira. She told me she was having lunch with you. I decided to come to the lie. To see the lies. To hear your lies about me this time. Now the whole thing is a lie. You got your daughter covering for your cheating ass as well?"

"Mom?" This time the person behind me was who I was expecting.

Sophia reached for her daughter's hand with both of hers. "Mira! Look who I found your father with now. Hudson's new girl."

Mira glanced around at the onlookers as she patted her mother's hand. "Mom, Dad's not with Alayna. He's with me. I told you I'd be here. I was the one who invited Alayna." She spoke to Sophia like she was a child.

Memories of helping my own drunken father swam to the surface of my mind. Public situations were the worst. At home, Dad could scream and cry and make a fool of himself. We'd let him pass out in his mess and clean him up later. When there were others around, we had to be responsible and hope he wouldn't be completely humiliating.

Mira's expression said she was hoping pretty damn hard for the same.

"*You* invited this whore?"

Too late—Sophia had already crossed to embarrassing. Though her attacks on me were fairly routine.

"I did invite her. I didn't invite you. Why are you here?" Mira waited only a second before going on. "Never mind. Mom, you're drunk. We need to get you home. Did you take a cab to get here?"

"No."

"How did you get here?" Mira signaled to the waiter to bring our bill. It was admirable how take-charge she was. I guessed it was a role she was used to.

"Frank?" Sophia paused as if not sure that was the right answer. "Yes, Frank's outside somewhere."

"I'll call him." Jack was already pulling out his phone.

Mira bent down to her mother. "I'm going to walk you to the curb, okay?"

Jack stood. "No, Mira. Let me. Frank?" he spoke into his cell. "Sophia and I are ready to go home. Fine. We'll be out there." He pocketed his phone then moved to help Sophia stand.

"Did you drive yourself, Daddy?" Mira's words were mundane, but her eyes were filled with gratitude.

"Yeah, my car's with the valet."

Sophia fell against Jack. She was passing out.

Mira gently slapped her mother's face. "Mom, you're almost there. Hang on 'til you get to the car." When Sophia roused, Mira said to Jack, "I took a cab. I'll drive your car home for you."

He reached in his pocket and pulled out a valet ticket. "Thank you, babydoll."

Mira took the ticket and nodded. Then she collapsed in her chair.

I watched as Jack led Sophia out of the restaurant. There was love in the kind way he held her up, the way he supported her journey.

When I turned back to Mira, I found she was crying.

"Don't mind me." She waved at her face as if she could fan away her tears. "I cry at everything these days."

"I think this was a valid thing to cry over." I shifted in my chair. It wasn't that I was uncomfortable with Mira's emotion, but I wished I knew how to soothe her. The best I could come up with was putting a hand on her knee.

"Why? I should be used to this by now, shouldn't I?"

I didn't say anything. I knew she didn't really want an answer—she wanted someone to listen. As for myself, I'd never gotten used to it. But Mira was older than I was when my father died. I probably would have expected to be used to it by then too.

Mira looked out toward the restaurant entrance. Even though her parents were long gone, I knew she was picturing them there. "I just keep thinking, this is going to be the grandma to my baby. Do I want my child to be exposed to this?"

God, I'd never thought about that. If Hudson and I had a kid…

I shook the thought off. "I can't imagine what that must be like. I do know how hard it is to have an alcoholic parent—how embarrassing it is. Has she ever been to rehab?"

"No." She laughed, like it was an inside joke of some kind. "She won't even talk about it."

"Have you forced her to talk about it? Like an intervention? I'm not saying they're fun, or easy, but they can work. I've seen them work firsthand, actually."

"With your father?"

"No. No one ever staged an intervention for him. I regret it often. I wonder if things would be different if…" How many times had I wondered if my mother could have changed something? If his boss and his friends and Brian and I and our mother had sat him down and demanded change. Could that have saved his life? Saved my mother's life?

I'd never know the answer. "Anyway. That's the past. But I was talking about me." I cleared my throat, surprised that I was sharing something so personal with someone I admired. "I had an intervention pulled on me."

"What? When? For drinking?" My confession seemed to shock Mira out of crying.

"For obsessing over relationships, actually. I didn't have many people in my life that cared for me at the time, but I'd gotten arrested, and—"

"Wait a minute—for *obsessing*?"

I watched my hands wringing in my lap. "For stalking." I peeked up to see Mira open-mouthed. "I know. Embarrassing." I swallowed my humiliation and focused on the goal of sharing my story. "Anyway, my brother and a couple of friends I had back then that have since all abandoned me because I was a total shit to each and every one of them, well, they sat me down and convinced me to seek help. Honestly, I only went because if I didn't agree, it would have been jail time. But having them gathered like that—hearing that people cared what I did and what happened to me—it meant a lot."

Mira put a hand to her mouth. "Alayna, I didn't know." Her eyes glistened still from her tears, but I could see something else as well—not disgust, like I would have expected, but compassion. "You've hinted at a rocky past, but…I didn't know."

"Of course you didn't. Why would you?"

"I guess I wouldn't."

"My point in telling you is that I've learned through all my therapy that most addictions are really just a cry for love. And the crazy thing is that the more you're addicted to something, the harder it is to look up and see all the love there is around you. For the one outside, it can be tough to break through. But sometimes you *can* break through. As long as you're willing to try."

I watched the wheels turn in Mira's head as she processed all I'd said. But she didn't say anything else. And then the waiter was there, telling us that Jack had paid for our bill on the way out, and our lunch was over.

"Monday for your fitting?" Mira asked as we parted.

"Yep. I'm looking forward to it."

I pulled out my phone, ready to text for my ride when I saw Jordan waiting for me across the lobby. With my bodyguard in tow, I walked to meet my driver. "Jordan, is there something wrong?"

"Not exactly, Ms. Withers. But I wanted to warn you that Ms. Werner is outside. She's been here throughout your lunch."

"Fuck." So much for thinking bodyguards and Pierce family members would protect me from Celia. "What is she doing?"

"Nothing. Sitting on a bench down the street is all. She even waved at me."

"Yeah, she's a very friendly stalker, isn't she?" I chewed on my lip, thinking. "Did you tell Hudson?"

"I texted him, yes."

"Would you take me to him?"

"Of course."

Maybe Hudson would share his plans for my stalker now. I just hoped he actually had something in the works.

MY NEW BODYGUARD, Reynold—who was only mildly attractive—insisted on coming with me into the Pierce Industries building. Having only had him around one morning, I hadn't yet gotten used to always having a shadow. Fortunately, Reynold was good at his job. He tailed me inconspicuously and made it easy for me to forget he was even there.

Reynold stayed in the lobby while I took the elevator up to Hudson's floor. As soon as I saw his secretary, I realized I hadn't called or texted ahead of time. I had a feeling my unannounced visits irritated her, but Hudson had never claimed to mind so I smiled and pretended my presence was no big deal. "Hi, Trish. Could I possibly stick my head in to chat with Hudson for just a minute?"

Trish returned my smile. "I'm sorry, Ms. Withers, but Mr. Pierce isn't back from his lunch date." She seemed a little too happy to really be apologetic.

I glanced at the clock on the wall. It was after two. Still at lunch? "Oh. Okay. Thanks."

Disappointed, I pushed the elevator call button to go back down. While I waited for it to arrive, I pulled out my phone and texted Hudson that I'd stopped by.

I had just pushed send when the elevator doors opened. Standing there was Hudson. With Norma Anders.

Immediately I tensed. They were the only two people in the elevator—was that who Hudson had been on a lunch date with so late in the afternoon?

"Alayna. I didn't expect to see you here." Hudson didn't seem put off by my presence, at least.

"I almost missed you."

"I'm glad you didn't. Come with me into my office." He began to usher me toward his door. Then he stopped. "Norma—"

She cut him off. "I'll email you."

Hudson nodded. "Good. Thank you."

Norma took off down the hallway, I guessed to her own office. I hadn't realized she shared a floor with Hudson. I'd never thought about it, really, but now that I did, it bothered me how close they worked together.

Once the door was shut behind us, Hudson put his hands on my upper arms. "Why are you here? Did something happen?"

The original reason I'd come to see him seemed like nothing compared to how I now felt at the sight of him and Norma together. My blood was boiling and my stomach was knit tight. "I don't know—*did* something happen?" Jealous accusations had always been one of my fortes.

Hudson leaned back, confusion on his face. "What do you mean?"

I wrapped my arms around his neck, hoping I'd sound less bitchy if I was in his arms. Also, I was sniffing for women's perfume. "Let me rephrase—was Norma your lunch date?" The only scent I came up with was the usual Hudson smell that tended to set my pheromones on overdrive.

"More like lunch meeting, but yes."

I'd hoped the evidence had been misleading. "Did you dine with her alone?"

Hudson withdrew from my embrace and pinned me with a stern stare. "Alayna, keep this up and I'm going to have to put you over my knee. Except I know how much you like that." He bopped my nose with his finger and headed toward his desk.

His patronizing attitude made me all the more infuriated. "I don't like that you had lunch with her. Alone."

He shuffled some papers, his attention obviously elsewhere. "Well, I don't like who you had lunch with either, so we're even." Before I could react, he looked up at me. "And no, that's not why I had lunch with her. It was business. We're working on a deal and we needed to hammer out details."

Of course it was business. Did I have any reason in the world to think otherwise?

I didn't.

I still didn't like it.

I walked over to the other side of his desk. Memories of our last encounter here helped take the edge off my emotions, leaving me sounding less accusatory but whinier. "Did you have to do it in a social setting?"

Whinier seemed to work in my favor. Hudson's eyes softened, though his tone was still straightforward and aloof. "I chose a lunch meeting with you in mind, Alayna. Would you rather that we'd stayed in my office with the doors closed and no one around?"

With the lingering images of the things I'd done with Hudson in his office behind closed doors, the question made me a bit ill. I slumped into an armchair. "You are not helping the situation."

Hudson sat across from me. "You know that Norma is one of my key employees. My business frequently requires me to interact with her. In person. Sometimes, we're alone."

The explanation of his working relationship with Norma made sense. And sounded familiar. I decided to suggest a one-size-fits all solution. "Maybe you could transfer her."

"With what reason?"

"The same reason you transferred David." It was the exact same deal, after all. In reverse.

Hudson pinched the bridge of his nose. "While I understand your comparison of the situations, I'm not transferring Norma."

I stood with a shriek of frustration. "This is really unfair you know." I paced as I spoke. "I can't work with someone you don't trust but you can work with someone I don't trust? And since you're the big business owner in this situation, you were able to just take care of things with David, transfer him, and if he refused, fire him. What can I do? Nothing. I'm helpless." I paused my walking and shook a finger at him. "Norma has a big fat crush on you, Hudson. I can see in her eyes that she's not afraid to make a move."

Hudson jiggled his mouse and focused on his computer screen. "She is quite aware that I don't return her feelings."

"How does she...?" The only way she'd know that was if he'd told her and the only reason he'd tell her..."Has she already made a move?"

"Alayna, this conversation is going nowhere. I have appointments—"

"Hudson!"

With a deep sigh, he leaned back in his chair and met my eyes. "She's told me that she wishes there were more between us. If that counts as making a move, then yes, she's made a move. But, as I've said, I'm not interested. And she knows it."

I gritted my teeth to insure my next words didn't come out in a scream. "Can you explain how this is different than me working with David?"

He blinked. Twice. "I can't. You're right. It's not different."

"But that's all I get? You won't change it?" It wasn't going to be much of a victory if he answered the way I suspected he would.

"I can't lose Norma. She's too valuable to my company."

And that was what I'd expected he'd say.

I leaned on the back of the armchair. There was nothing to say. Nothing I could say. He agreed with my point but was unwilling to do anything about it. Now we were at an impasse. Our eyes locked on each other as we each silently refused to back down.

After several long seconds, Hudson swore under his breath and looked away. When he turned back, he asked, "Do you want David to stay?"

My heart flipped in my chest. "Would you let him if I said yes?"

His eye twitched. "If that's the only way to make this right, then I would."

A thrill of happiness ran through me.

Until I remembered all the reasons why David staying wasn't a good idea.

"Dammit, Hudson." I couldn't believe I was actually going to say what I was going to say next. "No. I don't want David to stay anymore." I refused to meet Hudson's eyes. "It wouldn't be good for him. He's...he's in love with me."

"I know."

I already knew Hudson knew. It was me that was just now admitting it.

I turned away from the desk and plopped myself down on his couch. Hudson came and sat down next to me. I rubbed my hand across his cheek. "Thank you for offering, though. I know that wasn't easy for you."

"No. It wasn't." He ran his fingers up and down my arm, leaving goose bumps in their wake. "But it would be worth it to make you happy."

Man, he'd grown up in the last few weeks. I had to give him that.

But maybe I hadn't, because I still wasn't quite ready to let the subject of Norma Anders go to rest. "Have you considered that maybe it's not good for Norma to work with you either?"

Hudson chuckled. "No, I haven't. And I'm sure it's not."

I shifted to face him. "Could we make some sort of concession here?" I took his hand in mine, playing with it as I talked. "Like, could you not have meetings alone with her? Is there anyone else on your team that could join you in the future?"

With his free hand, he brushed a piece of hair out of my face. "On the project we're currently working on—no. But it's almost done, and I don't expect that this level of secrecy would be necessary in the future."

And on top of their private meetings, they were sharing a secret. Fucking great. "What project are you working on?"

"Nothing you'd be interested in." Before I had a chance to scowl, he corrected himself. "I'm trying to purchase a company from someone who would never sell if they knew I was the purchaser. Norma's the only person I can trust not to leak the information."

"Fine." I hated that there was no way around their working relationship. *Hated it.* But what could I do? "Fine," I said again, more for me than him. "Social settings only, please. Where there are people around. And when this deal's over, you won't need private meetings with her anymore?"

"No. I won't."

"I'm going to still ask about her. Like, all the time. Because I can't just let it go."

He nodded. "I understand."

Though I was pleased that we'd worked through our argument constructively, the resolution was still a bitter pill to swallow. "Do you know how much this hurts to let you keep her employed?" I squeezed his hand hard, digging my fingernails into the back of his hand to accentuate my pain level.

Hudson narrowed his eyes, tolerating my assault. "Believe me, I do."

"Okay then. As long as we're clear." I released his hand.

"Was there another reason you stopped by?" He rubbed the back of his hand. "Or was Norma the intended subject all along?"

I laughed as I recalled the ridiculousness of my day. "No. I came by because I just wanted to see you. Lunch was...interesting...and then Celia was there again."

His brow shot up. "Celia was there?"

"Jordan said he texted you."

Hudson reached in his pants pocket and pulled out his phone. He flipped through a few screens. "Damn. I left my phone on silent. I didn't know. She didn't try anything?"

"Nope. Just let me know she was there."

"Alayna. I'm so sorry." He pulled me so I was half on his lap and wrapped his arms around me from behind.

I sighed, settling into the warmth of him.

Hudson kissed the top of my head. "Maybe you should take some time off. I could send you out of town. Would you like another week at my spa?"

I stretched my head to see if he was serious. He was. "I can't leave now. Not with everything at the club. And she'll know she scared me off. I can't let her have that victory."

"That's a very brave response. I just hate that you're in this position." He tightened his arms around my breasts.

It was then that I remembered my other reason for stopping by. "Do you have a plan to deal with her?"

He was silent for a beat. "I talked to my lawyer today," he said finally. "As you said, there's nothing we can do legally. But we're looking into some other options."

"Illegal options?"

"How about you let me handle this? I'll fill you in when everything's sorted out."

I didn't have the energy at the moment to push him. Besides, it seemed he really didn't have anything worked out at all, and forcing him to admit that would be unkind.

So I let it go. "You require an awful lot of trust these days."

He placed a light kiss at my temple. "Too much?" His voice was strained and his body tight—it was his turn to need my reassurance.

So I said, "No. I trust you." Though sometimes my trust was more of a work-in-progress. I turned to kiss his cheek. "I know you'll take care of me."

"Always." His lips met mine just as his intercom buzzed. He sighed against my mouth. "I'm sure that's Patricia letting me know my next appointment is here."

I stood and then offered my hand to help him up. "Guess my blowjob plans are shot to hell then."

His eyes darkened. "Maybe I could make them wait."

Laughing, I swatted at his shoulder. "Shut up. I didn't have blowjob plans. For all that I'm conceding to, I think I'm the one who deserves the sexual favors."

"Tonight."

"I'm holding you to it, H." I reached up to give him a final peck on the lips. "Meanwhile, you should know that I hate you a little."

"You do not. You love me."

I shrugged. "Same thing."

Hudson walked me out so he could welcome his next client in as I was leaving. I'd almost made it to the elevators when Trish called after me.

I walked back to her desk, wondering if she meant to scold me for keeping Hudson occupied.

"This was delivered for you while you were with Mr. Pierce." Trish handed me a simple white envelope with my name written in block letters on the outside.

It didn't occur to me that I should have given the envelope to my bodyguard until after I'd opened it and found the same business card that had been stuck in my books at home. *Celia Werner, Interior Design.*

The knot in my belly tightened. She'd been on foot when I'd left her at the restaurant. How could she possibly have followed me so quickly? Did she simply guess that I'd come here? Why hadn't Reynold seen her coming up in the lobby?

"Who gave you this?" I asked Trish, aware that my voice was more demanding than would be deemed polite.

"I don't know. A courier. I didn't pay attention."

"Was she blonde, blue-eyes—"

Trish cut me off. "It was a he."

That explained why Reynold hadn't seen Celia—she'd had someone else deliver it. As for knowing I was at Hudson's office, well, wasn't that predictable of me too?

I closed my eyes and took a deep breath. All she'd left was a silly business card. It didn't hurt me. It was meant to scare me, that's all. Meant to warn me that she was watching. That she knew how to get to me.

Resolving to *not* let her get to me, I opened my eyes. I quickly scrawled a note to Hudson on the white envelope and put the card back inside. "Thank you, Trish. When Hudson is free, can you give this to him?"

I really wanted to burst through his doors and show him personally. Then convince him that both of us should leave it all behind and go to his spa.

But that would be running away. And running away never solves anything. Or so, that's what everyone always says.

— CHAPTER —
NINE

After I left Hudson's office, I decided to try to forget my tension by wrapping myself in work. I was successful for most of the afternoon, but the anxiousness and stress of the day lingered just under the surface. I had to be at the club to meet Gwen by eight and imagined it would be a late night. I longed for a run, but decided instead on a group therapy session. Thursdays weren't the day I usually went, but there was a session at six led by my favorite counselor. I could grab a bite to eat, hit the group, and be back in time to work that evening.

I shifted in my rusty folding chair in the Unity Church basement as I focused on listening to the others share. Most of the Thursday night regulars were strangers to me, and it seemed most of their addictions were hard to relate to mine. One person was a shopping addict. Another was addicted to social media. There was a gamer there too, a guy who was just as consumed with buying the latest system and game as he was with playing them. The only person that I felt even slightly connected to was the tattooed sex addict that I'd seen on other nights as well. I'd heard her speak before and recognized a lot of her same fears and frustrations as my own.

"Would you like to share anything, Laynie?"

I was more than a little surprised when the group leader called my name. Members weren't required to speak at each meeting—or ever, if they didn't feel comfortable—so it was odd for Lauren to call on me specifically. She knew me, though, having counseled me since the early days of my recovery. And if she couldn't tell from my demeanor that I had something on my mind, the fact that I'd shown up twice in one week had to be an indicator.

I gave the customary history of my illness and then paused. Since I hadn't planned on speaking, I wasn't quite sure what I wanted to say. After a breath, I said, "I've had some extra stressors in my life recently, and I'm here because I feel like it's causing me to backslide."

Lauren nodded, her long braids clicking with the movement. "Very concise identification of emotion, Laynie. Let's first talk about what kind of stressors you're dealing with. Is there anything you can eliminate?"

"Not really." I guess half of my stressors would be removed if I broke up with Hudson, but that wasn't an option I was willing to consider.

"And that's perfectly fine. Sometimes you can't eliminate stressors." Lauren turned her words to the whole group, using it as a teaching moment. "Most times you have to deal with them. Or we choose to deal with them because the reward is greater than the impact of the stress."

Boy, had she nailed it. "Yes. That's it."

"So what are these stressors?"

"Um." Now that I thought about it, I realized I'd had a lot in the last few weeks. "I recently moved in with my boyfriend." I didn't add that the relationship was still fairly new. At least not out loud. Internally, I marked it as another factor in my anxiety level.

"You have a new living situation." It was customary for the leader to acknowledge the information shared. "That's an adjustment."

"Yes. And I just took a huge promotion at my job."

The room buzzed as people shared congratulations. "Kudos to you," Lauren said. "But yes, another stressor."

"And my boyfriend..." How to bring up my current situation when I wasn't quite sure why I was in it in the first place was tricky. "He has baggage that I'm having some trouble dealing with."

Here Lauren took notice. "What kind of baggage?"

"Well, his ex—" Celia wasn't really his ex, but it was easier to call her that. "She's decided for whatever reason that it's her mission to destroy our relationship. She's been terrorizing us. Me, really. First, she accused me of harassing her—which I didn't do." I looked around at the other group members. "Honestly."

"Hey, no one's judging you here," Lauren reminded.

Which wasn't exactly true, because I was certainly judging myself. Admitting the next part was especially hard. I was about to complain about the thing people usually complained about me for. "And now she's harassing me. Following me places. Leaving me notes and things."

"Oh my god," the shopping addict exclaimed. "Have you been to the police?"

A few other people mumbled the same concern.

I shook my head, halting the talk. "She hasn't done anything worthy of reporting." I could go on about what was and wasn't worthy of reporting, but it wasn't relevant.

"That kind of harassment would be stressful to anyone." Lauren leaned toward me, her forearms braced on her thighs. "But I'm going to take a guess that it's been harder on you. Does it bring back emotions from your past?"

"Of course it does. I used to do these same things to other people. It's awful. It makes me feel awful." I'd been afraid I might cry, but surprisingly, the tears were absent. Perhaps, I was growing stronger or had become more reconciled with the situation.

With my emotions in control, I was able to delve further into analysis. "Also…I kind of feel like I deserve it now. Like it's my karma for the shit I pulled."

The red-haired sex addict piped up, "You know that's not how life works, right?"

"I guess." But hell, I didn't really know anything.

Lauren let us sit silently for a moment. She believed in a lot of quiet moments of reflection. They were often the worst and the best parts of the session.

I chewed on my lip as I processed. "Honestly, I know there are things that I need to work through in the area of self-worth. I'm journaling. I'm doing some meditation—yes, I need to do more. But really, those aren't the emotions that I'm concerned with."

"Okay," Lauren conceded, "as long as you recognize that you have some work to do there, we can move on. So you have these stressors—some of them good—that can't be eliminated. And you say they're causing you to backslide. How so?"

I ticked the list off on my fingers. "I'm agitated. I'm anxious. I'm paranoid. I'm accusatory."

"That sounds like me on my period." Again from the sex addict.

"Yeah, I call that being a woman." This came from the compulsive shopper.

I couldn't decide if they were attempting to relate or invalidating my feelings. Paranoid that I was, I assumed the latter. "You're saying these are normal emotions, and I need to just chill the fuck out."

"Maybe," sex addict said.

"Not necessarily." Lauren tapped her index fingers together. "They are normal emotions. But if they are impacting your daily life and relationships, then you need to deal with them."

"They aren't…yet. But only because I'm fighting them." At least I was trying. "The paranoia is the worst and it's unfounded. I'm suspicious of a woman my boyfriend works with. And I have no reason to be. Fortunately, he likes it when I'm jealous." I delivered the last part for the sex addict who winked in appreciation.

"Do you think you'd like to try medication?" Lauren preferred to stay away from drugs, but she always offered it as a solution.

I'd hated the numb zombie I'd become on the anti-anxiety pills I'd taken in the past. "No. No meds. I'd rather handle this on my own."

"Well, you know the drill."

"Yes. I do. Substitute behaviors." Though two of my go-to substitutes were running and reading—both had been compromised by Celia.

Lauren pointed a stern finger at me. "And communication. Make sure you talk through all the feelings you're having, no matter how unreasonable."

I tried not to roll my eyes. "That's why I'm here."

She smiled in a way that made me think she understood I'd felt patronized. "Being here is a great step, Laynie. Don't get me wrong. But it's not just us you need to talk to. Make sure you're communicating with your boyfriend too."

Communicating with Hudson…

God, I was trying. We were both trying. But if I really went there, really told him all the paranoia that lived inside, about the knot of dread that permanently occupied my belly—would he still be interested?

As she often did, Lauren addressed my unspoken concerns. "I know, it's scary. You're afraid other people can't deal with your thoughts and your feelings. And I can't promise that they can. But this is who you are. It's not going away. If you can't share who you are with the people who love you, then maybe they don't really love you."

That was the biggest question of all, wasn't it? Did Hudson truly love me? He'd shown me that he did, but he'd still never really said it. And I'd never really asked. Maybe there were still things left to be said—by both of us.

GWEN SHOWED UP to The Sky Launch fifteen minutes early, which would have been impressive if I wasn't running in just she arrived. And because of everything else on my mind, I felt off my game. Fortunately David was there with me to help fill in the gaps as we walked through the club and talked about what role Gwen might fill.

It turned out Gwen Anders knew her stuff. At every turn she had appropriate questions and innovative ideas. She was no-nonsense, enthusiastic, and forward-thinking. Though most everything she said was right on, I inexplicably bristled a few times at her suggestions. Maybe because she was tough. Maybe because she challenged me. Maybe because I was on edge in general.

After the tour, Gwen helped us open for the night. Then we moved back to David's office to wrap things up. More accurately, *my* office, since David was leaving. Maybe *our* office if I decided Gwen would be the one to help me with The Sky Launch.

"So," Gwen began, "right now the club is open from nine p.m. to four a.m., Tuesday through Saturday?" Gwen and I were settled on the couch. David had pulled the desk chair around to make an easy conversational area.

"Right," David confirmed.

"But we're moving to expand the hours and be open seven days a week." That had been one of my goals since I'd gotten my promotion to assistant manager.

Gwen frowned. "That doesn't seem the best idea right now. Eventually perhaps. But right now you aren't filled to capacity when you are open."

I tried to hide my scowl. It was refreshing that she was so direct, but attacking one of my ideas so blatantly didn't sit well.

Apparently not noticing my reaction, Gwen went on. "Why would you extend your hours? First step is to bring more people in, fill the club, then expand."

David looked hesitantly to me. "There's actually some good reasoning in that, Laynie."

There *was* good reasoning. Still, did I want to work with someone who was always so forthright?

I wasn't sure.

"Expansion was your idea, wasn't it?" Gwen finally caught on. She shrugged. "I stand by my opinion."

She was good. Real good. "Gwen, I have a feeling we're either going to be very close friends or bitter enemies."

"Do you want this job, Gwen? Because I'd suggest the close friends angle and then you're a shoe-in." It was sort of cute how David tried to smooth the tension over. He'd never been one to like conflict. He was more of a people-pleaser.

"Oh, I don't know." Gwen crossed her long legs. "Alayna's a smart woman. She strikes me as the type to know the value in keeping your enemies close."

I narrowed my eyes. The last time I'd heard that phrase it had been from Celia. Keeping her close hadn't benefitted me at all. Of course, I hadn't been aware she was my enemy at the time, and I wasn't sure that Gwen was my enemy either. I just didn't know enough about the woman yet.

"Tell me something, Gwen." I put my elbow on the arm of the couch and propped my chin in my hand. "Why do you want to leave Eighty-Eighth Floor?" The question had crossed my mind before, but I hadn't gotten around to asking until just then. "You seem to be an integral part of that club's success, and, not that I wouldn't love to steal you away from them, but why would you let me?"

"Sometimes a woman just needs a change of scenery." She ran a hand over her leg, smoothing out her pantsuit with deliberate focus.

"I don't buy it." If she could be hard-nosed, so could I.

"Touché." She sighed then met my eyes. "Personal reasons. Forgive me for not being more forthcoming, but it really doesn't have any bearing on why I should or shouldn't be hired. My boss at Eighty-Eighth knows I want to leave. He'll give me a good reference. Other than that, I'd rather not share."

People and their damn secrets. I wondered if Hudson knew Gwen's reasons. I wondered if he'd tell me if I asked.

Then, paranoia snuck in, and I wondered if it wasn't the reasons she wanted to leave Eighty-Eighth Floor that were important, but the reasons she wanted to work at The Sky Launch. "It's not because of Hudson, is it? That you want to work here."

"I'm not sure what you're asking. If you mean, do I want to work here because this club is the only one in town owned by the powerful business exec Hudson Pierce who also runs the hottest restaurant in town—Fierce—and the hottest club in Atlantic City—Adora—then the answer is yes. I want to work here because Hudson Pierce has the power needed to make this place live up to its potential. The Sky Launch is one of the few places that could rival what Eighty-Eighth is."

Of course that's why she'd want to work here. What other reasons would there be?

I scolded myself for thinking the personal reason had to do with Hudson. *Trust.* I had to remember trust.

Blowing a piece of hair out of my eye, I made my decision. "Then you're hired. Not because you're my friend or my enemy but because you're exactly who I need. I reserve the right to pass judgment on you personally in the future."

Gwen smiled slightly. "Fair enough."

David stood and held out his hand. Gwen stood up to shake it. "Welcome aboard," he said. "Sorry I won't be here to watch you kick ass. Or kick Laynie's ass. Either way, I think you're going to knock her off her feet."

"Hey, now. I can kick ass, too." I stood and put my hands on my hips, feigning indignation.

The look on Gwen's face said she doubted my statement.

"What's that expression for? You can't doubt me. You don't even know me."

"No, I don't." She narrowed her eyes. "But you have to be lacking something—or you *think* you're lacking something. Otherwise, you wouldn't have come looking for me."

Maybe we'd be enemies then. "I just don't want to do it all alone." My voice came out meek and I regretted defending myself. I didn't owe her anything.

To make matters worse, Gwen pointed out my unnecessary words. "No need for explanations. All I need to know is when I start."

"You'll accept the position then?" I was already somewhat regretting my decision.

Gwen raised a brow. "You accept that I might be a bitch to work with?"

"For some crazy reason, yes, I do." We had to work together, after all. Not be friends.

"Then I'm all yours." This time her smile reached her eyes.

"Fantastic."

HUDSON WAS ASLEEP when I arrived home hours later. It was disappointing—not just because he'd promised sexual favors, but because, after therapy, I'd been eager to connect with him. I considered waking him, but a part of me couldn't help feeling like he might be avoiding me. There was no reason to believe that. Just that he rarely went to bed without me and my insecurities were on high alert.

Instead of giving in to them, I sat on the edge of the bed, closed my eyes and ran a few mantras through my head. The repetition settled me, but I longed for more. From his breathing pattern, I knew he was sound asleep behind me. Still, I was eager to start the communication that Lauren had suggested. Without bothering to undress, I stretched out next to him and ran my fingers through his sleep-tussled hair.

"I'm scared, H."

His breathing didn't alter.

"About lots of things. Little things. Mostly, I'm worried about Celia—that I'm not strong enough to not let her get to me. Especially because she's always been the girl that you should be with. In my head, she's the one I picture you with. Everyone does. She's perfect for you, from her manicured nails to her pedigreed upbringing. And, at the moment anyway, she doesn't have a police record." I smiled to myself, fantasizing about Celia pushing far enough that she'd possibly get a restraint against her.

Of course, she was a Werner. Her money and connections would never let that happen. I shared that fear with Hudson too.

It was so simple to tell him these things when he was sleeping. Not because it was difficult to talk to him when he was awake, but because his presence dominated so completely that I didn't feel the need. It was when I was away from him that my thoughts tortured me most.

"I believe in us, H. More than anything. But do you? You used to tell me you were incapable of love. Do you still believe that? Or do you love me as much as I believe you do?" He curled into me, but it seemed like a reflexive move, not a conscious one.

As he turned, his phone fell into my lap. He must have fallen asleep with it in his hand. Had he been waiting for my call? I'd texted around midnight saying I'd be late. Had he gotten that message?

Curious, I swiped his screen to unlock it. My text message had been marked unread—he must have fallen asleep before that. No wonder he hadn't texted back.

It was mostly accidental that I hit the recent calls button. At least, I told myself it was an accident. Immediately, the name on the last call caught my eye—*Norma Anders.* They'd talked for twenty-seven minutes, the call ending at nine-fourteen.

I reached over Hudson to put the phone on the nightstand then settled into his arms. He'd probably been talking to Norma about Gwen and her new position at the club, I told myself. Except Gwen hadn't left the club until ten. She hadn't made any calls or dismissed herself during that time, so Norma and Hudson couldn't have known I'd offered the job to Gwen at the time of the call.

And the thing that really didn't fit into the equation—why was Hudson the one who called Norma?

They work together. They were discussing business, of course. Because wasn't nine at night exactly the time that a typical executive talked to his female financial manager? On a cell phone? From his bed?

— CHAPTER —
TEN

I woke up with Hudson's head between my thighs.

"Mmm." His breath along my folds sent chills down my spine. I peered down at him through half-open lids, wondering how he'd gotten me bare and spread without rousing me until now.

He caught my gaze. "You didn't wake me up last night." He licked along my seam. "And I owed you." His words were gravelly. I loved that I was the first person he spoke to most mornings—that his just-woke-up voice belonged to me.

And I loved what he was doing with his tongue.

I shivered as he caressed my clit with a long velvety stroke.

His head popped up suddenly. "Or would you rather I let you sleep?"

"No! Don't stop." I pushed him back down and stretched my arms above my head.

Hudson chuckled lightly. Then he attacked my nub with earnestness, in turns sucking and licking and swirling his tongue, exciting every nerve in my body. My insides clenched, and a trickle of moisture pooled in my channel. Overcome with pleasure, I wriggled underneath him, but his hands grasped under my thighs, keeping me still and at his mercy.

My breath came out in soft, jagged moans, and then in a gasp as his tongue moved lower, plunging into my hole. "Oh god, Hudson." My hands flew to his hair. Though I'd never dream to control his actions—he'd do a much better job than I would—I loved pulling and tugging at his strands while he drove me mad with oral attention. While he fucked me with his tongue.

Then his mouth was back at my clit, flicking and dancing along my tight ball of nerves, and it was his fingers inside me, rubbing along my wall, stroking me in just the right place.

"Fuck yeah, right there." My leg muscles tightened and my lower belly tensed as the pleasure built within me. The first wave of climax washed over me unexpectedly, much faster than I wanted it to.

"It's not enough," Hudson growled. "I need you quivering and out of your mind."

I couldn't argue if I wanted.

He renewed his assault with invigorated passion, adding a third finger, stretching and filling me with skilled strokes. He reached his other hand up to massage my breast through my clothes. I ached to feel him skin-on-skin but didn't want to interrupt his rhythm to undress. Instead, I arched into his kneading palm while my hips bucked under his artful ministrations.

Damn, I was soaring again, so soon. My legs shook, my knees knocking against Hudson's head as I tried to hold on. Then, with a half-sob, half-yelp, my orgasm burst through me. Stars shot across my vision and my entire body trembled while I came and came over Hudson's hand.

He fed on me while I settled, teasing my pussy until the last waves of my release shuddered through my system.

"You're welcome." Hudson was up and off the bed before I could regain thought process.

I reached after him. "Where are you going? I need to return the favor." Though my limbs were mush, and my mind already skirting the line between consciousness and post-orgasm coma.

"That wasn't part of the deal. And besides, as incredible as that sounds, I have an early meeting to get to." He leaned down and kissed me on the forehead. "What time did you get in last night?"

"Three-ish," I mumbled, still in a haze.

Hudson pulled the covers over me. "Go back to sleep, then. I'm sorry I woke you."

"I'm not."

I must have dozed because Hudson had already showered when I finally got up and padded into the bathroom. I yawned a, "nice view" as I passed Hudson shaving in a towel at his sink.

"You slept in your clothes."

"But I somehow seem to be missing my panties." I flashed my bare ass to remind him. "And yeah, I was too tired last night to get undressed."

He grinned. "You should have woken me. I would have helped."

"Nah, you looked so peaceful. I didn't want to disturb you."

"Trust me, it wouldn't have been disturbing. It's disturbing now because I can't have you the way I want you." His dark gaze met mine in the mirror. "I thought you were going back to sleep."

"I will. Nature called." And I wanted to see him. His phone call to Norma nagged at me, and, in an effort to take Lauren's advice, I thought I should communicate my feelings about it. Hell, even without Lauren's advice, I'd still be eager to confront him.

I started past him, figuring I'd talk to him when he was done in the bathroom. Or at least when he was dressed and the sight of his body with a measly towel around him wasn't such a distraction.

But Hudson reached his arm out and caught me. "Hey."

I could never resist his touch. I settled into his embrace, inhaling his just-washed smell.

He lowered a clean-shaven cheek to my head. "I missed you."

I smiled against his chest. "I missed you too." So much. Missed being in his arms, missed touching and cuddling, missed feeling like we were completely together and safe from the world.

My fingers trailed against his bare skin, and I felt the towel tent up between us.

"Christ." Hudson pushed me away with a reluctant groan. "I want you, but I really don't have time to deal with you properly this morning."

"I wasn't the one who woke me up." I sighed, recalling the good-morning delight. "Not that I'm complaining."

Hudson looked after me with clouded eyes. "Maybe I can be late."

"No, no. You be on time like a good businessman." I waggled a finger at him. "How about I follow you around while you get ready and we can just talk?"

"I'd like that. I've missed talking to you too." He returned his focus to the mirror, applying cream to the still unshaven cheek. "Oh, I got your note you left with Celia's business card. My lawyer said we should save anything we find like that. As potential evidence. So if you get anything else, let me know."

"Believe me, I'll tell you." I sat on the edge of the tub and braced both of my hands on the porcelain at either side of me. "There's nothing he suggests we can do about it, though?"

"No. Not yet." His tone was more serious than I liked. "Are you sure you don't want to leave town?"

"I'm sure." But I did think about it for half a second. Getting away had its appeal. But being apart from Hudson was the last thing I needed at the moment. Especially with all the women in his life that wanted me gone.

My thoughts flashed again to the name I'd seen on his call log. "Though I bet Norma wouldn't mind if I wasn't around."

"Norma again?" He grimaced. "What's brought her up?"

"You're going to laugh." Or he was going to be pissed off. Taking a deep breath, I let it spill. "You fell asleep with your phone and I checked to see if you had gotten my text. Then…oh god, don't hate me."

"What did you do?" His tone was curious.

I lowered my gaze. "I checked your recent calls. I saw you talked to Norma."

When I peeked up, I found he was smiling. "Let me guess—that bothers you?"

His amusement erased my hesitation. "You called her at eight-something at night. From your bed."

This time, he laughed. "Come here."

I didn't move, infuriated by his response.

He composed himself and turned to face me, holding his hand out as he had before. "Alayna, come here."

Sighing, I went to him. "I told you I was always going to ask about her."

"Yes, you did." Hudson wrapped his arms around my waist and settled his forehead against mine. "It was business. I needed to get some figures together for the meeting this morning, and the ones she'd sent me earlier in the day didn't add up."

"It was business," I repeated, relaxing into him. "Always business. Always the excuse." Asking him didn't really make a difference. I knew what he'd say. But it would nag at me whether I voiced it or not. Speaking up gave me the chance to hear his story stay the same, one of the bonuses of communicating.

I pulled my head back to see his face and found his grin was back. "Why are you smiling at me?"

"Because I adore it when you're jealous." He circled my nose with his. "You know this."

"Shut up. I hate it. I can't believe you like seeing me crazy."

"I like seeing that you care."

I didn't know if I should laugh or be concerned. Why would he need my reassurance? "I love you. You know that." Hadn't I proven that time and again?

"Yes, I know." He tightened his grip around me. "Your jealousy shows me your words are true. It's nice. Keep being jealous. Or crazy, if that's what you want to call it."

"You're so weird." I ducked away as he bent to kiss me. "You're going to get shaving cream all over me."

"I don't care." This time when he came toward me, I met his lips. He kissed me sweetly and tenderly, yet I could feel he was holding back, trying to not get carried away with his passion when he had a schedule to keep.

I wasn't on a schedule though, and I liked kissing him. I put my hands around his neck and pulled him closer, deeper, moving my tongue in further to play with his.

He had to push me away. "I can't have you this close anymore." He swatted my behind as I walked back toward my spot at the edge of the tub.

"I'm sorry I snooped." But I wasn't all that sorry. Not anymore. It had earned me a fabulous make-out session that I didn't regret in the least.

Hudson turned back to the mirror. "Don't be sorry. You know I have no secrets." He paused. "Well." He kept his eyes down as he washed his razor. "You know I don't care if you snoop."

My stomach dropped, as if I was coming down the hill of a roller coaster. "What do you mean by that?" I moistened my suddenly dry mouth. "Do you have secrets you aren't telling me about?"

Without looking up, he shook his head. "Of course not." He turned to face me. "I simply meant that we can never know everything about each other. Can we?"

"But we can try."

"Yes. We can try."

We sat a few seconds in awkward silence with him leaning against the back of the counter and I on the edge of the tub. There was something more beneath his statement. Something dark and heavy. I was both drawn to it and turned off all at once. Maybe he was referring to the details of the things he'd done to people in his past. I'd heard some of his stories—none of them pretty. I never expected he'd share each and every past guilt. It would be cruel to want him to relive his pain. I certainly hadn't told him every one of my past indiscretions.

But what if there was something else...something new, something present. Were there secrets that he kept from me that were relevant to us?

How could I ever know?

"Speaking of Norma—" He was the one to end the weirdness. "How did your interview with Gwenyth go?"

Talking business was the perfect escape from the worry that was edging into our pleasant morning. I jumped right in. "I offered her the job, and she accepted. She's leaving Eighty-Eighth Floor without notice. They knew she was trying to leave, it seems, so she's working today as her last shift there and will be at The Sky Launch tonight."

I hadn't realized how excited I was about having a partner until right then. Wow. I was going to be the manager of The Sky Launch. And I wouldn't fail because I had a good team—Hudson, Gwen, and a slew of other great assistants. Why hadn't I let this sink in before now?

"Congratulations!" Hudson caught my enthusiasm. "I'm glad you hit it off."

I thought back to the strange interaction Gwen and I had the night before. "I wouldn't say we hit it off, exactly. Challenged each other is more like it. But she'll be good for the club. Do you know why she wanted to leave Eighty-Eighth so quickly?"

"I don't." He turned back to the mirror and wiped off the remaining shaving cream from his neck with a face towel. "Did you ask her?"

I kept my eyes down and traced the floor's tile pattern with my big toe. "She said it was personal. I thought you might know more. Because of Norma." Was she the source of his secret?

"If Norma knows, she didn't share." He set down the towel and turned toward me. "Or if she shared, I wasn't paying any attention."

I grinned, somewhat mollified. "I like to hear that you don't always pay attention to Norma Anders." I slid my gaze over him. He was so hot. I didn't think I could ever get tired of how delicious his body was. And he was all mine. Wasn't he?

"Stop looking at me like that or I'll definitely be late."

I instantly longed for him to forget his meeting. He could stay and warm me up, fuck me good morning until the sun was high in the sky. There couldn't be room for doubts as long as he was in my arms.

But unfortunately, we couldn't live our lives in bed.

With strength I didn't know I possessed, I tore my eyes away. "Get dressed. It will help."

"Good plan." With an evil grin, he tossed his towel aside.

My eyes were glued to his naked behind until he disappeared into his closet. *Such a tease.*

While Hudson dressed, I undressed, trading the clothes I'd slept in for a t-shirt of Hudson's from the hamper. It smelled of him and I needed that—needed his presence to cling to me even as he was preparing to leave.

When he met me again in the bedroom, he was wearing one of my favorite suits—a dark gray Armani two-piece that intensified the color of his eyes. He looked sharp. Extra sharp. His meeting was obviously an important one.

"You look good."

He glanced at me in the mirror where he was straightening his tie. "Do I?"

"Mm-hmm." In one of my more passive-aggressive moves, I added, "I'm sure Norma will agree."

But though Hudson was good at games, he only played them when he was the one in control. His didn't say a word as he filled his pockets with his phone and wallet, didn't acknowledge if my guess was right.

Communication, I reminded myself. *This is who I am. I need to know.* "She will be there, won't she?"

Finally, he turned to me. "She will." In three quick strides he was at the bed, pulling me roughly to my knees. He wrapped his hand around the back of my neck, forcing my eyes to meet his. "And whether she thinks I look good in this suit or not is none of my concern. I only care that you'll be the one to take me out of it later tonight."

My breath caught. "Okay."

He brushed his nose down the side of mine. "You'll be home to undress me this time?"

I nodded. "I promise." I couldn't remember everything on my agenda for the day, but if there were a conflict, whatever it was, I'd rearrange it to be home.

"Good." He inhaled deeply and I sensed he was warring with himself. "I have to go. This meeting—"

"I know, I know. You're late."

He paused. "Kiss me goodbye?"

I moved in to give him a peck, not wanting to kindle any flames when he was running behind. But Hudson wouldn't settle for that. He plunged in between my lips, fucking my mouth with aggressive strokes of his tongue the way he'd fucked my pussy earlier. When he'd finished, I was breathless.

"That seemed a lot like a promise of some sort," I panted. "Whatever do you have up your sleeve, Mr. Pierce?"

"Now I can't give away all my secrets, can I?" He kissed my nose. "Going now. Get some rest. You're going to need it."

I climbed back into bed with the taste of him still on my lips and the smell of him on my clothes and the warmth of him in my heart.

I MADE IT into the club around eleven. With David training Gwen on most of the night shifts, I was alone with my bodyguard for most of the afternoon. It made it easier to be productive, but it was also lonely. If Jordan had been on duty, I'd at least have someone to talk to. But it was Reynold, and he wasn't the chatty type. It was silly to have him while I was at work. Hudson's money, though, not mine. If he wanted to pay for the guy to sit outside my office and play Candy Crush on his iPhone, then so be it.

Around four, I decided to get some coffee at the shop nearby. Reynold was talking on the phone this time so rather than bother him with my plans I let him think I was going to the bathroom and slipped out the back door. Stepping into the light of day, I remembered how much I loved the outdoors. Sure, I preferred the earlier hours before the heat and humidity became sweltering, but if it weren't for my recently acquired stalker, I'd definitely be in the fresh air more often. *Damn, Celia.*

Thinking of her made a trickle of sweat bead at the back of my neck. Perhaps I should have brought Reynold along after all. Traffic rushed around the circle next to me. A cab was idling at the curb. A limo pulled up behind it. I was surrounded by people—why did I suddenly feel so anxious?

As if spawned by my anxiety, a strong arm wrapped around my waist, while another covered my mouth, stifling my scream. I was hoisted and pulled into the back of the limo and onto the lap of Hudson Pierce.

"What the fuck?" I scrambled to a sitting position, my heart beating at a rapid pace. "Hudson! You scared the shit out of me!"

"Where's your bodyguard?" he asked pointedly. "You on the sidewalk without him scared the shit out of me."

I scowled. "Terrifying me isn't any way to prove a point."

"It isn't?" He grinned, pulling me into his arms.

I struggled, still fuming about his prank, but I wasn't a match for him. He easily restrained me against his chest. Besides, in the end, I enjoyed being in his arms. "What are you doing here, anyway?" I nestled into him.

"I'm kidnapping you. Obviously." His hand slid up and down my bare leg, leaving gooseflesh in its wake.

I wrapped my arms around him and beamed. A night out with Hudson was exactly what I needed. "Awesome. Are you taking me to dinner or something?"

"Or something." With his elbow, he nudged the intercom on. "Let's go," he said, and the limo pulled out into traffic.

My concern for the unattended club outweighed my usual concern about riding without a seat belt. "Wait! I haven't locked up the club or anything."

Hudson tightened his hand around my waist, holding me in place, and moved a finger up to my lips to shush me. "I was talking to Reynold when you left. He's taking care of securing the building. Why were you sneaking away?"

I stuck my tongue out and licked the length of his finger, the salty taste lingering on my lips. He pulled it away with a stern look. It seemed he wanted answers before he was willing to play. "I wasn't sneaking away." Okay, maybe I was. "I was only running next door for coffee. No big deal." The crease in his forehead said that he didn't agree with my assessment of the situation. "All right, I won't do it again." I leaned up and pecked him on the lips. "So seriously, where are you taking me?"

He smiled mischievously. "I said I wanted you out of town."

"What?" I bolted upright, straining against his hold. "I can't leave town, H. I work tomorrow night. And I don't want to leave town. We talked about this."

He grabbed my wrists and held them as if he feared I would push the intercom and ask the limo driver to stop. Which I was considering.

"Settle down, precious." He pulled my hands up to his mouth and placed a kiss on each one. "I simply thought a weekend away might be good for us."

"Both of us?" I'd been very much opposed to the idea of running away, but a weekend away with Hudson was an altogether different idea. Sweet. Romantic.

"Yes, both of us. I'd send you away if you'd let me, but I'm glad you won't because I can't bear to be away from you." He circled my nose with his before settling a kiss on the tip of mine. "I arranged for David and Gwen to cover The Sky Launch tomorrow. We'll be back Sunday night."

"I'm the main manager now. I can't just take off whenever I want." There wasn't any fight in my protest though. I was only pointing out the facts so that I wouldn't feel guilty.

Hudson had no such guilt. "I'm the owner. Yes, you can."

"I feel like I should be irritated at you about this." I grinned. "But I'm not. Thank you. I'd love to be away with you for the weekend."

"I think you need it. *We* need it."

"You've never been more right. And that's saying something since you're right an awful lot. But don't let it go to your head." I wriggled out of his arms, eager to get into my own seat where I could buckle up.

I snuggled as close to him as I could with my belt on. "Where are we going? Are we stopping at the penthouse so I can pack some clothes or did you take care of that, too?" Knowing him, he probably did.

"You'll see when we get there." He fastened his own belt, likely for my benefit, then threw his arm around my shoulder. "And precious," he whispered at my ear, "you aren't going to be needing any clothes."

"WAKE UP, PRECIOUS. We're here."

I must have fallen asleep leaning against Hudson, because the next thing I knew, we were stopped and he was gently nudging me.

I blinked several times, letting my eyes adjust to the light. "Where's here?" I yawned.

"Come on out and see." He tugged me out of the limo.

We were by a log cabin surrounded by lush green woods. A line of wildflowers bordered the stone walkway, butterflies dancing from blossom to blossom. The blue sky was clear and free from smog. Birds sang and a pair of chipmunks scurried up a tree nearby. A little way beyond the house, I could see a lake. The scene was so remote, and the limo and Hudson's two-piece attire were out-of-place. It completely satisfied the yearning for nature that I'd been experiencing.

"The Poconos?" I guessed. He nodded, his eyes watching mine as I took in the beauty. It was perfect. "It's absolutely gorgeous."

Hudson's face relaxed into a smile. He turned to the driver of the limo who was unloading a small suitcase from the trunk of the car. "Seven p.m. on Sunday."

"Yes, sir."

I watched as the driver got back in the car and drove off, leaving us alone in what I was calling paradise. Hudson picked up the suitcase with one hand and took my hand in the other, leading me to the door of the cabin.

I gestured toward the luggage. "I don't need clothes, but you do?"

He laughed. "It's essentials. For both of us. I assure you, if you're naked, I will be as well."

At the door, Hudson pulled a key from his pocket. "This cabin's been in our family for years," he offered before I could ask. "We have a hired manager that opens the place up once a week to keep it from getting musty. Other than that, Adam and Mira are the only ones who come up here on a regular basis. I thought it was time to get my own use out of the property."

"As I said before, H, good thinking."

He opened the door and swept his hand for me to go in first. The interior was as perfect as the outside. The design was rustic and homey—not typical of the Pierce's usual gravitation toward luxurious spaces. I could see why it wasn't a place that Sophia would hang out, or even Jack for that matter. The front room had large comfy sofas and leather armchairs. Two log columns separated the space. A stone fireplace broke up the floor to ceiling windows that overlooked the deck and the lake beyond. It was peaceful and breathtaking.

And we were alone—no coworkers with crushes, no bodyguards, no crazy stalkers. Completely alone.

I heard the click of the door and Hudson came up behind me. I felt it then—the crackle of energy that always existed between us. It kicked up to a high buzz, as if someone had just turned on a switch, and all my lingering fatigue and anxiety instantly left me, replaced with an intense, immediate need for him.

It wasn't just me that felt it. In one swift movement, Hudson had me turned around, one hand on my ass, the other pinning both of mine behind my back as he kissed me frantically. Mercilessly. His tongue tangled with mine, twisting in a dance that was new and consuming. He backed me up as he held his lock on me, leading me somewhere, leading me I-didn't-care-where. The only place I wanted to be was in his arms, in his mouth, in this bubble of frozen space and time that only contained me and him.

God, I was lost—Hudson's lips sent me spiraling into a haze of lust and desire. Then his hands were under my bodycon dress, gathering the material and shimmying it up my thighs and up over my breasts, over my head until I was free from the garment. He tossed it aside and pushed me against one of the log pillars. Again, he pinned my hands, this time over my head. His other hand stroked my skin at my hip. He broke away from my lips and lowered his mouth to my breast. He nipped through my bra, sending an electric shock through my body. The rough wood against my back, his teeth biting my sensitive flesh—it was a mix of such strong sensations, sending my nerves into full alert.

His fingers trailed along the skin at the top of my panties, then slipped inside to find my clit, already swollen and wanting. His hand slid lower through my folds. "Ah, you're so wet. I want to lick your lips clean. But I want to be inside you."

"Hudson." I wriggled against the post. "I need. My hands." I couldn't speak in full sentences. "Need to touch you. Need you naked."

His mouth returned to mine. He bit my lower lip and followed it with a soothing suck. Then he let my arms free. "Okay," he said.

He shrugged out of his jacket while I began on the buttons of his shirt. My hands worked so frantically, so urgently, that I popped a button. I paused. "Whoops."

With a groan, Hudson pulled at the material, popping all the remaining buttons. It was impressive. And hot. My hands flew to his chest. I pressed my palms along the smooth planes and down over the ridges of his abs. His skin felt like fire, the solidness of his flesh such a stark contrast to the softness of mine.

As I explored his torso, he explored mine. He pushed the cups of my bra down and plumped my breasts with strong, sturdy hands. My nipples stood at avid attention. A brush of his thumbs across them set my knees to buckle and my thighs to press together.

With another groan, Hudson let go of me and took a step back. "Fuck, you're so gorgeous like that. Your breasts standing up for me. Your legs begging for me to push my way between them."

I moved toward him, unable to bear the absence of his heat. As I reached him, though, he surprised me by picking me up and throwing me over his shoulder. "Time for a change of scenery," he said.

He spoke as we walked. "Mini tour. Kitchen's there. Bathroom. And here's the master bedroom."

I craned my neck to peek at each of the rooms as we passed, not really caring about them, but curious as to our destination. In the master, he plopped me onto the bed. "Though I plan to mark you in every room of this house, we'll be spending most of our time here."

I wasn't even tempted to glance around. I sat, propped on my elbows behind me with my eyes pinned on him while he undid his belt and pushed off his pants. His hard, thick cock poked from the top of his briefs. My mouth watered as I waited for him to take them off, too.

But he didn't. Not yet. "Turn around," he ordered.

I rolled to my stomach, my body obeying before my head could register his command.

"Up. On your hands and knees."

God, when he got dominant, I got insane. My limbs shook with anticipation as I pushed up to my knees, my head away from him. With his hands clutched at my hips, he tugged me to the edge of the bed and pulled my panties down until they were at my knees. He leaned over my body and undid my bra. The straps fell down around my elbows. I left it there, not wanting to move, enjoying the feel of his body pressed against my backside. His bare cock poked against my ass—he must have removed his underwear while I turned around. Instinctively, I spread my knees as far as my panties would allow them.

Hudson squeezed my breasts and slipped his cock between my legs, rubbing his hard length against my pussy. I moaned as he knocked against my clit, each jab sending me higher and higher. Yet he wasn't where I really wanted him—not yet.

"Hudson." It was half plea, half cry. "Please. I need you."

He continued rocking against my folds. "I know, precious. I know what you need."

And yet he wouldn't give it. I squirmed against his cock pulsing between my legs. "Need you. Inside."

"Say it again and I'll make you wait even longer."

"Please, Hudson." I couldn't help myself. The words tumbled out without my permission.

He pulled off of me. "I told you not to ask again." He slapped my ass. Hard.

A trickle of moisture pooled between my legs. He slapped me again on the other cheek, and I cried out from the pleasant sting. He rubbed away the burn with wide circular passes of his palms. If he spanked me again I thought I just might come right there.

But he didn't. His hands left me. My body shuddered from the absence of his warmth and the jolt of the strikes and the unease of not knowing what would happen next.

Then suddenly he was where I wanted him, inside me—not his cock, but his tongue. I cried out at the sweetness of it. I looked down between my legs and found his face there, his mouth poised over my hole as he plunged in and out with long, velvety strokes. His fingers came up to swirl across my clit. I squirmed, absolutely in love with what he was doing to me, at the same time desperate for him to fill me with his erection instead.

The torment drove me mad. It also made me come, hard and fast, a breathy cry escaping from my lips. I was still coming when he—*finally*—entered me. He thrust in, grunting as he pushed through the clenching of my orgasm. "Ah, Jesus, you're so goddammed tight."

Quickly he pulled himself out to the tip and bore into me again. I loosened around him as I settled down. He dug his fingers into my hips and hammered into me, pulling my whole body to his with each drive. My hands curled into the bedspread, another orgasm already beginning to gather in my belly like a storm.

With a frenetic pace, he continued to drill into me. "I. Can't. Get. Deep. Enough," he grunted a word in between each thrust. "I need. To be. Deeper."

Fuck, he was already so deep, each merciless jab hitting me in just the right place. Every exhale was a whimper, my hands and knees shaking as he assaulted me with enormous jolts of pleasure.

He withdrew again to his tip and paused as he flipped me to my back. Pushing my knees back into the bed, he leaned into me and resumed pounding into me with a fevered pace. "Come with me, precious." It wasn't a request. He meant for me to obey. "I'm going to go soon. Tell me you're coming with me."

"Yes," I panted. "Yes. Yes."

"Good." He pushed on the underside of my thighs, tilting my hips up, and bucked into me, hard and deep. Deeper than he'd ever been; I'd swear he'd never been that far inside of me. My orgasm began surging through me. "Wait, Alayna."

I widened my eyes, gasping in shallow breaths as I tried to hold on.

"Wait. Wait. Wait." His command matched the rhythm of his thrusts. "Wait." Then, "Now!"

At his permission, I succumbed to the force that had built inside, letting it rip through me with lightning speed. My pussy clenched around his cock as Hudson pressed into me with a long, deep drive. "Fuuuccck!" He elongated the word as he knocked against my pelvis, spilling into me fiercely.

He collapsed onto the bed next to me, his chest rising and falling in tandem with my own. "Well," he said after a few minutes. "That was…"

Holy, wow, I thought.

Hudson finished the sentence, stealing one of my other favorite terms. "…amazeballs."

WE SPENT THE evening in the bedroom, only leaving to make sandwiches from the supplies that the property manager had dropped off before we'd arrived. We made love late into the night and woke with a morning round as well.

Though we were in the middle of nowhere, I discovered we still had wi-fi. It was almost a disappointment—part of the beauty of the cabin was the remoteness of it. Yet it was nice for listening to music. After a breakfast of yogurt and fresh berries, I set up Spotify on Hudson's laptop, logging in as me, and turned on one of my favorite playlists. We lounged naked on the sofa, my head at one end, his at the other while he massaged my feet.

Phillip Phillip's *So Easy* came on. I hummed along for a bit, occasionally singing some of the words.

Hudson watched me with admiration. "You have a nice voice."

I blushed. It was funny to realize that I hadn't ever sung in front of him. Oh, the firsts we still had between us. Since I was already embarrassed, I admitted, "This song makes me think of you."

His nose wrinkled in surprise. "You have a song that makes you think of me?"

"Several. A whole soundtrack." We were listening to the playlist I had titled *H*, after all.

"Hmm. I didn't know that." He tilted his head and I could tell he was trying to catch the words.

I sang along, helping him hear the important parts, getting louder at the chorus where Phillip sang about making it so easy to fall so hard.

It was Hudson's turn to be embarrassed. He looked down at his hands working the sole of my foot, a small smile playing at his lips. The song ended, and he moved to my other foot. "How about a shower?"

I stretched my arms over my head and pointed my toes, noting the soreness of muscles that I didn't even know I had. "Yes. Definitely." A hot shower sounded good. But I didn't make a move to get up. Not moving sounded good too.

"Do you have any specific plans for the day? Besides the shower."

I groaned as his thumb worked at the knot in the ball of my foot. "You have me kidnapped in the mountains—I think I'm kind of at your mercy."

"That you are. In which case, I was thinking I'd like to spend the day inside you as much as possible."

I grinned. "I'm totally okay with that. Anything else you have planned?"

"I'd like to take you for a walk around the property. And perhaps some online jewelry shopping. I believe a new necklace or earrings for Mira's event might be nice."

Instead of automatically arguing about the idea of a gift like I usually did, I weighed the idea in my head. "That might not be bad. I don't have anything nice, and I have been through the wringer lately. Maybe I deserve a present of some sort." I smiled coyly.

"Alayna!" Hudson exclaimed. "I've never heard you care about any of that before."

I stared at my hands and shrugged, wishing I hadn't said anything.

Hudson abandoned my feet, crawled up to my face, and covered my body with his. "I'm very pleased. And a whole lot aroused."

Well, he was somewhat aroused. The new position made it evident.

"Why does my acting like a greedy bitch turn you on?"

"Because I love giving you things. It's something that I'm good at. I wish I could give you more but you never seem interested." He ran his fingers through my hair. "So anything you want, I'll give it to you. A shopping spree? A week in Nevis? A car?"

I rolled my eyes and tried to push him off of me. "You're making fun of me now."

He held his ground, both physically and conversationally. "I'm dead serious. Do you want me to buy you a company? Or an island?"

"Stop it."

"No. I won't." He tilted my chin up to meet his eyes. "Anything you want, Alayna. It's yours. And since you don't seem to know that, I'll have to work even harder to make sure you take advantage of my wealth."

Again, I tried to push him away. "I don't want or need to take advantage—"

"Now stop." He moved his hand to caress my cheek. "I know you don't. You never have. But I've told you before that you own me. Whether you take advantage of it or not, I'm yours."

I started to protest again, but he continued. "And thereby, all I own is yours." He met my eyes with stone-cold sincerity. "There are contracts that can guarantee that, you know."

I swallowed. Gulped, actually. The kind of contracts he was talking about…joint ownership…those were hints at wedding bells if I'd ever heard them. Petrified and a little bit thrilled, I tested the waters. "That's some pretty serious stuff you're implying."

"I'll do more than imply if you let me." His voice was quiet but genuine.

My heart pounded in my chest. He couldn't say I love you, but he could promise me the moon? He got intimidated when I expressed my feelings through a song, but he could offer a lifetime?

We weren't ready for that. I wasn't. He wasn't, even if he thought he was. "I think I'll just take a nice piece of jewelry for now," I whispered.

I waited with bated breath for his response, hoping I hadn't hurt his feelings.

It took a second, but he smiled. "Then it's yours."

Wanting to lighten the mood more, I added, "Also, some more books. And did you really say a car?"

He shook his head in disbelief. "You don't want a car. You don't like to drive."

It was true that I wasn't fond of being behind the wheel of a car. But there were other places that driving occurred. "No, I like to drive. You just never let me."

He narrowed his eyes. "You're not talking about cars anymore, are you?"

"Nope." I reached my hand down to circle his cock that was still semi-aroused. I stroked him, once, twice.

He groaned and flipped me so that I was on top of him. "How about you drive right now?"

I straddled him, positioned myself over his cock and slid down. "It kind of seems like I already am."

— CHAPTER —

ELEVEN

We returned to the city Sunday evening, rested and deliciously sore. At least, I was. I was also more excited than ever about our relationship. Still, as eager as I was to get back to our home and our lives, a sadness accompanied our arrival. Hudson and I had made great strides at connecting while we were alone. Could we hold onto our progress back in the real world?

I worried that the answer was no. Especially when, after setting the suitcase in our bedroom, Hudson headed straight to the library to get some work done. I was asleep when he went to bed, and he didn't wake me. Just like that, our vacation was over and we were back to life.

The next morning, I woke before Hudson left for the day. I sat up against the headboard, watching him as he laced his belt through his slacks. "I'm glad I caught you."

He lifted a brow. "You caught me? I was under the impression that I'd caught you."

I tossed a pillow at him. "I mean right now. I'm glad I caught you before you left."

He put his jacket on and turned to give me his full attention. "Why? Do you need to talk to me?"

"I don't *need* to. My days are just better when they start off seeing you."

His lips slid into a smile. He came to the bed, placing one knee into the mattress and pulling me into him. "I feel the same way. Completely."

I wrapped my arms around his neck and played with the hair at the back of his neck. "Let's try to make sure we start it that way more often, okay? And when we go to bed, the same thing."

He leaned his forehead into mine. "I didn't want to wake you, precious."

"We never want to wake each other. Let's get over that. I'd rather lose sleep than lose what I have with you. And sometimes I feel like with our work and day-to-day lives, we slip away from each other. This weekend reminded me how good it feels to be the center of your world."

His expression grew warm. "You're always the center of my world."

I melted. Would he always be able to make me feel this good? I had a feeling the answer was yes. As long as he took the time to tell me. As long as I took the time to listen. "Well, then wake me up and tell me that before you go from now on."

"Done." He captured my mouth, kissing me sweetly. "You're the center of my world, precious. Every minute of every day. Even when I'm not with you." He brushed his lips against mine. *"You make it so easy to fall so hard."*

He remembered the words of the song I sang him! My heart flipped in my chest and my eyes grew misty. I clutched onto him. "God, I love you."

He lingered another moment, his gaze fixed on mine.

A rush of...*something*...swept through my body. It was impossible to pinpoint the exact emotion, and I suspected it was a combination of a whole lot of stuff—melancholy and lust and love and adoration.

But, even with all the good stuff, under all that, there was a steady pulse of dread.

He narrowed his eyes, studying me. "What is it, precious?"

"I don't know." How could I explain this unwarranted feeling that the beautiful thing we had was right on the edge of shattering? I brushed my hand across his cheek. "Sometimes, when you go, I'm left feeling off kilter."

"Trust me, precious, the feeling is mutual."

I thought about his response long after he'd left, wondering what he'd meant. Maybe he hadn't realized that my statement wasn't exactly a compliment.

Or maybe I had him just as off balance as he had me.

MIRA TUGGED AT the waistband of the blue floral A-line I was wearing. I couldn't see myself in the mirror from where I was standing in the dressing room, but from what I could see, it looked pretty damn good.

"Turn," she demanded.

I spun half-heartedly. I was tired of spinning, frankly. It was nearly three and after trying on dozens of outfits, we still hadn't found the perfect one for her reopening. Scratch that. *Mira* hadn't found the perfect outfit. I'd found several.

"Hmm." She studied me with narrow eyes. "I love this one, but it's not as good on you as I thought it would be."

I swallowed back my sigh. "Maybe I'm not a very good model." I suddenly had a ton of appreciation for those who modeled for a living. I loved clothes. I loved trying new clothes on. I did not, it turned out, love being poked and prodded and scrutinized by a feisty fashion expert.

Mira shook her head. "That's the thing. You're too gorgeous and this dress dulls you."

Dulls me? That was a new one.

"There's too much material," she went on. "It's like I'm trying to hide beauty."

"Whatever."

"There's got to be something else." She rifled through the dresses on the rack that I had yet to try on, which was not many. "All of these have the same problem. We need a perfect balance between the dress and you. We need one that shows more skin."

"Don't make it too skimpy or Hudson will kill you. Or me. Or both of us." Thoughts of Hudson were never far away when I was in Mira's shop. We'd had amazing sex right in that very dressing room—my hands pressed against the mirror, his cock thrusting in from behind—

"Hudson can bite my ass."

Leave it to Mira to bring me back to reality. Sharply. Except now I was thinking about Hudson biting my ass…

Mira pulled a dress from the rack, looking it over. "Did you figure out if Hudson has any plans for Celia?"

"Unfortunately, I think he doesn't." That was what my heart was truly telling me. It was probably also why he wanted me out of town. "And did you see Celia was there at the restaurant last week?"

Mira whipped toward me. "Oh my god! She was? I didn't see her. With Mom and everything, I guess I was distracted. Did she say anything to you?"

"Nope." She'd skirted past the Sophia incident, so I took that as a sign she didn't really want to talk about it.

"Thank goodness for that." She turned to put the dress back in its place and began shuffling through the outfits we'd already been through. "I can't believe she has time to dedicate to that. I mean, she doesn't need the money, but she has a job. Does she just ignore her clients?"

I'd actually lost jobs in the past due to my own obsessions. But for once, I didn't want to compare. I decided to go for a lighter approach. "I know, right? Maybe she pays an assistant to do all her work."

Mira laughed. "Or she canceled all her projects this month."

"And put up a sign in her office that says: *Closed for Stalking*." We were both laughing now. The release felt good. It broke the ever-present tension sort of in the same way sex did. If I couldn't spend all my days in bed, I definitely should spend more of it laughing.

"Well, at least we can find the humor." Mira moved behind me, apparently giving up on the clothes rack. "But there's no humor in this horrid dress. Let's get you out of this lousy thing." She loosened the ties that threaded across my back, then started removing the pins she'd put in to tighten the dress at my waist.

There was a tap at the dressing room door. Stacy entered without waiting for an invitation. "Here's some for that one." She handed a pair of cherry red heels toward her boss.

I hadn't seen much of Stacy that afternoon. She'd stayed relatively busy with another customer, but as soon as she was finished, she had popped her head in. Mira had sent her on errand after errand, asking for a different bra, another box of pins, and so on.

But even just seeing her sporadically, it was enough to send my mind back to the video she'd offered to show me. I'd told Hudson I didn't need to see it—and I didn't—but that didn't stop me from being slightly curious. Okay, more than slightly.

Mira waved the shoes away. "We're scrapping this one. It's not quite right." Her eyes lit up. "You know what? We should try the Furstenberg piece. The new one. What do you think, Stacy?"

Stacy tilted her head and examined me, perhaps trying to picture me in the dress they were talking about. "It would look great with her skin tone. And the fit is meant to accentuate the bust line, which works with her body type. Is it still in the backroom?"

"Yes."

Stacy turned to leave.

"No, wait." Mira stopped her. "I pulled it for Misty to try on and then she chose something different." Her brow pinched. "Crap. I don't know where it is now."

"I can look around," Stacy offered.

"Let me go. I don't expect you to figure out where my hormone-influenced brain left it. Will you help her out of this one?" Mira handed the pin box to Stacy.

Maybe it was my imagination, but Stacy's expression didn't seem too pleased. "Certainly." And her voice was tight.

Mira didn't seem to notice. "Thanks. Be back shortly!" Under her breath, she added, "Hopefully."

Stacy kept her head down while she moved behind me, as though she were deliberately avoiding looking me in the eye. Waves of hostility rolled off her body. She'd been cold in the past, but this was different. More angry. Was she mad that I'd refused to see her video? How petty was that?

I debated whether I wanted to break the tension or not. Finally, I decided to try. "Are you excited for the renovation celebration?"

"Sure." Again, her response was curt.

And not a lot to work off of. "I imagine it will bring new business. Will you be hiring more help?"

"Probably."

Yeah, definitely some rage going on. I felt the waistband loosening as she removed the last pins.

"Lift."

I raised my arms for Stacy to pull the dress over my head. She was rough as she did, and when my hair got caught, she muttered an unconvincing apology. Then she turned to hang up the outfit on the rack.

I wrapped my arms around myself, feeling odd in my panties and strapless bra in front of a woman I barely knew. A woman who apparently was not very happy with me.

I considered letting it go.

But letting things go had never been one of my strong points.

Stacy remained turned away as she worked, so I had to address her back. "Are you mad at me?" She didn't say anything so I clarified. "Mad that I didn't want to see your video?"

"Don't be ridiculous," she huffed. Then, after a beat, "That's not why I'm mad."

"But you *are* mad?" *I knew it!* My paranoia wasn't always off-base. "Why?"

"Seriously?" She flew back around to face me. "I offered that video as a gesture of kindness. One woman to another—we're supposed to look out for each other. At least we are in my book."

I was completely lost. "I have no idea—"

She cut me off. "I told you Hudson didn't know that I had it. And then you went ahead and told him about it anyway. That was just…just low."

My head swam. "Wait, wait. I'm confused."

"What exactly is confusing about it? I went out of my way to help you and you pretty much betrayed my confidence." She leaned against the dressing room wall, throwing her gaze up. "I don't know what I expected. He's Hudson Pierce, after all. He gets everybody's panties in a wad with just a glance." Her head shot back toward me. "Hey, he didn't trick you into telling him about it, did he?"

"No. No, he didn't trick me." Things were starting to fall in place, but not enough of them. I took a step toward her. "Look, I'm sorry that—"

"Don't bother." She practically spit. God, she was mad.

"Please!" I put my hand up either to prevent her from stopping me or to shield me from any further assault. "Please let me finish."

I don't know why I waited for her permission, but she gave it to me. "Fine."

"I'm sorry I told Hudson, and that it betrayed your confidence." Honestly, it hadn't occurred to me that she wouldn't want me to tell him. Now that I thought about it, perhaps it hadn't been in good taste. "I wasn't trying to…hurt you…or piss you off in any way. I was just trying to be honest with my boyfriend. And I didn't tell him what it was, obviously, because I didn't know. I asked if he knew what you might have and he said he had no idea. End of discussion."

She started to open her mouth to say something, but I spoke before she could. "Wait, one more thing—" *The most important thing.* "How do *you* know that I told him?"

She tapped her finger against her thigh as though considering whether or not she wanted to tell me. "He's emailed," she said after a beat. "And called me, asking about it."

"Emailed…?" *Hudson had emailed Stacy about the video?*

"And called. Every day last week, in fact."

The color drained from my face, and I had to sit down on the dressing room bench. "But why would he do that? What did he say?"

"His email said he learned that I had a video with him in it, and he wanted to talk to me about it. He mentioned a bunch of legal things about privacy and libel and all that crap. Then he asked if I'd send it to him. His phone messages said the same."

"What did you say?"

"I didn't actually talk to him. He kept calling, though, so I finally sent it Thursday. There was really no point keeping it from him. He knows I saw what's on the video, even if he didn't know about the video itself."

If she sent it on Thursday, then Hudson had most likely already seen it himself. Was that what he'd been referring to the other morning? His *secrets*?

"Then he emailed me today and asked me if we could talk about what he'd need to do in order to ensure the video was gone forever." Her voice was thick with disgust. "Like I could be bribed."

"I don't understand." My eyes rested on my lap, my words for myself, not Stacy. "He said there was nothing you could possibly have that would interest me. He wasn't concerned about it. Why would he…?"

"Because he's lying to you, Alayna!"

Stacy's emphatic statement drew my focus back to her.

"That's exactly my point about him. You can't trust him or anything he says. He'll string you along, make you think he's interested, make you think he's available. But he's not. I don't know what the hell game he's playing, but he's good at it."

A game. Was that what the whole thing was about? Had Stacy been one of his victims? It would explain why he'd been so protective about the material.

I felt sick.

Though I knew about the things he'd done to people, it didn't mean I was comfortable with it. Didn't mean I wanted to have to meet face-to-face with the people he'd hurt.

And what if that wasn't what this was about at all? If he'd scammed Stacy, I could deal with that. It wasn't new information.

If it was something different…

I made a choice. One that I didn't know if I'd necessarily be proud of later, but the only one that would protect my sanity. "What's on the video, Stacy?"

"Uh-uh." She turned back to the dressing rack, busying herself with straightening the clothing. "I'm not playing this game. You didn't want to see it."

I still wasn't sure that I wanted to see it. But now I had to. "I was wrong. I shouldn't have...I don't know...dismissed it so easily. You have to understand—I was trying to trust him because..." Why was I trying to explain the details of Hudson's and my relationship? It didn't matter why I hadn't wanted to see it. What mattered was that I'd changed my mind.

I stood and stepped toward her. "Look, you wanted me to see it to warn me about him. Don't you think I need the warning even more now? Woman to woman. Please." I was desperate—grasping at whatever would speak to her. It was manipulative, perhaps, but I'd been learning from the best.

Stacy's face softened. "I'm off at four. Give me your email and I'll send it to you as soon as I get home."

"Thank you. Thank you." I dove for my purse on the floor where I kept my business cards.

"But I'm done. I'm destroying the damn thing like he asked and then no more. Whatever you decide about the man, you're on your own."

"Of course." I found the item I was looking for and handed it to Stacy. "Here's my card. The email is my home and work."

She took the card from me and tucked it in her pocket.

"Thank you, Stacy. And, again, I'm sorry. If I can make it up to you..."

"Found it!"

Mira's return interrupted me. I was grateful, actually. The sooner she had a dress chosen for me and her event, the sooner I'd be on my way home. And Stacy would be off soon. Maybe her video would even be in my inbox by the time I booted up my laptop at the penthouse.

As I put the latest outfit on and posed and smiled and succumbed to Mira's primping and ecstatic cries of "This is the one," I felt more comfortable with myself than I had in a while. Lauren was right—some things would always be in my nature. Needing to know everything didn't say anything about my levels of trust or distrust in Hudson. It was all about me and my compulsions. The things I could and couldn't live with.

And when it came to secrets, I would always have to uncover them eventually.

— CHAPTER —
TWELVE

The drive back to the penthouse was the longest I'd ever been on.

I'd left Mirabelle's at the same time Stacy had. Once again, she'd said she'd email me the file and once again I thanked her. Then she headed toward the subway and I slipped into the back of the Maybach. My hands were sweaty as I fastened my seat belt, but my heart was also beating with anticipation.

It didn't escape me that I was reacting like an addict getting her first fix in months. And wasn't that exactly what I was doing? The romantic obsessive girl about to indulge in compulsive snooping?

It was only Jordan and me in the car—Reynold had the afternoon off—and I'd intended to go back to the club for a while after Mira's. But I knew I'd be too consumed with the video to work. And watching it in a private location seemed like the best move.

Four p.m. on Monday in NYC, though, is rush hour. Getting from Greenwich Village to Uptown was a nightmare. I busied myself with trying to figure out how to set my email up on my phone—why hadn't I thought that was a good idea before now? But I couldn't focus enough on the steps to make it happen.

Instead, my mind buzzed with questions. So many questions beyond what was on the video. Like, how had Stacy happened to make a video in the first place? If it had been made with her phone, wouldn't she have been able to send it by phone? Was she carrying around a video camera and then just happened to tape this…this…*whatever* it was? Why did she think this particular moment was even worthy of preserving?

Which led to the question, what about the video made Hudson want it destroyed? That was a big one, the reason I'd ended up pursuing getting a copy for myself.

And then there was Stacy's comment about Hudson wooing people. She'd said it as if he had wooed her. Hudson had sworn they'd only had the one date. It was this detail that intrigued me the most. Because even if all the video ended up being was proof that his relationship with Stacy had been one of his scams, he'd at the very least lied to me about the extent of his interaction with her. That pardoned me from whatever trust of his I was about to break, didn't it?

I hadn't promised I wouldn't see the video, I reasoned. I'd told him I didn't have to. Well, things had changed. And now I did have to. No promise broken, simply a new set of circumstances.

That's what I convinced myself, anyway.

At the penthouse, I was out of the car before Jordan could open my door. "Remember to set the alarm," he called after me. That was the arrangement. When I was at the penthouse alone, Jordan or Reynold would wait outside until I'd set the security system. Then they'd get an automatic text showing a secured status and they'd leave. At the moment, Celia was the least of my concerns, but in general, it was nice knowing that even though I was protected, I still had some semblance of privacy.

Once inside, I set the alarm, ran to the library to get my laptop, and settled in on the couch. I muttered to myself as my email seemed to take longer than usual to load, and then held my breath while I scanned my inbox.

There it was. My only unread message. From *StacySBrighton.*

I clicked the email open.

There was a short paragraph above the video attachment. Eager as I was, I began the download then returned to read it.

Alayna,

As I said, I'm done with this now. Take or leave this information as you wish. In case you want to know the circumstances of the footage, I'll tell you this: Hudson had asked me to meet him for coffee. I'd shown up and found him like this. I shot them with my phone before he saw me. Later, I transferred it to my computer and I got a new phone, which was why I couldn't send it to you that way.

Anyway. Here it is.

Stacy

At least she'd answered one of my questions. But Hudson asking to meet her for coffee? More and more I was sure what I was going to find—Hudson playing a game on his sister's assistant. It was heartbreaking. For Hudson, for Stacy…and what about Mira? I wondered what she knew about it all.

My computer popped up with a message that my download was complete. My hand paused above my keyboard as, for half a second, I considered not watching. Once I saw it, I could never un-see it. What if it was something that embarrassed him? Was it fair that I see the worst of him? What if Hudson had learned *my* deepest darkest mistakes? How would that make me feel?

But he already *had* learned them. He'd gone behind my back before he'd ever really spoken to me, read my police record, done his own research. And in the end, he was still with me. How was this any different?

I wouldn't know until I saw it.

My finger clicked the file open. I enlarged the picture to full-screen. Then I sat back and watched.

The video swept across a building as it moved to focus on its subjects. Then it settled on the back of a head. It didn't matter that I only could see hair and shoulders—I knew that hair. Knew the color and the texture by heart. I even knew that suit jacket. A dark blue Ralph Lauren. Not one of my favorites but definitely familiar.

Hudson's head swiveled slightly one way then the other. He was kissing someone—making out with her. His body completely hid the other person. All I could see of the woman were her small hands wrapped around his neck.

Jealousy wracked my body. I couldn't help it. Sure, it was before I knew him, but this was my man, my love, kissing someone else. If Stacy had come to meet him, thinking they were about to go on a date—well, that explained why she'd been upset.

Then the kiss ended. And for a moment I was thrilled.

But he moved away, and there she was—her face flushed, her lips plump from the kiss, her blonde hair wrapped tightly into the chignon that was typical of her style.

I felt the blood drain from my face. Hudson and Celia. I'd thought about the possibility before, but seeing it for real was much worse than I could have ever imagined. So much worse.

The video kept on. Celia reached out to straighten Hudson's tie. He shooed her away, turning more fully to the camera. Now I could focus on his face. His expression made my gut wrench—he was smiling, laughing almost. Something he'd done so rarely before he'd met me. At least, that's what I'd come to believe about him. It was that happy, carefree expression that made it impossible for me to excuse the kiss as being one-sided. They'd both been into it.

Then, when she started to walk away, he pulled her back into another kiss. Slower, sweeter.

The video ended there.

Thankfully. Because any more and I was going to throw up. Except that didn't stop me from pushing play again.

I pulled my legs up to my chest as I watched this time. Each second of their kiss, my chest tightened in anguish. It would have been cliché to say my heart was breaking. As if it could actually tear apart from emotional pain and still allow a person to live. How trite.

Besides, it didn't feel like that. It felt like a vise-grip. Constricting. Like someone had taken the organ from my chest and squeezed.

All the times I'd asked, all the times he'd denied…

But if it had been a scam, a scam on Stacy—my hopes lifted for a moment as I reasoned that scenario. Maybe the kiss wasn't real. Maybe it had all been Celia and Hudson playing a game together. He'd never said he'd involved Celia in his charades, but knowing that she was also a player, wasn't it a good possibility?

It was marginally better. They'd still been kissing, but it meant he hadn't lied to me about their relationship. It meant they'd never truly been together.

It took the third time viewing the video before I realized the flaw in that theory. When I'd seen it enough to be able to catch the details and not just be focused on the kiss. Hudson had said his scheming had been over for some time before he met me. That he'd been in therapy and had been on the wagon, so to say.

But the sign on the building behind them—it was for the Stern Symposium. That had been the night of my presentation. The night Hudson saw me for the first time. The night he said he knew that I was special.

The night that began everything for me and Hudson, he'd been kissing Celia Werner.

Either he was still scheming when he met me or he'd been dating her. Either way, he'd lied.

Having an alcoholic parent, I'd chosen to never use liquor to settle my emotions. My addictions were of a totally different nature. But the emotions boiling inside of me needed something stronger. I went to the library bar and reached for a shot glass and a bottle of tequila.

"HERE YOU ARE."

When Hudson found me almost an hour later, I was outside on the balcony, looking out over the railing. I'd intended to be shit-faced by the time he got home, but had only managed four shots. For me that was enough to make me impaired.

But it hadn't been enough to stop the throbbing ache in my chest.

I glanced at him over my shoulder. I'd prepared several speeches, but at the sight of him, they all left me. "I didn't realize you were home."

I turned back to the view. It was far less devastating than looking at the man who'd betrayed me.

"I am." In my periphery, I saw him move up beside me. "You don't come out here very often."

I shrugged. "It scares me." I was cold to him—my tone, my entire demeanor. There was no way he missed it.

Tentatively, he attempted to figure it out. "You're afraid of heights?"

"Not really. It's falling that scares me." I gave a small laugh as I realized the relation of the fear to the feeling I was experiencing at the moment. "It's actually thrilling to be out here. Being so high up, feeling so untouchable, the wind rushing at you from below. I can see why so many people are intrigued by the idea of flying. Problem is, no matter how good the flight, you always have to come back down eventually. And lots of times, that return is a free fall."

"You're waxing poetic tonight." His frown was apparent in his voice.

"Am I?" I gathered up my strength and turned to look at him. "I suppose so."

Hudson smiled and took a step in my direction, his arms reaching for me.

I stepped away, or more like stumbled away.

He grabbed my arm to catch me. My eyes latched on to where his hand grasped. It felt like my skin was burning under his touch, and not in the amazing way that it usually burned, but in a way that left me wondering if I'd be scarred for life. Hell, he'd touched me everywhere in our time together—would all of my body be scarred?

At least my outside would match my inside.

Hudson leaned in to help me steady. He smelled it then, how could he not? "Have you been drinking?"

I pulled my arm away. "Is that a problem?"

"Of course not. You just don't usually drink. You're full of all sorts of surprises this evening."

"Ah. Surprises. It's certainly a day for that."

"Have there been others?"

"There have." I brushed past him to get inside. I was done with the small talk. There were things to be said, and saying them outside wasn't my preference.

He followed me in.

I waited until I heard the door shut behind me before I turned to face him. I'd planned to hit him straight up with the news that I'd seen his video. But those weren't the words that came out. "Hudson, why don't you ever tell me that you love me?"

"Where did that come from?" He looked like I'd slapped him. Considering that I wanted to, it was a pleasing outcome.

However, it wasn't the response I wanted. Not in the least. And I had enough liquor in my system to keep me pursuing the answer I wanted. "It's a valid question."

"Is it? My methods of emotional expression haven't seemed to bother you before—why now?"

"Hasn't bothered me?" I was incredulous. Did he really not know how desperate I was to hear it? "It's always bothered me. I've been patient, that's all. Letting you settle into our relationship. I realize it's all new for you—you've never let me forget it. But it's new for me too. I've bared all my heart to you. And you can't give me this one thing—three things, actually. Three little words."

"You know how I feel about you." He turned away from me and headed toward the dining room bar.

It was my turn to chase after him. "But why can't you say it?"

"Why do I need to?" He poured himself a Scotch. "If you understand, there's no point."

"Sometimes it helps to hear it."

"Helps what?"

He was so controlled, so even-mannered—it drove me insane. I raised my voice. "Helps everything! Helps deal with insecurity. With doubts."

He set the bottle on the counter and pivoted toward me. "What are you doubting? Us? What we have? I asked you to live with me. I changed my entire life to be with you. What is there to doubt?"

"Your reasons. Your motives."

"My reasons for wanting you with me are *I want you with me.* What more do you need to know? You want words? They can be changed and manipulated and misconstrued. But my actions—they speak everything that you need to know."

His words were calm and soothing and, at another time, would have melted me. There were many actions he'd shown that backed up what he was saying. Too many to do an inventory of in the space of a few seconds.

But there were other actions—the ones that were ambiguous and hard-to-interpret. Lunch meetings with Norma Anders. Purchasing the club for me before he'd even known me. And there was the video.

I wrapped my arms around myself, suddenly cold. "If I'm going by your actions, then right now what I know is that I've been lied to."

He took a swallow of his drink, his jaw moving the liquid around his mouth before he swallowed. "What are you talking about?"

I straightened my back for the moment of confrontation. "I saw it, Hudson. I saw the video."

"What vid—"

I punched my fist onto the dining room table. "Don't even fucking pretend you don't know what video I'm referring to, because after everything we've been through, I don't deserve the runaround."

His eyes were locked on mine, so I saw the brief flare of panic.

And then I saw the moment he resumed control.

"Okay. I won't run you around then." He wiped his mouth with the back of his hand. "Where did you get it? Stacy?"

Where did I get it? "Does it matter?"

"I suppose not." His tone was straight.

My gut clenched. I'd expected immediate denial or reassurance that it wasn't what it looked like. I'd expected answers. Not this. Not complete indifference.

"You were kissing Celia."

"I saw."

"Do you want to explain?"

"Does it matter?" He threw back my own words at me.

"Yes!" My composure was gone. Only he could fix me and he wasn't even trying.

He moved back to the bar and refilled his drink. "It was before I met you, Alayna. I haven't asked you to explain your actions before we met. I shouldn't be expected to either."

I gaped for a moment while he threw back his liquor. Of all the responses I'd imagined he'd give, downplaying wasn't one of them.

"But this is different," I finally managed. "Because you've already offered an explanation. You said there was never anything between you and Celia."

"There wasn't."

"I'm supposed to believe that after seeing what I saw?"

"Looks can be deceiving." His voice was a low rumble. The only indicator of emotion since I'd brought up the video.

It incited me. "That's all you got?"

"You've told me there's nothing between you and David, yet there's been many a time that it has looked like there was."

"It only looked that way because you were paranoid and jealous. You never saw me lip-locked with him. Believe me, seeing it is worse than you can imagine."

He placed his fingertips on the back of a chair and leaned toward me. "I'm sure if I went and looked at old security tapes I might see exactly that."

His words were cold and harsh and spiteful. It was times like these that Hudson's gift to manipulate showed itself. It was frustrating and unfair how he could mold a situation to his favor, but I understood that it was a part of him. He wasn't trying to play me.

Knowing that didn't make it any easier to deal with. "Yes. Once upon a time I was with David. I've told you that."

"After you let it slip and I figured it out."

"Jesus! Will I always have to pay for that mistake?" He didn't answer, but I didn't give him time. "Okay, I wasn't forthcoming. I kept things from you. But only because I didn't want to hurt you, and I admitted it when you confronted me. But this—you outright lied about this, Hudson. You told me there was nothing to see on Stacy's video. You told me I didn't need to go looking."

"And you went looking anyway."

"No. I didn't. I stayed away. Until I found out that you were deliberately trying to hide it from me—yes, Stacy told me you'd asked her for it. Was I supposed to keep trusting you then?"

He shrugged it away. "I didn't know what she had. I asked because I was curious. I wasn't deliberately hiding anything."

"You were deliberately hiding a whole fucking relationship with someone who you swore was never anything but a friend! And even now that I've figured out you and Celia were together, even now that I have proof, you still can't admit it." My eyes stung and my hands shook from the surge of frustration running through me.

Hudson pinned his eyes to mine. "I'm not admitting anything," he hissed. "You haven't figured out anything, Alayna."

"Then clear things up for me. Tell me what I can't seem to understand. What's going on in that video?"

"Nothing," he spit out. "Nothing's going on."

"Hudson!" My voice caught on the lump in my throat, but I kept on. "You're kissing her. Kissing her deeply. Passionately. Oh yes, I watched it several times, I could reenact the whole thing for you by now if you wanted."

Shaking his head, he started for the living room.

I was on his heels. "Not to mention that you were supposed to be meeting Stacy right then. And it didn't escape me on what night this whole thing took place."

He spun toward me. "*Meeting Stacy*? Is that what she told you? What else did she say?"

If he could withhold information, so could I. "That really doesn't have any bearing on this conversation."

"Well, as far as I'm concerned, this conversation is over." He headed for the library.

I stood stunned for a beat before following after. "It is not. I have questions and you've given me zero answers."

"I have no answers to give you. This subject is closed."

His dismissal infuriated me, and more, it left me feeling helpless. "Are you kidding me? You're not going to talk about this?"

"No, I'm not." He sat at his desk, reinforcing his refusal to speak further on the matter.

"Hudson, this is so not fair." I moved around to his side of the desk, not wanting this physical barrier between us. "We've said we needed to be honest with each other—that we needed to form a relationship built on trust. We agreed to be open. But you're hiding something with this. You lied! And not talking about it? How are we supposed to move forward when you're keeping such a big secret?"

He flew up from his chair and grabbed my arm with a tight grip. "Have I done anything to betray your trust before this?"

I was too surprised to try to pull away. "You went behind my back to transfer David…"

He yanked me closer to him. "That was *for us*." His eyes widened as he emphasized the last two words. "Have I done anything that makes you think I don't have our relationship's best interests in mind? Have I done anything to make you believe that I don't want to be with you? That I don't…" His voice cracked and he swallowed before continuing. "That I don't *care*…for you with everything I have?"

I shook my head, unable to speak.

He relaxed his grasp on me, but didn't let go. "Everything I've done since we've been together has been for you and me. Trust me when I tell you this isn't important." With his free hand, he brushed my hair off my shoulder. "This doesn't affect us."

"How can it not affect us? This was the night of the Stern Symposium. The night you said you first saw me."

"Yes, it was the night I first saw you." His voice was softer. Soothing as he cupped my neck. "But this was before that. Separate. You need to forget about this."

Separate. I held onto that word, absorbing it, searching for its meaning. But how could it be separate? It was the same night.

Looking into his eyes didn't clear up anything either. All I saw there was him pleading and begging to lay this video to rest.

But that wasn't the person that I was. He'd told me once that he would always be manipulative and domineering, even when he wasn't playing games. It was who he was.

Me, I would always be obsessive. I'd always question. Even when I was healthy. Asking to forget about this was defying my nature.

I swallowed. "What if I can't let it go?"

His expression filled with disappointment. "Then it means you don't trust me." He let me go, straightening his back. "And I don't know how we can continue on with our relationship without trust."

My knees buckled and I put my hand out on his desk to steady myself. "Are you saying that I have to choose? Trust you about this or we're over?"

"Of course not." His confidence was missing from his words. "But I have nothing else that I can say. Whether you can live with that or not is the choice you have to make."

I brushed my fingertips across my eyebrows and down my face. The situation felt so surreal, it was almost as if I had to be sure I was still physically there. How had I gone from a question about Hudson's past to an ultimatum about our future?

And even if I could bring myself to live with his terms, what kind of a future could we possibly have?

I shook my head. "That's a trap, Hudson. How could anyone live with that? How can we ever move forward when everywhere I turn there's a wall?"

"There are no walls." His jaw tensed and his voice tightened. "I'm here with you. I share everything with you."

"Except your past."

"Except this *one thing* in my past."

"No. There's more." My throat and eyes burned. "It's not just the video, Hudson. It's your secrets, the things you can't say. You can't tell me what that night was about. You can't tell me how you feel about me. You can't tell me what the true nature of your relationship is with Celia, with Norma—even with Sophia!"

"Jesus Christ, Alayna. I've told you exactly the true nature of my relationships and you—" he pointed a finger into his desk for emphasis, "refuse to believe what I've said."

"Because there's proof over and over again that says otherwise." I slammed my hand against my thigh each time I said *over*. "And if I'm missing the whole picture, than maybe you should stop leaving all the vital parts out."

He closed his eyes briefly. Then he stepped closer to grasp my forearms. "Nothing of what I've kept from you is vital to our relationship." His voice was low and sincere. "It has nothing to do with us."

I threw my arms in the air. "It does! It has everything to do with us."

Hudson slammed past me to the other side of his desk, but he didn't go far. He rocked on his feet, his back to me, and I felt he was deciding. Deciding what, I didn't know.

I circled after him until I was within an arm's length. I could reach out to touch him with my hands, but I kept them at my side. "Don't you see, Hudson? I want to know everything about you. I want to be everything with you. How can I when you don't let me in?"

"I've let you in further than any other human being I've known. You know things about me that I never planned to share with anyone." He turned his head to look at me. "Doesn't that count for something?"

"It does." I reached out to caress his cheek and he moved the rest of the way to face me. "It counts for so much. But see," I dropped my hand to my side, "that's where we're stuck. Because you're asking me to give up so much of who I am in order for you to keep your secrets, and that will tear me apart. I can't do it. I can't function. I obsess, Hudson. I've never kept that from you. Now, I've had a history of obsessing over things that weren't valid, but this time, it's not in my head. There are real things you're hiding and can you not see how I'm going crazy over it? Everything you fixed about me is unraveling and I don't know what to do." I took a deep breath. "And I'm not even sure you care."

"I care, Alayna." He brushed a tear off my cheek—funny, I hadn't even noticed I was crying. "I care more than I can stand it, and I will do anything to make this better."

He braced his hand behind my neck and leaned his forehead against mine. It would be so easy—so easy to lean up and let him kiss away my pain and insecurity. His lips on mine could erase all darkness, could soothe any pain. Until that afternoon, I'd believed that like some people believed in their religion—Hudson could fix me, every time.

Except this time he was the problem.

And it wasn't his touch that would fix me. It was words. Words he wasn't willing to give. "Then tell me what I need to know," I whispered.

He straightened and took a step away from me. "No. I won't."

He turned away, heading back toward the living room.

Once again, I chased after him. "Were you together? Did you fuck her? Did you fuck her that night? The night you met me?"

He paced the room. "No. No. No. And no. I've told you this before and if those words aren't enough, why should I believe that any others would be any different?"

"Because those words aren't the words I need. I don't need denials. I need truths. What happened, Hudson? What is she to you?"

"Alayna, leave it alone."

"I can't!"

He stopped suddenly. After a beat, he said, "Then I need to leave."

"What's that supposed to mean?" I swallowed. "Like leave to cool down?"

He shook his head. "It means that we need to take some time apart."

"What? No!" I'd thought my heart had hit rock bottom before. Apparently there was a whole chasm left for it to fall into—a chasm so dark that it obliterated my previous notion of darkness. And the cold and the ache of that place made every pain I'd ever felt pale in comparison. The death of my parents, my journey from crazy to sanity, even the betrayal from Hudson when he didn't choose me over Celia—those were flesh wounds next to this.

"It's for the best," he said as he retrieved his jacket from across the back of the couch.

It seemed I needed to say something—anything—to make him stay. But I couldn't figure out what that would be. All I could hear were his words repeating over in my head—*time apart*. Because why? Because I'd needed him to be honest?

This couldn't be happening. "You tell me you care about me more than you can stand and now you want to break up with me?"

He glanced over at me, his eyes filled with sadness. "No, not break up, precious. Just take some time apart. Time to figure out how we want to deal with this."

His words were compassionate and sweet, but they weren't enough to mollify my hurt and anger. "You mean time for me to get my shit together."

"Both of us, Alayna."

I swiped the tears from my face with the back of my hand. "I don't know where you get your definitions, but that sure sounds like breaking up to me."

"If that's what you want to call it."

"I don't want to call it anything. I don't want it to happen!"

"I hope it will be temporary." He swept past me, careful not to touch me as he did. He grabbed his briefcase from the hall then patted his pockets, apparently satisfied that he had what he needed.

Oh my god. He was really leaving. Really, really leaving. "Hudson!"

When he turned to me, I rushed to him. "Don't go. Please don't go." I clutched at him.

His body remained cold and impassive, his eyes not meeting mine. "I'm doing this for you, Alayna. For both of us." His words were warm, though he still wouldn't look at me or touch me. "I can't bear that I'm hurting you, and it will destroy me if I lose you. But there are some things that I can never tell you. And now we're at an impasse, as you said. Because you say you can't go on not knowing and I can't go on without your trust."

"I do trust you. I'll learn to live with this if I have to. I'll figure it out. I just can't lose you!" I was desperate, making promises there was no way I could keep.

Finally, he connected his eyes with mine. "You're not losing me. We're simply stepping away. Maybe I can…"

He trailed off and I grasped onto whatever alternative he might be offering. "Maybe you can…what?"

But he had none to offer. "I don't know. I need time." Gently, he unwrapped my fingers from his clothing and pushed me away.

"But where are you going? This is your home."

"It's your home too. I'll stay at the loft."

Without looking at me, he stepped toward the elevator.

"Hudson! Don't do this. Don't leave."

He reached out as if he were going to touch me then pulled his hand back. "This isn't forever, precious. But I can't watch you like this."

"Like, what? Like crazy?" While I'd always feared that Hudson wouldn't be able to take me at my worst, I'd begun to think he'd be with me always. Like he promised so many times.

I'd been wrong. Again. "Yeah, I'm crazy. This is who I really am, Hudson. You see it now. Here I am, exposed. It always scares people away, but I never thought it would scare you. Yet here you are running. No wonder you think I can't handle your secrets. Because you probably think I'd react just like you are now. But I'm not a coward, Hudson. I can take it. I won't run from you."

His face fell. "I'm not running from you, Alayna. I'm saving you."

"From what?"

"From me!" We stood in silence as his exclamation rung through the foyer. Then he hit the elevator button. "I'll talk to you later. Tomorrow, maybe."

"Hudson!"

"I…I can't, Alayna."

He stepped inside the elevator, his focus fastened to the floor as the doors closed.

Then he was gone.

— CHAPTER —
THIRTEEN

After Hudson left, I cried so long and so hard that it seemed like I should have passed out from exhaustion. But I didn't. I tried curling up in bed, but it felt too big. And no matter how many blankets I had, I felt cold. Eventually, I wandered out to the library where I had a few more shots of tequila to warm up and turned on a movie from my AFI's Greatest Films collection. I chose *Titanic*. I was already heartbroken, after all—might as well wallow in it.

Sometime before the ship sunk, I passed out on the couch. I woke the next day with swollen eyes and a splitting headache. My first thought was that I needed caffeine. But there was no smell of brewing coffee in the penthouse, and that's when I remembered that Hudson wasn't there. Every day before he left for work, he set the Keurig to brew for me. This simple missing gesture threatened to start a new round of tears.

But maybe he'd called.

I fumbled around for my phone and found it buried in the cushions. *Fuck.* It was dead. I'd been too consumed with grief to charge it for the night. After setting it up at the library charging station, I made my own coffee and found some Ibuprofen in the bathroom cabinet.

I showered then, hoping the warm water would relieve the swelling of my eyes. Perhaps it did, but I didn't feel any better. Afterward, I stood with a towel wrapped around myself and stared into the steam-clouded mirror. This was what it was like to see Hudson now—through this fog, knowing that something more lay underneath. If only it were as simple as stretching my hand out and wiping away the condensation to see the man beneath. If only he'd let me in, maybe it would be that easy. Maybe then my touch could finally bring him into focus.

But it wasn't that simple. Instead, all I could hope for was a message or a missed call. I dressed and settled back on the couch to power up my cell.

There was nothing.

So I sent one to him: *Come home.*

When I didn't have a response after five minutes, I considered sending another. He was at work. I shouldn't bother him. But I was supposed to be important. If he still cared at all, he'd answer me.

I battled with myself over it. In my past, obsessive texting and calling had been my biggest weakness. For more than a year after I started therapy, I didn't even allow myself to have a phone. The temptation was too great. In the height of my obsessing, I could fill a voicemail box within an hour. Paul Kresh had to change his number after I texted him nonstop for three days straight.

Even with Hudson, I carefully weighed each message I sent him. I didn't send everything I was thinking. It was hard, but I had managed to stay in control.

Today, I didn't give a fuck about control.

I typed a new message: *Are you going to avoid me now?*

Five minutes later, I sent again: *The least you can do is talk to me.*

I sent several more, delaying each by a span of three to five minutes:

You said I was everything to you.

Talk to me.

I won't ask about it if you don't want to.

This isn't fair. Shouldn't I be the one who's mad?

I was about to start another when my phone vibrated in my hand with a received text. It was from him: *I'm not mad. I'm not avoiding you. I don't know what to say.*

Hudson at a loss for words was the craziest thing I'd heard in the last two days. He always knew what to say, always knew what to do. If our separation had him so out of character, why were we apart?

My fingers could barely enter a response fast enough. *Don't say anything. Just come home.*

I can't. Not yet. We need time.

I had hoped the new morning would bring clarity. But I still wasn't even sure what I was supposed to be doing with the time that he insisted we needed. *I don't need time. I need you.*

We'll talk later.

You don't understand. I have to talk now. I'll keep texting you. I can't help myself.

And I'll read every one.

I almost smiled at his last message. After all the years of being ignored and called crazy, Hudson embraced my whacked out tendencies.

But one sweet little text wasn't enough to erase the hollow ache in my chest. I started to type out another message.

Then I stopped myself.

What the hell was I doing? Never mind old habits and what was healthy and what wasn't—why was I chasing after this man so desperately when he'd already clearly indicated it would have no effect on him? Besides, he'd said over and over that he liked my obsessing over him. It made him feel loved.

Well, fuck that.

If Hudson wanted to feel loved, he could come home and work things out. Yes, we had troubled pasts and were inexperienced with relationships. Still, sooner or later we had to grow up and take responsibility for our actions. More than anything in the world, I wanted to do that with Hudson. But if he wasn't ready, it didn't matter how much I loved him. I couldn't be the only one fighting. He had to fight too.

In one of the strongest moments of my adult life, I set down my phone and walked away.

Since I wasn't insane enough to believe my strength would last, I decided to get out of the house. And I needed a run.

I called Jordan. "Hey, you're a runner right?"

"Ms. Withers?"

"You were Special Ops. You had to stay in shape for that, right?" The idea had crossed my mind before, but since Hudson had been so opposed, I'd never pursued it. But now Hudson wasn't around. "And I imagine that makes you a fairly good runner."

"Yes, I suppose so."

"Good. I want to go for a run and Hudson won't let me go without a bodyguard. I'll be ready in fifteen."

He hesitated for only half a beat. "Be there in ten, Ms. Withers."

"Thank you." It had been surprisingly easier than I'd expected. Might as well see what else I could get. "And, oh my god, Jordan, please call me Laynie. Please, please, please. I know you're not supposed to, but I don't care about Hudson's stupid rules. I'm having a bad day and I could use a friend. Even if you aren't really my friend, pretend. Please."

"You should know me well enough to know that I'm not much good at pretending." The phone jostled as if he were getting ready while he talked to me. "But I am an excellent runner. Be ready to have your ass handed to you. Laynie."

I was almost grinning when I met him in the lobby. This was new for me—life actually going on in the midst of heartache. Who knew it was possible?

TRUE TO HIS word, Jordan handed me my ass on our run. The six miles we did around Central Park barely seemed to faze him, while I nearly had to be carried back to the penthouse. The physical discomfort was welcomed—it matched my sullen mood. The adrenaline and endorphin rush did little to improve my spirits, but it did make the act of living seem just a bit more bearable.

Back at the penthouse, I showered and got dressed. Then I did go to my phone. I scrolled through my texts looking for another from Hudson. The disappointment at finding none was hard to swallow. Even though he'd said he wouldn't respond, I had hoped. Wasn't it just the morning before that he'd said I was the center of his world? Was there any way he could still mean it?

I couldn't think about the answer. The evidence wasn't in my favor and it hurt too much to face.

Needing another distraction from reaching out to Hudson, I called Brian. We chatted for over an hour—a record for us. After that, I called Liesl. We were both working that night, which provided a perfect excuse for shopping and dinner beforehand. My heart wasn't in it, but I could fake it with the best of them. And being with Liesl helped keep the tears at bay.

It had already been a full day by the time Jordan dropped us off at The Sky Launch. "My shift's over, Laynie," Jordan said as he shut the car door behind me. "Reynold's waiting for you up there."

Sure enough, I spotted Reynold by the club's employee entrance.

Though I'd never done it before, I felt the urge to hug Jordan. So I did. "Thank you," I said, my throat tightening. "I needed you and you were there."

Jordan looked at me compassionately. "It's not my place, but you should know—Mr. Pierce is a complicated man."

"Yeah, yeah, I know." I wasn't interested in anyone defending Hudson at the moment.

Jordan continued anyway. "But no matter how complex the situation may be, it's easy to see how he feels about you."

I stuck my chin out, defiantly. "Is it?" I'd thought it was, but now all bets were off.

My driver patted my upper arm. "Perhaps not to you. But to me, it's obvious. I pray that he'll figure out how to show you before you're gone for good."

I watched Jordan as he got in the car and drove away.

Me, gone for good? It had been Hudson who'd left. Hudson who'd broken the promise he'd made to stand by my side through everything. Hudson who'd dropped not so subtle hints at a long-lasting future and yet he was now nowhere by my side.

With a sinking horror, I feared that Jordan was right—Hudson's feelings for me *were* obvious. Obviously gone.

I bit my lip to curtail any crying that latest thought might bring on.

Liesl wrapped her arm around mine and directed me toward the door. "Do you get sick of the bodyguard stuff?" She was excellent at deflecting. "I mean, I wouldn't get sick of that Jordan dude—he's hot."

"And gay."

"Figures. But maybe he's also experimental."

I laughed. "Not likely." My laughter quickly faded into a frown—it felt too strange to be amused when my heart was so heavy. "I don't usually mind having bodyguards around, though I do like my independence. And I don't really get why I need to have someone here while I'm at the club." An idea surfaced. "In fact—"

We'd reached Reynold by then. "Hey, stranger," I said in greeting. "Guess what. I'm giving you the night off."

He chuckled.

"I'm serious. Hudson is probably the only one who has the power to give you the night off, but here's the thing—Hudson's not around. And I'll be here at the club all night. We have security guards on staff and bouncers. I'm going to be fine."

I couldn't say why it was so important for me to send Reynold away, but it suddenly was. Perhaps it was an act of defiance. If Hudson wasn't willing to give in our relationship, then I wasn't willing either. Or not as willing as I had been, anyway. I was too pissed. Wasn't that a phase of grief?

Besides, I felt strong. I didn't need someone following me around. And Celia hadn't been around in several days—maybe she was bored with the game.

"So I'll see you when I'm off later. Okay?"

Reynold seemed dumbfounded. "Uh, sure. At three. I'll, uh, be here at three."

"Awesome."

The victory with Reynold bolstered me. I hadn't known how I'd be able to get through the night at work. Now I thought I might actually be able to do it. I hadn't forgotten my pain—more thoughts than not had been filled with Hudson—but the misery was almost tolerable.

The time with Liesl had been the most helpful. We hadn't seen much of each other recently, and there was a lot to catch up on. I told her everything that had been going on, including Celia's stalking and Hudson's secretive behavior. It was depressing but also therapeutic.

"Maybe Hudson is really, like, a CIA guy," Liesl said as I handed her a cash drawer for the bar. "And Celia's his partner. And he's abandoned his mission—defected, or whatever they call that, and she's trying to reel him back in."

Her crazy ideas were almost entertaining. "That one's definitely it."

She nudged me aside with her hip to take her place in front of the register. "I wish you'd be serious about this. I know I'm right."

I forced a smile. "Excuse me for being—what do they call it? Oh, yeah—based in reality."

Liesl ran a hand through her purple tresses and laughed. "Reality is so overrated."

"Isn't it?"

We got lost in the hustle and bustle of the night after that. David had trained with Gwen the night before, but it was the first shift that I really got to see her in action. She'd worked enough now that she knew what she was doing. I watched her as she managed the upper floor, keeping on top of change orders and unruly customers, not once missing a beat. She was good, and I'd never felt better about my decision to hire her. Especially now that my whole future at The Sky Launch felt in limbo.

With a shudder, I swallowed the sob forming in my throat. I couldn't think about that. Not here. Not now. In perhaps the same delusional manner I'd used in my days of Paul Kresh or David Lindt, I focused on convincing myself that Hudson and I were fine. This was just a blip. We'd recover and life would go on together.

Somehow it had been easier in the past. I hoped that said more about the current state of my mental health and less about my future with Hudson.

It was still early in the night, only a little past eleven, when I saw Celia.

I'd just come down from the upstairs to check in with the bartenders on the main floor. They were busy but not slammed. I slid behind the bar where Liesl was working and scanned the club, not looking for anything in particular—just getting a general sense of the scene.

The center of the club was surrounded by bunches of seating areas. They usually filled early in the evening. They were the best tables to get since they were right off the dance floor. She was the only one at her table, which was odd for a Saturday night, and that drew my attention. No one sat alone at The Sky Launch.

But there Celia was—alone, wearing tight jeans and a tight tank, her hair down around her shoulders. It was so uncharacteristic of her usual prim and proper look that I wasn't sure it was her. Then she caught my stare, and the wicked grin she gave me confirmed it.

I grabbed Liesl's forearm. "Oh my god."

"What? What is it? Did I fuck up the last order?" Her eyes were wide and alarmed.

"No. She's here. Celia!" I nodded toward the woman who still had her eyes locked on mine.

Liesl followed my gaze. "The stalker chick? Should I kick her ass?"

"No." Though the thought of the tall Amazon at my side kicking the ass of my now arch-nemesis was pretty entertaining.

Liesl squinted as she continued to study Celia. "No offense, but she's a knockout. Not like you're not a knockout, but I'd do her." She bumped me affectionately with her shoulder. "I'd do you harder, though. Of course."

"Wow. I can't believe she actually came here." *Maybe I should call Reynold to come back.* I instantly dismissed the idea. With everyone around, what could she do to me? Even her constant watch was nothing more than annoying.

Rows of goose bumps lined my arms despite my attempts to remain nonplussed. Well, I'd made it over three hours at work before having an emotional breakdown. That was something, right?

"What's going on?" David asked.

I turned to find Gwen and David had joined us. Which meant it was time to get back to the job. "Nothing." I certainly wasn't sharing my Celia story with my ex-boyfriend and an employee I barely knew.

Apparently, Liesl felt differently. "That girl over there is Laynie's crazy stalker."

"Liesl!" I smacked her shoulder with the back of my hand.

"I'm not going to stand by as the only one who knows about this. You need some backup. What if she does something to you? You know, roofies your drink or something."

"Right. 'Cause I'm drinking openly tonight." She was my closest friend, but sometimes she lacked in the intelligence department.

Gwen raised an eyebrow. "You have a stalker? You're cooler than I thought."

I rolled my eyes. "She's not…it's not…I don't even know why she's…" I let out an exasperated breath. "It's complicated. I'm going in the back room if you all need me."

Without looking back, I headed to the employee lounge behind the bar. Seeing Celia had thrown me, and in the shape I was in, that was enough to send me over the edge. I paced the room, trying to get a hold of the composure I'd had earlier in the evening.

Gwen and David followed.

I considered telling them I wanted to be alone. But I wasn't sure I did.

"Are you okay, Laynie?" David's voice was tentative and tender.

"No. Yes. I'm fine. I'm just…"I shook my head, unable to finish the thought. My chest was tight and my head felt like it was going to explode.

"Well, tell us something about her. Your stalker." Gwen genuinely seemed like she wanted to be helpful. "A name. How you know her. Anything."

"Her name's Celia Werner." I was surprised at my willingness to share, yet even more, I needed to talk.

"As in Werner Media?" David kept abreast of the who's who in the business world. Of course he'd recognize her name.

"That's the one," I confirmed.

David stepped closer to me, concern on his face.

"It's nothing to worry about, David. She's just not happy about me being with Hudson."

"Is she the ex?" Gwen asked.

"Yeah." When I'd said that in therapy, it was because it was easier. Now after the video, it was what I truly believed. "She is." For the millionth time, my mind went to thoughts of her kissing Hudson. What else had they done? How close had they been? Had he slept with her?

I swallowed the bile that threatened to come up. "So now she's trying to scare me by showing up where I am. Sending me messages. Stuff like that."

"Do you want us to kick her out? I can call Sorenson up from the door." Unlike Hudson, David's protective mode was subtle, but I recognized it in his face all the same.

"She's not going to hurt me."

"Are you sure?" David put a hand on my shoulder.

"No." I stepped casually out of his grasp. Despite its innocence, his touch felt like a betrayal to Hudson. "But I don't want her to win."

"Fair enough." His body language told me that my brush-off had stung. Another reason it was good he was leaving.

Gwen turned a plastic chair around and straddled it. "It's creepy how she just stares at you like she does."

"Isn't it?" I was still trying to decide how I felt about Gwen knowing about my private life.

"We could spike her drink."

Now this sounded interesting. "With what?"

"I don't know. Spit."

I didn't laugh, but I managed a genuine smile. Okay, Gwen was officially cool. And maybe I needed more people involved in my life—more than just Hudson and his family. The phone call with Brian, the run with Jordan, the day with Liesl—all of it reminded me that there was a whole world outside the one I'd been living in. A world with friends and interests that I'd forgotten about recently.

Whether or not Hudson and I had a future together, I had a future of my own. I couldn't ignore the people that belonged in that future anymore and just hope that they'd still be there when I needed them. And Gwen was now a part of The Sky Launch. That made her family. It was time to embrace her as such.

But just because they were family didn't mean I had to talk about everything with them. And talking wasn't calming me down anyway.

"You know what? I'm fine," I lied. "Don't worry about me. Let's get back out there where we can at least keep an eye on her."

With Gwen in the lead, we stepped back into the club, the flashing lights and thumping beat washing over me with a familiar comfort.

I ran into Gwen's back when she stopped short. "Ah," she said. "She knows we were talking about her. She's calling in reinforcements." She lifted her chin toward Celia. "See?"

I looked toward my stalker and saw she had her cell to her ear.

Just then Liesl walked over to me with the bar phone in her hand, the cord stretched almost to its max distance. "There you are, Laynie, phone call."

"Oh, shit." Gwen's eyes were wide, and I imagined they mirrored my own.

Was Celia calling me?

"Let me take it," David offered.

"And say what?" I shook my head decisively. "I've got it." What was she going to say to me, anyway?

I took the receiver from Liesl's hand, my own hand surprisingly steady. "Hello?"

"Alayna, where is your bodyguard?"

The voice on the line shocked me more than if it had been Celia. "Hudson." I said his name out loud, looking around at my coworkers so they'd know who it was. "Hello to you, too."

A mixture of disappointment and elation swept over me. I'd almost wanted the call to be from Celia—more and more, I was eager to confront her.

But on the other hand, it was Hudson on the phone. *Hudson!* I'd longed for his voice all day. I didn't even care about the circumstances for his call—*he'd called,* that was the point.

"Ah, it's not even her," Gwen said. "That was some mind fuck."

David agreed. "I think she must have been checking messages. I never saw her mouth move."

I looked back at Celia, who was, sure enough, pocketing her phone.

"Could you answer the question, please?" Hudson's voice in my ear drew my attention back to him.

It took me a second to remember what he'd asked—oh, about my bodyguard. As glad as I was to hear from him, I wasn't about to make things easy. "Why do you care?"

"Goddammit, Alayna!"

His voice was so loud that I had to lean my ear away from the receiver. Well, what had I expected? That Reynold wouldn't tell him? "I sent him home. I figured I didn't really need him at the club."

"How's that working out for you?" His sarcasm was lined with frustration.

"I'm fine! With the security guards and cameras and the bouncers..." It took a second for me to realize what his statement meant. "How do you know she's here?"

"Because I'm outside."

"You're outside? Why are you outside?" My heart sped up. He hadn't just called, he was here. I covered the mouthpiece with my hand. "Liesl, hurry, grab the cordless."

Hudson continued. "Thank god your bodyguard works for me and not for you. You don't have the authority to send him home."

Don't have the authority...? "Jesus Christ."

"And when he noticed Celia..."

Liesl handed me the cordless. "Thank you," I whispered.

"Alayna, are you listening to me?"

"Yes. I'm working here too, you know." I punched the talk button on the cordless and handed the other phone to Liesl. "Go on." Then, I bee-lined for the front of the club. If Hudson was there, I wanted to see him, wanted to see the look in his eyes and in his face. See if I could read the emotion that I needed to see from him.

"When he saw Celia entering The Sky Launch, he contacted me, as he's supposed to do, and asked me if he should go in as well since you didn't want him on the premises. I told him yes. So Reynold will be there whether you want him to be or not."

"Fine." I didn't really care anymore. "Send him on in."

"I already did."

"Of course you did." I was almost at the bottom of the ramp now. The club was picking up for the night, and I was fighting against traffic. "But why are you here? You could have arranged all that over the phone." Had he wanted to see me as much as I wanted to see him?

He paused. "I wanted to be sure you were okay." His tone was softer. It tugged at my chest.

"I'm okay." Well, since Hudson was still sleeping in another apartment, maybe that wasn't the right word. "I'm safe, anyway."

"Good." He cleared his throat. "Then I'll talk to you later."

"Hudson, wait!" I was at the front door now, the night air cool compared to the warmth of the club. Not wanting to be seen, I stayed tucked behind the doorman.

"What is it, Alayna?"

I scanned the circle drive in front of the club. There he was standing next to his Mercedes, the emergency lights flashing as he paced the sidewalk next to the car. He was in another three-piece suit. It was late, why was he still dressed for work? And had he really driven all the way out to the club just to leave without seeing me face-to-face?

My next words bubbled with the hurt I'd carried all day. "Is that all you have to say to me?"

"Right now, yes." He shoved his hand through his hair. "You're protected. That's what's important right now."

He'd been concerned—that much was obvious. His hair was tussled as if he'd ran his hand through it more than just the one time, and his agitation was present in his stride.

It wasn't enough. If he really cared, I'd be in his arms. He'd have come in and found me instead of the other way around. "Have you considered that if you just told Celia that you'd left me that she'd probably drop this whole thing?"

He shook his head, even though he had no idea I could see him. "I didn't leave you."

"It sure feels like you did."

He leaned his hand on the top of his car and looked toward the club entrance. "Is that what you want?"

"No!" *Never.* "No. I just want the truth. That's all." The doorman shifted, and my cover was blown. Hudson's eyes met mine.

We stared at each other, locked in our gaze, for several long moments. Even across the hundred feet of sidewalk, there was a current between us. An electric spark that ignited from so much more than chemistry or lust. It was an emotional charge that surged right from the heart of me. We were connected, so completely, that for the first time since he'd walked out of the penthouse the night before, I felt a flash of hope.

He broke the gaze first. He looked to the passenger window of the car, as if someone were inside, talking to him through the glass.

I stepped forward, squinting to see. "Oh my god, are you…?" My stomach fell. "Hudson, are you with Norma?"

Hudson threw his hands in the air. "Not now, Alayna."

I started toward him. "Are you fucking kidding me? One day gone and you're out with her?"

He circled around to the driver's side of the car. "It's for business!" The door slammed.

I picked up my pace, even knowing he'd be gone by the time I reached the curb. "At this time of night?" In a suit, by themselves. How fucking stupid did he think I was?

"It's…I can't get into this right now." He pulled out onto the road. "Why can't you ever just trust me?"

"Because you can never tell me the truth!" I watched the taillights of the car as they mixed in with the rest of the traffic. It was comical, really, to ask for his trust when I'd just witnessed him on what could be described no other way but as a date.

"I have to go. I can't talk to you while I'm driving."

I could hear Norma's voice in the background. I wanted his attention on me, not her. "Wait, don't—"

"Goodbye, Alayna."

"—hang up." The dial tone replaced his voice. "Dammit!" I screamed and threw the phone down on the sidewalk. Hard. It shattered into pieces. Seemed fitting, considering that's how I felt inside.

"Laynie, are you okay?" David's voice was neither surprising nor comforting. Of course he'd come after me. It was a nice gesture—I just wished he were somebody else.

"Yeah." Total lie. My entire body felt weak. Like I could just fall over there on the sidewalk, unable to walk or even crawl back to the club.

But I was strong. I could ignore the fact that I had died inside until I was alone at home. "Yeah, I'm fine," I said again. "I broke the phone." I bent down to collect the pieces off the sidewalk.

David squatted next to me to help. "It's technically Pierce's phone."

"Well, that makes me feel better." Marginally. "Funny, this is the second phone I've destroyed on account of that man."

"Maybe that means something."

"Maybe." I knew what David wanted it to mean. I didn't want to think about what it could mean for me.

When we'd gathered all the parts, David stood and held his hand out to help me stand. Reluctantly, I took it. He didn't let go right away, though. Worse, I didn't pull away.

David studied me with soft eyes. "I'm not going to ask because I know what you'll say. I'm just going to do."

"What?" Next thing I knew, I'd been pulled into his embrace. "Oh."

"It seemed like you could use a hug."

I hesitated for only a second. Then I gave in. For me, it was comfort from a friend, comfort that I needed. He may have taken it as more, but in that moment, my need outweighed his.

Except then he pulled me in tighter. And his arms felt strange and his scent was wrong. As gently as I could, I began to push away. "I think I better..."

David released me, his eyes pinned on the club door behind us. "Hey, look. She's leaving."

I turned to look. Celia was indeed leaving. She'd seen our hug, I was sure. It didn't matter. Even if she told Hudson, he'd been out with Norma Anders. I was certain his trumped mine in terms of disappointing a lover.

David's smile grew tight. "Man, I don't know anything about her, but that smile was wicked. What a bitch."

The pain and hurt of the past twenty-four hours subsided then, leaving in its wake a tidal wave of rage. I was angry, so angry. While a lot of my wrath was meant for Hudson, the greatest portion belonged to Celia. Without her, Hudson and I might be able to work through our differences. But how could we when she was always around, reminding us of our pasts, stirring up our distrust?

My hands balled into fists. "You know what? This is ridiculous. I'm confronting her."

"Laynie, I'm not so sure you should." But that was the extent to which David tried to stop me.

I'd covered more than half the distance between me and Celia when a figure stepped from out of the club and blocked my progression.

"Ms. Withers." Reynold put a gentle but firm hand up to stop me from proceeding. "Not a good idea."

He was right. As worked up as I was, I probably would have punched her. And though it would have felt good, it would be me with the restraining order then, not Celia.

Still, I had to wonder what my bodyguard's orders had been. Did Hudson mean to keep me from trouble, or was he worried if I talked to his ex that I'd learn things he didn't want me to know? "One question, Reynold. Are you protecting me from her? Or protecting her from me?"

"I don't catch your drift."

And even if he did, he likely wouldn't answer honestly. "Never mind."

By then, Celia had made it to the curb and was hailing a cab. Determined to not let her get away without some victory chalked in my square, I approached our doorman. "You see that woman? She's not to be let back in here. Permanently banned."

The doorman nodded. "Yes, ma'am."

"I'll hang her picture in the back room." I'd print something off the Internet. Maybe it wasn't a good move to let her know that she'd gotten to me, but honestly, I didn't care about her game. I simply wanted my life back. Kicking her out of my club was a good first step.

It was just past three when I crawled into bed. Though it still felt too big and lonely, I was pretty sure I was exhausted enough to sleep. It was worth a try anyway.

Even with my determination, I was still tossing and turning when four a.m. rolled around. My insomnia turned out to be a blessing. Otherwise, I may have missed his call.

"Alayna. I need you." The ache in Hudson's voice was new to me.

I sat up with a bolt. "What is it?"

"Mira. At the hospital." He couldn't even speak in full sentences. "The baby…"

I was throwing on my yoga pants and a t-shirt before he finished. "I'll be right there."

"Jordan's already on his way to get you."

— CHAPTER —
FOURTEEN

Hudson was waiting for me outside the emergency room when Jordan dropped me off at the hospital. He'd obviously dressed in a hurry as well. He was wearing jeans and a wrinkled polo I didn't recognize.

Though he didn't smile, his eyes seemed to light up at the sight of me. "She's not in the ER anymore, but this is the only entrance open at this time of the morning." He was already heading toward the elevator.

I trotted to catch up. "Have you seen her? What's going on exactly?"

"All I know is that she's having contractions. Adam called as they were checking in and he texted me when they were moved to the OB ward." He pushed the up button on the call panel. "I didn't want to see her without you."

I reached out and grabbed his hand. He took it without hesitation.

He let go though, when the elevator arrived, gesturing for me to go in first. He followed and hit the floor button, then stuffed both hands in his pockets. He glanced at me sideways, and I felt his ache to touch me. It echoed my own yearning. Still, he didn't reach for me again.

The elevator began moving. "Alayna, about Norma..."

I shook my head. "You don't have to do this now." Didn't he know that I didn't care at the moment? In the past few weeks, I'd grown to love Mira too. If anything happened to her or her baby...

But Hudson went on. "I need you to know—this business deal." He ran a hand through his hair. "It's very important and I've had to be sneaky about the whole thing. Tonight was about that. Norma was able to arrange what looked like a chance meeting with the sellers at a charity gala. When Reynold called and said that you sent him away and that Celia was at the club..." He trailed off and I knew he was imagining the worst. "I didn't even think to arrange a ride home for Norma. I simply grabbed her and we left."

A pang of guilt burrowed through my gut. "Is the deal ruined?"

"No. And it wouldn't matter if it was." He turned to me and brushed his thumb across my cheek. "You're safe, precious. That's all I care about."

I closed my eyes, savoring his caress.

Then the door opened, and his hand fell to his side.

We followed the signs pointing to OB, eventually reaching a set of doors that required us to buzz to get in. "Will they let us in at this time of night?" I asked while we waited for a response.

"It's my impression that babies are born twenty-four hours a day," he said. "And we're on her list."

Mira was only six months along, though. Hopefully her baby wasn't coming any time soon.

"May I help you?" a voice said through the intercom.

"We're here to see Mirabelle Sitkin. Hudson Pierce and Alayna Withers."

Instead of an answer, the door simply opened automatically.

I smiled lightly. "I guess we've been approved."

Mira's room was easy to spot because Adam, Jack, Sophia and Chandler were standing in the hall outside. Hudson went straight to Sophia. He put his arm around her and bent to kiss her cheek. "Mother."

"Thanks for being here, Hudson." Sophia's hand was shaking as she hugged her son, and I couldn't help but wonder if she was emotional about Mira or simply in need of a drink. Either way, she was with it enough to throw a glare in my direction. "You brought her?" Her tone accentuated her disgust.

"Yes, and you'll not say another word about it." At least Hudson was still defending me to Sophia. That had to mean something.

Jack gave me a warm smile, reaching out to squeeze my hand. "It's good to see you, Laynie."

Neither Sophia's insult nor Jack's welcome registered very high on my interest level. I only cared about Mira—my friend.

I peeked around Jack past the open door and found Mira lying in the bed surrounded by two nurses. They looked calm enough. Hopefully that was a sign that things weren't dreadful.

Hudson wasn't the type to simply hope. "What's her status?" he asked Adam.

"She's fine. Now." Adam's expression looked tired and concerned, but his words were only slightly strained. "When we came in she was having contractions every three minutes. But they got her hooked up on an IV, got lots of fluids in her, and everything settled down. She hasn't had any contractions now for almost forty minutes. Her blood pressure is still a little high, though, so they want to keep her here a bit. Fortunately, they don't think it's pre-eclampsia, but they'll watch her at her visits."

"We can go back in as soon as the nurses are done," Jack said.

Chandler nudged Hudson with his elbow. "Mira said Mom and Dad were making her too tense. She sent us here for a timeout."

The twinkle in Adam's eye said he had found as much amusement in the statement as Chandler had. "She is a bit feisty at the moment."

The nurses came out then. One stopped to talk to us, or Adam, rather. "She's doing better, Dr. Sitkin. I'm sure she'll be out of here in the next couple of hours. When you go back in, try to keep things light and relaxed."

"Thanks." Adam gestured toward the door. "After you, Laynie. I know she'll be happy to see you here."

I nodded, surprised and touched that he thought I meant that much to his wife. I made my way inside. Hudson followed close behind me, but not so near that we were touching.

"Mira." I offered a warm smile.

"Hey! You came!" She tried to reach toward me, but the cuff on her arm kept her trapped.

"Of course we did. Don't be silly." I stepped aside for Hudson to slip in, eager for him to get a chance to connect with Mira as well. Hudson was family. I was only the girlfriend. And maybe I wasn't even that.

"Hudson." Mira smiled up at her brother. "Thank you for being here."

He nodded and it struck me that he was too overcome with emotion to speak. I remembered then how hard it was for him to say how he felt—not just with me but with everyone. Mira had once told me Hudson never gave out *I love you*s. Even to her. But the look in his eyes said he felt it for her in spades.

Was that the way he looked at me? I wanted to say yes, but it was hard to be objective.

Hudson patted his sister's hand then stepped away, turning his back to her momentarily. He was getting himself together. More than anything I wanted to go to him, to reassure him. But his body language so far had shown he didn't necessarily want it.

My eyes stung. Again and again he shut me out. Even with something as normal as sharing concern over his sister, he couldn't let me in. Didn't he know how much it killed me?

This wasn't the time to dwell on it. Forcing my smile in place, I stepped near Jack and gave my attention to Mira.

"I have to tell you," she said to no one in particular, "this whole incident has proven one thing—labor is going to be a bitch. Those contractions hurt like a mother and when they hooked me up to this thing—" She gestured to the monitor. "They barely registered."

Sophia sat in the armchair next to Mira. "Has this finally changed your mind about taking Lamaze?" Her condescension suggested this had been an ongoing battle.

Mira rolled her eyes. "It's changed my mind about wanting drugs. I'd like them as soon as I arrive, please." She hooked eyes with Adam, who had slipped in on the other side of her. "Can you add that to the birthing plan, honey?"

"Add them? I'm demanding them." He brushed her hair from her forehead. "Sorry, but you're not a nice person when you're in pain."

Mira's eyes flared. "You keep that up and I'll exclude you from the birthing room." Adam hadn't been kidding when he'd said she was feisty.

Chandler laughed. "I don't think she's joking."

"Do they know what caused this in the first place?" Hudson's question drew the room's attention back to him. Though he was engaging now in the conversation, he still wasn't huddling close like the rest of us.

Mira's gaze flicked from me to Hudson. "A combination of dehydration and stress. *Stress*. Do you all hear that?" She narrowed her eyes and scanned the room. "So you two right there—" She gestured to Sophia and Jack. "You need to get your shit together because you are hurting me and my baby."

Sophia's mouth tightened, but she refused to look at Jack who stared after her tenderly. Man, he really did love her.

"And you two—" This time Mira pointed to me and then Hudson. "Don't think I don't notice how you're standing apart. And you're barely looking at each other. I don't even want to know what the hell is going on with you right now. Go work it out." The cuff on Mira's arm began clicking as it tightened around her. She turned her attention to the numbers on the screen next to her.

I froze, not sure if she was actually sending us away or if she meant for us to work things out later.

Chandler seemed to get the sense that she meant now. "Are you kicking out Mom and Dad too?"

"No. Their crap is too messed up to fix on demand. But those two—" She sent us both scathing looks. "You better not be that messed up."

"Might as well get comfy then." Chandler settled on the couch and began playing on his phone.

I exchanged glances with Hudson. *Shit.* He wanted to be with Mira—and she was wrong, our crap was too big to solve quickly.

Hudson stepped toward his sister. "Mirabe—"

"I'm not kidding, Hudson. Leave. I don't want to see either of you until you've got that happy glow again." The machine next to her flashed a read-out. "See? My blood pressure is spiking. Jesus."

"Mira," Adam said, "just take deep breaths. Settle down. Stop yelling at everyone."

"I'm not yelling at everyone. I'm yelling at them!"

Adam turned to me and Hudson, his expression apologetic.

"We're going." Hudson gestured for me to proceed in front of him. "But we'll be back," he said over his shoulder.

"Happy and glowing," Mira yelled after us.

We walked in silence toward the waiting room at the end of the hall. With each step, my heart grew heavier. This was wrong. I shouldn't be there at the hospital. Hudson should. As for working things out, it was going to take him opening up. And he was certainly not ready for that. His attitude to me since we'd arrived proved that.

At the waiting room, Hudson held the door open for me to go in first. It was a small room, completely enclosed with several couches and a counter with coffee supplies. It was empty, thankfully. Babies might be born at all hours, but no one was expecting one at the moment. At least that gave us privacy.

I turned to face Hudson as he shut the door behind him. "I know you want to be in there with your sister. I can leave. Or we can pretend things are all hunky-dory, if you'd rather. I'll under—"

Hudson cut me off. "Don't leave."

His desperation stunned me. Did that mean he *did* want me there? The man was a bunch of mixed signals. This signal I liked. I'd cling to it, if he'd let me. "Okay. I'll stay."

"For Mira."

My spirits plummeted. "For Mira. Of course." Not for him. He didn't want me to stay for him.

All of a sudden, I wasn't sure if I could do it anymore, if I could remain self-controlled around him. I turned away and made my way to a couch. With shaking knees, I took a seat.

Sitting was better. It made me feel stronger than I was. I thought about the reason we were there—the perky romantic sitting in the room nearby. Her faith and encouragement had been instrumental in reuniting me with Hudson. Even if she couldn't save us again, I owed her.

I lifted my chin and met Hudson's eyes. "Then we need to put everything else aside for right now and give Mira our happy face."

He held my gaze for only a second. "I agree."

There was plenty of room on the couch by me, but he took a seat in a chair instead. He couldn't even sit by me. The rejection rippled through me with excruciating pain. Every move he made, everything he said, hurt.

I wanted to do the same to him. Wanted to hurt him in all the ways he'd hurt me. My fists tightened into balls as I thought about ripping into him, telling him all the things that were barely under the surface of my composure.

But again, I remembered why we were there. Mira would be upset if we didn't walk back in her room together. The best thing I could do for her and myself was make a plan and get back to her. Back to the comfort of people who made me feel good rather than sad.

Obviously this would require some acting. A lot of acting. "So any idea how to give Mira a happy face? Because she read right through us in there."

"She is very perceptive." Hudson leaned forward, his elbows on his thighs, his chin in his hands. "But I think if we wait here for a while, give us time to supposedly talk things out, then if we go back in there with smiles and...holding hands, she'll believe it." His pause said that even holding hands sounded uncomfortable for him. "She wants to believe it, so she will."

I made a gruff sound in the back of my throat. "Pretending we're a couple. Just like old times."

His head spun toward me. He fastened me with a piercing stare. "We aren't pretending we're a couple. We *are* a couple. We're pretending that we're...that we're not..." He moved his hand in the air as he tried to figure out how to finish his sentence.

When he didn't come up with an end, I pushed him. "That we're not... what? Not fighting? Not completely confused and heartbroken? Not miserable and lied to?" My voice cracked, and I refused to cry. Biting my lip, I crossed one leg over the other and put all my energy into jostling my knee up and down. It helped to focus my pain.

Hudson stared at the wall across from him, refusing to respond or look at me.

I should have dropped it, but I couldn't help myself. "I don't understand how you can say we're a couple when you're living in one place and I'm in another. When you're on dates with another woman."

"I told you what that was," he said quietly.

I ignored him. "When you won't even let me touch you without acting like it burns." I shook my head. I was getting too upset. "I said I wouldn't do this here. I'm sorry." Except I really wasn't. "Sort of."

I wanted him to refute my words, wanted him to explain how things really were. But he didn't. Sure, it wasn't the time or place—I knew that in my head. My heart, on the other hand, didn't care. I was in so much pain, how could he not be? And if he wasn't, what did that mean?

It means he can compartmentalize, I told myself. That's all. God, what I'd give to believe that was all it was.

We sat in silence, the only sound the clicking of the seconds ticking by on the wall clock. Finally, Hudson spoke, his voice low and sincere. "Touching you only burns because it reminds me how much I want to touch you more."

A wave of optimism burst through me, so tangible and fierce that my whole chest felt on fire. "Then touch me more, H. Come home."

He raised a brow and his expression carried the same air of hope that I felt. "And you'll let the past lie?"

With everything in me I wanted to say yes. Yes, I'll live with it. Whatever it is. I'd find a way. I'd said that before, and I'd thought I meant it. But I'd been talking desperate. I couldn't live with it. There was no possible way.

Besides, I respected myself more than that. I respected our relationship more than that. Even if it meant losing him, I had to stand my ground on this. “No. I can’t let it lie. But you can tell me what it is you’re hiding.”

With a shake of his head, he dismissed it.

There we were again—at our impasse. “We might as well be broken up, Hudson, if you can’t believe that I’d love you beyond whatever this secret is.”

And if we truly couldn’t get past this, why were we even taking time apart? Weren’t we just postponing the inevitable?

It wasn’t something I could face. Not yet. Maybe the time apart was to help make that idea more bearable.

Apparently, Hudson felt the same way. “Let’s not do this here.”

“Let’s not.” *Let’s not do this at all. Let’s go back to where we were three days ago, lost and alone in the mountains.* Happy and glowing, as Mira put it.

If there were anything I’d ever wished for more, I didn’t know what it was.

But wishing wouldn’t get us through the next hour. I stood up and paced the room. “Okay. We’ll go in there. We’ll smile. We’ll hold hands. We’ll be happy and glowing. And Mira will never know the lie.”

“Yes,” Hudson said. “Thank you.”

“What if she asks what our problem was?”

“She won’t.”

I wasn’t so sure and the expression I shot him said exactly that.

“If she does ask, let me handle it.”

“Yes, I’ll do that.” The venom I was trying to bite back slipped past my lips. “You are the master manipulator, after all.”

He stared at me with sad eyes. I’d meant to hurt him, and it worked. But he didn’t argue, didn’t defend himself. He wouldn’t even fight with me. Wouldn’t fight *for* me.

It’s not the place, I reminded myself. The reminder didn’t change the hollow ache in my chest. I knew his indifference extended beyond the walls of the hospital.

Hudson stood. “Are you ready to go back?” He shoved his hands in his pockets, obviously keeping them from my reach.

Fucking asshole.

I didn’t let him know how much his simple gesture felt like a knife in the gut. “You think she’ll believe this was long enough?”

"Yes." He moved to the door and held it open for me. "If we convince her that all is well, then she won't focus on the timespan in the least. She'll have no reason to question what we're selling." He was so clinical about it. So proficient about the steps of pulling off a scheme.

And why wouldn't he be? "Tips from the expert," I said as I passed him.

"You're very good at lashing out, precious. It's interesting that I'm just learning this now." He was behind me, and he said it quietly, but I heard him all the same.

I held on to his endearment—*precious*—like it was gold. Like it was the last drop of water in a desert. Like it was a beacon in a dark storm. He couldn't still call me that and not feel something for me. Could he?

We hurried back to Mira's room, not speaking or looking at each other. Outside her door, Hudson paused. His hand hung at his side now. I placed mine in it automatically, as if it were the most natural thing in the world. Because it was that natural. The way it fit so snugly, so perfectly in his. As if we'd been made to lace our fingers in just that way.

He looked down at where we were joined, studying our hands for long seconds. There was sadness and yearning in his tone when he spoke. "Your hand fits so well in mine, doesn't it? Like it belongs."

I had to turn my head in order to fight the tears. He was so in sync with me. Why, why, why were we apart?

"I didn't mean to say that out loud," he said. "I apologize. Can you still do this?"

Forcing a smile on my face, I turned back to him. "Yep."

"Showtime, then." Hudson led us in, entering with much more zeal than he had earlier. "We're back." He headed straight for his sister, placing a sweet kiss on her forehead. "And everything's fine."

He was such an excellent liar. I'd known he had to be. I'd seen him pretend to his family about me before. Then I'd convinced myself that his acting was so good because he'd actually felt something for me. Seeing Hudson now, so easily falling into the charade—it stung. How much of the past had been a lie as well?

Mira narrowed her eyes. "I want to hear it from Laynie. I don't trust you." She swatted him aside.

Taking a deep breath, I pushed away my heartache and reminded myself this was for Mira. I gave her what I feared could only be taken as a fake grin and slid in closer to her. "Everything really is fine." I looked back at Hudson, hoping for a sign to make the lie easier. I received none. "Maybe not perfect, but things are definitely fine."

Mira frowned dubiously.

Damn. I needed to get my shit together.

Before I could, Hudson stepped in to save the farce. He wrapped his arms around me from behind, a major show of public affection for Hudson. "I don't know what you're talking about. Things are completely perfect."

He nuzzled his face against my hair and I shivered with an unwelcome tingle from head to toe. I sighed into him. How could I not? This was what I wanted—to be held by him, to be loved by him.

But this was fake. It had to be or he'd tell me what I needed to know. Right?

Either way, Mira bought it. She clapped her hands together. "Ah, see? The happy and glowing is back! Thank god." She cast her eyes around the room, stopping first at her mother beside her, then Adam and Chandler and Jack on the sofa, then to me and Hudson in front of her. "This is the best. Now my whole family's here."

I shifted, feeling a little uncomfortable at her declaration. I wasn't family. And at the moment, I was sure I never would be. The farce was going too far. I opened my mouth to protest.

Sophia beat me to it. "Well, not everyone here is family."

Mira glared at her mother. "She is. And right now I'd send you out before Laynie. Since I want all my family here, you can sit over there with your mouth shut and pretend you're shaking because you're cold and when you get home you can have the drink you wish was in that water bottle."

All eyes darted from Mira to Sophia to me. The tension was so thick and palpable. I felt I had to say something. "I should go, Mira. The sentiment is nice, but I'm not really family."

Jack met my eyes. "Yes. You are."

Hudson tightened his grasp around me. "Agreed."

I nodded, not daring to speak. My throat was thick and my eyes filled with tears. At least when Mira looked at me, she thought I was crying out of happiness. She had no idea she was watching my heart break even more.

— CHAPTER —
FIFTEEN

Mira was released shortly after seven a.m. under strict orders to take it easy and drink more water. We all walked out together, Adam and Jack fussing over Mira as an attendant wheeled her to the front door. While I'd both hoped and feared that Hudson would drive me home himself, Jordan was waiting as we exited the main doors. Hudson must have texted him while I wasn't watching.

The others had to wait for the valet to bring their cars up, so I was the first to say goodbye. I bent to hug Mira. "Take care of yourself, sister. I don't want to be back at Lenox Hill until you're pushing out a baby—and that better be months from now."

"I couldn't agree more. Thanks for coming, Laynie."

"Anytime." I straightened. "Well, my ride's here." After all the talk of being part of the family, leaving by myself felt extra lonely. My mixed feelings were no longer mixed—I wanted Hudson to drive me home. Desperately.

"Your ride…?" Mira looked from me to Hudson, obviously questioning the different cars.

"We're off to separate places," Hudson said. "Alayna gets to go home and crawl in bed. I'm off to work." Always prepared with an answer, he was. Except when I was asking the questions.

Mira scowled. "You're going to work after no sleep? And I'm the one getting yelled at about working too hard."

Hudson waved his hand dismissively. "I got enough sleep." He walked me to the Maybach, opening the back door for me. "I should kiss you goodbye," he said quietly so that only I could hear.

"I suppose you should. Do you want to?" I held my breath, afraid of the answer. I didn't know the answer for myself. It was like what he said in the hospital waiting room—kissing him only reminded me how I wanted to kiss him more. And knowing that I wouldn't kiss him more anytime soon felt like razorblades to my chest.

His response only heightened my pain. "I've never kissed you just for show, precious. I'm not about to start now." But his actions said differently when he bent in to deliver a partially open-mouthed kiss, no tongue. The type of affection suitable for onlookers.

Without permission, my hand flew to the back of his neck. I held him there, locking our lips for much longer than I believe he'd intended. When I finally pulled away, I made sure I had the last word. "That would be easier to believe if your actions matched your words. But, let me guess—you're not about to start that now either, are you?"

I slipped in the car and slammed the door before he could respond.

AFTER FIVE HOURS of restless sleep, I woke up with another throbbing headache, swollen eyes, and a plan.

I made two phone calls, right off the bat. One of them was productive, earning me an appointment for the next day with someone who, hopefully, could shed some light on Hudson's recent behavior.

The other call got me nowhere. Mirabelle didn't go into work, of course, so it was Stacy that answered when I called the shop. That was fine. She was whom I wanted to talk to anyway. But even though I pleaded and put on my sweetest voice, she refused to talk any more about the video she'd sent.

"I told you, I'm done," she said and hung up.

I bounced my knee as I thought about what to do next. Then I made one more call. "Can you come over for a bit? I need your help with something."

"Um, sure." Liesl sounded groggy, as if I'd woken her up. It was just after one p.m. I probably *had* woken her. "I need, like, twenty. And coffee."

"Awesome. I'll send my driver to get you. With Starbucks."

I got off the phone, showered and dressed in record speed, and then dove into my project. Projects, I'd learned in therapy, even ridiculously unnecessary ones, were excellent forms of distraction. They helped keep me from doing the crazy things I tended to do when I was hurting. It was possible that this project in particular was as crazy as the things it kept me from doing, but I was ignoring that.

More than an hour later, Liesl and I sat on the floor of the library surrounded by books—the books that Hudson had ordered for me through Celia. While most of them hadn't been marked at all, we were pulling those that were. They were easy to find. All of them were bookmarked by Celia Werner's business card. I planned on burning the pile when we were finished.

"Here's another one." Liesl read the highlighted quote. "'*Don't cry, I'm sorry to have deceived you so much, but that's how life is.*' It's from *Lolita*."

I cringed. Nabokov. One of my favorites. "Put it in the to-go pile." On the notepad next to me I scribbled down the quote.

She stacked it with the others that had been highlighted—the books I planned to get rid of. "What do you think it means?"

I shook my head and looked over the list in my lap. There were several from my favorite books and some from books I'd never read:

"People could put up with being bitten by a wolf but what properly riled them was a bite from a sheep." James Joyce, *Ulysses*

"He who controls the past controls the future. He who controls the present controls the past." George Orwell, *1984*

"Blameless people are always the most exasperating." George Eliot, *Middlemarch*

"Once a bitch always a bitch, what I say." William Faulkner, *The Sound and the Fury*

"There ain't no sin and there ain't no virtue. There's just stuff people do." John Steinbeck, *The Grapes of Wrath*

"It's not my fate to give up—I know it can't be." Henry James, *The Portrait of a Lady*

"There is no harm in deceiving society as long as she does not find you out." E.M. Forster, *A Passage to India*

There was another page, much of the same. If there was a hidden message, I couldn't find it. "I'm beginning to think none of them mean anything. They're simply ominous quotations intended to mess with my mind."

Liesl snatched the list from me. She scanned it quickly. "I think she's talking about herself. She doesn't think she's harming anyone, she's not going to give up, she thinks she controls stuff, and she's a bitch." She tossed the notepad to the ground and reached for another book. “So spill it. Why did you so badly want me here for this only mildly entertaining task?”

I twisted my lips. “I didn’t. There’s something else.” With a deep breath, I spilled the plan that had occupied my mind since waking.

When I was finished, Liesl sat back against the couch, her forehead pinched. “So let me get this straight—you’re going to obsess and stalk people on purpose?”

“Research,” I corrected. “Research, dammit! Not stalk.” Though the idea sounded much better in my head than when I said it out loud.

“You’re obsessed with your boy toy’s past. And you want to *track down* people to research whatever he’s hiding from you. Right? Or did I miss something?”

“That’s exactly it.” I nodded more enthusiastically than necessary. “That’s not stalking. That’s talking to people. People who have insight into Hudson. If he won’t tell me what I want to know, then I can ask them. Get a clearer picture.”

Liesl shot me a disapproving glance.

“Why is this not an ideal plan?” I’d hoped she’d be more supportive. Especially since parts of the idea were already in action.

“Because you have a history of being, you know…” She clicked her tongue and circled a finger in the air next to her head, the universal sign for psycho. “I’ll just say it. Cuckoo. You’ve been cuckoo. And I haven’t been to that many of your group thingies, but I seem to remember that snooping and prying and digging into people’s stuff are all on the no-no list.”

I shut my eyes so I wouldn’t be tempted to roll them. Liesl had been to a few of my meetings. I hadn’t realized she’d actually paid attention. “This is different.”

She nodded. “Yes, it is.” Then she stopped nodding and raised a brow. “How exactly?”

Inwardly I groaned. To me, the difference was obvious. “The other times it was a compulsion. I couldn’t help myself. This time, I’m choosing it. It makes it totally different.”

“Uh-huh. Totally different.” She didn’t seem convinced. “And why am I here? ‘Cause if you want me to tell you you’re not crazy, that’s not happening.”

“Then, well, fine. Think I’m crazy.” Liesl’s version of sanity wasn’t necessarily one for the textbooks anyway. “But I also need your help.”

Her eyes lit up. "You want me to take down that Selina bitch?" She punched a fist into her palm a few times.

"*Celia*," I corrected. "What is with you and getting names wrong?"

"It's fun to watch you get all I-know-everything and correct me." She smacked her gum with a wide smile. "I really will take Ms. Celia Werner down if you want me to. I'll kick her ass so hard she'll lose that cute bubble butt of hers." Without any guilt she added, "Yeah, I checked out her behind. Sue me."

"Um, no. No ass kicking. Please." Liesl could do it, though. She was a brute when she wanted to be. And wouldn't that be awesome to see Celia with her pretty little face bruised and bloodied?

But that hadn't been the help I'd needed from Liesl. I had another plan in mind. Perching on the coffee table next to where she sat on the floor, I put on my puppy dog eyes. "I was hoping you could come with me to see someone."

"Oh, Jesus. You're trying to convert me to stalking too?"

"There's no stalking." It wasn't in the plan, anyway. "I just need to talk to a lady that doesn't want to talk to me. I'm hoping if I'm not alone, she might be more amicable."

Liesl grinned, obviously flattered with the request. "You think I'm intimidating, don't you? You want me to intimidate the fuck out of her."

"Yeah. Sure."

Her smile widened.

Then it fell. "God, I don't know, I don't know!" She stood up and began walking in a circle. "The whole thing seems really fun. And I want to be a good friend. But I'm not sure if I should be supporting you or putting up a big fat stop sign in your path." She brought her hands to her forehead, massaging her temples. "What to do, what to do? Maybe we should call Brian."

I flew up from the table. "You should be *supporting me*. Please! And we don't need to call Brian." I heaved a lungful of air out, trying to calm down. My plan could work without Liesl's help, but I needed her to understand, at least. Needed her to realize how close to the edge I was, how, as far as I was concerned, this was my last chance. My last chance at sanity.

"Okay. You might be right—this might not be the healthiest of ideas." I waited until Liesl's eyes were on mine before continuing. "But here's the thing—if I don't take some control over this limbo state that my relationship is in, then I'm going to end up doing the stalking and obsessing and all of that anyway. I'm being proactive. I'm taking a stand for once instead of letting a guy walk all over me. Because if not this, I only have two other choices—let Hudson and me stay in this '*time apart*' mode, which is asinine and unproductive and really leaves me as a doormat. Or break up. And I'm not ready to lose him." My lip trembled with the raw honesty. "And I don't think he's ready to lose me. Or he would have ended things already."

Liesl's eyes grew compassionate. But also concerned. "You are so over-thinking this, Laynie."

I threw my hands emphatically to the side. "No! I'm not. I'm *fighting* for the guy I love." My eyes stung with the tears that seemed to be ever-present as of late. "Yes, I'm pissed that he's not fighting for me, but maybe he doesn't know how to fight for anyone. Maybe he needs me to show him."

If Liesl still had reservations, she hid them. "All right, I'm in. What else am I going to do with my afternoon, anyway?"

"Really? Thank you. Thank you!" I hugged her. Though her company wasn't crucial, I was desperate for it. Her presence helped with the unending loneliness that occupied my heart since Hudson had walked out the door.

When I let her go, she shrugged dismissively. "It's all good. Besides, this book project is pretty much done."

I looked around at the mess. There were still a few unmarked stacks that needed to be shelved. That could be done later. "Then I'm ready to go if you are."

"Yup." She grabbed her backpack from the couch. "Where we headed, anyway?"

"Greenwich Village."

I'd told Jordan that I'd be leaving later. I texted him now and found he was already waiting in the parking garage. After grabbing my purse and my cell phone, we stepped in the elevator.

We stood next to each other, leaning against the back wall. Liesl nudged my shoulder. "Have you considered that you might not like what you uncover with all this?"

The sinking feeling in my chest wasn't just from the descent of the elevator. "I'm pretty certain that whatever it is, it might kill me." That was the bitch about the situation—Hudson had confessed pretty shitty stuff already. If he couldn't tell me this, it had to be bad.

So why was I so desperate to find out?

Because that's who I was. And whatever this was, it was who he was too. "It might kill me, but I need to know. And then I can move on, preferably with Hudson."

It didn't fix the bigger problem—Hudson wasn't being honest with me. But maybe if he realized that I really would love him no matter what, he'd be able to let his last walls come down and we could finally start working on rebuilding our relationship together.

SINCE NEITHER OF us had eaten, we stopped to grab souvlakia from a food cart nearby before heading to the Village. By the time we got to Mirabelle's, it was nearly four. I wasn't positive that Stacy would still be there, or that she'd be available to talk. Or that she'd answer the bell when I rang. Their clients could only come by appointment. If she wasn't expecting anyone, would she open the door?

Maybe showing up unannounced was a long shot, but when she'd hung up on me, this was the only way I could think of to get a few questions answered.

At the door, a sudden flashback of the first time I'd been there flooded my memory. I'd been so nervous, standing there waiting with Hudson for his sister to answer. It had been our first outing as a couple—as a *pretend* couple. The fear that I'd mess up the charade had been immense, but more than that, the sizzling energy between me and the man that stood at my side had threatened to light me on fire. Threatened to consume me.

In the end, it *had* consumed me, and that was why I was there now—burned and blistered and broken.

Before ringing, I turned to Liesl. "This is where I need you. There's a peephole. If Stacy looks through it and sees me, I'm not sure she'll open the door."

"Cool. I got this."

I moved to the side of the building and made myself flush with the wall. At my nod, she rang the bell. The door opened almost immediately.

"Hi. Vanessa Vanderhal?" Stacy asked Liesl.

She must have been waiting for a client. Before Liesl could answer, I stepped into view.

"Oh, no. Not you." Stacy began to shut the door.

But Liesl wedged her shoulder in the entrance before the opening got too narrow. "Hey, she only has a few questions. Nothing that's going to take more than a few minutes. You're the only one she can ask. Can't you help a girl out? Woman to woman?"

I'd known Liesl could be intimidating. I didn't realize she could also be charming.

Stacy narrowed her eyes, considering. Considering was better than I'd expected, to be honest.

I looked to Liesl, mentally sending her signals to lay on more charm since it seemed to be working.

She apparently wasn't on the same wavelength. "If you aren't interested in doing this the easy way, I'm willing to go another route. I'll introduce myself—I'm Liesl. I have a triple black belt in karate and I do competitive boxing on the side. So come on. Let us in."

The extent of Liesl's fighting skills was kickboxing at a nearby gym. But Stacy didn't know that.

Stacy groaned. "Oh, all right. Come on in. But make it quick. I have a client in fifteen."

I was more relieved than I realized I would be. There were too many questions about the video that could only be answered by three people. And I wasn't about to ask Celia. "Thank you, Stacy. We'll be in and out. I promise."

She widened the door for us to come in. "Yeah, yeah." To herself, she muttered, "I knew there wouldn't be an end to this." As soon as we were in, she let the door slam and crossed her arms over her chest. "What is it you want to know? I didn't stage the video, if that's what he's convinced you."

Obviously we were having our conversation in the front entry of the store. At least she'd let us in.

"No, he didn't." I supposed he deserved credit for that—for not denying that the kiss had taken place. By avoiding telling me anything, he'd avoided making up a lie. Was that an effort to remain true to our promise to be honest with each other? If so, didn't he realize that concealment was just another form of lie?

"Actually," I said, "he won't tell me anything about the video at all."

"Ah, I see." Stacy rubbed her gloss-shined lips together. "And so you're asking me instead."

The judgment and superiority lacing her words irked me to no end. I wanted to shake the woman by her thin shoulders and tell her she didn't know. That she couldn't understand.

But I was trying to play nice. And why would she understand anyway? My best friend was having a hard time figuring out why it was so important to me to uncover Hudson's secrets, why would a practical stranger get it?

She wouldn't.

I gritted my teeth. "Yes, that's exactly what I'm doing. I'm going behind his back and asking you instead. It's definitely not one of my finer moments."

Stacy stared at me hard for several seconds. "Well, we've all experienced some of those, I suppose." Her shoulders relaxed ever so slightly. "So he doesn't know you're here?"

I shook my head.

"And you're not planning to tell him?"

"No." Guilt shuddered through me like a cold chill. Hudson hadn't asked me not to talk to Stacy again, but I'd promised to be open and truthful with him. Not telling him felt secretive. Sure, he wasn't living up to his promise, and he'd called for a fucking break—those facts probably excused me from the open-door policy. But I'd said I was done keeping secrets. Period. Either I meant it or I wasn't worthy of him in the first place. And if I wasn't worthy of being with him, why did this whole detective scheme matter?

I changed my answer. "Actually, that's a lie. I will tell him." If I ever actually had a chance to speak to him again. "I told you before—we're working on honesty. I can't betray him." Even if he'd betrayed me by not being forthcoming.

My transparency had likely cost me Stacy's cooperation, but my only other option was to lie to her. And that seemed shitty too.

She pursed her lips, her eyes darting back and forth between me and Liesl. Finally, she sighed, leaning back on the counter behind her. "What do you want to know?"

Knowing our time was short, I jumped right in. "Why did you film Hudson and Celia kissing? I mean, what did you plan to do with the video in the first place?"

"Prove he was lying." She said it matter-of-factly, as if I'd understand with just that much. When she realized I didn't, she expounded. "I was supposed to meet him that night. For coffee—I think I told you that before. As

I was walking up, I saw him with *her*. He'd protested so much about them being a couple that I knew he'd deny it again. So I filmed it. As proof."

My chest tightened. Oh, how the protest story sounded familiar. Still, there were holes. "But you never showed it to him."

She shook her head. "I didn't end up needing to. I walked up to them right after I filmed it. While they were still…like that." She cringed as if the memory of seeing them kissing hurt her.

I knew how that felt. And it hurt doubly that Stacy was upset about it. She obviously had something with him, even though he'd denied it. How many women had he been with that he'd told me he hadn't? Was Norma also on that list?

Well, that I'd find out tomorrow, if all went as planned.

Stacy brushed a strand of golden hair off her face. "I'd filmed them in case they stopped before I got there. In case he denied it. But he didn't."

No, denial wasn't Hudson's thing—redirection was. And avoidance.

Or maybe that was just with me. "What did he do when he saw you?"

Stacy's nose crinkled as she recalled the scene. "He acted surprised, even though I was supposed to be meeting him. Or maybe it was because he'd lost track of time or forgotten he was meeting me. I don't know. Celia apologized first, which was strange because I didn't realize she knew anything about me. Then Hudson apologized. Most of the explaining came from Celia. I guess he was shocked to have been caught or something. I really didn't listen to most of what she said. I was shocked as well. And too busy feeling stupid."

"Feeling stupid?" This was where I needed clarification. Hudson had seemed honestly perplexed when I'd mentioned Stacy had been there to meet him.

"Yes, stupid. He'd made me feel like he liked me, you know?" She seemed to be recalling an old ache that hadn't healed entirely. "And all the time he was with her. Why would he do that? "

"Why do any men cheat on their women?" Liesl asked then returned to biting the nail she'd been working on since we'd arrived.

I frowned. Of all the negative traits I was realizing about my lover, I sure hoped cheating wasn't one I had to add to the list.

Stacy protested the logic in that. "He asked me to meet him, though. Hudson Pierce doesn't seem like the type to mix up his dates. If anyone could successfully pull off an affair, that man could."

That's exactly why Norma scared me. But, like Stacy was saying, if Hudson were really with Norma—or back then, with Celia—wouldn't he be better at covering his tracks? That was the part that didn't make sense.

Maybe Stacy had misread his intentions. "How did he make you feel like he liked you? I thought you only accompanied him to that charity event last year." Taking a stab in the dark, I added, "I didn't realize you were together."

Stacy lowered her eyes. "We weren't. Not really." She ran her hands along the counter behind her. "After that charity event he never asked me out again. But we talked a lot—by email. He flirted. Sent me flowers a couple of times. That's why I thought there was a possibility. That night on the video was the first time he'd offered to see me in person again."

"Maybe they were dicking with you together." Liesl wiped her freshly "manicured" hand on her jeans. "You know. Like maybe the emails weren't from him."

"You mean Celia sent them?" I considered it. I'd certainly learned Celia wasn't to be trusted, that she'd manipulate information for her benefit. "Yeah, she could have." And I liked that scenario better than some of the others.

Stacy, on the other hand, didn't like the idea at all. She straightened up to her full height and narrowed her eyes in my direction. "Are you saying that you think Hudson couldn't possibly like me? That's pretty nervy to assume. What, you don't think I'm good enough for him?"

Man, that woman had claws. It wasn't even me who'd suggested the idea.

I put my hands up in an attempt to calm her. "No. That's not it at all. There's just details that don't add up. Like you said he seemed surprised to see you there. And when I mentioned you being there to meet him, he had no idea what I was talking about. Total deer in the headlights. Maybe he was faking his reaction—I'm not denying that's a possibility. But that's exactly why I wanted to talk to you. I'm trying to figure it out for myself."

Liesl poked me with her elbow. "And tell her about Celia WerWhore."

I ignored her jab though it inwardly made me smile. "That's the other thing, Stacy. Celia tried to pull a scam on me recently. And now she's messing with me in other ways. I may not be the first of Hudson's interests to get that treatment."

Stacy's posture didn't change, but her expression said she was pondering the new information. "So when he took me to the charity event, I showed up on her radar?"

"Possibly." I hoped that was it. Otherwise Hudson was lying to me about his relationship with Stacy. "And possibly not." That was the problem with secrets—anything was potentially the truth.

Stacy's eyes grew dim, as if the idea that all of it had been a hoax disappointed her more than catching the guy she liked with another woman. I got that. She'd wanted Hudson Pierce to be interested in her. Simply by being a woman, I could relate to crushing on a guy. Being me, I could relate to crushing on Hudson. If I'd discovered he'd faked being into me…well, that would have been more devastating than the current situation I was in.

I decided to give her some compassion. "But even if it wasn't Hudson who wrote those emails, Celia obviously thought you were a threat. That has to mean he showed some interest in you in front of her."

Stacy blew out a stream of air. "It's actually an interesting theory. It fits in some ways."

"Do tell." Liesl was as eager now for the information as I was.

"Like I said, he did act strange when I came up to him. And whenever he came in the shop, he ignored me. As if he hadn't said all the beautiful things he'd said to me online. He was very poetic. His emails were like long letters."

"I'm not claiming to know who the actual author was," I started tentatively, afraid of hurting Stacy's feelings more, "but from what I know of Hudson, he's not much of a letter writer. And Celia does seem to be comfortable around the literary world." The quotes she'd picked to highlight in my books indicated as such, anyway.

"What was the email address he sent from?" Occasionally Liesl came up with things I should have asked.

Stacy wrinkled her brow. "H.Pierce@gmail.com, I think."

I was already shaking my head when Liesl asked, "Is that his email?"

"I only know of his Pierce Industries account. He uses it for both business and personal, but he rarely sends personal emails." Or if he did, I wasn't aware.

The bell rang, announcing Stacy's next client. She looked to the door then back to us, as if she was torn.

I felt the same way. There was more to potentially uncover, but I'd promised we'd be in and out. Besides, there probably wasn't anything else I could know without reading the actual emails and that seemed like too much to ask from Stacy unless she offered. "Thanks again, for your time and your answers. I know you're busy now."

She nodded as she crossed in front of us to open the door. With her hand on the knob, she paused. "I should be thanking you too, I suppose. You've enlightened the situation." She opened the door before I could respond. "Vanessa? Welcome to Mirabelle's. Come on in."

Stacy's client walked in and we headed out.

"If I think of anything else," Stacy called after me. "I'll contact you."

It was a hopeful ending to the conversation. If she was anything like me—and very few people were, but it was possible—she'd go home and reread all the emails "Hudson" sent with the new scenario in mind. Maybe she'd find something there and send me a note.

I texted Jordan and discovered he'd found a meter down the block. He waved, letting us know his location.

Liesl linked her arm in mine as we walked toward the Maybach. "Do you think you learned anything?"

I shrugged. "I'd like to believe it was all a scam on Celia's part. But that doesn't answer why Hudson was kissing her or why he won't tell me the truth about it."

"Maybe she asked him to play along. Would he do that? Or he was in on it all along."

I bit my lip. "All of those options are possible." I thought he'd been well at the time he'd met me, but maybe he had still been playing people. Was that what Hudson didn't want me to know? That so recently, he hadn't been well?

Or was it Celia he was protecting? Yet again.

THE CLUB WAS already open to the public when I showed up for work that night, so instead of using the employee entrance, I went through the front doors. If I hadn't, I wouldn't have seen Celia waiting in line. So much for her being bored with the game.

The doorman asked before I had a chance to remind him. "Not her, right?"

"Right." I looked out toward the blonde once more. It was somewhat comforting to know she was still interested in tormenting me. To my sick mind, it proved that she thought I was still important to Hudson. Even if it wasn't true any longer, at least she hadn't gotten the memo.

As I stared at her, she waved. "Hi, Laynie." It was the first time she'd talked to me since she'd begun her stalking.

I didn't respond with words, but I did smile before going into the club. In about two minutes she was going to be turned down at the door. That was definitely something to grin about.

It was the last time I smiled for the remainder of the night. My shift was ho-hum and I worked my ass off keeping on top of the summer crowd, but the constant ache of missing Hudson ate at me. Everywhere I looked, I saw him—in the bubble rooms, in the office, at the bar.

By three a.m. when my shift was over, the idea of going back to the lonely penthouse had me in tears. I considered going somewhere else instead—Liesl's, a hotel. The loft. *I could go to the loft and see him.* Be with the man I wanted to be with.

But why would I want to be with someone who didn't want to be with me? That was proof that I wasn't the person I'd once been—the person who would have gone anywhere to be with the man she was into, whether he wanted her or not.

So I ended up at the penthouse. Alone. I managed not to cry as Reynold drove me there, but the tears started before I exited the elevator. They continued while I got ready for bed, and while I checked my phone that I'd left at home during the night. Then they turned to sobs when I read the one text message I had:

Sleep tight, precious.

Tomorrow, I thought as I cried myself to sleep for the fourth time in a row. *Maybe tomorrow I'll wake up from this horrible nightmare.*

— CHAPTER —

SIXTEEN

"Jordan, I need to go to Pierce Industries?" I asked when I got in the car the next afternoon. I paused, wondering if I should say that I wanted to see Hudson. It wasn't really a lie—I did want to see him. He just wasn't whom I *intended* to see.

"Certainly, Ms…Laynie." He corrected himself before I had to. After a moment he added, "I'm sure he'll enjoy the surprise."

I smiled and nodded as his eyes met mine in the rearview mirror. It bothered me that he knew enough about my life and my day-to-day schedule to know that Hudson didn't expect me. Had Hudson told Jordan he didn't want me to come by? Then he probably wouldn't agree to take me. But then I'd find my own way to his office—Hudson had to know that about me by now. Perhaps my driver was simply informed of my daily plans. Though it wasn't by me, so how accurate did he expect that information to be? I wasn't Hudson's prisoner, after all.

Whatever knowledge the two—three, if I included Reynold—shared about me, I was convinced that Hudson was always apprised of my whereabouts. Jordan would likely text Hudson the minute I got out of the car, telling him I was on my way up.

I couldn't stop my bodyguard from telling on me—it would risk his job. But I could buy some time. When we pulled in front of the Pierce Industries building, I leaned toward the front seat. "Give me a few minutes before you report me, will you? I don't want to ruin the surprise."

He didn't verbally agree, but Jordan's smile said he'd play along.

"Thank you." I kissed my driver on the cheek, surprising both him and me with the affection, and stepped out of the car.

Considering how destroyed my heart was, my spirits were actually almost good as I hit the elevator button for Hudson's floor. The talk with Stacy had gone well, and that boosted my confidence that today's appointment would follow suit. Even without Liesl accompanying me, I felt capable of accomplishment. And if all went well, I'd have answers.

Hopefully they wouldn't be answers that destroyed me more.

I panicked only briefly as the elevator opened on Hudson's floor. I peeked through the glass walls to Hudson's waiting room. Except for Trish at her desk, the room was empty. Hudson's office door was closed. If Jordan had already sent a text about me, Hudson either hadn't read it yet or wasn't in the building. Either way, it was good news for me.

I escaped down the hall free and clear.

Norma Ander's office was easy to find. There were only top executives on that floor so there weren't many to look through. I could tell from the outside that hers was smaller than Hudson's and didn't have a corner view. For some reason, that made me feel good. God, was I really such a spiteful bitch? No, I was simply a woman scorned.

I'd scheduled my appointment with Norma's assistant so I already knew I'd find a male at the desk outside her door. What I didn't know from his voice was how attractive he was. Not attractive in the dominating powerful way that Hudson was, but in the cute, nerdy way that was trendy lately. He seemed about my age or possibly a year or two older. His hair was light brown and unruly and his blue eyes were bright despite being hidden behind dark framed glasses.

How lucky was Norma to be surrounded by hotties? Maybe I needed to take a job at Pierce Industries after all so I could enjoy the view.

Like I cared about any guy besides Hudson. If I could just have that view back, I'd be happy.

The nameplate indicated his name was Boyd. I stepped up and introduced myself. "Alayna Withers to see Norma Anders."

"Let me just buzz her to see if she's ready for you. Please feel free to take a seat."

The idea of sitting made me want to puke—I was much too nervous. "No, I'll stand. Thank you." I circled the small waiting area, pretending to study the art on the walls while stealing glances into Norma's office. Despite her door being open, I couldn't see her desk, and the more time I had to myself, the more I thought I'd chicken out. The meeting with her could very well backfire, after all. She may not get the whole woman-to-woman thing. The possibility of security or Hudson being phoned was quite high. Both those scenarios were unattractive.

For good or bad, I didn't chicken out and Norma didn't keep me waiting. "Alayna, please come in." She stood aside to let me pass her and gestured for me to take a seat in front of her desk.

As she shut the door behind me I heard her say, "Stop it. You're being bad." At least that's what it sounded like she said.

I turned back to her before sitting. "Excuse me?"

"Oh, nothing. I was talking to my assistant."

As she crossed around to her side of the desk, I took in her space. Not only was it simpler and smaller than Hudson's, it also lacked any aesthetic form. The room consisted of a desk, three chairs, two bookcases, and several file cabinets. Apparently Celia Werner hadn't been hired to design all the offices—just Hudson's.

Norma cleared her throat. Since I hadn't initiated the conversation, it seemed she would. "I was surprised by your request to meet with me. I assume it's about Gwen?"

When Boyd had asked the reason for my appointment with Norma, I'd simply said, *"It's personal. I'm her sister's boss."* The implication was clear.

Also, it was totally misleading.

I sat up taller in my chair. It was lower than Norma's and I supposed that was a tactic to make her clients feel beneath her. I wouldn't let it affect my confidence. "No, I'm not here about Gwen. Though I may have led your assistant to believe that's what it was about. I apologize for that deception."

Norma blinked once. "Now my interest is piqued. Go on."

I leveled my eyes with hers. "I'm here to ask you about Hudson."

"Hudson?" She actually jolted in her chair from the surprise. "You couldn't have shocked me more if you said you were here to talk about the pope. Why on earth would you be asking me about your boyfriend?"

It was the most words she'd ever spoken to me directly. It occurred to me that I knew absolutely nothing about this woman—whether she was fun or serious or compassionate or mean. She'd always acted as though she disapproved of me or I disinterested her. Was that simply because I was with Hudson? She was a woman with authority—she'd likely learned over time how to be tough, learned to thicken her skin. Was there a girl beneath her exterior that I could appeal to with my jealousies and insecurities?

I hoped so. "I'm interested in your relationship with him. With Hudson."

Her mouth curled up on one side. "Call me a bitch, but why aren't you asking him?"

I'd already called her a bitch many times in my head, but I recognized the title hadn't been validated. Yet. And, just as when Stacy had judged me, I felt the urge to be defensive. That would get me nowhere though. "I have asked him. He's answered. I'd like your clarification."

She nodded, accepting my answer easily. "I have a business relationship with him. He's my boss. I'm his lead financial officer."

"Business only?"

"Business only."

I'd feared her answer wouldn't convince me, and it didn't. He signed her paychecks—for that reason alone, why would she disclose information to me? And if he had been her lover, or still was her lover, then she had doubly the reason not to be honest with me.

Still, I hoped that proceeding with the conversation would teach me something. Maybe she'd slip, or I'd see it in her face—anything. "You obviously find him attractive. You don't hide it when you look at him." She stared at him like he was Adonis.

Then again, wasn't he?

Norma let out a small laugh. "He's a very attractive man." *Well, duh.* "But I'm not interested in him that way."

There was no way that was true. Besides what I'd seen from her, Hudson had confirmed her interest. "He said you approached him about having a relationship."

Her eyes widened in surprise. "Did he?"

My heart thundered in my chest. *Why would he lie about that?*

But then Norma conceded. "Well, I did. Quite a while ago. I'm simply surprised it meant enough to mention. Things have changed now."

I tilted my head, trying to read her. Very few of my crushes had simply disappeared with time. Generally it took a new man to end my interest. But I obsessed, so I didn't have an accurate point of reference.

Hudson, however, believed she still liked him. "He doesn't seem to think things have changed."

She stared for two solid seconds before she narrowed her eyes and grinned. "Maybe I don't want him to think so."

I wrung my hands in my lap, determined not to slap the smugness off her face no matter how tempting it was. Instead, I pinned her with my eyes, hoping that my persistence would deliver.

After a brief stare-off, I won. Sort of. She offered an answer, albeit not a completely satisfactory one. "He's my boss. It pays to flatter him."

I leaned back in my chair. "There's more than that. What are you not saying?"

Her eyes flickered briefly with rage or panic. I wasn't sure which, but neither would get me what I wanted.

I backed down and tried another tactic—appealing to her sense of compassion. "I'm sorry. It's none of my business, I know. But I'm desperate for information. It would mean a lot to me. And with Gwen at the club now, I thought maybe we could find some sort of a bond."

Now her eyes definitely showed rage—and not just a flicker. "Are you threatening Gwen's job security if I don't answer your questions?"

Fuck! "No! God, no. I love Gwen." *Not exactly true.* "Or, I like her anyway. A lot. She's good at the job. Perfect for what I was looking for." Jesus, I was flustered.

I took a deep breath and centered myself. "I mean that I think of everyone at The Sky Launch as family. Gwen's moving her way into that category quite nicely. Even though she's sometimes blunt and overly anxious to speak her mind."

Norma chuckled. "That's Gwen for you." It was her turn to tilt her head and study me. "I appreciate you getting her the job, by the way. I thanked Hudson, but he says it's really you who hired her. She needed out of Eighty-Eighth. In many ways, she was as desperate as you say you are now."

She swept her tongue across her teeth and narrowed her eyes, considering. "And for that reason—because of what you did for Gwen—I'll share something with you." She pushed a button on her phone. "Boyd, can you come in here?"

Boyd's voice filled the room. "Certainly."

Norma focused her attention on her closed door. I turned in my seat and followed suit, curious and anxious about what her assistant could offer to my situation. Was this who would drag me out of the building?

Boyd rapped on the door and then opened it without waiting for a response. "May I help you?"

Damn, his grin was that of a schoolboy's, all sweet and contagious.

Norma's smile almost matched his. Definitely contagious. "Boyd, Ms. Withers wants to know if I'm having an affair with Hudson Pierce."

Boyd's mouth dropped open and his eyes flitted from me to Norma to me to Norma. He wiped his hand on his suit pants, suddenly nervous.

"It's okay, dear. Answer honestly. As honestly as you like." Her tone suggested an inside secret.

Did Boyd schedule trysts for his boss? I braced myself for his response.

At Norma's encouragement, he relaxed and met my eyes. "She is not."

The answer should have been comforting. But I was a cynical girl. "How can you be certain? Are you there when she has her meetings with him?"

"I am not. But I know that she isn't." He looked one more time to Norma for permission to continue. Seeming to believe he'd received it, he went on. "She wouldn't do that to the person she's involved with." He moved his focus from me back to Norma. "She's very loyal."

"Thank you, Boyd. That's all."

He nodded once and left.

The door wasn't yet shut when I spun back to Norma. "You're involved with someone?" The blush on her cheekbones said it all. "Oh my god, it's Boyd!"

Her blush and her smile deepened. Damn, the woman had it bad. "Now do you really think I would fool around with someone else in the office when my lover is right outside my door?"

I was speechless. "Why didn't Hudson just tell me you were involved?" It would have eased my mind. Of course, affairs could still happen, but her having a boyfriend diminished the likelihood. Especially knowing how gaga he was over Boyd.

At the mention of Hudson,though, Norma's giddiness evaporated.

"Hudson doesn't know," I realized. "Why? Is it a big secret or something?"

"Corporate policy is no dating within the same department. Boyd would be transferred. I don't want to lose him. He's worked for me for two years; we've been together for half that time. He's the best assistant I've ever had. In more ways than one."

"And perpetuating the idea that you're still into Hudson is to throw him off track." I was slow but catching on. "Gotcha." The woman wasn't a bitch—she was simply nervous her secret would be found out.

A wave of guilt rolled over me. "I feel like an idiot. I'm sorry to have assumed. And don't worry—your secret is safe with me."

She shrugged. "Thanks. It's actually fun to tell someone." Her smile reappeared.

"I'm sure." The true nature of my relationship with Hudson had started as a secret. I'd been busting to tell someone—anyone—what was really going on. I certainly could relate.

Plus, talking about being in love was one of the highlights of the emotion.

Despite my paranoid nature, Norma convinced me she only had eyes for her assistant. But that didn't explain all the time she was spending with my boyfriend. "So if there isn't any romantic interest, why are you with Hudson so much?" I was keen to hear if Norma would say it was a business deal as well, and if so, if she'd expand.

Norma's forehead furrowed. "He hasn't told you?"

I shook my head, and she took that in. "Well, maybe I understand." This seemed to be more for her than myself. To me, she explained, "It's a very complicated idea he's working on. He owns stock in a company but wants to purchase enough to have a controlling interest. But he doesn't want the board members to be aware that he has the controlling interest. So he's in the process of buying out another company that has enough stock in the first company to equal controlling interest when combined with the shares he already owns. Since he's doing this all under the radar, we've had to be covert about the purchase. It's all been like a game. Chess moves. We move, they move. I've had to research financial laws and tactics I've never encountered before. It will be a miracle if it goes through, but I'm beginning to believe in miracles."

Her eyes lit up as she talked about the deal and I realized it wasn't Hudson that turned her on as much as it was the work.

She paused, thinking perhaps that she'd gotten carried away. "Hudson's methods have been brilliant," she concluded. "He's a fascinating man to watch in action."

"It's obvious you love your job, Norma." I waited as she nodded. "Hudson's mind is certainly one of the most creative I've ever encountered. It must be a real thrill to get to work with him so closely." I loved it when he let me work with him. It was a real turn-on both mentally and physically. "And I'm not insinuating anything by that."

"I understood what you meant. And yes, it is." Her face grew serious. "By the way, I meant it when I said that I think you're a much better match for him than that Werner girl. She made him miserable. You make him almost happy."

I'd heard Norma insinuate that Hudson had been with Celia before. He'd dismissed it, saying she was as snowed as everyone, that he'd used the misconception to avoid Norma's advances.

Now that I'd seen the video, I wondered if there wasn't more to Norma's notion. "Why do you believe he was with Celia? Did he ever tell you he was? Did you see them together?"

She frowned as she recalled. "He never said they were. She accompanied him to many of the office functions. I simply assumed. Were they not?"

I ignored her question, eager for more information. "Did you ever see them intimate together? You know, holding hands? Kissing?"

"No, I didn't." She thought about it a moment, as if realizing that it was strange. "That's part of what seemed miserable about them as a couple—they were so unaffectionate when they were together. There was never the shine in his eyes like there is when he's with you. Even when he talks about you, he glows."

This surprised me. "He talks about me?"

"All the time." She said it as if it were the most matter-of-fact thing in the world.

My heart flip-flopped. "Hmm. I never knew."

I LEFT NORMA'S office feeling lighter than when I'd arrived. She'd assuaged my doubts about Hudson's fidelity and had even given some insight on his relationship with Celia. More and more, the video seemed to be a sham.

Walking to the elevator, my better mood quickly quieted as I remembered I had to get past Hudson's office again. If Jordan *had* texted him, he'd certainly be on the lookout for me. I wasn't sure if I wanted to bump into him or not. If I saw him, I'd have to explain why I was there.

But I'd see him. And that sounded both glorious and painful.

I walked cautiously down his hall, trying my best to keep my heels quiet on the marble floor, all the while keeping my eyes pinned on his closed office door. Which was why I didn't notice he was standing in front of me until I bumped into him.

"Alayna."

There it was, the sound I loved above all others—my name on the tongue of the man I loved. The way he said it, reverent like a hymn, like a lullaby—it kindled the emotions I'd been attempting to bury deep inside. Goose bumps scattered down my arms and my chest grew tight. So tight, so ready to burst.

I started to say something, but my voice was gone.

Hudson wrapped his arm around mine. "Let's talk in private, shall we?" He led me to his office. "Hold my calls," he said over his shoulder to Trish. Then he shut and locked the door behind us.

If the circumstances had been different, the whole dominating alpha mood he was in would have been hot. Okay, it was still hot. No matter the circumstances. And I'd been a bad girl—going behind his back and speaking with his employee. Maybe if I was lucky, I'd get spanked.

Wow, wasn't I feeling optimistic?

"Well, hello, H."

He released my arm. "What are you doing here, Alayna?" He looked and sounded tired. His eyes were bloodshot and rimmed with dark circles. Was he losing sleep over me? Or were work and an unfamiliar bed the more likely cause?

Even with the bags, he looked delicious. I'd wondered many times if I'd ever get bored of his devastatingly good looks. If so, it wasn't today. His simple presence affected me—aroused me, flustered me. Pissed me off. The combination of attraction, frustration and desperation put me in an odd mood—a cross between flirty and feisty with a whole lot of bitter on top.

"What am I doing here in your office? You dragged me in here, remember." I walked away from him, dragging my hand along the top of the couch.

"Don't be cute." Though I sensed a smile behind his straight-man routine. "I meant in the building."

I peered at him over my shoulder. "Maybe I came to see you. I tend to stalk when I feel dismissed by a man." It could happen. It had happened before. With him, even.

Hudson heaved a sigh. "You didn't come to see me. You arrived on this floor over half an hour ago and are just now coming by my office."

I spun toward him. "How the fuck do you know everything I do? Jordan? Your security cameras?" I knew it was my bodyguards, but I wanted his confirmation. And saying it out loud, I realized how much the situation ticked me off—if he was watching my every move, I didn't feel so bad digging into his life. As far as shitty behavior went, the two were on par in my book.

"I'm not going to feel guilty for the lengths I go to in order to protect what's mine." He crossed his arms over his chest, his already broad shoulders expanding.

And I didn't miss his words. I might have licked my lips.

"Alayna?"

I tore my eyes away from him, breaking the hypnotic trance he had me in. "Yours, huh? Don't make me laugh." I seemed to be back at the angry phase of grief. It was an interesting and a thrilling change to the constant pain I'd been experiencing.

My rage spurred Hudson's. "Jesus, how many times do I have to go through this with you?"

"I don't know." I shrugged dramatically. "Maybe a couple hundred more times. Because I'm obviously not getting it."

He turned his back to me, running his hand through his hair. When he faced me again, he was relatively calmer. "Why. Are. You. Here?"

I battled over telling the truth and keeping it to myself just to spite him. My bitchy mood was voting for spite.

But I was fighting *for* him, not against him. Honesty it was. "I came to see Norma."

His brows rose. "About Gwen?"

I covered my face with my hands then dropped them. "About you, you dummy. I don't give a shit about anything but you." My throat tightened with the truthfulness of my declaration. "Jesus, how many times do I have to go through this with you?" I threw his words back at him. Guess the spite was coming along with the fight. It helped keep away the tears.

"You came to talk to *my* employee about *me*?" His eye twitched and his jaw was tense. From my experience, that meant he was pissed. Beyond pissed.

And I'd been going for romantic.

I threw more of his words back. "Don't guilt me for protecting what's mine."

His eyes sparked. That remark hit him—in a good way. In a way I didn't know I could anymore. As if he were moved by my possessiveness.

I took advantage of his surprise and softened my approach. "I only wanted to see for myself if she was into you. If you had something going with her."

Bitterness crept back in. With a pointed finger, I said, "And don't you dare talk to me about trust because you know I get jealous about her, and you aren't around to help reassure me."

Every other word I said was pointed and harsh. I'd hated feeling so distraught. This new temperament wasn't any better, but at least I was getting it out. It was like shedding my skin and underneath was nothing but raw and rugged emotion.

Hudson leaned his hip against the couch, regarding me closely. When he spoke, he was calm and controlled. As always. "Did you get what you came for?"

"I did."

"And?"

I bit my lip, not wanting to give away any ground. Carefully, reluctantly, I answered. "She thinks a lot of you. She respects you and admires you and she recognizes you're physically attractive—don't let that go to your head."

"But..."

"But she's not into you anymore. I can see it in her eyes." It was a fair way to avoid spilling Norma's secret. Besides, I *could* see it in her eyes.

"Good. Then you believe the things I've told you." He appeared pleased.

"It was never the things you've told me that were the issue. It's the things you haven't told me."

"They aren't your things to know," he snapped back.

The sliver of composure I was maintaining disappeared. "What the ever living fuck?" I was infuriated. Enraged. Out of my mind with exasperation. "I could say the same thing about you—spying on me, digging into my history before you'd even met me—maybe I think those aren't your things to know. Still, you did and do whatever the hell you want with no regard to boundaries or personal space."

I squared my shoulders and faced him head on. "And while that's out there, let me be clear—since you aren't able to explain things to me, I'm digging on my own."

Concern flashed through his eyes.

It fueled me. I wanted him off kilter. Wanted him where he always had me—flustered and imbalanced. "That's right. I've been through all of the books Celia sent. I've been to see Stacy. And Norma. I'm collecting my own facts. Don't you think it would be better to tell me your secrets than have me find them out on my own?"

"Alayna, stop digging." He took a step toward me, his voice even but strained.

Why, why, why couldn't he just tell me what I'd find? "You're protecting Celia again, aren't you?"

"Celia's not who I'm protecting."

"Who then? Yourself?" I was yelling, not even caring if his doors were solid enough to absorb the sound. "Me?"

He reached for me, grabbing me at the elbow. "You need to leave, now."

With those five words the anger disappeared and the hurt returned full force. The air left my lungs. My chest constricted. My eyes filled. He wanted me to leave, wanted me gone. And the last thing I wanted was to leave.

We were at such odds. All there was between us lately was struggle. There was never any progress.

I wiped a renegade tear from my cheek. "Shutting me out again. Like you always do. Hiding behind your thick walls. What's the point of me even fighting for you if you're never, never going to let me in? Who are you protecting, Hudson? Who?"

His grip on me tightened. "Yes, you, dammit! I'm protecting you. Always you."

Before I could blink his mouth was on mine, crushing into my lips, bruising me with his abrasive kiss. He tasted of the same neediness that I felt deep in my own belly—of lonely desperation. Of lust and affection that had been bottled for far too long.

My tears halted and my hands flew to his lapels, pulling him to me. I lifted my leg around his, my skirt bunching around my upper thighs. Pressing against him, I tilted my hips, rubbing my core against his erection.

He groaned in frustration and I echoed the sound, eager to be even closer, not able to get close enough.

In a blur, he spun me toward the couch. I grasped the back as he removed my panties. He growled when his fingers dipped into my hole and found me wet—soaking wet. Next, I heard the sound of his belt, then his zipper. His palms settled on my ass. Then he drove into me, deep and hard, again and again. He grunted with each thrust, his balls slapping against my ass, his fingers curled around my hips like a vise-grip.

He was fucking me, bent over his couch, and it felt so good and I needed him like that so much. But I couldn't see his face—not in that position—couldn't look into his eyes. I knew that he was doing that on purpose, trying to avoid that extra level of intimacy, hoping to make the act just about sex and nothing else.

But it was never just sex with us. It was always something more—a complete and total union of him and me, where we became whole and healed and brilliant. I couldn't let him succeed in making it less.

Twisting my torso, I reached my hand back to his chest and clutched onto his shirt. His lids had been squeezed shut, but at my grasp, they popped open. I locked my gaze on his. With the contact of my eyes, his drive steadied—still fast, but no longer frenzied. It was the connection I needed. My pussy clenched and I began my ascent. The friction increased as I tightened around him, but he continued at his even pace through the tension until he was spilling his seed with a long stroke and spilling my name on a low groan.

As his orgasm tore through him it spurred mine to higher heights until my head was spinning and my vision blinded. I fell forward on the couch, panting and euphoric. Hudson collapsed on top of me, holding me tight for several beautiful moments while our breathing became regular.

The minute he pulled off and out of me, I straightened and turned into his arms. He welcomed me, tilting my mouth to his. He locked my upper lip in a hard kiss, holding me in place with his hand behind my head. It was different from any kiss we'd shared—our mouths not moving, our bodies held together in a desperate union, as we breathed in and out in tandem.

When we finally broke apart, I wrapped my hands tightly around his neck and kissed along his jaw. "Oh god, I miss you. I miss you so much."

"Précieux…mon amour…ma chérie…" He ran his hands down my face, caressing my skin with sweet sweeps of his thumb.

He was tender and perfect, and though I was afraid to break the moment, I was more afraid to miss out on the power of our junction. Barely above a whisper, I voiced the question I desperately needed to ask. "When are you coming home?"

He leaned his forehead against mine with a sigh and settled his hands at my neck. "I have to go to L.A. for the weekend." He tilted his wrist to glance at his watch. "I'm set to leave in about twenty minutes, in fact."

If it was possible to be both elated and disappointed at once, that's what I was. He wasn't pushing me away as he had been the last few days, but if he was coming back, it wouldn't be tonight.

I proceeded with caution, pressing him to let me in without scaring him off. "Part of your big business thing? With Norma?"

It wouldn't bother me if she were going. Well, not as much as it would have before I'd spoken to her. I just needed to know the answer.

Hudson stroked my nose with the tip of his. "Yes, with Norma. And after this, if all goes well, we'll be done."

I closed my eyes and inhaled him. So close…we were so close to working everything out…I felt it in my heart, felt it in my bones. Would we lose it all because he was leaving now?

Invite me to go with you. I willed him to say the words, *Come with me.*

He didn't.

With what felt like great reluctance, he pushed me away. He tucked himself in, zipped up his pants, and stood to face me, his fist on his hip as if trying to decide what to do about a problem that had arose unexpectedly.

It was surprising that I could still be hurt when I was already in so much pain. Wasn't there a limit? Where the ache would become so unbearable and my spirit would simply cease to go on? If there was a threshold, I hadn't met it yet. Because that look on his face—it pushed me further into the depth of the hell that I was in. It crushed me.

I didn't want to be his *problem*. I wanted to be his *life*. After all, he was mine.

Then, all of a sudden, everything changed. He dropped his hand to his side and his expression melted and transformed, and for the first time in days, the look in his eyes said I was the center of his world again. The crux of his universe. The core of his existence.

He reached for me, and instantly I was back in his arms. He clutched me tightly to him, with determined devotion. "God, Alayna, I can't do this anymore." It was almost a sob. "I can't bear to be apart from you. I miss you so terribly."

"You do?" I leaned back to look into his eyes, to see if they told the same story.

He settled his hand at my jaw, his thumb tracing the line of my lower lip. "Of course, I do, precious." His tone was uneven but sincere. "You're my everything. I love you. I love you so much."

My heart thudded in my ears and the world closed in around me as if there were only Hudson and me and nothing else.

He'd said it. He'd said it *twice*. Said it, and meant it. I felt the sincerity in every cell of my body.

And with just those three little words, the darkness scattered and the sky cleared. The heaviness that had cocooned me for days fell away, and I was left new and beautiful in its place. It was he who'd finally taken the step, had metamorphosed enough to deliver what I needed to hear, but it was me who was now the butterfly—me who could finally soar.

And still, as I was already flying, I needed to be sure. "W-w-what?"

His lips fell into an easy smile. "You heard me."

"I want to hear it again." I held my breath, afraid that if I stirred at all that the spell would be broken and I'd be alone in our bed at the penthouse, that all of this would be a dream.

But it wasn't a dream. And I wasn't alone. And I was in the arms of the man who was saying once again, "I love you."

"You love me?"

He brushed his lips over mine. "I love you, precious. I've always loved you. From the moment I first saw you. I knew before you did, I think." He tilted my chin to meet his eyes. "But there are things—things in my past—that have kept me from being able to tell you. And now…I have to do this…this thing. Finish this deal. Then, when I get back, we'll talk."

"We'll talk?" I felt like a parrot, repeating his last words, but I was delirious, my mind hazy with happiness. It was all I could manage.

"I'll tell you anything you want to know. And if you still want me, I'll come home." He swept a strand of my hair behind my ear, seeming to need to keep touching me as badly as I needed to be touched.

God, he's such an idiot! "Yes, I want you home. Of course I do. We belong there together. There's nothing you could say that would make me stop loving you. *Nothing*. I stick, remember?"

He sighed into me. "Oh, precious. I hope that's true."

"It is." It was the truest thing I knew, like the way the sun knew to rise in the morning, the way a rosebud knew to blossom in the spring. He was in my veins, in the innermost recesses of my heart and soul. I'd love him until I died—through death, even. Through fire, through hell. I'd love him through eternity.

And now I believed he might love me that way too.

I dug my fingers into his jacket and shook him softly. "Say it again."

"You're such a spoiled girl." He circled my nose with his. "And I love… spoiling you."

I leaned back and smacked his chest.

"And I love you." He pulled me back toward his mouth. "I love you, I love you. I love you."

— CHAPTER — SEVENTEEN

Hudson and I kissed and cuddled right until the moment he was supposed to leave, neither of us wanting to end our reunion. Hand in hand, we walked out of the building together. He invited me to ride with him in the limo to the airport. I considered it, but Norma was accompanying him, and the look in Hudson's eyes said he'd have his way with me, no matter who was present.

We did get a chance for a goodbye kiss. "I'll miss you," he mumbled against my lips.

If he wasn't going to say it, I would. "You could ask me to come to L.A."

"Someone keeps reminding me about a club that she has to run…" He ran a hand down my bare arm, sending chills down my spine. "And I'm going to be swamped. Though I'd love you there, you'd be ignored."

Briefly I wondered if he had an ulterior reason for not wanting me to go with him, but I didn't let the thought stay. He was right. I had responsibilities at home. His recognition of that was a big step on his part.

But I pouted all the same.

Hudson kissed my forehead. "Don't pout. Stay here, go to David's going away party on Sunday, I'll be back by Monday."

"Back to the penthouse?" I wanted his reassurance once more. I could bear a few more days if he'd come home for good.

"Back to our house, yes." He brushed one more kiss against my lips then got in the limo and rode away.

THOUGH HUDSON AND I were still apart in the literal sense, the fact that we were a couple again made all the difference in our distance. Finally, we were happy and in love. Happy and in love like we'd never been before. I fluttered around work all shift like I had wings. Gwen introduced herself to me, claiming we'd never met. David, on the other hand, spent the evening being glum. He blamed it on his impending move, but I knew it was me. He'd been hoping Hudson and I were over. Thank god we weren't.

Even across the miles, Hudson showed me things were different. He had flowers sent to work—a bouquet of wildflowers that looked exactly like the patches we'd seen in the Poconos. He also texted me, something he rarely initiated. I'd received several before I had the chance to look at my phone.

Just landed in L.A.

Did you get my flowers?

I had some sent to my room too, so I could think of you.

Are you avoiding me now?

I laughed at his repeat of what I'd said when he hadn't responded to my texts. Then I sent: *Not avoiding you, working. Thnx for the flowers. Keep texting. I'll read every one.*

His next message came immediately, as though he'd been sitting with his phone in his hand, waiting for it to buzz. *If that's a challenge, I accept.*

He continued texting me throughout the evening. I responded when I could between the busy Friday nightclub scene. Our messages varied from romantic to sexual to sweet to funny. We acted like a couple in that slap-happy, I-can't-get-enough-of-you phase that happened at the beginning of relationships. With our untraditional start, we'd never really experienced that. Then we'd had too many walls. But now they were all down—or nearly all down.

On Saturday, more flowers arrived at the penthouse. Then late that afternoon, he did more than text. He called.

I answered on the second ring. "I can't believe you're calling me." Hudson called as rarely as he texted. He was a no-nonsense type of guy. To him, chit-chat was a waste of time.

Now though, he was acting like I was anything but a waste of time.

"I wanted to hear your voice. Digital letters weren't cutting it any longer."

Talk about wanting to hear a voice…

His low tenor stirred butterflies to dance in my stomach. "I love hearing you too." I stretched on the bedroom floor, my legs raised to rest against the bed. "Did you sleep well last night?"

"I did not. I've slept horribly every night that I haven't fallen asleep inside you."

I couldn't hide my grin from showing in my voice. "So you're horny."

"No, Alayna. If I were simply horny, I could take care of myself."

That's something I wouldn't mind watching.

"It has nothing to do with sex—" He paused. "Well, it only has some to do with sex. It's connecting with you that I miss."

Damn, now I was horny. "I get it. I feel the same. When you come back, we'll connect for hours, how does that sound?" Knowing Hudson, it would be literally hours. We had lots of reconnecting to do.

"It sounds wonderful, precious." His tone grew serious. "But we still have to talk."

"We'll talk. We can connect first and then talk. And then connect some more." I shook my head as I listened to myself. Usually it was Hudson who was all about the sex.

"You're insatiable." He didn't sound like he minded. "You forget that you may not want to connect after we talk."

I waggled my eyebrows even though he couldn't see me. "Another reason to connect before. But I'm not worried about it. Just your willingness to talk is enough." That wasn't quite true. "Okay, not exactly enough, but it pleases me. A lot." And even though I knew whatever he had to say would likely rock me, I was sure that we'd get through it.

Hudson still didn't believe that. "Hmm," he said, and I knew he doubted the strength of my love.

Part of me wished he'd just spill his secrets now, over the phone. I was eager to hear what they were, but more than that, I was eager to put him at ease—to prove that I'd stick around.

But I had to start getting ready for work soon. There wasn't time. And I had the feeling we'd need *connecting* after his revelation, in whatever form that took.

We sat silently for several seconds, and I worried he was fretting. "What are you thinking about, H?"

"You. Bent over the couch in my office."

I laughed. "No, you aren't."

"Actually, I am. The sounds you made…the way you looked at me… your eyes when I made you come…God, Alayna, do you have any idea how beautiful and sexy you are?"

My face warmed and my toes curled into the comforter. How could he make me blush over the phone? "If I am, it's because you make me that way."

"That's a lie. I never want to hear you say that I'm responsible for your beauty again. I can't take an ounce of credit for your perfection."

"But you can take every ounce of credit for my happiness, and that's much more important to me than beauty."

He was silent again, and I feared I'd scared him. "What is it, Hudson?"

"I was just wondering what I did to deserve the responsibility of your happiness. I hope that I can live up to the honor."

Perhaps it had been an ill-timed remark since he'd so recently made me miserable. That was the fact of the matter though—Hudson had the power to lift me to heights I'd never imagined, and that meant he also had the ability to absolutely obliterate me.

Maybe it was a lot of pressure, but it was part of the romantic relationship package. "You deserve the honor just for loving me," I said softly.

"And love you, I do." He barely let a beat pass before switching gears. "What are you wearing?"

"Black lacy panties and a camisole." I pulled the phone from my face to check the time. *Shit*, I needed to wrap things up soon. "I was just about to jump in the shower when you called." I rolled to my knees and stood.

Hudson's next words were a gruff command. "Take off your panties."

"Oh my god, Hudson, I don't have time for this." Though, I was already stripping. For the shower, not for him.

"You have to undress anyway."

Such a man of reason. "For that alone, they're off. And now I'm getting off the phone. You're too distracting for me at the moment." I walked to the bathroom as I spoke.

"Fine." Tenderly, he added, "I miss you."

"I miss you, I love you."

"I love you first."

I held on to the handle of the shower door and closed my eyes, relishing his words, breathing them in. "I *said* it first," I teased.

"But I meant it first," he said with finality. "Get in the shower. Don't touch yourself unless you're thinking of me."

"Whom else would I think of, you silly man?" My nipples were already standing at full attention, and even though I was naked, it wasn't because I was chilled. "I'm letting you know now that I plan to text you throughout the night. Wicked, dirty things. You'll be desperate for me when you get back."

"I'm desperate for you now," he groaned. "Go, before I make you touch yourself with me on the phone."

With a reluctant sigh, I said goodbye and hung up, catching my face in the mirror as I did. The woman I saw was quite a contrast to the one who'd stood there only the day before. And there would only be one more day—maybe two—before Hudson would be home. I couldn't wait to see the woman in the mirror then.

BY LATE AFTERNOON on Sunday, I was stir-crazy. Minutes passed like they were wading in molasses. Every time I looked at the clock, it seemed the time hadn't changed at all. Normally in these situations, I could entertain myself with a movie or a book. But I was too anxious, too ready for Hudson to be home. His texts and calls had occupied the days before, but he'd texted while I was sleeping that he would be in meetings the entire day and unreachable.

I'd already put a run in on the treadmill, and though I considered doing some window shopping, it was Reynold on duty and he was not my favorite companion. At five, I was already completely ready for David's going away party—two hours early—and couldn't think of a single thing to distract me from my boredom.

I decided to fuck it.

Grabbing my laptop bag, I set the alarm to *away* and slipped down to the lobby. I knew a text went out to my bodyguards when I set the alarm to *home*, but I wasn't sure if it did anything when I left. I stood outside The Bowery for several minutes, waiting to see if Reynold would show up or message me.

He didn't. I scanned my surroundings. Seeing no pesky blondes lurking in the area, I set off for the French bakery on the corner of the block.

Being out on my own felt absolutely amazeballs. It wasn't that I minded having Jordan and Reynold in tow; it was simply such a pain to arrange outings that spontaneity had lost its place in my routine. The whole need to be protected was Hudson's idea, anyway. Celia didn't scare me.

Okay, she scared me, but there was no reason why she should. What the hell could she do to me anyway?

The bakery had very few customers when I arrived. Though I would have liked to sit at one of the outdoor tables, I took my iced tea and a pesto panini and settled in a seat near the side door. If I wasn't going to have my bodyguard, then I should at least take some additional precautions. Sitting inside was my version of precaution.

After finishing my food, I set up my computer and opened up my email. There were a few items regarding the club, a random e-card from my brother, and an unread message from Stacy. Ignoring everything else, I opened Stacy's email and scanned it.

I'm still not sure who wrote the emails. Maybe if you looked at one, it would help. Here's one of the longer ones.

Below her short note was a forwarded message from the H.Pierce email she'd told me about. Other women might have decided that reading the message wasn't necessary when Hudson was planning a tell-all.

I have never been other women. I read eagerly.

Before finishing the first paragraph, I was convinced the message wasn't from Hudson. It was too poetic, too flowery. Hudson avoided analogies and figurative language. Even when he was romantic—something he swore he never was—his phrasing was direct and to-the-point.

This letter was composed of everything Hudson wasn't. There were references to nature and popular music and relatives. The author spoke of his mother as *the rock of the family* and his father as a *compassionate patriarch.* Definitely not the Pierces I knew.

It was a section midway through the letter that confirmed without a doubt that the email was not written by Hudson. The paragraph read:

I've studied and learned about the world from books and tour packages arranged by and for the discontented rich, but I'd prefer to one day leave all my life and responsibility behind and travel the earth by whim. Right now, I can say that I love Paris and Vienna, but what do I truly know of these cities when I haven't lived *in them,* participated *in their culture? Words without experience are meaningless.*

I read the last line again. "*Words without experience are meaningless.*" It was a quote from *Lolita*. There were other lines that seemed familiar, certainly more quips from other literary classics. Hudson Pierce did not read the classics. His library had no books before I'd moved in. Celia, on the other hand…

A flash of movement out the window drew my attention.

I peered out to find that a couple sitting on the other side of the glass was leaving. What kept my focus was the woman at the table behind them.

Goddamn, speak of the devil.

As my eye caught hers, Celia smiled—the same old bitchy smile she always delivered.

I chewed on my lip, deciding what to do. I could continue sitting in the bakery and text Reynold for a ride. Or I could leave and see if she'd follow.

Or I could talk to her.

There wasn't anything I burned to say to the woman. I knew that any request I made to be left alone would only result in more harassment. And asking her reasons for her actions wouldn't get me anywhere. Anything she said to me couldn't be trusted, so what was the point in conversation?

The point was that I was curious. Curious what she'd try to convince me of, what her body language would say.

Before I could talk myself out of it, I threw my bag over my shoulder, grabbed my computer and walked out to the patio.

To her credit, Celia didn't blink when I sat across from her.

"By all means, Laynie, sit," she said, her tone pleasant and condescending and a little bit eager, as though she was looking forward to a confrontation. She probably was.

Without any preamble, I turned my laptop to face her and pointed to the email still on the screen. "This is you, isn't it?"

She scanned a few lines, recognition flashing in her eyes. "I don't know for the life of me what you're talking about, Laynie."

She liked to say my name a lot—it was a trick I'd learned in grad school. When said in the right tone, it made a person feel patronized. She certainly knew the tools of basic manipulation.

But so did I. "That email, Celia. You're the one who sent it to Stacy. I recognize your choice of literary quotes."

"Why, that's crazy." Her inflection was exaggerated. "This says it's from Hudson. Did you hack into his email? I hear that's typical of women with your condition. In fact, Laynie, should you really be sitting with me? I could still file that restraining order."

I tilted my head, studying her. She wanted me to threaten a restraining order of my own. But we were playing this conversation on my terms. "What I don't understand is how you got Hudson to go along."

"Go along with what?" She blinked innocently.

"The kiss." I turned the screen back to face me and loaded the video. I pushed play and spun it toward her. "This."

She watched silently, giving nothing away. When it was finished, she raised her eyes to meet mine, her expression suddenly serious. "So you've discovered our little secret."

She wanted me to assume the kiss was real. I didn't believe it was. "That you played together? Yes."

She laughed. "Is that what he told you? I suppose he wouldn't want you to know what we really meant to each other."

"Ha ha. I don't buy it."

"That I was Hudson's lover? Suit yourself." She pursed her lips. "It lasted beyond that, you know. Why do you think I had a key to his place? And when I picked him up at the Hamptons—there was no business trip."

Lies, lies, lies.

I didn't have any doubt that every word was meant to instigate me. "You've fucked with me too many times to believe anything that comes out of your mouth." I closed my computer and began stuffing it in my bag. There was nothing to learn from her after all.

Celia shrugged. "I could give you proof, if I wanted to. I know all his bedroom moves. Does he dominate you completely? Does he have a nickname for you? *Precious,* perhaps?"

Unwittingly, my eyes popped up at Hudson's pet name. How the hell did she know about that? Hudson had promised me it was private.

She caught my reaction. "He does, doesn't he? Don't you know that he calls all his lovers *precious*? Did you think it was just for you? He called me that when he plowed into me over and over on his office desk. *'My precious, my precious,'* he'd say. I'm sure he simply says it now out of habit."

It didn't matter if she was telling the truth or lying. Either way, she'd tainted something sacred. Something that meant a great deal to me. That combined with all the other shit she'd pulled?

I snapped.

"Maybe it wasn't just for me. But this is just for you." My hand curled into a fist and flew at her face before she could see it coming. From the cracking sound that accompanied my punch, I guessed that her nose was broken.

"You fucking bitch!" she screamed, her hands holding her nose.

"I was thinking the same about you. Though cunt would have been my choice of noun."

Blood oozed out from between Celia's hands. "You want a noun? Try *lawsuit*."

That was the last I heard before I darted out the patio gate. Afraid Celia would find someone to come after me, I headed straight for the subway.

A lawsuit, huh? Well, it was fucking worth it.

— CHAPTER —
EIGHTEEN

I jumped on the first train that was available and found an empty seat in the back, my hands shaking and my heart pounding.

God, what had I done?

I couldn't decide if I was scared or exhilarated. Probably an equal combination of both. Because, *damn*. I'd punched Celia Werner. And probably broke her cute little nose. That was surely going to get a cop or two knocking on my door. And, with her power and money, they'd take her charge seriously. I'd had trouble with the law in the past. Having another incident on my record was not something I was looking forward to.

On the other hand—I punched Celia *fucking* Werner. And holy fuck did it feel good.

I had to do something, tell someone. I considered my options—Brian had always been my go-to person for getting me out of sticky situations. That had been hard on our relationship, and now that we were getting along, involving him wasn't my ideal choice.

That put Hudson at the top of my list. He was better suited to go up against the Werners. While I was pretty sure that he would be one hundred percent supportive and take care of anything I needed, calling him with the news promised to be embarrassing. Especially since I'd ditched my bodyguard. He wouldn't be pleased with that.

Cell service was spotty underground, but I managed to get through. Unfortunately, I reached his voicemail. I tried a couple of times with the same result. Hudson had said he had meetings all day. I was sure that was where he was. I chose not to leave a message. Instead, I texted him to call me ASAP and hoped to heaven I got to him before Celia did.

Because she would try to contact him too. Of that I was certain.

And what about what she'd told me? As much as I didn't want to let her get to me, I couldn't help but think about the things she'd said. I didn't automatically believe her—why would I?

But her proof…

I shook off the idea. Somehow she found out about Hudson's name for me. That had to be it. There was no way he'd called her that too. And, yes, he was dominating in bed, but anyone who knew him would assume that.

The only reason it continued to nag at me was that I still hadn't heard Hudson's confession. Was this what he meant to tell me all along? That he'd been with Celia? That he'd slept with her while with me?

I didn't think so. I didn't *want* to think so. It was too easy, too predictable. Hudson was never predictable.

Except if that wasn't it…

The alternate possibility that had started to form in my mind was worse than what Celia had suggested. Much worse. Like, it would shatter my world to discover it were true. I couldn't entertain the idea long enough to work through it, even to try and discount it.

So I didn't think about it at all. Buried it until I had to deal with it. *If* I had to deal with it.

Meanwhile, I needed someone to give me some advice. Besides Brian, who would know how police handled battery charges? I considered David and Liesl. Mira and Jack were even possibilities. Finally, I settled on someone who I was sure would be able to handle the situation the best.

Jordan answered on the first ring.

"Hey, I know your shift doesn't start for a bit, but I'm sort of in a situation and I need your help."

"I can be at the penthouse in twenty-five."

He was already about to hang up when I stopped him. "Actually, I'm not there. I'm just walking off the subway at Grand Central Station."

There was only a minor pause before he asked, "Reynold's not with you?"

"No." I should have been more regretful, but I wasn't. "I'll explain when I see you. Can you come meet me?"

"Yep. In fact, if you're at Grand Central, I can be there in ten."

We agreed on a place to meet. Then I hung up and waited for him to show.

True to his word, Jordan was indeed only ten minutes away. *He must live nearby.* Funny how little I knew about the man.

We found an empty bench and talked without leaving the station. I caught him up quickly, leaving nothing out. Well, very little out. I didn't mention what it was exactly Celia had said to cause my fist to fly.

Jordan seemed neither surprised nor judgmental of my story. "Have you called Hudson?"

"I tried. I got voicemail." I'd tried again while waiting for Jordan with the same result.

"That's fine. It's really not urgent. Here's what's probably going to happen: Celia will likely have gone to the ER. Because of who she is and the pull she has, I'd assume she'd get the police to take her complaint there. With a simple one-swing hit, the cops will often forget the whole thing. They won't because she's a Werner."

"Could I be arrested?" It was the question most pressing on my mind.

He shook his head. "They'll track you down and give you a court date. No warrants, no arrests. There will be plenty of time for Mr. Pierce to get the whole thing dropped—which he will. You know that, right?"

"I do." I wrung my hands in my lap. "At least, I think I do. I also feel shitty about being a burden."

Jordan laughed—I'd never heard him outright laugh. He was nearly as serious and on-task as Hudson. "That man could never think of you as a burden, Laynie. He turned mountains over to get your last charge completely expunged. And the deal he's working on now has been much more problematic than it will be for him to get rid of any charge from Celia."

I'd known Hudson had buried my restraining order violation, but Jordan's last words were news to me. "What does the deal he's working on now have to do with me?"

He studied me carefully. "I'm sorry, Laynie. That's going to have to come from him. My point is that you're not his burden. You're his reason."

I savored Jordan's words. I needed them right then. Especially with Hudson out of reach, I needed the reminder that he was still there for me. "Thank you, Jordan. I appreciate that more than you can understand. Do you know when he'll be back?"

Jordan's mouth tightened, and I knew he was being careful how much he said. "Depends on how his meetings go today."

Why did it feel like everyone knew some big secret about this business deal that I didn't? Hudson, Norma, even Jordan. From what I'd gathered, it wasn't anything bad. Then why was I not allowed to know?

Hudson had promised me I could find out anything I wanted to know when we talked. This was definitely going on the list. I'd rather hear things from him than my bodyguard anyway, so I didn't press.

I checked the clock on my phone. There was only a little over an hour before David's shindig. Maybe I should just head there. Unless that was going to be a problem. "The club is closed on Sundays, but we're having a party for my coworker who's going away. Do you think the police will show up there? I don't want to ruin anything."

"Nah. They'll either show up at the penthouse or wait until normal business hours to find you at work. You'll be fine."

"I know I have to face them eventually, but I'd rather not today." Shit, I was such a coward.

If Jordan agreed with my assessment of myself, he didn't indicate as such. "Let's do this: we can take the train back uptown. I'll leave you at The Sky Launch—I don't expect Ms. Werner to show up and bother you tonight."

"No. Not likely." Though, I wouldn't mind seeing how much damage I'd actually incurred. Just thinking about it brought a smile to my face.

"The car is parked at the penthouse. I'll go and get it and come back to the club. Then we can leave whenever you want." Jordan casually watched the subway passengers as they walked past us. Or it appeared casual. The more I learned about him, the more I realized nothing he did was casual.

And he was always thinking. "I bet that the police will stop by tomorrow morning, Laynie. If you prefer to stay away from them until Mr. Pierce gets back, I could take you to the loft tonight after the party instead."

"That's not a bad idea. I'll consider it." Except I hoped that when I finally reached Hudson, he'd take care of things for me so I wouldn't have to hide out anywhere.

But even if Hudson could get rid of a battery charge, he couldn't protect us from her forever. He hadn't been able to stop her stalking. Surely now she'd up her game. I thought of Jack's advice from our lunch—*the only way to get rid of her was to let her think she'd won*. Punching her in the face definitely wasn't letting her win. By striking against her, had I made the worst move possible? More than ever I feared that Celia Werner would be a permanent fixture in my future. Could Hudson and I survive that?

THE PROBLEM WITH holing up at The Sky Launch was that I wasn't in the mood to be there. Fortunately, I didn't have to do anything for the party except open the doors for the caterers. Hudson had arranged the whole thing, including an open bar. It was beyond generous on his part—probably his way of apologizing for the circumstances in which David was leaving.

Everyone on staff had been allowed a plus one. With David's friends and the few regulars that had been invited, the total guest list numbered around a hundred. It was a true party. The whole thing might have been fun if my plus one was there. But he wasn't. And by ten, I still hadn't heard from him.

"Put the fucking phone down and boogie with me," Liesl urged. I'd filled her in on the day's events when she arrived. Her feeling was that if I was going to face policemen tomorrow, I should party harder tonight.

She and I were definitely different people.

"Laynie, I love you and I'm here for you if you truly need me. But you seem to have moping down on your own so I'm going to leave you to it and go have a good time." She tugged at a strand of my hair. "Forgive me?"

"Totally forgive you. Go. Have fun."

She gave me a peck on the lips and joined a raucous group in the center of the floor. I tried not to feel abandoned. It wasn't Liesl I wanted anyway.

Determined to not spoil the evening for anyone else, I sat curled up on one of the sofas that lined the main floor and nursed my champagne while I watched the crowd dance and mingle in front of me. It was probably a good idea for me to sit out anyway. Most of them were my employees, after all. There should be a level of separation and respect.

I wondered how much respect I'd get if they all watched me get dragged out in handcuffs.

Stop it, I scolded myself. Jordan said there'd be no arrests, and Hudson would fix everything before it came to a head, though it wouldn't surprise me if Celia reported my assault to the media.

God, the media!

I closed my eyes, wincing at the thought. *Please, Hudson, call me. Please!*

"Mind if I join you?" a voice shouted over the pulsing beat.

Opening my eyes, I found Gwen in front of me.

She was already taking a seat before I answered. "By all means, join me." I scanned the room again. Though not everyone was dancing, I appeared to be the only loner. Was that why Gwen had come over?

Fuck, I hoped not. I wasn't in the mood to be jollied up. Might as well let her know that right off the bat. "Why aren't you out there?" Maybe she'd get the hint and join the crowd on the dance floor.

She furrowed her brow and I realized that the drink in her hand had not been her first. If she wasn't drunk already, she was on her way. "I'm not really into…" She trailed off as if forgetting what she was saying.

I finished for her. "Dancing?"

"Actually, I was going to say *people*." She added an amendment. "Besides, they're our employees. It doesn't seem right to party hard with them tonight when I might be writing them up tomorrow."

Damn, she was a good manager. "Gwen? I'm starting to like you. What's up with that?"

She almost laughed. "I'm sure it won't last. Give it time." Her words were heavy, as if she had a sad story to back them up. Or perhaps she was simply a somber drunk.

If she wasn't outright going to share, I wasn't going to ask. I had my own problems. For the tenth time in fifteen minutes I hit the screen of my phone, checking for a missed call or text.

Nothing.

Jordan had already returned with the car and was now hanging out in the employee lounge watching something on PBS. I shot him a message: *Any word from Hudson?*

His reply came fast. *Nope. West coast is 3 hours behind. It's only six there. Give him time.*

It had already been five hours since I first texted Hudson to call me. How much time did he need?

Gwen interrupted my thoughts. "You keep checking that thing. Are you expecting a better offer?"

With a sigh, I stuffed my phone in my bra. "Just waiting for Hudson to call. He's in L.A. for a couple of days. I hadn't realized I'd been so obvious."

She groaned. "God, you're so lovesick, it's disgusting."

I tilted my head. "Do you not approve of me with Hudson?"

Gwen shrugged. "I don't give a flying fig about you and Hudson. It's love I don't approve of. I get it enough with Nor—" She stopped, catching herself before she finished her sister's name. "Anyway. Seems there's love all around. I'm over it."

She didn't know I was already aware of Norma and Boyd's fling. I didn't bother to tell her. It was her anti-romance attitude that intrigued me. Did she feel abandoned by her sister since she'd started fooling around with her assistant? Knowing almost nothing about Gwen, it was hard to say.

Then it hit me. "Ooh, Gwen's got a heartache story." Things were clicking in place. For the first time that evening, I felt slightly interested in something other than myself. "Is that why you were so eager to leave Eighty-Eighth Floor?"

Her eyes glossed over, whether from memory or alcohol, I wasn't sure. She opened her mouth to say something. Then her focus returned. "Nice try. I'm drunk, but I'm not that drunk." She took another swallow of her Wild Turkey and glanced at my half-full glass of champagne. "Speaking of which, why don't you join me on the intoxicatrain?"

"Not much of a drinker." With my low tolerance, I was already feeling a little tipsy, and I planned on being sober when I talked to Hudson.

"Hmm." She looked me over as if sizing me up. Then her attention went to the crowd tearing it up on the dance floor. She took another swallow of her drink. "I heard you saying something about addiction to Liesl. Are you a former alky?"

I laughed. She was as curious about me as I was about her. Perhaps if I spilled my story, she'd spill hers. Except at the moment, bonding wasn't exactly on my priority list. "Uh-uh. Not happening. You have your secrets, I have mine."

Gwen smiled. "I'm good with that."

"So this is where the party is." David leaned over the back of the sofa between our heads.

"Ha ha. Sarcasm. Nice." Gwen finished off her glass and set it on the table next to her.

David ignored Gwen and turned his attention to me. "This night is supposed to be my last chance with my favorite people. And my most favorite people is over here moping. What's up with that?"

His reference to me as his *favorite people* made me tense only slightly. He was on his way out of town. No need to worry about his intentions.

And he was right. This night was about him, not me. "Shit, I'm sorry, David. This is supposed to be a party, and I'm crashing it with my bad mood."

He crossed around in front of the sofa and sat on the low table in front of us. "Why are you in a bad mood, anyway? You were so...*peppy*...the last two days." His brows lifted, hopeful. "Trouble in paradise?"

It was sweet how he never stopped trying. "I hate to disappoint you, but I don't think so." Though telling Hudson about my lapse in self-control might alter that.

Why hadn't he called yet? And did Jordan really know how the NYC legal system worked?

I bit my lip with worry. "There is the fact that I could be arrested soon." It was easier to let info slip with David than Gwen.

David glanced questioningly at Gwen. "Don't look at me," she said with a shrug. "She doesn't tell me jack shit."

He wrapped his hands around the edges of the table on either side of him. "I think I need to hear more."

For half a second I considered spilling it all. But that wasn't fair to David. He'd been a good manager and a good friend. Was this any way to send him off?

"No, you really don't need to hear more. Forget I said anything. Please. I'm being melodramatic." *Hopefully.*

"Let me know if I can do anything?" That was David. Never the type to push or pry. At one time, I'd fooled myself into thinking that could be enough for me. That he'd be safer. That he was the guy that would keep me sane.

Now I knew differently. Though Hudson pushed and pried and drove me crazy, he was the nearest thing to clarity I knew.

That was why I needed him so desperately at the moment.

But sitting around lamenting his absence wasn't going to bring him to me. And it was a hell of a lousy way to say goodbye to my friend.

Putting on the happiest face I could muster, I set my glass down. "You know what you can do, David? You can cheer me up." I stood up and nodded toward the floor. "Let's dance, shall we?"

"I thought you'd never ask."

Instead of joining the rest of the crowd in the center of the floor, we stuck to an empty corner. A few minutes into the dance mix of David Guetta's *Titanium*, I felt better. It had been forever since I'd let myself loose, since I'd stopped worrying and fretting and just lived in the moment. I closed my eyes and let the beat overtake me, let my feet and hips move as they liked. Sweat gathered at my brow and my breath got short, but I was alive—alive in the way that only the club made me. Soon my anxiousness dissolved and all I was thinking about was the present—the music, the lights flashing around us, the friend standing in front of me. It was exactly what I needed.

I wasn't sure how long we'd been dancing or how many songs had played before the DJ faded into a slow song. The club never played slow songs. I looked to David, my brow raised.

"Someone must have requested it." He held his hand out for me. "Let's not waste it, shall we?"

A voice in my head nagged that it was a bad idea. If David had asked for the song to be played—and I was certain he had—then he'd meant it for me. He'd meant it as a means to get me in his arms. It would be wrong—I had a boyfriend that I loved with my entire being. Hudson wouldn't like it, and that was reason enough to not engage. Every impulse in my body said to walk away.

Except there was a flicker of emotion in my chest that I couldn't ignore—a need for closure, perhaps, or a touch of melancholy for what once was or what could have been. Or maybe it was simply the alcohol and the adrenaline and the need for someone to hold me after all the stress and anxiety of the day.

And Hudson wasn't there, so what could one dance hurt?

Without another thought, I took David's hand and let him pull me into his arms. He was warm in a way that I'd forgotten. Like a giant teddy bear. He wasn't nearly as cut or as trim as Hudson, but he was strong and easy to fall into.

I rested my head on his shoulder as we swayed together. Closing my eyes, I listened to the words of the song and relaxed into our final embrace. The singer was familiar, but I couldn't remember his name. He sang to his love, telling her that she was in his veins, that he could not get her out.

They were words that made me think of Hudson. He was so deeply imprinted on me that he'd seeped through my skin and into my veins. He was my life force, each pulse of my heart sending another shock of love through my body.

Was this how David felt about me?

A strange mixture of panic and sorrow and a little bit of contentment washed over me as I realized that it was exactly how David felt about me. If I had any doubt, it was cleared when he began singing the words at my ear. "*I cannot get you out.*"

I stopped moving with him and leaned back to look at his eyes. He knew, right? Knew that this was wrong, that I was spoken for? That I didn't feel the same way about him?

If he did know, he didn't care. He pressed forward, taking my lips in his before I knew what was happening. His kiss was shocking and unwelcomed. Immediately I pushed him away.

The sadness in David's eyes pierced through me. I knew that depth of heartache. It tore me up to know I was the cause of his.

There was nothing I could do for it but shake my head and bite back tears.

David started to speak—to apologize maybe, or to try to persuade me to give him a chance. Before he said anything, though, his eyes moved upward to a point behind me, his expression stricken with alarm.

I knew without looking who was standing behind me. Wasn't it fate's sick way of paying me back for all the shit I'd pulled in my lifetime? Put the person who I wanted most in the situation I wanted him in the least? That's why he hadn't returned my call, why I couldn't reach him—he'd been coming home.

Slowly, I turned toward him. His jacket was off, his shirt wrinkled from traveling. He'd loosened his tie and his jaw had a layer of end-of-day scruff. It was his face that I focused on, though. The pain in David's eyes was nothing compared to what I found in Hudson's. The anguish there was unbearable, his expression filled with so much pain I wondered if there could be any balm to soothe it.

For the second time that night I asked myself, *god, what have I done?*

— CHAPTER — NINETEEN

I swallowed back the panic that surged through me. I could fix this. I *had* to be able to fix this.

"Hudson." I took a step toward him. "It's not what it looks like." I didn't actually know what it looked like, having no idea how long he'd been standing there. Did he see that I'd pushed David away?

His face was stone. "Maybe we should discuss this in a more private setting."

"Okay." It was more a squeak than a word. But I headed toward the employee office and assumed he'd follow.

He did.

We took the stairs without speaking. I didn't feel his eyes on me as I walked. He didn't even want to look at me. Despair washed over me. I'd been so desperate for him, and now I'd fucked it up. Again.

I didn't turn to face him again until he'd shut the door behind us in the office. When I did, I almost wished I hadn't. The forlorn look I'd seen downstairs was even worse than I'd remembered. Was there really anything I could say to erase that?

With feeble words, I tried. "*He* kissed me, Hudson. I didn't kiss him. And when he did, I pushed him away." It was the truth. If he'd been there long enough, he'd have seen it.

"Why were you in his arms in the first place?" His tone was low and gravelly. It was more emotion than he generally displayed, and it killed me.

A tear trickled down my face. "We were dancing. It was a party."

His eyes flared. "You were in his arms, Alayna. In the arms of someone who has made no secret of his feelings for you. What did you think he'd do?"

He was right on many counts. I'd known it was dangerous, felt the wrongness of the embrace from the minute David put his arms around me.

But *my* intentions had not been to lead him on. It was a goodbye dance. My thoughts had been focused on Hudson the whole time. "It was innocent," I insisted. "I needed someone. He was here. And you weren't."

The memory of the anxiousness that had driven me to David's arms in the first place turned my tears bitter. "Where were you today, anyway? When I needed you?"

He matched my bitterness plus some. "What was it you needed, Alayna? Someone to keep you warm?"

I pressed my lips together, hoping to squelch the sob threatening to escape. "That hurts."

"What I just witnessed hurts."

That wasn't news, but hearing him say it twisted my heart all the same. I'd experienced that same hurt—when I'd seen him kissing Celia on the video, then again earlier today, when she'd suggested they'd had an affair. Perhaps it wasn't fair to compare her probable lies with what he'd witnessed in person, but he had to see where I was coming from. "Yeah, I know how it feels."

"Do you?" Even that tiny phrase was filled with enough venom to smart.

It triggered more of my own snark. "Yeah, I do. Let me see if I can explain it. It feels like your gut has been wrenched out of your body. At least that's what it felt like when Celia told me that you'd been *fucking her* for most of the time we've been together."

"What?" He seemed truly surprised, and not in the *I've-been-caught* way, but in the *what-the-eff-is-she-talking-about* way. It was the same expression he'd had when I'd mentioned him having more of an involvement with Stacy. "When did she say that?"

"Today," I grumbled, already regretting bringing Celia up this way.

"You saw her today?" His eyes narrowed. "Does this have something to do with the phone message she left me?"

"I *knew* she'd call you!" And if she had, why hadn't he called me? "What did she say?"

He shook his head dismissively. "She was raving nonsense. Something about you and her lawyer. I figured it was more of her shit from before so I deleted it."

Hudson took a step toward me, and I noticed his eyes had softened, that instead of pain the predominant feature was now worry. "What happened with her? Was she following you again? What did she do? And why didn't Reynold call me?"

I leaned on the desk behind me. "He didn't know." Guilt pressed on my chest, not only for ditching my bodyguard, but for Hudson's willingness to set aside his ache out of concern for me.

The expression on his face magnified my shame. "Please don't look at me like that. I'm sorry. I was stir-crazy so I grabbed my computer and went for coffee. I thought when I set the alarm to *away* that Reynold might notice, but I guess it didn't inform him."

Hudson's mouth tightened. "It only texts when you set it for *home*."

I was a little surprised that he hadn't set the system to monitor all my comings and goings. It wasn't like him. At a more appropriate time, I'd try to remember to be impressed. "Anyway, I just went to the bakery down the street. And Celia showed up. And I was sick of it. So I approached her."

"*You* approached *her*?" Not only was his eye twitching and his jaw tense, but his hand was shaking as well. I hadn't seen that from him before. Was he that angry?

"I did. It was stupid. I know it was stupid. But Stacy had sent me one of the emails that you had supposedly sent her, and I was reading it, and I could tell it wasn't from you. I recognized one of the quotes used from one of the books Celia highlighted, and I knew the email was from her. So I confronted her about it. About writing the email." The story spilled out in babble that I wasn't even sure he could comprehend.

Apparently he did. "And she told you then that I was with her? Just out of the blue?"

I cringed. He wouldn't like what I had to say next, but it was best to get it all out. "First, I showed her Stacy's video." After checking for his reaction, which I couldn't read, I went on. "Then she said that you were together. That you were a couple. That you fucked her that night and it wasn't the first time and it wasn't the last."

If Hudson's face grew any redder, steam would come out of his ears. "And you believed her?"

I squared my shoulders. "It pissed me off enough that I punched her." Yeah, I admit it, I sounded proud.

"You *punched* her?" There went the steam.

That hadn't been the reaction I'd wanted. "You know what? Keep acting like this is an interrogation and I'm out of here."

Hudson paced the room, pushing his hands through his hair. When he stopped to focus on me again, he'd regained some composure, though his shoulders were still tight and his voice strained. "I'm sorry if I sound a bit tense, Alayna. I assure you it's only out of concern for you."

I studied him for several seconds. It was out of concern—I saw it now. His eyes were pinned on me, his shaking wasn't out of anger; it was fear. Fear for me. The extent that he cared for me was limitless. It was as obvious as the color of his eyes.

The realization calmed me. I pulled back every ounce of snark and venom and gave him raw honesty in its place. "Yes, I punched her. I think I broke her nose. So I'm probably going to get some sort of assault charge for that. *That's* why I needed you."

"Alayna." His eyes radiated with love. "Why didn't you call me?"

"I did! Your phone was off. I could have left a message, but I didn't want to say all that over voicemail, and I didn't want to interrupt your meeting because I knew it was important."

"Not as important as you." He wanted to come to me—the urge was palpable. But there was still that other thing hanging in between us—the moment he'd walked in on—and so he sat on the arm of the couch instead, his hands playing with the bunched fabric of his slacks. "Have the police contacted you?"

I shook my head. "I was afraid to go back to the house so I came here to wait for your call."

His eyes settled on his shoes. "I got your text when I was already in flight. I didn't call because I knew I'd end up telling you I was on my way home, and I wanted it to be a surprise." He laughed gruffly. "I took a nap instead. I should have called."

Now it was my eyes that studied the floor. "I should have kept my cool."

"I'll take care of everything. Don't worry about it in the least. She's not going to bother you again."

He said it with such conviction that I had no choice but to believe him. He'd find a way to protect me from Celia. I simply had to comply with the parameters he set to keep me safe. If I'd done that to begin with, she wouldn't have had the opportunity to push me, and Hudson wouldn't have to bail me out of my mess.

Gratitude and relief swept through me, along with a twinge of regret. "Thank you."

And then a whole bunch more regret followed. If I hadn't punched Celia, would I have ended up in David's arms? Something told me probably not. Either way, the weight of what Hudson had witnessed was immensely heavy. "Hudson," my voice trembled. "I'm sorry."

"Don't be. Good for you, actually. She deserves worse." He even managed to smile as he said the last part.

I wanted to smile with him. But I couldn't. Not yet. "I mean, I'm sorry about David."

"Oh." His face grew grim and the pain from earlier resurfaced. His next words were careful and precise and burdened. "Tell me one thing—do you still feel anything for him?"

"No. No, I don't. Nothing. I've told you that before, and I meant it, though I'm sure it doesn't seem like it seeing me tonight. But the whole time he was holding me, it felt wrong. All I could think about was you. I was missing you, H. Needing you. So much. And I didn't think about what I was doing. I'm so, so, sor—"

He flew to me before I could finish, wrapping his arms around me.

Yes, that was how it was supposed to feel, that was what I'd been longing for.

He buried his face in my hair. "I missed you too, precious. Needed you. I was trying to get back here—"

"And I ruined your surprise." I nuzzled further into his chest. "I'm so sorry."

"I don't care. It hurts, but I've hurt you. And as long as you swear that he means nothing—"

"Nothing. I swear with every fiber of my body, it's only you." I tilted my head up to kiss along his jaw. "How about you—" The question threatened to stick in my throat, but I forced it out. "Do you still feel anything for Celia?"

His body stiffened. Leaning back to meet my eyes, he said softly, "Alayna...I've never felt anything for Celia."

"You mean, it was just sex?" They were things I had to ask, even if the answers were already clear.

He shook his head slowly. "I've never been with her at all."

"She was lying." It wasn't a question. I'd already suspected she'd made it up.

He confirmed anyway. "She was lying."

"That's what I thought." It should have been a relief. Why did my acceptance of this only bring a pit of dread?

Because if that wasn't what he had to confess to me about the video, then there was still a truth I had to learn. Something told me I already knew. The alternative explanation that I'd managed to tuck away earlier returned to niggle at me. And this time it wouldn't let go until I explored it fully.

Gently—reluctantly—I pushed my way out of his arms. "But here's the thing—I sort of wish it were true."

He raised a questioning brow.

"Not that you were sleeping with her while we were together—not that part. But the rest of it—that you were really with her when Stacy saw you. If that was the truth, I could accept it. Don't get me wrong—the idea of you with her, fucking her—it torments me. It really does." Like, actually produced bile in my mouth. "But I think I always knew you were never with her. It's in your eyes—both now and in that video."

Hudson's Adam's apple bobbed as he swallowed. "I wasn't. I was never with her."

I continued to stare at his neck. It was easier than looking at his eyes where dark storms were beginning to gather. "And that means that the thing with Stacy was a scam. Of course it was. I wanted to think it was just Celia in on it, and you were protecting her. But you said you weren't and you did go along enough to stage that kiss. You were part of it."

I paused, letting what I'd said sink into my consciousness, tasting the truth of the words that still lingered in my mouth. "I thought for a minute that might be your secret. Except it's not it. I mean, yeah, that's shitty that you did that to her, but I knew you had those things in your past. And *you* knew that I knew those things. If that were all there was to learn from that video, you would have told me. There had to be more you were hiding."

Finally, with great effort, I raised my eyes to his. "It's because of what night it was, the night of the symposium, isn't it? I considered that you didn't want me to know that you were still manipulating people for fun that recently, but now I don't think that's all of it either."

"Alayna…" Even though only a whisper, there was weight to his single word. It was cautionary, it was pleading. It said, *don't go here,* even though we were always headed there, from the second he first laid eyes on me. It was fated that we'd arrive at this moment, and whether we wanted to face it or not, here it was.

"It's not the video itself. It's what happened after." I spoke as if I was just figuring it out, but really, it had always been there, buried in my subconscious where I didn't have to deal with it. I knew. I'd always known what I was only now able to admit.

Hudson repeated my name, calling for my attention, but I was no longer focused on him.

"If Celia was there with you outside the symposium…then doesn't it make sense that she went in with you? And if she went in with you, she was there when you first saw me. And if you were still playing people together…"

My skin broke out in goose bumps as a chill ran down my spine and a wave of nausea wracked through my body. A ringing began in my ears, and somewhere behind that I could hear Hudson still speaking.

"I was going to tell you," he seemed to be saying. "I came back to tell you."

I searched his face, barely registering his fragmented explanation as the truth settled over me.

"It's my worst mistake, Alayna." He stepped toward me, his face twisted in anguish, his voice desperate. "The most horrible of all the things I've done. My biggest regret, although it's what gave me you and for that I'm forever grateful. But I never knew what I'd feel for you. I never knew that I could hurt you that much, and that I would care that I did. Please, Alayna, you have to understand."

I was beginning to understand. With shocking clarity. "That's what I was, wasn't I?" I wasn't really asking anyone. "A game. Your game. Together." My legs went weak and I fell to the floor. "Oh god. Oh god, oh god."

"Alayna—" Hudson fell to his knees and reached for me.

I scrambled away, my entire body shaking. "Don't touch me!" I screamed. I couldn't tell if he'd stopped moving toward me or not—my vision was blinded with fury and pain. My stomach twisted as though I might vomit and my head—my head couldn't process, couldn't think.

It didn't help that Hudson refused to let me have a minute to hear my own thoughts. "It wasn't what you think, Alayna. Yes, it started as a game. As Celia's game. But I only went along because it was you. Because I was so enamored with you."

I stared at him, blinking until my vision cleared. Then it was as if I were seeing him for the first time. I'd known this was his M.O. How could I have ignored that this exact situation was a possibility? Our beginning had been strange and unusual. He'd bought the club. Then he'd hired me to break up his engagement—an engagement that wasn't ever a real thing. Why had I not questioned the bizarreness of it before?

And now he was trying to reason with me. My stomach wrenched tighter and I began to dry heave.

"Alayna, let me—"

I held a hand out to stop him from coming toward me. "I don't want your help," I said when the heaving subsided. With the back of my hand, I wiped the spit from my mouth. "I want fucking answers."

"Anything. I told you I'd tell you anything." His words tumbled out as if he thought that answers might benefit him.

I already knew there was nothing he could say to fix this. That every answer would likely be more painful than the last. Still I had to know everything.

I bent my fingers into the carpet, trying to grasp onto something to give me strength. "You were enamored with me?" The phrase was sour on my tongue. "So you decided to fuck with me?"

"No." He sat back on his haunches and shoved both hands through his hair. "No, I wanted to get near you, and her plan was an excuse."

"And what was her plan? '*That girl presenting now. Make her fall in love with you and'*...what?"

He shook his head fiercely, emphatically. "No, it didn't happen like that. It wasn't like that."

I slammed a fist into the floor. "Then what was it like? Tell me!"

He clambered to find his words. I'd never seen him so lost, so off-balance, so miserable. "I saw you, like I've told you, and I was drawn to you. Completely drawn to you. I've never lied about that."

"Drawn to me so you decided to destroy me." And it had worked, hadn't it? Because here I was, completely destroyed.

Hudson shook his head again. "This isn't how I wanted to tell you. It's not coming out right at all."

"You mean if you told it another way, you could manipulate it to make it sound better." I was shaking so badly, my teeth chattered as I spoke.

He winced as if I'd slapped him across the face. "I deserve that. But that's not what I meant." He inched closer, then stilled when my expression told him not to dare move nearer. "Let me tell it the way it was. Please. It won't be better. It will still be awful, but it will be accurate."

I leaned my back against the desk front, not wanting to hear more, needing to hear it all. "I'm waiting."

He ran his tongue along his lips. "I saw you. And Celia noticed, I think. Noticed me noticing you. A few days later, she showed up with information about you."

"*She* showed up with information?" My interruption shook him from what I'd guessed was a memorized script. Too goddammed bad. I wasn't about to let any of it be easy for him.

"Yes, Celia had investigated you. It wasn't me. She had your police record and the restraining order, plus a copy of your mental health record."

Another wave of nausea rippled through me as I thought about Celia being the one to uncover my secrets. As I pictured her running to Hudson with the information of my worst sins.

He seemed to read my disgust, seemed to want to ease it. "It was in complete opposition to what I'd seen of you, Alayna. Everything she'd gathered—that wasn't the strong, confident woman we'd seen at the symposium. It was obvious those things existed in your past. You were better. I saw that."

"I was better." I said it defiantly, even though it was exactly what he'd just said. "I was."

"Yes. You were. It was evident." He took a breath. "Her theory, though, was that you could be broken again." His eyes flared. "*I didn't agree.*"

He let those words hang in the air, waiting for them to sink in.

But what did he expect that I'd do? Stand up and give him a fucking medal because he'd wagered on my side? Because he'd assumed that he *couldn't* break me?

He'd still tried!

Anyway, he'd been wrong. He had gone beyond breaking me. He'd shattered me.

He kept talking, my brain barely computing his words. "That was the bet. She made up the whole idea to have you break up our nonexistent engagement. After a time, I was to end things with you, naturally. Say that the farce was no longer necessary. Then we'd wait and see what happened." He paused to find his words. "But I didn't ever feel—"

I cut him off. "So all of it was a scam. Every single part of us was a lie." My speech was labored as I forced out words that I could never have imagined saying.

"No!" He was animated, passionate. "Even in the beginning, it was never about the game. Not for me. I wasn't supposed to seduce you. I wasn't supposed to fall in love with you. And I did both before you'd even agreed to play along."

I tilted my chin up, the only challenge I could muster besides my heated words. "But you didn't fall in love with me. There's no way, because you don't do shit like that to people you love!"

"I'd never been in love, Alayna! I didn't understand what I was feeling. I only knew I had to be with you and this was the way to do it." His voice cracked. "I'm not excusing what I did, but I'm explaining. I'm pleading for you to try to…to try and…"

"And what? See it from your point of view? Forgive you?" Bitterness dripped from me. There wasn't anything else inside me. I couldn't even cry.

I cocked my head and met his eyes, making certain my next words were clearly understood no matter how I stuttered to get them out. "This is unforgiveable, Hudson! There is no moving forward from this."

"Don't say that. Don't ever say that." His tone was urgent and remorseful. Pained.

I didn't fucking care. Let him hurt. I was glad for it, if that's even how he really felt. I'd hurt him further if I could. I did my best to try. "What is it exactly that you don't want to hear, Hudson? That I can't forgive you? I can't. I can't forgive this. Ever."

"Alayna, please!" He started for me again.

I kicked at him, managing to connect a foot with his upper arm. "We're over. Over! Don't you get it? There's no fucking way to ever trust you again after this!"

He sat back again. He could have easily overcome me if he'd kept trying. Even when I was upset and pumped with adrenaline, he was stronger than me. I couldn't even gather an ounce of gratefulness for it though. He owed me that. He owed me more.

I didn't trust that he wouldn't try once more, and the last thing I wanted was his touch. In fact, I couldn't even look at him. I had to go. Placing a hand in front of me, I pushed myself up to stand. "I'm leaving now. Don't try to stop me. Don't come after me." It took great effort, but finally I was on my feet. "We're done."

Hudson followed me up. "We aren't done, Alayna. This isn't over. We've rebuilt trust after you've broken—"

I spun toward him. "Don't even fucking compare what I've done to this! My mistakes are not even in the same category. This is the worst thing. The *worst* thing you could...I can't even...I can't breathe..." I leaned over, placing my palms on my thighs, trying to get air into my lungs.

He settled a hand on my back, leaning in to check on my breathing.

I shrugged him off. "Don't," I seethed with what air I could find. "Don't ever again. Don't touch me. Don't call. Don't try to reach out to me. This is over, Hudson. *Over*! I can't see you anymore." I'd been numb before, but now I felt volcanic, explosive. Everything inside—I wanted it out. Wanted to retch up every single speck of emotion I had about Hudson, good and bad. I yearned to be free of it all.

And yet the feeling went on. Endless and deep and unbearable.

"Don't say that, Alayna. Tell me how to fix this. Please." Hudson's despair echoed my own. "I'll do anything. There has to be a way."

I reached my hand out to the desk for support. "How? Tell me how there could possibly be a way to go on together after this?" I wasn't even sure I'd be able to go on at all after this.

"I don't have all the answers yet. But we can work on it together. We fix each other, remember?" Hudson curled his hands into fists, straightened them, then curled them again. "I love you, Alayna. I love you—that has to mean something."

For so long I'd waited to hear him talk of his love. Now, he said it freely, and it felt like a complete mockery of everything I'd yearned for him to express. "Right now it really doesn't."

"Please. You can't mean that." He reached for me yet again, his grasp circling my wrist.

With a scream, I yanked my arm away. "Get your fucking hands off me!"

He put his hands up in the air, in surrender. Then he let them fall to his side. He took a step backward. "You said," he paused, "you said you could love me through anything..."

I'd been waiting for him to throw that back at me. Honestly, I was surprised he hadn't mentioned it earlier. "Since everything you said turned out to be a lie, I don't feel like I'm obligated to honor my promise either."

Obligated or not, I did still love him. If I didn't, then I wouldn't feel this way. Every molecule in my body wouldn't be consumed in despair. That was the joke of the whole thing—I'd kept my promise. I did still love him through this horrible, fucked up thing he'd done to me.

But it didn't matter. Not anymore. Not when everything that my love was based upon was a sham.

There was a short knock followed by the opening of the office door. David stuck his head in. "Are you okay, Laynie?"

Had he heard me screaming a moment before? Or had he simply decided enough time had passed that he should check on me? Either way, I'd never been more grateful for the sight of him. "No. I'm not okay."

David looked from me to Hudson, not sure what to do.

Hudson tried once more. "Alayna..."

I had no more words for him. Nothing left to say, nothing left to give. I simply shook my head once. I was done. That was all.

He continued to plead with his eyes for long seconds. After a while, he lowered his head. "I'll leave." Hudson turned to David. "I'm sorry to put a damper on your party. Thank you for looking out for her."

He turned to look one last time at me, his expression filled with sorrow, regret, and longing. I knew he believed that I'd run to David after he left, and that the idea pained him even further. He was making a huge sacrifice leaving me with David alone.

But his sacrifice was a classic example of too little, too late.

So he was hurt? Too fucking bad. I was destroyed.

I turned away, not able to look at him any longer. I knew he was gone when David put his arms around me. I let him hug me for a moment, but contrary to what Hudson believed I'd do, I wasn't interested in seeking comfort from David. All I wanted to do was go somewhere and cry until the pain in my chest, in my head, in my bones, didn't threaten to pull me under anymore.

I wasn't sure it was even possible. I suspected that in reality I'd hurt—hurt hard—for a very, very long time.

"What can I do?" David asked as I pulled away.

I wiped a stream of tears from my face. "Get Liesl, please."

— CHAPTER —
TWENTY

Liesl was an angel.

She calmed me down enough to get me out of the building without drawing attention from the employees. I barely had the strength to walk, and she let me lean on her as we went to the curb and got into the cab that David hailed for us. She didn't make any jabs about being pulled away early from the party, nor did she try to get me to talk about what happened. Instead, she pulled my head into her lap and smoothed my hair while I cried all the way to her apartment in Brooklyn.

Once inside her place, Liesl tucked me into her bed with a glass of straight tequila. Though she had a futon in her living room, she stayed with me all night. She spooned behind me, and when I woke up from the little bouts of sleep I managed to get, her warm presence calmed my screams to sobs. I hadn't grieved and mourned that much since the death of my parents. Even then, I hadn't known the level of betrayal that I felt now.

That was the worst part of it, the betrayal. If I'd heard the story earlier from Hudson, at a point in our relationship where I hadn't put everything on the line, then I may have been able to survive it. I'd still have left him—I couldn't possibly be with him after that—but it would have been so much easier to survive. Leaving it as long as he did, especially when we'd talked at end about honesty and transparency—that was the ultimate betrayal. That was the deepest cut.

But the loss of the man I loved so desperately came as a close second.

The first two days were a blur. Liesl cooked for me and forced food down my throat. She listened to my story as I told it, in spurts, piecing it together as best she could, again without pressing. Throughout it all, she refilled my glass any time I asked. In a rare moment where I managed to focus on something other than my heartache, it occurred to me to wonder if that was why my father had spent his life drinking—had he been trying to block out some sort of pain? What had hurt him? Wasn't it sad that I'd never know?

The rest of my thoughts were mismatches of memories and realizations. Sweet recollections turned sour with the new information layered on top. I relived every conversation that I'd had with Hudson a dozen times. Sometimes all I could do was cry. At other moments, I became angry. I broke more than one glass throwing it in rage.

Once even, I considered taking a broken piece and slitting it across my skin. Maybe not too deep.

Or maybe exactly too deep.

Thankfully Liesl was there to clean up the fragments before I managed to steal any away. Besides, I didn't really want to end things—I just wanted to end the pain.

Eventually, I began trying to piece things together. Tried to figure out what was real and what wasn't. Imagined how and where Celia had fit into my relationship with Hudson. Like the way he'd condoned my jealousies, the way he supported my snooping. *Encourage her obsession*, I imagined Celia saying. *Don't get mad or upset if she shows any of her crazy traits.*

And the way she knew to throw his pet name in my face. Had that been her idea as well? *Give her a pet name. Something like* angel *or* precious.

I remembered Sophia's birthday—Hudson had spoken with Celia then, and when we came home he'd been distant. Had she reminded him of the game then? What he was really supposed to be doing with me?

To his credit, Hudson hadn't lied. His exact words came back to me with full force: "*I will be saying and doing things—romantic things, perhaps—that are not genuine. I need you to remember that. Out of the public eye, I will seduce you. That will be genuine, but it can never be misconstrued as love.*"

When had that changed? When had his false romancing become true? Had it ever? Was he at this very moment celebrating with his partner in crime—toasting to the complete and utter destruction of my soul?

That was the crux of my heartache—I'd never know. There was nothing to hold on to with fondness because the authenticity of every moment we'd spent together was up for debate. I couldn't believe anything he'd said or did.

He'd so expertly administered his manipulation it was impossible to see the real story underneath the formulated one.

That plain and utter truth was what kept me refilling my glass.

By Tuesday night, I sobered up enough to acknowledge some of my responsibilities. I propped myself against the headboard of Liesl's bed and called her from the kitchen into her room. "The club…" I started to say.

She leaned her head against the doorframe. "I already called in sick for you."

God, she was amazing.

She'd told the truth. I could barely get out of bed, let alone leave the apartment. And I'd cried so hard that I'd thrown up more than once. That had to count as sick.

Knowing that burden was off my plate, I considered resuming my drinking and sleeping. But as I scratched an itch at the top of my head, I discovered my hair was matted and dirty—I really needed a shower. And a change of clothes. Did I care? Yeah, I kind of did. That was progress, right?

But I had nothing of mine at Liesl's apartment. "Do you have something I can wear if I take a shower?"

She nodded encouragingly. "Anything in my closet's yours." Cleaning up would be as much to her benefit as mine. I smelled pretty rank.

The shower hurt as much as it helped. Though it made me feel better, it cleared my mind enough to worry about the future. Where was I going to live? Where was I going to work? Could I go back to The Sky Launch? I'd had the club before Hudson had come into my life—I didn't want to give that up. But even if he let me work there, could I be there anymore?

Maybe. Maybe not.

First things first. I couldn't stay holed up in Liesl's room. I moved to the futon that night.

"My bed is yours, babe," she said as I pulled the mattress into a prone position.

It was tempting to take her up on that. But I stayed surprisingly strong. "I already feel bad about overtaking your place. Besides, I need to start trying to function a little bit on my own. Even if that only means being in my own bed."

"Suit yourself." She threw me a pillow from her closet. "And you're welcome here as long as you want."

I wrapped my arms around the pillow and fell onto the futon. "I think it's going to be a while, Liesl. Are you sure about the offer?"

"Yep."

At least that took care of living arrangements for a bit. I'd have to arrange to pick up my things from the penthouse at some point. I didn't have much, but I needed my clothes. Not the items that had been bought by him—I didn't want those—but the rest of my stuff.

And I needed to get a new phone. My current one also came from Hudson. I didn't want anything to do with it. I'd already given it to Liesl and asked her to hang on to it for me. If Hudson had decided to ignore my request and call, I wouldn't even know. I didn't want to know.

Then there was Celia's possible lawsuit…

I sat up. "Have the police been looking for me?" Hudson had said he'd take care of it, but I didn't trust a word he said anymore.

Liesl sat down at the foot of the futon. "Nope, and they won't be." She answered my questioning look. "Hudson called me on my cell yesterday morning. He wanted me to tell you that he'd gotten the whole battery charge dismissed."

So he knows where I am. Of course he did. It wasn't that hard to figure out where I'd go. And I had the feeling Hudson wasn't the kind of guy you could hide from very easily.

I couldn't help myself. I had to know. "Did he say anything else?"

"He said lots of things. I decided you weren't interested in hearing any of it."

"Good thinking. I wasn't." I leaned back on my elbows. "But I am now. What did he say?"

"That he wanted to give you your space, but that he's anxious to talk to you when—*if*—you want to. That he'll do anything you want him to for the club, even if that includes doing nothing. That you're welcome to come back to the penthouse—he's staying at his other place."

"The loft." The offer of the penthouse was a waste of his breath. I had no desire to be anywhere I'd been with him. Except maybe the club. I still hadn't decided about that yet.

"Yeah, the loft." She lowered her eyes. "He also insisted that I tell you he loves you."

"I don't want to hear that." Even knowing it was a lie, it still had impact. My stomach tightened and my eyes watered. And some stupid little spot in my chest flickered with a spark of…I don't know…hope, maybe? It surprised me. Disgusted me. After everything, how could there be any part of me that still wanted his love to be true?

Liesl grinned. "That's what I told him." Her mouth straightened to a tight line. "He said it didn't make it any less true."

That night when I cried myself to sleep, it wasn't the betrayal that kept the tears coming—it was the loneliness. My lips burned for Hudson's mouth, my breasts ached for his touch, my entire body pulsed with isolation. And instead of wishing I'd never met the man, that I'd never heard his name, I wished I'd never found out the truth. Ignorance, it turned out, truly could be bliss.

"I TOLD YOU it sucks," Gwen said when I called in sick on Wednesday.

I didn't follow. "What sucks?" I should have had Liesl call in for me again. This talking to people thing was harder than I'd comprehended.

Gwen delivered her response in sing-song voice. "Love, darling. L-o-v-e, love. Worst thing ever."

Guess my claim of the flu wasn't fooling her. "Yeah. It really does."

THURSDAY I ALMOST seemed like a real person again. A broken, distraught person, but that was better than the sobbing lump that I'd been the days before. Now I could feed myself and I even managed to drink something other than alcohol.

Liesl had seemed to think I was ready to be pushed further. "You need a distraction. A release. Like maybe you should pet the pussy. I could loan you my vibrator while I'm at work tonight."

I cringed. "Um, no thanks."

"Then we could drive to Atlantic City this weekend and check out David's new place. You know he'd fuck your brains out if you asked."

"First of all, David doesn't fuck anyone's brains out." Though I'd never slept with him, I'd been with him enough in a sexual sense to know he was a total puppy dog.

"Secondly, I don't ever want to have sex with anyone ever again." Hudson had ruined sex for me—there would never be anyone better, no one more serving and demanding and fulfilling. It had been the place where things had been real for us—even now, with all the lies, I believed that. Anyone who tried to come in after would be a sorry comparison.

And there was a third thing—Saturday was the day of Mira's Grand Reopening. I couldn't go, of course. That would be ridiculous to even consider. But telling her was going to be hard. Since it was already Thursday, I probably couldn't put it off any longer.

With a deep breath, I held my hand out to Liesl. "Speaking of the weekend—can I borrow your phone? I need to call Mira."

She handed me her cell. I looked up Mirabelle's Boutique and pressed the button to dial. This would be a true test of my strength. Mira had been so pro-Alayna-and-Hudson that she was likely as devastated as I was. Well, not quite that devastated, but nearly. And knowing her and her love-conquers-all attitude, she'd probably try to convince me we could work things out.

Maybe I didn't want to call her after all.

"Mirabelle's. This is Mira." Too late to hang up now.

"Hey, Mira."

"Laynie!" she exclaimed with her usual bubbly, happy tone. "I was going to call you and check in. Great minds. I have your dress altered and ready for you—do you want to pick it up before Saturday or change here that day? Or I could have it sent to you by courier."

Dammit. Hudson hadn't told her the news of our breakup. What the fuck?

I definitely didn't want to be the one to tell her that. But now I kind of had to.

"I…Mira…" I was having trouble finding the words. I decided to start somewhere else. "I can't do your event. I'm sorry. I called to cancel." Then, after a swallow, "Hudson and I…we broke up." Why did it hurt so much more to say it out loud?

I swallowed again, bracing myself for Mira's reaction.

"I know," she said softly. Then she immediately perked up again. "Which is why I banned him from the store on Saturday. I don't give a shit if he makes it to my event. But you—Laynie, I have to have you here. Please say you'll still come. It would mean so much to me."

My mouth went dry. I was not emotionally equipped to handle shock. Or anyone being nice to me. "Mira, no," I floundered. "That's not right. You can't keep your own brother from your special day."

"Yes, I can," she insisted. "He doesn't care about fashion. He does care about me. And you."

Ah, there was the Mira I'd been expecting.

I clamped my eyes shut to ward off a new set of tears. "Please, don't say that. I don't want to hear about his supposed emotions."

"Okay, okay. That's fine. I wasn't trying to meddle. I was simply trying to tell you that he already offered to not come before I banned him. He said he wanted me and you to be happy and so he was bowing out. Yes, I'd rather have you both there. Of course I would. But if it comes to you or him, I definitely choose you. You're one of my models, and more importantly, you're my friend. You're like a sister, Laynie."

I warred with my options. When I called, there'd been no way in hell that I planned to go to Mira's event. I couldn't be there with him. It would be impossible to be a model under those circumstances.

But her speech…

We had become friends, and I had hoped that we'd one day be sisters. She'd done a lot for me and Hudson, but truly, she'd also done a lot for just me. And maybe doing this for her would help me with closure.

"All right. I'll do it." *Did I really fucking just say that?* "But you better swear to god that he will not be there. And this better not be a trick to get us together."

"I swear he will not be there. Swear on my baby." She paused. "Though that tricking you to get you together idea…"

"Mira—"

"I'm just kidding." Her smile was evident in her voice. "Yay! Thank you, Laynie."

"You're welcome." *Sort of.* "But don't expect a cheery model."

"You can do the serious/somber thing. I'm totes okay with that." She lowered her voice. "And for the record, I don't know what that fucker did to mess things up with the two of you, but he's a miserable wreck about it. I mean, completely and utterly broken up."

For half a second, I actually felt joy. Was it because I was happy the asshole was as miserable as I was or because I thought his misery said something about how he felt for me?

It would kill me if I kept wondering about the validity of any of his emotions. I had to stop thinking about it. "Mira, if you're going to keep telling me about him, I'm going to cancel."

"No! Don't do that." She sounded panicked. "Just had to get that out there. I'm done now."

"Okay, but no more." *Please, no more.* Another deep breath. "I'll change there on Saturday."

She squealed. "I'm so excited! See you then."

I almost smiled as I hung up.

"Well, look at that," Liesl said as I handed her phone back. "You have some color in your cheeks."

"It's not possible." I scrubbed my hands over my face. God, mourning was exhausting. And boring as hell. I had to find a way to move on. Mira's event was a good first step. But I needed to take some other steps.

Like figure out what to do with the rest of my life.

Just thinking the thought seemed overwhelming. A tear rolled down my cheek. Seriously? Wasn't I about fucking cried out yet?

But it had to be done. I grabbed a Kleenex and dabbed at my eye. "I, um, I want to go to work."

Liesl cleared her throat. "Are you sure?" My tears probably had her unconvinced.

"Not tonight. But tomorrow, yeah. I need to see if I can be there. I don't think I can make a good decision about my future at the club without trying a shift out."

Through all my struggles with obsessive love addiction, The Sky Launch had been my sanity. It had been the only thing to ground me when I'd been free falling. Now, as I was falling again, couldn't it be the place to save me again?

If not, I had to find out what could. Because already, I was getting that restless feeling in the pit of my stomach—that anxious tickle that marked me as an addict no matter how healthy I was. It was another sign that it was time to start figuring out my future.

When Liesl went into work that night, I forced myself to find something to do other than sleep and cry. Something other than remember. I turned on Spotify and found something to download on my Kindle app since Liesl had no books in her apartment.

But I couldn't get into the novel. And nothing else on the Internet or on TV was enough to occupy my mind. I couldn't stop thinking, and as I moved through the grieving process, my thoughts turned obsessive, as they always did when I was hurting. Some of them weren't even clearly formed but were instead only rough impulses. The urge to see him, for example. Not to talk to him, but to look at him from a distance. The urge to smell him again. The urge to hear his voice.

The yearning drove me mad.

And it pissed me off.

Because I was stronger than this. I was stronger than Hudson Pierce and Celia Werner. I would not let them pull me down to the person that I once was.

She thought she could destroy me?

Well, fuck that. I'd survived heartache before. I could survive it again.

Adrenaline surged through me, and I suddenly felt invincible. Or capable at least—invincible was going a bit too far. But "Roar" by Katy Perry came on my playlist, and I did jump around the room singing at the top of my lungs.

It felt good. Invigorating. Energizing.

Then "So Easy" by Phillip Phillips came on, and immediately my strength disappeared. *"You make it so easy..."* he sang, and all I heard was Hudson saying it to me.

And it was all a lie.

I dissolved into a mess of snot and ugly tears. Well, another night of crying wasn't the worst thing in the world. There was always tomorrow to be strong.

— CHAPTER —

TWENTY-ONE

The next day, I didn't feel stronger, but I did feel resolved.

Planning the future still seemed overwhelming, but I could handle today. *Baby steps*. It's what I'd learned in therapy. It was something I knew how to do.

On paper and in pencil, I broke down the hours. It helped to look at it written down so it didn't feel bigger than it was. I started at the bottom of the page since I'd already decided to go to the club.

8 p.m. to 3 a.m. work, I wrote.

Before that I'd go to a group meeting. I looked online and found one at six that evening. *Perfect*. I filled it in above my work shift.

At the top of the page I wrote in: *breakfast, shower, dress.*

Then: *sneak over to the penthouse to get some clothes.*

Even writing the last thing had been hard. To say it sounded daunting was an understatement. The Bowery had been the place where Hudson and I had really begun sharing our life. It would be filled with painful reminders.

But going through the memories, dealing with them—that was part of healing.

Getting through the first line of items was easier than I'd expected. Breakfast actually stayed down, and I managed to find a pair of drawstring shorts in Liesl's drawer that didn't fall off my waist.

"Do you want me to go with you?" Liesl offered around a bite of a bagel.

"No. I need to do this by myself." I threw my still wet hair into a ponytail. "I'll need you for the next time—when I get all my stuff. But this time, I'm just going to run in and pack a bag to get me through a few days. It'll feel good to finally wear panties again."

I stood up and looked at my bare feet. "Shit. I only have my heels from the party."

"I'll loan you some shoes."

"We don't have the same size feet." Liesl was much taller than me, with a larger frame. If it weren't for the drawstring, I'd be drowning in her shorts.

She kicked off the flip-flops she was wearing. "You can wear these. They're like one-size-fits-many."

"Fine." I slid my feet into them. They'd do. "Okay. I'm off. Wish me luck."

"You don't need luck. You got this." She pulled me in for a hug. "You're sure he won't be there?"

"Positive." I'd called Norma for that. She'd checked with Hudson's secretary and reported back that he had a meeting in his office all afternoon. And he'd told Liesl he wasn't staying at the penthouse. If I believed him, which I didn't necessarily, then he wouldn't be there no matter what. It was possible that he hadn't even been back there after L.A. I guess I'd find out soon enough.

Since it was still early in the day, I took my time getting to the penthouse. I took the subway instead of a cab and didn't rush to meet the connecting train. But as much as I dillydallied, I eventually arrived at my destination.

The memories started before I made it inside the building. I stood outside staring at the letters engraved on the stone above the door. *The Bowery.* In many ways it felt like the first time I'd been there, when I was nervous and anxious and unaware of what waited for me inside. Then though, my stomach fluttered with butterflies. Today it was filled with rolling stones. Though both had my tummy in motion, there was a definite difference in gravity. One feeling lifted me up. The other pulled me down, anchored me to my dismal reality.

With a final breath of fresh air, I headed in.

On the elevator ride up, I decided I'd be no-nonsense about my task. As soon as the door opened inside the penthouse, I headed straight to my closet. I put on some underwear and changed into a dress and shoes suitable for work. Then I packed a duffel bag with a few items to get me through the next week. I was done and ready to go in less than fifteen minutes.

But a sudden wave of nostalgia kept me from leaving without doing a final look around. I told myself it was the smart thing to do—in case I found something that I wanted to take with me.

Yeah, that was it.

The place was almost exactly the way I'd left it, except the cleaning lady had been through. The trashcans and dishwasher had been emptied. The only sign of disarray was the books I'd left out in the library. All clean and immaculate like that, the apartment felt empty, abandoned. Lonely. The warmth that had once filled it was gone. It seemed staged. Like a model home that no one really lived in. Like nothing special or beautiful had ever happened there.

It could be anyone's home. Nothing reflected us. How had I never noticed this before?

It was fitting, I supposed, to feel so empty.

Except it deepened my sorrow. I'd been prepared to walk in and be met with the ghosts of our past. That they weren't there rocked me.

Suddenly, I felt desperate to find a sign of us somewhere—anywhere. I set down my bag and ran back to our bedroom. I threw myself onto the made bed and buried my face in a pillow. It smelled clean. The bedding had been changed since we'd last slept there together. In Hudson's closet, I found only rows of clean clothes and an empty hamper. Finally, in the bathroom, I found a bottle of his body wash. I opened it and breathed in the scent.

My knees buckled. God, it was him and not him all at once. The smell permeated into my skin, reawakening every memory of him, rekindling feelings that I wanted to forget.

In that moment, though, I didn't want to forget. I wanted to embrace everything I had left of him. And this scent wasn't enough. It was missing the most important part. I wanted more, all of it. And I couldn't find it here.

I recognized the emotion immediately—the desperate urge. I could make it go away if I tried hard enough, if I refocused, if I concentrated on my substitute list.

But I didn't want to do that. I wanted to follow the urge, to let it lead me where I needed to go. For once, I wanted to give in to it instead of constantly fighting it. Wanted to fall into the comfort of the old pattern and let it swallow me.

Maybe, just today, I could let it take me away. I could go to the loft, slip in while Hudson was in his meetings, and feel him in the place that he'd been living. Look for traces of his existence. Smell him and sense him.

It wasn't healthy, but it would only be one time. One time wouldn't destroy me. And after that, I could move on. I'd go to my group meeting and get back on track and my new life—my life without Hudson—could really begin.

It sounded divine. Like a guilty pleasure. No worse than eating a whole tub of Ben and Jerry's straight from the carton. Without any more thought, I decided to do it. Then I flagged down a cab and headed to the Pierce Industries building before I could change my mind.

I was grateful that Norma had told me about Hudson's afternoon meeting. It made the chance of bumping into him not an issue. He'd be wrapped up in his business whatnot, never knowing I was right above him. It added to the appeal.

As soon as I opened the front door of the loft, I felt it. The thing I'd been missing—Hudson's presence. It lingered in the air, not just his scent, but the warmth of him. It made the hair stand up on my arms and made my skin tingle. It was exactly what I'd longed for.

Setting my duffel by the front door, I explored further, remembering and putting to memory the place where we'd shared our first time. I trailed my hand along the back of his leather couch as I passed. Then I trailed my other hand over the papers on his desk as I went deeper into the loft. At the back, I found the private elevator. It led to one place only—down to his office. That's how close he was. I placed my palm on the cool metal.

How close. How far away.

In the kitchen, I lingered over a half empty mug of coffee on the counter. *He drank from this.* His lips had touched the rim. I lifted the cup to my face, pressing it against my cheek. It was cold, but I could imagine it hot. Imagine him sipping at it gently, carefully.

I knew I was acting crazy, but I didn't care. I couldn't stop myself even if I did care.

Soon, I made it to the bedroom. The room he'd first taken me in. He'd been both amazing and overwhelming. I'd felt out of my league, and yet, I couldn't help but try to fit into his world in the way he'd wanted me.

My eyes glanced toward the bathroom. If I went in there now, would the scent of clean Hudson still be lingering from his morning shower? I'd go there next.

But first, the bed…

I fell across the mattress. This time when I inhaled, he was there in abundance. I wrapped my arms tight around his pillow and closed my eyes, breathing him in and out and in. And out. The scent soothed me, calmed me. The ache in my chest released ever so slightly. The tension behind my temples abated. For the first time in days, I felt okay.

Closing my eyes, I let the fantasy wash over me. Let myself forget the hurt and betrayal and pretended Hudson and I could be together again in all the ways we used to be. I imagined his lips on me—phantom kisses along my neck and down my torso that sent shivers down my spine and caused my toes to curl. Then his hands, caressing and kneading my body, reawakening my skin with his simple touch. Adoring me physically but with so much concentration and attention that the effort had to come from true and pure love.

I was still lying on the bed, lost in my daydream, when the private elevator arrived in the next room.

My eyes flew open. Had I imagined it?

Then Hudson's voice filled the air.

Fuck!

And he was talking to someone—he wasn't alone.

I scrambled off the bed and crouched by the floor considering what to do next. It sounded like he was still in the back of the loft, near the kitchen. I crawled to the wall next to the doorframe. There I could peek out and get a better idea of the situation and still stay hidden from the living area. As long as they didn't come in the bedroom, I'd be fine.

But if they did come in the bedroom…

Gathering my courage, I peeked out and saw Hudson standing in front of the open refrigerator. He grabbed a bottle of water and turned toward his guest—toward me.

I pulled my head back around the corner. *Did he see me?* No, I didn't think so.

Shit, shit, shit. All I could do was swear. And pray.

And eavesdrop.

"I haven't been here in a while." I hadn't gotten a chance to look at his visitor, but I knew who it was from her voice. "I'd forgotten what a good job I'd done with the place." *Celia Werner.*

My chest tightened and my eyes began to water.

I was gone barely a week, and he was bringing her to his loft? Why? To celebrate the slaughter of my soul? To plan their next game?

To *connect*?

Each possibility was worse than the last. This was heartache on top of heartache. Salt on the wound. A lesson to teach me not to give into my urges again.

Celia's heels clicked on the cement floor.

Where was she going? I held my breath, my heart pounding. Maybe I should hide out in the bathroom. Then they wouldn't see me if they came this way. But then I couldn't hear what they were saying. And, besides, if they did need the bed…

God, I couldn't think about that.

"Remember how I had to convince you to go with the leather couch?" she asked.

She was in the living area. If they stayed right there, I could pull this off.

"We're not here for a walk down memory lane." Hudson's voice was cold.

Her footsteps paused. "Why *are* we here?"

Yes, Hudson, do tell. Though I wasn't sure I wanted to know.

"Because we have some things to talk about, and they aren't suitable for my office."

"Then I can't help but think of old times. Other conversations that weren't appropriate for your office." Her heels clicked again and then stopped. Then the leather of the sofa creaked as she took a seat.

I let out the breath I'd been holding.

Now Hudson's shoes sounded on the floor. "If you want to relive those times, then do it on your own." His voice got nearer.

Shit, fuck, dammit! He was headed my way.

But then I heard the rattling of ice in a glass. Slowly, I turned my head to the side. He was there—not ten feet away, fixing himself a drink at the bar. If he looked over and down, he'd see me.

I froze, not blinking, not even breathing; willing myself to fade into the wall. My heart thudded so loudly, I was certain he could hear it.

Except he didn't. He finished making his drink, then turned back to face Celia.

"Come on, Huds." Her tone was playful, cajoling, in complete opposition to his. "You act like we never had any fun together."

"That was a lifetime ago, Celia." Though he was still merely steps away, his words were distant. "It's time to move on."

Celia laughed. "Because of her?"

"Who? Alayna?" A chill ran through my body. Jesus, even when he said my name to someone else, it had the same effect as when he said it to me. "Yes. And no." He paused. "We aren't together anymore."

And hearing him say that—it was as painful as when I'd said it to Mira. The verbalization of it made it so real. So final.

Celia seemed overjoyed with the news. "Am I supposed to be sad?"

"Why would I expect that? That was your intended outcome, after all." He moved forward, out of my sightline. Then there was another creak of furniture. He'd sat in the chair across from her, I guessed.

I struggled with listening to them talk as I debated with myself—should I scurry to the other side of the doorframe? If he came back to the bar, I'd be better hidden. But if one of them went to the guest bathroom, then I'd be easily seen.

"No," Celia said, "my intended outcome was that she'd go crazy after your break-up and end up back in her psycho obsession mode."

I decided to stay put.

"Well, that's not happening. She's stronger than you thought."

And yet, there I was, hiding in Hudson's bedroom because I'd done exactly as predicted and gone stalker. It crushed me that he could believe otherwise—that he had no understanding of how much he could break me. Did he not get what he'd meant to me?

If he didn't understand, Celia did. Perhaps it was a female thing. "Maybe. I'm not sure I agree. How long ago was this breakup?"

"A few days now."

"Oh, give it time. She'll be back. That girl was head over heels for you. She's not walking away that easily. Not that type."

I cringed at the accuracy with which she was describing me. It would fuel me to be strong, I decided. Otherwise, she'd win. Technically, she'd already won—I was here, after all. But if she didn't know, then she couldn't take it as a victory, right?

"Celia, stop it." Hudson's sharp command drew my attention.

"Are you still sticking to the story that you're in love with her?"

Her question made my hair stand on end. *He'd told her that he loved me…*did that mean there'd really been some truth to it?

He didn't answer her verbally, but his expression must have been in the affirmative because Celia scoffed. "That's ridiculous, Hudson. You've never loved anyone. It's not in your nature. You're fascinated with her for some godforsaken reason. But it's not love."

"What do you know about love?" He'd never spoke so harshly in my presence.

She laughed again. "Everything you taught me—it's a fleeting emotion that can be manipulated and fabricated. It's not real. It's never real."

"It's time you found another teacher. I no longer believe any of that."

I drew my knees into my chest. He believed in love now—because of me? The discovery tugged at my heart, begging me to reexamine the status of our relationship. Oh, how I wanted to fasten myself to his love. Wanted to turn it into a chance for us to be together.

But I couldn't. His deceit was too great. It didn't matter that he fell in love. It was deserved. His just rewards. His karma.

"Maybe I should be the teacher for a while," Celia suggested. "It's time to change up the game anyway."

There was a sound of ice rattling—Hudson shaking his glass, perhaps. Then a pause while he swallowed. "I don't want to play anymore, Celia."

"You said that before with Stacy. And you ended up coming around."

"That was all your game. I gave you a make-out session. That's all. And it wasn't for you, it was for her. I don't know the extent you played with her, but it was time you were done. I knew that the kiss would end it."

"Are you trying to convince me you had feelings for Stacy too?"

"You were using my name to fuck with my sister's assistant. It was going to come back and bite me in the ass eventually. And she was a nice girl. She didn't deserve it."

Their words had come fast, one statement on top of another.

Now they paused as Hudson perhaps took another swallow of his drink. Then he said, "Those are the only reasons I resorted to helping you with that."

His words hung in the air. They sunk over me slowly. They pissed me off. I didn't want to think of him as the hero of that situation, of any situation. So he'd participated in the scam to help Stacy. There were other ways he could have helped her. It wasn't enough to redeem him.

I heard the creak of the couch—maybe just Celia leaning forward, but I tensed, afraid she was on the move again.

But there wasn't any sound of footsteps, just her speaking, "And why did you agree to the Alayna game? Don't tell me that was an excuse to be with her."

Hudson must have nodded, because next she said, "Liar. You're you. Hudson Pierce. You would have found a way to be with her anyway."

"The minute I showed her any interest, you did too. Going along with your game was the only way to protect her."

"Whatever," Celia echoed my thoughts. "If it's true that your interest was what attracted me, then the way for you to *protect her* would have been to run from her. Far and fast. I don't buy it. You wanted to play."

I hated to admit she and I were on the same page, but we were.

It was Hudson's answer that surprised me. "You're right. I should have run. I couldn't. So I did the next best thing."

A memory flashed into my mind of the first time I'd seen Hudson at the bar of the club. I'd known immediately that he was someone I should run from. The words *far and fast* had even occurred to me. Against my own conscience, knowing my faults and my weaknesses, I'd gone after him anyway.

Could I blame him for doing the same?

"I didn't want to play the game with her," he said next. "And I don't want to play ever again."

More movement. Then Hudson returned to the bar.

I should have moved. I should have moved! My pulse accelerated, and again, I held my breath.

"You don't mean that, Hudson." Celia stood as well. Her heels gave her away.

God, please don't let her join him. Hudson was at least focused on his glass. She'd see me for sure.

Thankfully, she stayed where she was.

"Remember what it's like?" she asked him. "The adrenaline rush? To stage a situation, knowing exactly how it will play out because you studied the characters so well you understand what they'll do. There's nothing like it."

"You're destroying people's lives!"

"*You* taught me!"

"Then learn this next lesson well—it was wrong. I. Was. Wrong."

Their words flew back and forth again. My heart continued to thud in my chest as they sparred. It was thrilling, exhilarating to hear him fight her.

Did that mean I thought of her as a worse enemy than him? Because I wanted him to defeat her?

Until that afternoon, I'd thought of them as a pair. Two of a kind. Now, my feelings were changing ever so slightly.

Hudson turned again to face her. "And of all the lives I've destroyed, Celia, I'm most regretful for what I've done to yours. But I can't be responsible for that anymore. You have to decide now who you're going to be. This is not who I'm going to be."

Damn tears at my eyes again. Not wanting to move while I was still in his sightline, I let them fall freely. If it was true—if he really was done with his games—well, it made me proud.

Why the fuck I even cared, I couldn't say.

"Then you're out," Celia said, resigned. "That's fine. I'm not. And I'm not done with the Alayna Withers experiment."

My stomach sunk. My break-up with Hudson should have won me a reprieve from her games. I'd never be away from her, would I?

Hudson thought I would. "Oh yes, you are done with Alayna." He stepped further into the room, again out of my sight. "And don't give me the line that you play to win. I can think of some times that you've lost. You've lost big, if I recall."

"That's cruel." She actually sounded hurt. I hadn't realized the woman had feelings.

"Ah, but isn't that one of the requirements to playing the game?" His awful, caustic tone both frightened and elated me. It was scary to think Hudson had it in him, but it was delightful that he used it on my nemesis.

"Tell me, I'm curious," Hudson began now, "what exactly was your plan with Alayna, anyway? After I dropped out and refused to break up with her, you created your befriend-and-frame scheme. When that failed, then what? The books with the quotes, the stalking—what was that supposed to do?"

I swear I heard her shrug. "I don't know. Push her over the edge. Make her doubt you. Drive you apart."

Hudson chuckled. "It seemed like random flailing to me. Guesswork. That's not how we played."

"It worked, didn't it? You're not together anymore."

Oh, how I wanted to knock the glee out of her voice. It was another one of the worst parts of breaking up with Hudson—Celia took it as a victory.

He wouldn't let her take the credit, though. "Believe it or not, that has nothing to do with anything you did."

"Really? I thought for sure telling her we were lovers had been the final nail in the coffin. Especially when I gave her proof."

"What proof could you possibly give for something that never happened?"

Though he'd said they'd never been together, I'd still had lingering doubts. His word no longer meant anything. But now…now I knew for sure. They'd never been romantic together. At least there was that.

"I told her you called me the same pet name you called her. Tore. Her. Up."

"From the looks of it, it seems she tore you up."

"Battle scars," she said dismissively.

Her face! I'd almost forgotten. Damn, I wished I could see the results of my attack.

"What pet name are you talking about, anyway?"

His question alone meant he'd never told her. I turned my head toward the opening, eager to hear how this proceeded.

"*Precious*," she said.

"How the hell did you know about that?" He was furious.

So it *had* been only ours. Finally, I had something to hold onto. That—his name for me—that would be the memory I'd take away as pure and true.

"I borrowed her phone one day when we'd had lunch. I saw text messages between the two of you. You called her precious."

Such a fucking cunt. I wanted to stand up and shout it across the room. It was almost worth revealing myself.

Almost.

Hudson's expression must have indicated he wasn't happy about the information because Celia said, "Oh, come on. It was a good play. A fucking good play. And you're telling me that had no bearing on your breakup?"

"No. I think she could have survived that, honestly." *Yes, we could have survived that.* "It was the truth that did us in."

"The truth? You told her—?"

He cut her off. "Everything."

"That's against the ru—"

Again he broke her off. "There are no fucking rules anymore, Celia. It's over! I'm not playing. And I'm not discussing Alayna with you for another minute." He spoke with finality.

I pictured what he must look like—his shoulders broad and squared, his face stern and unmoving. There was no way to refute him when he looked like that.

Her heels clicked again.

I tensed.

Then the sound of the couch creaking. "Is that why you brought me here? To tell me that you're quitting?" Though she was trying to sound bored, I heard the disappointment in her voice.

"I haven't even really played in years. Except to be your pawn." Hudson's steps then movement as he sat in his chair. "But no, that's not why you're here. I'm telling you that *you're* quitting. You're done, Celia. No more games."

"You're joking, right? You can't decide that for me."

While I appreciated that Hudson believed he could simply talk Celia out of her ways, I recognized her fortitude. She was not one to give up easily. Or at all. Even if Hudson asked her nicely.

"You're right that I can't monitor you in every facet of your life," Hudson said, "nor do I have any intention, but I can tell you that you will not be messing with me or my family or my employees and definitely not Alayna."

There, again. The sound of my name from his lips. Said so carefully, so reverently, like carrying something fragile and precious. *Ah…precious.* His care for me was…it was deep. I couldn't deny that.

And the realization only hurt that much more.

Celia's response kept me from spiraling into a fit of sobs. "That's hilarious that you think you have any control over me in any measure. And your declaration is only begging for me to prove you wrong. Plus, even though I agreed to not press charges, I'm not finished with this Alayna game."

"You *are* finished, Celia." Again, he spoke with authority. "While I'd hoped you'd give it up for the sake of our friendship—or whatever it is that we once had—I had a feeling that you'd disagree. So I've attained some insurance."

"I'm intrigued."

So am I.

"Let me tell you about a company that I just bought." There was unusual pep in Hudson's tone. "Actually, I'll show you the paperwork."

Once more my heart raced as Hudson stood and moved. But he sounded like he was walking away. Then a shuffle of papers—he was at his desk. Then back to where he'd been—again, the chair creaked. I heard another shuffle and then individual paper movement as though someone was flipping through a packet and periodic silence as they paused to read. I could picture it—her French-tipped nails turning one page after another.

What was it? I itched to know. Though there was no way I'd be able to see what she was reading, I couldn't take it anymore—I had to peek. If they were buried in papers, they wouldn't notice me. I moved to my knees and peered around the door.

She sat, as I'd imagined, on the couch, a manila folder in hand, her brow furrowed. Her hair was up, as usual, and her nose was bandaged. Black and blue bruises extended underneath the tape.

I couldn't help but smile at her injury.

Her eyes widened and her head shot up to look at Hudson whose back was to me. I sat down quickly, not wanting to be seen.

"How did you…?" she asked.

"Very sneakily." He was proud; I could hear it in the edges of his even tone. "I'll admit, it wasn't easy. I had to convince another company to purchase a portion of the stock, and then I bought out that company—you don't really want the details, do you?"

The deal he'd been working on. It had to do with Celia?

"The contracts are signed now," he continued. "That's all that matters. I'm officially the majority owner of Werner Media Corporation."

I gasped, then slapped my hand over my mouth too late. *Fuck!* Had they heard my gasp? Had they heard my slap? And now my heart was beating louder than it had the whole time I'd been trapped in his bedroom—surely they could hear that?

But if they did, they gave no indication.

"And you said you'd quit playing the game." Celia's words were low and heavy.

"I had one final move to make," he said.

And what a move it was. Werner Media Corporation—Celia's family's business—Hudson had bought it? This was…this was *big*.

She let out a long, slow hiss of air—or I guessed it was her, I couldn't see for sure. "It's checkmate, is it then?" she asked.

"You tell me." Triumph hung in the texture of his words.

"What are your plans for Werner Media?" She fought to the end. Some people might be impressed with her dedication.

I imagined, once upon a time, that Hudson had been one of those people.

For me, it was Hudson that impressed me.

"At the moment, I have no plans. The company's doing well as it is. Warren Werner is definitely the right man to be in charge. However, if there were any reason that I felt his presence was no longer needed…" He let his threat trail off.

"He'd be devastated," Celia said softly.

"I imagine he'd be devastated just to learn he no longer holds controlling interest. For now, the fact is still hidden. He has no idea that he's no longer in charge. Would you like that to change?"

"No," she said.

"Do you plan on doing anything that might cause me to alter my current business plan?"

Defeat clung to her simple one-word answer. "No."

"Then yes, it's checkmate."

We sat silently, all of us, for several minutes after the game was declared finished. My skin tingled as Hudson's victory settled in the air. A smile graced my lips and a mixture of many, many emotions swept up and over me, very few of them sinking in with enough clarity to cling on to for long. Some, I could name—surprise, gratitude, relief, triumph. Others were more difficult to discern through the blanket of heartache that still covered me from head to toe. Was there some forgiveness toward Hudson in there? A touch of hopefulness, perhaps?

Love, there was love. There was always love.

"I guess it's time for me to go," Celia said eventually.

"It is. I'll walk you out."

They weren't going back through the office. The realization sent another stab of panic through me—was Hudson not leaving? And my duffel—it was at the door.

Once again, I held my breath as they crossed the floor. I heard the door open. If they were at the entrance, their backs would be toward me. I had to see what was going on.

I moved up to my knees again and peered around the frame. Hudson was holding the door open as Celia walked past. He started to shut it behind her—*dammit, he was staying*—then his gaze fell on my bag.

He paused there for half a second. Then his eyes rose to scan the room.

I didn't move—did I want him to find me?

He did.

Our eyes locked, and the intensity of his expression—it was all-consuming. Maybe I couldn't read all of my own emotions, but in his gaze I saw three with clarity. Surprise, elation. And, clear as day, I saw love.

If he came to me at that moment, I was certain I'd fall back into him.

But he didn't.

"Hold the elevator," he said to Celia without looking away. His lip ticked ever so slightly, delivering me a half-smile. Then he left, shutting the door behind him.

— CHAPTER —
TWENTY-TWO

Nine in the morning came awfully early after working until three a.m. I peeked from under my lids at the sun that suddenly filled the room.

"Hey," I groaned. "I had the curtains shut for a reason."

"Too bad. You got your fashionything." Liesl poked at my foot sticking off the bottom of the futon. "Get up."

"But, Mom, I don't wanna." I rubbed my eyes and sat up. I glanced at the time. It was actually after nine. I must have pushed the snooze button on the alarm clock a couple of times. "Why are you awake anyway?"

I'd worked a short shift but Liesl had stayed until close. That meant she'd probably only been home a couple of hours. Funny, she hadn't woken me when she came in.

Then I realized, her coming in was what *had* woken me.

"Got a ride from one of the regulars." She waggled her brows. "And when I say ride, I don't mean in a car."

Sex looked good on Liesl. Her cheeks were rosy and her eyes bright. Part of me had always been jealous of her ability to sleep with random people and not get attached. This morning, thinking about sex just made me sad.

My face must have given away my thoughts because next thing I knew, Liesl had crawled onto the bed and wrapped her arms around me in a giant girlfriend hug.

I sighed into her embrace. It felt so good to be touched, to be cared for.

She kissed my temple. "Are you going to be okay today?"

I shrugged against her arms. "Hudson's not supposed to be at the show. So yeah." Saying his name made my heart simultaneously flip and sink. After he'd left the loft, I'd expected him to come into the club during my shift. Or to call. Find me somehow. There was so much to say after all I'd witnessed. Maybe he wasn't interested.

Liesl released me and bopped me on the nose with her finger. "What's that frown about then? You're wishing he was coming, aren't you?"

Did I wish that? "I don't know." While I didn't want to see him, I wanted *him* to want to see me, if that made any sense.

I hugged my knees to my chest. "Why do you think he hasn't tried to talk to me?"

"Maybe he's respecting your space."

Memories washed over me, times Hudson had bullied his way into my life when I'd tried to push him away. "Hudson's never been one to respect my space." Maybe that hadn't been the real Hudson Pierce. It was preferable to think that than to believe he'd really given up on me so easily. "I guess I thought he'd fight for me. Especially after what he did yesterday. After he saw me."

Liesl tilted her head. "Wanna hear what I think?"

"Probably not, but I'm sure you're going to tell me anyway."

"I am." She tucked her legs underneath her. "I think that it's probably still too soon to figure out whether he's going to fight for you or whether you even want him to."

"I don't want him fighting for me." Except I sort of did.

She wagged a finger at me. "Uh-uh. Too soon."

Maybe she was right. A myriad of emotions had enveloped me in the past week. Which of them would endure? In a month from now, which feeling would dominate? In a year? Betrayal? Pain? Or would it be love?

Liesl *was* right. It was too soon to know.

She reached her hand out to squeeze mine. "I'm proud of you though. You made it through this week. And through work last night. And you're going to his sister's thingamabob. And you only had one obsessive breakdown. I think you've done pretty good."

It was amazing how she made just living sound like an accomplishment. Truthfully, it did feel like a success. A little bit of pride filled my chest.

But that ever-present ache didn't go away. I bit my lip. "I miss him."

Liesl leaned forward and kissed my hair. "I know. That might get worse before better."

"Yeah."

MIRABELLE'S BOUTIQUE WAS crazed when I arrived, even though the event wasn't due to start for more than another two hours. The place swarmed with florists and caterers and models and new employees. It took me a while to find anyone I knew in the crowd, but eventually I spotted Adam sampling—or stealing rather—a chocolate-covered strawberry from a Saran-wrapped food tray.

He paused to finish chewing. "Laynie, good to see you."

He gave me a hug, which was a little weird since he'd never been affectionate with me.

"I'm so glad you're here. Please, get Mira to stop running around, will you? She needs to sit and put her feet up. I swear to god, after today, if she doesn't start taking it easy, I'm going to chain her to the bed."

"That sounds a little personal," I teased. "Where is she now?"

Adam directed me to the workroom in the back. There I found even more models, more employees, and Mira fussing over everyone.

"You're here!" she exclaimed when she saw me. Though her expression and smile were bright, the bags under her eyes gave away her exhaustion. "I was afraid you'd bow out at the last minute."

I'd been a little afraid of the same thing. "Nope. I'm here. Do you have time to give me a tour?" Maybe getting her distracted would keep her blood pressure from spiking while she worried about the details of the event. "Or would you prefer I get dressed first?" I wouldn't want her stressing about that either.

"Get dressed first and then it's on."

The dress she'd chosen for me looked stunning with the alterations she'd had done. Looking at myself in the mirror of the dressing room, I couldn't help but remember when I'd first tried it on. It was the day Stacy had sent me the video. That had been the beginning of the end, hadn't it? If only I hadn't let my curiosity get the better of me.

I shook my head, tossing the thought aside. Today, I wouldn't be sad. It was Mira's day, and I didn't want to ruin it for her. Even though I had waterproof mascara on, crying didn't go well with makeup.

Besides, I couldn't wish for anything to be different. Sure, I'd been happy with Hudson, but it had been a lie. The truth would have come out eventually. Better now than later.

When I was dressed, I found Mira, this time seated in a chair as she yelled at people. Adam must have forced her to sit.

She jumped up when she saw me, though, her eyes wide. "Oh my god, you're so beautiful! You are definitely going to be the finale. Dammit, I wish Hudson could see you." She clapped her hand over her mouth before I could scold her. "Sorry. It slipped out. It's going to take a while to get used to the new situation."

"Yeah, I get that." I was still adjusting myself.

She wrapped her arm around mine. "Let me show you my baby. Well, one of my babies." The new addition was beautiful but simple. There was more space to display clothing, a few more dressing rooms, a bigger workroom for the staff and a small runway.

"The stage is where we'll do today's show. In the future it will be for private fashion selection," Mira explained as we finished up. "Some of these rich bitches are too lazy to try on their own clothes so we have models hired to do it for them."

I laughed. Mira was a Pierce—she was probably richer than any of her clients, and she was neither lazy nor a bitch. I could certainly see her mother being one of the women she was referring to, though.

"Speaking of Sophia," I said, looking around the shop, "where is she? Isn't she coming?"

"Um, no." She bent to pick a piece of lint off my skirt. "I banned her along with Hudson."

"What?" Not that I was disappointed about Sophia's absence. With as out-of-control drunk as she'd been the last time I saw her in a public situation, it was probably a good idea she wasn't here.

Mira straightened but kept her eyes down. "I took your advice. We staged an intervention."

"Oh, my god, Mira!" I reached my hand out to touch her arm.

She slid my hand into hers instead. "It was hard, but Hudson and Chandler and Adam and even Dad were there. We all sat her down and told her she needed to get help." She met my eyes and flashed a somewhat forced smile.

I squeezed her hand. "When did this happen?" *And how is Hudson handling it?*

"Last night. She didn't want to hear it, of course. But when I told her she couldn't be a part of my life anymore if she didn't get help, then she agreed.

She checked into a long-term facility upstate this morning. Hudson, Dad, and Chandler drove her out."

"Wow." My chest ached in a way that was different from the past several days. Instead of hurting because of Hudson, I hurt *for* him.

"You know, I've never seen my mother sober—she might still be a bitch. But at least I could trust her not to drop my baby."

I pushed thoughts of Hudson out of my mind yet again and studied the beautiful woman in front of me. Though I was twenty-six to her twenty-four years of age, she struck me as the most genuine, mature person I knew. Such a contradiction to her brother. Such a contradiction to myself.

She blushed under my stare. "What?"

"I'm just really amazed by you. That's hard to stand up like that for someone you love and today you have your event...how are you dealing with all of this?"

"Honestly, except for being tired, I feel really good." It was her turn to squeeze my hand. "The only thing I'm worrying about now is you and my brother."

I pulled my hand away from hers. "I'm miserable enough without the guilt trip, thanks." I studied my shoes, afraid that any more show of emotion might wreck me.

"He told us what he did to you."

My eyes flew back up to meet hers. "What?"

"During mom's intervention. He said that if we had any hope of being a family, then we needed to face our flaws and own up to our mistakes. He went back to therapy this week, and I think his doctor encouraged him to be open with us. So he owned up to what he did to you." Her expression grew serious and sad. "I'm sorry he did that to you, Laynie. Really sorry. I'm not going to defend him. But I will say that he is full of regret."

"I'm..." My throat tightened. "Dammit, Mira, you're making me cry."

She grasped my upper arms. "Don't cry! Then I'll cry and that will be a disaster. No more serious talk, except to say I love you. Thank you for being here."

"I wouldn't miss it for the world."

There was a little more to the modeling gig than standing and smiling. I also had to walk down the short runway, pose, and return. While the place seemed to be crawling with models, there were only seven of us in the show. We were able to run through it enough times in rehearsal that by the time the actual event started, I wasn't so nervous that I couldn't perform.

Frankly, I was happy for an emotion other than grief. I clung to it. Wrapped it around me like a blanket.

At two, the doors were opened and the event began. It wasn't a big hurrah like the charity fashion show Sophia Pierce had hosted, but was elegant and important in its own way. Mira was a beautiful bird, floating around the room, talking to big name fashion designers and top clients that had been invited.

Then there was the press—they'd been limited to invitation only and were sequestered in an area near the stage, which made them less intimidating. I never got close enough to them to be hounded with their questions. If they wanted to know about me and Hudson, they'd have to ask him.

Would they even ask? When the next girl showed up on his arm in the limelight, would they ask what happened to that nightclub manager the same way they asked about Celia in front of me?

There were so many awful things about that scenario that I had to block it out with a glass of champagne.

At a quarter to three, I lined up with the other models along the horizontal length of the stage. This is where we stood while each person walked the runway. My placement as last in the show made me wish we were walking on from offstage instead of waiting there the whole time. It felt like hours that I had to stand still and smile while the other women walked and posed. Stacy described each item, crediting the designer and then explaining the individual alterations done by the boutique to make the outfit perfect for the wearer.

Finally it was my turn. I walked to the end of the runway with a smile that was surprisingly authentic. Butterflies stirred in my stomach as I stood at the end while Stacy talked about my dress. Photographers were flashing bulbs at me, but the room wasn't dark as in a typical fashion show, and I could actually see the faces of the onlookers as I cast my gaze around the room.

That's how I spotted Hudson so easily.

There, in the back, leaning against the wall. His hair was mussed and he was underdressed in a t-shirt and jeans. His eyes were pinned on me—hell, the whole room's focus was on me—but his were the only eyes I felt. Even across that distance I could sense that electrical current, the simmer in my belly that spurred the butterflies to dance more frantically than before.

Our gazes locked and without thinking to let it happen, my smile widened.

God, it was good to see him.

Then Stacy finished her speech, the crowd applauded, and it was time to turn around and walk back to my place along the back of the stage. With my back to him, the momentary elation disappeared, and all the shit rumbled back over me like a Mack truck. The deceit, the hurt, the garbage—and he wasn't supposed to be there!

Though I was the final model, I had to remain on stage while Stacy introduced Mira, and then while Mira spoke about her renovations and made her acknowledgements. I was still in the limelight, but I couldn't stop fidgeting and wiping my sweaty palms along my skirt.

He's here, he's here. What do I do?

I tried to keep my attention on Mira, but my eyes kept darting back to Hudson. Every time, he was already looking at me. It wouldn't be easy to escape. Especially because I couldn't just run out—my purse and belongings were still in the back. I could leave my clothes, but I needed money for a cab or my subway card. He was across the room, though, and there were lots of people—perhaps I could sneak away before he got to me.

The minute the final applause began, I took off. As discreetly as possible, I slipped off the stage and to the back hall, hoping Hudson didn't see me and follow.

Or hoping he *did* follow. I couldn't quite decide.

Of course my stuff was in the last dressing room in the hall, but I made it there without anyone behind me. My hands were shaking as I gathered my clothes from the floor where I'd left them. Looking around, I realized I had nothing to carry them in. *Shit.*

I could change. Or get them later.

Later.

I should have at least folded them, but there wasn't time for that. Instead, I set them on the dressing room chair, grabbed my purse from the corner of the room where I'd stowed it under my clothing, and turned to go.

But there he was, filling the doorframe.

My shoulders sagged, but my stupid heart did a little dance.

Dammit, feelings were confusing.

He looked even better up close. Was it possible he'd gotten more attractive in our time apart? His blue-gray t-shirt hugged his muscles, which seemed more pronounced than I'd remembered. His faded dark jeans hung low around his trim hips. His eyes were soft and sad with bags underneath them that matched his sister's. Matched mine.

And the way he looked at me…as if I were more than a silly, emotional, broken girl. As if I were someone who mattered. As if I were someone he loved.

"Hey," he said softly. His voice was like the pied piper, calling goose bumps to the surface of my skin with just one word. Did he even know he had that effect on me?

The way his hands were stuffed in his pockets, making him look so boyish and innocent, I had to think he had no idea.

Except, no matter how he looked, he wasn't innocent. Not at all. It was even manipulative that he'd shown up here.

I folded my arms over my chest, as if that could protect me from his piercing gaze. "You're not supposed to be here, Hudson. Mira promised you wouldn't be."

He pursed his lips. "Mira had nothing to do with me coming."

I started to say something snarky, and then softened as I remembered where he *was* supposed to be. "Weren't you taking Sophia to rehab?"

God, that was blunt.

I wanted to say something more comforting, something to let him know I was feeling for him, but I was afraid my compassion might be construed as something else. So I left it at that.

"Already done. I hurried back." He took a step into the room. "So I could talk to you."

His quiet tone was so un-Hudson-like, it put me off-balance.

Or his presence in general put me off-balance.

I sighed, rocking from one foot to the other. I should leave. But there were things I wanted to hear him say, whether I could trust them or not. "If you wanted to talk to me so badly, why did you leave yesterday?"

"I had to be at my parents' for the intervention. If I stayed, I wouldn't have been able to leave. It was hard enough to leave as it was." He tilted his head. "And I thought perhaps it was best to let you have your space."

If he kept saying all the right things, I was screwed.

What am I thinking? I'm screwed anyway.

I leaned against the wall behind me. "But you're here now." *When he'd promised he wouldn't be.* "How is that letting me have space?"

Do I really want space?

It was hard to answer that question. On the one hand, the walls of the dressing room felt like they were closing in around me. On the other hand, the distance between Hudson and me seemed wider than the Mississippi.

"I couldn't stay away anymore." As far away as he was, his words found their destination, piercing through the ice around my heart. "Why were you at the loft?"

I couldn't stay away anymore. "Because I'm weaker than you give me credit for."

He stared at the blank wall to the side of us as he scratched the back of his neck. "I was hoping it wasn't weakness, but a sign that you still cared." His eyes swung back to me, searching for my reaction.

I almost laughed. "Of course I still care, you asshole. I'm in love with you. You shattered my fucking heart."

His eyes closed in a long blink. "Alayna, let me fix it."

"You can't."

"Let me try."

"How?" It was a rhetorical question because there was no answer for it. "Even if I can figure out how to forgive you, I can't trust you again. I could never believe that you were with me for any reason other than to continue your sick game."

He flinched only slightly. "I quit all that. You heard me."

I shrugged. "Maybe it was all a set-up. Maybe you knew I was there the whole time." He hadn't known I was there—his expression of surprise when he saw me was genuine. But there were still pounds of bitterness inside me that I had yet to expunge.

"You don't believe that."

I made a disapproving sound in the back of my throat. "It's hard to believe anything after being so totally lied to."

"For the record," he bent to catch my eyes with his, "I didn't lie to you about us. Everything I ever said and did with you was honest."

"The whole circumstance of our *pretend to be my girlfriend* sham was a lie."

"Yes, but that's all. Every touch, every kiss, every moment between you and me, precious…none of that was pretend. I didn't *want* to pretend with you. I wanted every experience with you, every moment to be completely genuine. You're the first person I have ever let in, the first person who's ever seen the real me through all the bullshit." His voice narrowed to a point. "You're the first person I've ever loved, Alayna. And I know you'll be the last."

His words hurt. They were everything I'd ever wanted to hear from him and more. But what was the saying? *Fool me twice, shame on me.*

"I don't know." I pressed my fingertips to my forehead. "I don't know, I don't know. I don't know how I can ever believe that you really feel the way you say you do."

He took another step toward me. "I'm sure that's true. But I thought of a way to prove that I'm devoted to you." Another step, and we were now only a handful of feet apart. "Alayna, marry me."

My gaze flipped up. "What?"

"Marry me. Right now. My plane's already ready and waiting on the tarmac. All you have to do is say yes and we're on our way to Vegas."

"What?" I was in too much shock to say anything else.

"I know you deserve a long engagement and a proper wedding—and we can do that again, whenever you want—but I know right now you need reassurance."

His hands were all over the place as he talked, totally out of character. Was he high? Nervous? Insane?

"You need confirmation that I am committed to you, Alayna, and there's no better way I can think of showing you that than to marry you. To declare in a written contract that I'm yours and that I promise to love you forever."

I settled on insane. "Hudson, you're crazy."

"And no prenup either." He wiped his palms on his jeans. Was he sweating? I sure was. "I'm ready to give you everything I have, to make myself vulnerable, just like you made yourself to me time after time."

"No prenup? Now I definitely know you're crazy." And I was crazy for simply continuing the conversation.

"I am crazy. Crazy without you in my life." He pushed his hands through his hair. "You're the only one who's ever made me better. And you have me by the balls now, Alayna, in so many ways. Because if you say no, if you turn me away, then I've lost everything that means anything in my pathetic excuse for a life. But if you say yes, I have to be the one to trust *you*—you could scam me if you wanted to. You could simply marry me now, divorce me later and half of all I have would be yours."

As if his money meant anything to me. "I have no interest in your—"

He cut me off. "I know. I know that you would never take advantage of me like that. But the point is you could." He paced the small room. "This is the only way I can think of to show you that I'm willing to be vulnerable to you. That I trust you." He turned to face me again. "And that, even though I don't deserve it, I'm determined to fight to earn back *your* trust. Even if it takes the rest of my life."

I was in shock. So many thoughts and emotions swarmed over me that I had no idea what to feel or think. Out of the plethora of reactions brimming to escape, I picked one at random. "Some romantic proposal—marry me so that I can prove you can trust me."

"No, Alayna," his voice deepened. "Marry me because I love you. More than life itself." He squared himself to me. "Marry me *today,* so I can prove I mean it."

"Hudson, this is insane." He didn't even have a ring. "You destroyed everything we had together. You can't just fix it by asking me to marry you out of the blue."

"Why not?" He was desperate, both his tone and his body language gave him away. "Why not?" He shook his hands in front of him for emphasis. "We belong together. For all the wrongs we've done—*I've* done—you can't deny that we make each other better." He shifted his weight to one hip. "You admit you love me. And I love you. What's keeping us apart? The fact that we hurt each other? Can you honestly say that you feel less hurt without me around? You came by the loft, Alayna. I know you're still thinking about me." He put his hands together, steepling his index fingers. "The only logical reason you can give for not being with me is that you don't trust that I'm really in it for love. Marry me and you'll have no doubt."

His voice lowered as he asked one more time, his eyes begging. "Please, marry me."

I'd thought about it. More than once. Thought about a forever with Hudson Pierce. And he'd hinted at it before. If I really believed him when he said that the majority of our relationship had been real, then his proposal wouldn't seem completely out of the blue.

And I did believe that most of it had been real. Not just because I wanted to, but because it had been real to *me*. The way I loved him didn't happen in a one-sided relationship. That was the false attraction I'd felt for men in the past, I knew the difference. No, this kind of love only grew from reciprocation. Whatever had been false between us, our love hadn't been.

But despite what I'd thought about and what we'd felt, there was more between us that hadn't had time to settle. More that hadn't healed. Falling into anything with Hudson again, let alone marriage—*marriage!*—would be like lying out in the sun while still recovering from a bad burn.

Baby steps.

Marriage was not baby steps. And, honestly, I didn't even know yet if the steps I wanted to take were in that direction. In his direction.

He was waiting for my answer.

I gave it. "No."

"No?" His expression was more confused than disappointed.

Hudson rarely heard the word no. It was likely shocking to hear it when he most wanted a different answer.

"No," I repeated. "No." I straightened. "You think you can fix everything between us by asking me to elope with you? It's hard for me to even look at you right now. Why would you think I would consider marrying you?"

He opened his mouth and I put my hand up in the air to shush him. "Don't talk. I don't want an answer. I need to say some things. Yes, I came to the loft because I missed you. Missed you desperately. But if I'd had any inkling you'd be there, I would have found a way to resist. I'm glad I was there because I found out some things that I needed to know. I'm grateful for what you did. But it doesn't change you and me. It just makes it easier for me to maybe one day find some closure."

"Don't say closure, Alay—" He stopped himself, realizing I wasn't finished. "Sorry. Go on."

His willingness to submit to me almost did me in. That had to be hard for him to give me the floor. He got a point for that one.

But he was so behind on the score that a measly point made little difference.

I took a breath and went on. "Even if I could trust you, Hudson, I wouldn't want to marry a guy just because he scammed me and now he feels bad. And not in Vegas. I'd want my brother and Mira and Adam and Jack. And even Sophia."

His expression turned hopeful. "You want my family at your wedding? Does that mean I have a shot at being the groom?"

"Once, you did. But now..." *Oh, this was hard to say.* "Now I can't see how."

Though it hurt for me to say the words, it was Hudson who appeared crushed. He closed his eyes and his jaw twitched as his entire body sagged. It struck me that the tables had completely been turned. Wasn't it usually he who had the emotional control while I was left floundering? He who was even and strong while I fell apart?

Strangely, it didn't feel any better to be on this side. Because though it seemed like I was in control, inside I was a mess.

Was this what it felt like to be Hudson Pierce?

I couldn't think about it anymore. None of it. It was time to get off the emotional roller coaster and move the fuck on.

There was no way to the doorway except through him. "I have to leave now, Hudson."

He made no effort to move. "Alayna, let's talk about this more. If not this plan, maybe we can talk about something else. Or no plan at all. Just talking to you is nice."

"I can't. I need to go." I was done.

"Alayna..."

"Please," my voice cracked, "let me go."

Slowly, reluctantly, he stepped out of my pathway. But just as I was about to step through the door, he slipped in front of me. He put his hands on each side of the frame, not touching me, but blocking my way. "No, I'm not ever letting you go." His words were raw with emotion. "I'll let you leave here right now, but I'm not giving up on you. I'll pursue you like I've never pursued anything in my life. I'll fight until you have no choice but to believe that I love you with everything I am."

He was so close. I could smell him, breathe him in the same way I had his pillow at the loft. But this was so much better because it was really him. Warmth rolled off him, calling me to his arms. If I simply leaned forward, I'd fall into him.

And the things he was saying—his vow to fight for me—it was hard to resist.

Then Liesl's advice from that morning came back to me. It was too soon. I needed more time. "Hudson," I kept my eyes down, unable to meet his gaze. "Let me go."

He waited a beat, but then he did step back and I slid past, careful not to touch him, though every cell in my body yearned to do just that.

I managed to hold my head high as I walked away from him, even when he called after me. "I'm never giving up, Alayna. I'll prove myself. You'll see."

— CHAPTER —
TWENTY-THREE

I went into work that night to find a package with my name on it waiting in the office. "What's this?" I asked Gwen.

"Beats me. A courier left it for you about half an hour ago. No message." She went back to counting the money in the safe.

No way to know unless I opened it. Inside, I found a brand new Kindle. I'd never had an e-reader, but I'd used the Kindle app on my computer. I turned it on and found the device was filled with books. Flipping through them, I recognized the titles as the ones on my bookshelves in Hudson's library. I picked up the wrapping, searching for a card, and finally found one—a simple note, handwritten:

In case you're missing your books as much as I'm missing you. – H

I stared at the card for several minutes while I tried to quiet my pulse. He was really going to fight for me, then. The realization thrilled me. Gifts weren't going to cut it though. I couldn't give a shit about material items. The note—that I'd cherish.

Gwen swung the safe door shut and came to glance over my shoulder. "Ah, so lover boy's trying to win you back."

"Supposedly." I tucked the note in my bra and waited for her traditional love sucks speech.

It didn't come. "There could be worse things," she said with more than a hint of melancholy.

It was possible she was right.

Sunday, a delivery service showed up at Liesl's with a new futon mattress, much thicker and of higher quality than the old one. The card this time read: *You should be sleeping well even though I'm not. – H*

I glared at Liesl. "How does he know I'm sleeping on a futon?"

She shrugged. "Maybe I said something in one of our texts."

"You're texting him?" Wasn't she supposed to be on my side?

"He had your phone charger delivered the other night to the club. Guess he figured that's why you hadn't been responding to him. So I plugged it in and holy Jesus, Laynie, that thing was filled with texts." She pulled her long hair over one shoulder. "Some of them made me feel a little bad for the guy. I texted him back."

I swatted her shoulder—or more like shoved. "What the fuck?"

"I told him it was me and not you." As if that were the reason I was pissed.

"That's private, Liesl."

Again she shrugged. "Someone should be reading them. That's all I'm saying." She turned to the deliveryman, who just walked up with his clipboard looking for a signature. She signed then looked back at me. "It's plugged in on top of the fridge if you're interested."

It was much later, when I couldn't sleep despite the comfortable new mattress, that I pulled my phone down from its hiding place. There were more than a hundred unread texts, plus a handful that had been marked read that I hadn't seen. Apparently Liesl had only viewed some of them.

I curled up on the new futon and began reading. Like the notes he'd been sending, most were sweet, but some were sexy, others desperate. I took my time absorbing each one, intermittently crying and smiling and sometimes even laughing.

Even though I'd responded to none of them so far, each was written as if I would. I rolled my eyes at one sent earlier that day.

I ordered a futon for me as well. Maybe sleeping on it will make me feel closer to you.

And then later, after eleven p.m., he sent several in a row:

God, this sucks shit. I wasn't sleeping before but at least I was comfortable.

I'll continue to endeavor, though. If this is how you're sleeping, I shall as well.

You know, we could both be together in the bed at the penthouse. If I remember correctly, the lack of sleep we got had nothing to do with the comfort of the mattress. ;)

Before I could stop myself, I shot a text back:

Hudson Pierce using an emoticon…will wonders never cease?

It was two in the morning and he responded immediately. He really *wasn't* sleeping.

I'm hoping they don't cease. If I ever have you in my arms again, that will certainly be a wonder. Goodnight, precious.

That night I slept with the phone next to me. Though I didn't often reply, I read the texts he sent from then on. Each and every one.

The gifts continued through the week with jewelry, tickets to the symphony, and a new laptop. On the days I worked at the club, the packages would be waiting there. Obviously Hudson was still monitoring my schedule, which was both irritating and sort of a turn-on.

Thursday, though, there was nothing on my desk when I arrived. I told myself it was silly to be disappointed. He didn't have to give me something every day to prove he was thinking about me. And I didn't want him thinking about me all the time anyway, did I?

I was still mulling around the question, still thinking about *him*, when the club opened for the evening. Since one of the bartenders had called in sick, I stepped in to help at the upstairs bar. We were hopping before the clock even hit eleven, so I was somewhat distracted when Liesl bent near me. "Did you see the suit at the end of the bar?"

"No," I said with a scowl. If she thought I would be interested in ogling man candy, she was wrong.

She winked. "Well, check him out then."

I finished topping the beer mug in my hand and, against my better judgment, shot a glance to the end of the counter.

He was sitting in the same seat that he'd been in the first time I saw him, wearing the same suit, if I wasn't mistaken.

And the way he stared at me? His eyes held the same heat as they had that night before my graduation. That burn that was more than lust, more than desire, it was possession.

Was it wrong that I smiled?

When I could finally tear myself away from Hudson's magnetic stare, I made a Scotch, neat, and delivered it to him.

"The service here is excellent," he said when I handed him his glass. As he took it from me, he brushed his fingers against mine.

Or had that been me that had done that?

Either way, the contact sent goose bumps running down my arms and warmth spreading through my chest. It had been so long since I'd touched him in any form. My body yearned for more while my head sent warning bells to run, run, run.

And my heart played some sort of Switzerland in the whole transaction, deciding not to make its desires clear.

With the war going on inside, I didn't know what to do or say. I stood frozen, my gaze locked on his. It felt so good—so *right*—to do nothing but get lost in his grays. Couldn't I find a way to do this every day of my life?

"Order!" a waitress called from down the counter.

I blinked, recovering from the trance Hudson had me in. "I have to go." Silly to explain. I didn't owe him anything. "Um, will you be wanting another when you've finished?"

"No, just the one. But I might sit here for a while, if you don't mind." His eyes moved down my body. "The view is stunning."

I turned before he could see my blush.

When he left, over an hour later, he settled his bill with Liesl. I only noticed he was leaving when she handed me an envelope. "This is from the suit."

I opened it and found a hundred dollar bill and a certificate to his spa in Poughkeepsie—the same gifts he'd given me that night in May.

"Liesl, I'll, um, I'll be right back." Maybe it was because I was disappointed to see him go, but I came up with an excuse to run after him.

"Hudson!" I yelled when I found him outside headed toward the parking garage.

He stopped and waited for me to catch up.

I held the envelope out toward him. "I can't accept this. I'm in charge here. I can't leave for a week to go to a spa."

It suddenly occurred to me that we hadn't talked about my job since our break-up. "Unless you'd rather I wasn't working here."

"Don't ever think that." His tone was harsh, final. "If you think you can't work with me as your owner, I'll give you the club." He would too, knowing him.

And that was definitely not a gift I could accept. "I just want to keep my job, thank you."

He softened. "It's yours as long as you want it." He pushed my hand that still held the envelope back toward me. "And the certificate—keep it. You can use it anytime you want. There's no expiration." His fingers lingered on mine.

Was this what we'd been reduced to? Stealing touches at any opportunity possible? Making up reasons to talk?

I pulled my hand—and the envelope—away from his. "Fine. Whatever."

A chill ran through me, though the night was warm. Frantically, I searched for something else to say. "There's another thing." I took a deep breath. There really was something I'd been avoiding. "I need to get my stuff from the penthouse."

His mouth tightened. "I wish you wouldn't do that."

I ignored him. It was the easiest way to deal with statements like that. Especially when I so liked the way they sounded on his lips. "I want to come get the rest of my things Monday."

"I can have it packed and moved for you, if you'd like."

"I'd rather pack it myself." If he packed, I'd end up with all sorts of things that didn't belong to me—things he wanted me to have. As sweet as it might be, I didn't want his gifts. I also didn't have any room for them in the apartment with Liesl. Even if we got a two-bedroom place together as we'd been talking about doing, we couldn't afford anything that big.

"At least let me arrange a truck." His tone was insistent, but his eyes were pleading. It was hard to resist.

So I didn't. "Okay. You can do that." Only because it was going to be a pain to do it myself. And he did owe me.

"It's done." His lip curled up at the edge. "This doesn't mean I'm done trying to win you back."

"I didn't think for a second that it did." Though I bit back a smile, my pleasure at his declaration showed in my voice.

Hudson tilted his head to study me. "You say that as if you almost enjoy my groveling."

I rolled my eyes and turned toward the club with a wave. But I couldn't resist calling back over my shoulder, "I couldn't say, H. I haven't really seen you grovel yet."

Friday and Saturday saw more gifts delivered—a coffee table book of pictures from the Poconos and concert tickets to Phillip Phillips.

"He's, like, recalling your entire relationship with this stuff, isn't he?" Liesl said on Sunday as I opened the box that had arrived that morning. "I hate to say it, but he's kinda good."

I wadded up the brown packaging paper from the box and tossed it at her. "Shut up."

"What's this one?"

"I don't know yet." I pulled out the John Legend CD I found inside and read the song list on back. I knew of the artist but had never listened to any of his music. The case wasn't sealed so I opened it easily and found Hudson's note.

This is the song that makes me think of you. Track 6. - H

R&B. Huh. Hudson rarely listened to music around me. When he did, he deferred to me to choose. I didn't even know what style he liked. Was this it?

I looked back at the song list and found track six. "*All of Me*," I read out loud. "I don't know it. Do you?"

"Never heard of it. Let's stick it in." She grinned and added her own, "That's what she said."

Shaking my head at her, I pulled out my new laptop, put in the disc and pushed play on the track Hudson had indicated. I leaned my head back against the futon and listened.

The song started with a haunting piano line. Then a tenor voice crooned about a beautiful woman with a smart mouth who had the singer distracted and spinning. He was a mess, but it was all good, because no matter how crazy she made him, she was still everything to him.

It was the chorus that had me in tears, when he sang about "*all of me*" loving "*all of you*" and offered to give all of himself to her in exchange for the same.

Sure, it was just a song, but if it really held the message that Hudson meant for me to hear, well, I couldn't help but hear it loud and clear. If he could really give all of himself to me—no more walls, no more secrets—then what was left holding us back? The past?

But my own history was imperfect. I'd even shown him my flaws on more than one occasion. He'd forgiven me and stuck around. Fixed me and found me and made me whole.

And now...

Not saying a word when I set the song to repeat, Liesl sat next to me and pulled me to her shoulder.

"Liesl, I don't care anymore," I sobbed into her shirt. "Even if I shouldn't be with him, I can't live without him. He makes me feel better about me. I don't care anymore about what he did in the past. I only care that he's around in my future."

She rocked me back and forth. "No one's telling you what you should or shouldn't do here. Either way, you got my support."

"Good, because I think I'm going to give him another chance." I wasn't quite sure what that chance would be yet—dinner? A date? Lots of dates?

That was a decision for tomorrow.

Though I didn't have a lot to pack up from the penthouse, I wanted to get started on it early enough in the day that we'd be long gone before Hudson arrived home from work. Getting Liesl anywhere before noon, however, proved difficult.

"Maybe I could join you later," she said, burying her head in her pillow at my first attempt to drag her out of bed.

"But I need you the whole time," I whined. "Please?"

The pleading worked, but she tried again to get out of going as we were getting in the cab. Then at The Bowery, she suggested that she make a coffee run and join me later.

"There's a beautiful Keurig inside. Best coffee ever. I'll make you as many mugs as you want." Maybe Liesl wasn't really big on packing.

"Fine."

It was much easier to go inside the building with Liesl along. As we went up in the elevator, I wrapped my arm around hers, grateful for the support.

Though I hadn't been living there for two weeks, moving out was big. It reeked of finality. And with my recent decision to let Hudson back in my life in some way, I wasn't quite looking for finality. I needed Liesl to talk me out of anything stupid.

Like deciding to leave my stuff there and not move out.

When the door opened to the apartment, I waited for Liesl to step out first. She didn't move so I went ahead of her. I turned around and put my hand on the side to keep the elevator open. "Aren't you coming?"

"Uh..." her eyes grew wide. Then she pushed my arm out of the door and pressed a button on the call panel. "Don't hate me!" she called as the doors shut.

What the fuck? I heaved a frustrated air of breath out of my lungs and closed my eyes. Either Liesl had somewhere else she wanted to be or she had something up her sleeve. And if it was the latter, there was no doubt Hudson was involved.

Might as well find out what was up.

I opened my eyes and peered around the corner of the foyer toward the living area. It was empty. Not just empty as in no Hudson, but empty as in no furniture. None. I wandered into the room to be sure I wasn't going crazy.

Well, if I were going crazy, the delusion I was having was of an apartment with no furniture. I glanced at the dining room. Also empty. Strangely, the place didn't feel any more cold and lonely than it had when I'd been there the last time. But the emptiness put me off. I couldn't understand what it meant. Was my stuff gone as well?

I backtracked and pushed the door open to the library. This room was only mostly empty. The sofa and desk and all the rest of the furniture were gone, but the shelves still contained all my books and movies. The books I'd pulled that Celia had marked were gone from the floor, but several boxes were stacked against the wall.

I walked toward the stack, intending to peek in and see if the books were there, but it was sealed.

"Those are new books."

Ah, there he is.

I turned slightly to find Hudson leaning in the doorframe. Again he was wearing jeans and a t-shirt. Dammit, he hadn't even planned on going to work if he was dressed like that. And he looked extra yummy. Somehow he had arranged that as well, I was sure of it.

He nodded again at the box I was still touching. "They're for you. To replace the ones that had been damaged."

"Oh," I said. Then I frowned.

"What is it?"

"I have nowhere to put all these." I hadn't intended to take them. They were beautiful and I loved them, but in New York City, that many books were a luxury.

He sighed softly and I could tell the rejection of his gift hurt, no matter what the reason. But all he said was, "I'll keep them for as long as you want me to."

"Thank you." I caught myself scanning his body. It was impossible not to. He was so good-looking, and I missed him so much. Though I'd planned my move on a day that he wouldn't be around, I was happy to see him. Elated, actually.

I wondered if he could see that in my smile. "I didn't expect you to be here." *I'm so glad you are.*

"You didn't say I couldn't be."

"It was implied," I teased.

He caught my eyes with his. "You don't seem that horribly pissed to see me."

God, the butterflies were stirring in my belly. Not the tug of fixation that used to make me act crazy, but the twitters I felt only with Hudson. It had confused me when I first felt it those months ago, but now I recognized it for what it was—a combination of nerves and excitement and attraction and anticipation. It was such a gloriously delicious feeling.

Surprisingly, it eclipsed the still fresh wounds from his betrayal.

Still, I was scared. And I didn't know what he was up to. His stuff was gone from the apartment. I didn't like what that had to mean. What *did* it mean? "Where is everything?"

His lips drew tight. "Your stuff is still all here."

"But where's your stuff?"

With another deep breath, he threw his eyes to the window then brought them back to me. "I can't live here without you, Alayna."

"So you're moving out?" I didn't know how I felt about that.

Strike that, I did know. I didn't like it. At all. The penthouse was where our real relationship had taken place. I hated the idea of someone else being in our space.

And Hudson moving out because I wasn't there—that meant he didn't really believe I'd ever be back.

I was too late. He was giving up on me.

But his next words tossed everything up in the air again. "Actually, I hope I'm moving in."

The twists and turns of this interaction had me flustered and on edge. I had to call an emotional timeout before I broke down. "H, you confuse me enough without you trying to be confusing. Could you say something I can understand?"

"I confuse you?" His eyes sparkled with satisfaction.

"Is this a surprise?"

He shrugged.

"So you're moving in?" I prompted. Dammit, why did he have to be so difficult?

Seeming to sense I was on my last nerve, he answered. "One day. I hope." He rubbed his lips together—ah, I missed those sweet lips. "But for now, I want you to live here."

"What?" One day a proposal, another *live in my million dollar penthouse without me.* The man certainly knew how to keep me on my toes.

He also had no idea what I really wanted or needed from him.

Hudson's expression grew serious again. "I can't live here without you, precious." His words were soft and low, but I could hear him clearly. "But I don't want to sell it, because I love being here with you. Someday, you and I will be here again. While I'm waiting for you—scratch that—while I'm groveling for your forgiveness, it's a shame to let it sit empty. You and Liesl should move in."

"I can't accept that, H." My eyes felt watery. But at least he'd said he wasn't giving up on me.

"I had a feeling you'd say that." He sighed, giving up much more easily than was characteristic. "Then it will have to sit."

I bit back the urge to say we could live here together and offered instead, "You could rent it out."

His brows rose. "I could rent it out to you."

I laughed.

"Best rent in town—only cost you a weekly dinner with the landlord."

"Stop it." I was still smiling.

"Biweekly then. I'm not above bargaining."

"Hudson." He had no idea that he already had me sold. Not on moving in, but on the dates.

"Fine, monthly. I'll take whatever scraps you're willing to give me." He studied me. "You're considering giving me scraps now, aren't you?"

"Maybe." How did he read me so easily? And why was it so easy to be with him when he'd hurt me so deeply?

The question scared me, so I skirted the issue. "Seriously, though, where's all your stuff? Did you get another place?" All his furniture wouldn't fit in the loft.

He shook his head. "I gave it all to a charity fundraiser."

"Lifestyles of the rich and famous." Though I couldn't say I'd miss any of it. It was beautiful furniture, but Celia had chosen it all. I was quite happy with the thought of the less fortunate benefitting from it.

It seemed Hudson felt the same. "I wasn't attached to any of it." He straightened and walked into the room, gesturing to the empty space. "This entire apartment was perfectly designed to my tastes and style, but it never felt like a home." He stopped a couple feet from me. "Not until you, Alayna. You made it come alive. The things that were here—they were chosen for me by someone I want completely removed from my life. Right now, the things here are the only things that made this house a place I'd want to live. Your things. You."

"I..." My throat was too tight to speak.

"And when I move back in, we can refurnish this place from scratch. Together. You and I."

I took in a shuddering breath. "You're so sure that one day I'll take you back." The outlook was getting better and better.

"I'm hopeful." He smiled mischievously. "Would you like to see how hopeful I am?"

"Sure." Really, all I wanted was for him to pull me into his arms. I was almost certain that was where we'd end up. But the game we were playing to get there was intriguing.

Hudson dug in his pocket and pulled out something small and silver. "I bought this."

He held the object by the jewel so I couldn't really see all of it at first, but when I realized what it was, my breath caught. Because it was a ring. *The ring.*

He dropped it in my palm for me to examine. It wasn't silver after all—it was platinum, if I guessed right. And the jewel was surrounded by two tapered baguette stones that led the eye to a round, brilliantly cut diamond in the center. It was at least two and half carats, maybe three. Maybe even four, for all I knew.

Tears gathered in my eyes and bewilderment muddled my brain. He'd handed it to me—it wasn't a proposal. What was this then? A way to mess with me?

"There's an inscription," Hudson said softly, as though he could read my confusion.

I blinked to clear my vision enough to read: *I give you all of me.*

Then he bent down on one knee.

It *was* a proposal.

I couldn't speak, couldn't think, couldn't even breathe.

"I realized something about the last time I asked this," he said from his place on the floor in front of me. "I did it wrong. First, I didn't have a ring, and second, I should have gotten on one knee. But more importantly, I didn't give you the right thing. I offered you everything I had, thinking that was the way to win your heart. That wasn't what you wanted at all. The only thing you ever asked for, the only thing I would never give you, was me."

A sob escaped my throat, but for the first time in days, it wasn't a sorrowful sob.

"But now I do." Hudson threw his arms out to the side. "Here I am, precious. I give myself freely. All of me, Alayna. No more walls or secrets or games or lies. I give you all of me, honestly. For forever, if you'll take it."

He took the ring from my grasp. With hands that were so steady compared to my shaky one, he slipped it on my finger.

I stared at it, shining brilliantly on my hand like a beacon in the darkness I'd been living in. Was he really asking me to marry him? Not elope, but marriage? Was this really something I could actually consider?

My plan to let him back into my life had been much simpler and less drastic—like a dinner and a movie type of thing. Not a proposal.

But that had always been Hudson. He moved fast and furiously, but when he truly wanted something, he committed with everything he had. If

I said no, if I turned him away, I knew without a doubt he'd ask again and again. And again.

That wasn't a reason to accept a marriage proposal.

The reason to accept was because I loved Hudson Pierce with every fiber of my being. Even his flaws and imperfections attracted me to him. They made him who he was. And I wanted all of him. I wanted to give him all of me.

And he had a lot of making up to do to me. Forever might just be the only way he'd get it covered.

"Alayna, I love you." He drew my gaze from the ring to his eyes—his wildly intense, passionate eyes that shown brighter than the diamond on my hand. "Will you marry me? Not today, and not in Vegas, but in a church if you like, or at Mabel Shores in the Hamptons—"

Somehow I found my voice. "Or the Brooklyn Botanic Gardens during the cherry blossom season?"

"Yes, there." His eyes widened. "Is that a—"

"Yes," I nodded. "It's a yes."

Hudson pulled me onto his knee and into his arms faster than I could blink. "Say it again."

"Yes," I whispered, placing my hand on his cheek. "Yes, I'll marry you."

His lips found mine, and it was like a first kiss—soft and tentative. Then our mouths parted and our tongues met and the kiss gathered from a fragile breeze into a raging storm. One of his hands tangled in my hair, the other cupped my face, holding me as if he feared I wouldn't stay, as if I might disappear.

And the way I held him was the same. I wrapped my arms around his neck, clutching onto him with all my strength. When our kiss began to metamorphosis into something bigger, something that required more of our body to be touching, and less of our clothing to be on, he grabbed his hand around my thigh, lifting it around his waist as he stood. I threw my other leg around him, hooking my ankles together at his backside and bucked my hips, rubbing against his crotch.

Damn, I'd missed this. Missed him—all of him. His touch was searing, his kiss burned me to my core. And the solidness of his body, his strong arms, his muscled chest—he was my foundation. Sturdy and fixed. Permanent.

Permanently mine.

We were halfway down the hall, our lips still locked when I realized I had no idea where he was taking me. If the house was empty, did it matter that we made it to the bedroom?

Asking, though, would require me to let go of his tongue, and the growl he made as I sucked on it made that not an option I wanted to consider.

I got my answer soon enough anyway. Hudson pushed into our bedroom and in my peripheral vision I saw on the floor, minus the bedframe, our mattress.

He toed his shoes off and then dropped with me onto the bed.

"You left the mattress?" I asked while he pulled my shirt over my head.

His shirt disappeared quickly after. "I picked it out myself. Besides, I couldn't bear to part with it. It has too many memories."

Yes, it does.

And more to be made. A lifetime of them, in fact. *Oh my god, a lifetime with Hudson.*

He bent down to nip my breast through my bra, bringing me sharply back to the present.

I moaned breathily. "Are you sure you weren't simply—" I moaned again as he nipped my other breast. "—being prepared for me to say yes?"

His mouth returned to mine. "There may have been a little bit of that," he said against my lips, his hands reaching behind me to undo the clasp of my bra.

"You know me so well, don't you?"

He grinned and lowered his gaze to my breasts newly released from captivity. "I want to know you better." He licked around one taut nipple. "I want to know you better right now. God, I've missed your gorgeous body."

And god, how I'd missed the things he did to it. Was there a manual somewhere entitled *How to Please Alayna*? If so, Hudson had surely memorized the thing. More likely, he'd written it. He knew how to please me better than I knew how to please myself.

As he teased and taunted my breasts, making me dizzy with desire, I reached down to cup his erection through his jeans. The warmth of it, the hardness, even through the thick denim material, had a geyser going off in my panties.

I stroked along the length of his imprisoned cock. "I remember this."

"Uh-uh. First we're focusing on you." He already had a hand traveling beneath the band of my yoga pants, determined to prove his point.

"But I like this." I petted him again. "There should definitely be some of this."

"Oh, there will be a whole lot of this." He bucked into my palm then turned his attention back to what his hand was doing. What his hand was doing so well. His thumb had settled on my clit, swirling across it with expert pressure.

I wiggled underneath him, wishing I was naked and that he was naked and that we were to the next part where he was inside me. I was desperate for that.

But Hudson made me wait. He dipped a finger inside me and I gasped.

"Jesus, Alayna. You're so wet. Do you know how hard that makes me? You're so wet and juicy that I'm tempted to lick you clean. But I'm anxious and missing you and I need my cock inside you as soon as possible. Tasting you will have to wait until the next round."

"Next round?" I was a bit delirious with the awesomeness of this round.

He added a second finger, bending them so that they rubbed against that magic spot that only Hudson ever knew how to find. Quickly my belly tightened and my legs began to quiver.

"You're so turned on—you're going to come fast, aren't you, precious?"

That was all it took to push me over. Pleasure washed over me in a tidal wave, and I let out a moan, digging my fingers into his back as he continued to rub me and finger me until the last spasm trembled through me.

Hudson sucked the lobe of my ear and then praised me. "Good girl. You're so fucking sexy when you come. It makes me so hard my cock throbs."

Fuck, his mouth alone was going to send me over again.

Hudson removed his hand from my pussy and pulled off my pants and underwear. "Remember our first night in the Hamptons? When I made love to you so many times that you were sore the next day?"

"How could I forget?" I watched in a haze as he stripped out of his jeans and briefs. His cock sprung free, harder and thicker than I'd ever remembered it being.

Hudson Pierce naked.

I had to swallow. Twice. There wasn't any sight on Earth that compared to the mouth-watering deliciousness in front of me.

And it was all mine. *Forever.*

Hudson climbed on top of me, covering me with his body. "That night is going to pale in comparison to today, precious. Today, I'm going to make love to you sweetly and tenderly. Then I'm going to fuck you so long and hard, your beautiful pussy is going to be raw. You won't be able to stand, let alone walk. After that, I'm going to go down on you until you're shivering and coming all over my tongue. And then we'll do it all again."

My pussy clenched at the promises being made. "You're such a big talker."

"I sure hope that wasn't a challenge," he said, settling between my thighs. "Because if it was, game on."

Now that was a game I didn't mind that he played.

I wrapped my legs around Hudson, ready for him to enter me. But he paused, his tip grazing my opening.

"Hurry." I tilted my hips up, prodding him. "I want you inside."

He ran a hand through my hair and laid a kiss on the tip of my nose. "Patience, precious. We have time, and I need to feel you."

He slid into me then, slowly and with great patience. I cried out at the agonizing sweetness as he filled me and stretched me and buried his cock inside of me. When I thought he couldn't possibly go any further, he bent my thighs up toward my chest and pushed in more.

Ah, he *was* throbbing. I could feel him pulse against my walls as he sank deeper, deeper.

"You feel so good, precious." He pulled out ever so slightly and thrust back in with a circle of his hips. "Rough, gentle—how do you want me?"

"You're giving me a say?" I blinked up at him.

His lip curled up slightly at the edge. "This time."

I loved him every way he gave himself to me. The only thing that mattered was that he did. "You decide. I trust you."

And I did trust him. Maybe not at the level that I could or once did, but we were a work in progress. We had time.

He seemed to like that answer. His eyes melted and his face softened. As he moved inside me, he clasped my hands in his and leaned his forehead against mine. "I love you, Alayna. My precious. My love."

We danced together, enjoying each other, loving each other as we took each other higher and higher. Pleasing each other in the ways we'd learned in the past and in new ways as well. It wasn't exactly sweet and it wasn't exactly rough and it wasn't exactly frenzied or passionate or gentle even—but it was all of that, rolled together. It was everything. And it was exactly perfect.

EPILOGUE

April

She's the most beautiful bride that's ever graced the Brooklyn Botanic Gardens. Hell, she's the most beautiful bride that's ever graced the Earth. I can't keep my eyes off her. Her dress hugs her gorgeous tits and her slim hips then trains out behind her. And the corset style in the back is fuck hot. I can't wait to undress her later. Though, when I finally get the chance, I have a feeling those ties will be more frustrating than sexy.

Though sometimes the frustration is half the fun.

And it's necessary. "Without struggle there is no progress," Alayna loves to tell me. It's a quote she learned in her counseling that she feels suits us fairly frequently. She's said it so many times in the last nine months that I was almost surprised it wasn't embroidered on our wedding napkins.

Honestly, the truth that lies in that simple statement is astounding. Though I am a man of commitment, a man who doesn't walk away from a challenge, I am the first to admit that the road from our engagement to our wedding was paved with boulders and potholes. Even though she said yes on that day back in August, there were many times I'm sure she was tempted to break it off afterward. Moments when I shut down and forgot how to let her in. Days when I pushed her away because I believed that I could never be worthy of her love.

Then there was the biggest issue of all—trust. I'd shattered every ounce of trust that existed between us, and rebuilding it took time. And therapy. Not just for myself, but for us as a couple. I'd thought working out my own problems was hard. Adding another person to the mix added a whole new dimension of struggle.

There was so much healing to be done, wounds that threatened to never scar over. Embracing Alayna's obsessive tendencies was natural for me, but I have had to learn how to not overly attach myself to her jealousies and insecurities. It can become enabling and as much as it's a turn-on to have her need me, I love her all the more when she's whole on her own. When she's strong and confident.

My healing has been much more tenuous. Abandoning the game I'd played for a lifetime proved the easiest part. With Alayna in my life, I have no desire to be cruel and heartless like that again. But my inclination to manipulate and master runs deeper. I don't even recognize when I'm molding a situation to my whims. Alayna, kind and forgiving woman that she is, often doesn't point out when I'm wielding and dominating. A great deal of the time, she even likes it. But she also doesn't wish to give too much power to my weaknesses. So she calls me on it more and more, and I in turn attempt to let go. To let things run their natural course.

That has been the most difficult part for me, the hardest component of recovery.

But the progress has been amazing. We wouldn't be here today if it hadn't been for the steps we took together to strengthen our relationship. And while I'm sure the struggle isn't over simply because I've slipped a ring on her finger, we know that we're worth the fight.

She's worth the fight.

Look what my reward has been? Even without our wedding vows, she's mine. And I'm hers. Completely and absolutely.

The ceremony was simple—that's how she wanted it, and her wish is my command. Mirabelle and Liesl and Gwen, who has become a surprisingly good friend to Alayna, stood as her bridesmaids. Their pale pink dresses exactly matched the blossoms on Alayna's veil and in the garden. How Mirabelle managed that, I'll never know. I'll thank her later for her contributions to my wife's day.

My wife.

I'll never get tired of saying that—*wife.* Who would have believed that I'd ever have one of those? I'd never been a man who intended to marry. My mother and father didn't present a pretty picture of matrimony, and I had no understanding of the concept of romantic love. It took Alayna to teach it to me. She's been the best teacher possible—patient and forgiving beyond what I deserve.

She hates it when I say that about myself—that I'm undeserving, and I suppose it's the same way I feel when she talks destructively about her own past. The difference, of course, is that her weaknesses and imperfections didn't almost destroy us as mine did. There are days it's hard to live with myself because of the lie that I wrapped her in. She soothes me then, fixing me with her love. "*We would never have found each other if it weren't for your game,*" she tells me.

I don't believe that, though. I would have always found her.

Always. Without a doubt.

It's not an exaggeration when I say I fell for her at first sight. If anything, I downplay. Not on purpose. The effect she had on me is simply beyond words, and when I attempt to voice it, the true experience becomes abridged and reduced. In all honesty, the woman who stood on that stage left me speechless. Her business ideas were only part of it. They were sound and innovative, but really, there are bright, intelligent up-and-comers around every corner. This went beyond that. I can't even pinpoint if it was her mannerisms or her pattern of speaking or the shocking depth to her chocolate brown eyes. Whatever it was, there was a definite recognition of her soul by mine. An awareness of something greater that tied us to each other upon first acquaintance. As if some part of me had always known she was out there, had been waiting for her to come and bring me to life.

It took me quite some time to label that as love. At first, I didn't know what it was. And now that I do, I still hesitate to call it that since the word fails to express the multi-dimensional way I feel for her. But it's the nearest thing I have, and I say it to her now as often as I can. Then I try to tell her what I really mean by that simple four-letter verb. That not only does my world revolve around her, but she is my world. That she's not just my reason for breathing, she's air itself. That she's the meaning behind every one of my thoughts, every thrum of my pulse, every whisper of my conscience. She's my entire everything. It's as simple and as complex as that.

I don't know that she'll ever understand, but I'll happily spend my lifetime trying to show her.

I gaze around the crowd of people that have shown up to celebrate our special day and think it's funny how, now that I know what it means to love and be loved, I see it everywhere. In the way that Adam tends to the baby and tags along behind Mirabelle as she flits from one person to another. In the way my father held my mother's hand during the ceremony. In the tender look that Brian had for his younger sister when he gave her to me to wed. Has there always been all this love in the world? How have I never seen it before Alayna Withers showed up in my life?

Alayna Pierce now. Doesn't that have a nice ring?

She's coming to me now, and my grin widens. I haven't stopped smiling since she walked down that aisle. I'm sure I look ridiculous.

"Hey, handsome," she says in that lusty voice of hers that makes my cock twitch. "It's time for the first dance."

I let her lead me to the center of the Esplanade. It's impressive how fast the crew we hired transposed the ceremony arrangement to a reception area. We could have moved to the Atrium or another venue all together as our wedding planner suggested, but Alayna wanted the whole event to be outdoors among the blossoms. It was a good decision. The Brooklyn Botanic Society doesn't usually rent out the whole garden for weddings. It's amazing what they'll do for a large donation.

The emcee announces our first dance as I pull my bride into my arms. "What will our first dance be to, Mrs. Pierce?"

I know nothing she has planned for the reception. Alayna took care of all the wedding details. I offered to help, but she preferred to surprise me. The tables will be turned when I get her on the plane to our honeymoon destination. She has no idea that we'll be staying in a private cabana in the Maldives Islands for three weeks. I'd considered Italy or Greece—both locations that she's mentioned wanting to visit—but out of my own selfishness, I chose a tropical setting. It will be easier to keep her naked on a private beach than at the site of an ancient ruin or in an art museum.

"Patience, Mr. Pierce." She's always so good at throwing my own lines back to me.

The music starts and I smile. *All of Me.* Of course.

She snuggles into my arms and I bury my head in her neck, breathing in the scent of her. Her cherry body wash mingles with the blossoms in the air, but none of it can completely cover up the delicious aroma of Alayna's skin—a combination of salt and sweet that I can't describe but would recognize anywhere.

Though I want to hold her and enjoy her in this tender first dance as a married couple, I feel that I've had so little chance to talk to her today, and I can't stop myself from doing so now. "It's a beautiful wedding, Alayna. You did an excellent job."

I feel her cheek tug into a smile at my shoulder. "Thank you. I had a lot of help, thanks to your money."

"*Our* money," I correct. As I'd promised the first time I asked her to marry me, I demanded no prenup. What's mine is hers, openly and without question. I wonder if she'll ever get used to it.

"*Our* money," she concedes. "And it's going well, I think."

"Very well." *Very well, indeed.*

"Did you notice Chandler's been following Gwen around like a lost puppy?"

I had noticed. Though there's too much lust in his eye for me to understand the puppy comparison. "She doesn't seem to mind." Gwen's gaze also holds a degree of desire. Can Alayna see it?

"No, she doesn't." Alayna giggles. *She does see it, then.* "And everyone seems happy."

"Everyone does at that." *And I'm the happiest.*

She places a kiss on my neck that sends a jolt to my cock. "Even your mother has managed to remain polite."

The mention of my mother has me limp. "She does seem slightly more in control of herself now that she's sober." Sophia's only been home from upstate since January. She missed Mirabelle's baby's birth, something that I believe she regrets deeply, but she's better now than she was, and I believe even Sophia thinks the sacrifice is worth it. "She still is a nasty old bitch, though, isn't she?"

Alayna laughs, her hair tickling my neck with the movement, the sound tickling my heart with its purity. "You said it, not me."

I hold her tighter and kiss her temple. This is everything I ever needed and never knew I wanted, wrapped up in the most beautiful of packages. Well, not quite everything. There's still one thing left on the list.

I broach the subject I've been avoiding in a passive way. Perhaps it's manipulative, but it's who I am. "I saw you with Arin Marise, earlier. You're so good with her."

Arin Marise Sitkin is Adam and Mirabelle's baby. My sister insists that she gave her daughter a name that couldn't be shortened so that I'll call her what everyone else calls her. But I've taken to calling her Arin Marise just to rile her up. She's five and a half months old now, all cheeks and grins. Arin's petite like her mother but feisty. You only notice her small stature in comparison to Braden, Alayna's nephew who's only four months old, but almost twice as big as Arin.

Alayna and I have never talked about children, not about our children, anyway. I've seen her with Arin and Braden and fallen in love with her all over again with the care and gentleness she gives them, but I've never brought up the actual topic. Perhaps it scared me, but it doesn't scare me now. Not now that I know she's mine truly and deeply no matter how this conversation goes.

I pull back from our embrace to look in her eyes, thinking I should probably put this off until a more appropriate time, but unable to wait another second to ask. "Do you…" I begin then start over. "Have you thought about children of your own?"

She leans forward to kiss my throat then, with her eyes cast down, says tentatively, "I'd probably fuck them up."

That had always been my fear, and if it weighs too heavily on her, I'll abandon the whole idea. I kiss her head again and then ask outright, "Would you like to fuck them up with me?"

She laughs again and meets my gaze, her eyes misty and her face aglow. "Yes," she says without any hesitation or trace of doubt. "I'd love to."

"Good." I draw her closer and spin her around. "We can get started tonight in the plane. Or right now, if you prefer. I saw a rather large oak in one of the smaller gardens. I'm almost certain we could hide there, even with this dress of yours."

"I'd love to see how you plan to get at me with all this material in the way."

I nip at her ear. "Oh, precious, I'm very resourceful. Need I remind you that I'm a man who gets what he wants?" Again I lean back to look in her eyes. "And anyone who ever doubted that only needs to look at me right now to know it's true. Everything I want is here, in my arms."

"I love you," she murmurs.

"I love you first." *And last. And everything in between.*

I kiss her, sweetly, chastely enough for our onlookers, but with just enough bite that she knows I mean it. Then our dance is over and it's time for her to dance with her brother and me with Sophia.

Reluctantly, I let her go. I can bear these few minutes apart. I have her for a lifetime.

THE END

ACKNOWLEDGMENTS

Here we are at the hard part. Seriously, writing 110,000 words is easy compared to writing the couple thousand that makes up the thank yous. I know I'll leave several people out. Please don't think that means I've forgotten you in my heart. Just my mind is a little fried.

First, as always, to my husband, Tom—I love you first. And last. And everything in between.

To my children who thought that mom writing full-time would mean they'd see me more—thank you for your patience and understanding. I love and adore you, even when I'm yelling at you to get out of my office.

To my Mom—thank you for raising me to be a person who goes after her dreams yet still thinks about others. I, too, hope I never change.

To Gennifer Albin for my covers and for understanding me in ways that many people never will. For sure, 2014 is your year.

To Bethany Taylor for editing and book-fairying and even a little for the moping because it makes me feel better about the amount of time I spend moping. And for teaching me so much about stick-to-it-ness and kindness (yes, I said that, you faux-blackhearted woman, you).

To Kayti McGee for being my plot partner and an excellent submissive. I fully recognize that I dominate all our conversations. Thank you so much for your ear and your suggestions. I will drive to Boulder/Longmont to see you even though the laws have changed; I swear it!

To my critique partners and beta readers. My, God! I would not have made it through this without you, especially when I was so behind. Thank you all for reading and suggesting so quickly. Specifically, thank you Lisa Otto for making time for me in your busy schedule and telling me how it is. To Tristina Wright for knowing my characters better than me and correcting their behavior. To Jackie Felger for always making me feel like I'm a better writer than I am while catching more comma errors than a person should possibly be able to catch. To Melissa B. King for always letting me know that the steamy scenes were working. To Jenna Tyler for last minute edits, even when I didn't ask—you are an amazing find of a friend. To Angela McLain for your passion and support—you're such a beautiful person to know. To Lisa Mauer for your enthusiasm and genuine love of my series; sometimes I felt like I was writing more for you than anyone. To Beta Goddess, you know who you are, but will never understand how grateful I am for "fixing" my book. I looked forward to your notes with a mixture of trepidation and excitement because I always knew you'd be hard, and that would make the story better. THANK YOU!!

To the people who make things happen for me: my agent, Bob DiForio; my formatter, Caitlin Greer; Julie at AToMR Book Blog Tours; my publicists at Inkslinger, Shanyn Day, and K.P. Simmons—both of you are amazeballs; Melanie Lowery and Jolinda Bivins for making me awesome swag; to my "other" editors Holly Atkinson, who has taught me to be mindful of comma splices, and Eileen Rothschild who is supportive of all my works and not just the one she bought.

To my FANTASTIC assistants, Lisa Otto, Amy McAvoy, and Taryn Maj. How did I get so lucky to have all of you working with me this past year? In many ways it's been the best part of the job.

To my soulmates and bandmates, The NAturals—Sierra, Gennifer, Melanie, Kayti, and Tamara. I honestly don't know what I'd do without you women. You love who I love, hate who I hate—you're my touchstones. I think Mel said this first, but I'm stealing it: If anyone had told me three years ago that I could love people I met on the internet more than people I knew in real life, I'd never believe it. But then I met you. Love and boobs to you always.

To Joe, last year was our year. So how much cooler will we be by this time next year?
To the authors who have helped out the newbie and inspired me with beautiful writing and so much amazing advice, especially Kristen Proby, Lauren Blakely, and Gennifer Albin. I'm really honored to know you all. Thank you for sharing your words and wisdom.

To the WrAHMs and the Babes of the Scribes—I can't wait to meet you at WrAHMpage and to hug the fuck out of all of you.

To the Book Bloggers and reviewers who have so enthusiastically shared my books. I can never hope to mention you all, but there are some of you I wouldn't dare miss: Aestas at Aestas Book Blog; Amy, Jesse, and Tricia at Schmexy Girls; The Rock Stars of Romance; Angie at Angie's Dreamy Reads; Lisa and Brooke at True Story Book Blog; Kari and Cara at A Book Whore's Obsession; Angie and Jenna at Fan Girl Book Blog; Jennifer Wolfel at Wolfel's World of Books. Though we have a symbiotic working relationship, I also truly think of you as friends. Thank you for your love and support.

To the Readers who make it possible for me to work full time as a writer and take care of my family with what I earn. I am so appreciative to you that I get choked up thinking about it. I know you have so many choices when it comes to picking up a book—thank you so, so much for picking up mine.

To my Creator who has given me more than I deserve—may I continue to understand what your role is for me in this life and to accept it with humility.

Did you know leaving a review helps authors get seen more on sites like Amazon? If you liked *Forever with You*, please consider leaving a review at Amazon or Barnes and Noble.

You can sign up for my email newsletter to receive new book release info at www.laurelinpaige.com. You can also connect with me on Twitter @laurelinpaige and Facebook www.facebook.com/laurelinpaige.

Enjoy a preview from Laurelin Paige's upcoming novel,

HUDSON

A full-length companion novel to the NY Times Bestselling Fixed Trilogy.

Told from his point of view, Hudson fills the holes in his love story with Alayna Withers. His past and relationship with his long-time friend Celia is further revealed and light is shed on his actions during his courtship with Alayna.

"I can easily divide my life into two parts—before her and after."

Chapter One

I sign in on the form and hand the clipboard back to the volunteer manning the desk.

The young man's brows rise in recognition of my name. "Mr. Pierce!" He stands from his seat and sticks out his hand to shake mine. "I didn't expect it would be you representing Pierce Industries. I thought you'd send someone."

I shake his hand, out of politeness, then force a stiff smile. "Surprise." God, I hate small talk. Especially from this twenty-two year old ass-kisser who likely hopes this interaction will earn him employment at my company. I'm afraid it's not that easy to even get an interview.

He lowers his focus to the nametags on the table, searching for the one with the Pierce Industries logo. He hands it to me, and I pocket it. I refuse to wear it. I'm easily enough recognized without advertising it.

The man—nothing more than a boy, really—seems disappointed. Whether it's because I'm not as charismatic or charming as he'd imagined or because I dismissed the damn nametag, I can't be certain. Frankly, I don't give a shit. Once upon a time, his emotions would have elicited more interest from me. Now, they're barely a blip on my radar. I'll never understand them. No point in wasting my time trying.

His smile is professional as he gives me the portfolio for the evening's presentation. At the same time, I feel a small hand press into my back. I tense. I know that hand.

I glance behind me, confirming my suspicion as I start toward the lecture hall. "What are you still doing here? I gave you what you wanted."

"I'm already here. I thought I'd stay." As she trots to keep up with me, Celia's heels echo on the marble floor of the Kauffman Management Center, the house of NYU's Stern School of Business.

I stop at the door to the hall and turn to her. "You weren't invited."

Her lids flutter ever so slightly, and I know my words have stung. "*You* could invite me. We rarely see each other anymore." She lowers her voice. "I miss you."

My jaw ticks, and I let out a slow breath. Celia is the one person I've been advised not to spend time with. She's also the one person who understands me better than anyone else. It's a war I wage daily—being with her is akin to being a drunk in a liquor store. She tempts me to indulge in wicked ways, even if she doesn't intend to. And I'm certain that usually she *does* intend to.

But she's my only friend, if that's what you would call our relationship. Without her, I'm all alone.

"Fine; you're invited," I resign. I open the door and hold it for her to walk through. "I don't know why you want to be here. These things are boring as hell."

I follow her down a row toward the back of the room and take two seats in the middle. The hall is small, and there are less than ten other corporate representatives currently seated. We could easily move closer, but Celia knows me well enough to understand that I prefer to be removed from situations such as these.

She leans toward me, the scent of her too-strong designer perfume pervading my space. "If it's boring, why do you even come? You could send someone who's twenty rungs down the ladder from you."

I pause, deciding if I want to explain. The annual Stern Symposium is the only event of its type that I attend. While the majority of the presentations are dull, I've found a handful of stellar students in the mix. A good find is rare and not worth the two hours I spend here every year, but that isn't the reason I continue to show up. Any of my execs could come in my place and be a better use of time management.

Still, I insist on coming myself. Partly, I'm curious. I want to know the ideas and trends emerging from the top schools. It's an attempt to stay in touch, to remind myself how to be fresh and innovative like the MBA graduates that will present tonight.

There's also another reason I attend, a reason that's less tangible and harder to put into words. It's been eight years since I finished my own business degree. Then I went straight to managing my father's company. I've become known for my cutting edge corporate decisions, my contemporary workplace vision. But the truth of the matter is that I was handed everything on a platter. I never had to fight for it or earn it like the students we will soon see. I'm ambitious and intelligent, but they have a passion and a fortitude that is intriguing. It inspires me. Most of them will do anything to make it to the top. They want to be me, to have what I have. They look up to me to show them how to get there.

And I look up to them.

Celia would never understand, so I simply say, "You never know what gems you might find." I pick up the portfolio from my lap and flip through it absently as I speak. "Don't blame me, though, when you have to fight to stay awake. And don't even think of trying to get me to leave."

"I won't do either. I'll be a good girl."

My eyes dart to her legs as she crosses one over the other. They're attractive, I'll admit. *She's* attractive. I'd be a liar if I said otherwise. But I am not attracted to her in that way. Not at all. It's likely a symptom of my inability to love, though I do take interest in other women. Women I don't know. I fuck them and have a good time, but that's all. Celia is the only woman besides my mother and sister that I know on any sort of intimate level. And as if she were a family member, I have not a speck of desire for her.

"I'm only here to be with you, anyway," she says now, wrapping her hand around my arm.

I flick my gaze toward her grasp, but don't shrug her away. "Stop saying things like that, Celia." As well as I know her, I've yet to understand her intentions by making statements such as this. She's smart enough to realize that I will never return any affection, and strangely, I don't think that's what she's after. She simply wants that same connection that I do—a kinship with someone who understands the dark fascinations that live inside her.

And I do understand her darkness. In fact, I'm fairly certain I birthed it in Celia. Time and again I try to remember if I saw it residing there before I subjected her to my cruel experiment. I can never be sure of the answer. How could I be expected to identify light when I dwell in total darkness myself?

Now, even though I'm *better*, though I've resigned from the game, there is only black everywhere around me.

Still pretending to focus on the portfolio, I feel rather than see her look away.

"I'm sorry," she says in a low voice. "I just…I don't know."

A moment of pity grips me. "You don't have to explain. I understand."

The lights dim, and the president of the business program takes the stage. I drop the folder onto my lap, having garnered very little information about the night's presentations. I won't learn anything from that, anyway. If there's someone worth my time, I won't know until I hear him or her speak.

After the president speaks, the first presentation begins. I know there will be six students in all. That doesn't vary from year to year. Only the top students of the graduating class are invited to present. They are the cream of the crop. Stern isn't Harvard, but it's a Top Ten business school. These students are some of the nation's best.

As I promised, though, the evening is a bore. Also true to her word, Celia doesn't complain. She appears to be deep in thought, most likely concocting her next scam. The temptation to join her in scheming is great, but I push against the pull and focus my attention on the event. International trade seems to be the topic of the night, but there are a few differentiations—one talk is about the newest tax codes and how they can better benefit corporations. Snore. Another presents a variation on an old business model. It's an original idea, but not practical.

By the time the fifth student finishes, I've met my limit. I nudge Celia out of her reverie. "I'm ready to go," I begin to say, but stop myself before I get the words out. The woman ascending the stairs to the stage has caught my eye, and all thoughts of leaving disappear. Something about the way she moves is captivating—the wiggle of her hips suggests an undercurrent of sexuality, and her back is straight with confidence.

Then she turns toward the audience, and my breathe catches. Even here twelve rows away, I can tell she's the most beautiful woman I've ever seen. Her dark brown hair falls just so around her face, accentuating sharp cheekbones. Her eyes are dark. Her short dress reveals long, lean legs. The modest cleavage of her outfit can't hide perfectly plump tits.

There's something else—something about her carriage that makes me sit up and take notice. And she hasn't even spoken yet.

"What?" Celia whispers, responding to the jab I'd given her. Or perhaps to the way I gasped at the sight of the angel before us.

"Nothing. Never mind." Our conversation was in conjunction with the introduction and I missed what the presenter's name is or what she's meant to talk about. I can't move my eyes for even a moment to check the program.

I'm mesmerized. Truly mesmerized.

She takes her place at the podium and begins her presentation, and I half expect my attraction to her to fade the minute her mouth opens. The opposite occurs. The sound of her voice sends a jolt through me, and I straighten in my seat. Her tone and demeanor ooze passion and authority, and also a touch of caution. For several minutes, I barely focus on her words. I'm too beguiled by her mere presence—by her smile, by her body language, by the way she furrows her brow when she refers to her notes.

And there's an air about her that I'm drawn to immediately. I sense that she's been downtrodden, but not broken. That she's known pain but emerged whole and strong. I scoff at myself—how can I know that from a few minutes of business talk? I can't. But I also can't shake the feeling that it's true. It attracts me more than anything else about her.

When I finally do catch her speech, I'm further impressed. Her topic is simple—print marketing in a digital age—but she's approached it with brilliant practicality, and I'm sure that every exec in the room is going to pursue her at the meet and greet after.

I make it a point to find her first. This, precious, precious, gem.

"Alayna Withers," Celia says quietly at my side.

"What?" I shake myself from the presenter long enough to see Celia reading from the portfolio folder.

She nods toward the stage. "Her name is Alayna Withers."

I bristle, irritated that Celia has noticed my interest. At the same time, a surge of gratification spreads across my chest. *I have her name!* It's a small thing and unfortunately everyone in the room has it as well. But I cling to it, this one bit of information I have about her. I say it quietly to myself. Let the sound of it settle in my ears. Let the texture of it swirl on my tongue.

The room is still dim, the stage the only place illuminated, but I feel the cloak of darkness around me start to dissipate.

Suddenly, I see light.

CHAPTER TWO

Before

"Your serve is terrible," I shouted to Mirabelle. Overall, my sister had gotten better since last summer. The private lessons she'd had throughout the year had strengthened both her backhand and her volley. Not that I planned on giving her the satisfaction of telling her I'd noticed.

Mirabelle's eyes sparkled as she bounced the tennis ball in front of her. "My serve is fine. I'm winning, aren't I?"

She'd won the first match because I'd gone easy on her. I hadn't expected her to be as good as she was. "Only because I'm paying more attention to your god-awful posture than to the ball."

Her lips curved up. "That's your problem. You're easily distracted." She tossed the ball up, but instead of swinging at it, she let her racket fall to her side and her attention shot elsewhere. "Oh, hey. I didn't see you there."

I followed Mirabelle's gaze and found Celia leaning against the side wall of our private court.

Well, what do you know?

I wasn't sure yet if I was glad to see her or not, but when she grinned, I returned her smile easily. I hadn't known she was in the Hamptons, but I wasn't surprised to see her. Of course, she'd stop by. Even if our mothers weren't the best of friends, Celia would find a reason to see me.

"I was enjoying your game," she said to my little sister, but her eyes never left me. "Hope you don't mind."

"Yeah, well, it's over now. Huds, we can play later." Mirabelle stomped to my side of the court where she left her racket cover and began packing up.

"Mirabelle," I said, low, with a hint of warning. I knew she didn't care for Celia, but she didn't need to be nasty.

She ignored me. Giving me a final scowl, she said, "Enjoy the rest of the day with your girlfriend." Then she took off through the opening in the hedges toward the main house.

"I'm not his girlfriend," Celia shouted after her. Then she turned to me, a fist on her hips. "Why didn't you correct her?"

I tilted my head to the side, waiting for my neck to pop. Honestly, I was surprised that Celia *had* corrected Mirabelle. I would have thought she'd be happy about the title. As for me, I preferred to let people believe what they wanted to believe. It made life far more interesting.

But my fascination with human behavior was one I kept to myself, so instead I said, "Mirabelle's a hopeless romantic. She'll form her own opinion no matter what I say."

Celia looked back after Mirabelle for a moment then walked toward me as I wiped sweat off my forehead with a towel. "She still doesn't like me." Disappointment was evident in her voice.

"Sorry," I said. I suspected that only-child Celia had always sought after Mirabelle as a surrogate sister. Our families were certainly entwined enough to make a bond between them seem inevitable. For some reason, it hadn't happened. Why was that? Curiosity tugged at my subconscious, but I forced it away. I would ponder that further at another time.

Celia didn't appear to think there was anything worth pondering. "She's fourteen. I get it. I wish it were different, but I understand."

"She needs to learn some manners."

"And you need to learn to relax. I'm fine. I don't have to be her friend. I'm your friend." She peered up at me with doubt in her eyes. "At least, I think we're still friends. It's been nine months since I left for San Francisco and not a single peep from you. What's up with that?"

I shrugged as if my neglect had been accidental. It wasn't in the least. Before Celia left for college, she'd made it clear that she was interested in more than friendship. I was not. I'd decided it was best not to lead her on. Not because I cared about how she felt, but because her infatuation was a hassle. I'd ignored her phone calls and deleted her few emails without so much as skimming them.

Yes, I was an asshole. This wasn't news to me.

Now, though, I was surprised at how good it felt to see her. Not in any romantic way, but in a familiar way. She was family. She was home.

I scratched along my jaw, deciding not to answer her question outright. Against my better judgment, I extended an invitation instead. "Millie should have lunch ready soon. I can grab a shower and then we can catch up over sandwiches."

Celia frowned. "Actually, I can't today. I only got away for a few minutes."

I raised an inquisitive brow. Why would she stop by if she couldn't stay?

She didn't expound. Instead, she asked, "Will you be here all summer?"

For as long as I could remember, both of our families spent the summer in the Hamptons. It seemed strange to think she'd assume differently. But I supposed, being older, things changed. I had already been thinking it was time to get a place of my own. I didn't need to spend all my time off from school with my parents. This would likely be my last season at Mabel Shores.

"Yes," I answered. "Will you?"

"I will. And I'd like to see you." She cleared her throat and moved her focus to her shoes. "I came by today to tell you something. Um, something that I thought might make it easier for you to want to see me again."

I folded my arms across my chest. She had me intrigued. "What is it?"

She forced her eyes up to mine. "I thought you should know that I'm seeing someone. I have been all year. We're quite serious." She fidgeted, obviously nervous. Did she think I'd be jealous?

"All right," I said. "Congratulations." I was schooled in how to respond in situations such as these though I didn't feel congratulatory. I felt nothing.

She took a deep breath. "I thought that might be the reason you hadn't returned any of my messages. Because you were worried that I…that I still…"

I cocked my head, fascinated with how she'd finish the sentence or if she'd finish it at all.

She didn't, and after a moment of awkward silence, I couldn't help myself. I wanted to push her, wanted to see what she'd say, what she'd do. "That you still liked me?"

Her cheeks went scarlet. *Interesting.* "Yes. You did know, then."

I laughed. "Everyone knew, Celia."

She shook her head as if reconciling herself with the idea. "Okay, everyone knew. But it was a silly schoolgirl crush. I'm over it now. I have Dirk, and—"

"Dirk? That's his name?" Immediately I pictured a long-haired hippy, though Celia would never be serious about anyone not in her social class. It wasn't in her. He was likely proper and well-mannered and from lots of money, just as she was.

"Be nice, Hudson." But her admonishment came with a smile. "Anyway. I have Dirk and I'm really in love with him. I think he might be the one." She blushed again, and this time I could see that she was indeed over me.

Fascinating.

"That's…great." This time, I wasn't really sure what else to say. Wasn't certain what Celia wanted me to say.

She seemed to sense I needed more. "So you and I can go back to being friends. No more weird puppy dog eyes from me. And it shouldn't be a big deal. Okay?" She smiled hesitantly, hopefully, as if my answer were important to her. As if my *friendship* were something she thought was important.

I licked my lips, salty from my earlier exertion. There was no reason to say no. And I did enjoy Celia's company. "Sure."

"Awesome!" Her relief was tangible. "I'll call you. Maybe we can play tennis later this week? Or take the Jet Skis out or something?"

"Sounds good." It also sounded dull. But she was proposing a routine summer in the Hamptons. It was what we always did and doing it again made sense. I'd find something else to occupy my boredom.

A moment of silence passed between us until it extended past comfortable to awkward. "Well, then," Celia said, shielding her eyes from the midday sun, "I'd better be going."

Chivalry returned to me. "I'll walk you out." I draped the towel around my neck and gathered my racket cover. Then we started up the path to the main house.

We were quiet as we traveled. I escorted her all the way to the circle drive where she'd left her car parked. After opening her door for her, I leaned in to give her a peck on the cheek. This was standard for us. She was, after all, practically my sibling.

She placed a hand on my arm, her expression melancholy. "Thank you, Hudson. See you soon."

I watched after her as she drove off, wondering about the change in the dynamics of our relationship. Our mothers had been best friends since we were toddlers. Every major holiday and family function had been spent with the Werners. Our parents had even enrolled us in the same elite private high school. We knew each other well, though I seriously doubted that we'd have become more than acquaintances had we not been thrown together as we were.

She should have been the perfect pairing for me. A match made in heaven. We both came from money, were already close. Yet, I had never had the slightest inclination toward her. What was wrong with me that I couldn't feel anything for her? For anyone?

"Do you like her?" Mirabelle's small voice questioned from behind me.

I turned to find her sitting on the front steps, her arms wrapped around her knees.

My jaw tensed with irritation. I didn't share the emptiness of my emotions with anyone. "It's really none of your business if I do." I strode past her, into the house.

Mirabelle jumped up and followed close at my heels. "She's not for you, Hudson. She's petty and shallow and not good for you at all."

I kept walking, heading to the main staircase.

Mirabelle continued after me. "And you don't like her. I can see it in your eyes. You have no interest in her at all."

That was true, but it intrigued me to think my sister had noticed. What else did she see? What did she know about me? I stopped mid-step and turned to her. "If you already know I don't like her, then why did you ask?"

"I wanted to be sure you knew too."

Well, I do. I didn't say it aloud. I turned away from her and jogged the remaining steps to the upper floor, then disappeared into my room.

For the rest of the day, I couldn't stop thinking about Celia and her supposed boyfriend. My chest knotted tighter and tighter as I spun the information in my mind. It wasn't jealousy—honestly I didn't care one way or another about her love life. It was intrigue. Obsessive intrigue. It wasn't the first time I'd felt it, nor, I was certain, would it be the last.

The idea of love and affection consumed me. I studied it on every occasion that I could. I didn't understand it. I'd never been "in love." I didn't believe it was even a real thing. I wasn't virtuous in any way, nor was I inexperienced. I'd dated a few girls. Or rather, I'd taken girls out to dinner and a movie with the sole intent of fucking them afterward. Sometimes I skipped the dinner and the movie and simply fucked. But I'd never had any inclination to spend any real time with anyone. I'd never had *feelings* for them.

And even though Celia had set her sights on me the year before, I'd never assumed that she felt anything deeper than the silly crush she spoke of. We'd both been cut from the same cloth. We knew the ridiculousness behind romantic notions.

Or so I'd thought.

Now, she said she'd found *the one*. The idea boggled me.

It also challenged me.

What was it that made someone think they loved another? Could the emotion be manipulated? Forced? I decided an experiment was in order.

It was unfortunate that the results might not be too favorable for Celia. But on the other hand, if love was truly a myth as I believed, maybe I was simply saving her from a lie.

I WAS SUNNING with my laptop by the pool when Celia phoned me the next day to set up a date to get together. Feigning previous plans, I pushed our meeting off until the next week. I needed time to plan before I saw her. I was meticulous with my experiments, and this time would be no different.

I tapped my fingers rhythmically on the keyboard as I schemed. After the failure of my last study, I was eager to find success. Perhaps *failure* was too harsh of a word. My results hadn't met my hypothesis, but I'd still gained information from the experiment, inconclusive as it was. I'd gotten the idea for the study after two classmates, Andrew and Jane, became engaged. They seemed to be lost for each other, dizzy in their haze of lust which they'd most likely mistaken for something more. I wondered—if they believed they were close enough that they should marry, did it mean their bond was unbreakable?

I set out to find the answer.

The three of us shared enough classes that it was easy to flirt with Jane in front of her fiancé. I did so casually at first, expecting some sort of reaction from Andrew. When none came, I upped my game. I touched Jane when we spoke, brushed my fingers against hers, played with her hair. I invaded her space. I whispered suggestive things to her—hell, dirty-as-fuck things that made her blush and her nipples stand at attention. A whole semester of this behavior and neither Jane nor Andrew had told me to stop. Shouldn't there have been accusations? If not at me, then at each other? Were they spoken behind my back, unbeknownst to me?

Or did the couple truly have enough trust and affection for each other to withstand jealousy?

Or maybe they were looking for a threesome.

The lack of a conclusive answer was why I'd considered the experiment a bust. This time I wouldn't settle for ambiguous results. Which meant I better start with a solid hypothesis.

I opened up my digital journal and started a new section which I titled *The Rebound.* It was a perfect follow-up to *The Engagement.* That study had tried to break up a couple without any prior history on my part. This time, the subject, Celia, had a prior infatuation with me. The question was, and I typed it in as I constructed it, *Could a prior infatuation affect the status of a new relationship, if the previous object of affection suddenly returned the emotion?*

Next I entered in my hypothesis: *If the subject truly believes the affection is returned, then yes.*

How would I be able to tell if I'd succeeded? I paused to watch my younger brother, Chandler, do a flip off the side of the pool as I considered. If Celia believed I was interested in her she'd likely either a) tell me to back off, b) consent to a summer affair, or c) break up with Dirk.

I would not sleep with Celia—that was non-negotiable. I couldn't have sex with women that didn't attract me, and I most certainly wouldn't have sex with a woman that knew me personally. That would mean letting her get close. And I never let anyone get close.

The only success, I decided, would be a break-up in the relationship.

I entered that into my document and sat back.

Now, I simply had to figure out my intended process. This was my favorite part—coming up with the plan. My heart rate kicked up a notch with the thrill. I'd have to put some study into it. Casual flirting would not cut it with this subject—she was only *The Subject* in my eyes now; to think of her as anything else would weaken my objectivity. I'd have to make a real attempt to show affection. It would be a challenge, but with true effort, I was sure I could win the subject over. Perhaps I could watch a few romance movies. Or ask Mirabelle—she seemed to think she was an expert on romance.

As if summoned by my thoughts, Mirabelle plopped on a deck chair next to me, her pink and black bikini seeming very mature for a girl her age. At least we were in the privacy of our own backyard. Were we to have company, she'd be wearing a cover-up, if I had any say in the matter. And I always had a say in the matter.

"Whatcha doing?" She peered toward my computer.

I swiveled slightly so that my screen was out of her view. "Nothing of importance," I said. Then I changed my tune. "Actually, I'm working on a project. For a friend. Perhaps you could help?"

"Sure." She grabbed the bottle of sunscreen that I'd brought out earlier and began slathering it over her petite body. "What is it?"

While I was sure she meant to sound aloof, I noticed the hint of excitement in her few words. If there were any reason in the world to learn how to love, it would be for Mirabelle. She adored me, as many younger sisters adored their older siblings. But unlike other big brothers, I did not deserve it. Yet she still persevered in her faith and affection. For that alone, I endeavored to try with her in ways I refused to try with anyone else. I went out of my way to give her attention—played tennis with her, took her for rides when the chauffer wasn't available, protected her from our mother's drunken ridicule. Asking her advice was just as much about boosting her as it was about helping me.

"Well," I began, "he wants to know the best way to woo a girl—"

Her eyes widened in surprise. "And he asked you? Anyone with half a brain knows you know nothing about wooing anyone."

I bit back the sting of her statement. It was true after all. "Exactly. So I'm asking you."

"This isn't really for you, is it? You aren't interested in someone, are you?" She stopped rubbing the lotion into her arm and stared at me point blank. "You aren't trying to woo Celia, are you?"

I made it a point to never lie. Even in my experiments, I had vowed to remain truthful. It was the way I maintained a bit of dignity despite my manipulative actions. So I spun my answer. "Now why would I try to woo Celia? You said yourself she wasn't for me."

"Just making sure." She returned to massaging her skin. "Let's see, women love the artsy, creative types of attention. Like write her a poem or draw her portrait."

I blinked. I wasn't artsy in the least. "Go on."

"Then there's the easy stuff—sending flowers, buying jewelry, giving gifts—"

I typed as she talked.

"But those are really lame if you don't personalize them."

I looked up from my screen. "What do you mean by *personalize*?"

"Don't just give roses. Those are boring. Give flowers that you know she'll like or that mean something to her. The jewelry should be unique to her or something she's admired."

God, it sounded like romanticizing was going to require more detailed investigation than I'd expected.

"Basically, all a woman wants is for you to spend time getting to know her," Mirabelle said, confirming my thoughts.

I chuckled. "As if you know what it's like to be a woman."

"Shut up. A girl, then." She smirked at me, an expression she had down to a T. "You know girls are just miniature women, don't you?"

"I've heard that somewhere." I scratched the back of my neck, noticing sweat had gathered while I'd been sitting in the sun. "Then all I—" I caught myself and started again. "All my friend has to do is spend time with this girl?"

"And then show that he's noticed who she is." She frowned. "Does that make any sense?"

"It does." Actually, noticing people was one of my talents. While trying to understand basic human emotion and behavior, I'd learned to study people with a fine eye. The application of my finds was what needed work. "I'm sure my friend will appreciate this advice."

Mirabelle put on her sunglasses and settled back into her chair. "I wish it were for you though. You'd make an awesome boyfriend."

I forced a smile, swallowing the nasty taste in my mouth. "Tell you what—I'll save the notes for when I need them."

I needed them now, but not the way Mirabelle assumed. I'd never need them that way. She was a bright kid, but she was absolutely wrong about one thing—I wouldn't make an awesome boyfriend.

But she'd never know that. I never planned to get close enough to a woman for her to find out.

Chapter Three

After

It's been two days since the symposium at Stern, and I'm still thinking of the brunette beauty who entranced me that night. I've returned to the portfolio over and over to read her bio and stare at her picture. Her face is ingrained in my mind and I've not even seen her close up in real life.

I had *tried* to see her, of course. After ditching Celia, I'd rushed to the meet and greet, eager to find Alayna Withers. I intended to offer her a job on the spot. Whatever position she wanted, I'd give it to her. It was completely crazy and like nothing I'd ever done before, but there was something about her. I couldn't shake it. I couldn't lose the desire to know her.

Then she didn't show for the meet and greet. To say I was disappointed was putting it mildly. I was also enraged and confused. Enraged because she'd wasted our time. *My* time. Who didn't show to meet with the top professionals in the business? There were six candidate and ten execs. She would have received an offer. Hell, she would have received five offers. Ten, even. And I would have topped each and every one to make her mine.

There was where my confusion lay—why did I give a shit? I'm not a completely emotionless man, but nearly. The feelings I do have are tame, controllable. Practical. This irrational desperation for someone I don't even know—it rattled me. It rattles me now, these days later when my desperation has increased.

Never in my life have I felt this way about someone.

Is it sexual? An overwhelming need to get laid? It has been a few weeks since I've had a woman in my bed. Maybe longer. I haven't had the interest lately.

But now, as I study her picture and remember her assuredness, her vivaciousness, my cock stirs.

I try to convince myself that's what my interest is—physical. Or that it's her mind. Maybe that's it—I'm intrigued by her ideas, her innovative way of thinking, so much so that it arouses me. Because what else can explain her effect on me?

I'm so consumed with figuring out the answer, so in need of exploring my fascination, that I called my investigator earlier in the day to look into her further. I told myself it was about business. Perhaps she didn't show up at the meet and greet because she'd already been offered a job. If I find her, I can counter.

But I know it's more than that because if she doesn't accept a job, I'll have to find another way to get close to her. I need to know if this preoccupation has staying power. It fleetingly occurs to me that the intensity of my fixation is very similar to the way I used to feel when starting a new experiment. I dismiss that notion immediately. This is different because for once I'm not interested in another person's emotions, but rather my own.

It's about damn time.

Though I'm not sure I like it.

Pinching the bridge of my nose, I lean forward at my desk and try to erase Alayna from my thoughts. My efforts are interrupted by the buzz of my secretary. "Yes, Patricia?" *Maybe it's my investigator now.*

"Your two o'clock is here. Dr. Alberts."

"Fuck." I hadn't meant to say that aloud. "Fine. Thank you. Send him in." I've forgotten about my appointment with Alberts, even though I've been seeing him regularly for over two years now. The truth is I don't want to remember my appointment. He's helped—I wouldn't be able to resist the temptations that I do if it weren't for him—but lately I'm restless. I miss the excitement of my old life. My days now are drab and endlessly the same. Perhaps it's why I'm so intrigued with Alayna Withers. Seeing her that night, I felt something for the first time in years. For the first time since I quit playing the game.

I stand and circle my desk to greet Dr. Alberts when he walks in. Though I don't need to, I gesture to the sitting area then take a seat on the edge of the leather couch, crossing a leg over the other. Alberts sits in the armchair as usual. This is our routine. He'll suggest I lie down, I'll politely decline. He'll pull out his electronic notepad and jot notes when I answer his prompts—the same prompts he gives me week after week. *How are you feeling? Are there any new life stressors? How will you deal with those? Have you had any inclinations to play?*

I'm bored before he's even begun, and I can't bear to go through the moves yet again.

He must sense my mood—or my constant shifting gives my anxiousness away—because he varies from the ritual right away.

"What's on your mind, Hudson?" he asks.

I run the tips of my fingers across my forehead, contemplating the answer. I could blame my anxiety on work. There is much to be concerned with there, such as the rumblings at Plexus, one of my smaller subsidiaries, where I fear I'm losing control of the board. Before the Stern symposium that was my major focus. After, Plexus is barely on my radar. How can I concentrate on silly business when I can't get the thought of deep brown eyes and a silky confident voice out of my brain?

That's what's on my mind—her.

But what could I tell Alberts about Alayna Withers? About a student I saw for twenty minutes at a business school event? Talking with him is supposed to help sort out my emotions, but these emotions are too vague and unidentifiable. Too intense and strange.

Instead, I choose to mention the detail of my last few days that will interest him the most. "I saw Celia."

"You did?" Alberts shows his alarm with only a slight raise of a gray eyebrow. "What were the circumstances of that encounter?"

"I'd like to say it was innocent. But it wasn't entirely." I run my hands through my hair while he waits for me to continue. "She called me. She's been using my identity to play someone—an employee of my sister's." I cringe thinking about how close to home Celia's game was with Stacy. And how I did nothing to stop it until the other night.

"Were you aware she was doing this?"

"Yes." I answer his next question before he has the chance to ask. "No, I didn't encourage it, but I was aware." I stand, needing to pace as I talk. "Celia asked me to help her wrap up the game. I agreed. I told her where I'd be and when. She made the arrangements for the rest to happen."

Glancing toward Alberts, I expect to see a look of disapproval. It's not there. The man is as careful with his emotions as I am.

Next he'll want to know why I agreed to help. It's an easy enough answer—the game needed to end. I didn't appreciate my name being pulled into her scheme and being available for her staged embrace was the easiest way to end it.

But that's not what he wants to know. "How did it make you feel? Playing again, after so long?"

I pause, considering his question. There had been a certain spark, a thrill that had run through my body as I'd kissed my childhood friend. Not because of the woman I'd been kissing or even because I'd been kissing at all, but because I knew the effect I was having on Stacy—on Celia's intended target. In the moment, I wanted to immerse myself in the feeling, wanted to grab it and hold onto it. It was feeling, for God's sake. Feeling, where I'd been void. All I'd have to do was stop fighting the impulse, and I could have the excitement back in my life. With Celia there, egging me on as she always did, it would have been so easy to fall back into our old patterns, to resume our games.

But all it took was the look in Stacy's eyes, the devastation she felt at my supposed rejection to remind me that my entertainment came at the price of others' emotions.

"There was a rush," I answer honestly. "Then it was over, and until now I hadn't given it a second thought." Even without the reminder of the consequences of the game, I would have abandoned any notion to play again when I went to the symposium. That brief spark with Celia had been completely obscured by the charge that jolted through me at the sight of Alayna Withers.

Alberts clears his throat and I look to find he's studying me. He narrows his eyes. "Then you aren't concerned that you'll be pulled back into the game?"

I let out a huff. I'm always concerned I'll be pulled back into the game. But am I worried that Celia will pull me back? "No, I'm not."

"Do you plan to see her again?"

My eyes widen when for a second I think that "her" refers to the brunette that's plaguing my thoughts.

But that's not who Alberts means.

"No, I don't plan to see Celia again." She'd like me to. She asks me over and over. I see her enough at family events as it is. Her presence isn't a temptation to me as my therapist believes, but seeing her is still not a good idea. She's a painful reminder of all the wrongs I've done in my life. Of all the wrongs I've done to her.

I resume my pacing, hoping not to go down that path of conversation today, not wanting to revisit my past.

"Hudson, sit down."

I'm surprised he hasn't requested this before. I sit, crossing my ankle over my bouncing knee. "Sorry. I have a lot on my plate at the moment." I take a quiet but deep breath that does nothing to relieve me.

Dr. Alberts leans back, a distinct contradiction to my own tense posture. "I don't sense that your anxiety has to do with your meeting with Celia. Is there something else you aren't telling me?"

It's on the tip of my tongue to bring up my strange reaction to Alayna Withers, but I'm again lost on how I'd phrase it. "It's nothing. Work is stressful." Work is always stressful.

Too late I realize I've opened the door to an old argument.

"I hate to beat a dead horse, Hudson, but if we met in my office instead of here, you'd have a chance to escape that stress, if even for a short time."

I throw him a glare. "If I had to meet in your office, I'd never pull myself away."

"That's a problem, Hudson. I've tolerated it for the past two years, but I feel we're at a point in your therapy that this will no longer work. If you want to continue with your recovery, you need to make it your priority. You must decide that pulling yourself away is more important, that your mental health is more important than the work you leave behind."

I feel my jaw twitch. I agree that my therapy is at a standstill. He's likely right that to progress further, I'd need to rearrange my current priority list. However, that's not going to happen. I have no desire to pull myself away. I don't believe that I am more important than the work I leave behind. I don't believe that I am more important than *anything*. And while working with Alberts has kept me from ruining other people's lives, it hasn't given my own life any more dimension than it had. I still haven't found a way to fill the emptiness that resides inside. At least the game was enough to distract me from that. Now I'm ever aware of my hollowness, of my inability to feel more than a dull hum of emotion.

In the past, when the topic to meet in his office instead of mine has come up, I've persuaded him to leave things the way they are. Today, I sense he won't let it go. And I'm not sure that I want to fight him any longer. I have the tools I need to continue on as I have without seeing him any longer. Could he fix me if I gave in? If I made more of the effort that he suggests I haven't before? I don't know. That's what I must decide. Either I play it his way, or I don't need him. I'm not ready to give a firm answer.

"Touché," I say. "I concede that this arrangement is no longer working. Perhaps we should end our relationship altogether." It's a manipulation technique, I know. Like a child pouting. If I don't get to play my way, I won't play at all.

But my psychologist is too good to fall for my tricks. "If that's what you want to do. You know this only works if you're a willing participant."

Part of me wants to cut him out of my life and move on, but I'm not comfortable with impulse-driven decisions. "I need to think about it."

"Do that. If you decide you want to meet with me again—in my office—than call my secretary and make an appointment." He stands, our session clearly over even though we still have another thirty minutes on the clock.

I suppose there's no point in continuing if I have no real interest in progress.

I get to my feet and shake his hand. "Thank you, Doctor."

"I hope I see you again," he says, the twinkle in his eye more of the look a grandfather would share with his grandson than a psychologist with his patient. He's fond of me. I wonder what he could possibly see in me to feel that way.

Maybe I haven't given him the chance I should.

Though I'm more concerned that if I did give him the chance, he'd still be unable to help me.

He's almost at the door when he turns to me. "Remember, Hudson, true progress only happens with work." With those words, he leaves me.

I shake my head in frustration. Of course I remember that. I've worked my ass off to get Pierce Industries to what it is today. If he thinks I don't understand the value of hard work, then he has no understanding of what I do, of what I am. But in the back of my mind, I know that he's talking about a different kind of work, and while I've already spent some time in the department of self-repair, I'm not sure that I'm willing to spend more.

At this particular moment of my life, the only thing I want to spend time on is finding out more about Alayna Withers.

The minute Alberts is gone, I pick up my phone and dial my secretary. "Were there any calls?" She knows not to interrupt me when he's here, and I'm hoping my investigator has called.

"No, sir."

I give a quick thank you and hang up, pausing only a moment before I'm calling him myself.

"Jordan here," he answers on the first ring. The man used to be Special Ops and I've found his skills are beneficial in many situations.

"Have you found anything out yet?" I realize I'm being impatient. I've only given him a few hours to look, after all.

"Not much. I'm still waiting for her medical history and complete background check."

Her medical history can't possibly inform me of anything useful, but the background check might. "What do you know so far?"

"The basics. Her full name is Alayna Reese Withers, born and raised in Boston. Her parents died in a car accident when she was sixteen. She lives between Lexington and Third, near the Waldorf. She got her BA in business at Boston University and is set to graduate from NYU with a Masters in Business next month. Right now she's working as an assistant manager at The Sky Launch."

The Sky Launch? I wrack my brain trying to place the name. "The night club?"

"Yep."

She can't possibly be planning to work at a night club after her graduation. She has to have another offer. "Can you tell if anyone else has pulled her information recently?" If she's got a job waiting, they'll have checked into her.

I hear muffled movement as if Jordan's cradling the phone on his shoulder while he looks for the answer. "The system says there was one other pull of her credit history. Yesterday."

"Dammit." I wonder which of my competitors was lucky enough to earn her *yes*. "Find out who ordered that." Then I'll prepare my counter proposition.

"On it."

"And call me the minute anything new comes in."

"Yes, Mr. Pierce."

I've just hung up when Patricia calls me again. I pick up the receiver to answer when my office door is flung open and Celia parades in.

"I'm sorry, sir," my secretary says in my ear. "I was calling to announce her and she just walked in."

"It's okay. I'll take care of her." I hang up, cursing under my breath. Celia's the last person I'm in the mood for, but Patricia isn't any sort of bouncer.

Celia slinks in and half-sits on the far corner of my desk. "You'll take care of me, will you?"

I ignore her suggestive tone. "Two days in one week, Celia. To what do I owe the *pleasure*?" I put enough bitterness in my final word that she can't mistake that there is anything pleasant about her visit at all.

Immediately I feel a pang of guilt. It's not Celia's fault that I no longer want to be around her, rather it's my fault. All of it, my fault.

She doesn't let my tone ruffle her. "Oh, come on, Hudsy. Don't be that way. I'm not the enemy."

No, she's not. I'm the enemy. She'll never see it, though, so it's my job to keep the distance. "Why are you here?"

There's a gleam in her eye when she smiles. "I have something that I know is going to interest you."

"Oh?" I sound bored, and I am.

"I'm serious. You're going to want in on this."

In on this? She can only be proposing a game. "Celia, I've told you, I don't play anymore." I shift my focus toward my computer screen, pretending to go back to whatever I was doing before she arrived.

She doesn't get that I'm dismissing her—or doesn't care. "You've told me, you've told me. Now I'm telling you, you'll want in on this."

I should kick her out now, pour out the bottle before I've even taken a sip, so to say, but I can't help myself. Even with my attention turned, my pulse has quickened and the moisture in my mouth has increased. Her eagerness is contagious. And I'm curious. Too curious.

I can't let her know. "I won't want in on anything. But since you're here," I casually turn back to face her, "what is it you're planning?"

Her grin kicks up a notch. "Look at you. You're dying to know. Your eyes blazed the minute you realized what I was offering."

I don't try to deny it—I *am* interested and even with schooled features, she can see it. I hate how well I've taught her to read people. I hate when she uses her knowledge to read *me.*

It pisses me off enough that I almost send her packing.

But curiosity wins out. She hasn't tempted me with her games in quite some time. Why now?

"Out with it, Ceeley." I cringe inwardly at the slip of her childhood nickname. She'll think I mean something by it that I don't. It's why I hate nicknames so much.

She stands and starts rummaging through her bag. "It's a basic scenario—make the girl fall for you and then deny her, watching her fall to pieces."

It had been our old favorite. No matter how many times we'd performed the experiment, it never failed to interest me. It was a marvelous study in the emotion called love, but somehow it never gave me any of the answers I was seeking.

I pretend the idea doesn't pique me in the slightest. "How original. What about that did you think would interest me?"

She smiles with confidence. "The girl."

I raise a questioning brow, but instead of answering me verbally, she retrieves a file folder from her bag and sets it on the desk in front of me. Then she waits for me to study it.

With a reluctant breath, I flip the cover open and move my eyes from Celia to the top sheet inside the file. Deep brown eyes and a warm smile meet me.

Celia's right—it is the girl that interests me. And I know before she says anything more that I will hear her out to the end. Because if Celia has the answer to getting closer to Alayna Withers, I am in.

All the way.

COMING SOON

FREE ME

Gwen Anders left her job as a top manager at Eighty-Eighth Floor to come work at The Sky Launch. She left suddenly and without warning. She hasn't told any of her new coworkers anything about her past or why she left.

Gwen Anders has a story of her own.

Lights, Camera...

TAKE TWO

Available now at Amazon, Barnes & Noble, and iTunes

On the night of her graduation from film school, straight-laced Maddie Bauers fell completely out of character for an oh-my-god make-out session with a perfect stranger. Complete with the big O.

Seven years later, that romantic interlude is still fresh in her mind. That stranger is now a rich and famous actor. And she's one very distracted camera assistant working on his latest production. She might consider another tryst...if he even remembers her.

Micah Preston does indeed remember Maddie. Too bad he's sworn off Hollywood relationships. He allows himself as much sex as he likes—and oh, he does like—but anything more is asking for trouble. For the woman, not for him. Yet knowing Maddie could want more than a movie-set fling doesn't stop him from pursuing her like a moth drawn to hot stage lights.

But as the shoot nears its end, it's decision time. Is it time to call, "Cut!" on their affair, or is there enough material for a sequel?

ONTO EVERY DIVA'S BACKSIDE, A LITTLE WOOD MUST FALL.

LIGHTS, CAMERA...

STAR STRUCK

Available for preorder at Amazon, Barnes & Noble, and iTunes

Hollywood actress Heather Wainwright was looking forward to a long, relaxing break before starting her next shoot. Except her assistant volunteered her for L.A.'s annual 24 Hour Plays.

Nervous about doing a good job for such a worthy charity, Heather falls back on "diva" mode, a defense mechanism that always carries her through. Until she encounters something that *really*gets on her nerves—a lowly carpenter whose Norse god eyes pierce right through her.

Highly sought-after production designer Seth Rafferty has little patience for A-listers with superior attitudes, which is why his attraction to Heather is absurd. Yet, sensing vulnerability beneath her screen-queen act, he lets her assumptions play out.

After the wrap party, Heather awakens with little memory of the night before—except that Seth gave her the best orgasm of her life, then disappeared. When he shows up on the set of her next movie, she winds up to give him a piece of her mind...and Seth shows her just how stinging hot "chemistry" can get.

Warning: Contains an outwardly snobby actress with a good heart, a delicious carpenter with a power drill, some much-deserved spanking, and an appropriately consensual—if tipsy—orgasm, as well as sex at an inappropriate time of the month.

THE AUTHOR

Laurelin Paige is the USA Today Bestselling author of the Fixed on You trilogy. She's a sucker for a good romance and gets giddy anytime there's kissing, much to the embarrassment of her three daughters. Her husband doesn't seem to complain, however. When she isn't reading or writing sexy stories, she's probably singing, watching Game of Thrones and the Walking Dead, or dreaming of Adam Levine. She is represented by Bob Diforio of D4EO Literary Agency.

Made in the USA
Lexington, KY
04 May 2014